Julie Highmore lives in Oxford and has three grown-up children. Her previous novels, *Play It Again?*, *Pure Fiction* and *Country Loving*, were warmly praised:

'So enjoyable . . . It's a lovely read' Catherine Alliott

'Compulsive reading' *Express*

'A funny and compulsive read' *Choice* magazine

'Classic, warm-hearted comedy' *Bookseller*

'Addictive . . . is basically a literary soap opera. Highmore manages to combine *Northern Exposure* and Rosamunde Pilcher with hilarious results' *Booklist*

'Welcome new life is breathed into a familiar scenario' *Woman & Home*

'This quick and enjoyable read is written in a refreshingly subtle understated style. It's perfect if you are looking for something light for a few hours of indulgent escapism' *Daily Record*

'Delightful . . . Witty and sharply observed tale . . . Pure enjoyment. It's funny and thoroughly entertaining' *Lancashire Evening Post*

Sleeping Around

Julie Highmore

headline
review

First published in hardback 2005 by REVIEW
An imprint of HEADLINE BOOK PUBLISHING

First published in paperback in 2005 by REVIEW
An imprint of HEADLINE BOOK PUBLISHING

A REVIEW paperback

1

ISBN 0 7553 2117 0

Typeset in AGaramond by Palimpsest Book Production Limited,
Polmont, Stirlingshire

Printed and bound in Great Britain by Clays Ltd, St Ives plc

Headline's policy is to use papers that are natural, renewable and
recyclable products and made from wood grown in sustainable forests.
The logging and manufacturing processes are expected to conform
to the environmental regulations of the country of origin.

HEADLINE BOOK PUBLISHING
A division of Hodder Headline
338 Euston Road
London NW1 3BH

www.reviewbooks.co.uk
www.hodderheadline.com

For Carol

Thanks to Sophie, Eliane and Justin,
and to Helena, Katherine, Nicola,
Joanna, Charlotte, Claire, Justinia,
Debbie and the wonderful Flora

FRIDAY

The man in the woolly hat was unloading his mud-coloured car. From her window, Jo watched him take out a rucksack, then a pair of hiking boots and a small suitcase. After contemplating the boots for a while, he chucked them back in. Jo pushed her glasses up her nose and saw that he was probably in his thirties – although hard to tell under the hat – and that his car wasn't mud-coloured, just covered in mud.

She let the lace curtain fall back in place and returned to her on-screen copy-editing. It was chapter three of Sergei's thesis, written in an interesting form of English and on the gripping topic of Russian Transport Law. So far as Jo could tell, Sergei's work contained neither original thought nor any attempt at an argument, but she guessed such things were waived when mega overseas students' fees were involved. Her eyes wandered back to the window.

She really couldn't see much through the lace, and wondered, as pretty as it was, if she should take it down and have a better view of the street. The idea was that it hid her monitor from passing burglars, but apparently they didn't bother with PCs any more. Too heavy. When number 7 was broken into, they just took the DVD player and Pippa's underwear.

With the tip of a finger, Jo eased the curtain to one side again and saw the newcomer's breath freeze as he locked his passenger door. The coldest March for decades, they were saying, which was why Lucy and Dom had shot off to their place in France, and why this person had come to house-cat-and-fish-sit for them.

She tried to remember his name. It was Mark or Marius, or something. Lucy and Dom hadn't been very forthcoming when Jo tried grilling them; appearing, in fact, to know nothing about him. Which was odd, considering how nosy Lucy was. 'We found him on the Internet,' she'd said. 'He gave us a glowing reference and we said yes. Who needs his life story?' Lucy and Dom were very trusting sorts.

After lugging his things up the path, the housesitter put his rucksack down and fumbled under a large and very obvious stone for the key. He then straightened up, turned, and with a broad smile beneath his snug-fitting hat gave Jo a wave before letting himself into the house.

'Oops,' she said, dropping the curtain and staring at it for a while. But then she shrugged, decided he was just being friendly, and set about chopping one of Sergei's interminable sentences into three.

Just before seven, she stopped work to focus on the lodgers' dinner. Would they notice if it was fish again? She was beginning to run out of ideas. Keiko, who weighed less than a small leaf, was the only person in the world still on the Atkins Diet while young Ernst refused to eat British beef, or even lamb – scrapie, apparently – and found vegetarian meals an enigma.

Having shut down the computer, Jo risked a peep over the road from her lamp-lit room. Back went the lace curtain again, very slowly, to reveal Lucy and Dom's house in total darkness. Mark or Marius must have gone out.

Marcus had woken a few minutes earlier to pitch-black, aware that he was in his coat and hat but with no idea of where he was. In his dream he'd been on the M6, but this didn't feel like the motorway. You wouldn't be horizontal on the M6. Not unless you'd been thrown from your car. Anyway, he was definitely stretched out on something soft and, what's more, it was pretty quiet. Just the sound of an engine running. But in the vicinity of his thighs? He stretched out a hand and encountered fur – lots of it – and the noise got louder. Cat, he thought, feeling whiskers. Cat . . . fish . . . house . . . Oxford . . . Oh, yeah.

After a noisy yawn that made the animal flee, Marcus eased himself up off the sofa and worked his way, arms waving before him, to where he thought the window might be. On hitting heavy hanging material, he tugged it first left, then right, before streetlamps and the last bit of daylight revealed the person opposite still looking his way from behind her net curtain. Oh, well. He guessed every street had one. When the phone gave a shrill ring on the far side of the room, he jumped out of his skin, then wandered into the darkness and found it.

'Hello?' he croaked, while the cat did a figure of eight around his ankles.

'Oh, good evening,' sang a familiar voice in soft Scottish tones. 'Would it be at all possible to speak to Mr Marcus Currie? If it's not too much trouble?'

Marcus cleared his throat. 'Yeah, it's me, Mum. I'll be the only housesitter here, so no need to ask for me.'

'Marcus, you don't sound yourself,' she said. 'Is your throat sore? It's not a dusty germ-filled place, I hope?'

'Um . . . no, I don't think so.' He peered into the darkness. 'I just fell asleep, that's all. As soon as I arrived.'

'I do worry about you, son.'

'There's no need, Mum. I am thirty-nine.'

'Not till next week. Listen, I'll put some vapour rub in with your prezzie, but don't overdo it, will you? Sheena McWhirter swears she got addicted. So, have you contacted her yet?'

'Sheena McWhirter?'

His mother tutted. 'No, *her*.'

Marcus was now keen to get off the phone. He really

didn't want to discuss Hannah, plus the cat had begun chewing his shoe leather. 'Not yet,' he said. 'I'll call her later this evening.'

'Good idea, love. You're not sounding yourself at the moment.'

'So you said. Listen, I've got a ravenous moggy here I should feed.'

'Oh, OK. I'll ring again soon. Is there someone I can leave a message with if you're not in?'

Marcus sighed. She never listened, his mother. 'Just the machine, Mum. Anyway, take care of yourself, won't you? And get those brothers of mine to pull their weight in the restaurant.'

'That'll be the day,' she said. Andrew and Fraser's hearts had never been entirely in the family business. But then Marcus couldn't say his had, either. He'd just been better at hiding it.

After putting the phone down, he made his way through to the kitchen, gradually lighting up the house as he went. 'Dry food only,' said the note – one of many – 'and change water daily. NO CANNED FOOD! (Creates problems for Maidstone.)'

Marcus scratched at his hat and wondered where a large town in Kent came into it, before pouring out a bowl of food for the short-haired tabby and putting the kettle on. It was then that he took a good look around and realised what a terrific place he'd got himself. They'd even stocked the fridge and food cupboards for him. The prospect of three weeks in such surroundings for no financial outlay filled Marcus with sudden and unreserved glee. He tried not to think that might be the Scot in him and helped himself to a biscuit.

Mug in hand, he went and inspected the rest of the house, saying, 'Veeerrry nice,' in each room. The décor was sleek, chic and beautifully finished. Modern, but never at odds with the original features of the house: fireplaces, shiny brass door furniture, curly architraves. What topped it all, literally, was the attic, where Marcus stepped into a vast wooden-floored, white-walled, dormer-windowed area with lots of electrical equipment and several plasma screens. Some sort of office, it seemed.

What on earth did these people do to afford all this stuff? A large three-storey period house – OK, Victorian – full of expensive items in a prime location, *and* they had a house in France they could take off to at the drop of a hat. They'd sounded young on the phone and looked young in all the photos of the tall blond couple scattered around. He sipped at his coffee and shook his head. Wealthy parents, maybe.

As he began a tour of the room, Marcus heard the distant ding-dong of a bell. He trotted down two flights and found a woman on the doorstep, shivering in a thin polo-neck jumper. She was slim and of medium height, and in the streetlight her long, straight and very shiny hair was Titian red, as were her jeans. She had that alabaster skin of certain redheads – either that or hypothermia was setting in. She was definitely pretty. If asked how old she was, Marcus would have put her between twenty and forty, because he was hopeless at telling ages.

'Hi,' he was about to say as she charged over the threshold and threw herself against a radiator.

'Jesus,' she said, teeth chattering, arms wrapped around herself, then, 'Oh, Christ,' as she bounced back off the radiator. 'Didn't they tell you how to put the heating on?'

Who was this woman?

'Marcus,' he said, extending a hand.

'Oh, yeah. S-sorry, I'm J-Jo.' She untucked a hand and shook his. 'I'm a n-neighbour.'

'Jojo?'

She shook her head. 'J-Jo.'

He still wasn't sure. 'Would you like my coat?' he asked. He started taking it off and she didn't protest. 'Here.' He wrapped it around her quaking shoulders and she slipped her arms in. 'Come on through. I'll put the gas rings on. You must have come quite a way to be this frozen.'

'Only from over the road. I just feel the c-c-cold a lot. It's a thin-skin thing.'

When they got to the kitchen, he lit up all six Smeg rings and offered Jojo his hat. She nodded and thanked him, but when he pulled it off she gave a start.

'Oh,' she said, her cheeks now rosying up nicely, 'I

thought you might have, er, dark hair, for some reason. And, you know, kind of thick and wavy . . . or something.' She looked a bit stunned.

Marcus raked fingers through his fair, some might say mousy, baby-fine locks in an attempt to bulk them up a bit. 'Can I get you anything?' he asked, aware of a curt edge to his voice. What was wrong with his hair, anyway? At least he still had some, unlike his brothers. 'Tea? Coffee?'

'No, thanks, I'm in the middle of cooking dinner. That's why I'm here, actually.'

'Oh?'

'I wondered if you'd like to join us. Me and my lodgers. Two foreign students. It's just fish.'

'Fish sounds good,' he said, putting the hair business to one side and smiling nicely at her. 'Yes, I'd love to come.'

'Great. I'm at number fifteen. Directly opposite.'

Marcus stared. It was the curtain twitcher. 'When shall I—'

'Eightish?'

'OK,' he said, and before he knew it she was flying back across the street in his coat and hat, shouting something about someone called Atkins.

Marcus closed the door with a frown and went back to look through Lucy and Dom's notes again. No, nothing about a care-in-the-community neighbour. Just one saying, 'Watch out for Pippa (No. 7) who will almost certainly ask you to remove large spider from bedroom whilst husband Ray is on car-factory night shift.'

Marcus shuddered at the words 'large' and 'spider'. Chances were he'd be calling Pippa in.

'At my home in Germany we are eating much veal but not so many fishes,' announced Ernst.

Keiko nodded and nodded and gave a quiet, 'Aaahhh,' then nodded some more and took a tiny sip of water.

Marcus nodded too but didn't say anything. Jo hoped he wasn't bored.

'Can I top up your coffee?' she asked.

'Thanks,' he said with a face-transforming smile. Not that he wasn't just as lovely at ease: blue eyes and that nice kind of dirty-blond hair. What a shock she'd had when he'd taken off the hat that had been hiding half his face. So good-looking, he'd taken her breath away. She'd blurted out something stupid about his hair, she remembered now. He seemed like a nice person too: talking football with Ernst; asking Keiko all about her family.

Jo filled his cup, but not Ernst's, and began clearing away the dessert dishes. 'Well,' she said, looking hopefully from student to student as she piled things up, 'I expect you two have lots of homework to do. Keiko?'

Keiko dabbed delicately at her mouth with some kitchen roll. She always wore red lipstick, even at breakfast. 'Yes,' she said. 'This weekend I must write essay

9

about dinner party for me and favourite six guests. Who I invite if I can choose anybody. Even famous persons. Even if dead.'

Marcus said, 'That sounds interesting. Who are you going to invite?'

'Ah.' Keiko held up her dainty left hand and pointed at its thumb. 'First, my best friend, Hiroko.'

'Uh-huh.'

'Second, my second-best friend, Nyoko.'

'Right . . . You can invite *anyone*, you say?'

'Yes. Anybody. Even if dead.' She moved along to the middle finger. 'Number three is my teacher at language school, Adam.'

'Ha!' exclaimed Ernst. 'Every girl in my class is wanting to have a baby from Adam.'

Jo laughed. She'd heard so much about this Adam, she was now keen to meet him herself. And maybe have his baby.

Keiko giggled. 'He is very handsome and very kind. Number four and five is my parents.'

Jo tried not to laugh, while Marcus said, 'Hang on a minute,' lurching forward and fixing his gaze on her lucky lodger. 'What about, oh, I don't know . . . Elvis Presley? No, not him, but Jimi Hendrix, say. Or Joan of Arc? I'm sure your parents make great dinner-party guests but I think this is meant to be a special occasion. Don't you want someone hugely talented there? Or a hero or idol of some sort?'

'Yes,' said Keiko, moving on to the pinkie of her other hand. 'So, number six. One very famous, very special guest. But dead. Princess Diana.'

'Good choice,' said Jo, smiling Marcus's way as he slumped back in his chair. 'What about you, Ernst?'

'Me, I have to learn pub vocabulary, then go at nine thirty to meet our teacher Jeremy and the other students in the Eagle and Child. Jeremy wants us to practise our contractions.'

'Sounds like an ante-natal class,' said Marcus, pulling a face.

'For example, "What'll you have?" not "What will you have?".'

'Oh, right.'

'Very useful,' said Jo, clearing more items off the table. 'Well, no need to help,' she told her lodgers. 'Maybe you should get cracking on your homework.' The two of them stared at her, so she explained 'get cracking' and Keiko wrote it down in her notebook, before they went off to their respective rooms.

'Fancy a drink?' Jo asked Marcus.

'Mm?' he said, looking at her but somehow miles away. Perhaps he was still working on Keiko's guest list. 'Sorry, I should have brought a bottle.'

'Don't worry. I never serve alcohol with dinner, anyway. Wouldn't make any money if I did that.'

He leaned towards her. 'The profit margin on Keiko must be huge,' he said, lowering his voice. His eyes were

11

a fabulous shade of blue. Deep blue. And the whites of his eyes were very white. Co-op store colours, she decided, while trying to think of a nicer comparison. A summer sky with cotton-wool clouds, a Hockney painting . . . 'I mean, what did she eat?' he continued. 'A forkful of salmon and a glass of tap water?'

'Yeah, well she makes up for it with long showers. Fifty minutes this morning. Poor Ernst had to pee in the frozen garden.' Jo tore herself away and found a bottle of vodka left over from her Christmas party. 'We could start with a short?'

Her guest looked at his watch – a gesture guaranteed to ruin an evening – and said, 'I should really make a phone call before it gets too—'

'Call from here, if you like.'

'Ah, no. Thanks, anyway. It's a bit, you know . . .'

'Personal?'

'Yes.'

'Right,' said Jo, feeling oddly disappointed that this relative stranger had a significant other. After all, was he really her type? On the whole, she tended to go for darker men, plus how keen was she on that checked shirt? 'You could always go home, then come back,' she suggested.

She watched his eyes swivel around before he said, 'Oh, sod it, I'll call her tomorrow.' He grinned. 'Why ruin her evening?'

* * *

'So how come you don't have much of an accent?' she asked him.

They'd moved down to the floor cushions in front of the illegal log fire she'd thrown together. Her fires tended to be a bit hit and miss, but this one was behaving itself, still alight after an hour. They'd talked about politics and war, and she'd filled him in on the neighbours and the neighbourhood, but so far they hadn't touched on anything personal. They were sitting facing each other. His legs were crossed at the ankle, not far from her knees, and she looked approvingly at his nice shoes: dark brown, soft leather. A man's shoes had always been a gauge for Jo. No amount of good looks and charm could make up for shiny, buckled slip-ons.

'I think I lost a lot of it at university,' he said, as Jo reached for the bottle of wine – their second – and filled the glasses. 'I went to Sussex. Mind you, it comes flooding back when I'm at home. You should hear me.'

'I'm the same when I go back to Wales. I mean Way-yells.'

He smiled then went quiet for a while. 'So,' he said finally, looking up from his drink. 'What do you do behind your curtain all day, Jojo?'

She was on the verge of telling him she was just plain Jo, but a fierce knock on the door prevented her.

'I am going off now,' announced Ernst. His head appeared in a fur-edged hood, making him look nine rather than nineteen.

'OK,' said Jo. 'You'd better hurry, though. It's gone ten. Know all your pub vocabulary?'

'No, I have been sleeping. I know only "Same again?", "What'll you have?" and "My turn to get them in". These are the three Jeremy wants us mostly to practise on him.'

Marcus laughed. 'Sounds like a clever bloke.'

'Well, have a nice time,' said Jo.

'And you also,' replied Ernst. His eyes bounced from her to Marcus and back again, before he winked and disappeared.

Jo cringed and grabbed the poker, then spent some time stabbing at the fire.

'What's that log ever done to you?' Marcus asked.

'Mm? Oh.' She put the poker down and composed herself, as much as was possible after a vodka and two-and-a-half – or was it three-and-a-half? – glasses of wine. Large ones. 'I copy-edit,' she said, remembering his question. 'And I proofread. Mostly academic stuff. Dissertations, theses. It pays the bills, but it doesn't pay the mortgage arrears, the overdraft or the maxed-out credit cards. Hence the lodgers.' She was telling him too much, she knew, but she was feeling loose and her tongue was quite drunk. Or maybe the other way round.

For a while she watched the mirror beyond Marcus's head do a strange little dance – jigging and swaying – before she lowered her gaze to his. He was definitely giving her a funny look. A bit like the looks her Italian boy, Gianni, used to give her before he pounced on her

14

that evening and she'd had to explain that landladies weren't supposed to sleep with their students. That if she started doing that, the school would stop sending people to her and she'd end up in Queen Street with only a blanket and a dog on a piece of rope. Gianni had said he understood and then apologised. He was just missing his mother, he'd explained alarmingly.

'You know, Jojo,' Marcus was saying, 'your hair's a fabulous colour. And so shiny.'

She blinked, taken aback at the turn in the conversation. Should she tell him it was hennaed? And what about the Jojo thing? 'Thanks,' she said, topping up their glasses again. 'And you?' she asked, deciding to keep to safe ground. 'What do you do?' She placed the bottle over by the wall, out of harm's way, and when she leaned back, Marcus was beside her, sharing her floor cushion, his arm resting on the seat of the sofa behind her. Actually, she thought, it was rather a nice shirt. And so very soft.

'Too boring to talk about,' he said. 'You know, I'm feeling what my mother would call "a wee bit merry".'

'Mm, me too.'

Something was trailing along her shoulder towards her neck. Marcus, now at very close range, looked at her with his one eye. Then with four. She blinked and he had two again. 'I'd love to kiss you,' he said.

'Would you?' she asked.

'Yes,' he said, and he did.

15

When he'd finished, Jo reached for her glass and gulped fairly furiously, then put it down, empty. What an unexpected evening this was turning out to be.

'I don't suppose I could stay here tonight?' Marcus asked.

She knew she should be shocked and wary, but Lucy and Dom had checked him out, sort of. And besides, her hand was in his lovely shirt now.

He stroked her hennaed hair. 'My house is so cold compared to yours. What do you say?'

'Erm . . . I don't know. Yes, I suppose so. But . . .'

'What?'

'Well, what about Maidstone?'

'Oh, no,' he said, now nuzzling her neck. 'Too far.'

SATURDAY

Robin woke to the sound – clomp, clomp, clomp – and then the feel – warm, slightly damp – of Freddie. It was dark, so he couldn't actually see him. As the little boy snuggled up under the duvet, Robin turned to the illuminated alarm and saw it wasn't yet six. Being the weekend, it was officially Hannah's turn to deal with Freddie, but she was dead to the world on the far side of their king-size bed, recharging herself after five days of abuse, more abuse and futile attempts to teach French at a bottom-of-the-league secondary school.

'Don't fidget, Fred,' whispered Robin. 'Just lie very still. That's it. Close your eyes . . . not too tight. And go back to sleep. That's what Daddy's going to do. Lovely, lovely sleeeep. Mmmm . . .'

'I spilled my water,' said Freddie. 'On my jim-jams.'

'Never mind. They'll soon dry off.'

'Daddy?'

'Sshhh, Freddie. Not so loud. What?'

'Why is water wet?'

Robin's heart sank. 'Well . . .' he began, still whispering, 'let me see . . .' Freddie's questions were always of this nature. Basically, impossible for Robin to answer. Never, 'Daddy, what's the connection between America's post-1945 international economic interests and its global political/military agenda?' In his forty-six years, Robin hadn't once wondered why water was wet. He doubted that Hannah, in her thirty-seven, had given it much thought either. Had they somehow freakily produced a little scientist, or had that paternity test been wrong, after all? 'It's because . . .' he said. 'Hey, want some breakfast?'

'Yeah, yeah, yeah!'

'Sshhh.'

'What would you like?' whispered Robin, lifting himself and his son up off the bed, as seamlessly as his back would allow. 'Yikes,' he said, straightening up. A recent rough and tumble with Freddie had left him, temporarily he hoped, with nasty back pain. He couldn't remember parenthood being so painful the first time round, but then he had been a lithe twentysomething when Theo was born. 'Creamy porridge again?' he asked.

'Yeah, yeah, yeah!'

'Sshhh.'

'Daddy?'

'Mm?' Robin felt around with an extended foot for

his slippers. He came across one but not the other so gave up and, without turning on any lights, carried his son down the stairs. 'What, Freddie?'

'Why is the dark a black colour? I want it to be red. Why can't it be red, Daddy?'

Robin thought he might be able to have a stab at this one, but not till he'd had a coffee.

Marcus woke to total darkness, aware of a thumping headache and the aroma of old joss sticks, but with no idea of where he was. A faint engine noise filled his ears, bringing to mind the cat, so he felt around for fur, first on top of what felt like a duvet, then beneath it. What he came across, though, was flesh: soft . . . round . . . human . . . almost certainly female. He jerked his hand away and lay for a while, staring at where the ceiling should be, while beside him the owner of the flesh purred loudly, or maybe snored quietly. Somewhere between the two. Jojo, he reminded himself. Neighbour. Very friendly. One whose hospitality, in fact, stretched to unusual lengths.

Oh Christ, he thought. Big mistake. He really wasn't in the habit of bedding people he hardly knew. Not these days, anyway. Was he coerced? And how come they'd got through so much alcohol? Did she have a drink problem? But more importantly, where was the bathroom? As his eyes began to adjust, Marcus could make out a fireplace, a cupboard or wardrobe and, thank God, a door. After gently peeling the duvet away from his body, he eased himself up and tiptoed across the room, hoping, since he was quite naked, that Jojo's students didn't rise too early on Saturdays. Outside, he found the bathroom door ajar and hurried in, gathering from the total silence in the house that no one else was up.

Back in the bedroom, down on hands and knees, he groped around for his clothes. How rude would it be to go home? He could leave Jojo a note saying he'd had to feed the cat and didn't want to wake her. Yes, that was what he'd do. She was still snoring – rather endearingly – and Marcus guessed she'd be out of it for a while. He dressed in the bathroom and crept down the stairs. It was only at the bottom, when he was slipping his shoes on, that he heard the radio.

'Good morning,' sang a cheery voice in the distance.

Marcus looked down the hallway and saw a perfectly groomed Japanese girl holding a teapot aloft. 'Would you like?' she asked, while he tried to remember her name.

'Um . . . yeah, why not?' He needed to find pen and paper, anyway. 'Thanks.'

Someone was playing old sixties numbers on the radio, Jojo's student was grilling bacon and whisking eggs, and Marcus was gradually sliding an airmail envelope towards him to read the name of the addressee. Keiko, that was it. He pushed the letter back across the table just as she came forward and dolloped the contents of the saucepan on his plate.

'Aren't you having any, Keiko?' he asked.

'Yes,' she said, scraping the last teaspoonful on to her own plate.

Marcus then received two rashers of bacon and helped himself to the toast done especially for him. 'Do you always make your own breakfast?'

'Only sometimes. Mostly when Bram stays here for night with Jo.'

'Bram?'

'Yes.'

'No, I mean, who *is* Bram?'

'Ah. He is part-time Dutch boyfriend.'

'Oh, right.' Marcus tried to work out if Jojo having a bloke was good or bad news. 'Why is he only part-time?'

Keiko swallowed a milligram of egg. 'He is sometimes away long time with job.'

'Oh? What does he do?'

'He is . . .' She put her fork down and picked up a notebook with Marge Simpson on the front, then thumbed through it. 'Ah, yes. Eco-warrior.'

'Really?' Marcus pictured a crusty with nose rings and a mohican. Jojo was still an unknown quantity; who knew what sort she went for?

While he worked his way through breakfast, he took a look around to get some clues as to who she was.

Everything was pretty tidy and clean and nicely painted. The house, he realised, was quite a bit smaller than his – he was thinking of it as *his* already – much narrower, definitely. Which explained why number 15 was opposite number 8, the houses on his side of the street all being larger. Jojo's kitchen was obviously part of an extension, with French windows overlooking a cheerful little walled garden, full of red and yellow tulips. Her modern table and chairs all matched and an old Welsh dresser had its shelves prettily lined with crockery and knick-knacks. Whatever else Jo was – seductress extraordinaire, lush – she wasn't sloppy around the house. The only messy thing in the room was a cork board covered in postcards. Many from Bram, no doubt. *Having a lovely time chained to Alaskan test-drill equipment. Weather nippy!*

Marcus asked, 'So is she Jo or Jojo?'

'Jo.'

'Oh.'

'But really Josephine.'

'Nice.' Marcus chewed on. 'Good eggs,' he told Keiko, and she thanked him for the compliment, then thanked him again. Once he'd finished and knocked back his tea, he borrowed a pencil, scribbled a note for 'Jo' on the back of an envelope and propped it against the toaster. He thanked Keiko for breakfast and, after a good hunt for them, left without his coat and hat.

* * *

'Hi, it's Marcus,' he said, holding his breath. Before phoning, he'd got the central heating going, soaked in a cast-iron bath that could take four more people, and fed the cat in a fresh bowl with 'Maidstone' written on it, so clearing up one puzzle.

'Oh,' Hannah said, rather flatly he felt. 'Hello.'

'How's things?'

'Fine.'

'And Freddie?'

'He's fine too.'

'Good,' said Marcus, raising his voice above the background noise. It sounded as though they were having building work done.

'And you?' she asked. 'I heard parts of Scotland are snowed in. Unusual for late March, I thought.'

'Actually, I'm not in Scotland.'

'No? Fred, don't do that to the cupboard, sweetie.'

Since when had he become Fred? 'I'm in Oxford,' he told her.

'Give the nail to Mummy, there's a good boy. And the hammer.'

Had she heard him? 'House-sitting in Jubilee Street.'

'Thank you, darling.'

'For three weeks.'

A silence followed and Marcus wasn't sure if she'd wandered off. 'Are you telling me,' she said, a small wobble in her voice, 'that you're two streets away?'

''Fraid so.'

23

'But how come? And why?'

'Well, the "how come" is I searched on the Internet for a house-sit in the Oxford area and found one. And the "why" is because I'd like to see Freddie.' And you, he wanted to add.

'Jesus,' she said. Then after a pause: 'What number?'

'Sorry?'

'Jubilee Street.'

'Oh, eight.'

'*What?*' she practically shrieked. 'Lucy and *Dom's?*'

'You *know* them?' he practically shrieked back.

'Yes, very well. I met them through Robin's friend, Jo. She lives op—'

'I know,' he said, wondering if he could have got off to a worse start. There he'd been, thinking he could quietly slip into Oxford for a few weeks and spend time with the little boy he'd thought was his son for two and a half years. Instead, he was in the house of some good friends of Hannah's, having shagged another one. Well, maybe he had. It was all a bit foggy.

'That's great,' she said unconvincingly. 'You must come round, but not just yet. Robin's gone back to bed. He was up early doing some carpentry with Fred and his new tools.'

'Right.' Hannah was still short in the sensitivity department, then. Didn't she remember how Marcus loved those early-morning sessions with Freddie? They'd watch *Teletubbies* videos and work their way through picture books, Freddie chewing messily on his Marmite soldiers. But how quickly they grow and change. Now Freddie and his real father were knocking up coffee tables at dawn. Well, Marcus thought, deciding not to be churlish, how nice that he had a proper DIY daddy.

Hannah tutted. 'Of course, Robin doesn't know a chisel from a wing nut. Look, I'll need to prepare Freddie rather than have you turn up out of the blue. It's been rather a shock for *me*, so . . .'

'That's OK. I'll come round later. I'm still settling myself in here. What do these people do, by the way?'

'Lucy and Dom? They're both graphic designers, doing brochures and marketing and that kind of thing, sometimes for quite big firms. They set up a business about five years ago with a couple of geeky guys who do all the website and software stuff. Anyway, it seems to have really taken off.'

'So I see.'

'It's a nice house, isn't it? Mind you, they deserve it. They're total workaholics, but every now and then they go off on a bit of a retreat.'

'Right.' That explained the mobile phones left up in the office. 'So how's your job going?' he asked.

'Oh, Christ, it's exhausting. I travel twenty miles to work each day, only to be given grief by these hormonal kids who don't want to speak French and wouldn't go to France if you paid them.' She attempted a laugh. 'It's hell.'

Marcus wondered if it was really that bad. He'd never known Hannah have a job she didn't moan about. 'Sounds awful.'

'Yes.'

'So, when shall I come round?'

'I don't know. Fourish? Fred sometimes still naps early afternoon. You know, I can't believe you're in Lucy and Dom's house. That's so weird. They said they were going away soon and might get a sitter. Sometimes I feed Maidstone, but he gets lonely if they're away more than a few days.'

'Right.' How tight Hannah was with them. 'Anyway,' he said, 'I'll see you around four.'

'Look forward to it.'

'Me too,' said Marcus, hanging up, then flopping against the wall, heart thumping. That could have gone worse.

I think I can recall . . .

Mary had a little lamb, its fleece . . . Marcus, just round the corner. Oh God. Everywhere that Mary went . . .

I think I can recall . . .

Dear Adrian . . . no, I'm not going to address this to my therapist. After all, I talk to him for a full fifty minutes every week. And what's more, he addresses almost nothing to me. No, I'll address it to myself. Or to whoever comes across it in the future

*and manages to break open the lock — not Freddie,
I hope.*

*Anyway, I think I can recall the exact moment I
knew for sure. It was when I collected the photos of
Freddie's second birthday party. I went through them
in the street and saw that one of me, Marcus and
Freddie, just as Fred was blowing out his two candles.
Fred with his thick dark curly hair. And those lips.
Very full, rosy lips. Robin's lips. There were signs, even
then, of a burgeoning nose. One that might one day
be the size of Robin's. Plus the heavy-lidded brown
eyes. Robin's best feature — still sparkling in his mid-
forties. Marcus's eyes are blue, mine hazel. Yes, it was
then. That photo. I stood staring at it outside the
chemist's — Freddie looking so unlike either of us, a
stranger would think he was adopted.*

*Ooch, he's so like his Great-uncle Robert, Marcus's
mother would often comment, reassuring everyone —
except me, of course — as Freddie entered his terrible-
two period. Eyes like polished chestnuts, she'd say. Just
like Robert's.*

*I knew I'd have to tell Marcus one day, but it never
seemed to be the right day or the right moment to
completely shatter his world. Our world.*

Apples, butter, bleach, jam. Silver foil, sausages

*But then, after months of guilt-ridden agonising
on my part, Marcus asked me if Freddie was his.
We were halfway up Lochnagar at the time —*

Marcus's second attempt at it and my first. I don't think so, I told him, and he went up the mountain and I went down and nothing was ever the same again. Prince Charles may love Lochnagar, but it's my least favourite place in the world – aside from the godawful school I work in, of course.

Four o'clock? I definitely can't wait that long.

Jo couldn't believe she'd slept till gone twelve. There were other things she couldn't believe she'd done either, like screwing a complete stranger.

'Shit,' she said, stepping into the shower. 'Shit, shit, shit.' And what's more it was someone she'd hardly be able to avoid for the next three weeks. Not unless she just stayed in the house. No, that was impossible. God, she was hungover. Not used to drinking, that was the problem.

But then she realised that staying home *was* feasible. The supermarkets could deliver everything the three of them needed, and she'd post her clients' work back to them instead of meeting up in a café to discuss the changes she'd made. Of course, she'd miss that human contact. It stopped her turning into another Len round the corner, who made exquisite leather goods in his basement all day but had completely lost the art of conversation.

Jo dried herself and dressed gingerly, every movement making her feel queasy, then, with a towel wrapped around her head, went down to the kitchen and found

Ernst reading a newspaper behind the congealed remains of a fry-up.

'Good afternoon!' he bellowed, and Jo's palms flew to her ears. He lowered his paper and grinned at her as she tried hard not to look at his plate. 'I think maybe you are . . . let me remember . . . pissed as a newt?'

She shook her head – ouch – and switched the kettle on. 'That was last night, Ernst. Now I have a terrible hangover. You know "hangover"?'

'Ah, yes. This we were also discussing with Jeremy in the Eagle and Child.' He folded the newspaper, very neatly, and placed it on the table. 'One moment,' he said, getting up and heading for the door. 'I will find you a . . . oh, what is the word?'

'Mm?'

He stopped and turned back. 'Do you have scissors?'

'Er, yeah.' She took some from a drawer and handed them over.

'One moment,' he said again and disappeared, not upstairs but through the front door, which he left open.

When it became too cold for comfort, Jo slid herself sideways along the hall wall so that Marcus wouldn't see her from his living room. Then, with a foot, she hooked the door towards her, put it on the latch and shut it with a sigh. This would be no way to live for three weeks.

Just as she was taking her first reviving sip of tea, Ernst charged back in and said, 'Here!' holding out a closed fist. 'It is the hairs of a cat.'

'Sorry?'

'Our teacher has taught us that in Britain the very best thing for hanging over is the hairs of a dog. But in Jubilee Street I think there are no dogs, and, besides, what can be the difference?' He put the scissors down and tipped a clump of cat fur, looking horribly like Maidstone's, into her palm. 'Don't worry, Marcus gave me permission.'

'What,' she began, very afraid to ask, 'did you tell him?'

'That you are needing some animal hairs for medicine. But I didn't tell him you were hanging—'

'*Hungover*, Ernst.'

'Ah yes, hungover. Because I am a gentleman.' He beamed at her and bowed from the waist.

'Thanks, but actually I wish you had explained what you were doing.' She looked down at the little mound of Maidstone. 'And he said?'

'Nothing. Just "Hello" and then one nod when I asked permission, and then maybe a kind of strange face, and then "Bye".'

Jo took all this in. She wasn't planning on seeing any more of Marcus, so did it really matter? He'd gone off without saying goodbye or leaving her a note or anything, which was rather *un*gentlemanly. 'Ernst,' she said, 'that was very thoughtful of you, thank you. But I think you took your teacher too literally. Now why don't you sit down and I'll explain "hair of the dog" properly. Yeah?'

When she'd finished and Ernst was looking suitably embarrassed, he jumped up and dashed across the kitchen. 'In that case you must have some wine.'

'Oh no, I couldn't poss—'

'But you must,' he persisted. He placed a disgusting-smelling half-glass of red in her hand, and the bottle on the table. 'Hair of the dog, yes?'

Jo was on the verge of retching when the doorbell sounded.

'I will go,' announced Ernst, and he did, returning seconds later with Marcus in tow.

'Hi,' said Marcus. He was looking remarkably well, considering. Remarkably attractive too. How silly of her to think she needed to hide from him. She wanted to unwrap her head but wasn't sure what horrors lay beneath the towel. She did, however, casually remove her glasses.

Marcus cleared his throat. 'I was just wondering if . . .' His voice trailed off as he took in the scene, then his eyes darted to the wall clock and back. 'If I could, um, have my coat? And hat? It's just that I have to go out later.'

With all the dignity she could muster, Jo put the wine glass down and said, 'Of course. Sorry.' She'd get in touch with the school on Monday and ask for Ernst to be repatriated. 'I think they're in the middle room.'

After he left, hurriedly, Jo decided it probably wasn't going to be her day, so took a deep breath, knocked back the hair of the dog, dried her own hair and returned to bed. She took Ernst's tabloid with her, and although tales of celebrity humiliation and degradation helped a bit, she couldn't help thinking she should let Marcus know, somehow, that she wasn't the trollop of Jubilee Street – up for it with any Tom, Dick or housesitter that came along. It was so unfair, she felt, when the whole world knew it was Pippa who held that crown.

As he was scooping a dead fish out of the tank, Marcus heard the doorbell and hoped it wasn't Ernst again, sent by his landlady for bits of fingernail or eye of goldfish. How he'd managed to get involved with an alcoholic white witch within hours of arriving, he'd never know. He dropped the fish in a plastic bag, praying it wasn't going to be the first of many corpses, and was still carrying it when he opened the front door and found Hannah and Freddie there.

'Hello,' Hannah said, nose pink with the cold, face half wrapped in a blue scarf that matched her eyes and complemented her long grey coat. Marcus looked down at an equally well-turned-out Freddie, then back at Hannah, and found himself shocked; not just by their sudden appearance on his doorstep or by how big Freddie had become, but by something in Hannah's eyes. A sadness or hollowness, or something.

'Hi,' he managed. 'What a nice surprise. Hello, Freddie.'

'Hello,' said the little boy, staring at him blankly.

The thing Marcus had been dreading – Freddie having

completely forgotten him – seemed to be happening. He did so want to bend down, pick the little boy up and give him a kiss, but instead he pointed at the large blue box in Freddie's gloved hand and said, 'What's that you're carrying?'

'My tools.'

'Oh, yes?'

Hannah said, 'He takes them everywhere. Anyway, we were just round the corner at the swings, so I thought—'

'Yeah, yeah. Come in. Great.'

'Thanks,' she said, and they stepped into the hallway. 'Gosh, it's lovely and warm in here.'

'Where's Lucy?' asked Freddie, looking confused.

That was it, decided Marcus. Freddie hadn't forgotten him; he was just having a problem with context. 'Lucy's gone away for a while, so's Dom.'

'Marcus is looking after the house for them,' said Hannah. She was staring at the bag dripping water in Marcus's hand.

'Dead fish,' he explained.

'Going to see the fish,' said Freddie, waddling off in his big outdoor kit, box still in hand.

When Hannah was taking her coat off and hanging it on the newel post, Marcus noticed that her brown hair was different somehow. Lighter? A touch longer? Nice, anyway. She might also have lost some weight. Not that there was much to lose. 'A wee slip of a thing' his mother used to call her, before she started calling her stronger things. Hannah was in a long skirt with a deep pink jumper that exactly matched her lipstick. Round her neck was an attractive silver necklace, and on her feet were expensive-looking black boots with a bit of a heel. He could smell that D & G perfume she liked so. What an effort she'd made for a walk to the swings.

She turned and smiled, and his insides did a spin. 'Some housesitter you are,' she said, nodding at the bag.

'You're looking very well,' she told him over Lucy and Dom's banquet-length kitchen table.

The boozy night had, he thought, left him looking unwell, but he thanked her anyway.

'Although a bit tired?' she added.

'It was a long drive down yesterday.'

'Must have been,' she said, one hand fiddling with a cork coaster, the other stirring her coffee. 'All on your own. I expect you made lots of stops?' Marcus nodded, then Hannah dropped the coaster and looked directly at him. 'How's your mother?' she asked.

'Fine. As energetic as ever.'

'I'm guessing she didn't send me her regards?'

'Mm? Oh, yeah. Yes, she did.'

'Liar.'

He shrugged and they took simultaneous sips at their coffees. Marcus then gestured to where Freddie was trying to unscrew the leg of a wooden footstool, his little face contorted with effort and concentration. The thing was beginning to wobble. Either the screws were already loose or Freddie had remarkable strength for a three year old. 'I'm not sure he remembers me,' Marcus said.

'Oh, he does,' said Hannah. 'We've just been talking about you. It's only been six months, after all.'

'Nine.'

'OK, nine. But still . . .'

'A fifth of his life.'

'Well, when you put it like that. Anyway, he does remember you, and the restaurant. How's business, by the way?'

'Not bad. Quiet at the moment, of course. Pre-Easter. Mum's running the show with help from my brothers. They *did* say to say hi to you.'

'Yes?' she said, a catch in her voice. 'Well, that's something.' Marcus saw her eyes flicker, and before she could get emotional and maybe vindictive – one of her less attractive traits – he turned his attention to Freddie and asked if he'd like some juice.

'Yes!'

'Yes, *please*,' Marcus corrected him. 'Sorry,' he said to Hannah. Her eyes were definitely filling up. 'Force of habit.'

'That's OK, he needs to be told.'

Marcus got up and went to the fridge. 'Come and choose what you want, Freddie. I've got . . . let me see . . . cranberry juice, orange juice, apple—'

'Apple!'

'Please.'

'*Pleeeze,*' said Freddie with that cheeky, full-lipped grin of his.

'OK, let's—'

'I just miss you,' Hannah suddenly wailed, '*so* much.'

Marcus's hand rested momentarily on the apple juice carton while he took in what he was hearing. He pulled it from the fridge door, poured some into a mug for Freddie, made sure Freddie was holding it properly, then sat on the chair beside Hannah and drew her towards him. 'Me too,' he said. 'Oh, me too.'

'Yeah?'

'Why do you think I'm *here?*'

She shuddered in his arms and mumbled something into his shirt.

'Sorry?' he asked.

She lifted her head. 'I said, what a horrible mess.'

He kissed her forehead – the only dry part of her face – and squeezed her harder, while Freddie looked on over the top of his mug. 'I know.'

When the phone rang, Marcus decided to let the machine pick up. Since arriving he'd had lots of calls for Lucy and Dom and only two for himself, from his mother.

'You wouldn't believe how much I've missed you two,' he whispered. The good times, anyway. Hannah rubbed a damp cheek against his, and when Freddie climbed on both their laps, the three of them went into a communal hug.

As he listened to Dom's pre-recorded message, Marcus felt close to blubbing too. He hadn't been expecting an emotional reunion. Just the opposite, knowing Hannah: forced and frosty, even. Jesus, what a nightmare all this was. A stupid situation they'd each brought about in their own ways: Hannah with her incomprehensible fling with Robin, and he by withdrawing emotionally when the truth came out about Freddie. Then Hannah, feeling frozen out by Marcus and his family, running to the safety of the newly divorced Robin. Marcus not following her and begging her to come back . . .

'What have I done?' Hannah was asking him.

'It wasn't just you, you know that. I was a total wanker for months.'

'*Lan*guage,' she said, managing a giggle.

'Oops, sorry. Cover your ears, Freddie.'

'Anyway,' Hannah said, 'you being a total W was understandable.' She looked up and settled her watery eyes on his. 'I still have such strong feelings for you, you know.'

Beep went the machine. 'Hi, Marcus,' they heard in their little human cluster, and Marcus froze. 'It's Jo. Listen, about last night, as they say. I, er, think it was a mistake, don't you? And it's certainly not the kind of thing I do, you know, often. I mean ever, really. I . . . um, look, if you want to talk about it some time, I'm here. Not that you probably do, only maybe I do . . . so . . . oh shit, this isn't coming out right.'

Click went the machine, and for a while no one moved. Not until the leg dropped off the footstool and made them all jump.

Robin woke from his nap to an empty house and a note telling him Hannah and Freddie had gone to the park. He made a pot of coffee and took a shower, then settled down in his office with *American Beauty: the benefits of US foreign policy for a fucked up world*, which wasn't quite the title he and young Bridget had settled on in their tutorial. Without thinking, he put a hyphen between the *fucked* and the *up*, then shook his head. What was he doing? He scored through the offending words and scribbled 'unstable?' as an alternative, then braced himself for a eulogy on the United States.

How often this happened. They'd arrive at university in Oxford – albeit not *the* Oxford University – intelligent and articulate but with a wonderful blankness about them, keen to absorb the informed and clearly *correct* views of their lecturers. Then, two years later, they'd go into rebellious mode: Thatcher prevented Britain becoming a Third World country run by the unions; Kissinger saved the planet from nasty old Communism, and so on.

Robin couldn't help thinking that he, Patricia, Bill and the others were going about things the wrong way, and had said as much in meetings. He himself had taken steps to temper his criticism of right-wing, imperialist actions and philosophies, but for a dyed-in-the-wool type such as Bill, that would have been on a par with rolling up at work in a mini-skirt.

Yes, Robin thought, flicking through pages fairly quickly, it was the usual stuff: 'Without US help these poorer countries wouldn't have made progress. Their impoverished inhabitants would still be living barbaric, archaic, superstition-filled lives, instead of watching satellite TV, phoning friends on mobiles and eating wholesome Western food . . .' Robin underlined 'wholesome' and wrote 'Debatable?' above it.

'Daddy!' he suddenly heard behind him, and with some relief put Bridget's work to one side.

'Hi, Freddie. Didn't know you were back. Let's get you out of your spacesuit, shall we? Did you have a nice time? Where did you go?'

Freddie put his toolbox down and came over to him. 'We went to the swings, then we seed my uvver daddy and Mummy cried.'

'Oh, yes?' asked Robin, wondering if he'd misheard.

'My uvver daddy killed a fish.'

'Uh-huh? Now, pull your arm out. That's it.' Hannah had probably been recounting some past event to Freddie. Keeping memories of Marcus alive, or something. 'Now the other one, there's a good boy.'

'And then he kissed Mummy and made her stop crying.'

'Oh, good.' Robin wasn't surprised to hear Hannah had been crying over a fish Marcus had caught, since she was totally soppy about animals. He'd never been sure she felt the same way about humans, though. Particularly the ones she taught. 'OK, Freddie, all done.'

'But best of all was when the leg falled off the stool. Which I done.'

Robin put Bridget's part-dissertation back in the pile he'd have to wade through over the weekend, then turned to his son, who'd opened his toolbox in the middle of the study floor and was rummaging through and humming to himself. Robin smiled. Although he some-times suspected Freddie had an obsessive nature, it was actually quite endearing in a three year old, and maybe not that unusual. He thought back to Theo at that age, listening to *Jack and the Beanstalk*, over and over, on his Fisher Price cassette player.

'What stool?' he asked, putting the tedious marking out of his head. But his question was drowned out by Freddie, nailing – for reasons known only to himself – one small strip of wood to another.

SUNDAY

Major cock-up, decided Marcus. He stretched himself out in the colossal bath, head back, ears underwater, and contemplated going home. If only he'd found a B and B instead of a house-sit, his first meeting with Hannah might not have ended with her spitting, 'This is some kind of revenge, is it?' – and his 'No, of course not!' being met with a slamming of the front door. How quickly she'd turned from loving and remorseful to dry-eyed and furious. But why would that surprise him? He'd just forgotten, that was all, how Hannah's mood could turn on the slightest of things.

Should he write her a note? Phoning could be scary. He might get Robin. Not that Robin was in any way scary, apparently. 'An absolute pussycat,' Hannah had once described him as, tactful as ever.

Marcus pinched his nose and went right under the water for a while, then surfaced for air. However much of a pussycat Robin was, Hannah didn't seem that contented. But then, for the length of their relationship, Marcus always felt he hadn't quite come up to scratch either. Contentment wasn't a state that came naturally to Hannah.

No, he wouldn't write a note. He'd just go round to their house. Today. Meet this Robin bloke at last. Be affable. Play at DIY with Freddie. Explain to Hannah, in a quiet corner somewhere, that there was nothing going on with Jo. That he suspected she had a screw or two loose, and had no idea what her crazy answerphone message was about. Yes, he'd do that. No point in giving up and going home now. Not with a bath this size to wallow in and all that food they'd left. Besides, he'd be letting Maidstone down.

The man who answered the door was like Freddie, but around six foot two. Same eyes, mouth and colouring. He was dressed in a denim shirt that had seen better days, and green corduroy trousers that had seen them even longer ago. He looked well into his forties and his hair was thick, dark, wavy and on the long side.

'Robin?' asked Marcus.

'Yes.'

'I'm—'

'Marcus?'

'Yes.'

'I've seen photos,' Robin said with a disturbingly

pleasant smile. 'Hannah told me you were in town. I'm afraid they're out, but do come in.'

'Thanks,' said Marcus, feeling this was all wrong. Shouldn't he be bopping this bloke on the nose? 'Nice house.'

'Thanks. A bit untidy, I'm afraid. Having a toddler can be—'

'I know.'

'Yes, of course. Sorry.'

Marcus was led through to the living room, where Robin removed toys from the sofa, then offered it to Marcus. 'Can I get you anything?' he asked. 'Beer, coffee?'

'No, I'm OK. Thanks.' With no Hannah or Freddie there, Marcus didn't intend to stay long.

'They're at a birthday party,' said Robin. 'Only just left, unfortunately.'

'Ah. Bad timing.' Marcus sank back in the cushions and looked around the room. There were photos on every surface and some on the walls. Hannah and Freddie. Robin and Freddie. Freddie on his own. There were lots of those. One picture was of all three of them wearing party hats. Christmas? Hannah was grinning broadly and looking beautiful, but there were those lifeless eyes again. Some photos were of a dark-haired, good-looking boy at different ages. Robin's other son, most likely.

'Good one of you over there,' said Robin, pointing.

So there was. He had a very young Freddie – six months? – on his back in a kiddie carrier. He remembered it well.

They'd been taking a walk round Loch Muick. It had been a great day out, ruined in the end by some casual remark he'd made about Hannah finding a job to help out until the restaurant got itself re-established. His uncle had let the place slide before his death and there'd been some costly refurbishing to do, then advertising and so on. She'd stormed ahead to the car and not spoken on the journey home.

'Are you sure you wouldn't like something?' Robin was asking. 'Lager?'

Would it be rude to refuse a second time? Marcus actually fancied a cup of tea, but did men do that together? 'Go on then,' he said, and while Robin was out of the room, he soaked up its cosy, slightly shambolic family atmosphere. Freddie must be happy here, he thought, even if his mother wasn't. Marcus's eyes scanned the CDs, spotting Hannah's favourites – Norah Jones, Dixie Chicks – slotted amongst what must have been Robin's – Bach, Pink Floyd, John Coltrane, Dvorak, Bob the Builder – Freddie's, hopefully.

'I'm really sorry,' Robin was saying. He handed Marcus a glass of beer, then took a seat opposite with his own.

'What for?'

'You know.'

'Oh. Right.'

'I didn't know at the time. About you.'

'No?'

'No.'

'I see,' said Marcus. He tapped at his glass, then took a long swig, hoping they weren't about to embark on a character assassination of Hannah, but suspecting Robin might not have the nature for it anyway. They could talk about Freddie, he thought, but that could be dangerous territory too. The room was very quiet.

'Any idea how the rugby's going?' he asked eventually.

'No, I haven't,' Robin said a little too brightly. He quickly reached for the remote. 'Let's find out, shall we?'

MONDAY

'Dear Jo, Thank you for a lovely evening' said the note she found beneath the toaster at nine o'clock Monday morning when she was giving the worktops a clean. 'Sorry for dashing off like this but must feed cat! See you later today, I hope. Love, Marcus.'

Jo slumped on to a kitchen chair in her usual morning gear: pyjamas, man's checked woollen dressing gown, socks, trainers and a long striped scarf wound twice round her neck. She tried not to use the heating during the day, so switched it off the moment the students left and, after a general tidy-up, worked in her bag-lady outfit until lunch and a hot bath. When it got really cold, as it had today, she added a back-to-front baseball cap.

'Bugger,' she said quietly. How she wished she hadn't left him that message. So insulting compared to this one he'd left her. No wonder she hadn't heard back from him. She'd have to go and see him; explain about the cat fur,

46

and the midday boozing and not finding his note. She'd have a quick shower, put her contacts in and nip across the road in time for elevenses. Everything could be sorted out by lunchtime, and then, well, who knew what path fate might take them down? Perhaps he could come and house-sit for her next? The only difference being she wouldn't go anywhere.

When the postman's jolly 'ring, ring-ring' brought her out of her fantasy, Jo clopped down the hall in her unlaced trainers to take whatever large package had arrived for proofing, but then stopped dead. What if it was Marcus? She couldn't be seen like this! The postman was used to it, but anyone else would reel back in horror. After the brass knocker gave several urgent raps, Jo crept to her living room-cum-office bay window, hooked the lace curtain to one side and saw the postman filling out one of his I-tried-to-deliver notes. She dashed back to the hall, opened the door and apologised, grateful that he was a very big man in a very big postman's jacket and completely hid her from view.

'I just wanted to explain about the cat-hair thing,' she said. He was staring at the kitchen table and chewing a finger. 'Marcus?'

'Mm?'

'I said . . . Oh, never mind. Are you all right?'

'Do you know who I am?' he asked, raising his eyes to hers.

Now it was Jo's turn to stare while she considered his question. He was famous and she hadn't recognised him? Was he a notorious ex-con, or the Duke of somewhere? She shook her head.

'Hannah's husband,' he said.

Robin's new partner? Jo didn't know another Hannah. 'Freddie's mum?' she asked.

He nodded. 'I expect Hannah's told you about the whole her, me, Freddie and Robin business?'

No, she hadn't, and neither had Robin. Hannah and Freddie had just sort of appeared. Moved in with Robin after his marriage broke up. Freddie was clearly his son, but Jo had never asked any questions. Robin had been an acquaintance, bordering on friend, for years – she was once his student and he now passed work her way – but Hannah she'd first met properly when she, Jo, had thrown a party the previous summer. Hannah had formed quite a friendship with Lucy over the road, so Jo occasionally came across her, but they hadn't exactly become bosom buddies.

'A little,' she told Marcus, hoping he'd feel it OK to expand.

Which he did.

'Crikey,' she said when he'd finished.

'And *then*,' he said, not quite finished, '*just* when Hannah and I were about to declare our undying love for each other, you piped up on the answerphone with your about-last-night message. Hannah left soon after that, twice as upset. She was still a bit frosty when I rang yesterday evening. I reassured her you and I weren't . . . By the way, did we actually . . . ?'

'I'm not sure, to be honest. I found a thingy, you know, still in its packet, which was kind of half ripped open. So I guess we didn't. *Hope* we didn't. Me getting pregnant would hardly help!'

'Might balance things, though?'

'True,' she said, grinning. 'But I'm too poor to have a child, sorry.'

Marcus laughed. 'Maybe Robin would take you in.'

'Actually, he's such a nice guy, he probably would. Oh, sorry. I don't suppose you want to hear that.'

'No, it's all right. I know he's a nice guy, that's what's making this all so difficult.' Marcus stared at the table again for a while before seeming to blink himself out of his gloom. 'God, how remiss of me,' he said with the trace of a smile. 'It's almost noon and I haven't offered you any alcohol. You must be gasping?'

Jo was back at work by two, sober and learning more than she'd ever need to know about limited liability insurance for foot passengers on Russian ferries. It didn't make sense, she kept thinking, about both Sergei's work and Hannah's behaviour. She tried to imagine what she might have done in that situation. Moved in with the real father even though she didn't love him? No, never. Jo had sensed something not quite right between Robin and Hannah at the party she'd thrown. Some couples gel – pass each other knowing little looks and eyebrow bobs in company, occasionally touch – while other couples . . . well, they were like Hannah and Robin. Almost formal. Perhaps they hadn't known each other that well when Hannah landed on his doorstep. Crazy. Still, it must have been tempting for Hannah. Nice man, nice house . . . No, Jo couldn't decide what she would have done in the circumstances, she just felt pleased she wasn't Hannah. As she checked through Sergei's table: 'Compensation Amounts Paying Compulsory by Insurers of River and Sea Companies of Ferry Boats for Foot Passengers Who are Losing One or More Limb in Accident' – a table that was shorter than its title – she decided she might, in fact, have stuck it out with Marcus and his family in Scotland; maybe had another baby with him. She also decided it might be worth taking a trip on an ill-fated Russian ferry, since the compensation figures looked astronomical. In roubles, anyway.

My parents were stunned by, rather than disapproving of, their daughter getting married in a Presbyterian kirk. Neither of them had ever been church-goers, so they doubtless assumed I'd do what they did – ten minutes in the registry office and an off-the-peg reception.

We all stayed in the castle-cum-hotel where the reception was to be held, and when Mum caught me throwing up in the morning and said that she too had been a bag of nerves on her wedding day, I told her I wasn't nervous, just pregnant. And while she stared at me before saying anything, I imagined the mixed feelings going through her head. Excitement at the prospect of a first grandchild, but distress at how far away it would be. Disappointment too, in that I'd only just finished my PGCE in Oxford and, after years and years of miserable office work, I could have started a real career teaching French.

That's fantastic, love, she said, suddenly hugging me. Marcus must be thrilled.

We're hoping to keep it a secret till after the wedding, I told her (it was a lie, Marcus didn't know). So don't say anything, I begged her. Not even to Dad.

Later, walking down the aisle in that ludicrous dress, amidst all the happy faces, then seeing my adoring and much-loved bridegroom waiting for me, I felt certain fate wouldn't be so cruel as to make the baby Robin's.

Little Jack Horner sat in the corner . . .

How fantastic Marcus looked on Saturday, and how very Marcus-like he still is. Funny, slightly diffident, caring (up to a point). I hadn't planned to sob like that, or had I? I've certainly played out the repentant, heart-broken, please-forgive-me scene in my head many times, but have never had it interrupted by a call from one of Marcus's girlfriends. No matter how much he assured me over the phone last night that nothing's happened between him and Jo, I can't help a sudden intense dislike of her.

Shit, ten to one already. God, I want to go home.

As Marcus was setting off for a late-afternoon stroll into town, he saw a woman steer her Ford Ka nose-first into a small parking space that any thinking person would have reversed into. Many a time he'd had to gag himself while his mother did this very same thing. It was always painful to witness: those endless forward and backward movements that were never going to resolve the situation.

Yes, back and forth the Ka went and, as excruciating as it was, Marcus felt transfixed. Sometimes, miraculously, these forward-parkers managed it. The woman, who looked somewhere in the thirty-to-fifty spectrum, made an embarrassed face at him when she saw he was watching. Once again she went forward a couple of inches, then reversed a couple of inches, but ended up where she'd started, more or less diagonal. Marcus politely looked away, flung his scarf over one shoulder and strode purposefully along the pavement, past the manoeuvring car.

'Excuse me?' a voice called out to him.

He turned and saw a flawless, faintly orange face protruding from the nearside window. 'You couldn't help me out here, could you? Always been hopeless at parking in small spaces.'

'Sure.'

The woman got out and walked the quarter-mile to the kerb. 'Sorry,' she said, throwing her hands up, and Marcus slid into the driver's seat.

'You trust me not to drive off with it, then?' he asked with a grin, before shutting the door and finding himself cocooned in perfume and listening to Mick Hucknall. After a few nifty moves, the car was as snug as a bug, right beside the kerb. 'There,' he said, getting out and handing the owner her keys, trying not to look cocky.

'Thanks ever so,' she said, slowly undoing the buttons of her suit jacket. She was dressed for the office but came across as more beautician than secretary: a heavy make-up job, shoulder-length very blonde hair and pointed shoes. 'I'm Pippa, by the way.' She gave his hand a lingering shake. 'You're house-sitting, aren't you?'

'Yes,' he said, when she finally let go. 'I'm Marcus. Marcus Currie.'

'Marcus. Great name.'

'Is it?'

'Mm, very strong. Listen, I'm at number seven,' she pointed at a house with a nasty glass porch, 'if you need anything.'

'Oh, right. Thank you.'

Her hand slipped into her shoulder bag and pulled something out. 'I don't know if you like massages?'

Marcus's mouth opened but was unable to form a response. What was it about Jubilee Street, he wondered.

Oestrogen in the water? He took the card being proffered and saw that she was, in fact, a qualified masseuse
with letters after her name; just a businesswoman
promoting a professional service. 'Thanks,' he said,
smiling. 'I've always found massages very therapeutic.'

'I'm at Top to Toe during the day,' she informed him
with a twiddle of her hair. She was quite attractive, he
realised, with a very full bottom lip that gave her an
alluring pout. Her eyes were enormous, although that
could have been the mascara. 'But am more than happy
to do a bit of extra-curricular at night,' she added. Her
voice was husky and peppered with South London
vowels, and managed to make 'curricular' sound pretty
exciting.

Marcus rubbed his chin and pretended to read the
card again. Once more he was confused and, in addition, he suddenly remembered Lucy and Dom's note.

'I think I should warn you I'm an arachnophobe,' he
said. It was all he could think of.

Jo had witnessed the whole thing, her lace curtains having
come down, for good, two hours before.

'Pathetic,' she whispered after Marcus and Pippa
parted. In a parallel-parking competition, Pippa would
beat her husband, and everyone else's, hands down.
What, she wondered, made a woman so desperate as to
pull a stunt like that?

The answer to Jo's question then appeared. Ray.

Overweight and underexercised, messy-haired and care-lessly dressed. He plodded across the road with his usual duck-like gait, spat on the pavement and got into the white van that was a throwback from his failed cowboy-builder days. Ray would return from the car factory in the morning, just before Pippa left for the salon. It was a perfect arrangement for the couple, once childhood sweethearts but now the Charles and Diana of Jubilee Street. They had a student daughter, Sasha, who still came home for all the holidays. Pippa said that, for the sake of convenience, she'd wait for Sasha to graduate before leaving her husband.

Although Pippa was incredibly energetic, Ray lay at the other end of the dynamism scale. Pippa said if they learned how to graft TV remotes on to men's hands, Ray would be first in the queue. When Jo called in, there was always a full ashtray and an empty plate or two in his vicinity, and a vacant pissed-off expression on his puffy unshaved face, as though whatever he was watching was truly annoying him. Jo had no idea how Pippa stood it, but still, that didn't give her permission to hit on the new housesitter. Not when two other women had a prior claim on him. Maybe a little chat was called for. She shut down her computer, grabbed a jacket and made her way to number 7.

'Well, I never,' said Pippa, who'd swept Ray's crumbs into a dustpan, plumped up his cushions and given the armchair a good spray of Haze while Jo had been talking. 'Poor old Marcus, eh?'

Jo had told her everything, but with only a hint of the Friday-night business at her house. 'Yes,' she said. 'Anyway, he still seems to be pretty hung up on Hannah, so, as cute as he is, I think it might be playing with fire if I got involved with him.' Was Pippa getting the message? 'Wouldn't be good for *his* psyche, either,' she added for good measure.

'Hard to know.' Pippa flicked off her shoes and fell from Jo's height to around five-two, then dropped into a chair and propped her feet on Ray's pouf. 'Golly, I'm exhausted,' she sighed. 'Two of my staff are off with flu. You know, it really takes it out of you doing nine waxings, four nail extensions and five massages in a day.'

'I can imagine,' said Jo. The extent of her daytime exertion was lifting the kettle. She did, however, do an awful lot of it.

'Not to mention all the paperwork, the phone calls . . .'

Pippa's eyelids were beginning to droop, which was a little unnerving for Jo, who'd never seen her neighbour the least bit weary before. She wondered about asking her to dinner, but Pippa had an incredibly healthy diet which, when combined with Ernst and Keiko's restrictions, would leave them nothing but their placemats to eat. Was Pippa asleep now? Her eyes were closed. Maybe she'd caught the flu too, which might explain why she couldn't park earlier.

Jo got up and quietly refilled her cup from the teapot. It was a flowery affair, as were the cups and saucers, the carpet, the curtains and three-piece suite. All a bit sickly really. Borderline tacky. Jo had often found Pippa an odd, possibly evolving, character: one foot in *Woman's Weekly* and the other in alfalfa and Qigong.

'That's better!' Pippa announced, eyes popping open scarily. 'Nothing like a power nap to revive you.'

'No?' said Jo, who regularly fell asleep over her work but always felt worse for it.

'So . . .' Pippa headed for the teapot, 'you say it's been nine months since Hannah left him?'

'Yep.'

'And he's still holding a candle for her, in spite of everything?'

'So it seems.'

'Hmm.' As she leaned against the dining table, Pippa tapped at her cup with a manicured nail, looking pensive. 'Would a massage help?'

'I'm fine, thanks.'

'I meant Marcus.'

'Actually,' Jo said, 'I had another idea. He let slip it was his birthday this Friday, and I thought maybe we could have a bit of a bash for him. You, me, Hannah, Freddie, my students.' The idea had, in fact, only just entered her head.

'And Robin?'

'If he wants to come.'

'Well, you can definitely count me in.'

'Great.' Jo was now quite warming to the idea. She'd get Keiko to make sushi and do some nice flower arrangements, and Ernst could go round saying, 'What'll you have?'

'You know, I think I'll give Marcus a home-treatment voucher,' said Pippa, running a chunky dried grass through her cupped hand, over and over. 'As a birthday present.'

Jo looked on suspiciously. One could never be really sure *quite* what went on in Pippa's home-treatment room.

'Then he can come when he pleases,' added Pippa worryingly.

To market to market to buy a fat pig . . . tea, porridge, shampoo. I read recently that the seven-year itch now kicks in after two and a half years, people's boredom thresholds having dropped considerably. Could that explain how I fell into bed with Robin so easily? Marcus and I had been together almost three years when I applied to do teacher training in Oxford and he decided to help run his late uncle's restaurant near Braemar and we had our temporary parting of the ways.

I'm not sure we'd grown bored with one another, though, just the life we were leading. Marcus, having eventually got himself a law degree, was doing his Articles with some stuffy solicitors in Wimbledon and hating every day, and I was working for a temping agency in Central London, bouncing from one dreary bitchy office to another, dreaming of more money, more job satisfaction. Anyway, we knew we had to part for a while in order to have a nicer future, but found we missed each other dreadfully and, during a weekend together in Durham, decided we'd get married.

I wanted something quick and private and secular, but Marcus – a product of his upbringing – talked me into doing the whole church thing, just as soon as my one-year course was over. I'm not sure I can ever forgive him for that. Not now, looking back. Me, head to toe in white. All that pretentious Scottish castle stuff. It just made what happened three years later much worse somehow.

The lead-up to the wedding was a happy time. I felt loved, secure. I did well in my teaching placements and couldn't wait to join Marcus in Braemar and be married and have a job. Then, at a party at some postgrad-friend-of-a-friend's house, a softly spoken, good-looking man with dark brown eyes said he'd noticed me the other day in the university bookshop, buying Foucault. Are you doing French? he asked.

It turned out this nice bloke, Robin, was a history lecturer. He was quite self-deprecating – which I liked then, but obviously can't stand now – and was also interesting and amusing, and I found myself flattered by his attention. Recently separated from his wife, he told me. I didn't mention Marcus. We talked about French colonialism which, to be honest, made a refreshing change from wedding plans. OK, I said when, as the party broke up, he asked if he could have my phone number. It's funny how you can go along making lots of right decisions and then suddenly begin a whole string of wrong ones.

I think it's the sex I miss mostly with Marcus. Robin's adept, in a perfunctory way, but I have caught myself planning lessons in my head. I stopped faking months ago. He and his ex-wife had amazing sexual chemistry, he told me once when he'd had a few too many drinks. I can't say it bothered me.

TUESDAY

Keiko was practising 'Happy Birthday' on the piano in the middle room; always fine until she got to the third 'BIRTHday', when she faltered and hit two or three wrong chords before finding the correct one. She still had a few days to perfect it, if Jo didn't throttle her in the interim.

'Dinner's ready,' Jo called out. She'd done a kind of Chinese pork thing with noodles and exotic vegetables, from which she was now fishing bits of pork to put on Keiko's plate. 'It's going cold!' she added before Keiko had one more run-through.

'Oh, that is plenty,' said Keiko, appearing at the door. 'Thank you.'

'Are you sure?'

'I am on At-kin Diet.'

'Yes, I know. But I thought the idea was that you could eat as much as you wanted of certain things. Like meat? Here, have a little more.'

'But . . .'

'It's OK,' Jo told her, thinking Dr Atkins should have kept the word 'diet' out of his regime, so as not to confuse. 'Honestly.'

The rumble on the stairs told her Ernst was on his way, so when the doorbell rang, she let him get it, and was somewhat shocked when Hannah followed him into the kitchen.

'Hey,' Jo said, 'what a nice surprise.'

Hannah stopped in her tracks. 'Oh. You're just about to have dinner.'

'No, no, don't worry.' Jo introduced everyone, then said, 'Let's go through to the front room, shall we? Leave Ernst and Keiko to it.'

'Aren't you eating?'

'No, not hungry,' Jo lied. 'Glass of wine?' she offered, suddenly in need of a prop. Hannah had surely come to confront her.

'OK. Thanks.'

While Jo poured out the Chenin Blanc, Ernst shot her looks that might have said, 'How nicely a glass of chilled white wine would go with this splendid Chinese dish,' but she couldn't be sure.

'I shouldn't be drinking, really,' said Hannah. She had her feet tucked beside her in the big armchair while she watched Jo light a fire. 'Got preparation to do this evening. Honestly, it's relentless.'

Jo had run out of logs and was using smokeless coal. The fire was taking ages to get going but at least it was legal. 'Poor you,' she said to Hannah, 'hating your job so.' As much as Jo would rather not share her house with others, she had to admit it was better than real work.

'Yes, poor me. Although some of the brats are *almost* human.' She tittered and tucked her immaculately cut hair behind a perfect little ear. 'Anyway, I just wanted to come and have a chat.'

Jo pulled a horrified face that Hannah couldn't see. Had Marcus confessed they'd spent an entire night together? 'Of course,' she said, turning with a smile. 'Are you OK?'

'No, to be honest.'

'Ah.'

'I know you and Marcus have become very friendly.'

'Nothing's happened between us,' Jo said, a bit too defensively. 'Not my type,' she added with a laugh, then wondered if that was a bit rude.

'No, I know nothing's happened. Not really. Marcus told me that you got him drunk and things turned a bit silly.'

Jo managed to stay composed. 'Oh, yes?'

'Mm. He also said you've got a boyfriend. Have I met him?'

Jo shook her head. If Hannah had met Bram, she'd have remembered. 'He's away a lot.'

'Ah. Well, I just wondered if Marcus has said anything

about, you know, *me*. Him and me? Sometimes I can't make out what's going on in his head.'

Jo breathed out at last and hoisted herself from the floor to the sofa. 'Only that he's absolutely potty about you.'

Hannah grinned. 'And has he mentioned being involved with anyone? You know, back in Scotland? Or someone he's keen on?'

'Nope.'

'Or has anyone got their eye on him?'

Jo chose to discount half of Jubilee Street. 'Not as far as I know.'

'Well, that's good. I'd hate to make some huge decision, only to find there's a bloody woman in Marcus's life.'

'No,' said Jo. 'I don't suppose you would, but what about . . .'

'What?'

'Well, Robin.'

'Ah yes, Robin. Look, I know he's your friend and all that, but to be honest, Jo, we're chalk and cheese. I messed up big time there. Anyway, he'd be all right. He could have Freddie for a while in the holidays, I suppose. If he insists. I mean, Robin did without Fred for his first two and a half years.'

Jo looked on stunned, trying to work out if Hannah was just a bit self-absorbed, or totally. 'Listen,' she said, 'I think I'll go and check on Ernst and—'

'Oh, don't worry, I'll be off now.' Hannah drained her

glass, slipped her feet back into her elegant boots, stood up and kind of swirled herself back into her classy long coat. Jo felt she'd give anything to be that graceful.

'Excuse me, Jo,' they suddenly heard Ernst say, his face poking round the door. 'But I have finished my first course, as well as Keiko's. And I'm not sure, but maybe yours too.'

Jo, made even more peckish by the glass of wine, gave a disappointed, 'Oh.'

'It was very good. Better than Shanghai House take-away.'

'Thanks,' said Jo. Quite a compliment.

After seeing Hannah out, Jo made her way to the kitchen and found Ernst helping himself to Ben and Jerry's, and Keiko helping herself to the washing up. She stood watching them for a while and a kind of maternal affection welled up in her, quite unexpectedly. This was what it must be like to have teenage children, she thought. Only not quite, because these two were helpful and polite and didn't say, '*Shit*, there's someone I know,' and dive down in the car when she took them out. How bad Jo felt at having done that to her parents so many times.

'Have you got homework tonight?' she asked.

Keiko shook her head and smiled. 'No. So, very luckily, I can practise more with "Happy Birthday".'

'Great,' said Jo, wondering where she could go. Marcus's?

* * *

'Come in. I'm just packing,' he said.

'What? Where are you going?'

'To the Cotswolds, tomorrow and Thursday. To do a bit of walking.'

'Ah. God, I'd love to do that.'

'Would you?'

'Mm, I adore going on long country rambles, but do you know how difficult it is for a woman to walk somewhere remote on her own?'

'I can imagine you might feel vulnerable. Well, why don't you come then?'

Jo's heart gave a leap. She wasn't sure if it was Marcus or the idea of a ramble. 'Yeah?'

'I was going to ask you to feed Maidstone but I suppose I can leave him masses of that dried stuff.'

'And I'm sure my students could look after themselves for one evening. I'll leave them money for a pizza or something.'

'It'd be nice to have the company. Got suitable footwear?'

'Yep,' said Jo, trying to picture where they might stay. A low-beamed inn with a log fire and a stag's head on the wall. There'd be a big old bed with huge pillows and a tapestry spread . . .

'Good,' he said. 'Nothing worse than walking with someone moaning about their feet all the time.'

'Don't worry. I'm quite hardy, as long as I'm wrapped up.'

'Oh, right, the thin-skin thing.'
'Listen, are you sure about this?'
'Absolutely. Are you?'
'Absolutely.'

Robin was trying to read a dense first novel that had received critical acclaim as well as Hannah's strong recommendation. He was about a quarter of the way into it and, so far, the book had involved unbelievable and unlikeable characters with ridiculous names, and not a whiff of a plot.

Hannah, sitting opposite, looked up from her writing. How she loved to scribble away in that new diary of hers, stopping occasionally to chew on her pen, deep in thought. The journal, or whatever, was always carefully locked after use, and the key secreted away somewhere Robin would never know. Still, as long as it worked. Adrian had suggested it as part of the therapy, apparently. Hannah was no doubt unleashing all sorts of bottled-up childhood anxieties on to those pages. Getting it out of her system. She looked up at him, perhaps sensing his eyes on her.

'Enjoying it?' she asked, nodding towards the hefty novel.

'Very much.'
'Terrific characters, aren't they?'
'Mm, terrific.'
'Don't you find Figgy Flybright totally fascinating?'

'Ah-ha,' he laughed. 'Yes.'

She went back to her writing and Robin frowned at his book, flicking it over to read the synopsis on the back. Who? He speed-read the blurb, but there was no mention of a Figgy Flybright. Oh well, with a bit of luck he or she would pop up later and turn this into his all-time favourite novel.

Robin had always had a problem with fiction. Even as a child he'd preferred books on the Second World War to Desperate Dan. Later, when all his friends were into *Portnoy's Complaint*, Robin would be devouring Pepys. And what, he'd often wondered, was the point of Dickens, when you had Booth's fascinating survey of life and labour in nineteenth-century London?

He turned a page – God, it was tedious – then looked up. 'Was that Freddie?' he asked Hannah.

She stopped writing and tilted her head to listen. 'I didn't hear anything, but I'll go, shall I?'

Robin snapped his book shut, not particularly caring that he'd lose his place. 'No, no, you stay put.'

Of course Freddie was dead to the world, all cherubic and adorable. Robin sat beside the bed for a while, just staring at his little miracle. What could he be dreaming about, he wondered. Having his very own shed?

Just write whatever comes into your head, Adrian said towards the end of our second session. Address it to me, or yourself, or to no one in particular. Try and do it every day. If you can't think of anything to say or if it becomes too difficult, too painful, just scribble a nursery rhyme or shopping list or something — anything to keep the writing going. But obviously we want it to be cathartic, so don't just be writing nursery rhymes. And do try not to avoid painful subjects or episodes.

Undoubtedly, the most painful episode of all was leaving, last June. Marcus went out for the day without saying where — he didn't take the car, so for a walk, presumably — and my parents came and collected us. We're going to stay with Granny and Granddad for a while, I told Freddie, and he got all excited at the prospect, standing on the sofa to watch for them through the window for a full hour before the two of them arrived, a lot later than planned, exhausted and bitterly disappointed in their daughter, but stoically trying not to show it. Sometimes I wish they wouldn't be so bloody British about everything.

Marcus's timing couldn't have been worse. Thinking we'd be well on our way, he returned just as the last of the toys — Fred's pedal car — was being squeezed into the boot. The look on his face said it all, and I almost told Dad to take everything out again, we'd be staying. But then Freddie and Marcus were having one last cuddle and tears were filling Marcus's eyes, and mine and my mother's, and it was just . . . awful. Jack and Jill went up the hill . . . Jack fell down. Poor

Jack. Poor me. I had to leave, didn't I? No one was speaking to me, least of all Marcus. But he never actually asked me to go. They all froze me out, though, the bastards. Soap powder, pan scourers, maple syrup. Maple syrup – would Freddie like that?

I think he must have gone back to sleep. Can't hear anything. I can tell Robin isn't into Divine and Conquered, *and is reading it, or pretending to, just to please me. When I tested him with a character I'd made up just now, he rather gave the game away. He's trying to be nice, but has no idea how infuriating I find that. What I once thought of as Robin's sensitivity, I now see as a kind of cowardice. He's back and picking up the novel again – my cue to yawn and say I think I'll turn in. If he offers to make us both a nice hot milky drink, I swear I'll scream.*

WEDNESDAY

As they headed west, Marcus wasn't exactly panicking, just fairly apprehensive about the venture. Jo, however, was chatty and excited as she pored over maps and walking guides, and it occurred to him that maybe she didn't get out of town much, what with the lodgers.

It was only for two days, he told himself. And, if they didn't hit it off for some reason, it would be just forty-odd miles back to Oxford. But no, that wasn't it. He was feeling bad about Hannah, that was the problem. Disloyal. Even though he'd called her earlier on her mobile and told her all about it. 'I'm sure Jo will be a great walking companion,' Hannah had said breezily. 'Have fun, won't you? Listen, got to go to class now. See you Friday.'

Fortunately, the further they got from Oxford, the more Marcus found himself relaxing and looking forward to a hike. They certainly couldn't have asked for better walking weather. It was all of a sudden bright and quite warm, as though someone – God? – had cleared his throat and politely informed the forgetful old sun that the first day of spring had come and gone.

The back of the car had been loaded with holdalls and rucksacks and, somewhat puzzlingly to Marcus, two carrier bags of food. 'I eat a lot when I walk,' Jo explained. 'Fuel.' Marcus had nodded and hoped he wouldn't gallantly volunteer to carry it.

'Anyway, listen,' she was saying now, head still bowed, 'I've found this brilliant-sounding circular walk. It's number twenty-four in my book, which means it's quite long, as they start with the shorter ones and—'

'How long?'

'Um . . . fourteen point five miles.'

'What!' No wonder she'd brought so many provisions.

'Too long?' she asked.

'I'll say.'

'OK, there's this other one that's ten point—'

'Down a bit.'

Jo reversed through the pages a way, then looked over at him and laughed. 'I thought you were a tough, energetic and adventurous Scot?'

'Well,' he said, taking the turning he'd planned all along, towards the B and B and the six-mile walk he'd planned all along. 'You'd be right on one count.'

'Scot?'

'Yep.'

*　*　*

The landlady assumed they'd be sharing a room, but Marcus explained they'd need two singles. He was very apologetic, having booked only himself in over the phone.

'Are you sure?' Jo whispered in his ear. 'Wouldn't it be cheaper to share? Twin beds, of course.'

'It's the same price,' he whispered back. 'And, anyway, you snore.'

'I do not!'

'You're lucky the schools haven't broken up for Easter yet,' the landlady was saying. They were following her upstairs for an inspection. 'We're fully booked from the end of next week.'

Marcus didn't quite get the connection, as they weren't exactly in family-holiday country, so could only assume lots of childless teachers headed Weston-on-the-Wold way.

'But I can certainly give you two tonight,' she added, opening a door with 'Lilac Room' on it, to a single room with a single bed and a single wardrobe, but not a single bit of space to manoeuvre. She'd obviously gone to an enormous amount of trouble with the décor, though, scouring the land for as many ruched things in different shades of lilac as she could find.

'Very nice,' said Jo. 'Why don't you take this one, Marcus?'

'Well, let's just see—'

'And here we have the Pink Room,' the woman said,

stepping across the landing and pushing open a second door.

Marcus popped his head in and saw that the Pink Room was, if anything, smaller and slightly frillier than the first, and that it lived up to its name admirably. He swung round and zoomed back to the first room before Jo had a chance to, and had his clothes strewn all over the lilac eiderdown by the time she entered.

'Oh, let's not bother unpacking now,' she said. She sat on the edge of the bed and began lacing up boots that looked as though they might have covered the whole of Nepal. How he'd got the impression Jo was a bit of a sloth, he wasn't sure. 'I'll just see if the landlady will fill my flask,' she added. 'See you downstairs in five?'

'Er . . .' he said, and she'd gone.

The lunch break is ridiculously short. We grab food, have a coffee, tea, smoke, or whatever, and are back in the classroom before you can say, 'It used to be an hour and a half when I was a schoolgirl!' I remember sometimes opting for 'home dinners' and would amble back to my house, share a leisurely meal with Mum, and still have time back at school for skipping.

Today I'm not hungry, so have just got a coffee in a corner of the staffroom, trying not to feel extremely pissed off by Marcus going away with Jo. It's platonic, I'm sure. And, anyway, who am I to object? Marcus, after all, is the one with all the Brownie points. Depressing that I can't possibly catch up with him. Going back to Marcus would gain me points, but in taking Freddie from Robin, I'd lose even more. Hopeless. And so unfair. Adrian told me to focus on the positive, but didn't get round to pointing out what that might be.

I suppose she's quite pretty, Jo, in a kind of gangling, pseudo-hippy way. Mid-thirties? Hard to tell, since everyone looks so young these days. But what a conniving cow, not even mentioning this Cotswold trip yesterday evening. Is the whole world duplicitous? You have to wonder.

Mustn't think about Marcus moving in with her when his house-sit is up. Bath cleaner, bread, Marmite, ginger biscuits, juice. Things we do need, in fact — must make separate list before that effing bell goes.

'So are you sure everything's all right?' Jo shouted at Ernst on her mobile. She wasn't sure she needed to shout, but something about Ernst made her do that. She could hear Keiko on the piano in the background, still not quite managing that chord. She thought she heard the doorbell too.

'Everything is fine,' Ernst told her. 'Danielle, hi! Mimi, hi! Go on through. Come in, come in, Ahmed. Good to see you.'

'Ernst?' called out Jo. She was in her very pink room,

stretched out on the bed after their walk and fairly surprised to find her phone had a signal.

'Cool, you have brought beers. Not such a good Muslim, ha ha.'

Jo heard the door slam. 'Ernst?'

'Sorry, Jo. Yes. Just go to the kitchen, Ahmed. Everyone else is in there.'

'What do you mean, "everyone else"?' asked Jo, when her phone suddenly died on her. 'Ernst?'

'I'm sure they'll behave themselves,' Marcus reassured her over their dinner. It was the usual simple menu of a modest country pub: *Roasted Quail with Juniper Berries, Grilled Shark Teriyaki.* Jo had gone for the *Armenian Pumpkin Stew* and wasn't regretting it, but Marcus seemed to be struggling with his *Chipirones en su Tinta*, which, if he'd only asked, he would have discovered to be squid in their own ink.

'I know, I know,' she said. 'They're all adults, of sorts. And I'm sure Keiko would scrub the place clean till dawn if necessary.' She took a swig of rip-off wine and watched Marcus's lemon-sucking expression. 'Look, we could swap meals, if you like?'

'Could we?'

She hadn't been expecting that response, but nevertheless handed over her plate and took his. She wouldn't have done that for just anybody, but they'd had such a lovely walk together. Well, not quite together, as his pace had often been slower than hers. Every now and then they'd level-pegged and chatted for a while. Yes, it *had* been nice. Too nice. And on top of that, this evening, amid flickering candles and the glow of firelight, he was looking so very shaggable.

'Thanks,' he said with that smile.

Jo was forcing herself not to be flirty with him, though. His response to her twin-bed suggestion had let her know the score in no uncertain terms, and she respected him for it. No way was she now going to stir up trouble and humiliate herself in the process. 'What kind of food do you serve in your restaurant?' she asked.

'It depends on who the chef is. They come and go. I don't get involved in that side of things. I just do the admin – ordering, marketing, the accounts. Anyway, we're doing Italian at the moment.'

'Don't customers get a bit confused? I mean, if you go back to a restaurant, it's because you liked what they offered, isn't it?'

'Well, the tourists don't care and the locals tell us they like the surprise element. Hey, this pumpkin stew's great.'

'Isn't it,' she said, quite wanting it back.

'It's not something I plan to do for the rest of my life,' he went on, 'helping run a restaurant. Tell the truth, I've pretty much had enough of it. That's part of the reason I'm taking this break. To have a think about what to do. Unfortunately, I'll have to go back, at least for a while. It's all hands to the deck in summer, right through to the Highland Games. We get a lot of royal watchers.'

'Balmoral?'

'Mm. And then there are all the walkers and climbers.'

'And where do you live?'

'Above the restaurant, which is a little way out of Braemar. It was my late uncle's restaurant. Well, more of a café when he had it. My mother inherited the lot when he died, but it was all a bit run down. We did the flat up, Hannah and I, when we were first married. She was pregnant and we made a great little nursery for Freddie. I think if they'd stayed we'd have had to move to something bigger eventually but, you know, it's fine for just me. All on my own.'

Marcus was sounding very matter-of-fact, but had stopped eating, Jo noticed, and was tapping the edge of his plate with his knife. She put a hand over his to stop him. 'I'm sure she loves you a lot.'

'Yeah, well, maybe.'

Jo uncovered his hand and picked up her wine. 'You know, Marcus, these things have a way of sorting themselves out.'

He raised a quizzical eyebrow at her.

'Yeah, yeah,' she said. 'I hate people who say things like that too. OK then, you've got yourselves into a horrible unsolvable situation, and it's going to make you miserable for the rest of your lives, so you may as well come to terms with it.'

Marcus looked down, stabbed at his food with his fork, then held up a piece of mouth-watering pumpkin between them. 'Actually,' he said, 'I'd prefer a platitude, if that's all right with you?'

She gave him a quick peck on the cheek outside his room, and said, 'Night. See you at breakfast,' before disappearing through her door.

'Good night,' he called out, surprised. He'd assumed they'd share the bottle of wine he'd packed, drinking it from the teacups provided in each room; carry on chatting till quite late. He hadn't imagined hitting the sack at – he checked his watch – 9.50.

Jo reappeared with a washbag and said, 'Bagsy first in the bathroom!'

'Yeah, go ahead,' he told her, still wondering what to do for the next couple of hours. He unlocked his door, thought better of switching the light on, and groped in his bag for the book he'd brought with him. He then locked up again and headed back to the pub they'd just left.

As he walked down the village's ancient main street, past tiny stone cottages and huge stone cottages, all of them weighted with history, Marcus wondered at the wisdom of picking *The Sexual Life of Catherine M* off Lucy and Dom's bookshelf. Incongruous, somehow. Plus, sad enough to be in a lonely corner of the pub with a solitary beer, but maybe entering perv territory to be reading erotica as well. He'd hide the cover, he told himself. Or, better still, get into conversation with someone.

When he approached the White Hart, he pushed Catherine deep into his jacket pocket and tried to recall if he'd ever heard anyone over ten say 'bagsy'.

'I *will* not go to his room on a pretext,' Jo affirmed one more time. 'Too degrading. And, besides, there's Hannah. Mind you, she's got Robin. No, no, I will *not* play second fiddle. Definitely not.'

She slapped another thick layer of face cream on as a kind of insurance, and carried on reading her whodunit. She thought it was probably Jason, the deceased's half-brother, who stood to inherit the Wiltshire estate and had a flimsy alibi. But then she always went for the red herring in these things.

After a while, she glanced at her travel alarm clock. It was 11.15 and her eyes were growing heavy, which was good. When she went back to the book, the words started swerving around and she gave up, closed it, switched off the light, clasped her hands and said a 'thank you' to God for keeping things simple between herself and Marcus. 'However,' she went on in a slow, deep-breathing whisper, 'if you have any of that potion, like, you know the one in *A Midsummer Night's Dream* – the stuff that makes people fall in love with the first person, or donkey, they see when they wake up – well, perhaps you'd see fit to use some on Mar . . .'

The next thing she heard was a tap, tap, tap at her door, and her heart thumped wildly from the shock of it. 'Sshhh!' she said, swinging herself out of bed.

His mother, Moira, drove me mad with her fussiness, and was always telling me things I was perfectly well aware of, thank you. Obviously, Freddie's cot should go against the inner wall of the nursery, away from the slightly draughty window. Yes, it was wise to take a first aid kit out in the car, when we were so far from a hospital.

She'd come round and tidy our kitchen cupboards, which left me gobsmacked the first time and fuming after that. But only once did I march her to the door with a 'Look, maybe some other time?' Mind you, I have to admit she had quite a knack for grouping things handily – for example, everything you could possibly want to make gravy or sauces on one shelf, pasta, rice and pulses on another. Herbs and spices would be graded from most used at the front to only used at Christmas at the back. When she stopped visiting the flat altogether – as they all did – I almost missed the interfering biddy sorting things out.

I shouldn't be up this late, not with work tomorrow, but am being tortured – despite taking two of Dr Maxwell's chill pills – by images of Marcus and bitch Jo making other-worldly love in an Elizabethan four-poster with flimsy curtains.

FRIDAY

Robin was in Jo's middle room, listening to Freddie rampaging over the piano keys. 'Very good,' he said, which encouraged Freddie to bash away more wildly and at greater volume. Robin got up and shut the door. He wasn't that keen on joining in the celebrations, anyway. Although he felt it was nice for Freddie and Hannah to still be part of Marcus's life, he couldn't help wishing the chap had had his birthday at a more convenient time. Two weeks ago would have been good.

He sat back down in a half-upholstered armchair, avoiding the pins, and carried on perusing the interesting things Jo kept in her middle room. Aside from the upright walnut piano, there was a tailor's dummy, an easel, a knitting machine and a collection of things for brewing beer in. On the windowsill were seed trays, and on top of the piano sat *Calligraphy Made Easy, Volume I*. Either Jo frenetically spent her leisure time making music, jumpers and lager, or she took up and dropped an awful lot of hobbies. On closer inspection, most things had a fairly unused look about them.

Freddie's discordant playing was beginning to grate, so Robin hoisted himself from the chair and went and sat beside him on the piano stool. 'OK, Fred, that's enough,' he said. 'Fred!' The little boy stopped at the unusual sound of his father's raised voice. 'Right,' continued Robin. 'Now, how would you like to learn "Baa, Baa, Black Sheep"?'

Freddie pulled a face. 'Can you learn me how to do "Wheels on the Bus"?'

'Sorry, Fred. Don't know that one.'

'It's like this,' Freddie said, and began singing it.

'Yes, I know the song, Fred, but let's play "Baa, Baa, Black Sheep", eh? It's nice and easy and you can play it with one finger. Like this. Watch. You put your finger on that key first. It's called Middle C.'

'But I want you to learn me "Wheels on the Bus". *Pleeze*, Daddy. It's my best.'

'*Teach* me, Freddie. Not learn me. Look, I'm sorry, but I only know "Baa, Baa, Black Sheep".'

'Mummy played me "Wheels on the Bus" when we went to Granny and Granddad's.'

'Yes, but Mummy's got her grade eight piano. Daddy hasn't. Daddy's good at other things. OK, let's have a go at "Baa, Baa, Black Sheep", shall we? Finger on Middle C. Finger, not thumb, Fred. No, just one finger.'

'Oh, I'm sorry,' said Jo's Japanese student at the door. 'Excuse me. But it is time for cake and "Happy Birthday" tune on piano.'

'Yes, of course,' said Robin, whisking his son off the stool as people wandered into the room carrying glasses, followed by Jo with a large cake ablaze with candles. Quite a lot, Robin was pleased to see.

Marcus was looking forward to a break from the women, if only for the time it took them to sing 'Happy Birthday'. Hannah had been surprisingly attentive and tactile, considering Robin was there, and the Pippa woman had stood behind him and massaged his shoulders for an entire, rather one-sided conversation on detox diets. As for Jo, well, she was being pleasant but a little distant. Maybe because Hannah was there, but more likely on account of the incident in the Pink Room the other night after he'd consumed way too much *Catherine M* in a corner of the pub. She'd responded to his taps at her door, let him in with a 'Shhh, you'll wake everyone else up too,' and led him the two steps to her bed in the darkness, where they'd fallen in a clinch and hungrily sought out each other's lips. But when Marcus found his cheeks, nose, chin and everything else swimming around in a sea of something unpleasantly warm and sticky, he'd pulled back with a 'Yeeuchh'.

'Oh, shoot, my face cream,' she'd said sleepily, before

heaving herself up and over him and leaving the room.

When she returned, cream wiped off, they'd had a laugh about it before chastely kissing each other good night again. No mention was made of the incident the following day during their gruelling nine-miler.

But now she'd unexpectedly come over and was clinging on to him as they all sang 'Happy Birthday'. She seemed tense, he noticed; her nails digging uncomfortably into his arm until the song finished, when she let go, rushed over to Keiko at the piano and gave her an inexplicable hug.

Everyone then grouped around the cake and Marcus managed to blow his candles out in one long puff, while the multi-tasking Keiko took photos. When someone put a knife in his hand he plunged it into the cake and, as he did so, his spare arm was hooked by Hannah.

'Did you make a wish?' she asked quietly.

'Oh yes,' he said, turning and giving her a tender look. He'd forgotten to, in fact, but was doing it now. Hannah and Freddie coming back to him, with Robin happily turning into a convivial visiting-uncle figure . . . maybe.

'Here, Marcus,' said Pippa, eyes wide, mouth somewhere between a smile and a pout. 'Happy Birthday.'

He put the knife down and took an envelope from her, expecting just a card but also finding inside a voucher for one massage at 7 Jubilee Street. His heart sank. 'Hey, that's great!' he said. He let her kiss his cheek, then added, 'You shouldn't have.'

'Come along any time,' she told him, kissing the other cheek. He felt the full force of her chest against his, before his attention was taken up by Keiko handing him a string of origami birds.

'I have made them especially for you,' she said with a giggle, a cocked head and a twinkle in her eye. Was she coming on to him too? He'd always been baffled by Japanese girls. Keen to bag a Western husband or just incredibly sweet?

'Thank you,' he said, while she snapped him – once, twice, three times – holding up the string of birds. 'How clever of you.'

Marcus was beginning to feel a bit overwhelmed, and after Pippa and Keiko wandered off, longed to go and join the fat bloke watching a gardening programme in the front room. When Jo came over he asked who the man was.

'Ray,' she said. 'Pippa's husband.'

'No!'

'Hard to believe, isn't it? She calls him her current husband, so watch out.'

Marcus slipped Pippa's voucher deep into his shirt pocket. If it went through a 60-degree wash cycle, she might refuse to accept it.

Seven people, a child and a couch potato did not a party make, decided Jo. It was all rather quiet and strained which, given the relationship tangles, wasn't surprising. If only she hadn't shot off to the Cotswolds for two days, she might have got round to inviting a few extra friends and neighbours. A bit insulting to go knocking on Conrad's door at this late stage, or to phone Jez and Alice. 'Hi, I don't suppose you'd like to come to a party? . . . Well, actually it's going on now. We're a bit short, you see.' Jo had an idea, though. She manoeuvred Ernst into the hall and had a word, and within seconds he was chatting away on his mobile.

'I know, Ahmed,' he chuckled. 'I am very lucky with my landlady. OK. Tell the others and bring more beers, yeah?'

'Thanks, Ernst,' Jo said, before rejoining the very quiet group in the middle room. 'Hey, does anyone play the piano?' she called out, then pretended not to see Keiko raise a tentative hand.

'Hannah's very good,' said Marcus. 'Aren't you?'

'Oh, no, I'd be far too rusty.'

'Nonsense,' chipped in Robin.

'Play "Wheels on the Bus", Mummy?' shouted Freddie.

Jo crossed to the piano stool and opened it up. 'I've got a Beatles songbook, somewhere.' She rummaged through her untouched-for-years sheet music and took it out. 'Here.'

'Oh, all right,' said Hannah with a shrug. She came over to Jo, gave her the meanest of looks – another one

– snatched the book and sat on the stool. 'But first "Wheels on the Bus" for Freddie.'

Freddie jumped on the spot with excitement and then, when the song began, everyone followed his lead with the words and the actions. It was great fun, and quite long, Jo was pleased to discover. After the wheels had gone round and the horn had beeped and the wipers had swished and the bell had dinged, and so on, all eight people in the room applauded. It was only when the noise died down and Hannah was flicking through the Beatles songbook, that they heard the very loud and agitated voices coming through the wall. Jo's heart raced, before she recognised the distinctive sound of *EastEnders*.

'Oh, for Christ's sake . . .' said Pippa, storming from the room.

After six of Ernst's classmates rolled up, the event went in a whole different direction. The Beatles songs had gone down well but had, at the same time, clearly hit the nail on the head, pressed buttons, and in the case of 'Yesterday', turned on the waterworks for Hannah.

Now, at ten past ten, after Ray had long since slouched home, they were all dancing to an ancient mixed tape of Jo's in a dimly lit kitchen. Even Robin, Jo was pleased to see. Marcus had an attractive Spanish girl gyrating in front of him, Pippa and Hannah dancing on either side of him and Freddie on his shoulders, and seemed to be having a pretty good birthday. Jo herself was dancing with Ahmed, who moved like a dream, but didn't stop her craving a slow dance with Marcus.

When, all of a sudden, Eric Clapton was singing about how wonderful she looked tonight, Jo excused herself and crossed the kitchen. But by the time she got to Marcus, he and several competing women had formed a sort of linked-arm dance. It looked somewhere between 'Auld Lang Syne' and a rugby scrum and didn't seem to be working that well, so when Robin hoisted Freddie from Marcus's shoulders and left the kitchen, Jo followed them into the middle room.

'I think I should get this little chap to bed,' Robin said. 'No, Fred. No more piano playing. Let's find your coat. And where did you leave your toolbox?'

'I put it by the front door,' said Jo, picking Freddie's coat out of a pile. 'I'm really pleased you came, you know, Robin. I wasn't sure . . .'

He gave her a warm smile. 'No, neither was I. But, it's been fun. I managed to chat with Marcus for a while, which was good.'

'Yes, I saw.'

'He called in the other day, but it was a bit awkward. Nice chap, though.'

'Yes.'

'Anyway, we talked about Scotland. My son's at Edinburgh. And a bit about sport.' Robin ran a sleeve up a tired-looking Freddie's arm. 'But not about why he's suddenly hanging out in Oxford. Nothing personal. Typical men, eh?'

Jo laughed. 'Yes.'

He eased Freddie's other arm into the coat and looked up at her from where he was kneeling. 'I don't suppose you know, do you?'

'What?'

'Why he's here?'

Jo, suddenly wishing she'd joined Marcus's entourage, said, 'I think he just wanted to see Freddie.'

'That's what Hannah says, but she's behaving weirdly.'

She certainly was. Hannah had elbowed Jo in the ribs during the cake-cutting, pretending it was an accident. 'Oops, sorry,' she'd said. 'Thought you were the curtain in that outfit.' Jo's stripy top did indeed resemble her stripy curtains, but anyway, what kind of a person went around jabbing at curtains? One who suspected the curtains of sleeping with her bloke, presumably.

'Is she?' Jo said to Robin. He was pulling Freddie's hood up and fastening a popper. Although keen to know more, she found herself slowly backing towards the door. Where were the guests wanting directions to the bathroom when you needed them? 'Well,' she said when she got to it, 'thank you so much for coming to the party, Freddie.' She held out a hand to him. 'I expect you'd like to say goodbye to Marcus?'

'Yes, let's,' said Robin enthusiastically. He probably wanted to break up the love-in as much as she did.

After he'd kissed Freddie's cheek and shaken Robin's hand, Marcus turned back to his fellow dancers. Why he'd been uncomfortable with all the female attention earlier, he didn't know. It was great. Of course, he couldn't be sure they weren't just being nice because it was his birthday. But, whatever, it was a great ego-boost, and to have a semi-dressed, black-haired young Spanish beauty cavorting before you was something to be appreciated. He was, in fact, having a ball. When had he last been touched so often and by so many people? Playing rugby seventeen years ago? Of course that was all blokes and these were all birds. A whole flock. All to himself! He stopped and swigged at his lager bottle, then looked around briefly for Jo. Still seeing Robin out, perhaps. It was a bit odd that Hannah hadn't left with him. But then maybe it wasn't, Marcus thought, throwing himself back into the dance he'd cultivated aged sixteen and stuck with ever since.

When someone put reggae on there was a big cheer and even shy Keiko, who'd spent most of the evening finding things to wash up, came and danced with him. She *was* very sweet, he decided. Hannah, beside her, looked gorgeous, and Pippa was being vampish, regularly running her hands over her buttocks in lap-dancer mode. Not that he'd ever seen a lap dancer. In fact,

Marcus was beginning to think he'd been leading far too sheltered a life. Could Oxford provide a new and exciting milieu for him? He slipped an arm around Hannah's waist and was making sexy eye contact with the Spanish girl when someone all of a sudden yelled, 'Bram!' over the music.

It was Jo, now on the far side of the kitchen. She dropped what she was doing and, with the biggest smile, hurried towards Marcus. Well, towards the door behind him.

'Oh my God, it's Bram!' cried Pippa, as Marcus spun round and caught sight of a very tall black guy – coffee-coloured, maybe – with a head of small tight dreads. Pippa handed Marcus her glass and was off. Within seconds, Jo was up in the man's arms, legs wrapped around his waist, and Pippa was planting a kiss on his cheek.

Marcus stood still and blinked, finding it hard to adjust to the sudden change in atmosphere. Only a minute ago he'd been in the midst of the sensual and highly charged, but now the music had gone down and someone had switched on a stark overhead light. Possibly Bram. Marcus heard Keiko sighing beside him. 'Aahh, Bram. Very handsome.'

'You think so?' he asked, but then saw that even the Spanish girl had stopped her dance marathon and was staring at the latest guest with *mucho gusto*.

'Hey, everyone,' Jo was saying as she untangled herself from her man, 'this is Bram.'

Bram beamed a very white smile and waved. 'Hello, everyone,' he said in a voice much too deep and resonant for Marcus's liking.

'Hello, Bram!' shouted all the foreign students.

Marcus then turned to Hannah on the other side of him and found that she too was glued to the newcomer, with an expression similar to the Spanish girl's. 'Wow,' she was saying as she groped, without looking, for her glass of wine on the worktop.

With Freddie tucked up and fast asleep, Robin settled in an armchair with *Divine and Conquered* and something of a heavy heart. Not so much heavy, perhaps, as unsettled. He turned over a page he hadn't really read and thought back to the relative stability he'd been enjoying just a week ago: his little family unit pottering along nicely. It was all so easy compared to his first attempt at living with someone. None of the high drama of his marriage to Judith. No affairs (Judith's), plates hurtling his way, or week-long sulks (Judith's again). He'd loved his wife with a passion he could never feel for Hannah, but how much better *not* to feel too much in the way of possessiveness or jealousy with one's partner. So much more relaxing.

Obviously, there was a physical attraction between himself and Hannah – a little more on his side, perhaps – and, despite their differing political stances, they could engage for hours in affable discussions about the state of the world. Conversations dotted with, 'Mm, yes, I see what you mean . . .' or, 'Good point!' They'd never rowed, as far as he could recall. Although Hannah would return from school some days and rant in a surprisingly foul-mouthed way, Robin had never personally felt the force of her venom. Whenever he'd caught the odd dismissive look from her that might have been interpreted as *God, you're a pillock*, or *Christ, you bore me, Robin*, he tended to put it down to Hannah's work-related fatigue and despair, and tried even harder to make her home life run as smoothly and pleasantly as possible.

A couple of days back he'd suggested she find another job, or maybe stay home with Freddie for a while. They could scrape by on his salary, even taking into account his having to support Theo at university. Also, he'd pointed out, if she wasn't teaching they might not have to fork out for the shrink she was seeing and those pills she took. He'd received one of her dismissive looks then, he recalled. 'You think teaching's the biggest problem?' she'd sighed before opening up her diary and going incommunicado on him again.

Anyway, their life together was relatively tranquil, and that was what he liked most about it. *Had* liked about it.

It was Freddie he was passionate about now, of course. With an emotional chasm and several hundred miles between Marcus and Hannah, Robin had felt relatively secure as he'd grown to know his son. Grown to love his son too, and wonder in his development and try to teach him things, such as – before they'd set off for the party today – basic time-telling. Freddie hadn't quite been able to distinguish the little from the big hand on Robin's Tissot, but it had been fun.

Now Marcus – still officially Hannah's husband – was a matter of yards away and dancing with her. Yes, it was all too unsettling. Where would he stand if she decided to go back to him? What access rights would he be given? What would be the chances that he could keep Freddie? Zero, probably, judging from those desperate disaffected fathers who'd mounted cranes and thrown condoms at the PM.

Robin turned another unread page and glanced at his watch again. The little hand was on the twelve and the big hand on the two. Funny. Most Friday nights saw Hannah wrung out and in bed before both hands reached the ten.

MONDAY

In the village of Laroche-les-Bois it was raining cold rain for the fifth day in a row, and Bertrand was still having trouble getting hold of the floor tiles Lucy and Dom wanted to run through the whole of downstairs. He'd be sure to find them in Montpellier, he'd assured them, and off he'd gone in his battered Peugeot. That had been early yesterday and there'd been no sign of him since. In Bertrand's absence the electricity had conked out again, owing to his recent wiring job, and there was still a sheet of plastic where the back door should have been, owing to his mismeasuring the first time and having to reorder. Lucy and Dom wanted to go home. Desperately.

'Any luck?' Lucy asked when Dom returned from using Madame Bouziges's phone, three houses along.

He shook his head. 'Still the machine. I'm beginning to wonder if we actually have a housesitter.'

'What an awful thought,' Lucy said, picturing

Maidstone all skeletal and scratching limply at neighbours' doors.

'I'll go back and try Jo. What's her number?'

Lucy wrote it down for him and he disappeared again,
leaving her in the semi-darkness of the house they'd had
such great plans for until the wonderful, skilful, super-
efficient young Claude had decided he'd rather be an air-
traffic controller than a builder and went off to
Clermont-Ferrand to train, leaving Bertrand in charge.
All Claude's work looked good and worked well because
he was painstaking and thorough in everything he did
– just the kind of person you'd want guiding your plane
in, in fact. But, with Bertrand having made zero progress
since their last stay, at Christmas, Lucy and Dom were
keen to pay him off and look for another local builder
with a good reputation. Unfortunately, they couldn't find
one and, added to that, there were feelings to be considered. Bertrand was the widowed Madame Bouziges's
father-in-law, and Madame Bouziges, Claude's aunt and
a total gem, had been promised the job of cleaner/keeper
of keys when Lucy and Dom started letting the house
to holidaymakers.

Some hope, thought Lucy, tugging a jumper of Dom's
on over her own and staring gloomily at the cold and
cavernous living/dining area with its fabulous beams and
wonderfully rustic walls. One day it would be terrific.
But when? They'd told all their friends about this amazing
place they'd bought and now there was a waiting list of

people wanting to stay there. 'Just needs a bit more work,' Lucy would say, but always held back on telling them just how much work, in case they lost interest and wandered off. They had to start getting rent for it soon as they were mortgaged to the hilt on both their houses. Their only hope was that Claude would fail some vital air-traffic controlling test and come hurrying home.

Lucy placed another log on the open fire – the one thing that had been keeping their spirits up – and settled back into her armchair with a torch and a deeply annoying book about some Brits who'd moved to southern Italy and found nirvana.

'Success!' shouted Dom, entering from the back of the house, then padding in socks over the concrete floor to kneel and warm his hands by the fire. 'Jo said she'll ask Marcus to give us a ring. Apparently, he's turned the volume down on the answerphone because all the calls were for us.'

'God, that's a relief,' said Lucy. She wondered how many calls were work-related. Although they'd come to France on a telephone- and computer-free retreat, she couldn't help yearning to get back to their business. Not to mention electricity.

'Anyway,' said Dom, plonking his bottom on the concrete, 'you'll never guess who our housesitter's turned out to be.'

'Who?'

'OK, who do we know who often mentions a Marcus?'

'Well, only Han—'

'*Monsieur Rrrrobson?*' cried Madame Bouziges from the region of the plastic sheet door. '*Le téléphone!*'

'Ah,' said Dom, getting up again and hopping back over the uneven concrete. 'Here goes.'

'Good luck!' Lucy called out.

'So let me get this right,' said Marcus, eyeing Jo's closed bedroom curtains through his living-room window. 'Are you saying you're coming back this week if you can get your flights changed and that it might be best if I vacated, as you do some of your work from home?' He squinted hard. Had those curtains moved? Maybe a tad?

Dom said, 'Um, yes, I suppose that sums it up.'

'Right.' Jo's downstairs curtains had also been closed for over two days, but Marcus knew the entire household hadn't been slain or asphyxiated because he'd seen Ernst and Keiko come and go. All weekend he'd wanted to thank Jo for the party – he'd even bought flowers – but decided to wait till she'd flung open those curtains, and maybe a sash window or two. He didn't want to feel he was intruding.

'And obviously,' went on Dom, 'we feel bad about doing this to you.'

'Uh-huh?'

'And that's why we'd like to offer you the use of this house, in France.'

'I'm sorry?'

'Here in Laroche-les-Bois.'

'Do you mean for a week and a half? The rest of the time I'd have been house-sitting in Oxford?'

'No, no,' chortled Dom. 'As long as you like. To be honest, Marcus, you'd be doing us a favour. We've got some last-minute repairs going on here, so it'd be good to have someone keep an eye on things. How's your French?'

'Well, I did it for six years at school.'

'Pretty ropey then?'

'Yeah. The thing is, I wanted to spend time in Oxford, not Latouche-the-whatever. Where is it, anyway?'

'The Auvergne. We're about an hour and a half north of Nîmes. In the mountains. Beautiful spot.'

Marcus thought of Freddie. He couldn't just shoot off now, not having really spent any time with him yet.

Unless . . .

'How big is this place?' he asked.

'Five bedrooms. We like to say it sleeps twelve. Well, it will.'

'Sounds spacious. And is there a garden?' Freddie would need somewhere to play.

'Big garden, yep. It's, um, in the process of being landscaped.'

Marcus spotted Jo's bedroom curtains being parted and his eyes widened. There in the window stood Bram – either naked or near naked – hands now clasped behind his head as he flexed and stretched various upper-body muscles, like a man who'd been horizontal for a long time. 'Sounds good.'

'So do you think you might be interested? We'd have to let Madame Bouziges know. She has the keys. Does a bit of cleaning.'

'Let me think about it,' said Marcus, as Bram hoisted a window and stuck his head out. Jo then emerged from the front door and looked up. They blew each other kisses and she bounced – yes, she was definitely bouncing – down Jubilee Street, swinging a straw shopping bag. 'And maybe check out flights. Can I call you back later?'

'Sure. Not too late, though. Madame Bouziges tends to retire early.'

'OK.'

Marcus hung up and was halfway across the room when he stopped in his tracks, turned, and looked back at the phone. He could almost feel the exclamation mark above his head as the contents and implications of the conversation suddenly sank in: Lucy and Dom returning . . . vacate house . . . south of France . . .

It sounded tempting but he wasn't sure he wanted to be there on his own. How he'd love to take Freddie with him, but then Hannah would have to come. Would that be possible? The Easter holidays were close. Hannah wouldn't be teaching . . . He checked his watch – it was probably her lunchtime – and found the mobile number she'd given him after the party. He dialled but was put straight through to voicemail, so left a call-me message.

'Adrian, it's Hannah. Just ringing in my lunch break, hoping you'd be there. Oh well. Listen, can I come and see you after school today, or maybe tomorrow? Text me or something and let me know? There have been developments since I saw you last week. You know how I was all wound up about Marcus and Jo sloping off to the Cotswolds? Well, nothing happened, according to Marcus, and anyway, it seems this mysterious bloke of hers does exist after all. Turned up on Friday, thank God, right in the middle of Marcus's birthday party. You'd think bloody Jude Law or someone had walked in from the reception he got. Nice-looking, though. After all the kerfuffle, I found Marcus slumped in front of the TV, knocking back some ghastly Schnapps-type drink one of the guests had brought along. Well, to cut a long story short, we went back to his place and cuddled on the sofa. It was a beautifully relaxing and peaceful platonic union, and I could have stayed like that, curled up all night, but then Marcus suddenly felt sick and had to go to the bathroom. I found him asleep, spreadeagled diagonally across the bed, so I covered him up and kissed him good night. He mumbled, "Night night, Jojo," which, as you can imagine, pissed me off. I haven't heard from him since. No apology or anything. Perhaps he doesn't remember, but all the same . . .

'Do you know, I feel better for airing all this, even if

it is to your voicemail. So . . . well, maybe I don't need to come and see you till Wednesday, now I've got it off my chest. But listen, Adrian, I'd prefer it if you didn't charge me again. You know, for having to listen to my message? I did feel that was rather mean of you last time.'

Jo was aware of a spring in her step as she went round the covered market. Spring was also in the air and, best of all, in Bram's vital organ. How many times had they made love in three days? A lot, as usual. But then there were his long absences to make up for.

She turned into the olive shop. It was Monday and she should have been working, but she'd catch up after he left on Wednesday. Off on a secret mission. It was all terribly romantic. Jo often wondered if she'd feel the same way about Bram if he worked in Dixons.

'Could I have some of the chilli ones?' she asked, pointing at a bowl through the glass counter. 'A large tub?'

For two years now they'd had this strange but exciting, semi-attached relationship. Mostly, he'd turn up out of the blue – she liked that – then disappear again, sometimes after only a night or two. His absences ranged from a week to, once, four months. It made it difficult to plan things to do together, which was a bit of a bore. Once, amazingly, he'd come to Wales with her to visit her parents, although most of the time they were there he'd rambled in nearby Snowdonia. The longest they'd spent in each other's company was three weeks. Not that this didn't suit Jo, in a way. Usually, by the time he was due to leave her place, the fact that he didn't always get her humour and liked to win every argument was beginning to tarnish Bram's prodigal-boyfriend appeal. Mostly, it was his certainty that got to Jo. He was clever and knowledgeable and stuck rigidly to his beliefs, so entering into an argument with Bram wasn't something she did lightly. But when, for example, he said people like her parents, who drove to the end of the road to post a letter, should be taken to court, well . . . she could hardly not go on the defensive. Her parents lived on a steep hill, after all.

When Bram wasn't being intense, though, he could be great company. He was informative and had lots of tales of daring to tell. That was what Jo liked most about him. Well, apart from the obvious.

'And a tubful of those with the peppers,' she told the assistant, pointing again. Bram loved olives.

She left the market and meandered around town, treating herself to a new pair of jeans, then bumping into a friend who told her she was looking really well. They went for a coffee and Jo told her *why* she was looking so well.

'How come I've never met this guy of yours in two years?' Jo was asked, and she laughed and said she'd barely met him herself. 'Don't you long to have someone around all the time?' said the friend. 'Isn't there anyone local you could go for?'

'Not really,' Jo replied, her head filling with Marcus.

She hadn't seen him for three days and suddenly found herself wondering how he was. Had he and Hannah got together after the party? Her stomach tensed slightly at the thought of that and she promptly excused herself and caught a bus home, where she showed Bram all the food she'd bought and said she might invite Marcus for dinner.

'Didn't you just throw a party for him?' he asked in the Dutch accent that made him sound vaguely American. 'Shouldn't he be inviting us over?'

'Marcus may run a restaurant but I'm pretty sure he never cooks. You know, like I never write a thesis and Richard Branson never mends a train.'

Bram came over and cuddled her from behind. 'You don't fancy him, do you?' he asked. 'He's very pretty, mind you. I could almost go for him myself.'

'Yeah, I'm sure,' laughed Jo, feeling him grow larger in the small of her back.

Robin's in his study and I'm at the kitchen table feeling tense and considering a trip to the supermarket. Freddie's watching TV. Washing-up liquid, milk, grapefruit. Sometimes mindless shopping helps. My first reaction to Marcus's suggestion was that he'd lost it. Freddie and I to come to France for the Easter holidays? Have you gone barking? I said.

But now I've had the slow, rush-hour drive home to think about it . . . well, Robin, after all, is plan-

ning a few days in Edinburgh with Theo, who would come to Oxford if he didn't have to work full time during the holidays to keep up his student lifestyle: iPod, clubbing, meals out and a wardrobe ten times the size of mine and Robin's put together. Theo, named after his Greek maternal grandfather, looks like Robin – a little less angular, maybe – but with all the same colouring. How Freddie might turn out, I expect.

I could just boldly march into the study now and say, Robin, I'm thinking of taking Freddie to France for a week or so. With Marcus. How would you feel about it? We need lightbulbs as well. It's funny how they all tend to blow around the same time. No, actually it makes perfect sense.

Might postpone the Robin encounter until I've aired things in my session tomorrow. Not that Adrian will offer any advice. After the initial How have you been feeling? he rarely says a word. Money for old rope, if you ask me – and all that professional prestige with it. Would love to see Adrian in a class of Year Nines, trying to get them to conjugate 'to be' for the umpteenth time, while they're chewing banned gum, sending banned text messages and asking with monotonous regularity whether he got shagged last night.

'No, thanks,' Marcus told Keiko when she waved the bowl at him again. 'I couldn't possibly manage another. I'll have olives coming out my ears soon.'

Keiko replaced the bowl and from the depths of her lap produced Marge Simpson and a retractable pencil. 'I am sorry. Could you repeat and explain? Olives out of ears? Is it idiom?'

'Um . . .' he said, but then Jo came to the rescue with a neat explanation and Keiko stopped staring at his ears, and Marcus, perversely, reached over for another olive. 'These are *really* good,' he told Jo.

'Aren't they?' She was dividing up a lasagne with a spatula. Marcus guessed the inch-square segment was for Keiko. 'Pass your plate, Marcus?'

'Sure.' He handed it to Keiko, who passed it to Ernst, who held it while a huge slab of steaming lasagne was slipped on.

'There's salad and bread to go with it,' Jo told him.

'Thanks. This all looks great.'

'I hear you never cook,' said Bram, turning Marcus's way. Being a large man, Bram had one long side of the table to himself. Keiko and Ernst shared the other, and Jo was at the head of the table facing Marcus, which pleased him as she was looking particularly radiant.

'I didn't say that,' Jo snapped at Bram.

'It's true, though,' said Marcus, sensing a little tension in the air. 'Well, hardly ever.'

'My father has never cooked one meal in his life inside his house,' said Ernst. 'But always he is the barbecue chef.'

Jo laughed. 'My dad's the same.'

107

'In Japan,' said Keiko quietly, 'women cook every-thing.' She took her tiny portion from Jo with a 'Thank you,' put it down and began fishing out the pasta.

'No, Keiko,' said Bram fairly forcefully. 'You don't mean women cook *everything*. That means women cook, you know, like the cat, the sofa, their mother-in-law. You mean women do all the cooking.'

Keiko covered her mouth and said, 'Ohhh,' behind her hand. 'My English is very bad.'

'No, it's not,' said Jo. She seemed to be smiling at Keiko and scowling at Bram at the same time. 'You're going great guns. One more term at the school and you'll be like a native speaker!'

Keiko giggled and thanked her. She carried on fishing out small strips of pasta, then stopped. Up from her lap came Marge and the pencil again. 'Please, could you explain why I have "great gun"?'

Jo did so with her usual patience, while Bram took his – quite a bit smaller than Marcus's – serving of lasagne from her.

Marcus warmed to Bram more as the meal went on; not a pedant after all, just a fairly straightforward, keen-on-facts, literal type of guy. He seemed to have an endless stream of interesting but fairly humourless saving-the-world stories and an opinion on everything. At one point Bram and Ernst discussed, in a quite heated manner, the subject of fining people for not recycling. Marcus got the impression Bram entered into such an argument on a daily basis, as he was pretty persuasive. In the end, he even had Ernst agreeing with the idea of cameras beside litter bins to catch those daring to throw away anything but the odd apple core.

'In Germany,' Ernst said, 'it would not surprise me for such a thing to happen.'

Bram gave an approving nod. 'Germany has definitely led the way when it comes to recycling. Along with Austria, New Zealand—'

'More lasagne, Marcus?' called Jo from the far end of the table. She looked great. She wasn't wearing her glasses, making her lovely brown eyes look half as big again. Her black top had a flattering neckline, and she wore a really pretty choker made of leather strips and beads; a present from Bram's travels, perhaps. The room was slowly growing darker, one or two candles were flickering and, all in all, the light was having a very flattering effect on her.

'Please,' he said, handing his plate to Keiko to pass on.

'I must admit recycling schemes have improved a lot here,' continued Bram. 'But, you know, you English still have a long way to go to catch up with more enlightened countries.'

Marcus realised he was getting a bit fed up with the topic now. 'Actually,' he told Bram with a curt smile, 'I'm Scottish.'

'And I'm Welsh,' said Jo, passing the heaped plate back. 'Is that enough, Marcus?'

'Plenty. I'll be stuffed if I eat all that.'

When Marge Simpson and the pencil appeared again, Marcus was quick off the mark. 'It means very, very full,' he told Keiko, patting his tummy.

'Aahh.'

'You know,' said Jo almost dreamily, staring at the bowl of olives, spatula dangling in the air, 'I can't think of anyone at the party last week who was totally English.'

'Robin?' asked Marcus.

'His grandfather was Greek, mother half-Greek.'

'Ah yeah. Forgot.' Freddie was part Greek and, on Hannah's side, a quarter Welsh. Obviously, he had no Scot at all in him. 'But surely Pippa's English?' Marcus asked.

'Brought up in London, yes, but her mother's Irish. Oh, I suppose Hannah might be—'

'Welsh mother. So, no.'

'Hannah's Welsh too?' said Jo. She looked vaguely annoyed.

'This is an explanation,' said Ernst while he chewed, 'for why the party was such good fun.'

'True,' they all agreed, laughing, and someone said, 'Down with the boring English!' and they clinked their glasses and went back to their food.

'Oh,' said Jo after a while, 'I've just thought of an English person at the party.'

Marcus looked up. 'Who was that?'

'Pippa's husband, Ray.'

'Are you sure?'

'Oh, yes. An Oxfordshire family through and through.'

He laughed. 'I meant are you sure he was at the party?'

Jo couldn't make out if it was the candlelight, the white wine or having too much sex over the past few days that was giving her these fantasies. Dark, almost glistening Bram was contrasting beautifully with Marcus and his Brideshead looks. Deep brown eyes/bright blue eyes. Big pale-chocolate biceps bulging from tight black T-shirt/slim golden-haired forearms below rolled-up sleeves. Raven chunky dreadlocks/soft blond flyaway hair. Ernst was saying something to her, but all Jo could think about was lying in bed between both men.

'Sorry, Ernst,' she said. 'I didn't quite catch that. Something about a member?'

'No. I said I re*member* the first time I was visiting England and it was raining for the whole week. It was a student exchange when I was twelve years old. My family I stayed with said they were sorry but that it rains a lot in Manchester. When I left to catch my plane I had a cold and the mother, her name was Mrs Ashby, she gave threesome Beechams Powders.'

'Threesome?'

'Jo, I think maybe you are not listening. Mrs Ashby gave me some Beechams Powders. They were very disgusting but maybe magical. When my parents met me I had no cold. I told them I'm never wanting to go to England again, but that we must find Beechams Powders in Germany!'

'And did you?' she asked, her eyes fixed on Bram's earring. Why the earrings? And why those coloured braided whatnots on both wrists? What she'd once thought was a part-hippy, part-African-roots aspect of Bram was now looking a shade immature. She noticed his head was gradually moving towards Marcus's, and while Ernst talked German pharmacies in her ear, she tried hard to hear what was being discussed animatedly at the far end of the table. When Ernst paused for breath she said loudly, 'Could you pass the white wine, Bram?'

Both beautiful faces looked her way and, once again, she saw herself sandwiched between the two men. Which one would she most want to be facing? She swallowed hard and took the bottle being handed her. 'What are you two deep in conversation about?' she asked with a big smile.

'Gaia,' said Bram.

'Ah.' Jo had never quite got the Gaia theory, which sees Earth as a living being; an organism that will inevitably reach the end of its life one day. Hopefully, not before her three-in-a-bed event.

'It's an interesting proposition,' said Marcus, bobbing his eyebrows at her over the top of his glass. Had he been reading her mind, or was he talking about Gaia?

'Excuse me,' said Keiko, who'd been awfully quiet. She raised her pencil in the air and turned to Jo. 'But what is meaning of threesome?'

Jo decided to pick nonchalantly at the salad on her plate. 'It just means, oh, three people, well, doing something together.' The other end of the table was eerily silent. Were they still looking her way?

'Ahh. So, when me and my friends Hiroko and Nyoko go to downtown Tokyo for shopping, we are doing threesome?'

Marcus said, 'Let me know next time you do that, Keiko. I'd like to come and watch.'

'It's not an expression we use much,' Jo said hurriedly. 'Honestly, I wouldn't even bother writing it down.'

'No?'

'No.'

There followed a bit of a silence when everyone went back to eating and drinking, until Marcus said, 'I haven't told you my big news, Jo.'

'Oh?' She didn't like the sound of this. Was that her alarm clock going off upstairs or something inside her head? 'What news?'

'Dom called. He and Lucy are coming home on Friday. Cutting their holiday short. They, er, want their house back.'

'What!'

He nodded.

'But . . .' said Jo.

'They have, however, offered me their house in France. For as long as I want it, apparently.'

'But . . .'

'I think I might go for it. Although I'd feel a bit bad as it's going to be busy in Braemar. Easter always is. Anyway—'

'On your own?' asked Jo, finding her tongue again. *Please say yes.*

Marcus shrugged. 'I don't know yet.'

Jo glued a smile to her face and said, 'Sounds great,' as her head moved on to a quite different fantasy. She, Bram and Marcus were in a hot-air balloon and rapidly losing height over treacherous terrain. Someone was going to have to go overboard to lighten the load. The men were saying she should decide.

'I was hoping Hannah and Freddie might join me,' Marcus said. 'But it looks like that might be tricky. You know . . . Robin.'

'Right.'

Bram reached for an olive and said, 'Which part of France?'

'Sort of the Auvergne, Cévennes area. Do you know it?'

'I know *of* it. Not such a good recycling record down there. Better in the north of France.'

'Well, it's pretty mountainous where I'm going, so perhaps they can be forgiven.'

'There's never an excuse,' replied Bram, wagging a finger at no one in particular, or maybe the whole of humanity, 'for squandering the world's resources.'

Jo sighed and her eyes went from Marcus to Bram,

to Marcus again. Back in the basket, above the Alps or wherever, Bram's ankles were now firmly clasped in her hands and, with the sudden strength of an ox, she was heaving him over the side.

'Excuse me,' she said, standing up. 'Back in a tick, then we'll have dessert.'

On the way to the bathroom, she crept into her front room to check that her passport was still valid. On her way back she checked it again.

That settles it, thought Marcus, on arriving home and listening to Hannah's whispered message. She'd spoken to Robin and he'd flipped, apparently, so no way could she and Freddie come to France with him.

He flopped on the sofa and Maidstone immediately jumped up and demanded food. Others might have seen all the purring and rubbing and pummelling as a friendly greeting, but Marcus knew better. Maidstone showed zero affection when he wasn't hungry, just buggered off out to do cat stuff until his next feed.

'In a minute,' Marcus said. 'Let me just have an existential moment, would you?'

Maidstone carried on pawing at his chest with his sharp claws, while Marcus contemplated his own place and purpose in the world and how he alone must be responsible for his actions. Ignoring the fact that Maidstone was actually hurting him, he then moved on to Jeremy Bentham's 'Greatest Happiness Principle', and how he, Marcus, ought not jeopardise Hannah, Robin and Freddie's welfare for the sake of his own selfish yearnings. What sort of a cad would do that? But then, what sort of a cad would impregnate a woman on the verge of getting married to someone else? Mind you, Robin claimed not to have known.

As the ethics of it all began to get blurry round the edges and it felt as though Maidstone might be drawing blood, Marcus gave up on his ruminations. There'd be plenty of time for that, all alone in France. It briefly flashed through his mind that he could invite Jo and her bloke to Laroche-la-thingy, if Lucy and Dom didn't mind. But would Bram be easy company? Doubtful. Jo on her own might be another matter. He conjured up the image of her over dinner, all soft round the edges in the candlelight. Lovely. But partnered. Like all the women he fancied.

When, ten minutes later, well-fed Maidstone shot through the catflap for the night, Marcus decided to turn in. He tidied up a bit, switched off lights and made his way up to the large bedroom he was going to be reluctant to give up, what with its TV, stereo and ensuite bathroom. As he closed the curtains he spotted Jo, also at her bedroom window, just standing there with the light behind her. Looking his way? It seemed so. Now he felt a bit awkward. Should he continue drawing the curtains, or acknowledge he'd seen her? He decided to wave. She waved back. They both closed their curtains.

WEDNESDAY

'Bye!' Jo called out to Bram. 'Bye! Have a good trip!'

He disappeared round the corner, on his way to the bus he always insisted on taking to the railway station if he had the time. She'd often go with him but today was feigning a headache. She stepped back into the hall and began counting. 'One, potato, two, potato . . .' When she got to twenty, she grabbed her keys and strode across the road.

'Hey,' Marcus said, looking pleased to see her.

'Hey,' she said back, and he let her in.

'How's it going?'

'Fine. When are you off?'

'Friday.'

Invite me to go with you. 'Looking forward to it?'

'Don't know, to be honest.'

'I'm sure it'll be great.'

'Yeah, yeah.' He led her through to the living room

where she plonked herself on a sofa. He came and joined her as she hoped he would. 'And if it's not . . .' he said, 'you know, if it gets a bit lonely . . .'

'Yes?'

'Well, I can always go back to Scotland.'

Invite me to Scotland. 'Be a shame not to make the most of it, though.'

'True. Although I'm still hoping Hannah and Freddie will be able to come.'

'Oh?'

'Mm. She's going to sound Robin out once again this evening, so keep your fingers crossed.'

'Will do.'

'Where's Bram?' asked Marcus.

'Gone.'

'Already? I didn't get to say goodbye.'

'No,' said Jo. If she told him Bram was still at the bus stop, he'd be bound to leave the sofa. And she didn't want that. 'On his way to . . . wherever,' she said with an apologetic shrug.

'That's a shame.'

'Mm.'

Not for the first time, Marcus checked his watch. Then checked it again. 'She said she'd ring,' he told Jo. 'And let me know.'

'Ah.'

'I'm not very hopeful.'

'No.'

'You know, if Hannah and Freddie can't come, I was wondering if maybe you—'

The phone rang and he sprang across the room and grabbed it. 'Uh-huh,' he said after a while. 'Oh. Well, only to be expected . . . Mm? . . . Listen, try not to be too upset, Hannah.'

Jo got up and went to the loo, just to be out of the way for a while. On returning to the living room, she expected to find Marcus holding a miserable head in his hands, but he didn't look particularly miserable at all. In fact, he seemed quite chipper and was even humming. 'They can't come,' he said.

'Shame,' said Jo, placing herself back on the sofa. 'What were you about to say before Hannah called?'

'Um . . .'

'You said if Hannah and Freddie can't— *Christ*, what was that?'

They'd both jumped at the sudden rapping on the window. Jo turned and there was Bram mouthing something. 'What?' she said, while Marcus hurried from the room. Jo followed.

'I just missed a bus,' panted Bram on the doorstep. 'Now I'm worried I'll miss my train too. You couldn't give us a lift, could you, Jo?'

Get a taxi, I'm busy! 'Yeah, I sup—'

'I'll take you,' said Marcus, picking up keys and unhooking a jacket. 'Got nothing else to do.'

* * *

119

While Bram nattered away beside him, Marcus tried to understand why he was feeling relieved. Borderline happy, even. He felt sorry for Hannah, who was distraught, by the sound of it, but he couldn't feel sorry for himself. Just pleased, in the end, that they weren't going to go upsetting Robin, causing unnecessary friction. Of course, a little 'family' holiday would have been nice, but had it been a selfish request on his part? Surely not, after all he'd gone through. Or maybe it had been. Hard to know who deserved what in such a weird situation.

'She's a wonderful woman – Jo,' Bram was saying.

'Yes.'

'Bright. Fun.'

'Yes.'

Another explanation might be that his feelings for Hannah had become . . . what? Murkier? Less clear, anyway. How easy it was to build someone up in their absence, only to be horribly reminded of their flaws as soon as you were with them again. She could be very bossy; he'd forgotten that. And her mood could change in the blink of an eye. On the plus side, she was gorgeous to look at. And clever. Well, in some ways she was. Running to Robin hadn't perhaps been the cleverest of moves.

'I'm very lucky to have her,' said Bram.

'Yes, you are.'

'But why she doesn't get herself a proper boyfriend beats me.'

Marcus turned to Bram. 'She could just like the lack of commitment?'

Bram shook his head. 'I don't think so. If the right person came along and wanted happy ever after, she'd jump at it. I'm sure she would.'

'Oh?'

'And he'd be one lucky guy, I tell you.'

'Well, here we are,' said Marcus, slowing down and wondering where to park. 'Shall I just pull in by the entrance and you can jump out?'

'Cheers,' said Bram. 'I owe you one!' He got out, hauled his bag from the back seat and ran into the station, leaving Marcus with the notion that it might also be Bram's departure that was lifting his spirits.

SATURDAY

At Freddie's request, Robin was being a trampoline. Like the one at nursery, Freddie said as he bounced on his father's spine, that Mrs Jessup let them go on if they did good colouring-in. 'But we have to promise to do little jumps,' he puffed, 'like this, and this and this.'

'Aarrgh,' went Robin again and again, and Freddie laughed because he knew his dad was only pretending it hurt. Robin was, in fact, pretending to pretend it hurt. But a bit of a sore back for a few more days didn't seem much in the scheme of things, so he carried on pretending to pretend until Freddie bounced off him and whacked his head on the coffee table, cried for a bit, then went back to his woodwork.

Fairly glad the game was over, Robin lay recovering, trying to think of something fun for the two of them, or even the three of them, to do. It was the first day of Hannah and Freddie's Easter holidays and Robin was experiencing a certain lightness of heart. Marcus had left Oxford. Had left the country, even. Things were back to normal.

Almost.

When Hannah stopped being watery-eyed and mono-syllabic, then things would be back to normal. Had she really expected him to agree to her taking Fred on holiday with Marcus? What was to say they'd ever come back, he'd asked, and she'd said not to be ridiculous, of course they would. What kind of a person did he think she was?

Robin had been quietly furious and more than a little shocked that she should suggest such a thing. It seemed out of character, but then Hannah had been very out of character over the past week or so. Definitely more miser-able and short-tempered, very weepy, snapping at both himself and Freddie for no apparent reason. Anyway, this had been their first major confrontation, even though neither of them had exactly shouted and ranted, what with Freddie still being up. All the emotions of previous marital discord came flooding back to Robin and had left him shaken and drained for a full four days – between Monday evening when Hannah had first made her crazy request, and last night when Marcus popped round to say goodbye. Hannah had been teary afterwards, taking herself off to bed at 9.30.

Robin sat up and rubbed at his middle back. 'What are you making now, Fred?' he asked.

'A clock. So you can learn me the time on it.'

'*Teach* me, Freddie, not learn me.'

'I made a big hand, look.'

'Oh, yes.' The hand was actually bigger than the clock itself but perhaps Freddie could take a saw, or whatever was needed, to it. Robin picked it up. Aha, balsa wood. In that case, he thought, a sharp kitchen knife should do the trick. But when he got up and tried sneaking out of the room with it, Freddie protested and waved a nail at him.

'I need it *now*, Daddy, to hammer it on.'

Robin knew better than to stem the flow of his son's creative genius, so gave him the very *big* big hand and said, 'How would you like to go and see Theo?'

Freddie hammered while he thought about it, then stopped, but still held the nail in place. 'Do you mean Feo at nursery? Or do you mean Feo my bruvver?'

'Half-brother,' Robin said, then wished he hadn't. Too hard to explain. 'Theo, in Edinburgh. I know he'd love to see *you*.' A slight exaggeration, maybe.

'Alright. But can we go to the zoo again?'

'I expect so.' Even as he spoke, Robin knew he should have consulted Hannah first. Hadn't she said something about taking Freddie to see her parents while he was away visiting Theo? Damn.

When she came into the room, still in her dressing gown, Freddie stopped work and said, 'Daddy said we can go to the zoo!'

'Which zoo?' Hannah asked, frowning Robin's way.

'Er, Edinburgh. It was just an idea. I thought maybe you could both come with me? We could find a B and B.' He forced a laugh. 'Save me having to stay at Theo's place.'

The look Hannah gave him was a resigned and miserable one. 'But I told my parents Fred and I would—'

Robin smacked his brow. 'God, sorry. Forgot. Maybe next time then, Fred. Hey, it'll be fun staying with Granny and Granddad, won't it?' What was fun about an ornament-filled semi in a publess sprawling village twelve miles from Leicester was beyond Robin, but his son seemed to think it was Heaven on Earth. Maybe if Ruth and Vic didn't treat Robin with undisguised contempt – understandably, some might say – he'd find it Heaven on Earth too. Robin had been cold-shouldered throughout his one overnight stay at the confusingly named 'Copse View' – it looked out on a dozen starter homes – and vowed not to repeat the experience. Most phone conversations between himself and Hannah's parents consisted of, 'Is Hannah there?' 'I'll just get her.'

'I want to go to the zoo,' Freddie was whining. 'Mummy, *pleeze* can we go to the zoo with Daddy?'

Hannah rolled her eyes and left the room, and Robin wondered if he ought to go after her.

'My best thing in the zoo is the grillas,' Freddie said. He placed a nail and a very short hand on his clock and began bashing.

'They were great, weren't they?'

'Will the grillas be there this time?'

'I expect so. Listen, Fred, perhaps we could go and see Theo and the zoo one weekend soon. After you've been to Granny and Granddad's. In the meantime,' he lowered his voice, 'it might be best not to mention it to Mummy again.'

Freddie stared up at him. "Cos she might cry?'

'Yes,' said Robin, rubbing his wonderful little son's head. What a fantastically sensitive and caring little boy he was.

'Mummy cries even more than Millie at playgroup,' said Freddie. 'And Millie at playgroup cries even if you just do this.' He put his hammer down and pinched the skin near Robin's wrist, long and hard. It was a very thin pinch, the type that hurts a lot.

'Ouch!' Robin cried. 'Stop!' He pulled his arm away and examined the growing red mark. Christ. Was there another side to Freddie that only little girls saw? 'You absolutely *mustn't* pinch anyone like that *ever* again. OK?'

Freddie continued to hammer.

'OK?' repeated Robin.

'Ok*aay*.'

'Good boy.' Robin stood upright, rubbed at the pain and wondered what to do with himself while Fred was happily occupied.

'But anyway,' said Freddie, 'now I don't pinch Henrietta or Lara any more, 'cos they always kicked me really hard.'

'Good for them.' This was terrible. Could three year olds be excluded? He'd have a word with Mrs Jessup.

On his way out of the room, Hannah passed him. 'When were you planning on going to Edinburgh?' she asked.

'The day after tomorrow.' He'd told her several times, he knew he had. 'Monday,' he added. Was she now considering joining him?

'Back when?'

'Well, it depends on Theo. And how long I can bear the lifestyle. Saturday, I expect.'

'Right,' she said, and headed for an armchair. She held her locked diary flat against her chest, which meant she too would be occupied for some time.

There was nothing for it, Robin decided, but to go and read Bridget's next chapter on US foreign policy, entitled 'Military Intelligence'. Would he write his usual 'Oxymoron?' wisecrack next to her heading? Maybe not.

'*Monsieur Kewrrriee!*' Marcus thought he heard outside his window. His eyes sprang open. Kewrriee? Curie? Currie? '*Monsieur Kewrriee!*' came the voice again. Marcus waited for a rap on the door, then remembered there wasn't one.

'Coming!' he called back, hauling himself from the bed. He opened the nearest window, pleased he hadn't closed the shutters as well, and stuck his head out.

'*Le téléphone!*' said Madame Bouziges, holding an invisible receiver to her ear in the back garden.

'Ah,' said Marcus. '*Un momento!* I mean . . .' God, this was far too early in the day to attempt French. He tugged on jeans, grabbed a jumper, found his shoes, stepped over a pile of floorboards on the landing, went past four empty bedrooms, down the stairs – careful with the missing one – then over the pot-holed concrete floor, under the dangling electric wires and through a plastic sheet. Madame Bouziges – trim, dark-haired, late forties and in chic red wellies – was charging homeward through the decidedly unlandscaped garden and Marcus hurried to catch up.

'Oh, hi, Mum,' he croaked once inside an interesting room: ancient beams with dried herbs hanging from them, sepia photos of ancestors on a dark and heavy sideboard, two small yapping dogs and a huge TV. 'How are you doing?'

'Ooch, are you all right?' she asked. 'You're sounding a bit poorly. It's not a dusty, germ-filled place you're staying in?'

Well, now she came to mention it . . . 'I'm fine,' he said. Had he been a bit hasty in giving his mother this contact number? He was sure he'd stressed it was for emergencies only. 'I need a *café au lait*, that's all. Just woken up.'

From the doorway, Madame Bouziges gave him a

knowing nod and before Marcus's mother had finished telling him about the large party they'd had in the restaurant, all the way from South Africa, the dear woman was back with a bowl the size of a chamber pot, full of strong milky coffee. If he'd known her a little better he'd have kissed her.

'No, Mum,' he said as he took sips and felt the caffeine hit. 'I'm *not* thinking of making house-sitting a way of life.' If she could see his present house she'd know why. 'I'm just sort of doing these people a favour, keeping an eye on their useless builder.' Madame Bouziges's eyebrows shot up and Marcus, horrified, wondered if her lack of English had been a ruse. But then she took a gentle swipe at one of the terriers who'd jumped in an armchair and Marcus relaxed again.

'So long as you're keeping warm,' said his mother, who'd always put that as her number-one priority in life. Being a petite woman in Scottish climes, it was understandable.

'Well, it'll be a bit more comfortable when the electricity's on again.'

Marcus laughed but his mother didn't. She just tutted and told him what a worry he was, then said, 'Have you got your sweater with you? The one I sent you for your birthday?'

'Yes, I have,' Marcus could answer honestly. He'd packed it at the last minute, guessing he'd be able to wear it in the French wilderness with no fear of bumping into an acquaintance. And, who knew, maybe red-and-yellow tartan was the new black in Laroche-les-Bois. 'Anyway, it's a beautiful spot, so I'll be out walking a lot. Keeping warm. However, the lady who looks after the house says the weather forecast is good.'

At least he *thought* that was what she was telling him at a rate of knots when he arrived last night, knackered from the long winding uphill drive. It could equally have been, 'Five stamps for England, please,' he realised later, flicking through his phrase book in bed. Or, 'Open wide, I'm going to give you an injection.' The sentence he'd been searching for – 'What the fuck have I come to here?' – was nowhere to be found. Thank *God* Hannah and Freddie hadn't come, he'd just kept thinking, until sleep took over.

'OK, Mum,' he said, raising his voice to add authority. 'I'll speak to you soon. Not too soon, though, eh? We don't want to keep disturbing Madame— . . . Mm? . . . Oh, I dunno. My car's booked into the airport car park for a month but I might cut it short; come back to Braemar. Although you seem to be coping without me.'

'Vinko says to tell you there's no hurry.'

'Who?'

'The new chef.' She chuckled. 'Actually, I think he's rather enjoying your flat.'

'What! Since when are we giving the chefs my flat?' The caffeine was well and truly kicking in now, and all Marcus's senses were coming alive. Particularly his sense of outrage. 'What's wrong with the room out the back?'

'Oh, Vinko said that in Slovenia he was used to a little more comfort, so—'

'Are you saying we're doing Slovenian food now?'

'Aye. Going down a treat it is. Anyway, son, as I say, there's no need to rush back. But do let me know how you're keeping, and how the sweater washes up, won't you? No higher than thirty degrees. Short spin.'

'Yeah, OK. But first I'll need electricity, don't forget.'

'And a quick press with a tepid iron wouldn't do it any harm.'

'Right,' he sighed. Sometimes his mother's inability, or unwillingness, to listen was a worry, sometimes a blessing. Often he *thought* she'd heard something he'd said, only to discover, next time they spoke perhaps, that she hadn't absorbed it at all. But at least she was like that with everybody. At one point, Hannah had started referring to her as Granny Groundhog Day, until Freddie began using it in his grandmother's presence but leaving off the 'Day' bit, making it sound plain rude.

'Don't worry,' he said. 'I'll take good care of the jumper. Anyway, gotta go. Madame Bouziges needs to use the phone.'

Marcus thanked her for calling and hung up, then went to find Madame Bouziges. She was plucking something in the kitchen, and through a combination of his limited comprehension and a lot of gestures on her part,

Marcus gathered that he was invited to partake of whatever was dangling from her hand, at eight that evening.

I should be over the moon – no teaching for two weeks – but am feeling shitty. Marcus has buggered off, having totally disrupted our lives and spent almost no time with Freddie. How thoughtless of Lucy and Dom to return like this. According to Lucy, they were happy to let Marcus stay on for the weekend, since they'd decided to shoot up to Dom's parents for some family event. But Marcus had already booked his flight by the time they offered. Sometimes I despair of those two. So up themselves.

Had I really thought Robin would be cool about me taking Fred to France? Go on your own, he said, if you feel you and Marcus have got things to resolve, but you're not taking Freddie. I've never seen Robin seethe as he did on first Monday, then Wednesday. He shook, and actually scared me a little, so I backed down – charmingly, I think – and said I understood and pecked him on the cheek. Just thought I'd ask, I said, then went and sobbed into the phone to Marcus. I keep catching sight of myself in mirrors and shop windows, crying. Unaware that I have been. Are you all right? people keep asking me at work. Fine, I say, then dash to the loos and there they are again, those red teary eyes.

It's all such a muddle, but also strangely clear – I don't love Robin, I do love Marcus. But maybe the gods are conspiring to keep me and M apart — keep me with Robin — keep things stable for Freddie.

Maybe the gods are conspiring to do my head in too, although Robin thinks it's the antidepressants that are fucking me up. Why not ask Dr Maxwell to review your prescription? he said. So I did. Yesterday afternoon. Maxwell took my blood pressure, checked my throat and ears for some reason, put his cold stethoscope on my bare back, gave me a clean bill of health and suggested I double the dose when I feel the need. I didn't tell him I was already doing that. He's hopeless — close to retirement and looks at his watch a lot, as though counting the minutes till his sixty-fifth birthday.

One thing's for sure — I'd recover quickly, flush the pills away and be my old self, if only I were with Marcus, as in with Marcus. Shall I go and see him, anyway? If Fred and I went for just a couple of days, Robin need never know — or I just deal with the consequences when we get back.

Last night I went online and checked flights to Nîmes and Montpellier, thinking they'd be fully booked as it's Easter. Not the case, it seems. Potatoes, honey, newspaper, oh, fuck these stupid shopping lists. Adrian's such a prick. Things to do: warn my parents we might not be visiting; put on a better front for Robin before he has me sectioned; go and feed Maidstone.

Keiko was being terrific, bringing her mugs of tea and saying, 'Don't worry, Jo. Bram will be back soon.'

Eventually, Jo said, 'It's not him I'm missing, Keiko.'

'No?' said her surprised lodger. She held out Ibuprofen and Jo took them from her. 'Then are you sad because Ernst has gone to see family?'

Jo sniffed and shook her head. 'Uh-uh. But I'll let you have one more guess.'

Keiko put a finger on her red, red lips while she had a think, then stared at Jo and said, 'Aaahh, it is Marcus?'

'Mm,' nodded Jo. 'Marcus. Listen, Keiko, you couldn't fetch the Milk Tray, could you?' She decided she might as well make the most of this. 'You know, the chocolates I wouldn't let myself eat? They're in the recycling cupboard, hidden in a cardboard box behind the bag of cans.'

Keiko headed back towards the kitchen. 'In Japan,' she said, 'girls eat many chocolate when boyfriend is unkind.'

Jo laughed. 'Yeah, it's the same here. Or even when they're not unkind.' She took a couple of painkillers, hoping they worked on heartache, and realised she *was* missing Ernst: his funny off-key wailing when plugged into his personal CD player; the way he ran not just up, but *down* the stairs two at a time, without even holding the handrail. How was that humanly possible? Ernst added a bit of young-male zing to the household, which was complemented by Keiko's sweetness and calmness. A nice easy couple of students, once you disregarded their dietary quirks. Unlike the two girls she'd had for a term before Christmas; close friends from the same Austrian town. Both had boyfriend-back-home problems they liked to share with her, mobiles that never stopped, a tendency to come home pissed at two a.m., and a daily stack of laundry for her to do. How she'd like to keep Keiko and Ernst for ever, but they'd be gone by July, when she'd be forced to have some of the younger summer-term students, many packed off by parents wanting a break.

She sighed and took the Milk Tray from Keiko. 'Thanks. Want one? Oh no, I forgot.'

While she worked her way through the chocolates, starting with her favourites and planning to end with praline, Keiko sat across the room examining a large book on her lap at very close quarters. 'What's that?' Jo asked.

'It is your map book of Europe.'

'Oh?'

'Middle and south of France pages.'

'Really?'

'To find where Marcus has gone.'

Jo put the chocolates down and joined Keiko on the sofa. 'Do you know the name of the place?' she asked.

Keiko produced a piece of paper. 'I ask Marcus for address to send photos of dinner to. Very good photos.' From the back of the atlas came a set of prints. 'Especially one of you in middle of Bram and Marcus.'

'Pardon?' said Jo, grabbing them. She went through the ten or so pictures and felt small pangs each time she came across Marcus, and something else altogether when she saw Bram: not much, in fact. What she couldn't get over was how good *she'd* been looking that evening. Irresistible, she'd say. How Marcus hadn't thrown caution to the wind and begged her to come to France was most puzzling. There was one hideous shot of her, though, taken when she was shovelling something in her mouth. Jo sneaked that beneath a buttock, plus a particularly dreamy one of Marcus, and handed the rest back to Keiko. 'You must send them to him. They're great.'

'Thank you.'

Jo helped Keiko check the address against the map, and eventually spotted the nearest town. 'Gosh, looks pretty remote,' she said. It looked pretty high too, if Jo was reading the contours correctly. What on earth was Marcus going to do there? He'd be able to roam in the hills, of course, but she knew from experience that he wasn't a fanatical walker. It was a great-looking house, though. She'd seen photos of the outside: an imposing stone building, covered in shutters. Really spacious, Lucy had said. Something like five bedrooms. So many bedrooms, thought Jo, that maybe you wouldn't even notice if you had a guest. Or two.

'Have you ever been to France?' she asked Keiko.

'Only once to Paris with my parents on whistle-shop tour of Europe. But not any more parts of France.'

'Do you mean whistle-stop?'

'No. Definitely whistle-shop. It was special shopping holiday for Japanese persons.'

'Ah. Well, do you think you'd like to see more of France?'

Keiko nodded and looked wistful. 'Yes. Very much.'

'This week?'

The thing Madame Bouziges had been plucking turned out to be a duck, now tender and tasty and accompanied by beans and assorted vegetables in a delicious cassoulet. Marcus thought about asking for the recipe for his restaurant in case they went French, but two things were stopping him. What were the chances of a French chef who *didn't* know how to make this national dish turning up in Braemar? And, even if Marcus made himself understood, would he grasp Madame Bouziges's reply? The past fifteen minutes had been spent delving into the depths of his brain for annoying little words he kept hearing, such as *donc, devant, depuis*.

'*C'est très bon*,' he said again and was rewarded with another dollop of cassoulet.

Marcus, Madame Bouziges and her father-in-law, Bertrand – a bulging and undulating man who'd clearly enjoyed many a cassoulet – had, in mostly one-word sentences on Marcus's part, covered the weather, the local towns and villages and the two family dogs. But now it had gone very quiet. After telling them the food was *très bon* again, Marcus wondered where they could go next, conversationally. He ruled out twentieth-century French feminist criticism and the films of Jean-Luc Godard and opted, instead, for making appreciative noises as he ate, just to fill the void.

It was a silence that seemed to go on interminably. He continued with the occasional 'Mmmm', and Bertrand's teeth clattered a bit, but that was all that could be heard. Surely he knew more French than 'Mmmm', Marcus kept thinking. All those years of study. Although he'd holidayed in France several times before, he'd been with the fluent Hannah and hadn't needed to say more than the odd *merci*.

However, he decided, this might be a golden opportunity to improve his language skills. Beginning now. In his head he started forming the French version of, 'Bertrand, are you thinking of pulling your finger out and getting my electricity back on?' – *Excusez-moi, Bertrand, mais quand*— when the dining-room door flew open and a shortish, muscular young man with dark hair, olive skin and a big smile burst in. Madame Bouziges exclaimed something, dabbed at her mouth with a napkin and accepted three kisses from him.

After receiving a wordy explanation as to whom Marcus was, the newcomer was then introduced as Claude. Marcus gave a slightly Del Boy, *'Bonsoir, bonsoir,'* as the two of them shook hands, then Claude sat down on the next chair and lifted the casserole lid to inspect.

'*C'est très bon*,' Marcus informed him.

Claude turned and nodded. 'Yes, it would be. My aunt is famous for her cassoulet, you know. Some consider it unsurpassable, although I personally think she overdoes the beans and underdoes the garlic.' He smiled at Madame Bouziges as he took a plate and a wine glass from her. 'Don't worry,' he murmured. 'She doesn't understand a word.'

Rather than fall off his chair with shock and gratitude at hearing English, Marcus said, 'Tastes perfect to me.'

Dinner went swimmingly after that, with Claude interpreting deftly and amusingly. He'd been an only child, Marcus learned, orphaned aged eight and brought up by his mother's sister and her husband. 'Tragically, we lost my uncle in a wild-boar shooting accident in Languedoc,' Claude added. 'Just last year. My aunt was inconsolable for months.' Marcus expressed his commiserations. He told Claude his own father had passed away too after a long illness. Then they moved themselves on to less painful matters. Claude was training to be an air-traffic controller, but was home on three weeks' leave and, to Marcus's joy, intended to make Lucy and Dom's house 'spick and span' before he went back.

'How come your English is better than mine?' Marcus asked as he passively enjoyed the post-prandial, continental-smelling cigarettes fugging up the room nicely.

'Years and years of classes,' explained Claude, taking

another long drag. 'And many a misspent night reading English dictionaries.' He exhaled all over Marcus. 'When I do something, I like to do it well, you see. Plus, you have to have a good command of English in my chosen profession.'

'I'm sure you do. I mean, you don't want to be getting your "Left a bit"/"Right a bit"s mixed up, do you?'

Claude laughed. 'Not forgetting "Watch out behind you!"' He drew on his cigarette again. 'I take it you don't know any French?'

'What gave you that idea?'

'My aunt. She said you have slightly less vocabulary than Piaf.'

'Well, I'll take that as a compliment.'

'Piaf is one of her goats. Her favourite, as a matter of fact. She's sweet-natured and very productive but no, she doesn't have a great command of our language.' Claude smiled. 'I expect it's just a vernacular problem you're having. The vowel sounds are quite different around here.'

'Ah,' Marcus said, not totally convinced and reeling slightly from Madame Bouziges's comparison. She seemed too nice a lady to be comparing him with a goat. 'That could be it.'

Later, when Madame Bouziges produced grapes and a living, breathing and possibly thinking slab of Brie, Marcus said a self-conscious, '*Oui, merci,*' when offered some, but skipped the '*C'est trés bon*' as he ate.

MONDAY

For such a little person, Keiko certainly packed a big suitcase. It was 8.15 and a bit of a shock to Jo's system to be up, dressed and ready for a holiday so early on a Monday morning. 'You know it's only for a week,' she told her lodger, 'not the rest of our lives?'

Keiko giggled as she bumped her luggage down the last stair. It was mostly her language books, she explained, because she wanted to work hard and impress her teacher, Adam, next term. 'But also mountain clothes from sports shop and climbing boots. Very expensive boots. More than one hundred fifty pounds, but man in shop said essential.'

'I'm sure he did,' said Jo, wondering what kind of walking companion Keiko might make. Tough and speedy, or like Marcus?

Once Keiko had made it round the corner and along the hallway, Jo opened the front door to Pippa, who was calling in on her way to work for housecare instructions: plant watering, picking up emails and passing on anything really urgent via Madame Bouziges's phone. 'Feel free to stay here,' said Jo, 'if Ray's driving you nuts.'

Pippa beamed and clasped hands under her chin. 'Great! I'll bring my stuff over tonight.'

'Are you being serious?' Jo had meant it as a throw-away remark. Did she really want Pippa living in her house? What if she refurbished it as a nice surprise for her?

'Deadly.'

'Well, OK. But—'

'Sasha's home for the holidays. It'll be nice for her to have a bit of bonding time with her dad.'

Jo said, 'Oh, I see,' but didn't see at all. Surely it would be like trying to bond with a table leg? Harder, maybe. 'Let me explain the heating to you, then,' she insisted. 'You know, the timer, where the thermostat is . . .' Pippa was looking at her blankly, as though she'd never heard of such things. Someone who kept her house at constant Dubai temperatures probably hadn't. 'It's best to light a fire if it gets chilly,' Jo added, wishing it was August and not early April. 'Nice and cosy and saves on the bills.'

'I think taxi has arrived,' said Keiko, squinting through the frosted glass of the front door.

'Look, here are the keys,' Jo told Pippa. 'I'm sure you'll work everything out for yourself. And remember, if Bram rings, I've gone to stay with an old friend.'

'Yeah, yeah,' said Pippa, casually rearranging the hall table and looking awfully at home. 'Off you go.' She air-kissed Jo's cheeks, then Keiko's. 'And have a *fabulous* time.'

Keiko yanked at her suitcase. 'Thank you.'

'We'll try!' said Jo, grabbing her stuff.

Pippa held the front door open for them, then waved them off down the short path. 'Oh, and tell Marcus there's no expiry date on that voucher!' she called out.

Once inside the taxi and gliding down the Iffley Road towards town, Jo flopped back in the rear seat and pictured the surprised and hopefully thrilled look on Marcus's face when she and Keiko rolled up at around seven or eight o'clock that evening. She'd tried Lucy and Dom's door a couple of times over the weekend, to ask if it would be OK to go, but they'd obviously shot off somewhere on Saturday and still weren't back. She couldn't get them on their mobiles either, so had put a note through the letterbox an hour ago, hoping they'd be cool about it. They'd told her enough times she should go to their place in France when it was done, so Jo didn't feel she was taking liberties. Neither was she going to feel bad about Hannah after that elbow in the stomach.

Jo smiled to herself, thinking of Marcus. Just before leaving on Friday, he'd hugged and squeezed her and caressed her back, shoulders, upper arms – a grope, in fact – ending with a kiss slightly to the left of her lips and a stroke of her cheek with a finger. 'You are wonderful,' he said. 'I'm really going to miss you. If only you didn't have the lodgers to feed, you could—'

'Actually, Ernst has gone back to Germany for the holidays. And Keiko's more than—'

'But, who knows,' he said, burying his face in her hair, 'maybe solitude will be good for my soul.'

'Maybe . . .' Jo had replied, considering herself invited.

The one thing she was now hoping was that Lucy and Dom wouldn't get back soon and ignore her request not to call France and spoil the surprise.

On the other side of the taxi, Keiko was quietly humming to herself. How great this trip would be for her. The language school was always encouraging host families to take their students out and about. They probably meant ten-pin bowling rather than the south of France, but Jo couldn't see it would do her landlady rating any harm. Once again she checked she had everything: passport, detailed directions to Laroche-les-Bois gleaned from the Internet, emailed confirmation of flights and car hire and, finally, the beta-blockers she resorted to every time she had to endure air travel.

'Do you enjoy flying?' she asked Keiko.

Keiko shrugged and pulled a face. 'Usually I sleep. Japanese always fall asleep on travel. Sometimes even when we stand up on train or bus.'

'I've heard about that. One theory is that Japanese babies are carried by their mothers all the time, so that kind of rocking, rolling movement sends you off.'

'Aaahh,' nodded Keiko. 'Interesting. But my mother doesn't like rock and roll. She is big fan of Dolly Parton.'

'Right.'

Claude began work at 9.30, blasting Marcus from sleep with a series of short sharp drillings that resounded painfully through the walls, floors and everything else of the bare and ancient house. There followed some tapping and a good deal of cheerful whistling, and before Marcus had formed the entire thought that he'd rather like to be home in Scotland, a bulb lit up, not far above his head.

'Yes!' he said, punching the air.

He then lay for a while contemplating the coffee he could now make and the bath he'd be able to take, but also considering what he was going to do with his days in Laroche-les-Bois. From his first couple of forays down the hill and into the village centre the previous day, he'd discovered the only lively place – apart from the male-filled and fairly scary 'Sports Bar' he'd popped his head into – to be the church. More of an abbey really. It was a huge affair, which the board outside explained the history of, in great detail and no doubt interestingly. The abbey had a vast car park and people poured into the village to pray and sing there; then in the evening, returned to pray and sing again. Meanwhile, the shop across the square was totally shuttered up and looking as though it hadn't seen any business since Vichy days.

He'd have another stroll down later, Marcus decided. Maybe Sunday hadn't been the best time to check out where it was happening in a deeply Catholic community. He'd try the shop again and watch the boules. There were bound to be boules. If only he had a string vest and a suspicious stare, he could get to know the guys in the Sports Bar.

'Hold that, would you?' asked Claude.

Marcus put his coffee down and steadied the top end of the back door, laid on its side, while Claude planed the very bottom.

'So what is there to do around here?' Marcus asked. 'For fun.'

'It depends. Do you like water sports?'

'I've been known to fish.'

'Only the canoeing's terrific over in the gorges. You should come with us some time. Give it a go.'

'Great,' Marcus said as Claude blew sawdust in both their faces, then planed a bit more. After a while they tried the door in its frame and it seemed to fit, so Marcus continued holding it as Claude worked away at screws and hinges.

'Of course, it's unutterably dull for adolescents in the village,' Claude continued, 'and they sometimes get into trouble. Intemperance and so on. But most of them leave for the cities as soon as they can. Nice, Montpellier, Paris even. Some stay, though, and get married and procreate.

The guys learn trades and repair the houses for the Germans and Dutch and British who buy up all the decrepit properties around here. It's not a bad life, and family is very important, you know. Big extended-family meals are *de rigueur*, especially at weekends.'

'Is that so?' Marcus was still pondering on 'intemperance' – bad temper or drunkenness? – when someone hooted loudly out in the road.

'It's the bread van,' explained Claude. 'You'd better hurry. She doesn't hang around for long.'

Marcus grabbed some change and went and bought himself two baguettes from a charming young woman who clearly had the fresh-bread market cornered in the area. When he returned, Claude was shaking his head at the door.

'It's still sticking a little,' he said. 'I think it's this small protuberance here, by the hinge.'

Marcus looked closely. 'I could always just give it a bit of a kick when I need to shut it.'

Claude tutted and began unscrewing things. 'No, no. I tend to be punctilious in my work, I'm afraid. Just my nature.'

The door came off again, Marcus held it again and Claude planed again. When it shut perfectly the second time it was screwed in, both men gave a little whoop and Claude took a fag break. 'The thing is,' he said, after they'd talked more about the exodus of young people from the area, 'I could do with a mate.'

'Oh?' said Marcus. 'Aren't there any nice women in Clermont-Ferrand?'

'No, I mean now. On this job. Perhaps I've used the wrong word. Um . . . an assistant?'

'Ah. Sorry. No, mate was the right word.'

'I don't suppose you'd be interested? Bertrand is of no use.' Claude grinned. 'My aunt always says he is as indolent as de Gaulle.'

Rude? wondered Marcus. No, that was *insolent*. Two days abroad and he was already losing his language. 'President or goat?' he asked Claude.

'Her least favourite goat. I'd pay you, of course, out of my remuneration from Lucy and Dom.'

'Well!' Marcus gave an embarrassed laugh and didn't quite know what to say. A builder's mate? It was an idea, actually. Give him something to do. Bit of exercise. There was one drawback, though. 'I have absolutely no skills,' he told Claude.

'Can you hold a ladder?'

'I guess so.'

'Carry stones and tiles?'

'Possibly.'

Claude lifted his coffee cup in the air. 'In that case, you're hired!'

Marcus lifted his too. 'Great!' he said, not certain he meant it but hoping he could help speed up the building process, just in case Hannah changed her mind. Or rather, Robin did. And, hey, he told himself, he might even improve his English if he hung out with Claude long enough.

Earlier, I gathered up Lucy and Dom's letters from their doormat, including a hand-delivered one, and tried not to get maudlin about Marcus no longer being in the house, as happened each time I fed Maidstone over the weekend. After all, I'll be seeing him tomorrow!

This evening we're booked on a flight to Montpellier, where we'll stay the night in a hotel and pick up a hire car in the morning. After rifling through drawers and papers in Lucy and Dom's attic office, then tapping into their Word files, I finally found the address of, and even directions to, their place in France.

Their two mobiles were charging up, side by side next to the computer, which explained why I hadn't been able to ring them yesterday. Actually, I was quite pleased not to get through, just in case they were a bit anti me joining Marcus. Lucy, I know, is particularly fond of Robin. The whole world's fond of Robin – apart from my parents and possibly his ex-wife. I left them a note telling them my plans and asking them to keep it under their hats as I wanted to surprise Marcus. And definitely not to tell Robin. All would be explained when I got back, I promised. I poured a second helping of dried food into Maidstone's bowl, then popped Lucy and Dom's key through Jo's letterbox, with a note asking her to feed the cat till they got back.

So, everything's sorted. Now what I have to do is talk Freddie out of taking his cumbersome toolbox to France. He'll never let it go into the hold with our cases, suspecting everyone of wanting to run off with his mini hand-drill. He's even begun tucking the box under his duvet at night. Cute or weird? I asked Adrian last week and he managed a few words. No doubt it's to do with loss, he said, making me feel fairly crappy for the rest of the session.

Just the thought of getting away from here and being with Marcus has lifted my spirits. So much so that I'm considering not taking this diary with me. Why would I need to sit in a corner and scribble my heart out if I'm with Marcus?

I have to say, Lucy and Dom's house looks stunning in the photos I found. So romantic. Has Lucy ever mentioned a pool? Freddie would love that, and it's bound to be warmer down there, even in April. Mustn't forget suncream.

Even with the beta-blocker it was white-knuckle time for Jo. The engines were making that 'Hold tight, we're about to explode!' roar, as the plane raced along the runway with the ridiculous idea that it could get off the ground if it only went fast enough. She turned to Keiko to utter a few last words, but found her companion already dead to the world – as opposed to dead, which they all would be soon. 'Please God, make me Japanese next time?' Jo said out loud, just to make sure He heard.

When the great overloaded hulk of a thing dragged itself into the air – the most dangerous time in any flight, apparently – and Jo had squeezed all the life out of her armrests, the white-haired man in the window seat to her left said, 'It's OK, don't worry,' in a French accent. 'I used to be joose like you.' He covered her hand reassuringly with his in a way an Englishman wouldn't dream of.

'Did you?'

'*Oui*. But then my wife was knocked from her *bicyclette* and killed by a madman in a Peugeot. And now I see ow safe flying is compared to our roads *en France*.'

'I'm so sorry,' she said, a bead of sweat trickling over one eye. He really wasn't helping, just confirming how fragile life was.

'But why?' the kindly man asked. 'You were not driving.'

'No. It's just what we say. It means I'm sorry to hear your story.'

'You would rather I did not tell you?'

Yes, actually. 'No, not at all.'

The man laughed and Jo realised he was joking. 'I am tugging your leg,' he said.

'Pulling.'

'Of course. Pulling. I think of tug of war.' He lifted his hand and replaced it in his lap but carried on reassuring her with his warm, twinkling eyes. 'You have far too many words to say the same thing.'

'I know. I help foreign people with their English and they can't believe how many ways there are of saying, oh . . . "look" for example. Peer, glance, glimpse, peep, stare, gawk, gawp, and more, all with a different meaning, sometimes just a subtle one. You know, we can't just "walk", we're ambling or rambling, or strolling or striding. Sauntering, tramping, shuffling, meandering.' Jo laughed. 'I could go on,' she said, and she did. All the way to Nîmes.

When everyone but Jo was preparing for landing – she'd been ready from the word go, belt buckled throughout – she couldn't quite believe how quickly and painlessly the journey had passed. Clearly, the thing to do on all future flights was to bore a neighbour rigid on the intricacies of English.

When the plane taxied to a halt beside the terminal, Keiko's eyes popped open, as though the hypnotist inside her head had counted down from ten and arrived at one, just as the engines shut down. 'Ah,' she said, leaning forward and peering, peeping or possibly peeking through their little window. 'We land in France. I am very happy!'

'Not as happy as I am,' said Jo, releasing herself at last and breaking her long-held record by, for once, not being the first to stand up.

* * *

On leaving the building to search for their car, Jo and Keiko were hit by a disappointing chilliness and slight drizzle. They stopped, groaned, opened their bags and took out coats – in Keiko's case, a brand new Scott-of-the-Antarctic affair – but then found their gleaming, plum-coloured, latest-model Renault and immediately cheered up.

As usual, it took a while to get the hang of driving from the wrong side of the car and on the wrong side of the road, but by the time they reached the dual carriageway Jo found it coming easily. How crazy and perverse of the Brits to drive on the left, she decided. Such an unnatural place to be. She checked the car's clock: 4.50. They'd have to stop somewhere and eat, as there wasn't much point in relying on Marcus for dinner, but even taking that into account they ought to be with him by eight at the latest.

'Are you OK to map read?' she asked Keiko, who was holding the large road atlas in front of her, staring hard at it.

'OK. First I find Nîmes, yes?'

'Yep. Got it?'

'Um . . . it is very hard.'

Jo glanced over again, then looked back at the road as cars overtook her at aircraft speed. 'Here,' she said, reaching across and turning the map 180 degrees. 'See if that helps.'

* * *

When Theo said they were going clubbing, Robin hadn't expected to be listening to Herman's Hermits, Procol Harum and, twice, Perry Como. It was fifties/sixties night, a favourite with students, apparently. Robin thought Edinburgh would be empty of undergraduates, but according to Theo almost everyone he knew had a job they couldn't leave in the holidays for fear of it being snapped up by some other student.

What serious and unrecognisable lives these young people lived. All for the sake – well, in Theo's case at least – of yet more CDs, when he already had a wall covered in the things. Robin thought back to the half-dozen played-to-death LPs that had seen him all the way through university. And how he'd eked his grant out by making one potato into an entire meal and drinking mostly shandy. Had Theo and his friends even heard of shandy? Robin sipped at his Backwards Blow Job – a cocktail Theo had talked him into – and watched, with some astonishment, as the mere children around him mouthed the words to 'Catch a Falling Star'.

'Can I get you another one of those?' Theo shouted in his ear, just as the DJ announced that the next track was for the First Polo Team and everyone in their group broke into a cheer.

'You play *polo?*' Robin asked.

Theo said, 'Yeah,' although it bordered dangerously on a 'Yah'. He tapped his foot and bobbed his head in time to 'Puppet on a String' without any apparent embarrass-

ment. 'Terrific fun and a bit of a chick magnet,' he added
with a nudge that sent some of Robin's horrible drink on
to the floor.

'I might have something different this time,' Robin said,
and he turned to the list of cocktails. He'd heard of a Gin
Sling, but what was a Pan-Galactic Gargle Blaster? Or an
Anne Robinson? He worked his way down the menu,
hoping to find Pot of Tea for One at the bottom. 'Actually,'
he shouted, raising his almost empty glass. 'I think I'll be
off soon.'

'You can't do that,' Theo shouted back. 'We've only
just got going. Take advantage of not having Freddie
with you. How is he, anyway? Still taking that fire engine
everywhere?'

'It's his toolbox now,' Robin said, laughing but getting
a sudden Freddie pang. He thanked God he'd booked
himself into a B and B. As much as he enjoyed hanging
out with Theo, he felt he'd learned all he needed to know
about the price of clothes for one day, and wanted to
hit the sack. It was now past ten o'clock and he was keen
to get back to the amiable but very elderly landlady he
felt sure would accidentally lock him out after eleven.
He gave this excuse to his son.

'Oh right,' said Theo. He didn't look too disappointed
that his dad wouldn't, after all, be grooving till dawn
with him. 'But come and see me in the shop tomorrow,
yeah? I can give you my staff discount on any of the
clothes.'

'Great. Will do.'

Robin pretended to knock back the last of his drink then shouted goodbyes to Jasper, Joss, Jonty and others. After weaving his way through a sea of young bodies, he reached the exit just as 'Tears' came on and the whole place erupted – as indeed it would have done in Robin's day, should anyone have played a Ken Dodd record.

Out in the street, he checked his phone and listened to a message from Hannah in a call box, telling him she'd dropped her mobile and it no longer seemed to be working. Robin swore. It was his main lifeline to Hannah and Freddie when they stayed with her parents. Now, when he got desperate to talk to them – Fred in particular – he'd have to call Ruth and Vic's number. But, dammit, he didn't have it with him. And weren't they ex-directory owing to Vic having been a copper?

'Bugger,' he said, switching off his phone, then looking up at the castle, towering majestically over him. He'd always thought of Edinburgh as a very masculine city, rather like Oxford but more so. All that granite, no doubt. Cambridge was feminine, as was Lincoln. Durham was definitely masculine. He continued this train of thought as he strode towards his guesthouse – Warwick masculine, Chichester feminine – but when he found himself deciding Brighton and Bristol were androgynous, Robin began to wonder what the hell they put in those Backwards Blow Jobs.

*   *   *

'*Oh. My. God,*' said Lucy.

'What?' Dom called out. He was rushing around, drawing curtains, turning the thermostat up, pouring food into Maidstone's bowl.

'*Shit.*'

'What?' he said again, appearing in the hallway with wine in his hand. 'Huge phone bill?'

Lucy shook her head and reread the note. 'Hannah's taken Freddie to Laroche-les-Bois.'

'Oh, bloody hell. To our house, I take it?'

'Yep. Looks like they left some time today.'

'Christ. Has Robin gone with them?'

'It seems not.'

'We should phone. Apologise for there only being one bedroom in operation and no electricity or hot water.'

'No point in trying Hannah's mobile; she wouldn't have a signal. Madame Bouziges will be asleep, so we shouldn't phone there. And anyway, Hannah's asked us not to let Marcus know they're coming. Wants it to be a surprise.'

Dom snorted. 'I think Hannah will be the one getting the surprise. Jesus, all those bare wires and missing floors. Pretty dangerous for a kid.'

'Well,' said Lucy, 'there's nothing we can do about it. Not from here, and certainly not tonight.'

'True. Maybe we should try and get some cash to Marcus as soon as poss.'

'You mean the money your parents just lent us? I think I'm going to cry.'

'No choice,' sighed Dom. 'Anyway, fancy a glass of wine?'

'Yeah. May as well celebrate our last hours of freedom.'

'Actually, I'm quite looking forward to going back to the office. Seeing the boys.'

'Me too.'

Dom headed back to the kitchen. 'Red or white?' he called out.

Lucy began working her way through the stack of letters they hadn't bothered looking at on Friday. Bills, bank statements, junk, and one with just 'Lucy and Dom' written on it. 'Red,' she shouted back, ripping open the envelope, taking the single sheet of paper out and immediately checking the name on the bottom – 'Jo'.

At first she couldn't quite take it in. Then she did take it in, and thought maybe Jo and Hannah were playing some kind of practical joke on them. But it wasn't April the first and, really, how amusing a prank would it be? No, Lucy realised on a third reading, Jo too had gone to Laroche-les-Bois to stay in their uninhabitable house, and, what's more, had taken her Japanese student with her. She made no mention of Hannah.

When Dom came back with her glass of wine, she said, 'It just got worse,' handing him the note. '*Much* worse.'

TUESDAY

Marcus woke to a combination of sounds: a familiar purring-cum-snoring, a page being turned, then another, and someone clearing his or her throat. He felt far too knackered to open his eyes and tried to drift off again, only the person doing the throat clearing continued to make noises, so he couldn't. He opened one eye and saw a blurry Claude, with hands on hips and a startled expression.

'I wondered whose the car was,' Claude said. 'I'd no idea you were expecting two, er, guests. I'm so sorry. Do excuse me, I will leave you to it.'

Not a dream, Marcus realised as he slowly came round. He *was* lying between two bodies; all three of them were fully dressed, by the feel of it. To his right he saw the back of Jo's head as she slumbered, and when he turned to his left, there was Keiko holding an English coursebook aloft. 'Present Perfect' was the heading on the page she had open and Marcus thought: no, not exactly perfect.

'Good morning,' whispered Keiko.

'Hi,' he said. 'Did you sleep well?'

'Yes, thank you. Although very short sleep.'

'Mm.'

They'd got to bed at around three, after much hemming and hawing about sleeping arrangements. Marcus had offered to curl up in the one proper armchair, so the women could have the double bed, but they seemed to think that a bit unfair. He said he'd be OK on the floor in one of the other upstairs rooms but then realised there wasn't any spare bedding to put either under or over himself.

They'd carried on discussing the matter and drinking wine until eventually Jo said, 'I think there is only one solution,' and they all trundled up to the one bed, in the one proper bedroom, and crawled under the one duvet.

While Marcus was attempting to slip back into sleep, the bread-van hooter honked loudly, making Keiko jump and then quietly gasp as Marcus hauled himself over her and hurried from the room to catch the impatient baker. There was nothing more miserable and rock-like than yesterday's baguette, he'd discovered.

He found some money then queued behind the van for a while and told an inquisitive Madame Bouziges that the new *voiture* in his drive belonged to his *amies*, who'd come to *rester à la maison pour une semaine*.

Feeling pleased with himself, Marcus then grew ambitious and tried to formulate, 'You wouldn't have a spare room you'd like to let to them?' when he found himself at the head of the queue, having to concentrate instead on loaves and euros and a short interaction on the prospects of a sunny day. As a concerned-looking Madame Bouziges, bread in hand, accompanied him up the path towards where Claude was tinkering quietly in the kitchen, Marcus hoped there wasn't going to be a confrontation of any sort.

But, after a short conversation, Claude said, 'My aunt has a spare mattress you can borrow, but stipulates that it must not be put directly on the hideously filthy floors upstairs. However, I have plastic sheeting, which will solve that problem.'

'Great. Maybe I can go and buy some duvets and pillows and things today.'

'Ha! My new assistant is taking time off already?'

'Is that OK?'

'Well,' said Claude, leaning towards him, 'that would depend. I mean, if you ever find having *two* beautiful lovers a little debilitating . . .'

Marcus grinned. 'Yeah, yeah, I'll let you know.'

Later, as he drove along the narrow winding roads on his way to civilisation and bedding shops, Marcus wondered what had motivated Jo's spur-of-the-moment journey. Was it the prospect of a cheap holiday for herself and her student? Did she just feel sorry for him, all on his own? Or was she more keen on him than she'd let on? She'd definitely been up for it on his first day in Oxford, and she hadn't spurned him the night he almost drowned in her face cream. But didn't Jo have every woman's fantasy as her boyfriend? Marcus was decidedly short of glistening coffee-coloured muscles and hadn't intercepted a single thing on the high seas. It didn't make sense.

As yet another vehicle to his rear waited for a blind bend to appear before overtaking him, Marcus sighed, not just at the daring of French drivers but at how irritating it was that women were so hard to read. It had been lovely to see Jo when she and Keiko arrived around ten last night – a fantastic surprise, in fact – but there'd been no polite way of asking, 'So why exactly are you here?'

'But I thought cords were making a comeback?' Robin said to Theo.

'Not ones with ink on them and bald patches on the knees and that elephant-bum look at the back. Honestly, Dad, you could fit another set of buttocks in there.'

Robin peered over his shoulder at the mirror. Theo was right. Did corduroy expand when spun twice a week for fifteen years, or had he simply lost weight? 'I see what you mean.'

'Here, try these,' Theo said, handing him a pair of

black trousers in a synthetic material that Robin might have marched against at one time.

'Well, OK,' he said reluctantly, while his son whooshed a changing-room curtain back for him. 'But I'm happier sticking to cotton and wool, as you know.'

'These are eighty per cent cotton,' said Theo, closing the curtain.

Robin pulled a doubtful face and checked the label. So they were. He stripped off, and before he'd got the trousers done up, Theo was back with a kind of grey/black shirt and a light-coloured jacket that had something of the lounge lizard about it. 'Thanks,' Robin said, and proceeded to pour himself into the ridiculously stylish items, thanking heaven he wasn't in Oxford and likely to bump into a friend or, worse still, one of his students. He put his shoes back on and tried to get a good view of himself, but the cubicle was too small, so he courageously stepped out into the shop, where Theo and another male assistant both cried, 'Oh, yes!'

'Are you sure?'

'Absolutely,' said Theo.

'*Quelle transformation,*' said his camp colleague.

Robin found himself being spun round to face a full-length mirror, in which was the image of a hip middle-aged guy who'd probably partied at many a Soho loft. It was a man who spotted and bought the work of up-and-coming artists and who hadn't dated anyone over thirty, ever. It definitely wasn't Robin, but he nevertheless slipped his hands into the trouser pockets to see what the effect would be. Pretty cool, actually, but how they'd mock him in the department if he pranced around looking like a lost graphic designer.

'I could arrange a great haircut for you with Crispin at Snip 'n' Tuck,' Theo was saying. 'Get rid of those ageing-hippy locks. What do you think?'

Robin wasn't sure what he thought. He was fond of his old look. He and it had been together a long time. And, what's more, he'd only had a haircut last week.

'I'm not sure,' he said, swinging his shoulders as he carried on checking himself out in the mirror. 'Hey, where are you going with my clothes?' he called out to Theo's retreating back.

'I'll bag them up for you, shall I? You could always drop them off at the Save the Children, next street on the right. How did you want to pay? Debit card, credit card?'

'Look, I'm not so sure it's *me*,' said Robin, as a thirtysomething couple were sifting through shirts on a nearby rail.

'What do you think of this blue?' the man asked his partner, but the woman was looking Robin's way and smiling quite beautifully at him. She gave his outfit an approving nod and Robin mouthed, 'Really?' and she nodded again and he decided he'd stick it all on the credit card.

Once Theo had removed all the labels, he put the transaction through the till and asked his father for £285.

'Bloody hell,' Robin said, wavering with his card. He lowered his voice. 'What happened to the discount you promised?'

'That's been taken off.' Theo raised an eyebrow. 'Style doesn't come cheap, you know.'

'Cheaply,' corrected Robin, trying to get at least one up on his son.

'I was told to ask for Crispin?' he said to a girl of around ten. All members of staff were ten years old and all were dressed in black but with lots of bare bits showing. There was no excess flesh on any of them.

'Do you have an appointment?' she asked, all wide-eyed and clear-skinned and silky-haired.

'No, but I think my son may have phoned him.'

'Just one moment,' the girl said, and she slinked across the room to a skinny boy who was tousling a woman's hair with a serious-looking dryer. The girl said something to him, the boy nodded, and the girl slinked back again. 'Crispin's going to squeeze you in,' she told Robin. 'He won't be long.'

'Great.'

'Would you like a coffee?'

'That would be nice.'

'Filter, cappuccino, latte, espresso, mocha?'

'Filter, please. Black.'

'Decaff?'

'No, thanks.'

'Fairtrade?'

'Why not.'

Robin took a seat and flicked through magazines aimed at the kind of men who wore the clothes he himself was wearing, only they'd be a good deal younger, he suspected. Sport, women, music, cars, women, gadgets, movies, fitness, women . . . The magazine posed lots of questions. 'Is this the sexiest woman on TV?' it asked of someone he didn't recognise, straddling a chair in the altogether. Robin's answer was, 'Almost certainly.' Next came, 'Is your shower gel letting you down?' Robin, a confirmed bar-of-soap man, moved on to what he thought was a sports article – 'Boxer comeback?' – but which turned out to be an underwear feature. Having discovered the joy of boxers only last year – Hannah had insisted – Robin was quite pleased to see they'd be around a bit longer.

'Do you want to come through?' he was suddenly being asked. 'Jade will shampoo you, then I'll bring you your coffee.'

Robin took one last look at the sexiest woman on TV, closed the magazine and prepared to be cruelly ejected from his floppy-fringed comfort zone. How had he let his son talk him into this? 'May as well go for the whole look,' Theo had said loudly enough for the lovely woman shopping with her chap to hear. Once again she'd nodded at him.

Robin got up and made for Jade by the washbasins.

Just a tidy-up was what he'd insist on with Crispin. Bit of a trim, no more.

Jo pulled her arm out from under the duvet and swivelled her watch around. It was late. Past eleven. She rolled over to discover the rest of the bed was empty, and for a while luxuriated in being able to stretch in all directions after the sardine-can night. She heard a man and a woman speaking French somewhere nearby but couldn't catch what they were saying. There were bumping noises and rustling noises and what might have been the odd swear word.

She lay for a while thinking she ought to get up, but inspected the room instead. Unlike the rest of the house, it was very pleasant. It had a nice wooden floor and its wonderfully uneven walls had been painted white. There was an antique chest of drawers and an equally old-looking mirror, and on two of the walls hung primary-coloured bits of modern art. The bed itself had a frame of good, solid wood and had no doubt cost a fortune. Light filtered in through thin orangey-red curtains, giving the room a cosiness that was going to be hard to leave. But leave she must, for the sake of politeness. She reached for her glasses, got out of bed fully clothed, put her shoes on and approached the French voices.

'*Bonjour*,' said a dark-haired woman holding one end of an upright double mattress.

'*Bonjour*,' replied Jo. She stood still while the mattress

bent itself round a door frame and the person at the other end came into view.

'Good morning,' puffed the man, who was younger than the woman but just as dark-haired and olive-skinned. He was a couple of inches shorter than Jo. 'Excuse us. We've just got to get this through . . . ah, success. I'm Claude, by the way. And this is my aunt, whom Dom and Lucy always call Madame Bouziges, so you may as well, too.'

'*Enchantée,*' Jo said to the woman. '*Je m'appelle Jo.*'

'Yes,' Claude said. 'We know.'

With the mattress settled on top of a large sheet of plastic, Jo went over and shook hands with first Claude, then Madame Bouziges, who told her Marcus had gone off to buy bedding and wouldn't be back for a couple of hours, so why didn't she and her friend join her for lunch? Jo said they'd be delighted, but that she'd like to have a shower first, and Madame Bouziges wandered off with a smile and a wave, apologising in advance that it would be a plain meal of bread, cheese and fruit.

'That's very kind of your aunt,' Jo said.

'I think she's just delighted to have someone here who understands her.'

'Oh? Marcus told me he spoke French quite well.'

Claude sniggered, then said, 'Look, I'm afraid the shower isn't yet connected, however the bath *is* functioning at last.'

'It wasn't when Lucy and Dom were here?'

'I believe not.'

'Blimey.'

'Tell me,' said Claude, pushing the door to, 'your friend, Keiko – does she have a paramour?'

'You mean bloke?'

'Yes.'

'Not so far as I know.'

'Excellent. Well, I must be getting back to work. When you've finished your ablutions I'll take you to my aunt's house.'

'Pardon?'

'After you've bathed, I'll—'

'Oh, right.'

The bath was surprisingly brand-new-looking and clean, and from where she lay up to her chin in bubbles, Jo was able to enjoy a spectacular view of the distant hills and forests, thanks to a hole in the wall where a first-floor outside door had been, and where a window would be. Apparently, the old cast-iron bath had exited the building that way.

It was a glorious day, much better than the previous one, and now that the bed situation was getting sorted, Jo was sure the holiday would work out well. Poor Marcus. So flummoxed last night. Although he'd appeared genuinely pleased to see them, he'd been embarrassed by the state of the place, and talked about finding them accommodation in the nearest town, fifteen kilometres away. Now what fun would that have been?

Jo could hear Claude talking as he sawed at some-thing beneath the window – or hole – then Keiko giggling, then Claude talking again and sawing. All the while, the aroma of his Gauloise hung in the air, confirming for Jo, as no other smell could, that she was on a continental holiday.

After dressing in shorts and T-shirt and applying lots of sunblock, just in case Madame Bouziges liked to lunch in the garden, Jo headed for the stairs saying, '*Don't* forget the missing one,' over and over to herself. Last night, she and Marcus had had to lift small Keiko over the gap.

Thanks to a fairly generous credit transfer from Lucy and Dom, Marcus had not only gone to town, but he'd also gone to town. In the back of the car were the required sheets, pillows and duvets, as well as a hammock and a badminton net to set up in the garden, and table foot-ball for indoors. Did women like table football? Well, he'd find out. In addition, he'd bought a portable tele-vision with built-in DVD player, a stack of DVDs – all either French or dubbed in French – several French board games and half a dozen French novels. If his grasp of the language didn't improve after that lot, he'd be amazed.

Obviously, they wouldn't spend all their time playing games and watching films. If he put in a few hours each morning with Claude – something he felt he was pretty much committed to now – then he and the women could go out on trips, see the gorges and caves, that kind of thing. How brilliant that Jo and Keiko were here, he found himself thinking and, fairly guiltily, how good that Hannah and Freddie weren't. He'd more or less decided before leaving Oxford not to rock that particular boat any longer. Or put all his eggs in one basket. Messier still, of course, would be to rock the boat *with* the basket of eggs in it.

As he pulled up outside the house in Laroche-les-Bois, Marcus continued the maritime theme, telling himself that time and tide wait for no man and that there were plenty more fish in the sea besides Hannah. He took the boxed TV from the passenger seat and carried it past a strange car – a friend of Claude's? – and through to the living room, where he stopped and blinked several times at what he saw. Either Claude had shrunk to half his size in the past three hours, or Freddie was crossing the floor with an enormous hammer in his hand. Marcus blinked again and had the wherewithal not to drop the brand-new television on to the concrete beneath him.

'Freddie?' he said nervously, as though waiting for the spooky apparition to fade away.

'I'm going to be Claude's mate,' said the ghost. ''Cos his old one's buggered off.'

'No, no,' Claude called out from a far corner. 'I said "bunked" off, Freddie.' He looked over at Marcus. 'Isn't that the right expression?'

'Hello, Marcus,' came Hannah's voice from some-where. He turned and she rushed towards him, then managed to hug both him and the TV. 'I couldn't not come,' she said.

Claude was giving him a kind of ooh-la-la, aren't-you-the-lucky-one smirk, but as Marcus kissed Hannah's cheek and said how great it was to see her, his head filled up with rocky boats and baskets of eggs.

Jo was learning all there was to know about Laroche-les-Bois. How the local mine had closed down – she hadn't quite caught what kind of mine – and how that had led to high unemployment and a general deterio-ration in the area. Homes needing so many repairs they were often simply abandoned, young people fleeing the moment they were old enough. When they'd all finished eating and Madame Bouziges and her father-in-law, Bertrand, stopped talking to light cigarettes, Jo translated for the excluded Keiko.

'Ah yes, Claude told me,' Keiko said. 'But he also said many foreign persons come to buy houses and have holiday, and so local economy is now . . . uh . . .' she delved into the bag at her feet for her notebook, opened it up and said, 'relatively buoyant.'

'Really?'

'And that many rural place who rely on farming and mining must expect, er, vi-cissi-tu-di-nous times.'

'Sorry?'

172

'I look up. It means changing fortune.'

'I know,' said Jo. Of course she knew.

Madame Bouziges had her eyebrows raised as though waiting for a translation, but Jo didn't feel she had the energy, so told her Keiko had enjoyed the lunch very much and said to thank her. Keiko, abandoning her diet, had launched into the bread with gusto and practically ignored the cheeses, pissing Jo off somewhat after the lengths she'd gone to over the months.

Madame Bouziges said they were both welcome, then asked, pointing at Keiko, if she was from a wealthy family.

'*Je ne sais pas,*' said Jo with a shrug, although she thought perhaps she was. Keiko was quite a shopper and two terms at the best language school in town would have set the family back a bob or two.

It was just that her nephew could do with a rich wife to help him through air-traffic school, Madame Bouziges went on. She and her father-in-law gave throaty laughs and Keiko began to look a bit uncomfortable.

'Madame Bouziges says the mining was a dangerous and filthy job,' Jo told her, suddenly keen to get back to the house. She liked Madame Bouziges and Bertrand very much, but she liked Marcus more. 'And that most people were glad to see the industry die out.'

'Ah.'

After profuse thanks and the promise to cook some Japanese food for Madame Bouziges if they could find the ingredients, Jo and Keiko headed back, hoping

Marcus had managed to find them some bedding. His car was in front of the house, parked behind another Jo didn't recognise. While passing, she stopped and peered through one of its windows and saw assorted comics and children's books strewn over the back seat. All of them English. At the far end of the seat sat a small blue box, open and spilling mini-sized tools. 'Keiko,' she said, steadying herself on her lodger, 'it might be time for chocolate again.'

Keiko opened up her bag and dug around. 'I have only energy tablets, which man in mountain clothes shop said hikers must carry all times.'

'They'll do.'

WEDNESDAY

It was Theo's day off and they'd done the castle and were on their way to an art gallery, when Robin, missing Freddie quite badly, said, 'How do you fancy going to the zoo?'

Theo gave a snort. 'I am twenty, you know, Dad.'

'Is that a no, then?'

'I vote we skip the modern art and go and meet up with Joss and Jonty at Va Va Voom. You'll love it. Cocktails to die for and the fittest women in town serving you. What do you say?' He looked anxiously at his watch in a way that indicated he'd prearranged the Va Va Voom thing and they were running late. But it wasn't yet one o'clock and the last thing Robin felt like was a drink with a rude name. On the other hand, he wasn't that bothered about the modern art either. He just wanted to be at the zoo, with a wide-eyed, loving-it-all Freddie. And he wanted to be there *now*, before Freddie grew old and cynical and took up polo.

'Tell you what,' said Robin, 'why don't you go and meet your friends and I'll nip round the gallery and catch up with you later? Text me to let me know where you are.'

'Yeah?' said Theo, taking small backward steps away from his father. 'Are you sure?'

'Quite sure. Plus, I need to buy a hat to cover this hair.' Robin laughed. 'Or rather, lack of it.' Young Crispin had obviously misheard 'Just a bit of a trim' as, 'Take it down to an inch and nice and spiky on top.'

'You look great,' Theo called out, now well on his way. 'Very De Niro!'

Oh sure, thought Robin, but he nevertheless wandered over to the nearest shop window to check himself out, hands in trouser pockets, stomach tucked in. Yes, in actual fact there was something of the younger Robert De Niro about him, although his colouring was more Pacino, perhaps. As the new look began to grow on him, Robin noticed someone waving at him from inside the shop. He stepped back, looked up, and saw that he was outside Snip 'n' Tuck, so waved back at the person in black – Crispin or Jade, he wasn't sure – and, suddenly getting his bearings, realised he was very close to Theo's clothes shop.

He took a jacket, two pairs of trousers, two shirts and a couple of nice ties to the young woman at the till, and she removed the big plastic tags and scanned the bar codes, all the while making pleasant conversation about the weather, the number of visitors in Edinburgh and how Oxford was one of her favourite cities. Robin had found nothing but the utmost courtesy and friendliness since his arrival in Scotland and told her so.

'Why thank you,' she said graciously, then asked him for five hundred and something pounds.

'Really?' Robin leaned forward and, behind a hand, whispered, 'My son Theo works here, and yesterday passed on his staff discount to me. I don't suppose . . .'

He stopped because the young woman's demeanour was changing. Her eyes narrowed, her lips pursed themselves, and she finally said, '*Did* he indeed? Well, I shall be having a word with him about that tomorrow.'

'Oh dear. Are you the manager?'

'Yes. As I said, that'll be £594.50 please.'

'Of course,' said Robin, handing over his card. 'Cheap at the price. And such excellent quality. As Theo is always saying.' He would have carried on but could see from her face that his attempts at damage limitation weren't working. His son would be out of a job tomorrow. Should he track him down and tell him, or just quietly slip out of town?

While the till made its processing noises, the woman said, 'It's just that I'm sure he gives all those poncy uni friends his discount, by pretending he's buying for himself.'

'Actually, I could verify that Theo does have a remarkably extensive wardrobe,' Robin told her. 'You know, if it ever went to court.'

She laughed and looked friendly again. Very friendly.

'Listen,' she said, 'if you fancy meeting up for a drink later, I could overlook what he did yesterday.'

Robin – truly stunned – took in the person before him. Mid-thirties at most. Pretty. Slim, but at the same time curvaceous. Dark hair held back in some kind of comb thing. Interesting grey eyes. It seemed to Robin that, for the sake of his son, he had no alternative but to accept her invitation.

Hooray. In spite of fly-in-the-ointment Jo – Jesus, what a shock to find her here – am feeling happy, happy, happy. This morning I found myself missing the daily writing habit, so managed to pick up this little notebook in the village shop. As I sit here on a bench in the middle of Laroche-les-Bois, under a fabulously clear April sky (praying Freddie isn't electrocuting himself up at the house) I'm wondering – despite current cheerfulness – which would be the best method of eliminating the opposition. Poison, strangulation, or a knife in the middle of the night?

The trouble is, apart from the sneaky, duplicitous side of Jo's character, I do almost like her. Even when she walked in yesterday afternoon and found that Freddie and I had turned up to spoil her party – her face was a giveaway – she came and gave us both a hug and immediately went to talk to the caretaker woman about getting more beds. Hard to push someone like that down one of the steep inclines round here.

*Well, she didn't actually succeed on the bed front, so
Fred and I slept with Marcus in the one decent room
in the house and Jo and Keiko shared a double mattress
in a shell of a room nearby. (Hannah 1 – Jo 0.) During
cuddles – no more, unfortunately – and whispers in
the middle of the night, Marcus assured me he and Jo
weren't an item. That Jo had turned up out of the blue,
and that he wasn't sure why but thought maybe she
just fancied getting away and having a cheap holiday.*

I wonder what it is that makes men so unperceptive?

*With Lucy and Dom's permission, Claude has gone
off in his big van to buy dining chairs and crockery
and other stuff. I suppose some of us could move out
to make things easier, but then there'd have to be pistols
at dawn to sort out who goes.*

*Jo and Keiko are walking in the hills – here's hoping
they get terminally lost – and Marcus is doing one or
two little jobs in Claude's absence – with Freddie's
help. Or hindrance. Maybe I should get back and
check they're OK. It is glorious, sitting here in the sun,
but I do feel I've been examined enough by those two
guys outside the Sports Bar, silently drinking beer and
watching the minimal village activity. These are the
things I love about rural France – the almost stand-
still pace of life, the lack of materialism . . . Heaven.*

It was a punishing walk. A good thing, Jo told herself.
She needed punishing for coming to France in the first

place, when there'd been, if she'd only stopped to think, a strong chance of Hannah turning up. She also needed punishing for letting herself get carried away on the Marcus front, and for bringing her lodger to a place with a lot of tension in the atmosphere, not to mention a missing bathroom wall and barely a place to sit.

Hopefully, Claude was sorting out the seating problem as she and Keiko lost, then found, then lost again, the footpath that was on Lucy and Dom's map but wasn't always on the ground. Many of the hill paths were excruciatingly steep, and some became fairly precipitous ledges that turned her knees to jelly. It was hell. And it was hot. Far too hot for their altitude and for April, *and* she'd foolishly worn a jumper.

She cupped hands around her mouth and yelled, 'Keiko!' to the figure a long way ahead and growing smaller. 'Lunch!'

'OK!' Keiko shouted. She arrived back, in sleeveless T-shirt and no perspiration, to where Jo had thrown herself and small rucksack down and was now fishing around for water.

'I'm not usually like this on walks,' she told Keiko. 'Honestly. Normally, I've got bags of energy and enthusiasm, but at the moment I just want to go back and read a book in a very dark place.'

'I think maybe you are tired. Last night, all the night, you were like this.' Keiko did an imitation of someone flailing in their sleep. She even shut her eyes.

'Was I?'

'Yes. Very much. Is it because Hannah has come to house?'

'*No.*'

'Claude and me think you and Marcus is perfect couple.'

'Oh, yeah?' chuckled Jo. 'When did you discuss this?'

'Today, before he went to buy marbles.'

'Actually, I think he went to buy furniture.'

'Yes, marbles. It is French word for furniture.'

'Of course. So, listen, what else did Claude say about Marcus and me?'

'That Hannah is very beautiful, but you have . . . uh.' She took a book out of her bag – a new notebook that didn't have Marge Simspon on the front – and turned to the first page. 'Ah yes, *joie de vivre*, and also handsome *derrière*.'

Jo laughed. 'Are you sure he said handsome?' It made her bottom sound a bit too substantial.

Keiko nodded.

'Not sexy or alluring?'

'No.'

Oh well, handsome was probably better than nothing. 'So he thinks Hannah is beautiful?'

'Yes. But also he says he has looked into her eyes and seen . . .' she checked her notes, '. . . aggrieved and tormented soul.'

'Really?' said Jo, suddenly worried. Aggrieved and

tormented souls were probably the most trouble. But then who was to say Claude was right? It did occur to her, as she glugged back delicious water, that if he stopped ogling people's rears and peering into their souls, the house might get finished a whole lot sooner.

Marcus had given up trying to keep Freddie from potentially live electrical wires and other tragedies waiting to happen, and was walking him into the village when they met Hannah on her way back to the house.

'We thought we'd try out the Sports Bar,' he told her. 'Fancy?'

'Are you sure women are allowed in?' she asked with a chuckle.

How lovely it was to hear Hannah laugh again. Her fair complexion had already managed to catch the sun, and she radiated a kind of contentment Marcus hadn't seen in her for years.

'Shall we go and find out?' he asked, and she immediately hooked an arm through his, then took hold of Freddie's hand, and the three of them sauntered down the road and into the square, like a perfectly perfect little family unit. Which Marcus had to keep reminding himself they weren't. So far, no mention had been made of Robin and how he felt about them coming to France. Marcus decided he'd bring it up, though, and when they were all seated beneath a screen showing football, digging into their *Croque Monsieur*

– served by the elderly proprietress – he did just that.

'He was fine about it in the end,' said Hannah with a wave of a hand.

'Yeah? Well, that was good of him.'

'Mm. Freddie, eat up there's a good boy.'

'He didn't want to come with you then?' asked Marcus.

'Look, ham and cheese. Your favourites. If you eat this, Fred, we'll get you something nice in the shop.'

'Can I get a lectric drill like Claude's?'

'No, I meant an ice-lolly or something.'

'I'd rather have a lectric drill.'

'I know you would.'

'So what's he doing?' asked Marcus.

Hannah was busily cutting up Freddie's food. 'Who?'

'Robin.'

'Oh, he's gone to see his son in Edinburgh. Having a great time, I expect. Theo will have him out clubbing.'

Marcus laughed. 'Hard to imagine.'

'Yes. Good boy, Fred. There, it's yummy, isn't it?'

'And you're leaving Tuesday, did you say?'

Hannah began brushing invisible crumbs off the table, then she straightened out the plastic checked cloth and brushed at nothing again. 'That was the original plan but I'd love us to stay longer.' She looked up at him. 'I'm sure we could change our flights. If that would be OK with you?'

'And Robin?'

'Of course.' Her eyes flickered, just slightly. 'I'll give him a call.'

'Great,' Marcus said, managing a smile.

Something about it wasn't great, he knew that. Hannah had gone from calm to tense in a matter of minutes, and Marcus felt a growing sense of unease. As much as he adored them, he wished he hadn't suggested Hannah and Freddie came out to France. How could Robin – so furious at first, according to Hannah – have had such a change of heart? Perhaps he hadn't, and in that case the gods were bound to make them pay for this in some way. He suddenly saw Freddie falling from the hole in the first-floor bathroom . . . through that gap in the stairs . . . 'Oh God,' he whispered at the thought, and Hannah asked him what was wrong. 'Are you absolutely certain you want to stay?' he said. 'It's such a dangerous place for Freddie. And surely Robin—'

'*What?*'

'I only meant—'

'Come on, Fred,' she said. Her eyes had grown wild and unfriendly, her cheeks went from lightly tanned to crimson. 'No, leave that. Come on, we're going.'

'To the shop to buy a drill?' said the ever-hopeful Fred as he was lifted from his chair.

'Hannah?' Marcus called out to their backs. 'Hannah?'

He would have run after them but he needed to pay, and the man in a tight vest, propped on folded arms behind the bar and glued to the football, didn't look the understanding type. Marcus went over to him with bill in hand but then thought better of leaving, and with a resigned sigh said, '*Une bière, s'il vous plait.*'

The man cranked himself to attention, took a bottle from a cold cabinet and knocked the cap off below the bar. '*Les femmes,*' he said to Marcus with a nod towards the door, then a shake of the head and a shrug of his hairy shoulders, 'enigmateek, *oui?*'

'*Oui,*' said Marcus, surprised to hear the guy could speak English.

He took his beer outside and sat with a couple of men of indeterminate age at an old metal table that could have done with a Claude paint job. They nodded, he nodded, and then they all watched a tiny old lady, possibly dressed in mourning, work her way steadily down the incline towards the village shop. After five minutes or so, she emerged from the doorway and Marcus and the others followed her progress back up the road and into her house with her bag of groceries.

Two vehicles in a row passed through the village, but after that there wasn't much excitement for a while and Marcus sat sipping his rather good beer until a vision of sweatiness appeared round the corner of the Sports Bar.

It spotted him, climbed the three steps to the terrace and said, 'Get me one of those beers, will you, Marcus? I'm completely shagged out. Do you want one, Keiko?'

* * *

Could Marcus have made it clearer he didn't want us here? Now he's concerned about Robin's feelings. Why didn't he think of that before rolling up in Oxford, let alone inviting us to France? Jesus, what a mess. What to do, what to do . . . moules, crêpes Suzettes, escargots à la bourguignonne . . .

Really wished I hadn't stormed out of the café like that – Freddie was upset, I could tell. And, actually, now I've popped a pill, Marcus's words don't seem quite so hurtful. Anyone in their right mind would be worried about Freddie's safety in this place. He's currently watching Claude assemble flat-pack dining chairs, following him around in total awe. So sweet. I'm sure he'd love to add Claude to his list of daddies.

How to play it, though. That's the thing. Marcus hasn't returned, so is probably licking his wounds. I can't believe he's lost all feelings for me. Can't believe the Jo thing isn't just a one-sided crush. I should stay and see how things pan out. Definitely. How ghastly and defeated I'd feel if Fred and I went back home early. And besides, I'd like to get Freddie practising the French I've tried hard to instil in him over the past three years, with little success so far.

There's Jo walking up the path and past the window now. There's the top of Keiko's head and there's Marcus. He and Jo are chatting and laughing. Shit. Could it be I'm wrong about them? That Marcus lied?

OK, fix smile to face, say a cheerful 'hello' to everyone, act as though the café business didn't happen, then go and hide notebook under upstairs floorboards.

'*Je soupçonne le Colonel Moutarde d'avoir commis le crime dans la Salle de Billard avec le Poignard,*' announced Hannah.

Marcus said, 'Pardon?'

Keiko and Freddie just stared.

'She means "Colonel Mustard in the Billiard Room with the Dagger",' said Jo.

Hannah feigned embarrassment. 'Sorry. I just assumed we'd all want to practise our French?'

'Ah yes, what a good idea!' said Marcus, who was being ultrasycophantic with Hannah, for some reason Jo couldn't make out. Insisting on taking over the cooking of dinner from her while she lazed in the hammock in the last of the day's sun. He'd bring her a G & T, he said, and apologised for there being no ice yet.

Marcus cooking had been an unsettling sight and involved a lot of fumbling, swearing and head scratching. In the end, Jo couldn't hold back any longer and went to help. After dinner, he'd suggested Hannah choose an evening activity for them all. It was to be Cluedo, she announced after giving it some thought, as Freddie might find it fun. How much fun the three year old would find an entirely French Cluedo was questionable. Already he was fidgeting on his chair and shooting at

Mademoiselle Rose – alias Keiko – with the tiny revolver he'd taken a liking to.

Jo revealed her *Colonel Moutarde* to Hannah, making sure none of the others saw, then Marcus showed Hannah a card and the game continued, in French and quite painfully.

When Marcus, finding himself in the *Salle à Manger*, decided to accuse *Madame Leblanc avec la Clef Anglaise*, Hannah straightaway pounced on him for pronouncing it 'cleff' instead of 'cleh'.

'Sorry,' he said with a big apologetic smile, when really, Jo thought, he must have wanted to stretch across the table and slap the woman. She certainly did. And poor confused-looking Keiko might have been induced to join in.

'Hey!' shouted Freddie, suddenly spotting the potential murder weapon and grabbing it. The revolver was dropped from his other hand. 'A monkey wrench like Claude's got!'

'It *is* a monkey wrench in English – well done,' said Hannah, still in annoying schoolmarm mode. 'But while we're playing this game it's a *Clef Anglaise*. Can you say that, Fred? *Clef Anglaise*.'

'It's *not* a clay onglez,' Freddie insisted. 'Claude calls it a monkey wrench and he knows everything about tools.'

'Well, Claude likes to practise his English but we want to practise our French.' Hannah looked up at the others. 'Don't we, everybody?'

Jo watched a muscle tensing in Marcus's beautiful jaw. His blue, blue eyes met hers and were saying something; she had no idea what, but it was making her feel funny. She picked up her glass of wine and drank half of it in three gulps. Then she finished it off, excused herself and went through to the kitchen and topped up. Deep breaths, she told herself. Deep breaths. She drank half the glass, filled up again and wandered back to the game, which they seemed to have abandoned.

'We're going round the table saying whole French sentences,' Teacher informed her. 'Your turn, Keiko.'

Keiko put a hand over her mouth. 'Ohh,' she said. 'My French is very bad, but I learn from whistle-shop tour how to say, "*Est-ce que vous avez la taille en-dessous?*" It means: Do you have it in a smaller size? Very important phrase for Japanese persons.'

Hannah applauded and sang, '*Très bien!*' while Jo took another swig of wine and quietly vowed to thrash her at table football later.

'Your turn, Fred,' said Marcus, that muscle still twitching.

Jo wanted to lean over and caress his cheek and calm him down. No, kiss his cheek and calm him down. Kiss his cheek, calm him down, undo his buttons and somehow pin him to the back of the chair with the shoulders of his shirt. Would that be possible? She took another swig while Marcus's attention was on Freddie, and tried to work out the logistics.

'*Pipi*,' said Freddie with a giggle. 'It means wee.'

'Very good,' said Marcus.

Hannah didn't look so impressed. 'That's not really a sentence, is it, Fred?' She turned to Jo and smiled stiffly. 'Your turn.'

'Oh,' Jo said, caught on the hop. She'd just been securing Marcus to the chair with his leather belt. 'Sorry. Um. Not prepared. Er . . .' Oh hell, why couldn't she think of anything? She could speak French. Was it just too much wine? 'Um . . .'

'The first French sentence that comes into your head?' suggested Marcus, making unsettling eye contact again.

Jo thought she'd forget the chair and the shirt and the belt, and just drag him up to that bedroom bathed in orange light. '*Voulez-vous coucher avec moi?*' she heard herself say, and in the quiet that followed, Freddie asked his mum what it meant. Hannah didn't answer, but calmly told Jo she should really have used the familiar *veux-tu*.

'Yes,' said Marcus, either answering Jo's question or agreeing with Hannah.

THURSDAY

Robin had chosen to cut his stay short for a number of reasons, the main one being that he hadn't heard a word from Hannah since the message about her damaged mobile. He wasn't panicking, but felt on edge and basically wanted to get home, look up Ruth and Vic's number and be reassured everything was OK. Separation anxiety, he told himself. Perfectly natural in a parent. Hannah no doubt thought he had her parents' number with him and was probably wondering why he hadn't called *them*. He tittered to himself at the silliness of it all and got on, as best he could, with the cryptic crossword in a packed train that was going to take for ever to reach Birmingham, where he'd then have to change for Oxford.

He'd also pretty much exhausted Edinburgh's tourist attractions, and as Theo was back at work again – God willing – Robin didn't see the point of hanging around and expanding his waistline with those full English – or perhaps Scottish? – breakfasts he could never resist. His new clothes would stop fitting him for a start. He filled in 4 Across, picked a couple of hairs off his jacket and wondered how Freddie would react to his new-look daddy. Hannah, too. Would it bring a spark back to the relationship, or was it simply the Robin inside Robin that Hannah didn't find very exciting? It had often occurred to him that he might not have what it took to be exciting.

He filled in 12 Across and told himself he surely wasn't terminally dull. Something had attracted Hannah to him in the first place. However, yesterday evening, with Theo's boss, Phoebe, he had sensed he might have gone on a little too long about what an absolutely ace character his son was. It was just that he wanted to supply her with enough examples of Theo's trustworthiness and conscientiousness – even as a child – to convince her she should keep him on.

Eventually, she'd said – snapped? – '*Look*, I wouldn't have sacked him anyway. He's such a charmer with the customers, and has that wonderfully upper-class voice and air of authority. Do you know what I mean?'

Robin knew exactly what she meant about the voice, but had no idea where his son got it from. He himself had deliberately toned down his accent when first becoming a poly lecturer, and had continued to keep it that way. As for the air of authority, well, Theo had obviously got that from his mother.

'Believe me,' Phoebe continued, 'it's rare to find that kind of class and style in part-time staff.'

'I can imagine,' he said, then after fetching them two more drinks from the bar, steered the conversation to the plight of the Highlanders in the eighteenth and nine-teenth centuries, a topic he felt a lot more comfortable with, and one he was sure would interest the very Scottish Phoebe. He'd been mistaken. While he gave not just his views, but also actual shocking figures on the abominable Highland clearances, her eyes began skipping around the room. 'So what are your interests?' he'd asked at this point, sensing it was time to drop the subject.

'Shopping mostly,' she'd said, looking at her watch, 'Listen, I'm going to have to dash. Sorry. Early start tomorrow. Stock-taking. It's been great chatting with you, though.'

'Yes,' he'd replied limply 'With you too.'

Robin had sat and finished his beer, feeling a little foolish. No, not so much foolish as deceptive. In the shop, earlier, Phoebe had obviously seen what she assumed to be an urbane, slave-to-style type of guy, only to discover over drinks that she'd got . . . well, Robin. Still, it hadn't been a date – not to Robin's mind, anyway. He wouldn't do that to Hannah. 'Pathologically faithful' was what a particularly debauched colleague had once called him. He'd only gone for a drink with Phoebe to make up for his gaffe, and because he thought it might be nice to have a conversation with someone over twenty.

Afterwards, he'd caught up with Theo and his friends in a stark, metal-and-white restaurant, where everyone ordered extravagantly, then Robin ended up paying. Still, it had been nice to spend a few days with son number one, but now it was time to get home and find out how the other one was.

When, at Birmingham, he changed trains and found himself opposite an attractive woman of around forty, who half-smiled each time their eyes met, he tried not to encourage her and decided he really ought to attach a 'Beware – Sheep in Wolf's Clothing!' badge to his new gear.

Something unnerving was happening to Marcus. Something to do with Jo. There. It happened again when she passed close by on her way to the garden. A *frisson*, he'd call it, since he was in France.

He pondered on it as he helped Claude with the tiling. The first time was at the Sports Bar when she'd appeared so suddenly, shattering the tranquillity – or tedium – and shaking him from the gloom Hannah had left him with by chattering on about the disastrous walk she and Keiko had just attempted. Laughing about it, with what was a bit of dirt or squashed bug endearingly stuck to her damp forehead, until he'd reached across and wiped it away. Then wiped again, unnecessarily. He'd just really wanted to touch her.

Marcus handed Claude another tile.

He'd always found her attractive, of course, but you could be attracted to someone and not always find yourself having *frissons*. It was all very odd and surprising. Three times now he and Jo had ended up in or on a bed together, and although at those times he'd felt certain things – drunk, horny, knackered – he'd never felt particularly romantic.

'It's something of a metamorphosis, isn't it?' said Claude.

'Sorry?'

'The floor. Don't you think the tiles are transfiguring the room?'

'Oh, right. Yeah. Definitely.' Marcus wasn't sure 'transfiguring' was the right word but didn't feel confident enough to challenge Claude's English. The tiles were large and a warm orangey brown, and were exactly right for the living/dining area, a place that was out of bounds for the duration of the screeding and laying. The kitchen was next on the list but that was going to be harder not to use. They'd probably all have to go and impose on Madame Bouziges's cassoulets for a couple of days. 'Quite a transformation,' he told Claude, passing him another tile for his fifteen euros an hour.

Marcus briefly wondered if he was being overpaid, but then his thoughts went back to Jo and how, quite unexpectedly during Cluedo, he'd found himself getting all churned up over her. What had triggered it off, Marcus didn't know. It was a cumulation of things, maybe. The way she'd pronounced '*bureau*' without making that throat-clearing noise Hannah went in for whenever she came across the French 'r'. The way she'd occasionally gazed his way during the game with a faraway look in her eye. The way she asked him if he wanted to sleep with her . . .

'You seem a little distracted today,' Claude was saying. He made sure the tile lay absolutely straight then took another from Marcus. 'Please tell me to mind my own business, if you wish, but I'm most intrigued by this harem of yours.'

Marcus laughed. 'It's not quite that.'

'Hannah introduced herself to me as Mrs Currie, but I was under the assumption you were single.'

'She and I are married but separated. Divorce proceedings are in progress. Hannah now lives with Robin, who is Freddie's father.'

'Ah, so you have been apart a considerable time?'

'No. Just nine, ten months.'

Claude looked puzzled, so Marcus checked everyone was in the garden, took a deep breath and explained the paternity business, the house-sitting in Oxford and how he'd rashly invited Hannah and Freddie to France but Robin hadn't been at all keen on the idea.

'You know,' said Claude, 'people outside the Cévennes lead such interesting lives.'

'More like complicated and hellish. I wouldn't recommend it.'

'And Robin?' asked Claude, lowering his voice. 'He finally acquiesced to this holiday?'

'I'm not sure he did.'

'Oh,' said Claude, eyes widening.

'Quite.'

'And Jo?'

Marcus shivered. There it was again, at the mere mention of her name. 'What about her?'

'Well . . . once more, pardon my inquisitiveness, but is it a *ménage à trois* we have here?'

Marcus sniggered. 'To be honest, it's pretty much a *ménage à un* at the moment.'

'Hard to believe!' Claude cried, then said, 'Ah, but I forget, you *are* English.'

'Scottish, actually.'

'Even worse. The further from the equator a man is born, the less romance he has in his soul.'

'Rubbish!'

'What's rubbish?' came Jo's voice from behind, making Marcus start. She was close. He could smell her sunscreen. He turned round and smiled dumbly. Claude repeated his preposterous notion to her and she laughed a little too loudly and for a little too long – almost as though experience had taught her the very same thing – and wandered away again.

'Actually, do you mind if I clock off soon?' Marcus asked his boss. 'It's just that we've planned a picnic by the river. That spot you told us about. For Freddie, really.'

'No, no,' said Claude. 'You go and have fun. I do believe you deserve it after the tribulations and utter wretchedness of your recent life.'

'Yes,' agreed Marcus.

'Were you planning to swim?'

'If it stays this warm.'

'Keiko too? She's brought a bikini with her?'

'Er . . . presumably.'

'You know,' said Claude, eyes twinkling in the direction of the garden, 'the ladies are not required to wear the top halves of their swimwear. Do tell them. And perhaps I may join you later?'

'Sure.'

The tribulations and wretchedness of the past couple of years was not something Marcus liked to dwell on. But as he lay in the bath soaking off the smell of tile glue, he flashed back to when he first began to wonder where Freddie got his looks from. The way Hannah would casually laugh it off whenever he brought up the subject. The growing unease he'd felt, mental and physical. At last, when they'd been walking up Lochnagar, he'd said to Hannah, 'Is Freddie mine?' and she'd broken down, confessed to her affair with a lecturer in Oxford and begged his forgiveness.

He felt it all over again, lying there in the bath. The sickness in the stomach, combined with a kind of relief at knowing for sure. He'd carried on alone, made it to the very top of the mountain and looked down on the loch, exhausted but, after a great deal of thought about the situation, resigned to a business-as-usual approach. For Freddie's sake.

Marcus felt tears sting his eyes and put it down to the shampoo trickling from his hair. He filled a big plastic jug from the taps and rinsed the suds off, then lay back and took in the spectacular view through the missing wall. But business as usual hadn't been that easy. No doubt he should have just forgiven and forgotten and carried on loving Hannah the way he had before. Nobody's infallible, after all.

His feelings for Freddie underwent a slight shift, though. That was what he couldn't forgive her for. He still adored him and intended to do everything to protect his little boy and give him a great life, but something of the invisible bond had gone. Once again the tears pricked, so Marcus shook away the memories and turned his thoughts to the forthcoming picnic. It was just what they all needed, he decided, pulling the plug out, then standing up as the water drained away noisily.

He was reaching for a towel from the nearby rail when he spotted a small colourful movement by a tree towards the end of the garden, part-way up a slope. An exotic bird? No, not in this area. A peacock, maybe? He stood still, hand resting on the towel rail, waiting for it to reappear. But when nothing happened he shrugged and got on with the business of drying himself.

* * *

Shit, had he seen her? Jo stood quite rigid behind the tree, watching him through the cleft in the trunk. She should have been more careful. Not moved at all and worn tree-trunk brown instead of pink and blue. She pushed her glasses back up her nose for better vision and carried on staring.

Yesterday, when Marcus had been bathing, she'd accidentally caught sight of him standing in the bath towelling himself. She'd been searching for dropped pegs in the grass around the washing line and happened to look up at the house. Today, though, she had to admit it was deliberate – no matter how much she told herself they were still short of pegs.

'Lovely,' she sighed when he finally stepped out of the bath and out of sight. She meandered back to the house with a smile and had installed herself next to Keiko, filling baguettes, by the time Marcus walked in and asked if he could help.

'Here,' said Hannah, handing him a bag. 'Take this to the car. And Fred's going to need his bucket and spade if you can find them in the garden.'

'Right.'

Hannah then turned to Jo and Keiko. 'You couldn't go easier on the cucumber, could you? It tends not to agree with me.'

'Ahh,' said Keiko. 'So sorry.'

Marcus reappeared. 'Anything else for the car, Hannah?'

'Yes, here's our swimwear. Has everyone else got theirs?'

Yes, miss.

Marcus nodded. 'You know, you can go topless there, according to Claude.'

'It's pretty much the norm in France,' said Hannah, as though telling them something they didn't know. 'However, I've only brought a one-piece with me.'

'I have two-piece,' Keiko whispered to Jo. 'But Japanese girls don't like sun on body much. We prefer skin light as possible. Like supermodel skin.'

'What about Naomi Campbell?' asked Jo, slipping extra cucumber into each and every one of the sandwiches. 'She's black.'

'True. But anyway, if I go back to Japan more darker than my friends, I will be odd one out. Not good.'

'Are we almost ready, then?' asked Hannah. 'We'll miss the best of the sunshine if we dawdle much longer.'

'Yep,' said Jo, mustering a smile. Just a one-piece, eh? She wrapped the last of the chunks of baguette in foil, put it in with the others, wiped the work surface and rinsed her hands.

Everyone then gathered the last of the things and filed out the door, shouting, 'See you later,' to Claude.

'Indubitably!' he called back.

Before reaching Hannah's car – the only one with a child seat – Jo said, 'Oh! Forgot something. Sorry.' She dashed back to the house and up the stairs to the bathroom, where she inhaled the remains of Marcus's steam and popped her contact lenses in. Topless, but still wearing glasses, wouldn't have been a good look.

'Uh-oh,' said Lucy. She'd nipped back to Jubilee Street with some dried food for Maidstone, his having run out way ahead of schedule. Either Marcus had resorted to eating the stuff himself, or he'd horribly overfed the cat. Through the living-room window, she carried on watching Bram delve into pockets and bag for his keys. He finally found them and let himself into Jo's house.

Interesting.

According to Pippa, Jo didn't want Bram to know where she'd gone. Also according to Pippa, Jo was 'hot' for Marcus. This, combined with the fact that Pippa was 'hot' for any man but her husband and was for the time being staying in Jo's house, could mean nothing but trouble ahead. Lucy couldn't wait to tell Dom.

She pottered about for a while, suddenly not that anxious to go and do some work on the top floor. She took clothes out of the washer/dryer, watered the plants, checked Jo's house for signs of activity. It all looked pretty quiet. Pippa was probably at the salon. When the phone rang, she hurried to answer it before the machine did. Maybe it was Dom calling from the office.

'Hello?' she said.

'Hi,' said a slightly warbly Hannah. 'We've found a spot with a mobile signal so I thought I'd give you a call.'

'Great. How are you? How's the house coming on? Did Claude go and buy the things you needed?'

'Yes, thank God. We can all sit down now.'

'Look, I'm really sorry. We weren't expecting—'

'That's OK. Anyway, this is just a quick call to say Freddie and I might stay on a while, if that's OK with you?'

'Yes, of course.'

'Look, um, Robin's going to be back from Edinburgh on Saturday and he thinks we're at my parents'.'

'Oh?'

'He didn't want us to come to France.'

'I see.'

'He may have contacted Mum and Dad and found out we're not there, and . . . anyway, I'm sure he'll be fine about it.'

'Really?'

'It's just that I thought I ought to warn you.'

'Warn us?'

'I've just left him a phone message at home, telling him where we are and for how long. He, er, may well come round and see you, and it occurred to me he might think you colluded.'

'Ah.'

'So let him know you didn't, won't you?'

Too right they would. What the hell was Hannah doing? 'When will you be back?' Lucy asked, all of a sudden feeling she *was* colluding. Other people's stormy lives were fascinating, but she didn't want Dom and herself to be part of them.

'End of next week. Ish. I haven't changed our flight yet.'

This wasn't sounding good. Was Hannah not coming back at all? 'Right,' Lucy said. 'Well, I'm not sure what you want us to do with Robin. And, to be honest, Hannah, I'm a bit pissed off that you've got us implicated in all this, or at least involved. I mean, how's Robin going to react? We'll be here dealing with the fallout, no doubt, while you're swanning around . . . hello? Are you still there? Hannah?'

Cut off. Oh well, maybe for the best. She was probably being a bit hard on her. Lucy replaced the phone and checked Jo's house again. Yes! Pippa's car was outside and the bedroom curtains were at that very moment closing! She grabbed the phone again and settled herself into the armchair with the best view. Work could wait, she decided, as she tapped out Dom's number.

'Hi, it's me,' she said, and told him about Hannah, then about Bram turning up and the curtains and everything.

'She might just be giving him a massage,' said Dom. Almost, but not quite, spoiling her fun.

What is it with cucumber? I thought I'd fished it all out but must have missed a bit, for am now in indigestion hell. Will lie down in a bit. That always seems to help.

How amazing Keiko's being with Freddie. She's playing with him now, with the ball he can't fail to catch because it's so big. She's praising him every time, then pretending to miss it when he throws. I told her she's a natural nanny and offered her part-time work when we get back to Oxford. Totally illegal, of course. She seemed keen but said she has lots of work to do on her English next term as she wants to find a job in the Japanese hospitality industry, which sounded quite dodgy till she said 'like hotel receptionist'.

We were very lucky to find this small beach-like bit of bank, and to have it all to ourselves. Slut Jo is lying on her front, sunbathing in unnaturally tiny shorts and an undone top. Obvious, or what? I want to kill her. However, Marcus is taking absolutely no notice of her, and is some distance away to our rear, deep in a book.

I'm quite concerned about Lucy's sudden onslaught over the phone, and am wondering what she went on to say after I switched off. I knew she'd take Robin's side. Knew it. She just has no idea what it's been like for me, living with a man I have few feelings for. Trapped. A bit like this wind. Ouch. Must lie down.

Marcus was having an out-of-body experience, caused by what, he didn't know. Perhaps it was because the sun was hot and he wasn't wearing a hat. He looked down on himself reading. There in front of him, some way to the left, was a pretty woman in a deep-blue swimsuit, tucking a red notebook under her bottom for some reason. She then lay flat on her back with a small groan. Hannah. Marcus watched Marcus's eyes go back to the page, then stray again to another woman with shiny reddish-brown hair spread around her head on the towel beneath her. She was to Marcus's right and closer to the river. Jo. Jo was sunning herself on her front, her top unhooked at the back.

Marcus could see that although Marcus was giving the appearance of reading, he was in fact taking in the sleekness of Jo's back and the enticing bulge of her right breast, squashed beneath her. *Turn over!* his out-of-body head was willing her, and at last she did. Marcus then saw himself raise his book in order not to be caught ogling while she slid the straps down each arm and flung the top to one side. He swallowed hard, re-entered his body and shifted himself back a couple of feet, until his head was in the shade of a tree. *Calm down,* he told himself. *Read your Flaubert. They're just breasts.*

Jo rolled back on to her front and caught Marcus's eyes darting back to his book. She smiled to herself, propped her chin on her hands and took him in while he read. For such a fair-haired man he was actually quite brown, in that kind of nice even Scandinavian way. He certainly didn't look like someone who'd burn easily. He just looked good. Firm chest and squared-off, rather than sloping shoulders. She liked that in a man.

Jo sighed and wondered how things would have been if Hannah hadn't turned up. She was just about certain Marcus and Hannah weren't having sex. First, Freddie was sleeping in with them, and secondly, Jo had lain as still as a corpse two nights in a row in the bedroom next to theirs, listening out for tell-tale noises. None. Only the odd whisper. This morning, she'd overheard Hannah tell Marcus they ought to get hold of a single mattress for Freddie. 'Is it really worth it?' he'd said. 'Just for a few more days?' His response was met with silence, while Jo punched the air and carried on past their bedroom.

Ah well, she thought, her gaze now fixed on his solid, nicely shaped thighs. No point in dwelling on what might have been.

But then his eyes rose over the top of *Madame Bovary* again and fell upon her. She smiled and he lowered the book and smiled back, then lifted a hand and started doing something with his fingers. A gesture of some sort. Definitely aimed at her, since Hannah was flat out and the other two were busy building a mud castle. Now he was beckoning her with his head. His fingers, she realised, were suggesting a walk.

She nodded and pulled on her T-shirt. As quietly as she could, she stood up and crept past Hannah in her flip-flops until she reached the grassy bank where Marcus held out a hand to her and lifted her up to the riverside path. They walked along fairly slowly for a while in a companionable silence, very gradually speeding up. Then, after looking over his shoulder, Marcus grabbed Jo's hand again and almost broke into a run as he led her to a small wooded area, away from the riverbank. Once there, they ducked behind the first substantial tree they came to and kissed hungrily, despite being out of breath.

So sudden, Jo thought, stopping to gasp at air. But so nice.

'I don't know what's going on,' Marcus panted.

'What do you mean?'

They kissed again.

'I don't know if it's the sun or France, but I can't stop thinking about you.'

'Probably the sun.'

'Yeah.'

His hands roamed inside her T-shirt then down her back and over her bottom. It felt good, and so did he. She slid fingers inside the back of his shorts. So smooth, so firm . . .

'I love your body,' he told her, hands circling her buttocks.

'Really?'

'Mm.'

'Would you call it handsome?' she asked, nibbling his ear and tasting Summer Fruits shampoo.

'Definitely not.'

'I'm glad.' They kissed some more, then she said, 'We shouldn't be too long.'

'No.' He rubbed his cheek against hers. 'Don't leave on Monday. It's Easter Monday. There won't be any flights, any trains. Don't go.'

She kissed his neck. 'Yes, there are. Anyway, I have to go back.'

'Why?'

'Work to do, mortgage to pay.'

'I'll pay it.'

'Ah, there you are!' they heard Claude call out, and they turned to stone. 'I was beginning to despair of locating you! Hello, Freddie.' His voice was becoming more distant. 'What's that you're building? . . . Oh really? . . . Ah, such a wondrous day for April . . . Are you OK, Hannah? . . . Sorry? . . . No . . . No, I didn't see them anywhere. Perhaps they're exploring. Here, Keiko, let me help you with that.'

They both breathed out and Marcus continued his exploring. 'I really want you to stay,' he said.

'Yeah?' she replied, then his lips were locked on hers again and she was sliding down the tree and leading him with her, until they tumbled sideways on to the mossy twiggy ground. She pulled back. 'So much that you'd pay my mortgage?'

'And your council tax.'

'God, that's so romantic,' she said, the palm of her

hand on the front of his shorts, while he was unzipping hers.

'Your water rates . . .'

'Mmmm, tell me more. I love it.'

Marcus pecked her on the nose as he tugged at her clothing. 'So much for Claude's equator theory, eh?'

FRIDAY

It was three in the morning and Robin was listening to Hannah's message for the umpteenth time.

'Hi, Robin. You'll probably have discovered by now that Freddie and I didn't go to my parents' after all.'

He took another sip of whisky. Yes, now that she'd told him, he'd discovered it He'd been picking up messages every day, but she'd left this one only yesterday.

'Sorry for not ringing your mobile and telling you, but I didn't know your number. It was in my mobile but I left that behind as it was broken.'

He'd searched the house and not found the phone. He did, however, discover her diary and had snapped the lock apart with the secateurs.

'What happened was, Jo and Keiko and Freddie and I all thought we'd come out to Lucy and Dom's place. Keep an eye on the building work for them.'

How Hannah loved to insult his intelligence.

'Freddie's having a ball with all the tools and equipment. You can imagine . . .' forced laughter . . . *'We should be back some time next week.'*

Should?

'Listen, give all the plants a thorough soaking, would you, Robin? They'll be parched by Saturday. Anyway, hope you had a good time in Edinburgh. Better go now and check on Fred.'

If he came to any harm, he'd kill her.

'Lots of love.'

Yeah, right.

Robin put the receiver down. When he'd first listened to the message at 10.30, he'd tried calling her mobile but with no luck. Perhaps it was broken after all. She'd left no contact number. Deliberately, of course. But he'd go and see Lucy and Dom in the morning, find out where the hell his son was and how he could get to talk to him.

The whisky was helping, but on the whole, Robin was feeling hurt and livid and a thoroughly bad judge of character. Not to mention cuckolded. Of course, if Hannah could sleep with *him* when she was about to marry someone else, she clearly didn't take any of her partnerships that seriously. Which would be bearable – they could just drift apart like zillions of other couples – if it weren't for Freddie. Dear, sweet little Freddie. How he'd been looking forward to seeing him.

Draining his glass, Robin got out of the chair he'd

been in for hours, picked up the empty bottle, swayed a bit, then meandered to the kitchen, slamming a photo of Hannah face down along the way. Time for bed and sleep. He needed a respite from his thoughts, if only for a few hours. God, how empty he was feeling. Should he force himself to eat something? Have a comforting nightcap? *If he offers to make us both a nice hot milky drink, I swear I'll scream.* No. No more Ovaltine. Ever. Instead, he downed two tumblers of water to prevent a hangover, then plonked up the stairs on leaden legs, aimed for the smallest bedroom and got under a duvet with dinosaurs on it.

'Oh, hi,' said Marcus. 'How are you?'

'I'm fine, but it'd be much better if you rang *me*, son. That lady who picks up the phone doesn't seem to speak English.'

'That's because she's French, Mum. Anyway, how's things? Restaurant OK?'

'Busy. Easter holidays now, you know. Did I tell you we've gone Slovenian?'

'Yes, you did.'

'Vinko's been a godsend.'

'Good.'

'And such a lovely man too.'

'Great.'

'Charming, good-looking and terribly romantic.'

'Romantic?'

'Your brothers call him my toyboy,' she said with a quiet chortle. 'He's fifty-six, you see.'

Marcus laughed. She was obviously charmed by this character. 'How's the weather up there?'

'Oh,' she said, 'fair to middling. By the way, we've taken down those blinds you had up in the living room. I don't know, I always think a window's not a window without curtains. Vinko agrees.'

'But I really liked—'

'Picked up a lovely set in Edinburgh, that Vinko was particularly fond of. Deep red with a gold thread. Reminded him of home, he said.'

'Well, so long as you haven't thrown the blinds out. When did you go to Edinburgh?'

'Vinko and I went for the weekend. I showed him all the sights and we had a whale of a time. He's terribly romantic.'

'So you said.'

'Oh, aye, and we've made a few changes to the bedroom. Vinko and I found we couldn't look at that Kandinsky without feeling giddy.'

Marcus frowned and drummed fingers on the receiver. What was with all this Vinko and I? 'Mum,' he said, half tittering, 'are you, er, trying to tell me something?'

'Well, yes,' she said. 'I suppose I am.'

'Not that you and this chef are . . . ?'

'Aye,' she said with a giggle. 'It's been what you might

214

call a whirlwind romance.' He heard her glug at something. Dutch courage? No, his mother only drank at weddings and funerals. 'And, well, now we're a bit of an item, as they say.'

Marcus slumped into one of Madame Bouziges's armchairs. True, his mother had been widowed seven years now, but this was truly outlandish. 'What do you mean, a *bit* of an item?' he asked.

'We're keeping it casual for now. No point in rushing into marriage, we thought, so we're having a little trial.'

'In my flat?'

'Yes. Sorry about that, son. Only it didn't seem right for him to move in with me. Not with all the memories of your father around.'

'No, of course not.' What was he saying? His mother had a boyfriend. Unbelievable. 'But you've always been so . . . so Presbyterian, Mum.'

'Yes. Talking of which, your Aunt Janine hasn't spoken a word to me for a week. Not since I told her I'd most likely be converting.'

Marcus threw his head back and stared at bunches of dried things dangling from a ceiling beam, expecting to wake up any minute next to a wriggling Freddie. Converting? What religion were they in Slovenia? And where the hell was it? 'To Islam?' he asked nervously.

'Oochh, don't be so daft. Catholicism. Anyway, are you keeping warm in those mountains? How's the sweater?'

'Er . . . it's fine, yeah. And anyway, it's very warm here. Look, Mum, are you sure you know what—'

'Not too lonely there in the middle of nowhere?'

'No, no. Not at all. Actually, Hannah and Freddie are here.' A silence followed while he waited for a response. 'Just for a week or so.' More silence. 'Mum?'

'Can't talk for much longer,' she said. 'Vinko and I are off to the cash-and-carry.' She sometimes did this with things she didn't want to hear. A coping mechanism. Either that, or she hadn't been listening again.

'OK,' sighed Marcus. 'Well, don't work too hard. Get those lazy brothers of mine to help.'

'Aye, will do. Mind you, Vinko has the stamina of ten men.'

Marcus wasn't sure he wanted to hear this. 'Well, thanks for ringing,' he said. 'I'll call you back in a couple of days.' If he hadn't flown home to confront the gigolo. Marcus didn't want to cast doubts on his mother's attractiveness – she was a lively blonde who'd just turned a mere sixty-two – but it could be the guy was just after a free lunch and a stake in their business.

'You're not back together, are you?' she was asking.

'Sorry?'

'You and her?' It was always hard for his mother to say Hannah's name. 'After all you went through? *We* went through.'

'No, we're not,' he said, wishing someone would tell

Hannah. She'd just changed her flight to Thursday. 'Don't worry.'

'And don't you worry, either. He's a good man, Vinko.'

'I'm sure he is.'

After hanging up, Marcus asked Madame Bouziges, very nicely and with the aid of gestures, if he could make a very quick overseas call that he'd pay for. She took the wad of euros he proffered and he dialled his oldest brother, Andrew, who told him he'd never seen their mother so alive and happy.

'So what's this guy like?' asked Marcus. 'He's not a gold digger, is he?'

'Well, he'd be digging in the wrong place if he were,' laughed Andrew. 'Actually, he seems pretty loaded. Talking about extending the restaurant and their upstairs accommodation.'

'*My* upstairs accommodation.'

'What? Oh yeah, of course. You wouldn't recognise it now, though.'

'But I've only been away—'

'Beautiful Slovenian crockery. Vinko had it sent over. And these amazing rugs.'

'How nice. But where exactly am I supposed to live when I get back?'

'Ah. Yes. I'm not sure Mum's thought that through, what with all the excitement of it all.' Andrew laughed. 'There's always her house, of course.'

'I thought you might say that.' Marcus saw the heavy

sideboard, ageing Regency-stripe wallpaper, Dralon three-piece suite with wings, and that swirly carpet that made you feel hungover even when you weren't. The brown patterned kitchen tiles . . .

'Anyway,' Andrew said, 'it's a good excuse for a tart-up.'

'But she's attractive as she is,' said Marcus dreamily, his mind on the turquoise bathroom suite.

'The house, thicko. Get it all done up. Modernised. You know she's been thinking of it for ages.'

'Oh, right.'

Madame Bouziges had begun hovering by the door, looking as though she might like a few more euros for the call. Marcus gave her a won't-be-long nod and wound down his conversation.

'Gotta go,' he told his brother. 'Things to do. You know, looking for a home and stuff.'

'Well, have fun.'

'Thanks.'

'Everything OK?' Jo asked a dazed-looking Marcus as he passed her in the kitchen.

He said, 'Yeah,' and stopped. 'I mean, no, not really.'

She looked over both shoulders then slid an arm around his waist and rubbed at his back inside his T-shirt. 'Have you had bad news?'

He nodded miserably. 'My mother's living in sin with a Slovenian she's known a fortnight.'

Of course she laughed.

'And what's more, they've appropriated my flat.'

'Ah.' Should she get in quick and offer him a home? No, no, no. 'Does that mean your mother's house is empty?'

'Yep.'

'So you could always house-sit her place?'

'I could,' he said, throwing his arms up. 'It's a lovely old place. Big and rambling. But it's not really me. I mean, my mother's not very old, but the house just has an elderly person's feel. And that kind of . . . aroma. Do you know what I mean?'

'Cabbage and Germolene?'

'No, that was my grandparents' house.'

'Mine too.'

'More Sunday roast and lavender polish.'

'Sounds OK to me.' Should she jump in with an offer now? What if her house had an aroma he didn't like?

Marcus said, 'Jesus, you can see how people lose their homes and are living in doorways before they know it. Could so easily happen to me.'

'Mm, scary.' Jo kissed his chin, he kissed her brow, then they gently rubbed cheeks. Come and stay with me! she wanted to urge him. Please, oh please. I'll turf a student out and you can have your own room. But instead she said, 'Don't worry. I'd bring you bottles of meths and fresh cardboard and stuff.'

'Thanks.' He embraced her and kissed her full-on, but

Jo began to feel tense. Hannah could appear any moment and kill them both with a frying pan. 'You're too good to me,' he added, his hand roaming upwards. 'But, more importantly, you've got great tits.'

Jo giggled and slowly pulled away. 'This is no place to talk dirty.'

'Fancy a walk?' he asked, bobbing eyebrows.

'Uh-uh. You've got to help Claude, remember?'

As though hearing his cue, Claude then rumbled up the drive in his van and gave Marcus two honks to come and help him unload the tiles.

'Just think,' said Marcus. 'If we get the living room finished today we could be playing French Cluedo again tonight. How good would that be?'

'Don't like Cluedo,' came a small voice from somewhere. Under the sink? Jo and Marcus blinked at each other, jumped apart, then slowly bent down to look. 'It's boring,' said Freddie as he continued to work at something with a screwdriver in the space where a cupboard should be. The thing he was screwing – or unscrewing – looked like it might be holding the sink up. 'My best game is Simon Says.'

'*There* you are,' cried Hannah, flying through the door. 'I've been looking everywhere for you, Fred.' She rushed past Marcus and Jo and scooped him up in her arms. 'Madame Bouziges is going to take us to her favourite town to do some shopping and visit the caves. Keiko's coming too. Doesn't that sound like fun, sweetie?'

Jo's heart skipped a beat. She'd have Marcus all to herself! If she didn't count Claude. She could see from the look he was giving her that Marcus was having a similar thought.

Freddie dropped the screwdriver on the floor in a resigned way as he and his mother headed towards the door. But before she got there, Hannah halted and turned. 'Coming, Jo?' she said. Her piercing gaze seemed to say, 'Don't even think about staying behind.'

'Er, yeah, why not?'

Robin had obviously got Dom's mobile number from their answerphone message. He'd called Dom at work, and then Dom and Lucy had tossed a coin to see who would go home and deal with things. Robin had said he'd be at their house in thirty minutes for the *exact* location of their French place and a contact number. Dom won – or rather, lost – the toss, but Lucy had nevertheless volunteered to go, believing she was less likely to be pinned against the wall and punched under the ribs. Well, that was what she told Dom. The truth was, she'd hoped Robin would feel free to open up and bare his soul, and she wanted to be there to catch it all. Any juicy bits of information would have vacated Dom's head the moment he heard them. Or, more likely, he'd hand over the Laroche-les-Bois details and the two of them would straight away move on to interest rates.

'Robin?' she was saying now to the man on her

doorstep. He wore a very nice blue/grey jacket, a dark
blue shirt with a loosely knotted blue-and-green tie, and
his hands were tucked in the pockets of beautifully cut
trousers the colour of a tropical beach. 'Robin?' she asked
again. She wasn't going to believe it till he said something.

'Ah yes, sorry. My son talked me into a haircut.' He
tried to laugh but Lucy could see it was an effort.

'Come in,' she said, and he did, wafting something
delicious her way as he passed. She took a deep breath.

'Lacoste eau-de-Cologne,' he informed her. 'Something
else Theo foisted upon me.'

'It's very nice.'

'Thank you.'

'Coffee?'

'Love one. Strong would be good.'

She led him through to a kitchen chair where he sat
and quietly stared into space while she busied herself.
But the silence began to unnerve her. 'What a surprise
Hannah's note was,' she said.

It seemed to bring him round. 'You mean you didn't
know she and Freddie were—'

'No. We didn't know Jo and Keiko were going either.'

'They've gone there too? God, you must be a bit pissed
off with them all?'

'Not really. We just feel sorry for them. Honestly, you
should see the state of the place. Nowhere near finished
and, well, totally hazardous, really.'

Robin sprang from his chair just as Lucy realised what she was saying. 'No, no,' she said, grabbing his arm as he passed her – presumably on his way to Laroche-les-Bois. 'Don't worry. Our wonderful French builder has taken control in the past few days. I'm sure Freddie's perfectly safe.'

Robin sat himself down again, heavily. 'Do you know when they're coming back? Or even if?'

'Well, I just called Hannah on her mobile. Miraculously it worked, as they were in a built-up area. Shopping, apparently. Anyway, she . . . Robin, you're not crying, are you?'

'Hay fever,' he said unconvincingly.

'She told me they'd be back at the end of next week, unless . . .'

'Unless what?' he sniffed.

'Unless they . . . weren't, I think she said.'

Lucy poured a cup of very strong coffee for Robin and a watered-down one for herself. 'Milk?'

'Please.'

She handed him the jug. While he stared at his mug and tipped so much milk in that coffee overflowed on to the table without his seeming to notice, Lucy went for a cloth and wondered if she wasn't making a complete balls-up of this. Dom's approach might have been better after all. She rinsed the cloth, squeezed it and bounced back to the table.

'Bad news about that latest interest-rate rise,' she said,

lifting his mug and dabbing away. 'A quarter of a per cent makes a *huge* difference when you've got a mortgage the size of Carfax Tower.' She laughed, hoping he'd join in. He didn't.

'Freddie loved Carfax Tower,' he said, 'when I took him up that time. He thought if he waved hard enough, his mum would see him from our attic window. I secretly phoned her and told her, and she said, "Freddie, that was a lovely big wave you gave me!" the moment we got back.' Robin looked up at Lucy with his wet eyes. 'She's a good mother, you know. Just a lying and deceiving partner.'

'In what way?' Lucy asked tentatively.

'Huh. Where would I begin? You see, I've only just . . . do you know, I feel quite sorry for Marcus now. I'm ashamed to say I've never given his feelings too much thought. I was just so thrilled to discover I had a fantastic little son.'

'That's understandable,' Lucy said. While Robin gulped his very milky coffee, she leaned over and wiped the bottom of his mug. Those new clothes were much too nice to dribble on. What a makeover he'd undergone. She didn't know Robin that well, but couldn't recall seeing him in anything that might have been made this century.

'I must have some rights,' he croaked. He sniffed and blinked away tears. 'Being Freddie's father?'

'I'm sure you do,' Lucy said, although she wouldn't

have held out too much hope. 'But listen, Robin, it's just a little holiday they're taking. I bet you they'll be back on Thursday or Friday. I mean, Hannah does have to teach the following week. Although, obviously, that wouldn't be her only reason for coming back. I'm sure . . .' She stopped, aware that Robin's so-called hay fever was getting worse. Tears now filled his reddening eyes. How vulnerable he looked. And tired. Kind of attractive, though. 'You know,' she began, certain that Hannah would kill her for what she was about to say, 'you're very welcome to go and join them.'

Robin raised his eyebrows at her in a questioning, hope-filled way.

She nodded. 'But I'd take a sleeping bag.'

'I'll think about it,' he said, sniffing again and taking something from the inside pocket of his nicely lined jacket. A packet of pills, by the look of it. He took two out, popped them in his mouth and washed them down with coffee, then held the box up. 'Antihistamines,' he told her with a wipe of his eyes. 'Bloody tree pollen.'

'Between you, me and the gatepost . . .' said Claude.

Marcus laughed.

'Sorry? This is not a commonly used colloquialism?'

'Yes, yes, it's fine. What?'

'Well . . .' Claude said, lowering his voice, 'I've been a little economical with the truth with regards to my three weeks' leave.'

'Oh?'

'Mm. Not long after I started the course, I began to suspect I might find a career in air-traffic control a trifle unfulfilling.'

'Really?'

'Not to say laden with mind-boggling responsibility.'

'I can imagine.'

'So I packed my bags and left.'

Marcus passed Claude a tile and stared at him. 'I'd call that being *very* economical with the truth.'

'I know.' Claude shook his head. 'Only my aunt would be vexed. Will be. When I tell her. There were costs involved, which the family rallied round for.'

'I see. So what are you going to do now?'

'Well,' said Claude grinning, 'my immediate plan, once this tiling is finished, is to repair the missing stair. I promised Keiko it would be fixed before she returns today. Apart from that, I have no idea. I'm looking for a position, so if you hear of anything . . .'

'You could always come and teach English to the British?'

'Ho ho, I think not.'

Marcus handed over another tile. They'd almost reached the door, thank God, then the room would be usable again. It looked fantastic. Very welcoming. Very Mediterranean, too. All it needed was some comfortable seating to add to the dining table and chairs. Marcus thought he might call Lucy and Dom and get permission to go and buy a sofa after lunch. And a bookcase. One or two small tables. He could look for some lamps and nice prints for the walls. Anything to keep his mind off his flat, his mother, his mother's lover, and how careful they were being with his hi-fi.

After Claude had put down the very last tile and taken his cigarette break, he said, 'I thought I'd utilise those old boards in the smallest bedroom to repair the stairs. That room's going to need a new floor eventually. Just as a temporary measure, you understand. Could you assist?'

'Sure.'

The two of them headed for the bedroom with saws and planes and hammers and nails – Marcus thinking how Freddie would have been in his element – and before long they were pulling up the loosest of the floorboards in a room that was nowhere near fit for habitation.

'Here,' said Claude. 'You hold that end steady whilst I measure and saw.'

'OK,' Marcus said, his eye caught by a red notebook lying in the gap where the floorboard had been. Was it the one Hannah was always scribbling away in? Lesson plans, she'd told him when he asked. It looked just like it. He leaned across and picked it up, flicked it open with one hand – yes, Hannah's writing – and tucked it in his back pocket to give to her later.

'I've been feeling quite drawn to catering lately,' said Claude. 'As a business venture.'

'Can you cook?' asked Marcus, wondering why Hannah would hide her lesson plans under the floorboards.

'No, but my aunt can.'

Marcus held the board with one hand and tugged the notebook from his jeans pocket. 'What do you mean?' he said, peering down at an open page where he instantly spotted the word 'Jo'. *Slut Jo is lying on her front, sunbathing in unnaturally tiny shorts and an undone top. Obvious, or what? I want to kill her . . .*

'Have you noticed the *A Vendre* sign on the Sports Bar?' asked Claude.

'Uh-huh.'

'It's been for sale for a while now. Madame Durand, the owner, is eighty-one and feels she may have produced enough *Croque Monsieur* for one lifetime.'

'Really.' Marcus flicked back . . . *best method . . . Jo . . . poison, strangulation, or a knife in the middle of the night?* 'So what . . . you and your aunt are thinking of buying it?'

'Well, first I have to mention it to her. You couldn't hold the board a little more steadily, could you?'

Marcus apologised and put the notebook down, a nasty dread filling his insides. 'Is it going for a reasonable price?'

'Fairly. My aunt might not be compelled to sell her house even.'

When Claude finished sawing, Marcus put the board down. With the hope that Hannah had been making notes on some classic French novel or play that just happened to have a 'Jo' in it, he picked the book up again and his fingers and eyes began darting hither and thither. *Jo and Keiko are walking in the hills – here's hoping they get terminally lost . . .*

'I think I'd like to take the café upmarket,' Claude was saying.

'Well, you couldn't really take it down,' Marcus managed to quip as he read on. *Hard to push someone like that over one of the steep inclines round here.* The book fell from his hand. He squeezed his eyes shut and pictured them all wherever they might be just then . . . underground somewhere. Jo 'accidentally' wandering down the wrong tunnel and suffering a mysterious but fatal blow to the head. *Mrs Currie, in the Cave, with the Large Rock.* His heart began pounding and he felt sure he'd never set eyes on Jo again.

'Completely refurbish the place,' continued Claude as he rubbed at the newly cut piece of wood with sandpaper. 'Then find a superlative chef.'

Marcus nodded thoughtfully. 'You wouldn't like a Slovenian one, would you?'

SATURDAY

No more Mr Nice Guy, Robin had decided, but already he'd apologised to two people who'd carelessly crashed into his supermarket trolley. Just a bit of training, that was all that was needed. Learning how to glower, for example. Or to pause, stony-faced, for a little too long before answering a person. Small gestures that managed to unsettle or undermine people, and so gain their respect.

'Sorry!' he said again to a hulk of a man who'd suddenly pulled away from the beer shelves and smashed into him. 'I mean . . .' The man gave him a watch-where-you're-going-you-cretin look and moved off.

Robin stood amid the heaving mass of shoppers and yearned for that golden age of retail when all shops shut at the stroke of one on Saturdays. Why was he here anyway? Just because tomorrow was Easter Sunday? With only himself to feed and no appetite, there really was no need to endure this hell. He abandoned his half-full trolley and was almost out of the building when someone said, 'Robin? Christ, wouldn't have recognised you! What have you done, gone on one of those makeover programmes?'

It was Paul, long-time law lecturer and great talker.

'It's a bit mad here today, isn't it?' he went on. 'No doubt they think they'll starve to death because some of the supermarkets aren't open tomorrow. Mind you, we're doing the same. Seemed to have lost Brenda in the mêlée. How are you, anyway? Enjoying the break? How's the family?'

Robin stared at his law-teaching friend. 'What do you know about fathers' rights?' he asked.

Paul said, 'Beg pardon?' and Robin ushered him to a quiet area beside the cookery books and sagas.

'Unmarried fathers' rights. You're a lawyer. Sort of. I need to find out about them. If I have any, for a start.'

'Well, is your name on the birth certificate? Were you present at the birth?'

'Uh . . . no, and no.'

'Ah. In that case have you and Hannah set up a Parental Responsibility Agreement?'

'Doesn't sound familiar.'

'Hmm. Is she about to leave you? Or making decisions about Freddie you don't approve of?'

'Something like that.'

'Right. We'd better go and grab a coffee then.'

They queued in the café, got their drinks and sat as close to the store as they could, so that Brenda would spot Paul, or vice versa. 'I like the new image, by the way,' Paul said. 'You look a bit like what's his name. Robert De Niro.'

'So I've been told. Anyway, these parental agreements. Fill me in.'

Paul took a deep breath and did. It appeared that without a PRA – why had no one told him about them? – Robin had no say in where Freddie lived, couldn't sign a medical consent form for him, and had no automatic right to look after him if Hannah died. Which, if Robin didn't watch himself, might be fairly soon. In addition, he would find it very hard to take Freddie abroad unaccompanied, and was entitled to no say in his schooling.

'OK, where do I get one of these things?' he asked eagerly.

'You can download the form from the Internet. Easy.'

'Great. I'll do it when I get home.'

'Unfortunately, you both have to sign it. You and Hannah. And signatures have to be witnessed by a court official.'

'Oh.' Robin stirred at the coffee he didn't really fancy. 'Damn.' Although she might have been willing to sign something like that six months ago, Hannah was altogether more deranged now and, as he'd learned from her diary, had nothing but contempt for him. If she was planning a move back to Braemar, the last thing she'd want would be for Robin to assert his right to have Freddie living within ten miles of him. 'Stupid sodding law,' he said quietly.

Paul agreed. 'So where is she?' he asked.

'France.'

'With your son, I take it?'

'Mm.'

'On their own, or with another—'

'Man? Yes.' Robin gave Paul a potted history, having always been pretty circumspect about the situation with his university colleagues. 'I tried calling last night and she couldn't, or wouldn't, come to the phone. Sent a message saying she'd ring back, but then didn't.'

Paul let out a long, 'Hmm . . .' which Robin didn't like the sound of. 'Is she staying, or is it just a holiday?'

Robin shrugged. 'God knows.'

Paul gave him a sympathetic look. 'I'd recommend a good lawyer but, to be honest Robin, without this agreement . . . hey, there's Brenda.' He promptly stood up and waved his wife over. She was an average-looking woman, whom Robin had met several times over the years and always found very friendly. Make-upless, pleasantly plump, and didn't bother too much with her short mousy hair. She spotted them, wheeled her overladen trolley into the café and when she arrived at their table, she and Paul did something very surprising. They kissed on the lips. In the supermarket. After only seeing each other ten minutes or so ago. How Robin suddenly wanted what Paul had.

He bade the happy couple farewell, left his undrunk coffee and got to his car just as someone was bashing it with her driver's door.

'Watch it!' shouted the reformed Robin, only to be ticked off by the young woman for parking 'much too fucking close'. 'Oh dear,' he said. 'So I did. How thoughtless of me. Sorry.'

Marcus is being very attentive. Following me around everywhere. Barely leaving my side, in fact. As I prepared lunch today, he was extremely helpful and terribly interested in the ingredients and so on. So that's definitely salt you're putting in the soup? he asked. Yes, I said, laughing. He insisted on making the salad dressing himself. All rather encouraging, particularly after I'd begun to suspect he and Jo of having something going.

During this afternoon's walk, which we all went on – it being such a lovely day and Claude wanting to screed the kitchen floor ready for tiling – Marcus was, almost embarrassingly, right beside me the entire way. Once, I slipped an arm around his waist but he had to dart off to show Freddie something interesting. However, he was soon back, matching his steps with mine again.

We kept getting the evil eye from Jo, not surprisingly. She must be feeling a complete loser and looking forward to going home now. I know I'm looking

*forward to her going home. Monday. Can't wait.
Freddie can be moved on to the spare mattress and
Marcus and I can make love at last. I'll have him to
myself for four whole days. More perhaps, if he talks
me into staying longer. My teaching job can go to hell,
and I'm sure Freddie would love to spend the rest of
his life watching Claude at work.*

*Although the days are gloriously warm, the evenings
cool quickly and I'm now feeling quite chilly. I suppose
I should go in – especially as Marcus has just popped
out for the fourth or fifth time to check on me, as he
put it. But first must think of another place to hide
this diary, as it seems Claude is pulling up floorboards
willy-nilly. Wonder what they're all doing in there.
Perhaps I'll suggest another game of Cluedo. I think
they thoroughly enjoyed it last time.*

EASTER SUNDAY

Marcus woke with an arm still stretched firmly across Hannah's body – psychologically, if not actually, pinning her to the bed. He wasn't sure he'd be able to keep this up for another day, but he knew he had to. One more day and one more night, then Jo would be off in the safety of her hire car.

Why he felt unable to confront Hannah, Marcus wasn't sure. He could only think that when his mother found and read his diary when he was fourteen, it had been *the* most embarrassing experience. He squirmed again, recalling her saying she'd never have believed such filth could exist under her roof. Mostly, he'd been guessing at some of his classmates' bra sizes, but to a strict Presbyterian, now clearly lapsed, it was obviously shocking stuff. Anyway, telling Hannah he'd found her little diary was somehow beyond Marcus. He'd read it all eventually, and was left with the impression she probably wasn't homicidal. Still, he thought, lifting his arm off her, no point in taking risks.

'Morning, sweetie,' she said, rolling over and kissing his cheek.

'Morning,' he replied.

'Morning,' said Freddie from beyond Hannah.

'Morning,' they both sang back.

Hannah stretched herself with an, 'Mmmm . . . I think I'll take a bath before breakfast.'

'Really?' asked Marcus. Hannah always had a bath *after* breakfasting. What was she up to? Keiko would have risen early, as usual, and left Jo a sitting duck – or rather a horizontal, possibly snoring duck – for anyone wanting to place a feather pillow over her face. 'Sounds good,' he said. 'Maybe I'll join you.'

'And me too,' said Freddie, suddenly on top of Marcus and bouncing a lot.

'Oh, I don't think all three of us will fit in the bath,' laughed Hannah.

'Yes we will,' insisted Marcus.

'Happy Easter!' said Lucy.

Pippa, head-to-toe in Lycra and glistening with perspiration, said, 'Happy Easter to you too,' with a big smile, but didn't look as though she was going to invite her in.

'We were just wondering if you've heard from Jo recently,' Lucy said. She heard Bram singing along to loud music, then caught sight of him flitting across the kitchen. 'About when she's coming back?' She knew really, but was just dying to discover what was going on over the road.

Pippa glanced wistfully over her shoulder, then back at Lucy. 'Tomorrow, apparently. Unfortunately, Bram's off then too. His trip got postponed, but now he has to go. Shame. It's been lovely having him. I've had *the* best week.'

'Yeah?'

'Mmm. Back home tomorrow, if I haven't topped myself at the prospect.' She rolled her eyes and laughed.

'Well, better be off,' Lucy said. 'Things to do.'

'Are you sure you wouldn't like to come in for a drink?'

Lucy was halfway to the kitchen saying, 'OK,' before Pippa had shut the front door.

'Hi,' Bram said, turning down the radio. 'Haven't seen you for ages.'

'Something smells good,' Lucy said.

'Pan-fried organic, free-range chicken. My favourite. Unfortunately, Pippa won't touch anything fried. But then, that's how she keeps her amazing figure.'

Pippa went up to him and dangled a hand over his shoulder. 'But maybe Lucy would like some, darling?'

Did Pippa call everyone darling? Lucy couldn't remember. 'Well . . .' she said. She'd left Dom sweating over spreadsheets in the attic. He wouldn't emerge for hours. 'Why not?'

Pippa went back to her workout while Lucy sat at Jo's

kitchen table and watched Bram chopping and flinging and stirring and tasting – all in his body-hugging T-shirt. It wasn't an unpleasant experience. 'Jo knows you're here?' she asked eventually. He'd brought her a glass of organic wine.

'Yeah,' he said. 'We've spoken on the phone a few times. Why?'

'Just wondered.'

'Shame we missed each other. She's visiting some friend, apparently.'

Pippa swanned back into the room covered in perspiration. She came over to Bram and ran a hand up and down his back. 'You've hardly been lonely, though. Have you, lover?'

Did Pippa call everyone 'lover'? Lucy couldn't remember.

'I have date tonight,' whispered Keiko. They were in the garden, Jo on a sunbed and Keiko in the shaded hammock, fully clothed and holding a brolly.

'No!' said Jo. 'With Claude?'

'Yes,' giggled Keiko.

'That's great.' And far more than Jo could expect. Marcus had gone distant on her over the past forty-eight hours. Strangely so. Yesterday, he'd steered her into the bathroom and said, 'I'll explain later,' then kissed her passionately but briefly, before hurrying off and gluing himself to Hannah again.

'We will have dinner in gourmet restaurant after church,' said Keiko.

'Sorry?'

'Today is big church day in village for Easter. Claude must go this evening and I go with him. He says service is very beautiful with big famous choir who has recording contract.'

'Wow. Maybe we should all come along?'

'Ah yes. That would be very wonderful. Why don't you ask Hannah and Marcus?'

'Tell you what,' said Jo. She rolled herself on to her front and caught Marcus rubbing sunblock on Hannah's skinny back. He didn't look happy, which was some consolation. 'Why don't *you* ask them?'

'OK.' Keiko tipped herself out of the hammock, then smoothed extra cream on her face for the trip across the lawn. When she returned she said, 'They think good idea. Especially Marcus.'

Jo looked across at the two of them and Marcus gave her a secret thumbs-up. What for she wasn't sure but, since she was beginning to feel grateful for any scraps of attention he threw her way, it did cheer her up a bit.

'I am very exciting,' said Keiko, diving back into the shade.

Jo smiled. 'I think you mean excited.'

'Ooohh, my English is—'

'No it's not, Keiko. It's excellent.'

'I like Claude very much. He is so kind.'

'Yes.'

'And handsome.'

'Yes.'

'And I learn much English from him.'

'We all do.'

Keiko sighed, like someone in love. Jo sighed too, like someone in love.

'I am very exciting,' said Keiko.

'Good,' said Jo, giving up and going back to her whodunit. Two of Giles Donne's lovers had died after dining with him, and Chief Inspector Grenville was confounded. Meanwhile, Betsy the cook, who loved Giles in an unrequited way, was off on her bicycle to purchase more poison for those pesky rats . . .

Can't recall when I was last this happy. When Marcus and I first got together? I really, really don't want to leave here. Ever. Would Lucy and Dom sell this place to me, I wonder. To us? If not, Claude might be able to find us a property. Freddie would go to the village school – become a little French boy. I could teach English. Conversation classes. Or do translation. Marcus would find an occupation. He's a bit short of skills – failed lawyer, mediocre restaurateur – so something like a little market gardening maybe. Growing courgettes and things. I keep dropping hints about settling in France and he says Yeah, great idea. I'm certain he'd like us to stay. He's constantly asking when

Fred and I are going home. Friday, I tell him each time, and he says, Oh right, so you haven't changed it then? – obviously hoping I'll postpone our departure again. Sweet.

Just tonight to get through, then slut Jo – who seems incapable of fastening that bikini top – will be gone. An early afternoon flight, apparently, so they'll have to leave around 9.00, 9.30. We're all off to some tedious church service this evening – bound to be in Latin and a bore for poor Freddie – but we'll go because Marcus was surprisingly keen.

3.30. Might get Keiko to play with Freddie while I go and have a nap. Sexual frustration and a rather cramped bed are definitely not conducive to a good night's sleep. But hey ho, one more day to go.

While Jo sunbathed and Freddie was passing on to Keiko all he'd learned from Claude about pivots and fulcrums, Marcus crept upstairs with a dining chair and positioned himself on the landing, just along from the bedroom door. If Hannah suddenly awoke and came out, he planned to jump on the chair and pretend to be changing a lightbulb. Ridiculous behaviour, he knew, but Hannah having been in a fantastically good mood for days didn't mean she wouldn't slip a black widow spider in Jo's bed.

He stretched out his legs and opened *Madame Bovary* in his lap, but couldn't concentrate too well on the words, his eyes growing heavy in that four-in-the-afternoon way.

He yawned, closed the book and was placing it on the floor beside his chair when, in the room opposite, he caught sight of a speck of bright red under the battered old chest of drawers Claude sometimes used as a work-bench. Marcus knew immediately what it was, but wasn't sure if he was feeling strong enough to examine it again. He took a deep breath, shook off his fatigue and tiptoed into the room, slowly closing the door behind him.

'What?' he kept whispering as he read Hannah's latest entries. '*What?*' This was far worse than he'd imagined was going on in her head. Courgettes? Turning Freddie French? He finished reading, vowed he'd give Robin a call, and slid the book back under the chest of drawers – or 'chiffonier' as Hannah insisted they call it.

'Oh dear, should we be dressed formally?' Jo asked Claude, who was smarter than she'd ever seen him, in a beige suit and no workmen's boots.

'Just a touch more demurely than usual,' he replied. 'Ah, here comes Keiko, perfectly attired.'

Keiko slowly descended the stairs looking truly glam-orous in red dress, red lipstick, black jacket, black shoes and one or two bits of gold jewellery. She was followed by Hannah in pastels: a chic calf-length dress and scarf. Behind her was Marcus in nice jacket, tie. Jo felt giddy at the sight of him.

'Look,' she said, conscious of her jeans and sandals, but aware she hadn't brought anything dressy with her either. How come they'd all packed church-going clothes? 'I'm a bit behind,' she explained. She passed the others on the stairs as she went up two at a time. 'Haven't changed yet. Sorry! You lot go ahead and I'll catch up.'

'Demure, demure, demure,' she said as she rummaged through her things in the bedroom. Perhaps Keiko had something? She went over to where her roommate had cleverly converted the deep-set window and its curtain rail into a wardrobe, having wisely thought to bring hangers with her. Everything was small, of course, and after several attempts at squeezing herself into tops, skirts and, on her, half-mast trousers, she almost gave up on the idea of going to the abbey. But then she went back and tugged some creased black linen trousers from her case, gave them a shake and decided no one would be looking at her anyway. Not with a famous choir and a dazzling Japanese woman in the building.

When she guessed she looked presentable – white top, a dark grey suit jacket of Marcus's she'd nicked from his room, and some of Keiko's expensive earrings – she set off for the village centre with a kind of end-of-holiday malaise hanging over her. In two days' time she'd have to face not only life without Marcus but, worse still, Sergei's next chapter.

Robin was in the Sports Bar, wired up after driving all night and all day, then consuming three welcome but awfully strong cups of *café au lait*. He was seated by the window overlooking the square, aware of how to get to the house but, owing to not quite feeling himself, determined to leave that till tomorrow. The charming old lady who'd served him had given him the name of a small guesthouse in the next village, which was sure to have vacancies, and he'd thanked her profusely in his best French.

All around him were empty tables and chairs, so with nothing else to distract him and no mental strength to rehearse his opening lines to Hannah any more, Robin watched the football on a large screen near the ceiling. Until, that was, a burly man in a tight-fitting suit came and switched it off apologetically. The café was about to close, he explained. He and his mother had a church service to attend. He pointed through the window at a large, cathedral-like building.

'Ah,' said Robin, who'd wondered why so many cars were pouring into such a small village. He drained his cup, chucked euros on the table and went out on to the small terrace, wondering if he was feeling better or worse than when he'd arrived. Just different perhaps.

He breathed in the cooling evening air and checked that he'd put the address of the guesthouse in his shirt pocket. Out of the village and turn first right, she'd said, then second left. Or the other way round. Oh well, he'd find out. He swayed slightly with fatigue, slipped an arm in his jacket, then caught sight of Hannah, Marcus and

Freddie walking down a narrow road towards the square. They were behind Jo's Japanese student, who was on the arm of a swarthy young man not much taller than herself. Robin's knees buckled and, as luck would have it, his bottom landed on the seat of a metal chair.

Freddie – dear Freddie – was skipping in an ungainly way, holding his mother's hand on his right, and Marcus's on his left. Every few steps they swung his little boy up in the air and down again, and from across the square, Robin could hear him giggle. It was a sound and a sight that cut to his very core. In all his years with Judith, dealing with her dalliances, he'd never felt the kind of jealousy he was experiencing now. As he watched Hannah, Freddie and Marcus follow the other two into the church, his head and heart felt close to exploding. Why was Hannah going to church? She didn't do that. Must be Marcus's influence. This was terrible. He could be influencing her and Freddie in all sorts of ways.

Robin sat for a while feeling a strange combination of powerless and galvanised before leaping from his seat. '*Papier?*' he demanded, charging back into the café. '*Je voudrais le papier, s'il vous plait.*'

The barman held up a pad.

'*Non, non. Plus grand!*' cried Robin, stretching his arms wide. '*Comme ça.*'

The man shrugged a couple of times, murmured something under his breath then disappeared and returned with what looked like a roll of wallpaper.

'Perfect,' said Robin. '*Et une plume? Une* felt tip, *peut-être? Ah, merci.*'

He left the café again, apologising in English because he couldn't think of the French, and sat himself on the terrace while the barman shook his head and very swiftly and firmly locked up.

Contact lenses, thought Jo. Definitely. She turned around and went back to the house, unlocked the front door, ran up the stairs and exchanged glasses for lenses. That was better. She hated getting all dressed up to go out, then ruining the whole look with the same old specs she wore day after day. It was a bit like always wearing the same necklace, or hat or something. When she became rich, she'd have a different pair of glasses for every day of the week. Better still, laser correction. She locked up again and walked as fast as she could, almost trotted, so that she wouldn't have a thousand heads turn as she arrived late through a huge creaky, squeaky wooden door.

But there it was when she got there, the big wooden door. Shut. Through it, she could hear the vague muffled sound of a priest chanting in that Johnny-one-note way. Damn. Should she go in now, get the humiliation over and done with? Or wait for a few more stragglers to arrive and slip in with them? She looked around and saw not a soul. A couple of dogs barked and whined in a lonely-sounding way, as though the only inhabitants of Laroche-les-Bois' houses at that very moment were its pets. What a field day a burglar could be having. Suddenly, the choir struck up, ethereally but loudly, providing a better opportunity for her to steal in unnoticed.

Here goes, she told herself and was lifting the door's enormous iron latch, when something fluttered down from the heavens and landed noisily at her feet, frightening the life out of her. It was a large sheet of paper – five or six feet long – now half-curled up on the ground and with something written on it. She let go of the latch and approached the ghostly thing with apprehension. 'FATHERS' she read, gradually untangling it, 'HAVE FEELINGS!'

What fathers? She looked up at the sky. Not *the* Father, surely? But then it was Easter Sunday, and didn't Jesus ascend to his dad on that day? Things were getting spooky, but maybe this was some kind of sign, sent especially for her. One of those incredible religious moments that change people's lives for ever. Crikey, she thought. All she needed was to understand it.

'Yes?' she called out hopefully, when something else fell at her feet. A small box. She bent down and examined it. Hay fever tablets. What could this all mean?

'Fathers have feelings!' came a distant voice, and Jo swallowed hard and stepped back from the church to get a better view of heaven.

'Pardon?'

'Fathers have feelings!' she heard again and there in

248

the bell tower – or half on it, half in it – was a figure. It was a man who sounded a lot like Robin, and looked like him too. Only better groomed. Short hair, smart jacket.

'Who are you?' she shouted, just as the big door opened and a man in a gown came out. He must have heard her fiddling with the latch.

'It's me!' yelled the guy above, and the priest or whatever ran to her side and stared upwards with her. 'Tell Hannah I want my son back!'

More people were coming through the door to investigate and the priestly chap tried ushering them back in, unsuccessfully.

'Don't do anything stupid!' Jo shouted through cupped hands as a crowd gathered round. 'I'll go and get her!'

Robin hadn't intended to draw attention to himself, only his message. Scaffolding along one side of the building had eased his passage to the top, but what he'd not thought of in his haste and haziness was something to attach his message to the church tower. He'd managed to wedge one end into a gap in the stonework, but then, when steadying himself for a moment, the whole thing had come adrift and fallen from his grasp. When he looked down and spotted Jo, his plan underwent a slight change and he'd voiced his message instead.

Now more and more faces were staring up at him, though not the one he wanted to see. But then, he wondered, ought Freddie to be subjected to the sight of his daddy clinging precariously to a bell tower? If his son were older, he'd understand that Robin was doing it out of love and desperation, but this could simply scar the little boy for life. Oh, well, too late now. In for a penny, he decided, and again shouted, 'Fathers have feelings!' to the congregation below. 'Give us all PRAs! Give us our due rights!'

Someone began yelling at him in French. A man. He had no idea what the chap was trying to tell him, but he was shaking his fist in a very French way. Robin shook his fist back. 'Fathers have feelings!' he called out. If he hadn't been so fuzzy-headed he'd have tried to translate it. *Les pères ont . . .*

'Daddy!' he suddenly heard to a background sound of an angelic choir.

He peered over the edge but couldn't see Freddie anywhere. '*Fred?*' he pleaded. 'Where are you?'

'Dadd*eeee!*' he heard again. The voice was echo-like and near.

Robin manoeuvred himself right back inside the surprisingly spacious bell tower to see a little face appear on the internal stone staircase that led up to it.

'I want to get to the top,' Freddie puffed. 'Like in Carfax Tower.' He heaved himself up the last step and stood proudly and breathlessly just inches from Robin. Behind him was Marcus, looking understandably concerned.

'Well, you're at the top now,' Robin said, a lump forming in his throat. He picked his son up and the two of them took in the view through a large hole in the round tower. There below, with hands on her hips and, Robin imagined, an appalled expression, was Hannah. He kissed his son's deliciously chubby face and said, 'Why don't you give Mummy a nice big wave?'

MONDAY

At 1 a.m. they decided Keiko might not be coming back to share their mattress, and began to get passionate under the duvet.

'So are you going to explain now?' asked Jo, stopping mid-kiss.

'What?'

'Why you've slavishly followed Hannah around and snubbed me for days.'

'Oh, that.'

Marcus tried kissing her again but she wasn't having it. 'Well?'

'Look, I thought she might try and kill you.'

Jo laughed, much too loudly but she couldn't help it.

'Shhh,' Marcus said, pulling the bedding over her head. 'I honestly did.'

Jo bit hard on the duvet until she calmed down. 'What on earth made you think that?'

'I can't say.'

'What do you mean, you can't say? Did she tell you she wanted to kill me?'

'Does it matter?'

'Yes, it does rather.'

'Anyway,' he said, 'it turned out I was mistaken. So let's just forget it, huh?'

'I want to know.'

'It really isn't important.'

'It is to me.'

Marcus sighed. 'Tell you what,' he said. He ran a hand up her leg and kissed her. 'If you put that jacket of mine on again, I'll let you know why I didn't trust her.'

'Really?'

'You looked so great in it.'

'Well, OK then. Pass it over. It's on the floor, by you.'

'My best suit!'

'Sorry.' She took the jacket from him, sat up and slid it on over her nakedness, trying to think of something she'd like Marcus to dress up in. Nothing came to mind. How strange men were. 'Anything else?' she asked.

'Definitely not.'

Jo was still awake at 2.30, promising herself that if she and Marcus one day got together properly she'd *never ever* keep a diary. She rolled on to her side and tried once again to get to sleep. Eyes shut tightly, focusing on her breathing. But it was impossible, and so annoying as she knew she had to be up early to do the packing she hadn't got round to. The more she dwelled on how awful it would be not to sleep at all, the more she seemed to be making that happen.

Maybe a milky drink would help. She slipped out of bed – well, off the mattress – and crept through the room to the landing where moonlight through a window lit her way and where she heard the sound of someone crying, or at least sniffling. She stood still for a moment and listened to what was almost certainly a very upset Hannah. Sniff. Sniff, sniff.

Robin had come to reclaim her and Freddie, and was now lying beside them both, no doubt completely out of it after his long journey. Jo couldn't pretend not to be relieved at this development, while at the same time feeling pity for screwed-up and possibly dangerous-to-know Hannah. She was just thinking that Robin might be able to knock some sense into the poor woman, when he loomed out of the darkness, making her yelp.

'Aaat*chooo*,' he went loudly before seeing her and jumping himself. 'Aaat*choo*!'

'Bless you.'

He sniffed, thanked her and plodded down the landing, saying, 'God knows what I've done with my antihistamines.'

* * *

'Is that them?' she whispered.

'I think it's a stone,' sniffed Robin. 'But let me check. Yes, just a white pebble.'

The church forecourt-cum-car park was part paving, part gravel, and despite the light of an almost full moon, in ten minutes they'd spotted only false alarms.

Jo said, 'Shame the torch conked out.'

'Yes.'

'I expect Lucy and Dom had to use it a lot when they had no electricity.'

'Hey, look,' Robin said, charging away from her and bending over. 'Is this . . . ? Yes!' He stood up, kissed the box in his hand, then took a couple of tablets out. 'They're a bit squashed, but well done, Jo.'

'I should have picked them up when you first dropped them, but in all the excitement . . .'

'Oh God, don't remind me. What on earth was I doing?'

'Apart from scaring the life out of us?'

Robin sneezed, then said, 'It won't get into the papers, will it? You know, the *Oxford Times* and so on.'

'Don't be silly.' She pointed at the tablets. 'How long do they take to work?'

'About fifteen minutes.'

'Let's sit on that bench while they kick in.'

'Are you sure? I mean, this is very good of you.'

She shrugged and they sat in their coats, side by side in the deadly quiet but very chilly village and talked in hushed voices, mostly about Robin's tenuous position. 'Well, Marcus is clearly determined to get them back,' he said eventually.

'I think he may have come to Oxford with that fantasy in mind,' said Jo. 'But the thing is . . . and he's talked a bit to me about this, he . . . well, this sounds terrible, but he seems to have gone off the idea. Kind of slowly.'

Robin sniffed and his face lit up. 'Has he?'

'I think it dawned on him, once and for all, that Freddie wasn't his son. Sort of emotionally.'

'Oh?'

'And on top of that, he and I are, you know . . .'

'You and Marcus are . . . ?'

She nodded.

'That's wonderful.'

'Yes. Yes, it is.'

'But Hannah must be gutted?'

'We're not sure she's aware. Marcus has been putting on a remarkably good act for her.'

'Oh, right.'

'To be honest, I think you've saved his bacon turning up like this, just as I'm about to leave.'

'When are you going?'

Jo looked over at the church clock. 'In about five hours.'

'What? Oh God, I'm sorry. Keeping you up like this.'

'Don't worry. With a bit of luck I'll sleep on the plane. I hate flying.'

'Maybe Hannah would give you one of her magic pills. I talked her into taking three of the things, to completely knock her out.'

'Sounds severe.'

He smiled and looked very attractive with his new hair and clothes. His eyes had stopped watering at last. 'Maybe,' he said. 'But you don't think I'd be here having a nice chat with you if there was a chance she might be conscious, do you?'

Jo laughed. 'No, I suppose not. She could have been packing Freddie into his car seat, or anything.'

Robin turned to her goggle-eyed. 'Let's get back, shall we?'

'Yeah, OK. Hey, wait for me . . .'

Robin didn't wake until almost midday, and the first sound to hit him was that of Freddie, singing an unfamiliar song. It wafted up from the garden, through the window as Robin slowly emerged from sleep. Such a sweet little voice. He wondered if they should do something about it. Get him in a choir? He pictured Fred in the dear little uniform of Christ Church Cathedral School, down in the heart of Oxford, becoming a chorister by age seven, eight. But then, when he came round properly, Robin remembered he was an athiest and ardent socialist. He got up and stuck his head out the window.

'What's that you're singing?' he called down.

Freddie stopped and looked up. '"*Il était une bergère*",' he said. 'It's my best song.'

'Oh, yes?'

'Claude learned me it.'

Taught, Freddie, *taught*. 'That's nice. Where's Mummy?'

'Asleep.'

'Oh. So who's looking after you?'

'Marcus and Claude,' Freddie told him. 'We're airplaning the shelves 'cos they don't fit. Look.' He pointed to a plank of wood as long and wide as himself. In his other hand was a small plane from his kit. 'And my second best song is "Fairy Sharker".'

'Uh-huh?'

While Freddie went through the first verse of '*Frère Jacques*', Robin's head remained outside the window. It might have been rude to disappear. 'Lovely,' he said when he'd finished. Which it had been.

'It's French.'

'Yes, I know. Where's Mummy sleeping?'

'In the car,' Freddie said matter-of-factly.

'Really?'

Robin went and checked. Hannah was upright and dead to the world in the passenger seat of her hired car. He hoped it was because she hadn't wanted to disturb him, not because she couldn't bear to come and doze beside him in the bed. After checking Freddie was still happy, he had a quick shower, then headed for the kitchen where he found Marcus gathering Freddie's things together.

'I'm assuming you'll want to all leave today?' Marcus said.

'Er, yeah. I suppose so,' said Robin. 'Hadn't thought that far ahead, actually. Listen, are you OK with all this? I mean, I can't be sure what Hannah's told you, but I was adamant I didn't want her to bring Fred here.'

'I guessed as much,' said Marcus. 'Dreaded it, should I say.' He held up a pot. 'Coffee?'

'Please. You know, I'm determined not to lose Freddie. Not now I've discovered him, as it were. I know it's been tough on you, the estrangement and everything . . .'

'Oh, don't worry about me,' Marcus said as he filled a large cup. 'Yeah, it was hard at first, but not so much now. Take them home. They belong with you. Freddie especially.'

Robin took the coffee cup from Marcus just in time, for a streak of something human flew into the kitchen and slapped Marcus's face, causing him to take two unsteady steps back. 'I'm sure I deserved that,' Marcus told a retreating Hannah, while Robin found himself thinking, just fleetingly, that it might be quite nice if Hannah disappeared from both their lives.

'I'll go and help her pack,' he told Marcus.

'Cheers.'

THURSDAY

Marcus and Claude were sitting at the dining table. Claude was chain-smoking and Marcus was drumming his fingers. With Lucy and Dom calling a halt to the repairs and refurbishment, there really wasn't much else for them to do. They'd pretty much exhausted table football, Marcus having thrashed Claude over and over, as he always did. He may have been a mediocre restaurateur but he knew how to smash that ball into the goal. It was the only thing he'd ever seen Claude truly annoyed by. They couldn't even go out and walk or fish or canoe or anything, since the weather had decided to be typical for April again: squally showers all over the region; sky the colour of slate most of the time.

'It's just that the building society have rejected our top-up application,' Dom had told Marcus over the phone. 'And the bank won't increase our loan. So we can't pay Claude any more. Apologise to him, would you?'

'Sure.'

'You can stay on as long as you like, though.'

'Thanks,' Marcus said, not sure he wanted to.

It was all pretty miserable really. The high drama of the previous week had left him feeling first horribly guilty – poor old Robin, and poor Hannah, so cross she'd actually hit him – then plain empty. The house certainly felt empty, especially at night. And he missed Jo badly.

'We could play a word game,' suggested Claude.

'Mm?'

'There's this one that's terrific fun. You see, I say a letter. The first letter of a word I've thought of. Then you say the second letter, with a word in mind. You always have to have a word in mind, and the longer you make it the better. The loser is the one who completes the word.'

'I'd rather not,' said Marcus. Play Claude at a word game? He'd be mad to. 'Do you mind?'

Claude took out another Gauloise. 'No, of course not. I just thought it might distract you from your erroneous affiliations.'

'You mean crap relationships?'

'Yes.'

'I am feeling bereft,' said Marcus. 'That's for sure.'

'Me too.'

'Bummer, eh?'

'Mm, most dispiriting.'

'What's more, neither of us seems to have a job or any prospects.'

'No. Not since my aunt pooh-poohed my Sports Bar idea.'

'And I haven't even got a home.'

'No?'

Marcus explained about his mother and the gold-digger.

'How awful,' said Claude. 'But perhaps you could go and live in—'

'Her house? Yes, it's been mooted. The place needs a lot of work, though. General updating. New kitchen. Things she's been talking about doing for ages but didn't want the disruption and, anyway, couldn't afford. Mind you . . .' Marcus stopped swinging back on his chair and the front two legs thumped to the ground, 'she was telling me one of her insurance policies has just matured . . . plus, easier to have the work done while she's not living in the house.'

'That's true.'

'And better if she had a couple of blokes she could totally rely on doing it, not bottom-of-the-barrel builders who have six jobs on the go and don't finish any of them.'

Tut tut tut, went Claude. He took a drag of his cigarette and exhaled. 'How can people be so dishonourable?'

Marcus smiled to himself. Should he remind Claude he'd left Bertrand in charge of things? 'There are loads of cowboys around, that's for sure.'

'Well, you must ensure your mother doesn't use any of these dubious characters.'

'You mean, find her someone more like you?'

'Why, thank you. But yes, that is what I'd recommend. Someone . . .'

'Punctilious?'

'Exactly.'

'Got a passport?'

'Of course.'

Ernst, bless him, was trying his best to cheer them up. Telling jokes about Bavarians, making Jo and Keiko a late-afternoon snack neither of them could eat. Not because it was inedible, they just couldn't eat.

'And did you hear about the Bavarian on the train?' he asked.

'No,' said Jo, and she didn't want to. As long as she lived she wouldn't get his humour.

'The sign on the train it said, "Do not lean out of the window." But the Bavarian leaned out of the window and his head was knocked off by an electricity pilot.'

'Pylon.'

'Sorry. Pylon.' He laughed while Jo waited for the rest of the joke. 'It's very funny, yes?'

'Mm. Have you got homework tonight, Ernst?'

'Unfortunately, I have. I must write an essay called "What I did in the holiday".'

Original, thought Jo. Would teaching EFL be a doddle compared to copy-editing? She'd spent most of the day close to tears with one of Sergei's chapters. But then it might have been Marcus rather than convoluted English upsetting her.

'Ah yes, I have remembered another excellent one,' Ernst was saying. 'A Bavarian man he walked into a bar . . .'

'How about you, Keiko? Any homework?'

'Yes,' she said heavily. 'But my heart isn't on it. My heart is on Claude.'

'. . . and he asked for a beer. The barman said, "I'm sorry, we cannot serve people who are wearing leder-hosen."'

'Maybe the homework would take your mind off him, Keiko?'

'Do you think so?'

'"That is OK," the Bavarian said, and in the middle of the bar he took off his lederhosen and was only in his shirt and knickers.'

'Underpants,' said Jo. This one was sounding almost promising.

'Sorry, underpants. "*Now* I would like a beer," said the Bavarian. Ha ha. Actually, maybe not so funny as the train joke.'

'No, just as funny.' After a quiet moment Jo said, 'So what *did* you do in the holidays, Ernst?'

She tried to listen but found it hard, lost in thoughts of France and Marcus and their sad farewell. She and Keiko had had to leave early. Robin wasn't even up and Hannah was ambling around like someone who'd taken three sleeping pills. She'd said a cursory goodbye to the two of them then, oddly, gone to sleep in her car. Jo too had been groggy after just a few hours' sleep, which was good because it numbed her a bit when it came to parting with a very huggy Marcus. 'Call me in a couple of days?' he'd said, looking forlorn. 'Tomorrow, even?' Claude turned up to see Keiko off, and they'd cuddled a lot too. Keiko was shedding tears that didn't stop until she fell asleep on take-off. So now, they were here and the men were there and Ernst was embarking on another joke.

Jo jumped in with one of her own. 'What's the difference between an onion and an accordion?' she asked.

'Ha,' said Ernst, 'I think there are a lot of differences between an onion and an accordion. For one, an onion does not have all those small buttons.'

'Ernst, you're just supposed to say, "I don't know. What *is* the difference between an onion and an accordion?"'

'Oh. Sorry. What *is* the—'

'Yeah, OK. Keiko?'

'I don't know. I'm so sorry.'

'Well,' said Jo, puffing herself up for the punchline, 'nobody cries when you cut up an accordion!'

Ernst rubbed his chin. 'But wouldn't it be difficult to cut up an accordion? I think they are very strong.'

Jo groaned and went back to staring at the phone. Should she call Marcus again? It would be the fourth time in two days. Would Madame Bouziges get pissed off? This morning, he'd said he'd buy a card to use in phone boxes. It was a nice cheap way of calling and he'd be able to talk to her without Madame Bouziges listening in. 'I'm sure she understands more than she lets on,' he'd added in a whisper.

'But maybe a Bavarian would try to cut up an accordion!' said Ernst, finally laughing.

The phone continued to do nothing. Had Marcus got hold of a card? He said he thought they sold them in the Sports Bar. If he had, he'd be bound to call this evening. But then, he and Claude had no doubt been busy working on the house all day, or driven miles to get supplies. He could be knackered. The place was going to be great when it was finished, though. Fabulous, even. Perhaps she and Marcus would holiday there again. Often. She looked around her and sighed. It was nice coming home to a house where everything worked and there weren't holes and things, but her little Victorian terrace definitely lacked something. Probably Marcus.

'Excuse me,' said Keiko, holding up her retractable pencil, notebook open. 'But please explain, who is Anna Cordion?'

He called around 5.30. She pictured him in the phone box in the square; the shape of him, what he might be wearing. 'How's it going?' she asked.

Not so well, he told her. The weather had turned filthy,

and Lucy and Dom had been forced to let Claude go, due to lack of money.

Jo said, 'Well, he'll be going back to air-traffic school soon, so I don't suppose he's too bothered.'

'Actually, he quit that.'

'Oh dear. Anyway, what about you?' she asked, crossing fingers. 'Any plans?' *Come to Oxford, come to Oxford.*

'Well, Claude and I had this crazy idea of doing my mother's house up for her. I just rang her, and she's well into the idea.'

'Really?' said Jo, trying not to feel miffed that he'd called his mother before calling her. 'What a good idea.' But then if he hadn't called his mother first he wouldn't have been able to tell Jo his news. Bad news, as it turned out. Back to Scotland?

'Claude's thrilled because he'll be much closer to Keiko. You'll both have to come up.'

'Yes,' said Jo miserably. It was hardly a day trip and there was Ernst to take care of. 'Tricky, though.'

'Hey.'

'What?'

'Cheer up. We'll work something out.'

'Yeah, yeah.' Another long-distance relationship? She wasn't sure. 'Look,' she said. She was close to tears but didn't want to go girly on him. 'I was just on my way out. Call again tomorrow?'

'Jo, are you al—'

'Bye. Must dash. Sorry. Bye.' She put the receiver down with a 'Shit', and went and made herself a calming herb tea, then sat back at the kitchen table, wiping her eyes. There were some people, she decided, who were destined never to experience a live-together relationship. Strange thing was, up to that point she'd never wanted one. Of course, it might have helped if she'd told Marcus the future she had in mind for them.

'Guess what,' she said to Keiko, who'd wandered in with her long face and what looked like a homework query in her hand.

Keiko shrugged and sat down. 'I don't know.'

'Claude is coming to work in Britain.'

Keiko breathed in sharply. 'In Oxford?'

'Well, no. Scotland.'

'Ohh, I want very much to see Scotland. Adam, my teacher, said it is very beautiful.'

'Yes, it is.'

Keiko jumped up and beamed. 'I will get map.'

Jo said, 'Good idea,' feeling mildly cheered up by her lodger's exuberance.

When Keiko came back with the British road atlas, Jo pointed out Braemar and Edinburgh, and Loch Ness and Aberdeen. 'Does Scotland have airport?' she was asked.

'Several,' said Jo, laughing for the first time in days.

Keiko clapped. 'Then it is easy. I go Heathrow then Scotland?'

'Well, yes . . .'

'For a big weekend.'

Jo said, 'I think you mean long weekend.' Or maybe she did mean big.

'Ohh, my English is very—'

'No it's not.'

'I am so exciting!' Keiko said, just as the phone rang again.

Jo reached over and picked it up. 'Hello?'

'I thought you were going out?'

'I lied. I was upset.'

'I know,' he said, then they talked and talked on his cheap-rate phone card. He didn't feel it was right to be in Oxford, he told her. 'Not right now.' He was hoping Hannah and Robin would patch things up. Repair all the damage he, Marcus, had done. 'I kick myself every day over it.'

Jo tried to say all the right things. She understood. She didn't think he had anything to blame himself for. Look at what Hannah had done to him, for goodness' sake. Yes, she'd come to Scotland to see him. Yes, she'd wear his suit jacket again . . .

'Oh, and one more thing,' he said, 'before the card runs out.'

'Mm?'

'Well . . . Bram. I was hoping you wouldn't—'

'I wouldn't.'

* * *

They were playing a fun game. Robin was diving under-water, swimming around for a bit, then surfacing next to Freddie and giving him a fright. Freddie, floating in his armbands, never knew where his dad would come up and say, 'Boo!' or 'Raarrrghh!' and was finding it hilarious. Each time Robin tried to stop the game for fear he'd give his son a lifelong water phobia, Fred would say, 'One more time, Daddy. Pl*eeeze*.'

'OK, this is absolutely the last time,' Robin said, needing a rest and meaning it. 'Down I go!' He arched his body and dived under, thinking this time he'd play a different trick. He swam around counting to ten then slowly ascended and, grabbing Freddie's foot, had a little nibble on it, before bursting through the surface right beside a blond-haired, blue-eyed boy with a terrified expression. 'Oh, I'm sorry,' Robin said. 'I'm *really* sorry. No, don't cry.'

'Feo's a cry baby,' sang Freddie, leaping on Robin's shoulders.

'Who?'

'This is my friend Feo, from nursery.'

'Are you all right, Theo?' asked a woman swimming over. Robin recognised her as a nursery mum.

'I think I gave him a bit of a fright,' he said. 'Sorry. Thought he was Freddie.'

'Hello, Freddie,' said the woman. She stopped swim-ming, stood up and turned to Robin. 'He seems fine now. Don't worry.'

'Yes,' he said, trying not to stare at her lovely shape in her pale green swimsuit. Blonde – naturally, he thought – and blue-eyed like her son. Great teeth when she smiled, which was what she was doing now, watching the boys. Freddie and Theo were having a race but not getting very far in their armbands, just splashing a lot and looking ridiculous.

'I've booked Theo in for lessons,' the woman said. 'Is Freddie going to take them . . . um, I'm sorry, I don't know your name.'

'Robin.' How come he'd never noticed how attractive she was?

'I'm Sadie. Hi.'

'Hi,' he said, the Beatles' 'Sexy Sadie' coming to mind. They shook hands, which felt like an odd thing to be doing in a toddler pool. 'I don't know about the lessons. Sounds like a good idea, though.'

'Yes. The earlier they learn the better, they say.' She sank down into the warm water and floated on her back for a while. 'You know they get on like a house on fire, those two.'

'So I see.'

'Freddie should come round some time. For tea.'

'I'm sure he'd love that.'

Sadie gave him her toothy smile again. 'They're back at nursery on Monday, so how about then?'

'Yes, OK. One of us usually collects Fred around four, four thirty . . .'

'I'll give you our address and phone number,' she said, swimming breast stroke towards the boys, 'before we leave here.'

'Great.'

'The thing is, Adrian, I honestly don't think these sessions are doing a bloody thing for me. If anything, I've got worse and am having to take more antidepressants. Floating round in this half-awake state all the time. I mean . . . What did you say? . . . Oh sorry, I thought you said something. Chance'd be a fine thing, eh?

'Anyway, I *was* feeling thoroughly betrayed by Marcus. Tricked. Stupid. "Take them home," he said to Robin on Monday. He didn't know I was listening outside the back door. "They should be with you. Freddie especially." How utterly cowardly, I thought. Do you know what I did? I went into the room and slapped his face. Quite hard. He went out somewhere – just like him – and I didn't really get to see him again before we left.

'Robin's been typically Robin. Very understanding. But, God, you should have seen him on the top of that bloody church. I couldn't believe it was him at first. Not just because risk-taking isn't his thing, but because he looked so different. For the better, that is. His son talked him into a change of style. I even noticed heads turning in Paris. We stayed there overnight, Monday. Robin turning Parisian women's heads!

'He's a great partner, that's for sure. He's kind and loyal

and involved, and, as I discovered in France, he can be extremely passionate when roused. I'm not talking sex, I mean over Fred. Yes, a wonderful loyal partner . . . but not for me, Adrian. Not for me. You see . . . I realised, after giving it thought on the way home, that it wasn't cowardice on Marcus's part, but altruism. He was willing to give away the two people he treasures most in life, for well . . . our sakes, and Robin's sake. An amazing gesture, but a mistake.

'No, there's only one man for me, Adrian. And he and I both know it. Adrian, are you still there? Oh, right. Anyway . . .'

So this is how it happens, thought Robin while he dried first Freddie, then himself. A chance encounter – or a chance nibbling of the wrong child's foot – a slight dizziness at the sight of the person . . . and then *pow*, you're suddenly considering infidelity for the first time in your life. She hadn't been wearing a wedding ring. He'd checked. Beautiful hands with long tapering fingers. Piano fingers.

'So tell me about Theo's daddy,' he said to Freddie.

'What.'

'Well, does he come to nursery and collect him sometimes? Does Theo talk about his daddy at all?'

'I don't know. Can we come swimming tomorrow?'

'I expect so.'

'And the day after, and the day after, and the—'

'No, Fred. Not every day.' Was this going to be his new obsession? Could be a lot more exhausting than DIY, though maybe easier on the ears. 'But we might see if we can get you into beginners' swimming lessons.'

'Aaww,' groaned Freddie. 'I don't like lessons. At nursery, Millie pretends she's a teacher and we're her children and she tells us off all the time. Specially me.'

'Well, maybe if you didn't pinch her? Anyway, they won't be anything like Millie's lessons, and Theo's going to be coming to them.'

'Feo my bruvver?'

'No,' said Robin patiently. 'The other one.' How strange – or indeed fateful and significant – that he and Sadie had sons with the same name. 'Here, can you put your trousers and socks on by yourself? We need to be quick because we're going to meet Theo and his mummy by the door. You're going to go and have tea at his house next week.'

'Hooray,' said Freddie.

And Robin thought *Hooray* too, but didn't know why he was getting so excited. Sadie was far too young for him, and now that he and Hannah were settling back into what they had before, this would hardly be the time to begin living dangerously. However, there was this unfamiliar fluttering going on in his tummy and his head felt light and carefree. Even if it was for only one afternoon, he'd enjoy it while it lasted.

FRIDAY

They decided to drive. Well, Claude did.

'My tools are of inestimable value to me,' he told Marcus. 'And, knowing what I know about the aviation business, I'm disinclined to hand them over to baggage handlers. What do you say we take my van? It'll hardly be first-class travel, but there's a CD player and I've got a great collection of French pop music.'

Marcus would have to pick his car up from Stansted. French pop all that way? It could be less painful to walk and swim to Essex. He said, 'Let me have a think about it.'

But Claude pulled a face. An apologetic one. 'I believe my aunt has already booked us on to a weekend ferry.'

'Oh?'

'Midday Sunday.'

'Jesus. So we'd need to set off . . . ?'

'Tomorrow, yes. Spend the night in Le Havre.'

'Will that be fun?'

'I think not. Anyway, my aunt has also booked us into some very reasonably priced accommodation. One star. But one star in France is equivalent to three or four in Britain. No offence meant.'

Marcus couldn't believe so much had been organised before he'd had his first cup of coffee. 'None taken,' he said, and as he tried to wake up properly, he began to question if he really wanted to go and do this huge exhausting job for his mother. Particularly as the sun had reappeared. Why didn't he just stay in France and write a brilliant novel? No, even harder work. His least favourite things at school had been composition and cross-country running. He'd never seen the usefulness of either. 'I'd better pack then,' he said. 'Can we fit the table football in?'

'No,' said Claude emphatically.

Pippa was on the doorstep in masses of make-up and with an enormous wheelie suitcase. For a moment Jo panicked. Did she want to move back in?

'I'm off to, er, Italy for a week or maybe a bit longer,' Pippa said, 'with . . . a girlfriend. Jane. Yes, Jane. But anyway, just thought I'd let you know I've had an email from Bram. Several, in fact.'

'Have you?' Jo hadn't had any.

'His boat's been delayed, so he's got a couple of weeks to kill.'

'Uh-huh.'

'Says to give you his love.'

'Right.'

'Could be away a couple of months this time.'

'OK. Would you like to come in? I found a couple of things of yours you left behind.'

'Oh, keep them,' said Pippa with a wave of her bejewelled hand and wrist.

'Well,' Jo said, 'have a great time with your . . . girlfriend.'

'Oh, I'm sure we'll have a ball. Jill's never been to Spain before, so . . . oh, there's the taxi.' Pippa waved at the driver, crawling along the street as he checked house numbers. He stopped and pulled in, then sat with the engine idling, looking up Pippa's short skirt as she leaned forward to kiss Jo goodbye.

'See you when you get back,' said Jo. 'In fact, when will you—'

'Bye!' Pippa said, rushing at the taxi. 'Bye!'

Jo closed the door and went straight to her email. No new messages. She decided to write one herself. 'Hi Bram,' she typed. 'When Pippa arrives, could you tell her thanks anyway, but I probably won't have any need for two second-hand thongs and *Great Breasts After Forty*. Love, Jo.'

She sent the message then wondered if she might, in fact, hang on to the book. She stared at the screen, deep in Marcus thoughts. He'd be on his way back to the UK

277

now. How tempting it was to jump in her car and drive to Stansted for a quick kiss and cuddle before he set off for Scotland. But maybe not. He'd said why didn't she and Keiko come up next weekend, so she'd just have to wait. And anyway, she was snowed under with proof-reading, as was often the case in the summer term. No, she'd go at it all week, then fly up to Aberdeen with Keiko on Friday.

It'd be great. Maybe.

She was slightly worried that things wouldn't be quite so passionate and romantic in the cooler temperatures of mid-Scotland, and without Hannah's presence to make it all deliciously illicit. But still, no point in speculating when there was a dissertation on the South American feral parakeet to get going on, and two students to feed. Keiko's appetite had increased alarmingly, which was good. Would her lodger like Scottish food? Jo was remembering her stay in the Highlands and wonderful red-deer stews, when her screen told her she had mail. She opened the new message.

'Will do!' it said. 'Love, Bram.'

SUNDAY

I absolutely don't understand it. I'm so certain I put my diary in the bottom of the wardrobe, under that unused fondue set Marcus insisted I take with me. A long-ago Christmas present from my parents. I'm positive that's where I left it, but who knows? I was in quite a euphoric state when I set off for France. Perhaps I put it there, then moved it somewhere less accessible? Mind you, I've scoured the place for a week now. Robin said he hasn't seen it, and Robin tends not to lie. So very strange.

I went back to the same shop and got another one. I need to plan, that's why. Writing helps crystallise my thoughts, in a way that talking to Adrian doesn't. You always feel he's being judgemental. Silently, of course.

OK. My plan. My plan is . . . no idea. But I'm sure inspiration will come. I believe Marcus will come too. Just now I rang Madame Bouziges, who told me he and Claude were crossing the English Channel this very minute! Claude was desperate to see his new Japanese girlfriend, she said.

Marcus, on his way to Oxford – yes!

It all must have been so hard for him, poor thing. We'll have a little talk when he gets here – where will they stay? Lucy and Dom's? Yes, we'll have a talk. Work something out. With Robin. Some kind of Freddie-share arrangement. As we'll probably live in Scotland – Oxford's way too expensive to buy or rent in – it'll most likely be a case of Fred spending one weekend every couple of months with Robin. Maybe a bit more in the holidays. Yes, I'm sure we can come to some arrangement like that. Amicably. Behave like sensible, rational adults. None of this scaling church towers nonsense. Honestly, what was he thinking?

They were at the pool for the fourth day in a row.

'Daddy, can we play the diving game?' asked Freddie. '*Can* we?'

Robin was fed up to the back teeth with the diving game, and couldn't understand why his son wasn't. Robin simply wanted a quiet time, lying on his back watching the entrance to the women's changing rooms, waiting for Sexy Sadie to appear. He hadn't seen her since their first encounter on Thursday, but he lived in hope. Even if she didn't turn up today, there was always tomorrow teatime at her house. It wouldn't be *quite* the same, though. She wouldn't be wearing her swimming costume – presumably – and there might well be a partner in residence.

'Aren't any of your friends from nursery here?' he asked Freddie.

'Only Jasper, but he smells. Please dive, Daddy.'

'No, Freddie. Which one's Jasper?'

'There,' said Freddie, pointing.

'He looks nice, and I'm sure he doesn't smell in the water. Let's go and see him, shall we?'

'No.'

'Come on. It'll be someone for you to play with, instead of wearing your poor old dad out.'

'But Jasper's smelly.'

'He won't be smelly in the water, I promise you.'

Freddie said, 'Oh, all right, then,' and followed his father across the pool.

'Hello, Jasper,' said Robin. Jasper looked puzzled. 'Freddie's come to play with you.'

The little boy's face lit up and he said, 'Goodie,' and the two of them began splashing around and leaping on each other in the way boys do; Freddie clearly forgetting all about the personal hygiene thing.

Robin relaxed at last and lay on the top of the water, locking his eyes on the women's changing rooms again, just as Sadie walked out with her son. Yes! Robin manoeuvred himself on to his front and swam a few yards. 'Hey, Freddie,' he said. 'Look who's here. Theo. Come on, let's go and say hello.'

'No, don't want to,' said Freddie, giggling. He and Jasper were giggling a lot, bashing each other with their big armbands.

'Please?' said Robin, taking hold of Freddie's hand and attempting to guide him to the far side of the pool, where Sadie and Theo had slipped into the water.

'No!' shouted Freddie. 'Jasper's my best friend now and I *don't want* to go to tea with Feo after nursery tomorrow. Feo's a cry baby.'

'Yes you do, and no he's not. Come on.'

'No!' screeched Freddie, yanking his hand away.

Behind them a voice said, 'Everything OK?' and Robin spun round. 'Hello, again,' Sadie said, and catching sight of her pretty smiling face, Robin couldn't think of a single thing to say. Instead, he grinned at her and hurriedly ducked under the water to hide the smattering of grey hairs on his chest, telling himself he was being ridiculous. How old was she? Thirtyish? Crazy. And what's more, he was a happily partnered man. Hannah was behaving normally again, and certainly being nicer to him since the whole France escapade. Partly due to remorse, he suspected, but he'd also wondered if his new look had anything to do with it. Whatever it was, things were much calmer at home and Robin was feeling relatively safe, especially after that little chat with Jo. So, he told himself, *behave*. Be *good*. Stop looking at Sadie's golden legs, flapping gently while she treads water. Think, instead, of something tedious. Marking essays . . .

But it was hard, because Sadie was staring long and hard at him with a definite glint in her eye. 'I was hoping you'd be here,' she said, before swimming in a circle all the way round him.

If he hadn't already been crouching, Robin felt sure his knees would have given way.

MONDAY

Marcus woke to the aroma of old Sunday roasts and lavender polish and a worrying hissing noise. No light was coming into the room, owing to the dark and heavy mock-patchwork curtains, plus their linings and the net curtains beneath. He stretched out an arm for a switch, and the tasselled bedside lamp was soon illuminating two pictures of his father: one when he was young and dashing, and one when he was older and dashing. More than ever, Marcus could see how much he resembled him. On the other side of the double bed, his mother's ancient tea-maker was doing its business. She'd always believed in starting the day as she meant to go on – drinking tea.

His mother also believed in blankets, and Marcus was weighed down by three of the things, in addition to a candlewick spread in faded lemon. He was hot, he realised. Very hot. He threw sheet, blankets and everything else aside and got out of bed. When he reached the window he prayed hard, then quickly tugged at the curtains to discover his prayer had been answered. It was a beautiful day. And a beautiful day in Scotland was hard to rival. He opened one of the larger windows and breathed in the clear air. Home again, he thought. Fantastic.

The contraption beside the bed began gurgling and burbling excitedly, then filled its little teapot and alerted Marcus of its accomplishment with a high-pitched alarm. 'Yeah, OK,' he said, rushing over to press the off button. 'Very clever.' He poured tea into a mug, added milk and got back into bed to admire the view of the Cairngorms, wondering what Claude would make of them.

They'd arrived in the dark last night, following a journey that had been painfully slow after Stansted, what with having to stick together in the inside lane most of the time, so Claude wouldn't get lost. The winding and weaving mountain roads had been tricky too. Several times, Marcus had stopped to check they were still Claude's headlights behind him. They'd arrived around midnight to a warm welcome from both his mother and a handsome, late-middle-aged man with fairly Slavic features, an incredible head of grey hair and a thick accent. 'Sossor about yr flet,' he said to Marcus.

'Pardon?'

His mother helped out. 'He says he's so sorry about your flat.' She kept looking at Vinko adoringly, touching his arm territorially.

'Oh, don't worry,' said Marcus.

'Pliss leave in flet's sparoom?'

'Sorry?'

His mother smiled. 'He says, "Please live in our flat's spare room".'

Freddie's old room? The one that took a cot and a chest of drawers, but only just. 'No, no, we'll be fine here,' Marcus told them both before hinting that he'd rather like to turn in for the night.

Claude had collapsed in the second-largest bedroom soon after they'd arrived. 'Please excuse me,' he'd said to the three of them. 'I'm feeling enervated from the rather protracted journey.' After he'd gone, Marcus's mother commented on what a beautifully spoken young man he was, but then she had spent almost a month listening to Vinko.

As he enjoyed his tea on the bed, gazing out at the majestic hills and mountains, Marcus pondered on the strange twists and turns of recent weeks. He'd left Scotland with one definite aim in mind: spending time with Freddie; and one small dream that he hadn't been that optimistic about: getting Hannah and Freddie back. He'd had no idea, setting off on that long drive to Oxford, that he'd end up in France and in love with someone else. Nor that it wouldn't be Hannah and Freddie he'd be returning to Scotland with, but a Frenchman with better English than the Queen.

It had been an eventful time, to say the least, but this

probably wasn't the way someone fast approaching forty should be living. If only he'd stuck at his Articles, he'd have been a lawyer by now. A solicitor of some sort. He was just wondering why 'lawyer' sounded so much sexier than 'solicitor', when Claude put his head round the bedroom door and said, 'I'm sorry to disturb you, but I can't find the fresh coffee.'

'You'll be lucky,' laughed Marcus. 'Here, have some tea.'

Claude looked as though he'd been offered a nice cup of hemlock. 'I think I would rather die of thirst. Or at least drive to the nearest café.'

'Again, you'll be lucky. I've got an idea, though.'

It was dark and thick and kind of Turkish tasting, with lots of grainy bits in the bottom, and Marcus was guessing from the expression on Claude's face that he was wishing he'd gone for the tea.

'It's very . . .' began Claude.

'Slovenia has bescoffee in wirld,' said Vinko, pouring more sludge into everyone's tiny cups.

'Mmm,' said Marcus, who quite liked it. 'So where's all my stuff?' he asked, turning to his mother. It certainly wasn't in their flat. His flat. How weird it felt, sitting surrounded by these alien items, with his mother and her *new boyfriend*. Surreal. Not that the past couple of weeks had been unsurreal.

'It's all safe and sound, don't worry. Your Aunt Janine

offered to take care of it all, now we've kissed and made up.'

'Have you? That's good.'

'But, as you know, her house never sees a duster, so your brothers put all your stuff in my loft.'

'Oh, great. Half the roof tiles have slipped.'

'I'm sorry, son,' she said, taking her hand from Vinko's knee and placing it on Marcus's. 'But be happy for me, won't you? Eh?'

Marcus nodded and smiled and tried not to think about his six-hundred-pound stereo. His mother pinched his cheek playfully before returning her hand to Vinko.

They were here not only to get Claude a cup of coffee, but also to discuss with his mother what she wanted done to the house. Claude had already got the ball rolling and had pen and paper out to write down instructions.

'I thought nice sliding glass doors between the lounge and the dining room,' she was saying.

'But, Mrs Currie,' said Claude, 'don't you feel—'

'Ooch, call me Moira.'

'Moira. You don't think sliding glass doors are a little, how shall we say . . . *passé*?'

'And one of those wall-length, teak-effect units Janine and Bob had put in. You know the one, Marcus?'

'Yes,' he said with a shudder.

'With compartments for your television and video and whatnots. They're grand, they are. Do you have them in France yet?'

'I don't believe so,' said Claude. 'And what about the floors, Moira? A good durable hardwood, perhaps?'

'Janine and Bob have a wee slot for their phone directories too. Very handy.'

Marcus could see Claude was writing it all down, but in a slow, reluctant hand, as though not quite believing what he was hearing.

'And Vinko would like a bit of a bar to make cocktails on his evenings off. Nothing too showy.'

'Well, if you're sure . . .' said Claude. He scribbled something and surreptitiously passed the sheet of paper to Marcus. 'What time's the next ferry home?' it said, and Marcus chuckled while his mother talked about some nice kitchen wallpaper she'd seen in a house makeover programme.

'A lovely wee pattern it had on it. Winter vegetables and kitchen utensils.' She shook her head. 'Heaven knows why they were ripping it off.'

'I have to say,' said Claude, as Marcus drove them both back to the house, 'as stunning as the scenery is, I do find your Scottish mountains a little denuded.'

'Huh!' replied Marcus, insulted. But of course Claude was right. Deforestation and intensive grazing had left them nowhere near as lush and tree-covered as those of the Cévennes. Marcus explained, then said, 'Luckily, there's quite a bit of reforestation going on these days,' but Claude didn't seem to be listening. He was examining the notes he'd taken earlier and shaking his head.

'Here, give that to me,' Marcus said. He took the piece of paper and tore it in two while he steered with his arms. He then crumpled the two halves into balls and chucked them to the back of the car. 'I think we can ignore all that. She'll never remember what she said, anyway.'

When they pulled up outside the charming old former farmhouse that Marcus had called home since the age of seven, they sat and took it in for a while, engine off.

'White walls and sanded floors?' asked Marcus.

'I think so.'

'Stainless steel and wood kitchen?'

'Absolutely.'

'Swirly carpet the first thing to go?'

'You're reading my mind.'

Ernst had cycled back in the school's lunch hour to eat with Jo. He occasionally did this and she found it touching, especially when lunch was on him. Exotically filled rolls from town, or fish and chips from just round the corner. Today, though, she'd made a salad, stopping work at 12.15 to do so, knowing he'd charge through the front door at around twenty to one. Which was just what he'd done a minute or so ago, breathlessly and carrying fresh orange juice.

'Today, I had some bad news,' he said, settling himself at the kitchen table.

'Oh dear.'

'Our teacher, Sue, has said that we must prepare a presentation for next week about our impressions of a part of this country, but not Oxford. Somewhere we have visited. But me, I haven't visited anywhere. Only Heathrow airport, twice. I don't like to go on the school's weekend trips to Brighton and Stratford and places, because some of the other students are . . . is there another word for "arseholes"?'

'Not really.'

'This means I must go to London at the weekend, but I have heard that it is dangerous and expensive. Ahmed has had his phone stolen in London.'

Jo helped herself to salad. 'Honestly, Ernst, London's not that scary. And, besides, didn't you go to Manchester on an exchange?'

'Yes, but it rained so much and all the time we were in a little house with only a small concrete garden. To speak for fifteen minutes on Manchester would be impossible for me.'

'Here,' said Jo, handing over the salad spoons. 'Help yourself.'

'Thank you.'

'It's a shame you're not coming to Scotland with Keiko and me.'

'Ah!' he cried. 'What an excellent idea!'

'But . . .' she said. Was this what he'd been fishing for all along? She and Keiko had been talking about

291

their trip all weekend. Poor Ernst must have felt left out.

He took scoop after scoop of salad and suddenly seemed much happier. 'I will look on the Internet for my own accommodation, then I won't be playing . . . oh, what is the word? When you are alone but the others they are a couple. I think it is a berry.'

'Goose?'

'No. I don't think it is playing goose. Not a bird.'

'I meant gooseberry. Playing gooseberry. And anyway, you wouldn't be.' Much. 'Let me check it out with Marcus, yeah? Wangle you an invitation.'

'I like this word "wangle". What does it mean?'

'Oh, to be a bit devious to get something. Manipulative, even. Someone who wangles is a wangler.'

He looked puzzled and a little shocked. 'Is not a wangler someone who is very annoying and stupid?'

'Different word, Ernst.'

'I don't suppose Marcus is here?' asked Hannah.

At the sound of the doorbell, Lucy had charged down from the top floor where she'd been working on a brochure. She was still out of breath and, without thinking, said, 'Shouldn't you be at school?'

'I've taken a sickie. Terrible thing to do on the first day of term, but there you are. Well . . . is he?'

'No. Why?' Lucy toyed with the idea of inviting Hannah in, but there was the brochure to get on with.

Mind you, she had wanted to ask if she'd feed Maidstone over the coming weekend. 'I thought he and Claude were going straight to Scotland.'

'What?'

'So Jo said.'

Hannah coloured up. '*What?*' she asked again, before doing an about-turn and crossing the road towards number 15.

Lucy didn't shut her door; just stood glued to the bristly mat beneath her bare feet, thinking maybe the brochure could wait.

'Is she in?' Jo heard. It sounded like Hannah, but it couldn't be. Not on a school day.

'Yes,' Ernst said, and then the front door closed and Hannah followed Ernst into the kitchen. 'It's your friend,' he told Jo.

'Hi,' she said. 'We're just having lunch. Would you like—'

'Where's Marcus?'

Jo went cold inside, but not as cold as Hannah's eyes. 'I'm not sure,' she said. It was true. She had no idea where he was at that precise moment.

'Isn't he coming to Oxford? With Claude? Claude's aunt said he desperately wanted to see Keiko.'

Hannah was wringing her hands and Jo imagined her neck inside them. If only Marcus hadn't told her about the murder plan. Jo wanted to alert Ernst to her current danger, but he'd ploughed back into his lunch and was quietly humming as he munched.

'I don't understand,' Hannah went on. 'Why aren't they here? Claude's aunt said he desperately wanted to see Keiko.'

Wringing her hands *and* repeating herself. This wasn't good. 'Why don't you sit down, Hannah?' Harder to kill someone when you're sitting down. 'I'll put the kettle on.'

'Fuck the kettle.'

At this, Ernst stopped humming and looked up at the two women.

'Or . . . there's this really nice orange juice?' Jo murmured.

'How *come*,' said Hannah, her voice growing louder with each utterance, her face redder, 'nobody *ever* tells me what the *fuck*'s going on?'

'Ah,' said Ernst, piercing a bread roll with his knife, then smiling Hannah's way. 'It's easy. Marcus and Claude have gone to Scotland, and me and Jo and Keiko will go to visit with them at the weekend. Simple. Unfortunately, I am going to be playing gooseberry, ha ha.'

Jo jumped behind Ernst and his chair for protection. Now *her* hands were itching to get wringing, being so close to Ernst's neck.

Hannah said, 'Eeaarrghh,' or something similar, thumped a fist on the table, and before Jo could plunge a hand in Ernst's shirt pocket for his mobile, two doors had been slammed and Hannah was gone.

For a while, Jo stayed where she was and the two of them stared at the closed kitchen door.

'Perhaps,' said Ernst, 'you could wangle for your friend to come to Scotland, too? I think maybe she needs a holiday.'

It was incredible what you could get done in only a few hours, thought Marcus, when there were two of you and you both hated the carpet. They were burning it now, in the garden, protecting themselves from noxious fumes with Claude's masks. Luckily, there weren't any other houses for miles; something Marcus resented as a child, but loved now. It really was a picturesque spot, even with bits of burned, swirly patterned carpet raining all over it.

'You see the top of those buildings over there?' he asked Claude, lifting his mask. 'Buried in the valley?'

Claude brushed smoke aside, lifted his mask too and said, 'Yes, I think I see them.'

'That's Balmoral Castle. The Queen's Scottish home.'

'Huh,' said Claude, clearly unimpressed. 'And how many homes does she have?'

'I don't know. Quite a few.'

'Why?'

'Because she does, I suppose.'

'You don't ever question the ethicalness of such an arrangement?'

Was ethicalness a word? He'd check later.

Claude was staring at him. 'You don't consider your royal family greedy and lacking any social conscience? Surely, such spacious and sumptuous homes could be made available to, say, the impoverished children of single parents, or battered women or asylum seekers, on occasion? What delightful short breaks they could take there.'

'Hm,' said Marcus. 'Nice idea, but I'm not sure the tabloids would go along with that.'

Claude rolled his eyes as if despairing of Great Britain, then handed Marcus the stick he'd been prodding the fire with and said, 'I'm just going to phone Keiko, if that's all right?'

'Again?'

'I'll reimburse you for the calls.'

'Oh, don't worry about that,' said Marcus, laughing. 'You're putting me to shame, that's all. I've only called Jo once today.'

'I'm sure the ladies don't compare notes,' Claude said, but Marcus wasn't so sure.

He watched Claude walk back to the house, through the old vegetable patch that no one had kept up since his father died, over the vast overgrown lawn and past the flowerbeds his mother had always attended to lovingly, but not these days, it seemed. Marcus had always assumed that he and his brothers would inherit all this – large farmhouse, large garden, large barn ripe for conversion – but now, of course, it could all go to Vinko, should his mother recklessly throw herself into marriage. Maybe he and Andrew and Fraser should have a word with her. Or, better still, a word with Vinko. At night. In a quiet alley somewhere.

When Claude traipsed back ten minutes later, he told Marcus there was a 'jocular' answerphone message from Jo for him.

'Oh, yeah?'

'I listened only superficially,' Claude said, 'not wanting to feel like an eavesdropper, but I did catch the words "Hannah", "homicidal" and "help".' He tittered, poised to put his mask back on. 'British humour can be very dark, I've found.'

Robin had lectured, seen a couple of students one to one, and was now hurrying from the building before anyone else accosted him. He walked briskly towards the staff car park, head down to avoid eye contact. It was twenty past four and, although he'd hoped to go home first and freshen up a bit, he realised he ought now to go straight to the nursery. Anyway, he knew he looked OK because so many people had told him so today. 'Robin, great outfit.' 'Love the hair, Robin. Knocks years off you.' He'd had his leg pulled too. 'Who is she?' Bill had asked with a smirk. Robin had been tempted to tell him.

'Sadie, Sadie, Sadie,' he said to himself as he pulled out on to the main road. *Whatever you do, don't call her*

Sexy Sadie. He put the car radio on, tuned it into Radio 2 and listened to some blasts from the past, requested by Pete from Rochdale. Pete from Rochdale was obviously of a similar age, since Robin was able to sing most of the lyrics to all three songs, though they wouldn't have been his choice. When was the last time he sang in the car? Not counting 'Wheels on the Bus'. Decades ago, that was when. Wow, he thought, how great it was to be alive sometimes. Even Headington's London Road shops looked good today, plate-glass windows shimmering in the late-afternoon sunlight.

Robin parked as close to the nursery as he could, being in a bit of a hurry. He checked himself in his rear-view mirror, just in case Sexy Sadie was also collecting her son – *don't call her that* – then got out and dashed into the building.

Right, where was he? Fred, Fred, Fred, he said under his breath, scanning the room of twenty or so children: some busy, some dozing, two having a small battle over an item. Fred, Fred, Fred . . . Perhaps he was in the toilet, Robin thought, and was on his way to check when Mrs Jessup looked up from where she was helping with a jigsaw and said, 'Freddie's mum collected him earlier.'

'Sorry?'

'During quiet time.'

No, this couldn't be right. 'Isn't quiet time straight after lunch?' Hannah would have been teaching.

'That's right. One thirty till two thirty. As I expect

you know, we prefer not to have mummies and daddies calling in then. Perhaps you could remind your wife.'

'Are you sure it was her?' Robin asked. A chill ran through him at the thought of a mentally ill child-snatcher picking Freddie up. 'Not some stranger?'

Mrs Jessup gave Robin a withering as-if-I'd-let-that-happen look and went back to her chunky puzzle.

He got home in record time, ignoring all speed cameras. Hannah's car wasn't there. Where could they be – the swimming pool, the supermarket? He rushed into the house, didn't find a note, so picked up the phone and dialled her mobile. It was switched off. He took the stairs two at a time and, once in Freddie's room, opened drawers and cupboards. Had things been taken? It was hard to tell. Fred had so many clothes.

Perhaps he was overreacting, Robin kept telling himself. But no, Hannah would have called him at work to tell him she was collecting Freddie, if she hadn't been up to something. Up to what, though?

He went to their bedroom and more or less ransacked it, hunting for her new diary. Next he searched the kitchen, but with no luck. Then the living room. It was there, casually slotted into the newspaper rack. 'Ha!' he said, and went out to the shed for the secateurs that had quickly done the job last time.

Once again, Robin felt his world fall apart as he sat on the brick floor of the shed, not caring if his expensive new trousers got oil or whatever on them. One weekend every couple of months? Was that the morsel he'd be thrown as a so-called 'absentee' father? Unbelievable.

It appeared from Hannah's jottings that Marcus was going to be in Oxford again. Perhaps he'd arrived and they'd gone to see him. Perhaps they were having this 'little talk' she mentioned. Perhaps, perhaps, perhaps . . . *Lucy*, thought Robin. They were all at Lucy and Dom's house having tea. Tea . . . Oh, *Christ*. Sadie. He checked his watch: 5.15. She'd be wondering where they were.

He found her number and dialled, and after he'd apologised and explained that there'd been a mix-up, she asked, 'Are you all right, Robin?' in such a very tender way. 'You sound a bit low.'

'Well,' he said, and then he was off, pouring it out. All of it. Marcus coming to Oxford, France, even the embarrassing church business.

'Oh, how awful for you,' she kept saying, sounding so kind and as though she really cared. Then, when he'd finished, she said, 'You know, you couldn't be more different from my ex-husband.'

Ex? The day was looking up. 'In what way?'

'He doesn't have much time for Theo, unfortunately. Bit of a drifter. He's in Ireland now. The benefits are better there, he says.'

'So . . .' began Robin, thinking of how to word things without sounding predatory, 'you're available, then?' No, not right.

She laughed quietly down the phone. 'Not for just any old body, I'm not.'

Robin wasn't sure how to take that, or indeed how to respond to it.

'Why don't you come round?' Sadie said. 'And we'll talk over what we should do about Hannah.'

We?

'OK, see you soon,' Robin said abruptly, aware he was getting all choked up. He put the phone down, blinked tears from his eyes – hayfever, still? – then climbed the stairs to have a shower. Quickly, before she changed her mind. When he got to the bathroom he received a jolt. Freddie's little toothbrush and special toothpaste weren't there.

'Hi, Adrian, it's Hannah. I'm afraid I'm not going to make it to tomorrow's session. Thought I'd better leave you a message, even though you're bound to charge me anyway.

'I'm on the M6, you see, on my way to Scotland. No, I know I shouldn't be using my mobile phone while driving, but how often do you see police cars on a motorway these days? Freddie's asleep in his seat, luckily. He won't last the whole journey to Braemar, so I'm planning on stopping overnight somewhere. We'll take pot luck. Cumbria, maybe.

'The thing is, I'm having to do what Marcus wasn't able to. He being a good person and me being . . . well, me. Honestly, you should have seen how close we were before Robin showed up in France. Marcus couldn't stay away from me. I hope you believe that. It was almost like a second courtship, only without all the rampant sex we had first time round. Owing to Fred sleeping in with us, you understand. Anyway, I expect I've told you all this.

'Once Freddie and I left France, Marcus left too. What does that say? Mm? Claude has come over with him. According to his aunt, it's to see his Japanese girlfriend. You know, Jo's lodger. I told you about her. But the odd thing is, they went up to Scotland instead of coming to Oxford, and I think that must have been Marcus's idea. I think he's avoiding Jo. She's not getting the hint, though, and has already got a trip to Braemar organised. Would you believe it?

'Do you know, talking to you like this – leaving you a message – doesn't really feel any different from one of our sessions. You're being just as responsive. Think, Adrian, of all the time you could save yourself if your clients would only phone in their troubles! Not only would you not have to say anything, you wouldn't have to listen either, if you didn't feel like it. Fuck, cop car looming in wing mirror. Gotta go. I'll call again in a minute.'

TUESDAY

Robin woke to an empty house and a sense of impending doom. Then he remembered Sadie, and the whole ghastly situation didn't seem quite so terrifying and impenetrable. Sadie, Robin had been relieved to discover, was quite a bit older than she looked. And, as luck would have it, was a part-time social worker. Exactly what Robin was in need of. She was caring, a good listener and had a practical, organised approach to life. If the gods had made him fall for a sculptor or accountant or something, he not might have been feeling quite so hopeful this morning.

Sadie had made a short list. He reached for it now; it had been the last thing he'd read before going to sleep. Number one was *Stay calm*. Easy to say, hard to do, when your son was God knows where. On his way to Scotland, presumably. This fact Robin had discovered on returning from Sadie's last night, when he'd gone to his study –

the one room he hadn't searched for Hannah's diary – and found a note resting on his keyboard. She and Marcus *had* to be together, apparently. This contradicted what Jo had told him, or Marcus had told him, but God knows who'd got the right or wrong end of the stick. Alternatively, Marcus could have been stringing them all along. The note had been scribbled hurriedly by the look of it, and talked of lawyers and sorting out access. She'd call once she got to Braemar, she promised, but Robin thought he wouldn't put money on it.

Secondly, *Get a good family lawyer.* Yes, he'd do that this morning. There were fathers' organisations that must be able to recommend a local solicitor.

Third on the list was, *Keep up the contact with Freddie.* It was all too easy, Sadie had told Robin, to become distanced from your child just by not being involved on a day-to-day basis. Robin protested, saying, 'No way. Not me.' But Sadie, apparently, had seen it happen time and time again.

Finally was, *Don't stop going to work.* The last thing he needed, according to Sadie, was to lose his job, however all-absorbing the fight for reasonable access was. 'Reasonable access?' he'd cried. 'It's custody I'm after, not reasonable access.' Sadie had pulled a dubious face and told him the mother would have to be off her rocker and a drug addict not to be named primary carer in this country. In that case, Robin said, he thought he stood a good chance.

He read through again. *Stay calm.* Yes, he felt reasonably calm compared to last time. Hannah running off with his son was almost becoming a way of life. *Don't stop going to work.* OK. He wouldn't do that. Today, he had a late-morning lecture on Mosley – something he could now do backwards should anyone request it – and two afternoon seminars. There was also that paper on Britain's embryonic, pre-1914 welfare state to be working on but, considering the current crisis, perhaps that could wait.

Robin got up and made coffee, then went to his study. *Get a good family lawyer.* He switched his computer on, picked up one or two emails from students, impressed himself by replying to them immediately, then started searching for a website that would point him in the right direction. He found one, jotted down a couple of phone numbers, switched off the computer, picked up the phone and mentally thanked Sadie. Sensible Sadie. What a lifesaver she was. Just look at how rational and together and methodical he was being. He tapped out the first number and a youngish-sounding man answered. Another dispossessed father?

'Ah, hello,' Robin said, when his eyes fell upon the rectangular wooden clock on the bookcase. It was the one Freddie made. The one with the very uneven, funny-shaped hands that always said twenty past six, because that was the time when he'd made it.

'Hello . . . ?'

Freddie had written the numbers all the way round the edge with a black marker pen that Robin told him to be very careful with. But he hadn't quite got the spacing right, and so at the top, where a 12 should be, was the number 9.

'Hello?' the man repeated. 'Can I help you?'

'Yes, sorry. I . . .' Robin's heart was thumping, his eyes still on the clock. He felt something sear through him. Anger, panic, a horrible sense of bereavement. 'I'm sorry, I . . . wrong number,' he said, putting the phone down. Bloody, bloody Hannah. How *dare* she?

Before he knew it, Robin was grabbing his keys, double locking his front door, and in the car. He checked he had a road atlas, started the engine and headed north.

Marcus had left Claude to the floor sanding and was helping his mother lay tables for lunch. Vinko was singing something Slovenian in the kitchen, in a really-not-bad voice.

'He's pretty good,' said Marcus.

His mother smiled proudly. 'Aye, beautiful voice. Friday night is music night now. Vinko on vocals and your Aunt Janine on keyboard.'

'*Here?*'

'Over there in the corner. We have to move a few tables, but I can tell you it gets packed. And everyone leaves in great spirits.'

'I'm not surprised,' said Marcus, who'd been checking

306

out a menu. *Young Goat in Wine, Carp in Wine, Wine Cake*. 'They're probably completely pickled.'

'It's not all Slovenian music. He does a lovely "My Way".'

'Ah.' Just when Marcus was thinking they'd come along on Friday.

Better to leave it till Saturday, perhaps. The four of them could come. No, five. He kept forgetting Ernst. It should be fun, he decided, and a lot more relaxed than things had been in France, now everything was sorted. Sort of sorted. Yesterday, Jo had seemed worried about Hannah, but he'd reassured her that it was *him* she was livid with. He told her about the face slap in France, but that didn't seem to help. 'I just want to get up to Scotland this weekend and feel safe,' she said, and Marcus had understood what she meant. Since arriving north of the border, he'd felt much safer.

'And a wonderful "Jumpin' Jack Flash",' his mother was saying, as she did things with napkins Marcus wouldn't master in two lifetimes. 'Does all the actions. One customer swore she wouldn't be able to tell Vinko and Mick Jagger apart.'

'Is that right?' said Marcus, laughing. Perhaps they would come along on Friday. He'd give the Young Goat a miss, though. Was that even legal?

Jo was trying very hard to concentrate on feral parakeets, but every now and then she'd lean forward and peer round the curtain, just to make sure Hannah wasn't coming up her front path. And occasionally, she'd look at the time and see that she was an hour or maybe half an hour closer to Friday morning, when they were all going to skip the day's work and fly to Aberdeen.

A domestic flight!

Jo pictured the small aircraft. A tiny cramped fuselage, overloaded with people and their luggage. Rickety wings and an under-the-weather-sounding engine. Ernst and Keiko might have to knock her unconscious and carry her on, but how great it was going to be to reach Marcus and his waiting car in just a few hours. It would take an entire day to drive up there. Who'd be mad enough to do that?

When the phone rang she hoped it was Marcus, but it was Lucy calling from her office to ask if she'd feed Maidstone over the weekend.

'Can't, I'm afraid,' Jo said. 'I'm going away.'

'How about one of your students?'

'They're coming with me.'

'Damn.'

'What about Hannah?' asked Jo. 'Doesn't she usually feed him?'

'Yes, but I think she must have gone somewhere. I've been trying to get hold of her at home and at her school. They say she hasn't been in at all. And she's not answering her mobile. Did she say anything to you yesterday?'

'No, she didn't.' Nothing repeatable. 'How about Robin?'

'He's not home either. Or at work.'

Jo frowned. Could the two of them have gone off somewhere to patch things up? It was a best-case scenario, and way too much to hope for. She put it to Lucy.

'You could be right.'

'Pippa's away too,' Jo said, 'but you could ask Ray to feed the cat.'

'Yeah, right. The walk would kill him. Listen, don't worry, I'll find someone. Where are you off to, by the way?'

'Braemar. To see Marcus.'

'Oh, he's back already, is he?'

'Mm.'

'So . . . let me get this right. Marcus is in Scotland, and Hannah has disappeared?'

Jo put her head in her hands and took a few deep breaths. 'I'd better phone him, hadn't I?'

'Hi, Adrian. Me again. Just felt the need to speak to an adult. We're in our bed-and-breakfast place, killing time till the pills I took to sleep last night wear off. Two when we arrived, two when I went to bed, and two when I woke up feeling anxious at four o'clock.

'We were supposed to be out of our room by eleven a.m. What's that, forty minutes ago? But the landlord's being understanding. I told him I had a bad headache.

'Freddie's moaning a lot, which doesn't help. Keeps saying he wants to be at nursery because he's got a new best friend, Jasper. And Theo might steal Jasper, or something. What I need is a good strong, decent cup of coffee. Of course, there's nothing resembling that in this establishment. Will make a cup of something with these sad little sachets they put in your room. Why are these places so hopeless? Freddie asked for apple juice at breakfast and they didn't even have that. Anyway, will love you and leave you. Thanks for listening. If you have.'

'Oh *hell*,' said Marcus. Hannah on the loose again? 'She wouldn't come here, would she?'

'I don't know. As I told you, she was pretty angry yesterday.'

'Well, no sign of her yet. But you say Robin's disappeared too?'

'According to Lucy. I just called his department and he hasn't turned up for a lecture this morning.'

'They could have just gone away somewhere. The three of them.'

'That's what Lucy and I hoped.'

'Yes, of course,' said Marcus, breathing out again. 'That's what they've done, I'm sure. Gone off to do a bit of bonding.'

'Probably.'

'How are you, anyway?' Marcus asked. 'You must be excited at the prospect of seeing me?'

'Uncontrollably. But not excited at the prospect of flying.'

'Oh, you'll be all right. Take one of your beta-thingies. And remember, more American airline pilots die from chainsaw accidents than in plane crashes.'

'Actually, I'm not sure I find that very reassuring. I mean, if they couldn't control a saw, what were they doing flying planes?'

Marcus laughed. He was so looking forward to seeing her. '*If* you make it, I'll be at the airport to meet you,' he said. 'I'll be the tall, blond, healthy-looking, hand-some one.'

'Yeah, and I'll be the one with the Munch *Scream* expression still in place.'

'Can't wait.'

'Me neither.'

'Hi, Adrian. Just to let you know I'm feeling a lot better. Fred and I took a stroll around the village. Such wonder-fully fresh air up here in Cumbria. Beautiful views. Well, it's cleared my head and lifted my spirits, so now we can get back on the road. Just a couple of hours and we'll be in Braemar. Home again. Might call you en route.

'Over and out.'

Jo was half dozing over parakeet distribution charts. It was almost always a mistake to proofread in the comfort of her favourite armchair. She put the work to one side, heaved herself up and went over to the computer screen to check the time: 16.12. She picked up the phone and dialled Marcus's number.

'No sign of her?' she asked.

'Nope. I think I'm probably safe.'

'Good. How's the work going?'

'Very well. Not that I'm doing much. Just watching Claude sand floors. I had a go at it, but the machine ran away with me.'

'Call yourself a man?' she said. 'Anyway, better get back to the parakeets. Let me know if . . .'

'Don't worry.'

'Hi, Adrian. I'd like to think you're listening to all my messages, but hey, what the hell . . . it works for me. We're fast approaching Scotland. Just passing Carlisle. Freddie's chatting away in his seat, glad to be back on the road again. It's a fabulous day, and I am *so* looking forward to seeing Marcus. The very first thing I'll do is apologise for slapping, oh, *shit* . . . what the . . . ?'

Ten hours after leaving Oxford, Robin was settling himself in the corner of a restaurant with the unfortunate name of MacDonald's. He guessed, looking around him, that this one had been here long before the Mc variety arrived. He was in a large high-ceilinged room with a tiled floor and cream walls. There were a dozen or so tables – four occupied – all nicely adorned with fresh flowers and starched, artistically arranged napkins. The tablecloths were a very white white and the chunky silver cutlery gleamed under modern, twisted-metal chandelier affairs.

He'd asked for the table in the far corner, in order to keep an eye on the door. If they came in that way, he wanted to see them before they saw him. He presumed, however, that there was a back way in from the flat upstairs, which was where the three of them probably were. Their flat. The one Freddie had spent his baby-hood in. For some reason, Robin pictured it still full of his early photos and tiny Babygros and teething rings.

The small blonde woman who'd accompanied him to the table came over and asked if he'd like a drink while he perused the menu. Since he was in Scotland, he asked for a whisky.

Leaning back in his chair, he studied the menu without really seeing it. It had been a long day. He'd stopped three times on the way, twice for nourishment and a pee, and the third time for a nap in a service station car park. On arriving in Braemar, he'd booked himself into a large hotel in the centre and made enquiries with an old-timer as to the whereabouts of the Currie family, only to be told there were dozens of Curries in the area. 'They've got a restaurant,' he said, and the chap's face lit up with recognition.

Robin's eyes began to take in what he was reading. Slovenian, it boasted at the top. He looked up at the

pictures and posters surrounding him. They all seemed
to be views of, or advertisements for, Slovenia. It all looked
rather lovely. He and Judith had once been on holiday
to Yugoslavia, before it became 'the former' and they'd
been very impressed by the country and the friendliness
of the people. Perhaps he'd return one day. Take Freddie.
'*Brodet,*' he read. 'A Mediterranean fish stew.' In the wilds
of Scotland? Maybe not. '*Struklji . . . Belokranjsko Curtje
. . . Matevz . . .*' English descriptions were given, but
Robin couldn't be bothered with them. He wasn't even
hungry, but he knew he'd have to order food if he intended
to sit watching the door for what might be a while. So,
when the nice lady came back with his whisky, he pointed
to the most recognisable item on the menu – Leg of Lamb
– hoping it wasn't an entire one.

'I don't think you'll regret it,' she said, jotting it down.
'Have you come far?'

'Lincolnshire,' said Robin, aiming to stay incognito
for as long as possible.

'Oh, aye? A lovely part of the country, I'm told.'

'Yes. A bit flatter than round here, though.'

'Most places are.'

'True.'

Robin was amazed at his ability to converse so
normally, when any minute now Hannah, Freddie and
the unfathomable Marcus might walk in. Had Marcus
asked her to come back? He'd seemed certain in France
that Hannah and Freddie belonged with Robin. Was

he just two-faced and devious, or was Hannah so screwed up that she couldn't see clearly? Robin had asked himself these things for the length of the journey and was now tired of pondering on the business. He'd just have to ask the chap outright.

'Moira!' someone called out from the kitchen, and the waitress turned and said, 'Coming,' and Robin suddenly realised who she was. He'd heard a lot about Marcus's mother, Moira. Never seen a photo of her, though. She looked normal. Nice, even. Nothing like the fussy, inter-fering witch Hannah had described.

A man in an apron and white hat appeared from the kitchen. He was grey-haired, tallish and dignified-looking. Definitely foreign and, guessing from the menu and décor, Slovenian. He slipped an arm around Moira's waist and kissed the top of her head, and Robin thought perhaps it was another Moira after all. Lucky he hadn't said anything.

The chef handed the waitress a mobile phone, and Robin heard her say, 'Oh, aye, son, I've kept you a table, don't worry. And tell Claude the dish of the day is a nice French cassoulet, Vinko style.'

Claude?

'OK, Marcus. See you in about ten minutes.'

They were the longest ten minutes of Robin's life, even though they turned out to be just seven. Marcus walked in first, followed by Claude, and while Robin's heart raced, waiting for Hannah and Freddie to appear, the door closed itself behind them. Marcus kissed his mother's cheek, then Claude did the French three-kiss thing on her, a bit of jolly chat was entered into, and the two men were directed his way.

Robin stood up, his chair scraping back over the tiles and Marcus stopped dead when he saw him, clearly shocked. 'Robin?' he cried. 'What are you doing here? Are Hannah and Freddie with you?'

Robin was thrown. This wasn't right. Not the way the script should be going. He suddenly felt awfully tired, so lowered himself back on to his chair.

'This gentleman's come all the way from Lincolnshire,' Moira was saying. She was straightening cutlery on the table next to Robin's, removing the Reserved sign.

'Aren't they *here*?' Robin asked quietly and Marcus shook his head.

'He's ordered the Leg of Lamb, but I'm wondering if he might like Vinko's cassoulet.'

'They set off from Oxford yesterday,' said Robin. 'She left me a note saying she was coming back to you. That you and she *had* to be together.' By the look on Marcus's face, this was news to him. 'I take it you didn't . . . ?'

'Absolutely not. I haven't heard from her since she slapped my face in France.'

'I can vouch for that,' chipped in Claude. 'Is it not possible that Hannah stopped overnight somewhere, procrastinated, then returned home?'

'Perhaps I should ring her mobile phone,' said Robin. 'Or home even.' He could feel himself beginning to shake. Fatigue and anxiety were the worst mix.

Marcus stood up. 'Use the phone under the counter,' he said, then led Robin to it.

He thought he'd try the mobile first. No luck. Then he rang home. Please answer, he willed her. Please answer, then let me speak to Freddie. Wish him good night. But Hannah didn't answer, so at the appropriate time he tapped in the pin number to pick up messages. He had four new ones, he was told. The first was received at 12.58 that afternoon.

'Robin,' said a strange voice. 'This is Adrian Lillis, Hannah's therapist. I was hoping to get you in person, but still . . . I'm concerned, you see. Hannah was driving to Scotland, and she rang me from her mobile just now, while she was driving, somewhere near Carlisle, and then, gosh, I'm slightly shaken . . . well, she may have been in some kind of accident. She screamed, you see. And then there were these ghastly . . . Look, I may be completely wrong and, golly, I do hope so. Perhaps you'd give me a call and let me know she's OK?'

Adrian started to reel off his number, but by then Robin was halfway to the floor, where his fall was broken by the chef, who said, 'Efter only one whisky, yes?' and laughed.

Marcus took hold of the receiver. 'Press *one*,' Robin managed to tell him, while he was being hoisted upright.

317

'And it'll play the message again. Quick. Oh God, they're dead, I know they are. And it's all my fault.'

He was helped to a chair by Moira, the chef and Claude, and as Marcus listened in he turned pale.

'There's one from the police,' Marcus whispered, and Robin covered his face with his hands. This was truly the most horrible moment of his life so far, but he had a feeling there'd be worse to come. 'Oh, please, *no*,' he whispered. '*No.*'

Marcus asked his mother for a pen and she whipped one from her blouse. 'Now it's the hospital,' he said while he listened and wrote on an order pad. He pressed a button to replay the message, then scribbled more things down.

A customer came up and asked of no one in particular where their desserts had got to.

'Ooch,' Moira said. 'I'm terribly sorry. Let me fetch them now. Two Wine Cakes, wasn't it?' She hurried off, the grumpy customer returned to his table, and Marcus finally put the phone down.

'Well?' asked Robin shakily, even though he knew the absolute worst had happened.

'They're in the Cumberland Infirmary,' Marcus said. 'Carlisle. There was an accident, involving another car. Someone from the hospital rang at five thirty this evening. There's a number to call. Here.'

Robin couldn't bring himself to take it from him. 'Would you?' he asked, and Marcus nodded and picked up the receiver again.

'I see,' Marcus kept saying, when he got through to someone who seemed to know something. 'I see.'

Robin still shook, but he also began to feel icily cold inside. Even the large whisky the chef had just handed him wasn't warming him. Why had he wished Hannah out of their lives? Such a terrible thing to do. His head spun, his palms sweated, his insides got even colder. He felt as though he were in a dream, or a film. Something not real, anyway.

'Yes,' said Marcus. 'We'll be there as soon as we can.' He put the phone down. 'Freddie's absolutely fine,' he said, which was, deep down, all Robin wanted to know.

They arrived just after eleven and a young woman in ordinary clothes, who could have been a doctor, an administrator or the tea lady, took Robin to one side while Marcus was outside parking the car. 'She's going to be OK,' she told him. 'Couple of fractures and some bruising. As far as we know, there are no internal injuries, but we've got her on a starvation diet and a saline drip, just in case. We found high levels of antidepressants in her bloodstream. Very high. Could have contributed to her veering into an oncoming car.'

Robin found himself forming a fist.

'We also believe, but can't be certain, that she was talking on her mobile phone.'

Although they'd already guessed this, Robin now found himself forming a second fist. It might not be beyond him to go and pummel a defenceless woman on an intravenous drip. 'I know my son's OK, but how are the other people?' he asked, perfectly normally. 'The couple in the other car.'

'Fine,' she said. 'A few bruises. Hannah's mobile phone came off worst, completely smashed, while young Freddie, as you know, emerged unscathed, due to having a decent kiddie seat.'

Thank God they'd gone for quality, thought Robin. 'Can I take him home?' he asked her.

'Yes,' said the tea lady or doctor, and with that he was off down the corridor, checking out side wards. 'Excuse me!' she called out to him. He turned and she was beckoning. 'This way.'

When Robin caught up with her, she said, 'I take it you are her husband?' and laughed.

'No, no. He's just parking the car.'

She came to a sharp halt. 'But you called Freddie your son?'

'Long story,' he said.

She frowned but nevertheless led him to a room with a dull clanging sound coming from it. Inside was a sleeping Hannah with tubes attached, her plastered leg in traction. There were three other beds in the room, all empty, although on one sat a battered and crumpled toolbox.

'Fred?' called out Robin, and his little head appeared above the bed.

'I'm fixing the wheels,' he said, before going back to work. ''Cos they don't work, 'cos the bed won't move. Only the nurse wrapped my hammer in my pillowcase, so I don't wake Mummy.'

Robin swallowed past the lump in his throat and said, 'Uh-huh?' He ventured towards his son, hoping not to see any unexpected damage – a missing limb, or something – but he found him all in one piece and gently picked him up, then squeezed him and kissed his soft plump cheek. Freddie smelled of antiseptic and beef stew, but then the whole place did. 'I expect the nurse has put the brakes on,' Robin explained, moving the toolbox over and lowering them both on to the bed.

Freddie turned and pulled a face at him. 'Like Mummy put the brakes on when she screamed and said that word that Mrs Jessup makes Nathan go and stand in the naughty corner for?'

'Yes, Fred. Just like that.'

FRIDAY

'The food it seems very interesting,' said Ernst. He was looking through the menu and pulling a face. 'But I didn't realise garlic was so very different from German and English. It has many consonants, yes?'

'Gaelic,' said Jo.

'Yes.'

'But actually, it's Slovenian.'

Now he was looking more confused, so Jo explained about Vinko, who was at that moment hoisting himself on to a stool, next to Marcus's Aunt Janine and her keyboard.

'So . . .' said Ernst, 'I must get this right for my presentation. Vinko is a Slovenian chef who cooks Slovenian food in a Scottish restaurant called MacDonald's, but which does not have one single burger on its menu. *And* he not only cooks, also he does the cabaret. Do you think he will sing "My Bonnie Lies Ofer the Ocean"?'

'Maybe,' she said, very much hoping not. Jo thought she wouldn't add to Ernst's astonishment by filling him in on Vinko's love life.

On her left sat Marcus. He had a hand in her lap under the tablecloth, stroking her thigh through her trousers while he chatted away to Robin, directly opposite him. They were talking about salmon farming, for some reason. Jo guessed it was easier than discussing important things, such as Hannah, who was now on her way to Leicestershire with her parents for the 'couple of days' rest' suggested by the hospital. Beside Robin, propped on cushions, was Freddie, who'd opened his menu, turned it on its side and was flying a fork into it with a 'Yeeeoowww'.

Beside Freddie was Keiko, deep in a one-sided conversation with Claude. She was throwing in the odd, 'Ahh, interesting,' staring at her man lovingly, as though he were reciting Keats rather than talking EU subsidies. 'There's bound to be misappropriation,' Jo heard him say, while Keiko nodded, wide-eyed.

'So, does everyone know what they want?' asked Marcus. His mother was hovering with an order pad.

Freddie shouted, 'Chips and ketchup!'

'I'm sure we can find some of those for you,' said one of Marcus's brothers from behind the counter. The two brothers looked similar and a lot like Moira, but neither resembled Marcus much. They were quite a bit shorter and both were receding. Last night, Marcus had shown her photos of his father; a gloriously handsome man who may have just pipped his son in the looks department.

Jo quite fancied chips and ketchup but, because she was an adult, asked for the lamb. Claude said he'd like the catfish, so Keiko ordered that too. Ernst ordered chips and ketchup.

As Moira was taking Robin's order, the keyboard struck up an intro. It was vaguely familiar. Jo knew she knew it, but because of the way it was being played – each note exactly the same length – she couldn't name it. Dah, dah, dee, dee, dah . . .

After Robin had ordered the lamb from the charming Moira, who seemed to have warmed to him despite his past misdeeds, Vinko began singing 'Every Breath You Take' by the Police. All at the table cheered and gave him a round of applause, as though Vinko himself had taken the song to the top of the charts. He bowed and continued, moving on to the second verse with his idiosyncratic diction. Robin drank in the words, bringing a whole new interpretation to them. Yes, he'd be watching his son. Every move, every breath, every step . . .

'Nice voice,' said Jo, and they all agreed. 'Are you OK, Robin?' she added.

'Fine,' he said, and he managed not to lose it before the song came to an end, at which point he excused himself, went to the Gents, blew his nose and told himself off for being so soft.

Returning to the restaurant, Robin saw Freddie's chair was empty and his insides seized. Where . . . ah, there he was, on Vinko's knee. Centre stage, if you could call it a stage. Robin took his place and wondered if he'd ever feel secure enough to let Freddie out of his sight again. Even leaving him at nursery was going to be hard. Not that Hannah, with a broken arm and leg, would be able to steal Fred for a while yet. Perhaps, when she was well on the way to healing, he'd accidentally trip her up.

'Freddie had a request,' explained Jo.

Robin laughed. 'Now there's a surprise.' His son was lapping up, and now taking advantage of, all the attention he was getting from his former family. Moira, who'd been desperate to see Fred when she heard he was so close, had been spoiling him rotten for two days. The day after tomorrow, though, they'd head south again, going via Leicestershire to pick Hannah up. How Robin wished they didn't have to do that detour. How he yearned to go straight back to Oxford with Freddie, set up home with Sadie and little Theo, and never look back.

Freddie was waving and beaming at him, still perched on Vinko's knee and, by the sound of the keyboard intro, about to sing 'Wheels on the Bus'.

His Aunt Janine's version was the old politically incorrect one, and whenever she sang about mummies on the bus going yack, yack, yack, or daddies reading the newspaper, Freddie scowled at her and sang the words he'd been taught.

At last it was over, and the applause died down and Freddie was back at the table. Marcus watched his brothers flying through from the kitchen with steaming plates and bottles of ketchup and bottles of wine, and eventually, everyone had their food and Vinko moved on to his next song.

'Is very special song,' he told his audience. 'From Net King Cole, many years go. Is for very lovely lady. Moira.'

Marcus looked over at his mother, who blushed as all eyes fell on her, then did a little curtsy.

'Is called "They Try to Tell Us Wirr Too Young",' said Vinko, and the restaurant gave a communal, 'Aaaahhh.'

He sang it beautifully, and in a heart-felt way, and when he'd finished Marcus's mother wiped tears from her eyes with her waitress pinny. Vinko got off his stool and went over and gave her a hug.

'Aaaahhh,' went everyone again, and Marcus suddenly found himself feeling extremely happy for his mum and not caring a jot about his lost inheritance. In fact, he was feeling generally good about everything and every-body. He was pleased for young-and-in-love Claude, so very relieved that Freddie was still in one piece, happy for Robin and thrilled for himself at having Jo for a whole weekend. Marcus even began feeling goodwill towards poor old Hannah. Yes, she'd treated first him, then Robin, abysmally, and she'd taken risks with her son's life, but she wasn't all bad. And maybe now she'd been weaned off the antidepressants in hospital, the fog would clear and she'd see that her place was with Robin. Good old Robin, currently showing Freddie a conjuring trick with a 10p. The little boy was amazed every time the coin popped out of his father's ear, or sometimes his own. Marcus hoped that one day he'd be a dad like that, then remembered he already had been. How lucky Hannah was in her choice of men, but how unlucky in other ways. Poor old Hannah, he thought and, in an overwhelming moment of fondness, found himself standing up with his glass of wine.

'I'd like to propose a toast,' he said above the hubbub. Everyone round the table raised their glasses. 'To Hannah. May she recover quickly and be back with us soon.'

'To Hannah,' the others said, with the possible exception of Jo.

'Oh, Marcus, that's so sweet,' came a voice from behind.

He turned and saw his wife, on crutches, just inside the doorway. Next to her were her stony-faced parents.

'I am back,' she said, her eyes intensely on his.

Marcus looked at her parents for support. 'She made us turn round,' her father told him apologetically. 'Threatened to throw herself out the bloody car.'

No one spoke. They'd stopped mid-chew. Mid-sip. Even the other customers. Vinko's 'It's Not Unusual' had ground to a halt. Marcus sensed the entire room was holding its communal breath.

'You know,' said Ernst loudly, and all eyes swung round to him to save the situation. 'These are the best MacDonald's French fries I have tasted in my life, ha ha. Ah yes, that reminds me about the Bavarian who went into a burger bar.'

'Ernst,' said Jo.

'Yes?'

'Not now.'

SUNDAY
SPRING BANK HOLIDAY

Jo was at her computer, literally propping her eyes open over Sergei's concluding chapter. Almost at the end, she told herself. Only five pages left, so try to keep going. But then she thought, hell, five whole pages. She saved the changes and checked her emails again. Another one from Pippa. Jo had the feeling her friend was being communicative out of guilt. Maybe she'd reply to this one.

'Hi, Pippa,' she typed. 'Congrats on preventing the GM maize delivery. It did rather sound as though you turned that ship around single-handedly, though I'm guessing Bram was there to help!! Hope the bone knits itself together soon. Yes, I'm sure the comfrey tea will speed up the process. Talking of broken bones, I've noticed Hannah's walking normally again now – as gracefully as before, damn her!'

For weeks she'd been hobbling past Jo's window, on

her way to the playground with Freddie. At first on crutches, then with a stick, now unaided. It wasn't far to go, from Pippa's house to the swings, but it could turn into an afternoon excursion for the two of them. She'd never call in on Jo, even though they were now neighbours.

'Lucy said to tell you Hannah's taking great care of your house, even with Freddie there half the week! Oh, and that Ray came back the other day for his armchair. Said his parents' three-piece didn't do it for him.'

A major disadvantage of house-sitting, Jo realised, must be that the owners could whip bits of furniture away when they felt like it. Or come home early, as Lucy and Dom had done. But Pippa, it seemed, wasn't intending to come home early. After their GM heroics, she and Bram had gone to rest at his Amsterdam home. If they kept that up it would be good for Hannah. With no rent to pay, she could save for her own place. Hopefully not in Jubilee Street. She'd be back teaching after the half-term break, according to Lucy. Everything was according to Lucy, or occasionally Robin when Jo bumped into him.

'Anyway, not much other news here. My two students will be leaving in a couple of weeks' time, which is gutting, but on the other hand, it means I can go and spend time in Scotland with Marcus. They've just about done up Marcus's mum's house now.'

Finished by the end of June, he estimated. Keiko was

hoping Claude would fly out to Japan with his earnings, but Claude talked of putting the money towards buying the Sports Bar now his aunt had had a change of heart. Marcus also thought Claude's head had been turned by Vinko's visiting niece, a Slovenian beauty. Poor Keiko. Jo had been dropping small hints by telling her how long-distance relationships were impossible to sustain, and giving her new definitions for her notebook: 'love rat' and similar.

She went back to her email. 'I can't wait to see Marcus again. Of course, he'd come here if it wasn't for a certain neighbour – but please don't feel bad about that. You needed a housesitter, she needed a home. Besides, Marcus and I have had two lovely weekends together in the Peaks.'

And a whole glorious summer ahead of them. Then what? Jo had already got Lucy and Dom's guys to make her a website, so she could pick up work should she find herself living elsewhere. She pictured herself proofreading by email in a cosy croft by a lofty mountain. Marcus throwing peat on the fire . . . or was that just an Irish thing?

'Anyway, must get on,' she typed. She signed off, sent the email and turned her thoughts to dinner. Would they notice if it was pasta again? Keiko had gone high-carb/low protein, which was proving more of a pain than Atkins, although cheaper – 'Would you like more bread with your bread, Keiko?'

OK, pasta. She'd make a separate protein-packed sauce for Ernst, who swore Keiko's new diet was giving him smaller 'muskles'. 'When I arrived I was like Popeye after his spinach, now I am Olive Oyl!' Best not to send the students home malnourished, she thought, and decided on a tuna sauce.

Robin had the Parental Responsibility Agreement in front of him again.

'Sure,' Hannah had said when he'd brought up the PRA issue. 'Seems only fair. Let's wait till I'm back at work, though, shall we? Just in case my being on sick leave and having counselling negates the agreement?'

Although he could see sense in what she was saying, Robin had been champing at the bit for weeks now, just desperate to get her signature on the damn thing. Anyway, having dumped Adrian for Belinda, a wonderful woman counsellor a few streets away, Hannah did appear to be making a lot of progress. She was always pleasant these days. Good-humoured. Almost eager to please. He couldn't foresee any problems with getting the thing sorted once and for all.

Late Friday morning was the time they'd set aside for getting it witnessed by a court official, after they'd both finished teaching. Freddie was to go to Sadie's for tea again. Safe Sadie. Port-in-a-storm Sadie. Robin looked at the photo beside his computer. They'd been at Cotswold Wildlife Park and she was kneeling with one arm round Theo, the other round Freddie. Robin had managed to get most of the llama in too. A nice day. They'd had lots of nice days out. What he and Sadie hadn't had, though, were lots of romantic and steamy nights in. None, in fact. It just hadn't happened, somehow. As much as Robin still hoped for more with Sadie, he knew he was guilty of holding back. Afraid a new entanglement would upset Hannah and set her off again? He certainly sneaked to his study every time Hannah called in, and put the photo in a drawer. It could be that he and Sadie had got past the point of starting up a physical relationship. He guessed that happened.

Meanwhile, Robin watched the real love of his life splashing around in the paddling pool with the little boy from next door but one. It was a gloriously hot Bank Holiday. Sadie and Theo had gone off to her parents on Friday but – Robin checked the time again – might actually be back by now.

He put the PRA down and called her number.

'Oh, *hi*,' she said warmly.

He invited them round and she said yes, that would be great. 'I've been thinking about you a lot,' she added, 'over the weekend. About us.'

'Oh yes?'

'Mm. I quite missed you, you know.'

'That's nice.' Why couldn't he say 'Me too'?

'Anyway, we'll be there shortly.'

'Good.'

'Um . . .' she said quietly, 'I was wondering if a sleep-over would be OK?'

'Yes, of course. Freddie will love that. Bring all Theo's night things.' Robin waited for a response. 'Hello?'

'See you soon,' she said in quite a different tone, and he suddenly realised what she'd meant.

He felt terrible. But no, they couldn't. Not now. Too risky with only a couple of days to go. 'Great!' he said, far too jovially. 'I'll put the kettle on.'

Marcus was listening in to a second message from Hannah, receiver in hand, heart in his boots. He and Claude had been clearing a vast area of garden and had come in for a rest and a beer. 'Unfuckingbelievable,' he said as he took in what she was saying.

Claude frowned and reached for Marcus's mum's dictionary.

A few days before, Hannah had left a message thanking him for his get well card and apologising for not contacting him sooner. She'd wanted to get completely better first. 'Anyway,' she'd said before hanging up, 'I'll call you again. Or ring me?' She reeled off Pippa's number and said goodbye.

He hadn't tried calling her. Hadn't seen the point. But here she was again, this time saying something about a form Robin was going to force her to sign. How that meant she and Fred couldn't live more than ten miles away from Robin. How it would put paid for ever to 'you, me and Freddie being together again'. How she had to get away from Oxford a.s.a.p., and how Freddie was coming back to her tomorrow, and so that might be a good time for them to make their escape. 'What do you think?' she asked.

Marcus couldn't possibly put into words what he thought. He pressed a button and forced himself to listen again, just in case he'd missed something vital, such as 'Only kidding!'

He wrote down Pippa's number, replaced the receiver and gulped back his beer.

'You've had some irksome news?' asked Claude.

'Yes,' said Marcus. 'I'm definitely feeling irked.'

He told Claude the latest and Claude shook his head and swore in French. 'It's like sitting through the same horror movie,' he said. 'Over and over. I believe it may be time to tell her about you and Jo. Make it clear and unambiguous. Get straight to the point. No shilly-shallying.'

'Yeah, you're right,' Marcus said. 'No more sparing Hannah's feelings for fear of what she might do.' He picked up the phone again and Claude slipped out of the room. Actually, he probably would shilly-shally a bit, out of sensitivity. Break it to her gently. Tell her how he and Jo had sort of slowly grown on each other.

'Hello?' she said.

'Hi,' said Marcus warmly.

'Oh, thank God. I was beginning to worry that—'

'Jo and I are an item,' he said, suddenly going for blunt.

'Pardon?'

'We're in love.' Marcus screwed up his face, waiting for whatever was about to be blasted his way.

'Hmm, well. I guessed as much.'

As his features gradually relaxed, Marcus said, 'Really? Then why the message?'

'Oh, I don't know. Last-ditch attempt maybe.'

Marcus couldn't believe this was going so well. Had they finally achieved closure? Hard to believe. Hard to trust Hannah, either. He needed more convincing. 'What will you do?' he asked.

'I don't know. Go back to teaching, I suppose. Find a place to live. Sign that bloody form for Robin.'

It was worrying Marcus, how resigned she was. He said, 'Are you sure you're OK about all this? No more wanting to push Jo over a precipice?'

'I never said I . . . Hang on, have you been reading my diary, Marcus?'

Whoops. 'Just had a bit of a flick-through. Once.' Or twice.

'Bastard!' She chuckled good-humouredly. 'Anyway, you must realise it was all written in the heat of the moment.'

'Of course.'

'Good. Jo didn't read it, did she?'

'No, but . . .' Marcus paused. 'Well, I did tell her I thought you had a contract out on her.'

'Really?' said Hannah, clearly amused. 'That must have made her a bit on edge?'

'Just a bit.' Marcus thought he'd get out while the going was good, and began winding down the conversation. 'Look, we must keep in touch,' he said and she agreed. 'Send me photos of Freddie?'

'Will do.' She promised to let him know when she moved, and they said their goodbyes, and then Marcus stared into space until Claude popped his head round the door.

'How was she?' he asked.

Marcus turned and blinked at him. 'Friendly, charming, totally accepting of the situation.'

'Oh,' said Claude. 'How very disquieting.'

'Yes.'

Jo was watching the pasta boil, thinking about Marcus's call just now.

Of course Hannah had to be told some time. And how great that she'd taken it so well. Now everyone could move on. Great. She lobbed some herbs into the pasta, just to give Keiko something to taste, then grabbed the garlic and was about to pull off a clove when the doorbell went. 'Bugger,' she said, turning down the heat.

It was Hannah, on her doorstep for the first time in

months and this time with large, very sharp-looking scissors in her hand. Jo's first instinct was to slam the door in the woman's face, but then she saw a bunch of white roses in her other hand, so instead took a small step back and subtly held the garlic up between them. 'Hi,' she said nervously.

Hannah smiled. 'Sorry to disturb you. I was just out the front picking roses when my door slammed behind me. Pippa said you had her spare key?'

'Oh, right. Yes. Now where did I . . . Ah, I know.'

'Phew,' said Hannah, stepping into the house. 'Lovely day, isn't it?'

'Yes.' Jo had begun walking backwards down her hall towards the kitchen, feeling her way along the walls, eyes riveted to the scissor points aimed at her heart. 'Bank holidays are so often a washout,' she added. There was a step down to her kitchen, which she thought could be her undoing if she wasn't careful.

Hannah said, 'Lovely in Scotland too, I hear.'

'Yes.' There was nothing for it but to spin round and hurry to that kitchen drawer, so she did.

Now breathing heavily, Jo rummaged through all the things she'd thrown in there over the past five years. Pippa's key was on a key ring. An Eiffel Tower, if she remembered rightly. She heard Hannah step down into the kitchen and waited for the scissors to plunge themselves into her back. She thought about the will she'd made recently, sitting on her desk waiting for two witnesses to sign it. She hadn't been able to use Ernst and Keiko because they were to be beneficiaries: Keiko the piano, and Ernst her dumbbells, so he could get his muskles back. Gestures, rather than serious bequests, although she could see Keiko having the piano shipped.

Jo's hand fell upon the distinct shape of a small tower. She could hear the pasta boiling away much too energetically. Did she have time to turn down the heat before she died? 'Here we are,' she said, pulling the key out and turning to face whatever Hannah had in mind for her.

'Oh, thank God,' said Hannah, looking relieved. 'Just think what I'd have had to pay a locksmith to come out on a bank holiday!'

'Yes,' said Jo, exhaling. 'A fortune.'

Hannah gave her another big smile. 'Thanks. Listen, we ought to get together for a cuppa or drink some time.'

'Er, yeah.'

'Or I could cook you some supper?'

Jo tried to nod. Supper she wouldn't be so keen on.

'Let me know when's good for you,' said Hannah, making her way to the door.

'Sure,' said Jo, following her, eyes still firmly on the scissors. She saw her out and dashed back to the kitchen to find the pasta – the last of it, unfortunately – had boiled itself to liquid form.

'What is for dinner?' asked Keiko, now behind her.

Unlike Ernst, she could glide down those stairs without making a sound.

'Pasta, er . . . soup,' said Jo, giving the saucepan a loving stir. 'It's a traditional Whitsuntide dish.'

'Aahh.' Keiko nodded. 'Like very burned pancakes is traditional for Shrove Tuesday?'

'Yep.'

This is going to be such fun. Her face when those scissors were coming her way! Now, what was that fish Keiko was trying to tell us about at the restaurant . . . fugi? The Japanese delicacy that can cause instant death to diners if not prepared absolutely correctly. Fugu, maybe. I could buy some cod or something and pretend it's fugu. No, no, I'll say. Don't worry, Jo. I know what I'm doing.

Perhaps I'll suggest Friday evening to her. It'll give me something to look forward to after I've signed away all my parental rights. Maybe. Belinda says I should sign it. Thinks I've been presented with too many choices over the past couple of years and, having a 'planner' personality, the PRA might provide me with much-needed structure. I think she's right. Belinda's right on most things, really. Thinks I should look for a man who'll stand up to me. Answer back. Marcus would bottle things up, then explode at me, which isn't the same thing at all. Passive/aggressive, Belinda called him. Said Robin probably is too. Or that I bring that out in them, anyway. Yep, she's pretty good, Belinda. Her 'directional' therapy definitely suits me better than Adrian's lazy approach – but, my God, can the woman talk!

When the doorbell chimed, Robin's heart gave a little leap. Sadie was here. He jumped up from his office chair and made for the stairs, but then turned around, went back into the study and picked up the two letters he'd been poring over. One was from Adrian Lillis stating that Hannah had been on the phone to him at the precise time she'd crashed, and the other, signed by Mrs Newby, said she'd seen Mrs Hannah Currie talking on a mobile before she'd collided into their car. Both 'witnesses' had been induced by Robin, for Freddie's sake, not to say anything to the police. Not yet, anyway. Hopefully, never. If Friday went according to plan, he'd tear the letters up, of course. The doorbell rang again and Robin tucked everything into a file with 'PRA Insurance!' handwritten on it, then charged down the stairs to let Sexy Sadie in.

As soon as he opened the door, he stepped forward, slipped an arm around her and kissed her on the lips. Theo, meanwhile, had charged into the house. 'You know that sleepover you suggested?' he said, pulling back a little.

'Oh well, I . . .' She waved a dismissive hand and coloured up.

'Friday would be good.'

* * *

Ernst, bless him, was making out it was perfectly OK to be drinking pasta. He did, however, give the impression he was very much looking forward to German food. '*Knackwurst*,' he said with a sigh. '*Wienerschnitzel, Schinkenwurst . . .*'

Such poetic names, thought Jo.

Keiko nodded to herself. '*Miso* soup,' she said quietly. '*Onigiri . . .*'

Jo rolled her eyes. 'Look, why don't we abandon this and go and eat in town?'

'Special treat?' asked Keiko.

'Yes, special treat. It is a holiday, after all. Come on. It's such a nice day, we could walk.'

'Shall I change to walking boots?' asked Keiko, who'd only ever bussed in before; asleep, no doubt.

'Not necessary,' Jo told her. 'It's not far.'

By the time Jo had gathered bag, jumper and keys, Ernst was at the front door holding it open for her. 'Have I told you the joke about the two Bavarians who were walking along the road?' he asked.

'Don't think so.'

'Ah. Well, one Bavarian he said to the other Bavarian, "Look at that dog with one eye." So the Bavarian . . . not the first one, you know, the one he was with . . .'

'Yes, yes,' said Jo, slamming the door behind them. Had she closed the small kitchen window? Was it wide ~ugh for Hannah to slither through?

covered one of his eyes and said, "Where?"'

Jo, striding down her path, stopped in her tracks.
'Ernst, that's almost funny.'

'Thank you.'

You can buy any of these other **Review** titles
from your bookshop or direct from the publisher.

FREE P&P AND UK DELIVERY
(Overseas and Ireland £3.50 per book)

Country Loving	Julie Highmore	£6.99
Pure Fiction	Julie Highmore	£6.99
Play It Again?	Julie Highmore	£6.99
Green Grass	Raffaella Barker	£7.99
Atlantic Shift	Emily Barr	£7.99
On Dancing Hill	Sarah Challis	£6.99
Secrets of a Family Album	Isla Dewar	£6.99
Single Men	Dave Hill	£6.99
The Distance Between Us	Maggie O'Farrell	£7.99

TO ORDER SIMPLY CALL THIS NUMBER

01235 400 414

or visit our website: www.madaboutbooks.com

Prices and availability subject to change without notice.

TRUE
DECEPTION

PATRICIA
WADDELL

tor paranormal romance

A TOM DOHERTY ASSOCIATES BOOK
NEW YORK

This is a work of fiction. All of the characters, organizations, and events portrayed in this novel are either products of the author's imagination or are used fictitiously.

TRUE DECEPTION

Copyright © 2007 by Patricia Waddell

All rights reserved, including the right to reproduce this book, or portions thereof, in any form.

A Tor Book
Published by Tom Doherty Associates, LLC
175 Fifth Avenue
New York, NY 10010

www.tor.com

Tor® is a registered trademark of Tom Doherty Associates, LLC.

ISBN-13: 978-0-7653-5465-5
ISBN-10: 0-7653-5465-9

First Edition: November 2007

Printed in the United States of America

0 9 8 7 6 5 4 3 2 1

True Deception

one

"THE MOMENT YOU leave this room, Aedon Rawn, as you and I know him, will cease to exist," Cullon Gavriel said. The Korcian Enforcer and Joint Commander of the Directorate was seated behind a desk in an office buried deep in the lower levels of the Registry Building. "There will be no record of your service in the Fleet, no documentation of your rank as Squadron Commander. Only Ambassador MacFadyen and myself will know your true identity, your true purpose. If you have any doubts, now is the time to voice them."

Aedon smiled, but it didn't reach his eyes. "Is that your way of saying now or never?"

"It's my way of saying that all Directorate missions are strictly voluntary. Once you enter the outer regions you will be beyond the reach of the Empire. Beyond our help. And our intervention. Whatever situation you find yourself in, you will be *alone*."

Aedon's enigmatic smile remained in place. He liked and respected Cullon Gavriel. His fellow Korcian was a trained professional, a calm man with an organized mind and incredible willpower. His determination and courage had made him an expert Enforcer during his days in the field.

"Infiltrating Rendhal's domain won't be easy," added a female voice. It belonged to League Ambassador Danna MacFadyen, the other half of the Directorate Command. "When you get to Hachyn, make contact with a man by the name of Eiven Jein. He's the leader of the Hachynite Citizens for Freedom. Offer whatever assistance you can. There are unsubstantiated reports that a new consortium is being formed; Hachynite factories are being retooled to produce weapons. I don't have to tell you that it's an upsetting rumor."

"And if the rumor turns out to be fact?" Aedon asked, already confident of the answer.

"Hachyn was originally colonized as an industrial planet," Danna said. "If its factories are being converted to produce weapons, they have to be destroyed."

Aedon nodded, knowing as well as the two Directorate leaders what the consequences would be if the outer regions, united under a Conglomerate banner, were to become a military force. The peace that the galaxy currently enjoyed would be drastically threatened.

Three months ago, when he'd first been approached by Cullon to join the Directorate, Aedon had been surprised to discover that the League of Planets and the Korcian Empire had joined forces, albeit clandestinely, to fight the encroaching threat of the corporate colonies. The two most powerful governments in the galaxy rarely agreed on anything. Up to now their intergalactic policy had been one of tolerance.

He'd been doubly surprised when he'd been introduced to Cullon's counterpart—a beautiful Terran female with an intellect to match. But the most astonishing thing about the lovely ambassador was her psychometric skills.

Danna possessed the uncanny ability to reach into the

past by holding an object in her hand. If the emotions attached to the object were strong enough, they pulled her into what she described as a *dreamscape*.

During their first interview she had used her skills to determine Aedon's suitability as a Directorate agent.

Afterwards, there hadn't been any further need to convince her that the Directorate's first undercover agent would give everything he had to make sure the Conglomerate's plans for military supremacy were stopped cold.

In Aedon's case, "everything he had" was considerable. The Fleet's best pilot, he was a professional warrior with simple tastes and ambitions, a quiet and friendly man when regarded by his comrades, an extraordinary weapon of war when used by his government.

His combat experience revealed nerves of steel, a remarkable instinct for guerilla warfare tactics, and a self-sufficiency that made him a natural for the special role the Directorate was about to thrust upon him.

Aedon's private war with the corporate colonies known as the Conglomerate had begun like so many wars, as an act of rage and frustration. At first, he'd been out to collect a blood debt, repayment for the murder of his wife and child. Since then, time had cleared his thinking. He still wanted revenge, but he was smart enough to realize that the war he was fighting wasn't just about one man's pain. It was about putting an end to the secret cartel that fed on greed and power, a malignant cancer that was slowly eating the galaxy alive.

"There's a shuttle waiting to take you to the transport station. I've arranged passage to Laconia. Once you're there, see the docking master. His name is Landon Almuller. He'll have a ship waiting for you."

"Make sure it's a fast one."

"Don't worry. Almuller knows how to fine-tune a stellar drive."

"Any last words of wisdom?" Aedon asked as he reached for the few belongings he'd packed.

Cullon extended his hand. "Just good luck, old friend."

Aedon gave Cullon's hand a firm shake, then turned and left the room. The time had finally come to avenge his family's murder.

Revenge.

The word stirred inside him like a living thing, growing to fill his mind and heart before slowly dissolving into what it really was—justice.

two

AT MIDNIGHT THERE was no blinding sunlight to reveal the shabbiness of Melgarr's neglected inner city. Instead, the streets were mottled with shadows while fingers of gray fog stretched through the narrow alleyways. A few sparsely spaced streetlights offered weak respite against the surrounding gloom, and passing figures appeared indistinct, like phantoms from the planet's ancient past, shifting in and out among the faded facades and sagging balconies like lost souls.

The port city was one of the most corrupt dens in the outer regions—a sanctioned corruption, promoted by the Conglomerate's very existence.

Ironically, patrols of gubernatorial police marched through the streets on a regular basis. They were there to enforce the law, which more times than not meant arresting Melgarr's citizens rather than protecting them. It wasn't healthy to question Avis Rendhal's method of governing.

The patrols walked rapidly and with purpose, their

ever-present weapons strapped to their shoulders, their
heads moving sharply to the right and left as they followed
any unusual sound or movement. Constantly aware, their
eyes focused on the people they passed with suspicion.

In times past, Melgarr had been a bustling metropolis.
Now it sat like a sagging skeleton on the cliffs overlooking the Jovian Sea. The people on the streets came in
every size, shape, and color, and spoke a variety of galactic dialects—immigrants from other worlds, a people
placed and displaced over centuries by the exploration of
the galaxy.

Aedon took a pedestrian bridgeway that connected
Melgarr's business district to an even more dilapidated
section of the city. The factory district had long ago
earned the scorn of the upper city's bourgeois. It was a
place where the poor and the working classes congre-
gated, a place of disenchantment, a place where the insur-
rectionists of the Hachynite Citizens for Freedom found
popular support.

His destination was a tavern called the Black Abyss.
Tonight's visit would be his third in a row.

"Go to the tavern," he'd been told by his contact on
Pecora. *"On the third night, pay for your drink with this
coin. You need say nothing. When they are ready to take
delivery of the goods, you will be found."* Tybalt had
pressed an ancient gold coin into Aedon's palm. *"When
you are asked where you got the coin, tell them a friend
from Pecora gave it to you."*

Aedon hoped it would be that simple.

He'd spent the last six months working his way across
the galaxy, establishing a reputation as a freelance pilot who
wasn't all that choosey about the cargo he transported—a
man who could be trusted for the right price.

Shedding his old life and putting on the new hadn't
been easy, but in the space of six months he had absorbed
the new Aedon Rawn with such totality that he'd been
forced to turn down more than one profitable cargo.

He had been on Pecora, in the Magras system, when he'd been approached by an old scholar with Hachynite roots and loyalties. As a result, Aedon had smuggled three crates of percussion grenades to Melgarr. Delivery was to be arranged tonight.

The gold coin was a signal to the people expecting the goods—a message that Aedon Rawn could be trusted.

The tavern occupied two floors of a building that was suffering from age and neglect. The inside wasn't much better. Dark and seedy, the curved bar was warped from years of being leaned on by weary customers, the chairs and stools nicked and dented from careless use and the occasional brawl.

Crowded with workers from the Conglomerate factories, the odor of spilt liquor, burning incense, and human sweat permeated the air.

Aedon lowered the hood of his tunic and walked directly to the bar where a middle-aged man with blotchy skin was serving drinks to the locals.

Aedon met the man's gaze. *"Observe the small things,"* Danna MacFadyen had told him. *"The way a man walks, the way he holds his head, the steadiness or lack of it in his eyes. His clothing, his posture, the quality of his voice. The small things will paint the picture."*

If the bartender recognized him from his previous visits, the man's dull eyes gave no sign of it. If the tavern employee was more than a messenger, for the resistance, nothing about his behavior revealed so much as a hint of it.

Aedon ordered an ale, and following Tybalt's instruction, paid for it with the gold coin.

The bartender fingered the embossed coin for a moment before looking up to meet Aedon's steady gaze. "Don't know as if I've ever seen one of these before," he said, his placid demeanor unchanged.

"A friend from Pecora gave it to me," Aedon replied casually.

The bartender tucked the coin in his pocket, then poured the ale without further comment.

As he'd done for the last two nights, Aedon carried his drink to a table in the far corner of the tavern and sat down.

All emotion suspended, all pain erased from view, he sat quietly and remembered why he'd traveled halfway across the galaxy to this particular planet.

Four years ago, his wife and three-year-old daughter had been passengers on a transport, traveling from Korcia to Tamis Four to visit his wife's family. The transport had stopped at Bellago Station to take on passengers. Six hours after the routine stop, the captain of the transport had refused to stand by and be boarded by Hachynite pirates. The ship had been attacked and destroyed. No survivors.

Afterwards, the Fleet and the void of deep space had become a narcotic for Aedon's pain . . . until Cullon Gavriel had offered him an avenue to avenge the wrong that had been done.

The promise of finding the men responsible for his family's death was a beckoning siren. A call Aedon couldn't refuse.

The realization didn't set him free. Instead, it bound him to the truth of his current life more fiercely than ever. If the Directorate theory was correct, and Hachynite factories were being used to build an arsenal that would one day supply a Conglomerate-controlled army, then Governor Rendhal's pirates were the prelude to an armed fleet commanded and crewed by men who cared nothing about honor or duty.

Aedon wasn't an altruist, but honor and duty did mean something to him. The age-old concepts had guided him since entering the Fleet.

He also believed in responsibility. His people had been exploring the galaxy for generations. Like the Conglomerate, the Korcian Empire had expanded by colonizing the new worlds it had discovered. But unlike the Conglomerate, the Korcians who had colonized those new worlds had been able to fulfill their dreams.

As Aedon looked around at the other customers in the tavern, it was easy to see that the Conglomerate had stripped away whatever dreams the Hachynite colonists had brought with them into the outer regions. Beneath the alcohol-induced laughter lay a gauntness of spirit that couldn't be disguised. Dull smiles, cynical eyes, and bone-weariness could be seen sitting at every table.

Draining the last of his ale, Aedon left the tavern.

"You need say nothing. When they are ready to take delivery of the goods, you will be found."

The night was black, the moon breaking only intermittently through a thick cover of clouds. Walking at a leisurely pace, Aedon repeated his behavior of the previous two nights.

He was nearing the bridgeway when footsteps moved in behind him, pacing him across the darkness. His keen hearing quickly identified them, slowing when he slowed, quickening when he increased his pace. If he was right, there would be another pair ahead of him to close the box.

He'd be trapped.

He paused in front of a building that was too distressed to excite anyone's admiration. Looking at it, Aedon could see the bones of a once-elegant hotel in the crested windowsills and doorway. He used the few seconds to think.

Spontaneity was an important part of any warrior's arsenal, but premeditated calculation was a better option. He wouldn't have to improvise if he was prepared for whoever was waiting to trap him on the bridgeway.

His hand was sliding inside his tunic for the dagger he carried when the commlink strapped to his left wrist hummed softly. Aedon engaged the link and answered with his name.

"Turn left at the next street. When you reach the plaza, take an air-taxi. Tell the driver that you want to go to the

Lontmastre," he was told by a voice with a thick Hachynite accent. "You'll be met by a man who will give you further instructions."

"What about the parade following me?"

"They are there to see that you do what you are told to do." The link was terminated.

The *Lontmastre* was a granite statue, originally erected in memory of the planet's first colonists. It marked the entrance to the city's only park. Beyond the silent slab of stone, the tiny section of trees and shrubs lay shrouded in darkness.

Aedon stood near the base of the forty-foot monument and waited. A short time later, leather-gloved fingers touched his arm, and a voice whispered from the shadows behind him.

"Turn around slowly. Keep your hands at your side."

Recognizing the voice from the commlink call that had directed him to the park, Aedon did as he was told.

The man had a meaty face, dark eyes, heavy brows, and a distrusting expression. His hands jabbed into both sides of Aedon's chest. Strong, nimble fingers spanned the cloth of his tunic in rapid movements, descending to his belt and trousers, then lower, leaving no part of him untouched as he was searched for weapons.

Aedon didn't resist when the dagger was found and confiscated, or when he was ordered to remove the commlink from his wrist.

It was understandable that anyone connected to Eiven Jein and his freedom fighters would be cautious of strangers, even someone who had smuggled in the weapons they needed to fight the tyrannical Avis Rendhal.

The resistance fighter stepped back. His expression was still cynical, but there was a slight, momentary flicker of curiosity in his eyes. Aedon assumed it was because Korcians weren't all that common on Hachyn.

"Walk due east until you reach the square," the man said as he slipped Aedon's dagger into his belt. "Take a table at the outside café and order a drink. You will be contacted there. Do you understand?"

"I understand."

The man turned on his heels and disappeared into the park.

When Aedon reached the square, which was modestly populated with late-night carousers and couples strolling arm in arm under the moonlight, he sat down at one of the café tables and hailed a waiter. His drink had been served and tasted before a young woman approached the table.

Slender and graceful, she moved toward him with a smile on her face and a sensual promise in her walk. Her hair was curly and shimmering with highlights of burnished copper. Barely constrained by a clasp at the nape of her neck, it spilled riotously down her back. Her eyes were a matching caramel, flecked with gold.

Aedon watched her with an admiring eye, just as every other man in the square was doing.

She stopped at the chair where he was sitting, leaned down, and greeted him with a casual kiss to the cheek as if they knew each other, then walked around the table and seated herself. Aedon found himself gazing into wide, almond-shaped eyes set in a face of delicate beauty. For a brief moment, he felt as if those eyes were taking measure of his very soul.

She smiled a smile full of promises, then reached across the table for the drink he had ordered. Raising the glass to her mouth, she tasted the amber-colored liquor, then she looked at him over the rim of the glass. Her gaze was wary. It was several moments before she spoke.

"Reach out and take my hand," she said in a casual whisper. "Hold it while we talk."

Aedon reached across the table and folded her hand in his. It felt warm and soft, and he quickly realized that the affectionate gesture was one he hadn't performed since his wife's death.

"Tybalt said I would be paid upon delivery," he told her, keeping his voice low pitched, as if he were the lover she wanted him to appear to be. "I've already waited three days."

Slender fingers moved to entwine with his. The touch was coolly executed, but there was nothing cold about the feel of her skin next to his. Warmth filled his hand.

Moonlight brushed her features, accentuating their delicate lines and eyes the color of an autumn storm. The contradiction matched the moment.

"First things first," she replied with a soft-spoken annoyance that belied the outward appearance of a man and woman enjoying each other's company. "The weapons. How quickly can you deliver them?"

"As soon as I've met Eiven Jein," Aedon replied with an ingenuous smile.

She tried to pull her hand back, but Aedon stilled the movement. When she spoke, the whispered words were sharply punctuated. "You will be paid for the weapons when they are delivered. Nothing more."

Aedon kept his smile in place as he lessened the pressure on her hand, allowing her to withdraw it slowly. Skin gliding against skin preceded his proposition. "You can have the grenades in exchange for an introduction to Jein."

"Do you think we are fools?"

"No."

"Why should I take you to Jein?"

He leaned across the table toward her, as if exchanging a lover's secret. His smile was intentionally innocuous and misleading. "Because you're a smart lady."

She smiled in return, not at what he said, but because anyone watching them would expect her to smile. "Return to your lodgings. I'll see what can be arranged."

Aedon shook his head, but kept his expression friendly. "No. Tonight. Now!"

"That's impossible."

Aedon gave a soft chuckle. "No introduction, no grenades."

She shifted her attention to the square, as if she were looking for someone, then back to Aedon. The mixture of moonlight and artificial light from the café's lanterns turned her hair to midnight fire. With each breath she took, her chest rose and fell softly, accentuating the fit of her dark dress over pale, firm breasts.

When she met his gaze again, it was to look at him with eyes as golden as firelight. But unlike fire, there was no warmth. Only distrust and suspicion.

Her smile was just as cold when she asked, "Who are you?"

"A friend."

For a brief moment, she looked as if she were about to bolt. Aedon reached for her hand again, applying just enough pressure for her to know that she wasn't going to be able to walk away that easily.

Wanting the physical exchange to appear natural, he slowly rubbed his index finger over the pulse beating in her wrist. His intention was to continue the game, to give anyone who might be watching them the impression that they were simply lovers. What he didn't intend was to enjoy touching her.

When he looked into her eyes, he found them watching him just as closely. Measuring. Gauging. Questioning.

Aedon couldn't recall ever seeing such raw, naked intensity in a woman's eyes before. Automatically, he raised the liquor glass to his mouth and took a drink, hoping to drive away the persistent feeling that had begun with his first look into the woman's eyes, a feeling that had been growing ever since.

The liquor didn't help. The feeling was still there, still gnawing at the pit of his stomach.

The feeling that he'd found more on Hachyn than he'd expected.

"Let's go," he said suddenly. Impatiently.

She sat motionless for several long moments, and Aedon knew she was frantically searching for an excuse to end their meeting. He wasn't going to give her the time to find one.

He stood up and held out his hand.

"Casually," he warned her. "We need to appear as if we have nothing but time. Walk with me out into the square."

Committed to seeing the night through to its conclusion, Aedon left the café with the woman's fingers clasped lightly around his arm. When they stepped into the shadows of a covered portico fronting one of the square's shops, she removed her hand and looked up at him.

"I don't have any reason to trust you. Can you give me one?"

Aedon placed his hand on the wall above her shoulder, pinning her in place without touching her. His lips smiled, but there was no humor in his eyes. "Why not? You've got your friend along."

"I don't know what you're talking about!"

"The man in the square. I saw him earlier in the café."

With practiced detachment, she ran her hand up his chest and onto his shoulder, pushing him slightly aside so she could see the man he'd mentioned.

The only thing that allowed Aedon to see the change in her expression was their proximity. He was standing close enough to count the heartbeats that pulsed in her pale throat.

Her breath came in audibly and held. Golden eyes went dark and narrow as they moved to meet his gaze. She didn't say anything, but he could sense the change in her.

Distrust had turned to fear.

"I assume we have a problem," he said, stepping in closer to feign an embrace. He caught the hint of perfume on her skin.

"Rendhal's spies," she said in a loathsome whisper.

To run, to make any sudden move that made them stand

out from the other couples in the square, would be to draw attention to themselves, and they both knew it.

They stood quietly for a moment, their bodies touching as the summer night took on a sudden chill.

In his peripheral vision, Aedon could see the man from the café slowly measuring the square, his gaze shifting in their direction. Something cold and sharp danced along his spine, making his instincts shudder.

"Kiss me," he told the woman. "Then take my arm and start walking."

She did as he asked, resting her mouth lightly beneath his. It was a benign kiss, a kiss given because the game had to be played, the man watching convinced.

But it wasn't convincing enough.

Aedon wrapped his arm around her waist, pulling her onto her tiptoes, bringing her body into intimate contact with his.

"Is he still watching?" he asked, moving his lips against hers as he spoke.

"Yes," she breathed the word into his mouth.

His mouth settled more firmly against hers.

Then the incredible happened, incredible because neither expected it, incredible because it shouldn't have happened.

Not here. Not now.

The kiss turned real; parted lips seeking, desperately needing the contact only a kiss could give, a momentary release from reality, a brief reprieve from a world gone mad.

Unleashed hunger consumed them for several long, breath-stealing moments. Thoughts drifted, logic forgotten, wrapped in the heat of human bodies touching as intimately as a public square and clothing allowed.

"Now," Aedon said when their mouths finally parted and logic returned. "Laugh as if you're scolding me for being impatient. Then take my arm and start walking."

She did as he asked, offering him a bright smile and a throaty laugh, then linking her arm through his.

They walked three blocks without speaking, their bodies brushing casually against one another as they moved. Each wishing the kiss hadn't happened, each grateful that it had, because it had convinced the watching man that they were lovers.

The woman paused near a dark alleyway to finally look at Aedon. There was nothing readable in her catlike eyes.

"Is he still behind us?" she asked.

"No. He didn't follow us out of the square."

She stepped into the alleyway. "This way. Quickly!"

Aedon followed her through a maze of dark passageways, turning left and right on her command, sensing she was trying to confuse him as much as anyone who might be following them. When they reached an avenue lined with small shops, she slowed her pace.

"This way," she directed him. "The air-scooter is on the right. Near the corner."

Air-scooters were the customary mode of transportation in the city. This one looked powerful though undistinguished by any markings or bright colors.

"Get behind the controls," the woman told him. "I'll give you directions."

Aedon straddled the scooter and started the engine. The vibrations caused the entire chassis to tremble. It had an oversized motor, guaranteeing speed once the throttle was engaged.

"Go south, toward the sea," the woman said as she climbed on behind him. "I'll tell you where to turn."

The next fifteen minutes were a blur of city scenery and a series of sudden turns. The traffic was a combination of similar, less powerful air-scooters, taxis, and the occasional air-bus. The woman intentionally issued directions at the last second, forcing Aedon to use all his skills to keep them upright and moving forward.

They sped into a major thoroughfare from a twisting avenue, nearly colliding with an air-taxi. Aedon cursed, maintained control, straightened the scooter, then darted between two parallel vehicles ahead of them.

"Faster!" demanded the fiery-haired female in the backseat. Her arms were wrapped around his waist. "Go faster!"

"You're going to get us killed."

"Tybalt said you were the best pilot he'd ever seen," she shouted to be heard about the whine of the scooter's engine. "Prove it."

Aedon drove on, the wind and the steady high-pitched hum of the air-scooter a maddening sound in the otherwise quiet night. He remained focused, avoiding any traffic they encountered, but it didn't keep him from feeling the woman's body poised on the seat behind him. With her arms wrapped around his waist, and her hips tucked close against his own, it was impossible to forget that his passenger was a young, softly curved female.

"Turn right!" she said as they neared the outskirts of the city.

Aedon barely had time to brake and turn the air-scooter into the narrow street before she was telling him to turn left at the next corner.

"Keep going," she urged when he throttled down the sleek little air machine to keep them from careening off the side of a building. "Out of the city."

The moonlight that had washed over the buildings of Melgarr soon revealed stretches of rock-hewn fields and barren meadows rimmed by gargoylelike trees with twisted branches and snarled roots that protruded above the dirt. The few houses they passed were locked tight for the night, an occasional hue of light showing at random windows. In the distance, an irregular silhouette of ragged hills outlined the horizon.

Above them, a million stars decorated the sky.

"Another ten kilometers, then south," the woman prompted from her perch behind him. "Don't slow down."

Aedon maintained the breakneck speed that wasn't
nearly as dangerous now as it had been while moving
through city traffic. When the distance gauge measured
off the ten kilometers, he took a turn to the south, following the plummeting landscape as it dipped toward the sea.

"Stop!"

The air-scooter glided to a halt under his experienced
hands. Once the engine was shut down, Aedon could
heard the stark melody of angry water slapping against
stone-faced cliffs.

"Get off," came the next command, but it wasn't spoken in the indifferent voice that had shouted in his ears
for the last fifteen minutes. This voice was softer, more
solicitous.

Aedon got off the air-scooter. He took a breath of sea
air before turning to stare through the shadows at the
woman. Her delicate features were accented by the same
moonlight that gleamed off the muzzle of the laser pistol
aimed at his heart.

three

KALA LOOKED AT the Korcian, knowing the truth would be in his incredible eyes. Unfortunately, she couldn't define any emotion in their ever-changing depths.

Gleaming in shades of blue, gray, and silver, their chameleon quality identified him as a member of the greatest warrior race in the galaxy. His body had the tautness that came with discipline and training. The breadth of his shoulders, the long muscular neck, and the convex line of a chest that stretched his leather tunic were evidence of physical precision and strength. Combined with his facial features and dark hair, the result was striking, yet cold.

No. Not cold, Kala decided. Resigned. As if living or dying were the same thing.

"Is this how the HCF treats its friends?" he asked.

"You've yet to prove yourself friend or foe," Kala pointed out, watching his reaction carefully. When she realized that she was being slowly trapped by the shimmering depths of his eyes, she forced herself to remember all the reasons she dare not trust anyone whose loyalty hadn't already been proven.

Life had taught her that a man could look honest, and sound honest, without being honest.

She knew the Korcian was hiding something; the question was whether or not that something threatened the resistance.

"I smuggled your grenades through Rendhal's security net." His voice was firm, not angry. "Your people have watched my every move for the last three days. What more do you want?"

"Proof that you're not a Conglomerate spy."

His reply was a crisp, mirthless laugh. "You'll just have to trust me."

Kala almost laughed in return.

How long had it been since she'd been able to trust anyone at face value? When she hadn't had to look over her shoulder. When she hadn't had to worry that someone would overhear what he shouldn't overhear, see what he shouldn't see, and turn her into the governor for the bounty put on every freedom fighter's head.

How long had it been since she'd fallen asleep to peaceful dreams, or had the luxury to dream at all? Time and space to be herself. The freedom to act openly and honestly.

Governor Rendhal had taken all those freedoms away.

Now there was only survival.

Being a freedom fighter made every move a risk, every person a potential enemy.

The thought quickly brought her back to the man standing tall and darkly dangerous in front of her. He looked toward the sea for a moment, and the moonlight on his sharply-angled face made him appear almost savage, like a hunter from primeval times in search of a mythical dragon to slay.

Standing well over six feet tall, his body encased in black leather, eyes an icy blue that threatened to bore into and through anyone who stood too long under their piercing gaze, Aedon Rawn wasn't a man to be ignored.

It was just as apparent that his strength went beyond the physical. Kala could see it in his face, in those incredible Korcian eyes. She could sense it. Confidence. Determination. A predator's prowess. It radiated from him like light from a star. Silent and powerful.

She scolded herself for the fanciful thought. After a lifetime of living under the Conglomerate's rule, she should know better than to wish for miracles. There was no easy solution to the problems her people faced, no quick fix that would bring her world into balance. There was only the hope of freedom.

But living on hope was dangerous: it implied that you had a future.

The governor's police were growing bolder every day, arresting anyone they suspected of being even remotely connected to the Hachynite Citizens for Freedom. As a result, the prisons were filled with innocent people who had committed no crime beyond that of sympathy to the cause.

Three days ago, the governor had personally attended the execution of a resistance leader from the western province. The freedom movement was dangerously close to being extinguished.

But Kala refused to give up hope. It was all she had.

"If you aren't who you say you are, you won't live to see tomorrow," she told him, meaning every word.

"Fair enough," came his reply.

Kala motioned for him to start walking.

The ruins lay on a rocky tongue of land that jutted out into the ocean. The front chamber of the building lacked a roof but otherwise it was intact, its carefully fitted stones untouched by the five or six centuries that had passed since it had served as a monastery for a now-forgotten religious order.

The scent of the sea and ancient stones mingled into a

fragrance that belonged to the past as they made their way through the dark.

Every time Kala visited the ruins, she found herself hoping that any lingering gods were friendly ones.

Before the monastery was reached, the path narrowed to little more than a ledge dampened by sea spray and assaulted by a relentless wind, while far below, whitecaps crested on jagged rocks. Beyond the shoreline, moonlight painted the water with a ghostly sheen.

"I hope you didn't bring me here to shove me off a cliff," the Korcian said, sounding more amused than worried.

Kala could see the glimmer of his chameleon eyes and the subtle flare of his nostrils as he breathed in the cool night air. The memory of his unexpected kiss came rushing back, and she promised herself not to be caught off guard again.

"Keep moving," she said.

She guided him to a circular room that had once been used as a chapel. The Korcian stood silently to the side while she dislodged a small stone to reveal a sensor panel, then watched as she pressed her left hand to the scanning plate. A short second later the silence was broken by the ragged crunch of a stone wall sliding open.

"You first," she said.

The room they entered had once been a small vestibule where monks had gathered for evening prayers. Now it served as a scanning booth.

There was no comment as the Korcian moved to the scanning plate embedded in the floor. After the body scan that told Kala he had neither weapons nor an implant that could transmit his location, she motioned him toward a heavy blast door.

The door required both fingerprint and retina confirmation. When it opened, Kala followed the Korcian into an ancient storage chamber that had been converted into a personal residence.

The furnishings were simplistic but comfortable, taking

second place to the sophisticated surveillance and communications equipment that kept the room's occupant in constant touch with the outside world.

An emaciated man, belted into a gravity-chair, looked up from one of the monitors. In spite of his gaunt appearance and physical disabilities, his face was strong, his wizardlike eyes sharply alert. His smile instantly soothed Kala's nerves.

"Good evening, Mr. Rawn," he said in a raspy tone that demanded its listeners pay attention. "I hope the evening has been a pleasant one."

Aedon watched as the elderly man maneuvered the gravity-chair toward a serving bar, using a hand that lacked two of its five fingers. Moments later, the chair floated back across the stone-walled room and a drink was offered.

"My name is Eiven Jein. The young lady who brought you here is Kala Char'ari."

The woman who hadn't had a name until this moment stepped to her left, revealing the laser pistol that was still aimed at Aedon's chest. "I don't trust him."

Jein exhaled a raspy laugh. "Don't be offended, Mr. Rawn. Kala doesn't trust anyone. An unfortunate reaction demanded by our circumstances. May I ask why you're here?"

Aedon hid his surprise at finding the Hachynite rebel leader resulted to a gravity-chair. He answered Jein's question with one word. "Conversation."

"Conversation." Jein pressed the fingers of his deformed hands together, his eyes riveted on Aedon. "What precisely it is that you wish to converse about?"

"Our common goal."

"And that goal would be?"

"The dethroning of Governor Rendhal."

Jein leaned back in his chair, seemingly impressed, but not noticeably surprised by the remark. "I know a thousand men with the same ambition."

"Now you know one thousand and one."

Jein laughed, the sound a low rumble in his thin chest. "If eliminating Rendhal were an easy task, it would have been done by now. The governor is never left alone, and his personal guards are paid handsomely to see that those in the lower ranks, those who might be persuaded to betray him, never get close enough to accomplish the task. He rarely appears in public, and when he does, he's protected by specially trained police. He calls them his Honor Guard, but they're nothing more than programmed psychopaths with a lust for bloodletting."

Aedon remained silent, sensing that Jein had more to say.

The underground leader studied him for a long moment, before continuing. "You intrigue me, Mr. Rawn, but trust is not given easily by those who fear betrayal. You say that you came here to dethrone Rendhal. If he's killed, the Conglomerate puppet-masters will only appoint a new governor. We will simply be exchanging one tyrant for another. If Rendhal is replaced, it has to be by a representative lawfully elected by the people."

"I'm not an assassin," Aedon replied. "I'm here to offer my services."

The woman named Kala interjected with a harsh laugh. "Your services as what? A spy who reports to Rendhal and helps to destroy us?"

"You've been fighting Rendhal for over twenty years, but there's little evidence that you're making progress," Aedon said, unscathed by her cynicism. "Rendhal still lives in the governor's mansion and your people are still forced to kneel to his authority. You're outnumbered, outgunned, and outfinanced."

"How very astute of you," Kala said sarcastically. "And I suppose adding one *Korcian* to our ranks will change everything. We'll be victorious overnight."

Aedon looked at Jein. "Even the strongest fortress can be toppled, if the right brick is dislodged."

"A poetic philosophy," said the rebel leader. "How do you plan to implement it?"

"With your help," Aedon said, taking his drink to where a frayed leather chair sat near a reading table. He sat down. "You know the governor's strengths and weaknesses."

"Just as you know mine," Jein said, looking down at the twisted flesh and bone that had once been his legs.

"Any man who can organize a resistance movement on a Conglomerate colony and keep it alive as long as you have isn't weak or crippled," Aedon said with conviction. "Let me help you take the fight where it belongs—into the enemy's camp."

Before Jein could comment, a perimeter alert sounded, echoing off the walls of the stone chamber like an ancient bell tolling the hour.

Kala keyed the surveillance monitor to full screen. A team of eight heavily-armed gubernatorial policemen were approaching the ruins. "They followed us!"

"Not followed, *tracked*," Aedon said coming to his feet. "The air-scooter."

The police team was getting close. In minutes they'd be in the front chamber. Although the initial entryway into the ruins was camouflaged, the locking mechanisms still emitted a low-frequency signal that could be picked up on their police scanners.

"Get out of here," Jein ordered. "Now!"

"I won't leave you," Kala argued. "I'll stay and fight."

Jein looked to Aedon. "Take her and keep her safe."

"No!" Kala screamed as Aedon grabbed her around the waist and lifted her off the floor because it was the only way she was going to move. "I won't leave him!"

"Go." Jein's crippled hand pointed toward a narrow, dimly lit corridor that led deeper into the ruins. "There's a passage that will take you down to the sea. Kala knows the way. Hurry. You only have a few minutes."

Aedon didn't argue. He and Jein both knew a man dependent upon a gravity-chair had limitations. One of those restrictions was his inability to move quickly and with stealth. He looked at the leader of the resistance and saw the inevitable in Jein's wizard-green eyes.

The rebel leader had known when he'd chosen the old monastery as his headquarters that the ruins would one day become his tomb.

He'd known it and prepared for it.

"Hurry!" Jein shouted at them from the control panel.

Kala kicked and squirmed, but Aedon held fast. He grabbed the laser pistol from her hand and started moving down the length of the corridor, away from the room where Eiven Jein was programming his epitaph into a computer.

"No, please," Kala pleaded with him.

Aedon kept moving until there was nothing but darkness and stone around him. "Which way?"

When she didn't answer him, he set her on her feet, blocking any escape with his body, and gave her a firm shake. "The tunnel, Kala. Which way do we go?"

She looked at him for moment then pointed to her right, accepting the circumstances for what they were—life or death.

She chose life. "This way."

The tunnel was a claustrophobic nightmare.

Little more than an airshaft drilled through solid rock, it angled slowly downward. In the darkness, Aedon couldn't see Kala, but he could hear her. The sound of shoes and clothing rubbing against cold, damp granite told him that she was only a few inches in front of him. Once his hand slipped away from the damp rock and onto her shoulder. She flinched at his touch, but she didn't stop moving.

It seemed like an eternity, but it was only a few minutes before the sound and scent of the sea reached them.

"I hope you can swim," she said when they reached the end of the shaft.

Aedon inched his way to where she was crouched in an opening no larger than a starjet hatchway. The tunnel ended abruptly, some twenty feet above the whipping currents of the Jovian Sea.

Aedon looked down at the vague shape of dark, silent danger. A curtain of fog rolled in and the huge boulders vanished like a bad dream. The sound of waves slapping against rock was all that remained. Not the option he would have liked, but the only one available.

He listened for another few seconds, gauging the time between one rolling wave meeting the submerged boulders and another. Mere seconds.

Aedon hoped it would be enough.

"Once we get into the water, swim out to sea," he told Kala.

She nodded, acknowledging what Aedon had suspected. Jein was going to blast the monastery, himself, and his enemies to smithereens. If they weren't far enough out in the water, they'd be buried under the cliff as it caved into the sea.

He reached for Kala's hand. "Ready."

"Yes."

The next second a blast, erupting like a volcano from the top of the cliff, shook the very ground they were standing upon. The shock wave rushed through the tunnel in a boiling cyclone of flaming heat and toxic fumes, flinging Aedon and Kala out into midair, then down toward the water.

Kala was a dark shape sailing over Aedon's shoulder. He grabbed for her and missed. Then they both were caught in the churning waves.

Aedon hit bottom and drove upward with all his strength. There was no clear direction in the dark water, nothing but the relentless push and pull of the current. When he broke the surface, it was just in time to see and hear a secondary blast.

Black smoke mushroomed into a ball of orange and red flame, sending ash and rock hurling toward the heavens and shadows dancing across the face of the moon. The scent of sea water and cool, clean air was replaced with the acid smell of death and destruction.

From the corner of his eye Aedon saw something break the water's rough surface. It was Kala's head. Eel slick, her hair formed a dark helmet around her pale face. Aedon saw her gulp down a lungful of air. Then he had his own worries.

The placement of the rocks along the shoreline caused the waves to form chaotic patterns. Concealed boulders altered those patterns. There was no logic to the water. The unremitting force of the waves drove him back toward shore. Kala yelled something at him, but the words became a sound without meaning.

Slowly at first, then with increasing speed, Aedon regained the advantage. Using all his strength, he kept swimming until he was close enough to see Kala. Her eyes were riveted on the shore—to the place where a huge hole had been gutted out of the rock.

"We've got to get out of the water," he shouted at her, but she didn't respond. He swam closer and shouted louder. "Kala!"

She turned toward the sound of his voice. Then, without being told what needed to be done, she did it. Her arms and legs began to move, to pull and stretch, to swim.

"Don't fight the current. Use it," he yelled at her. "Let it draw you down the beach."

They swam for ten minutes or more, each concentrating on staying afloat, each glancing at the rocky coast, each seeking a place where they could exchange cold dark water for firm dry land.

Finally, as Aedon's muscles began to ache, he saw it. A small alcove in the rock. He reached out and grabbed at Kala, his hand skimming down the length of her slender leg. "There," he pointed.

Together they swam, and together they stumbled through the swirling surf and immovable rocks to collapse on the hard discomfort of the stony beach.

Kala drew half a dozen long, sobbing breaths. Aedon put his hand on her shoulder. Beneath the sodden fabric of her clothing, muscles jerked and danced in the rhythm of exhaustion.

She looked up at him with eyes as mysterious as the sea behind them.

"I'm okay," she said without being asked.

He nodded, then sank down beside her.

They had shared a crisis and survived. Aedon knew it wouldn't be their last.

four

"WE NEED FOOD, shelter, and weapons," Aedon said after he'd caught his breath. "The authorities will be swarming over the coast in a few minutes."

Kala looked from his face to where sea met land, to where the phosphorescent surge of waves crawled onto the beach. Beyond the cresting whitecaps, moonlight bathed the horizon in a cool luminousness. The piercing loneliness of the scene touched the very depths of her.

She turned to stare at where the ruins had once stood, rock built upon rock, and the enormity of what had happened finally struck home.

No one was there.

Jein was dead.

"Kala," Aedon said, forcing her to let go of the images in her mind and return to the present. "We have to go. Is there anyone you can trust? Anyplace you'll be safe?"

The ruins had been safe.

She'd always been able to trust Jein.

There were other thoughts, as well. Desperate thoughts

that she tried to control and keep in perspective, pushing away the panic that could so easily engulf her, causing her to do the wrong thing, make a wrong move that could harm other friends, other comrades.

She searched her memory for anyone who could help her, constantly rejecting every name and every face that came to her, because in one way or another each could have been part of the horrible strategy that had killed Jein.

"No," she said, letting the truth take root. "I don't dare trust anyone now."

He reached for her arm and pulled her to her feet. Anger and grief battled inside her. Anger because everything that should be wasn't. Grief because the man she had loved like a father, and respected as a friend, was dead.

With tight motions, she jerked her arm away from the Korcian's grasp and took a step back. "How do I know that you didn't bring the police to the ruins? You insisted on meeting Jein. You said you recognized the man in the square. Was it some kind of ploy? A way to make me panic? You said they put a tracker on the air-scooter, but there's no way for me to be certain. I can't trust you. I don't want to trust you."

Anger accumulated into a split-second decision. Kala propelled herself toward him. At the last second the Korcian dodged her outstretched arms. She seized his wet tunic instead, and hammered her knee toward his groin. He torqued his pelvis back defensively, she flexed her wrist into a slap block, and sent him stumbling backward.

She instinctively assumed a classic self-defense stance: her left arm out and perpendicular to her body, a barrier to any rush he might make at her. Her right arm was extended straight down and held a small knife. It had been boot-holstered, and the Korcian hadn't seen it until it was drawn.

Well trained, Kala choreographed the next few seconds in her mind. Aedon Rawn might be bigger and stronger, but she had the advantage of being faster, more agile, and armed. The blade was small but sharp.

She gripped the knife handle firmly, knowing better than most how to wield it with slashing force.

Then, without so much as a blink of his incredibly colored eyes, he moved on her, delivering a sharp blow to her right wrist. Momentarily unable to control the nerves he had struck, her hand opened and the knife fell to the ground.

He grabbed the weapon, but not before her left hand shot out toward his shoulder. Kala dug her thumb deep into his muscle, jolting the nerves that ran beneath the skin and temporarily paralyzing his arm. She saw a bolt of pain stretch across his face, but it didn't keep him from swinging his leg out and toppling her backward.

He fell on top of her.

"I don't want to hurt you," he said.

The sound of Kala's sarcastic laughter was carried out to sea by the wind.

She could feel the heat of the Korcian's body, feel his muscles tense as she squirmed and thrashed beneath him. With powerful thighs, he pinned her legs, but her hands were capable of hurting him just as much. She struck at his brachial plexus, the bundle of nerves that reached from the top of his shoulder to the vertebrae of his neck. He pushed his elbows down into the wet sand and pinned her to the ground.

She was held in place by his greater weight and pure brute strength.

His breath was warm against her face. "Stop fighting me."

Another writhing attempt to throw him off passed through her body like a powerful shudder.

The Korcian stayed right where he was, covering her from head to toe.

Their foreheads were pressed together, nose to nose, mouth to mouth in a strange, unsettling intimacy of combat.

"Look at me," he demanded.

Kala looked into eyes as dark as the tide that had swept them onto the beach.

"I'm the one person you *can* trust," he said.

His hands moved, not to hold her in place, but to brush back her hair.

Kala felt their warmth stealing past the damp cold that had seeped into her body. She felt it, and she fought it.

She didn't want to feel warm, she didn't want to feel comforted. She didn't want to feel anything.

Jein was dead.

She deserved to be cold and miserable. To have her stomach tied in knots. To feel unmoored, set adrift.

"You've got to put it aside for now." His voice was quietly soothing as he rolled away from her.

Kala knew he was right. *Understanding* Jein's death would have to wait. There was no time for grief now.

He found the knife and tucked it into his own boot.

Kala remained on her back, her eyes staring upward into the night, her mind racing with possibilities. It was the perfect moment to strike, to take the advantage, but beneath the anger that had spurred her into fighting the Korcian a few minutes ago, common sense seeped to the surface.

The Korcian had the knife now, plus size and strength. She'd gain nothing by challenging him again.

She sat up and raked her hands through her wet hair. She needed time to think. Time to organize her thoughts, make plans. Where could she go? Who *could* she trust? What would happen to the resistance now that Jein was dead? Who would lead the fight?

"The man at the monument," Aedon said, interrupting her thoughts. "Did he know that you'd have the airscooter nearby?"

"What?" Her eyes closed, but only for a moment. The images lingering in her mind, waiting to be relived, weren't what she needed to be seeing now. She looked at the Korcian instead. Into the quicksilver depths of his eyes.

"Whoever tracked us to the ruins wasn't looking for Jein," he said intensely. There was no anger in his voice, but retribution shimmered in his eyes. "No one knew I wanted to meet him. That I'd *insist* on being taken to him. We were tracked because they wanted to intercept the grenade shipment. Jein wasn't the target. We were."

Kala's spine stiffened at the idea of being betrayed by one of her own. Everyone she knew in the resistance was as committed as she was, willing to forfeit their lives if necessary. Many already had.

"Circumstances change and loyalties shift with them," he said. "Someone alerted the police that you were arranging for a shipment of weapons to be delivered. They knew I would be at the café. They knew you'd be meeting me in the square."

Kala tried to block out the Korcian's accusations only to hear Jein's words of counsel echo in her mind. *"If you can't see a way out, take the time to see things differently. See what you don't want to see, and the picture will become clearer."*

Her eyes came to rest on Aedon's strong features, his high cheekbones, full mouth, and extraordinary eyes.

"See what you don't want to see."

The rush of contradictory emotions was like being buffeted by a strong wind. Emotions. Not facts.

There was no real proof for or against the Korcian. No facts meant that Kala was left with nothing but her instincts. Tutored instincts that had kept her alive and beyond the governor's reach for years.

The deepest instinct, one that ran soul deep, told Kala to believe the man, not the circumstances.

She looked toward the ruins again, then said, "The man who met you at the *Lontmastre* is named Selwyn, but I can't believe he would turn traitor."

"Someone did."

"You can't be sure of that," she protested. "They've been looking for Jein for years."

"Who else knew he headquartered in the ruins?"

The thought of how much Jein had trusted her, the faith he'd invested in her loyalty, did little to lessen Kala's guilt about being alive when he was dead.

"No one," she answered softly. "I was his only personal contact. That's the way he wanted it. He coordinated everything from his console."

"Someone helped you get him there," he said. "Someone built the safe room and set up the equipment."

"Branson. Max Branson," she told him. "He was Jein's friend, a subordinate in the colonial government. He's also the one who risked his life to get Jein out of prison."

"Where is he now?"

"Dead. He was killed during a skirmish with a police patrol six months after Jein was moved to the ruins."

Kala knew her answer confirmed the Korcian's assumption rather than contradicting it. She didn't like it, but she had to agree with him. If she was the only one who knew Jein's whereabouts, and she didn't tell anyone, then they had found the ruins because they'd been tracking the air-scooter.

"Who else knew about the grenades? About me?" he asked, wiping away the water that was dripping off his dark hair and down his face. "How many people were involved into tonight's meeting?"

Kala forced aside her emotions and concentrated on the last twenty-four hours. Objectively. Abstractly.

"Jein, myself, and three others . . . Selwyn, Černak, and Ryze."

"The men who shadowed me when I left the tavern."

Kala nodded. "Once Selwyn gave you instructions, he moved ahead to be in position at the *Lontmastre*. Černak and Ryze kept you in sight until you got into the air-taxi. They were to stay in position until I confirmed that the delivery would be made tonight."

"And if you didn't contact them?"

"An unforeseen delay or an abort," she said with a neutrality that didn't quite mask her emotional state.

"Are those unusual?"

She looked up at the night sky. The fumes and smoke of the explosion had joined the clouds, darkening them to an angry gray.

When Kala answered the question, her voice was as flat as the hope she'd clung to for years. "They happen from time to time."

"I lost the laser pistol when the blast sent us flying into the ocean," he said, looking toward water. "If you don't know who to trust, then we trust no one. We take care of ourselves. It's a risk returning to the city, but it's the only place where we can get food and weapons."

Kala came to her feet, then dusted the wet sand off her clothing. She started walking toward the rocky incline that fenced off the beach from the roadway that led into the city.

She'd made her decision, now she'd live or die with it.

She didn't look back to see if the Korcian was following her. From this moment on, there was no looking back at all.

One of the good things about Melgarr was its kaleidoscope of cultures. Aedon and Kala didn't have any trouble blending into the city's morning crowd after they stopped on the outskirts to purchase a change of clothes.

Aedon chose a loose-fitting brown robe, worn over his now dry black tunic and trousers. He kept the hood up to conceal his unusual eye color.

Kala's disguise was more elaborate. She decided on a multicolored shawl in shades of bright blue and green tied around the shoulders of a white dress. The shawl's white fringe was long and silky, like the hair she had covered with a blue turban. As strange as she looked stepping out of the dressing stall, she blended in perfectly once they were back on the street.

The took an air-bus into the inner city. Kala tucked the canvas shopping bag, filled with her dark clothing, under the seat.

"I assume you have some sort of plan," she said to Aedon once they were seated.

"First stop, my lodgings," he said. "As soon as it's dark, we'll find a way out of the city."

"Until they know for sure who was killed in the blast, they'll be watching your lodgings and my apartment."

"They'll be watching what they *think* were my lodgings," he replied with a crooked smile. "Don't worry, I know how to cover my tracks."

She digested the remark, then said, "I can't leave without warning the others. If there is a traitor in the unit, their lives are at risk."

Aedon looked around. The other passengers were concerned with their morning commute and the day ahead, nothing more. He and Kala hadn't so much as drawn a glance since boarding the air-bus. "How are you going to warn them? If they're watching our lodgings, it's a sure bet that they're monitoring the communication frequencies."

"I'll send out an alert the same way Jein would have."

She pointed out the window at a digital air-bus schedule mounted on the face of a building. There were similar ones all over the city, constantly updating scheduled stops along the mass transit routes that were used by thousands of the city's populace. Between updates, the boards were consumed by advertisements.

Aedon watched the display for a moment, picturing the console he'd seen in the ruin's stone chamber.

"Jein was tied into the transit computer," he said, admiring the simplicity and the audacity of the communication channel. The resistance leader had maintained contact with his people in full view of the police. "Did he use a code, or a change in sequence?"

"One or both, depending on the circumstances," Kala told him. "The explosion had to have made the morning announcements; even the police can't keep something that noisy out of the daily updates. Everyone will be watching the transit boards, waiting for Jein to give them instructions."

Aedon gave the woman sitting next to him an approving smile. Whatever the reason, Kala had apparently decided to trust him. "If you post an alert, everyone in the unit, including the traitor, will assume that Jein is still alive."

"I'm buying time."

"Smart move. How do plan to make the announcement?"

"From one of the computer ports in the maintenance tunnel." She looked toward the front of the air-bus where several passengers had come to their feet. "We should get off at the next stop."

That put them across the street from a massive office building in the heart of the city. Kala led him into the cavernous lobby, holding onto his arm and chatting casually, as if they were simply reporting for work like everyone else who had departed the air-bus.

She was a polished performer. Anyone watching her would see a young woman behaving like a young woman, not a freedom fighter on the run.

Midway in the building, a secondary hallway bisected the main corridor to form an inverted T. Kala took the minor corridor to a door at the rear of the building. Once the door was shut behind them, she turned to Aedon. "These stairs will take us to the basement. There's an access tube to the maintenance tunnel."

Fortunately, they didn't encounter anyone on the stairs. Once they were inside the basement with the hum of air-recyclers and utility generators, Kala led him through a maze of pipes, cables, and junction panels. The access tube was marked with a yellow-striped lid.

Aedon bent down, gave the lid a hard turn to dislodge its locking arms, and lifted it open.

"Down we go," Kala said as she stepped onto the ladder's first rung.

He followed her down the ladder, closing the lid behind him. The darkness was an impenetrable black. The tunnel was musty and oppressive. Aedon had a feeling of entombment as the hatch slid into place above him.

Using nothing but the feel of metal rungs under his feet and the smooth, cold texture of steel gripped in his hands, Aedon made his descent. He stopped when he reached the bottom and waited for Kala's cue to turn left or right.

Her touch alerted him to her closeness. Her fingers lay on his arm for a brief second before sliding down to take his hand.

"The tunnel makes a sharp turn to the right just ahead," she told him.

Aedon let Kala lead him slowly forward. When she stroked her fingers lightly over the top of his hand, Aedon told himself she was only trying to reassure him that while he was walking blind she was as much at home underneath the streets of Melgarr as she was strolling on their scarred pavement. But despite what he told himself, Aedon couldn't ignore the warm sensation of her skin against his. The contrast between the softness of her touch and the pitch blackness of the tunnel was disorienting.

For an instant Aedon's pulse quickened in a purely sexual response. Man touching woman. Woman touching man.

He forced himself to remember that despite Kala's gender she was a warrior just like him.

A wounded warrior.

Her emotions had been slashed to ribbons when she'd been tossed into the ocean by the explosion that had killed Jein. On the beach, she had struggled with those emotions and come to grips with them. But only temporarily.

Shock could be postponed, but it couldn't be erased.

Sooner or later the emotions caged inside Kala were going to explode. When they did, it could come boiling out of her in a fit of anger or a flood of tears.

Whatever the reaction, Aedon had to make sure she was safe when it happened. The reasons were twofold. First, his protective instincts wouldn't allow him to do otherwise. Second, like it or not, Kala Char'ari was now his only link to the resistance movement—the key he needed to unlock the door. Without her, without the resistance, without its people and its knowledge, he wouldn't be able to complete his mission.

The simple fact made the young woman with soft golden eyes and hair the color of a Korcian sunset the most important person in his life. The irony wasn't lost on Aedon as he felt Kala's delicately boned fingers move over the back of his hand.

He'd traveled halfway across the galaxy to avenge the murder of one woman, only to find himself partnered with another.

"Wait here," she told him when they'd moved about a hundred yards. "I'll get the lights."

She released his hand and moved forward on her own.

Suddenly the tunnel was aglow with an eerie orange light cast from illumination tubes mounted on the arched ceiling. Running underground for miles, the faint light made the tunnel seem less like a coffin and more like a mine shaft.

"There's usually a trolley at the next junction," Kala said. "It's faster than walking, but not by much."

The trolley was a railed platform mounted on a conveyor belt. Kala climbed onboard and reached for the controls. A few seconds later the cough of an engine coming to life filled the tunnel, followed by the grunt and groan of the conveyor belt as it began to move sluggishly forward.

Aedon joined Kala on the platform. The pulsing power

of the trolley's engine reverberated through the metal deck and into his bones.

He ducked his head to keep it from colliding with a knot of cables that crisscrossed the tunnel's roof. The movement put his mouth a scant inch from Kala's ear. The brush of her hair against his face caused him to release a broken breath before asking, "What is the message going to say?"

"The truth," she said. "We've been compromised. Get out of the city."

"Where will they go?"

"Everyone has an exit strategy; it's one of the things Jein insisted upon."

It took them half an hour to reach the computer port, and another fifteen minutes for Kala to perform her computerized sleight of hand.

"I programmed the code to run for a full six hours. I hope it's enough."

His smiled gleamed against the bronze coloring of his skin. "One of the first rules of war is to live to fight another day."

Kala climbed back on the trolley. "There's more than one rule of war."

Aedon didn't have to ask what she was thinking—her tone of voice said it all. "You want to go after Selwyn."

"I have to know," she said. "If he betrayed me, he'll betray others. I can't let that happen."

five

"WHAT MAKES YOU think you can find Selwyn?" Aedon asked her as the trolley began moving forward again.

Kala stared into the depths of the tunnels, remembering when they had been her home. There were times when she could almost forget having to hide belowground to avoid the police patrols that were little more than rape gangs if they happened upon a young woman foolish enough to be walking the streets alone at night.

This wasn't one of those times.

Being underground, hearing the echo of activity from the streets above, wondering what would happen to her if she made a mistake, if she got caught, brought the memories rushing back. Memories that had been her silent companion for years.

But they also served as a reminder of the present. If she'd made the wrong decision in trusting the Korcian, she could find herself underground permanently.

Trusting him was difficult.

Kala couldn't subtract her emotions from the equation. She couldn't forget the sizzling moment of fire that had been his kiss, or the warmth of his hands on her body. Even now, with him riding on the trolley behind her, she was acutely aware of his strength. His masculinity.

Without her objectivity, all she had was what she'd started with—her instincts.

And her instincts told her that Aedon Rawn had a very special reason for hating Governor Rendhal. He may have been telling Jein the truth, but Kala knew it wasn't the *whole* truth. There was more, but whatever the Korcian's truth was, it was the second question on Kala's mind. The first question was Selwyn's loyalty to the resistance.

She let out a harsh breath and flexed her hands on the trolley controls.

"I won't have to find Selwyn," she said, glancing over her shoulder to where he stood. "He'll come to me."

Eyes that had been silver-blue moments before now glowed like black onyx. "How can you be sure, and if you are sure, where?"

Kala slowed the sluggish trolley to a complete stop. The conveyor belt had come to an end. Aedon helped her off the platform and onto the damp concrete floor of the tunnel. In the artificial light she could see the strong tendons in his neck, the beard shadow on his face, and the steady pulse beating in his throat.

His eyes had changed again, this time to silver-blue rimmed in black. It was unnerving. Each time she looked at the man it was as if she were seeing a variation, a part of him, but never the whole.

Never the complete man.

And then there was the other—emotions she couldn't completely define.

Each time she looked into Aedon Rawn's uncanny eyes, Kala discovered something about herself. She realized that being physically attracted to a man could make her pulse quicken and her blood run hot, that it could make her concentration splinter and her thoughts go wild. But what really troubled her was that she wanted him to kiss her again. She wanted to experience the blinding sensation of not being able to think at all.

Grimly, Kala tried not to think about the strong hands that had controlled her so easily on the beach. The same hands that had gently brushed her hair away from her face.

Taking a quick breath, Kala managed to subdue the elemental need the Korcian aroused in her.

"If Selwyn turned traitor, then the explosion and our deaths are a victory," she said. "Men celebrate victories."

"It's a little early for visiting a tavern."

Kala flashed him a smile. "Not a tavern, a brothel."

He tilted his head slightly, studying her in a way that made Kala's pulse quicken and her skin tingle to be touched.

She waited, expecting him to come back with the remark that it was never to early in the day for sex, but he didn't. Instead his eyes gleamed, changing color yet again at he looked to where the tunnel ended in a T-junction a few hundred feet in front of them. Cables crawled up the walls and ceilings like black snakes.

"Left or right?" he asked.

"Left. The tunnel will bring us out in the alley behind the pleasure house. Selwyn has a particular fondness for one of Yahaira's girls."

The brothel was actually a sex club where pleasure suites could be rented by the hour and the gambling tables operated around the clock. The building had no distinguishing signs or markings when seen from the rear alley. It looked like all the other buildings, its windows opaque glass, its rear door made of dull metal with a comm panel to announce visitors or deliveries.

Kala pressed the announcement button on the comm panel. "Yahaira, it's Kala. I need to speak with you."

The lock was disengaged and the door opened.

Aedon followed, stepping into a storage room where bottles of liquor were stacked neatly on shelves alongside clean linens and vials of the enhancement drugs that were frequently used to increase a customer's pleasure. The sound of music and muffled voices drifted in from the gambling room.

"We'll use the back stairs," Kala said. "Yahaira's office is on the third floor, above the pleasure suites. A lot of policemen favor this club, and Yahaira is an excellent listener. Whenever she hears anything interesting she passes it along."

"Another link in the chain," Aedon said. "Does Selwyn know Yahaira is one of your informers?"

"No. I didn't discuss my contacts with anyone but Jein."

When they reached the third floor of the building, Kala walked to a set of double doors and gave the top panel a soft knock. Activated from within, the doors slid open with a shushed whisper.

Aedon followed Kala into the room that was part office, part living quarters. The woman sitting behind a scarred metal desk lifted her gaze from the monitor she had been studying.

Yahaira was middle-aged with blond hair and hazel eyes. Her face had been pretty at one time. Now stress lines creased her forehead and her skin sagged into loose jowls around her mouth. Her attire was a loose-fitting, multicolored robe that concealed a body that was no longer profitable.

She stepped out from behind her desk and greeted Kala with an affectionate hug.

"I didn't expect to see you today," she said, holding Kala at arm's length. "You look tired, honey. And why are you wearing that ugly turban? Your hair is beautiful. Don't hide it."

Before Kala could answer, Yahaira turned her attention to Aedon. Her hands dropped away from Kala's upper arms and came to rest on thick hips covered by cheap synthetic silk.

Yahaira's eyes raked Aedon from top to bottom. "Well now, if I was twenty years younger, I'd be glad to get back into the business. I hear Korcians have lots of stamina."

Hazel eyes shifted back to Kala. "If you want to use one of my rooms, it's your. No charge."

"I'm here for information," Kala said. She didn't introduce Aedon to the brothel owner. "Is Selwyn here?"

"Let me check the register." Yahaira returned to the computer pad embedded in the desk's scratched top. "No. Not this morning. He paid for a double session last night, though."

"What time?" Kala asked.

"Early evening. He was done and out the door by nine."

Aedon watched Kala absorb the information that Selwyn had *celebrated* hours before Aedon had visited the tavern. Her facial expression didn't change but her shoulders stiffened as she prepared herself to carry the heavy weight of betrayal.

"What girl?" Kala asked.

"His usual. Leaha."

Kala stepped closer to the desk. "Is she working this morning? I'd like to speak with her."

Yahaira pressed a button on her console.

The groggy voice of a young woman who had been awakened from a sound sleep replied with, "Yeah, what is it?"

"I need to speak with you," Yahaira told her.

"Why? Did some jack file a complaint against me?"

"No lip," Yahaira snapped. "Just get your ass in my office."

"Okay, okay. I'm coming."

A few minutes later, Leaha walked through the door. She was wearing a gauzy pink robe that fanned out behind her naked body, leaving nothing to the imagination. Limp brown hair framed an unremarkable face.

When she spotted Aedon, she smiled. Her gaze barely touched on Kala before moving on to the brothel's proprietor. "What's the problem?"

"No problem," Yahaira told her. "Sit down."

The prostitute did what she was told, but not before she cast Aedon a sideways glance that spoke volumes. She sat down in a chair and crossed her legs. Her foot swung impatiently as she waited for her employer to explain why she'd been summoned to the office.

"You had a double session with Selwyn last night," Yahaira said.

The prostitute shrugged. "He's one of my regulars."

"But double sessions aren't regular," Kala said, stepping into the conversation. "Are they?"

Leaha looked at her. "No, but he was in a bull of a mood last night. Said he wanted to make sure I didn't forget him since he wouldn't be visiting me anymore."

"Why?" Kala prompted. "Was he going somewhere?"

Another shrug. This one brought the shoulder of the gauzy robe down the prostitute's arm. She didn't bother to right it. "He told me that he'd gotten a promotion."

"What kind of promotion?"

"A new factory in the western province. A shift foreman. More money. An apartment of his own." Leaha snickered. "He asked me to go with him. Can you imagine that? Me working in a factory."

"When was he leaving?"

"This morning. Why?"

Kala stepped back, letting Yahaira know that she'd gotten the information she needed.

"You can go back to your room," Yahaira told Leaha. "Get some sleep. Your shift starts in two hours."

Yahaira looked to Kala as the door closed. "I take it that wasn't good news."

"Let's just say it wasn't a total surprise," Kala said as if the news hadn't shaken her very foundation. "I'm leaving the city for a while."

Yahaira came to her feet. "I won't ask why, but I will ask you to be careful."

Kala smiled slightly. "I'll send word as soon as I can."

Aedon and Kala were outside in the rear alley before Kala's energy gave out. She slumped against the wall, her expression blank, her eyes staring straight ahead. The truth about Selwyn held her in its power.

"Selwyn's reward for betraying us was a factory promotion."

Aedon wanted to pull her into his arms, but he knew his embrace couldn't protect her from the reality she'd been forced to face. Yet even as he told himself that his touch couldn't cure what plagued her, his hands were rubbing up and down Kala's arms, warming the chill that had her trembling.

When she looked up at him, his body tightened with a heat he hadn't felt for years. Her expression was a mixture of confusion and conflict. Aedon knew it was only a matter of time before she collapsed on her feet.

"Yahaira was right. You need some sleep," he said knowing his voice was communicating more than words. Fortunately, Kala was too stressed to recognize the emotion under the statement.

Her lips were drawn and pale, yet nothing could hide the sensual promise they held. As for the rest . . . she was everything a man could want.

Everything he couldn't have.

A woman who became more intriguing, more desirable, the longer he knew her. The contrast of female sensuality and warrior courage fascinated him.

"What about Selwyn? Betrayal shouldn't be rewarded," she said. Her voice was strained but it wasn't weak.

"It won't be," he promised.

There was no such thing as an actual hotel in Melgarr. People were recruited to work in the factories that churned out everything from agricultural machinery to food processors. Their lodgings were dormitory-style buildings built to house as many workers as possible. The right amount of money could get you a small apartment. An additional bonus could bribe the landlord into keeping your name off the housing register.

The workers who lived in these buildings had believed the promises of the corporate recruiters, the pledge of a new life on a new world. But the Conglomerate was a harlot, making sweet promises it had no intention of keeping, offering huge recruitment bonuses, and drawing in unsuspecting souls with the hint of treasures that lay waiting to be discovered in the outer regions. A liar and a cheat, but tempting nevertheless.

Once they were snared, the colonists quickly found themselves on a world where they were paid just enough to afford the necessities of life, all of which were supplied by the Conglomerate. Profits from the exorbitant prices paid for these necessities lined the pockets of stockholding merchants and landlords. Colonists who wanted to leave had to petition the colonial governor, who could grant permission once their recruitment bonus had been repaid in full.

The likely outcome, however, was that discontented workers found themselves out of work, without the wages they could have saved to repay the bonus. The result was a network of industrial planets fueled by cheap labor and ruled by egoistic tyrants like Avis Rendhal.

Aedon's lodging house was across the street from a distribution warehouse. He swiped his entry card through the scanner, then motioned Kala inside. A tube-lift took them to the twentieth floor. The interior hallways matched the building's overall blandness—dingy gray walls, scuffed floors, and metal doors marked with numbers. Aedon's apartment was at the end of the hall, close to the emergency exit.

"It isn't very impressive," he said once they were inside.

Kala looked around, then smiled sadly. "It's bigger than the one I called home for twelve years. All my father could afford was a two-room unit."

She tossed her turban on the bed, fluffed out her hair with trembling fingers, and walked into the kitchen. Once there, she checked out the food he'd stocked, and without being asked, began preparing a meal.

Aedon watched her, realizing three things. First, Kala needed the simple activity to keep her focused. Second, they needed food since neither of them had eaten for hours. Third, he enjoyed watching her.

He couldn't stop looking.

She was beautifully made, supple and graceful, essentially and exquisitely female. He wondered what she would be like as a sex partner. The way she moved suggested that she was comfortable with her sexuality. Would she enjoy slow, easy sex, or did she prefer it hard and fast and furious?

Hastily Aedon looked away from the kitchen, settling his sights on the single bed that filled most of the front living area of the overpriced accommodations. He hadn't thought about sex for a long time, but looking at Kala made him regret his self-imposed monasticism.

There were times, like now, when his body demanded him to put aside his mourning.

He knew his initial decision to keep Kala at a distance was the right one. The problem was keeping that distance when they were forced to hide in a cell of an apartment.

When the simple meal of rice, steamed vegetables and bread was served, Aedon directed his attention to refueling his body and his mind.

Kala did the same.

"The northern provinces are our best bet," she said midway through the meal. "Lots of open country and less police."

"Off world would be safer," Aedon said pointedly.

"No." Her tone was adamant, her golden-brown eyes fierce. "I've spent my life watching the Conglomerate rape Hachyn to fill the pockets of their shareholders. The factories pollute the air and the water, and the mines turn our mountains into rubble, while we're forced to watch the very life being leeched from the planet. When we win it back, and we will, it will take generations to undo the damage that's been inflicted."

Aedon wasn't surprised by her reply. The short time he'd spent with Kala had told him that she was embedded in the resistance movement up to her pretty neck.

"You said Jein coordinated the units from his console," he said conversationally. "Individually or jointly?"

"Individually. Each unit operates independently of the others. Jein was the only channel of communication, the only one who knew names, places, and contact codes. If one unit required the assistance of another, Jein arranged it. If one discovered something another unit needed to know, Jein was the conduit that information passed through. He *was* the resistance movement."

Aedon knew Kala was oversimplifying the facts, but to call her on it now would only provoke more distrust. The events of the last twelve hours had created an alliance between them, but it was still a fragile truce.

"What about your unit? The one operating here in the city. Was Selwyn the leader?"

"No."

Aedon arched a brow. "You?"

"Yes. Surprised?"

"No."

The show of respect wasn't what Kala had expected. She paused before voicing whatever retort she'd had poised on the tip of her tongue, then changed the subject.

"Jein was a man with a conscience," she said quietly. "He came to Hachyn with Rendhal, but after a few years his eyes were opened. By then he knew it was useless to object to the governor's way; others had, and it had cost them. Sometimes they paid with their lives. Jein used his rank as one of Rendhal's advisors to countermand orders, hiding his compassion beneath the bureaucracy of the colonial government."

Aedon remained silent, knowing Kala needed to purge her system of the emotions she'd been holding in check since the explosion.

"He did what he could behind the scenes," she said, continuing Jein's eulogy. "When Rendhal found out, he had Jein stripped of his rank and his property, and tossed into prison. He was tortured almost to death. Rendhal called him a traitor, but the people he had helped called him a savior. They risked their lives to free him, and he became that savior. Now, he's dead."

Moisture pooled in her eyes, but she didn't shed a tear. "If we can break away from the Conglomerate, it will prove that they're not infallible. Other worlds will follow."

"That's why Rendhal is doing everything he can to crush the movement," Aedon said. "Freedom is contagious."

He stood up and shed the robe he'd bought. Now that they'd eaten, it was time to get some sleep. An exhausted body led to an exhausted mind, and he was going to need his senses intact to get them out the city.

"You're hurt!" Kala said, leaving the table to come to where he was standing. She touched his back, just below the right shoulder, where blood was caked onto a jagged cut in the black leather.

"I'm fine," he said shortly. "A chunk of rock grazed me. It's not serious."

"It's serious enough to need attention."

She motioned for him to sit down at the table where she immediately set to work dressing the wound on his back, cleansing it with a mild antiseptic she'd found in a medical kit in one of the cabinets, then applying a regeneration ointment. She worked quickly, with the practiced skill of a field medic.

Outside the single, narrow window, rain was coming down in angry gray sheets. The darkened sky cast the illusion of twilight over the cramped apartment. Inside, Aedon was using up his self-control. Having Kala's delicate hands moving over his back and shoulder was sweet torture.

"Time to get some sleep," he said, standing up and stepping away from the soft hands that had branded his skin with each careful touch. As her silky hair had done each time it brushed over his bare arm. And her breath had done each time she leaned in close to make sure she had cleansed the wound properly.

He watched from across the room as she put away the medical kit, picked up the shawl she'd discarded, and walked into the bathroom to take a shower.

Alone for the first time in hours, Aedon mumbled a string of Korcian curses to himself, then poured himself a drink. It wasn't what his body wanted, but it would have to do.

Moving to the window, he sipped the worst whiskey he'd ever tasted and watched the storm release its fury on the city. Thunder rumbled and lightning arced. There was barely any light left in the sky. The storm cast everything into shades of gray.

Wherever he looked, factory buildings and exhaust stalks crowded the horizon. Aedon found himself thinking of the wild, restless jungles that covered his homeworld and the wild scent of the sea that blew inland whenever a storm was brewing.

Thoughts of Korcia and the life he'd left behind filled his mind only to be slowly replaced with the reality of the current world and the unexpected woman who was standing naked under the shower.

When Kala came out of the bathroom, her hair was a mass of damp curls that fell midway down her back. The features of her freshly scrubbed face were exquisite. Her nose was strong yet delicate, her lips full, her face dominated by wide, amber-colored eyes that were as intense as they were intelligent.

The only thing she was wearing was the fringed shawl. It was wrapped around her like a towel, leaving her shoulders and arms and legs bare. She had very nice legs, ending in narrow, high-arched feet.

"I know nothing about you," she said as she sat down on the side of the bed. There were no meals to prepare, no wounds to attend, no busy work to occupy her hands, so she crossed her long legs and looked to where Aedon was standing near the window. "Rendhal had murdered your family. How?"

"They were on a transport his pirates attacked," Aedon said, keeping the reply simple but truthful.

He wished he didn't understand another truth. Kala was beautiful and highly intelligent. Beyond that intelligence she was intimately familiar with the workings of the resistance. Aedon needed that familiarity, but he didn't need the complications of having a beautiful woman within easy reach. It was going to make for a complicated night and a complicated mission. His first goal had been to contact Eiven Jein.

The goal had been reached, but the circumstances had changed. Now, his link to the resistance was the beautiful woman sitting in front of him.

"My father was killed in an industrial accident," she

said. "When my mother couldn't afford to pay the land-lord, she was put out on the street. I was twelve."

"How did you manage after that?"

"My mother moved in with a factory supervisor who could afford a paid companion," she said solemnly. "I didn't like it, and I didn't like him. After a few years he decided that since he was paying for two females, why shouldn't he enjoy them both? I tried to get my mother to leave, but she was afraid he'd put her on a blacklist. You don't get hired again after that."

She looked away for a moment, then shook her head as though she were physically ridding her mind of the memory. When she looked at him again, her eyes were soft, her expression still distant, still turned inward. "I ran away and lived on the streets. I know every alleyway in the city, every deserted warehouse, every maintenance tunnel. They were my home before I joined the resistance."

A sad smile came to her face. "Yahaira was the one who introduced me to Jein. She found me stealing food. I hadn't eaten for days. She took me in."

Aedon clenched his fists and listened despite the overwhelming need not to see Kala the way he'd seen Leaha, a woman bought and paid for by the hour. He tightened his jaw against the turmoil of emotions rippling through him, the all-too-familiar feelings of anger and despair.

Kala wasn't his wife. She wasn't his woman. And despite what he wanted, he couldn't undo the past. Not hers. Or his.

She noticed the change in him and shook her head slowly. "It wasn't that way. Yahaira was hiding Jein in one of the suites. I became—"

"His eyes and ears and legs," Aedon said. His hands relaxed as he began to understand how Kala's life had unfolded. "Why didn't you tell Yahaira that Jein is dead? Still buying time?"

"Partly," she said. "But mostly it's because I couldn't bring myself to say the words. Yahaira and Jein were lovers before he was put in prison."

She folded back the coverlet on the bed. "So now you know my life history. Care to elaborate on yours?"

"I'm a pilot with decent soldiering skills," he said. "There isn't much more to tell."

It was obvious that Kala didn't believe the part about there being nothing much to tell, but she didn't press the issue. Aedon poured them both a drink, setting hers on the small table by the bed.

He knew he was playing a dangerous, dishonest game with her, and he despised having to do it. By telling her only part of the truth he was effectively lying to her, playing on her hatred of Avis Rendhal, playing on her quest for freedom and her love for her people. Yet he had no choice. Nothing could link him to the Directorate.

"You mentioned the northern provinces. Why?" he asked.

"It's where the resistance is the strongest." She sounded slightly surprised that he didn't know the fact already. "When the Conglomerate colonized Hachyn, they divided it into development quadrants. The northern provinces are in the fourth quadrant, the one scheduled to be *developed* next. The people who colonized there have had plenty of time to see their future unfold."

"And they don't like what they see," Aedon said dryly.

"Would you?"

Whatever Aedon expected, it wasn't what happened next.

Kala walked to where he was standing, then reached up with both hands and cupped his face, her fingers gently caressing his cheeks, his eyelids, his temples.

Aedon could feel the tension in her body; the aftershock had finally arrived—anger, grief, and uncertainty were demanding acknowledgment. Needing release.

Aedon understood the need. It was mirrored inside him.

The need to touch and be touched.

A need that required little more than a spark to ignite an explosion.

six

HE HELD HER at arm's length. "Do you know what you're doing?"

"Yes."

Emotion rippled through the single word as soulful eyes searched his face, and Aedon saw what Kala had refused to let him see until now—loneliness.

He had lived with the same emotion too long not to recognize it in another.

When she moved toward him again, Aedon hesitated for a moment, waiting for her to step away, giving her a last chance to withdraw.

She didn't.

He kissed her with a ferocity that spoke of a long-held control quickly disintegrating. His mouth was hard against hers, his strength overpowering. He could feel the loneliness that clung to her like a shroud, a loneliness he understood all too well.

Fire against fire, she fought him; not to be free, but to be closer. To possess and be possessed.

Then she was moving, backing away and reaching for the knot that held the shawl in place.

He watched wordlessly as the silky fabric rippled down her body, over her hips, and onto the floor, imitating the unveiling of a statue. Naked, she came to him, sliding into his arms, raising her mouth to be kissed again.

Her hands moved slowly, dawdling over the muscular planes of his chest, idling at the waistband of his trousers as if disrobing him were all part of an ancient ritual. She drew his mouth to hers and kissed him deeply. Then she lightly kissed his eyelids and the line of his jaw. Her hands moved to his chest, caressing and teasing the flat, hard nipples.

Logic told Aedon to stop, but arousal came to him like a long-lost friend, beckoning him to take what she was offering.

She guided him to the bed and he lay down. The rain-soaked day cast long shadows over her slender body. Aedon moved his hand caressingly up the length of her outer thigh. She was delicately formed, but there was strength under her pale skin, muscles tuned by years of surviving, running if she had to run, standing and fighting if there was no other way.

Not a word was spoken as she climbed astride his legs and began to touch him, her hands moving gently over his stomach and chest. She rose above him, her eyes bright with passion. When she leaned forward to kiss him again, Aedon was treated to the pleasure of silky hair cascading over his chest.

Her lips explored him. Her tongue found the hollows of his body and caressed each one, licking him, sucking on his skin.

Her hands teasingly skirted his groin before she grasped him between her hands. Her touch was slow and languorous, yet insistent. Aedon's body answered the way it had been designed to respond. He grew even harder under her touch.

He heard her breathing change and gently began to return her touch, running his hands over her, exploring her, indulging her. What titillated him the most was her unbridled passion, her uninhibited movements, her unashamed pleasure in what they were doing.

She was slender, but her body was sturdy and sleekly muscled, her breasts small, but firm, with dark aureoles circling pink, responsive nipples. Her skin was cool and smooth, glowing with an alabaster luster. Her long fingers stroked him, making him shiver with sensual anticipation. Her fingernails lightly grazed his inner thighs while her lips and teeth nibbled at his stomach, her thick, silky hair brushing against him with every move.

They explored each other in the heavy silence, prolonging the anticipation, heightening their desire. Her eyes were closed now, her head tossed back, her wetness teasing him, sweeping over him until Aedon thought he'd lose control and climax before he was inside her.

She moved until her hips were directly above his, her body open and waiting to be filled. Aedon slid into her and stopped. Her channel was moist silk around him, hot and warm and snug.

She moved with the insistence and rhythm of a ballet dancer. It was all Aedon could do to control himself, but he did. He stayed with her, rising and falling, sensitive to the pitch and roll of her need.

He whispered her name only to have her fingertips press against his lips. She continued to move, slowly, rhythmically, and he moved with her.

She arched her back and moaned softly, pinning her hips even more tightly against him, taking him completely, caressing his shaft with every glide and clench of her body. Unable to stop himself, he pushed even deeper into her.

Her climax came in a series of tiny, intense convulsions that drove Aedon with increasing passion to find the same sweet release, the same hot rush of pleasure.

All control ebbed away. Sharp prickles needled his spine. It was coming. Soon. His legs stiffened. His breath caught in his throat. He wanted to prolong the sensation, but he couldn't.

And then it came. The shudders. Muscles stiffening to contain the pleasure. The thick wetness of his orgasm. The final spasms of release. Joy and pain so intimately bound they were a single emotion.

In the aftermath, he saw the glint of tears in her eyes and felt the faint, uncontrollable trembling of her body. Gently she drew his head to her shoulder, and with light fingers she stroked his hair, traced the contours of his neck and shoulders.

"The family you lost," she whispered, ending the silence. "It was your wife, wasn't it?"

When he didn't answer, she leaned upon one elbow, watching him, running a fingertip across his chest, tracing his chin, then resting one finger lightly upon his uncompromising mouth. "Aedon."

"Yes," he admitted after a long moment. "And our child."

"I'm sorry." She kissed him tenderly.

For a moment Aedon's mouth stayed hard and ungiving beneath hers. Then his lips parted and he returned the kiss. In spite of everything, he felt the tension drain away. He closed his eyes.

"Her name was Nazlean," he said. "My daughter's name was Cassandra. She was three years old."

When the uneven thumping of his heart had settled to a quiet rhythm, and the arm that held her relaxed, Kala turned her mouth to his ear and said, "Nazlean and Cassandra are beautiful names."

"They were my life," he said, his voice strained as the past drifted over him in a painful cloud.

He had thought that losing his wife and child had hollowed out his soul, eviscerating him, leaving a void that couldn't be filled by another human being.

He'd been wrong.

Tonight a beautiful young woman had broken through the bars of his personal prison with a single kiss, opening the door he had thought securely locked.

He'd dreaded this moment for four years. Consciously, he had avoided it. Subconsciously, he had always known that temptation and desire would eventually win—that the need to be a living, breathing man would override the celibate existence of a grief-stricken widower.

He'd left the Fleet for the Directorate because it was a way to extract vengeance for Nazlean and Cassandra's deaths, and yet it had been more. He'd also come to Hachyn to help its people find a new way of life. A new beginning. But he hadn't expected that beginning to touch him so personally.

Outside, the storm was subsiding, reduced to a steady drizzle. The rain and wind became a lullaby, and Kala drifted off to sleep in his arms.

Aedon lay awake, feeling Kala's body surrender to the comfort of sleep. He looked down at her relaxed features, soft and vulnerable as she slept. Their innocence was at odds with the strong-willed presence she radiated when she was awake.

Right or wrong, he had cast aside the cloak of mourning. Holding Kala in his arms was proof of that.

Enjoying the feel of her soft body, the brush of her breath against his bare shoulder, and the pleasure that still soaked his senses told him that the past was behind him. Replaced by the future, but not forgotten.

Never forgotten.

Kala's eyes opened. A sound, a scrape—an intrusion on the silence of the room that had nothing to do with the sounds of the outside world. It was closer, more personal. She blinked at the indented pillow beside her, and despite everything that her mind was putting together, she felt a sudden sadness that Aedon had left the bed.

The reason she had chosen to trust a man whom she had the least reason to trust was inexplicable, and yet Kala realized that she had come to the same conclusion Jein had reached the previous night.

"Take her and keep her safe."

Jein had entrusted her to Aedon Rawn with his final words. Hours later, she had given herself to the man with unique Korcian eyes and a haunted heart.

For most of her twenty-six years, Kala had felt like Sisyphus pushing the boulder up the highest mountain only to have it roll back down. Personal satisfaction had eluded her. She had reached for it, stretched for it, yet she'd never really captured the sweet sensation of fulfillment.

The closest she'd ever come was Eiven Jein.

She had loved Jein, fought by his side, shared in his hopes and dreams, and yet she had never allowed herself a single moment of personal happiness. She had always told herself that it would come later—after Hachyn was a free world. Her life could wait.

Jein had argued with her, insisting that life had to be lived in individual moments. That doubt and opportunity had to be grasped with equal fervor. Nature had a way of demanding order, he'd told her. For each loss, there was a gain. For each death, a birth. For each separation, a coming together.

Kala finally understood what he meant.

Oddly, she felt at peace with herself. She knew that peace would end soon. She also knew that making love with Aedon had been a reactionary response to the desperate feelings Jein's death had aroused. But for now, this hour, this moment, in this place, she was at peace.

She got out of bed and wrapped the shawl around her nakedness, then looked toward the bathroom. Aedon was standing in the doorway, studying her. There was so much she wanted to say, so much she wanted to ask, but she was hesitant to break the spell their lovemaking had created.

She smiled instead, deciding to leave words for later.

"It's almost dark." He paused by the bed. His fingers played with her hair then stroked her cheek. Gently, he bent down and kissed her lips. She wanted to wrap her arms around his neck and pull him to her, but he backed away. "Get dressed, and then we'll talk. We need to get out of the city tonight."

She went into the bathroom and adjusted the shower temperature to a steamy hundred-plus degrees. As the water washed over her body, Kala couldn't keep from turning events over and over in her mind, categorizing the ensuing emotions because they had to be dealt with one at a time.

Grief for Jein first, anger at the suppressive political arena that had caused his death, and still that indomitable remnant of hope that one day Hachyn would be a free world, enjoying everything that freedom implied.

As for Aedon Rawn, she had no idea where her feelings for the handsome Korcian would take her. There was so much about him that puzzled her—so many unanswered questions. He had barged into an empty space in her life and the possibilities he brought with him were impossible to resist. One of those possibilities was to seize the moment before it disappeared.

Kala knew better than to view him without faults or flaws. He had lost his wife and child to the Conglomerate the same way she had lost Jein. Last night they had used their bodies to express that common grief. Still, Kala couldn't ignore the feelings that remained.

Aedon had awakened something in her that she had no idea she possessed. She was still in awe of the flowing undercurrent of femininity that surged within her.

When she returned to the kitchen, wearing the black leggings and dark dress, she'd saved from the previous night she found him sitting at the small table, sorting through an array of hand weapons.

He looked up, then pushed a cup of hot tea across the scarred tabletop toward her.

"You smuggled more than grenades," she said. The two laser pistols, three easily concealed daggers, and a tranquilizer gun looked small in comparison to the high-power laser rifle. "How did you get them past the guards at the docking station?"

His smile was pure predator. "That's the one good thing about a corrupt corporate colony; it isn't hard to find a dishonest guard willing to take a bribe."

"Did you get the grenades off the ship, too?"

"No. Too bulky. But they're safe where they are for the time being. I paid my docking fees for a full month," he assured her. "Besides, they wouldn't have been tracking us to intercept an arms transfer if they thought the grenades were still onboard my ship."

"You're right." Kala sank into the chair opposite him.

"What?" he asked, seeing her expression turn sour.

"I should have known that without being told."

"Don't be too hard on yourself."

Kala couldn't keep her shoulders from slumping any more than she could keep the doubt from her voice. "Jein was the glue that held us together," she said in a near whisper. "When the others find out that he's dead . . ."

He looked at her, his eyes gentling to a soft, shimmering gray. "Commanders die on the battlefield in any war, but the armies they lead aren't necessarily doomed to failure. A well-trained, well-disciplined army keeps fighting because there's always a commander in the wings. Someone ready to step forward and assume responsibility."

The calm, factual tone of his voice brought Kala's head up to meet his gaze. He was inspecting the laser rifle, his hands strong and capable as they slid out the rechargeable cartridge, checked it, then snapped it back into place. He performed the task as easily as breathing. It was an automatic reflex, an extension of his survival skills.

At that moment, sitting in the near dark, his eyes gleaming silver and blue, his face etched in shadows, Aedon Rawn looked to be exactly what he was—a man made for war.

"Are you thinking to take Jein's place?"

He dismissed the remark with a shake of his head. "I'm not a Hachynite. Your people won't accept an outsider as their leader, nor should they. Jein trusted you more than anyone. And I suspect that you know more about his methods than you're willing to admit. Who better to take his place than the person he trained to lead the resistance here in the capital?"

"Me!"

Her astonishment made him laugh. Eyes that had softened to a gray as crisp and clear as polished metal were now a brilliant midnight blue. He laid one of the laser pistols on the table in front of her. "Warrior queens have been leading their people to victory since the beginning of time."

Kala sat, looking at the pistol, knowing she had to think clearly. It was more than meeting the challenge in Aedon's eyes, it was defining what was before her, what would be expected of her by others. Above all, she knew she couldn't give into the panic of losing Jein, even the perception of panic—a panicked mind made mistakes. She had faced down fear and uncertainty before. She could do it again.

Aedon was right. She knew much more than she'd told him. She knew everything that Jein had known—the placement of the resistance units, the location of their hidden munitions, the name of each provincial resistance leader, and more important, she knew the enemy. Not just through her eyes, but through the eyes of a man who had once been one of them.

Kala reached for the pistol, then lifted the hem of her dress to slip it into a thigh holster. She added one of the daggers, placing it in the holster where it could be slipped out when needed.

Doubt had been replaced with determination.

"We can use the maintenance tunnels to keep us away from the police," she said, "but they won't get us out of the city."

Aedon left the table and walked the few feet to where he'd discarded the brown robe he'd bought on the outskirts of the city. Its loose folds would conceal the laser rifle.

Kala inclined her head slightly, observing him. How attractive he was. How strong and confident. She longed to reach out and trace the wrinkles at the corners of his eyes, to smooth the taut line of his mouth. God, she was so tempted.

His eyes shifted to meet hers and she could almost feel their caressive warmth.

"Lejan is the largest city in the northern province. There's a resistance unit we can contact," she told him. "The air-buses run on a regular schedule, but passengers are scanned for weapons."

"A shuttle would be faster."

"The only shuttles on Hachyn belong to the police and the governor's Honor Guard."

He returned to the table to take up his own weapons. Once they were concealed in the various pockets sewn into his black trousers and tunic, he lifted his head to smile at her. "Then we'll just have to steal one."

Kala made an exasperated sound. "That's not exactly what I'd call keeping a low profile."

He shrugged off the cautionary remark. "The authorities expect us to play it safe."

His uncanny, chameleon gaze had a hypnotic effect that quenched any argument Kala had against his daring plan. She suppressed the urge to kiss him. What didn't fade from her mind was the ironic fact that they were both armed to the teeth with a war waiting just outside the door.

Kala communicated her decision with a flash of golden-brown eyes and her own shrug. "Why not? We've been doing the unexpected since the moment we met."

seven

THEY LEFT THE maintenance tunnel a few hundred yards from a shuttle platform used by the police brigade assigned to the northernmost sector of the city. Metal barricades and "knife nests" of barbed wire surrounded the platform, allowing a narrow entryway onto the elevated landing tarmac. Two armed police officers stood on either side of the gateway, perfunctorily examining the faces and IDs of their fellow officers as they passed.

The rain had stopped, but the moon was still hidden behind a bank of charcoal clouds. The muted moonlight that filtered through the clouds was eerie, lending a somber cast to the end of a long, overcast day. The air was humidly oppressive. The night itself seemed to exhale the hot, moist breath of a predator lying in wait.

Aedon crouched in the darkness next to the maintenance hatch, his eyes scanning the area, his mind swept clean of all thought but the task ahead of him.

The guards were human ornaments. The precinct's nighttime illumination was glaring, silhouetting the outside guards like targets on a firing range while simultaneously impeding their ability to see anything in the surrounding darkness.

Off to his left, glinting in his peripheral vision, was what Aedon had hoped to find—a newly fueled shuttle, fresh from the hangar and waiting for a pilot.

A few hundred yards beyond the hangar, another building crouched low on the horizon. Faint shadows appeared and vanished—sentries on patrol.

The chemical exuberance of adrenaline seeped into Aedon's veins, bringing his body to a heightened awareness of his surroundings. He closed his eyes for a moment, letting the night envelop him, letting new energy spill into his body for the upcoming fight.

He could feel the wind blowing inland from the nearby sea, smell the mixture of salt air and factory fumes, and sense the treachery that came with a world where corruption was the norm, greed the rule of law, and death a certainty for anyone who tried to change the status quo.

Kala knelt next to him, the soft sound of her breathing the only hint that he wasn't alone. She leaned in close and whispered in his ear. "I think it's time for you to tell me how this is supposed to work without us getting killed."

Aedon surveyed the area once again, this time as a tactician. His military training had taught him that the simplest approach often proved the most successful. Each additional twist added at least one, if not more, opportunity for failure.

Like everything, combat fighting followed certain rules. The advantage went to the soldier able and willing to surprise the foe. But once advantage was achieved, it had to be maintained. That was the tricky part.

"Surprise," he whispered in reply. "Shock and hit."

Kala looked at him for a long moment, but whatever she was searching for—a flicker of doubt, a blink of fear—wasn't there.

Aedon had grown up on a planet with a landmass that was 80 percent tropical jungle. He'd played in that jungle as a child and trained in it as a Fleet recruit. A man could survive the violent domain if he was strong enough, quick enough, and fast enough to think on his feet.

Aedon had learned to survive.

His gaze drifted magnetically to the beautiful woman kneeling beside him in the dark. While he watched, Kala drew the laser pistol from its holster, revealing the soft skin that he had caressed so lovingly only a few hours ago, but there was nothing soft about the expression on her face. The lady had grown up in her own kind of jungle, and like him, she knew what it took to survive.

"Stay here," he told her. "When I give the signal, run like hell for that shuttle."

"What signal?"

He gave her a hard kiss, then flashed her a bright smile that could barely be seen in the dark. "You'll know it when you see it."

With that, he was gone, disappearing into the darkness, becoming black on black as he crawled on elbows and knees into the grass at the edge of the tree line to get a closer look at the hangar. The guards were three stout men who made no attempt to hide their weapons.

Aedon had an edge-on view of the platform about two hundred yards across a carefully cleared no-man's zone. Beyond that, a series of outbuildings clustered around the police precinct headquarters. Two more guards chatted idly by the front entrance.

So far he had counted nine guards, and he would bet that there were at least as many more inside the headquarters building. However, they weren't taking their work seriously, obviously relying on safety in numbers, trusting bulk and brawn rather than brains.

There was almost no cover between Aedon and the hangar, just a few trees and shrubs trimmed into obedience.

He took advantage of what was available, making his approach to the front of the hangar on an angle, weaving from cover to cover. At each point, he paused to observe the guards, but saw no sign that they were aware of his presence. They were content to chat, laser rifles slung over their shoulders.

One more silent rush brought him to the hangar.

Time to do it.

Aedon tossed back the front flap of his robe and the laser rifle came out of hiding. But it wasn't his weapon of choice. He needed to get inside the hangar without being seen or heard. Putting the rifle down on the ground, within easy reach, he pulled the tranquilizing gun out of its hidden pocket, took aim, and sent one hangar guard staggering to the ground.

Another dart was delivered a few minutes later, hammering a nerve-dulling dose of nerve juice into a second unsuspecting guard.

The third hangar guard caught a full load of the toxin in the neck and went down with a groan that left his mouth gaping open.

Aedon inserted a fresh clip of darts on the run, pausing by the downed bodies just long enough to make certain the drug was doing its work.

A shadow made its appearance on the hangar's outside wall.

Aedon swirled around and dropped to the ground. Target acquisition took a mere second, and the guard flopped hard onto his back, his eyes staring emptily at the night sky.

Aedon listened for other guards, but the only sound that came to his ears was the whisper of wind and an occasional muffled word as the platform guards continued talking among themselves.

From where he was poised in the dark, just outside the hangar door, Aedon surveyed the area again. The closest guards were at the platform and the precinct building.

Close enough to use their laser rifles, but not close enough to realize that their numbers had just been substantially reduced.

After a few moments of studying the lay of the land, Aedon eased to his right and into the hangar. Cat-footing noiselessly, he inspected various items used to perform maintenance on the shuttles before stopping at the fueling tube that protruded above the floor, its source an underground tank.

He turned the valve, allowing a small steady stream of the highly flammable fuel to dampen the hangar floor.

He was headed for the shuttle when a side door opened with a jerk. The guard took one look at the man in black and raised his weapon, intent on making a quick kill. Aedon threw himself forward, striking the guard in the knees and knocking him off balance. The two collapsed in a tangle, with the guard momentarily on top and the Korcian intruder flat on his stomach.

No stranger to unarmed combat, Aedon could kill a man with his hands as readily as he could with a pistol or a knife.

Experience had taught him that it wasn't always the strongest or even the quickest who survived a hand-to-hand clash. All the strength in the world did a man little good if he didn't know how to use it the right way.

As the constricting weight of the guard held him down, Aedon let himself go limp. The man's grip loosened and he shifted to get a better hold. In that instant Aedon struck.

He flipped over in a wrestler's roll, bringing the tranquilizer gun around to bear on his opponent. Aedon's left hand automatically clutched for the guard's throat, but he wasn't giving up easily. The guard swung his fist in an arc that connected solidly with Aedon's wrist, knocking the dart gun from the warrior's hand. A second later, the guard's look of satisfaction changed to pain as Aedon's knee exploded into his groin.

The guard collapsed on his side, all interest in Aedon lost as he struggled with the agony of having his testicles hammered into his body. Aedon sprang to his feet, retrieved the dart gun, and put a dose of tranquilizer into the man's shoulder. The guard twitched, then went limp with both hands still cupped between his legs.

Again, Aedon turned toward where the shuttle was parked on the maintenance tarmac.

Right now, the trick was to get to it while appearing as if he had every right to board the shuttle. The distance from the barricade guards and the platform was enough to disguise his true appearance.

He began walking, moving with the air of a man with a task to perform, showing just enough speed to indicate that the job was important, but not enough to extract interest from anyone who might be watching. It was a fine line, and Aedon knew he was walking it as he got closer to the shuttle's open hatch.

He could see several heads turning his way, but no one called out to challenge his right of passage.

Once inside, he stripped off his robe and leaned his laser rifle within easy reach of the pilot's chair. It took only a few minutes to familiarize himself with the navigational controls and the shuttle's weaponry. The inventory was impressive—two laser cannons and a powerful Gatling gun that could fire in excess of five hundred rolls a second.

The Conglomerate used these armed shuttles against Hachyn citizens. People foolish enough to demonstrate their grievances in public would be mowed down by the shuttles' powerful guns. This provided yet another reason for Hachynites to form the underground resistance.

Aedon's next task took a good five minutes. He had to locate the shuttle's tracing registry and erase the program.

Aware that time was passing and that Kala would be getting impatient, Aedon reached for the ignition control and began a ten-second countdown that would end with the gravity-thrusters lifting the shuttle free of the tarmac. By second three, he was at the hatchway entry, laser rifle in hand.

At T minus five seconds he saw Kala running toward him, her slender legs eating up the ground as she raced to be onboard before the thrusters ignited.

An alarm sounded at T minus seven. Someone had noticed that the shuttle was preparing to take off without clearance. Guards scrambled out of the precinct buildings, some heading for the hangar, others running toward the deployment platform and their own armed shuttles.

A second later Aedon fired at the guards who had headed for the maintenance tarmac, laying down cover for Kala as she sprinted the last few yards to the mesh catwalk that would fold up at T minus nine because the shuttle would be airborne two seconds later.

Laser fire chewed up the ground around her, spitting scorched dirt into the air. Aedon returned the fire, then held out his hand and pulled Kala inside, instantly pushing her behind him.

He squeezed off another series of deadly blue-light fire before the hatchway buzzer sounded and the catwalk began to fold inward. The guard closest to the shuttle screamed out in pain, then crumpled as blood erupted from a severed femoral artery.

"Get strapped in," Aedon ordered Kala, shouting over his shoulder as he moved to the shuttle's rear hatch used primarily for loading and unloading supplies.

He manually bypassed the safety lock, then eased the hatchway open just enough to get his rifle in position. One carefully aimed shot and the fuel that had leaked onto the hangar floor burst into a stream of sparkling flame.

In his mind's eye, Aedon followed the fire through the underground tanks and into the flex-lines that led to the fueling station on the main platform.

He started a second silent countdown in his mind as he

climbed into the pilot seat and took the shuttle up and away in a sharp turn toward the open ocean.

Behind them, the platform exploded into a pyramid of flame.

eight

AEDON PROGRAMMED IN a course that would take the shuttle due north, along the coast. The precinct explosion hadn't only eliminated the shuttles attempting to launch in pursuit, it had destroyed all evidence that one of the governor's prized airships had escaped.

"Tell me about the factories," Aedon said, letting the shuttle's autopilot maneuver them through the dark-bellied storm clouds that had poured out their wrath over the city hours earlier.

Kala looked at him, then shook her head. "You just stole a shuttle, blew up an entire police precinct, and you want to talk about factories?"

"Humor me." He was checking his weapons, always the conscientious warrior. "Are they all like the ones I saw in Melgarr?"

"No. The ones in Melgarr were the first factories built. The ones being built now are manned by robot workers. I guess the word's gotten out that Hachyn isn't the utopia the recruiters make it out to be."

Aedon smiled as he connected robot-manned factories to the rumors of Conglomerate arms production. Robot workers didn't gossip about whatever was being made on the assembly lines.

Aedon took back manual control of the shuttle just long enough to make a minor correction in their course. Within minutes the clouds gave way to clear skies.

"Have you ever been inside one of the new factories?" he asked.

"You've forgotten you're on Hachyn," she said laughingly. "Half the signs on this planet read Authorized Personnel Only."

Kala studied the man sitting in front of the control panel. She had been on her share of raids, but she'd never seen anything like the Korcian in action.

He had been fast, accurate, and deadly.

Having spent most of her life in a world of probables and improbables, possibles and impossibles, she had a keen sense for what was real and what wasn't. Kala knew that tonight she'd seen the *real* Aedon Rawn—a man who carried the detachment born of self-control. Total control. A patina of authority that had nothing to do with his status as a freelance pilot.

She had seen that detached authority throughout the previous night and day—when he'd met with Jein; when he'd confronted her on the beach; when he'd left her in the dark to take on a precinct of police single-handedly.

Even now, piloting a stolen shuttle, he wore the assurance of self-control as easily as his clothing.

The image of the black-clad warrior didn't completely blend with the identity of a freelance pilot, and yet the two could easily overlap. A loner trolling the galaxy for profitable cargo would have to be able to take care of himself, especially here in the outer regions.

"Were you in the Korcian Guard or the Fleet?" she asked

without preamble, watching him as she gauged his reaction to the unexpected question.

"The Fleet," he said. "Once I got into deep space, I was hooked."

The answer came smoothly from his lips, Kala thought, almost too smoothly, as if it were a practiced response.

In spite of what had happened between them, she still retained the caution life as a resistance fighter had brought to her. She trusted Aedon, but she wasn't entirely sure that she believed him. An odd paradox, to be sure, but one that served to reinforce her initial feeling that there was more to the Korcian than he was willing to share.

"Do you really think the factories are the path to Rendhal's destruction?"

"What do you think the robots are manufacturing?"

Kala shrugged. "I'm not sure. Whatever it is, it's not being manufactured and assembled in the same place."

His eyes took on a piercing quality. "What makes you say that?"

"Too many transports," she told him. "They load at one factory and unload at another. That means components, not a finished product. Why? What do you think the robots are making?"

"Weapons," he said succinctly. "I think the Conglomerate has decided it's time to move out of the boardroom and onto the battlefield."

A chill ran the length of Kala's spine. She looked at Aedon's face, hoping that he was making an off-the-wall assumption. Nothing she saw reassured her. His eyes were a clear, chilly gray. The man who had made love to her earlier in the day was gone, replaced by the warrior who had taken on a precinct of armed guards.

A second shiver of trepidation followed the first. If Aedon was right, there was more than trouble ahead. A Conglomerate-controlled military would be the overture to total control of the outer regions and the end to any hope of independence.

"If you're right, it explains why new factories are being built in the third quadrant much faster than they were in the first and second," she said. "It also explains why Rendhal pushed up the development schedule for the fourth quadrant."

"The outer regions take up half the galaxy," he said. "That means a big army and a hell of a lot of weaponry."

"You can't honestly believe that the Conglomerate plans on taking on the Korcian Empire *and* the League of Planets."

"Only if they're convinced that they can win," Aedon said dryly. His eyes took on the color of a midnight storm. "The Conglomerate may appear invisible on the surface, nameless men in corporate offices, but those corporate offices are *in* the League and the Empire. Bribery and blackmail are powerful weapons. If you want to influence something as crucial as the debate over the outer regions, money can grease the wheels, and no one has more money than the Conglomerate. Money can certainly buy weapon schematics, and that's all they would need. The colonies provide the raw materials."

Kala exhaled sharply. "And the factories."

She sat back and thought about what Aedon had just said. It was vaporous speculation, theory with no solid foundation, and yet, the hypothesis rang true. The Conglomerate was money hungry, it would stand to reason that they were just as power hungry.

A navigational sensor, set to alert them when their designated coordinates had been reached, chimed softly.

Aedon assumed manual control and began gliding the shuttle out of the night sky and down toward the planet's surface. The coordinates Kala had given him put them two thousand kilometers north of Melgarr in the northern province.

Not wanting to risk landing the shuttle in Lejan, she had selected a secluded area near the foothills of the Moviash Mountains. At the highest elevations, the mountains were swept by winter snow and assaulted by arctic winds, while far below, the fertile valleys sprouted wildflowers and leafy saplings.

"There." Kala pointed out a flat plateau that was more rock than dirt. "Land there."

Aedon did as she asked, bringing the shuttle to the ground. The foliage that rimmed the plateau would shield the small vessel from being seen from anything but a direct overhead view.

Kala unfastened her safety harness and began searching the shuttle's storage bins. When she found a laser rifle, she added it to her personal arsenal.

"Where to from here?" Aedon asked.

Kala gave him a smile dampened by the thought of a Conglomerate army with millions of rifles like the one she had just slung over her shoulder. "To friends, I hope."

They exited the shuttle to find clear skies overhead. Long streamers of moonlight illuminated the rural landscape. Dawn was still several hours away.

Kala took a moment to soak in the serene scenery, needing the peacefulness of the rolling hills and lush valleys to suspend the memory of what had happened at the precinct platform. She'd spent almost half her life at war with the colonial government, but she had never gotten used to the destruction and death.

Still, she'd never taken well to watching and waiting. If there was a choice, she preferred to join the fight. Being forced to hide in the dark while Aedon had made his way to the shuttle hangar had put her nerves on edge. Having laser fire lick at her ankles when she'd made a run for the shuttle had pumped an abundance of adrenaline into her bloodstream.

She needed a few deep breaths of fresh air.

Stepping away from the shuttle, she found a place where shadows and moonlight merged, where the soft whisper of the wind caressed her skin. A place where she could momentarily put reality aside and concentrate on nothing more than inhaling and exhaling clean, cool air.

She stood for a while, staring out over the rugged land, trying to imagine that it was as free as it looked.

Shrugging off the laser rifle, she leaned it against a tree trunk, then sat down on the cool grass. Aedon joined her, sitting down beside her and using the tree as a backrest.

"There's a small town a few kilometers due west of here. There's a resistance unit there. Alexander Ginomi is the leader," Kala told him. "He was born in Melgarr, but his family applied for rights to join an agricultural commune. With a growing population to feed and acres of empty land waiting to be cultivated, the Lejan province filled up quickly."

"I'll bet it did," Aedon said. "This is the first clean air I've breathed since arriving on Hachyn."

Kala looked toward the snowy peaks that gleamed arctic white in the pale moonlight. "The first time I saw the mountains, I cried. I'd never seen anything so beautiful."

"The key to winning any objective is to focus on what you want, then go after it—one small step at a time until the objective is gained," he said, reaching out to take her hand. "Don't worry, you'll keep the mountains beautiful."

Kala smiled, realizing that Aedon had immediately understood why she had cried the first time she'd gazed at the pristine beauty of an untouched wilderness. The Moviash Mountains were the last remaining refuge of her world, the only place where the poisonous sting of the Conglomerate hadn't been felt.

Dawn was a hint of color on the horizon when they left the shuttle and started out for the village. A sturdy bridge spanned the swift waters of the Naud River that originated in the mountains and flowed eastward to the open sea. Once the bridge was crossed, they passed through a tree-notched maze of forest trails before Aedon got his first look at the village of Vinsenia. Around them, mountain peaks reached toward the sky.

Light fingers of dawn stroked the horizon, painting a pale blush over the slate rooftops. Tucked into a snug alpinelike valley, the small town had a fairy-tale quality about it. The land rising on all sides was upholstered with greenery and wildflowers that gradually gave way to bare stone, sleek gray-pink granite that gleamed surreal in the first light of day.

There were mountains on Korcia, but not like the ones towering here. Not bare stone peaks crowned with sparkling ice crystals and billowy white clouds. Here on Hachyn things were different—different colors, different smells, cooler breezes.

As Aedon stood staring down into the valley, sunlight began to pour over the mountains in a brilliant avalanche. With it came a vivacity in the air that was almost palpable. He could see the river from where they stood. It ran with color, violet and green and shimmering blues, curving and broadening into a small delta before narrowing again to pass out of the valley and on to the sea.

His first thought was that Hachyn could indeed be a beautiful world if left to its own devices.

"How strong are the police forces in the village?" Aedon asked.

"A small contingent," Kala told him. "Twelve men at the most. There's a full garrison at Lejan, but the outlying villages are deceptively peaceful. Jein was adamant about not drawing attention to ourselves. Ginomi coordinates the entire province, with units in Lejan and Marous."

"How many men altogether?"

"Two thousand," Kala said. A soft breeze tugged at her hair and flattened the cloth of her dress against her firm breasts.

Aedon forced his mind to stay focused on the business at hand instead of recalling how responsive those breasts had been when he'd licked his tongue over and around them.

But even while the professional soldier in Aedon remained pragmatic, the man in him couldn't forget the passion that had filled a rainy day with pleasure.

He set down the backpack they had filled with supplies from the stolen shuttle, opened it, and took out a pair of high-powered binoculars.

Turning his back to Kala, he focused on the village. It appeared quiet, its residents still inside their homes. His gaze swept the main street, looking for police patrols. No men wearing the easily recognizable gray and red uniforms of Rendhal's police force were moving about, but he counted at least four surveillance scanners mounted on various buildings. Aedon assumed there were more, watching every route into and out of the sleeping township.

Turning slowly to his right, he exchanged his magnified view of Vinsenia's streets for one of the majestic Moviash Mountains.

Without a topography scan he couldn't be certain, but he suspected that the roughed range of granite slopes that paralleled the northern coast weren't as solid as they appeared to be. Like most mountains, they had been formed by primeval volcanic activity, the violent push and shove of planet mantles. The pristine snow capping their peaks was evidence of another force of nature—water.

When snow and ice melted, it seeped into every available crack and crevice, tunneling its way to lower elevations. Eons of water trickling and percolating its way through rock created underground caverns—the perfect hiding place for a band of rebels.

"I'll go into the village alone," Kala announced. "I know where the surveillance scanners are, and I know how to get around them. If I can, I'll bring Ginomi back with me. If I can't, I'll bring whatever help I can."

Aedon's dislike for the plan showed on his face.

"You asked me to trust you. Now, I'm asking for your trust in return," Kala said.

"I trust you. It's the people I don't know that I don't trust."

"The people you *don't* know encompasses the entire population of this planet," she said laughingly.

"Exactly."

"I'll be careful." She stepped closer; her hands cupped his face and she stared into his eyes.

It was an unexpected moment of intimacy that felt completely natural, part of the complex, passionate Kala he was slowly coming to know. He kissed her eyes closed, eyes made more golden by the early morning sun, and her mouth curved into a smile.

Then he kissed her for real, tenderly at first, then deeply. His arms encircled her lithe body, his hands exploring her as his mouth and tongue did the same, knowing all the while that they had crossed a line each had drawn for their own individual reasons, a boundary between natural impulses and pragmatic necessity.

Their relationship as lovers was uncharted territory, very possibly dangerous territory, but as Kala returned his kiss, Aedon knew there was no going back.

Kala made her way into the village from the south end. Her destination was a small café. After ordering a light breakfast, she paid for the meal with a gold coin.

The message that she wanted to meet with Alex Ginomi had been delivered.

Exactly fifteen minutes later, she entered a small shop that specialized in therapeutic tea and herbs. She spent another ten minutes browsing before gradually working her way toward the rear of the shop.

Making sure no one saw her, she used a small service door to slip into the working area of the store where Alex Ginomi was waiting for her.

He was a plump man of medium height. There was nothing distinguishing about his features except for a red birthmark on his left cheek. He greeted Kala with a nod of his balding head, then led her down a corridor that ended at a steel door. Once they were inside, he methodically keyed in a locking code that would keep them from being disturbed.

Still not speaking, Ginomi pointed toward a second door. It looked like a utility closet, but Kala knew it was actually a soundproof chamber—a narrow, shallow space with steel-lined walls, acoustically engineered to keep any sound waves from escaping that might register on a police scan.

Once Kala was inside the closet, Ginomi shut the heavy door behind him and locked it. Only then did he allow himself to smile and give Kala an affectionate hug of welcome.

"What is going on that Jein sends you to me personally?" he asked.

There were no chairs inside the tiny room, so Kala had to remain standing as she gave Ginomi the news of Jein's death.

The older man swayed on his feet. He braced his hand against the cool steel wall to hold himself upright as the devastating announcement hit home. "What will we do?"

"What we have always done," Kala said firmly. "We will continue to fight. No one else knows of Jein's death. I didn't even tell Yahaira. No one can know until we've had time to plan."

Ginomi was silent for a moment. The only noise was the faint sound of two people breathing shallowly inside the snug soundproof closet.

"Plan what?" he finally asked, straightening his shoulders as he realized what Kala had accepted on the beach. The past couldn't be undone.

She told him about Selwyn's suspected betrayal.

"If he is in the western province, we will find him," Ginomi replied angrily. "I have men there. Good men."

"Find him, but don't do anything that will alert the

police," Kala warned. "Selwyn wasn't privy to any information about the western provinces or about you and your unit here in the north. Jein made sure of that. Security was his paramount concern. Stay alert, be careful, and have your people watch Selwyn once they find him. If he's killed, the police will know that I escaped the ruins."

Sweat gleamed on Kala's skin. The closet had no ventilation. It was an airtight steel cage.

Her heart drummed inside her chest. This was the moment she'd been waiting for—would Ginomi agree with her decision? Take her orders? Accept her as the surrogate leader of the resistance now that Jein was dead?

"What more do you require of me?"

Kala exhaled the breath she'd been holding and smiled. "Food, a change of clothing, and a few days to piece together a plan to get inside one of the new western factories."

"What is in the factories that interests you?"

Kala told him about Aedon and his theory that the new factories were producing weapons.

Ginomi looked both shocked and impressed. He mumbled something about the gods helping them, then asked, "You believe this Korcian? You trust him?"

Kala's mind flashed over everything that had happened between herself and Aedon Rawn. She still had her doubts about him not being completely truthful with her, but her gut instincts hadn't changed.

"Yes. I trust him."

nine

AEDON HAD USED the binoculars to watch Kala enter the village, then watched again as she exited the café. She had disappeared from his sight when she'd taken a narrow avenue that led deeper into the small business district.

Now, unable to do anything but wait, he sat in the shadows of a thick thousand-year-old tree on the rocky slope above the village. As he waited, Aedon forced himself to relax, to take deep breaths of cool morning air, to decelerate his physical and mental processes. To rest.

Despite his efforts to clear his mind, thoughts of what his life had once been kept colliding with thoughts of what that life had now become.

The past melted into the present—and the future.

If there was a future.

He had no guarantee that he'd leave Hachyn alive. No guarantee that anything he did on the planet would make one iota of difference in its future, but the risk didn't frighten him.

Life was an unequal combination of risks and rewards.

Like the risk he'd taken yesterday when he'd pulled Kala into his arms. And the reward she'd given him by wiping away years of loneliness.

Like the risk he was taking now by keeping her at his side.

The reward of feeling that he was a part of something important, a fight that desperately needed to be won.

Risk and reward.

Life.

Three hours came and went before Aedon heard, then saw, Kala returning. She was carrying a backpack, as was her companion, a heavyset man who was puffing from the exertion of climbing the steep hill.

Standard tactical protocol, ingrained from years in the field, brought Aedon to his feet. He slung the laser rifle over his shoulder and pulled the strap taut, then tighter still so it became a fixed but flexible appendage to his upper body. The binoculars came up, and he studied the area behind Kala and the man he assumed was Alex Ginomi to make sure they hadn't been followed. When he was satisfied they were alone, he relaxed his hold on the laser rifle.

"I brought food," Kala said, smiling at him.

She put the backpack down within his reach, then turned to help her companion rid himself of the extra weight he had carried up the hill. "This is Ginomi."

The older man acknowledged Aedon with a nod and a grunt of relief as he sagged to the ground to catch his breath.

"I used to run up and down these hills when I was a boy," he said. "That was a very long time ago."

Kala opened one of the backpacks and handed Aedon a thermos of hot tea. "Ginomi doesn't think it's safe for us to stay in the village."

"It is a small town," the resistance leader explained. "Many of the policemen have been here as long as the residents. They know people by name and by sight.

Kala has been seen before. If asked, she is simply visiting an old friend of her father's—a brief respite from the noise and confusion of Melgarr. But a Korcian . . ." Ginomi shook his head. "There is no easy way to explain you."

"I understand," Aedon said.

Ginomi looked toward the village, his expression solemn. "Kala told me what you think is being manufactured in the factories. If you are right, the production must end."

"That's my plan," Aedon said. "But the only way to know for certain is have a look."

"It will be difficult." Ginomi's mouth curved into a crooked smiled. "Difficult. But not impossible."

"I'll need building schematics and topography maps. Detonators and explosives," Aedon said. "Can you supply them?"

Ginomi looked to Kala. She passed him a cup of cold water. "Tell him, Ginomi. If anyone can get inside, it's Aedon."

The resistance leader quenched his thirst before meeting Aedon's steady gaze. "We are not as ill-equipped as the governor would like to think," he said. "There is a camp in the mountains, near Marous. Many of the men worked in the western provinces, building the robot-factories. Perhaps they can help."

"How far?" Aedon asked.

"Four hundred kilometers. I will send word ahead and join you as soon as I can. You are a good pilot, yes?"

"Yes."

"You will need to be," Ginomi said. "The camp is not easily reached, even from the air."

Not easily reached was an understatement. The Marous camp was surrounded by a wall of granite that didn't have an inch of give in any of its four sides.

As Aedon made his decent from the clouds that permanently rested atop the western ridge of the Moviash Mountains, he throttled back on the shuttle's controls until the booster engines were sputtering from lack of fuel. The only way to bring the aircraft down was to turn it into a glider and hope like hell that the unpredictable winds didn't toss them into the mountainside.

He concentrated on the navigational panel where a series of green dots told him that the canyon was several thousand meters wide and over twelve hundred meters deep. The viewing port was useless. The wind was whipping snow in every direction. Visibility was zero.

"Six hundred meters," Kala read off their altitude as the shuttle bobbed back and forth as if it were riding on water rather than air. "Five hundred meters."

The wind lagged for a moment and Aedon caught a glimpse of sturdy evergreens dressed in snow and icicles. And lots and lots of hard, unforgiving rock.

The rock was too damn close.

He revved the starboard thrusters, edging them away from the canyon wall and creating a small cyclone of snow. The heat from the thrusters vaporized the snow into steam, making visibility even worse.

"Three hundred meters."

Aedon mumbled a Korcian curse.

"Two hundred meters," Kala said. "Almost there."

"No wonder the governor's men haven't found this valley," Aedon complained as he cycled just enough fuel through the thruster engines to keep them away from the cliffs. "They'd have to be suicidal to bring a craft in here."

"That's the idea. Eighty meters."

Aedon gritted his teeth, cut back the revs on the main engine, watched the altimeter, counted to ten, then cut the fuel to the thrusters.

They didn't land gently, but they landed in one piece.

"Amazing," said Kala as Aedon disengaged the controls. She reached for the warm jacket Ginomi had provided and slipped it on. "You're to be congratulated. Terk has always sworn that no one could land a shuttle in this canyon."

"Who's Terk?"

"The camp leader," Kala replied, tossing Aedon a jacket of his own. "He's one of the men Ginomi mentioned. Before he joined the resistance, Terk was a tech rigger at several construction sites in the western province."

"Tech rigger. Is that what I think it is?"

"Probably. His job was installing the computer equipment that keeps the robot assembly lines moving."

"Just the man I want to meet," Aedon replied as he headed for the exit hatch.

The voice-activated hatchway irised open and a cold blast of arctic wind swept in. Kala pulled up the hood of her jacket and gave a shiver. "I'd forgotten how cold it can get up here."

"How did you get in before?"

"The same way Ginomi's going to get here. An airscooter to the southern pass, then a long walk."

The world shifted sharply as Aedon stepped out of the shuttle and into the boxed canyon that hid a resistance camp from view of everyone but God himself.

He saw ground that was more ice than earth, a sky thick with clouds and swirling snow, and towering canyon walls that had witnessed the beginning of time itself.

Aedon admired the natural habitat only slightly more than he admired the camp's camouflage. A long-forgotten river had carved deep alcoves into the lowest strata of the cliffs, creating cavernous recesses that couldn't be seen from the air. Those natural depressions had been given fake stone walls that would insulate the people living behind them from any scans the police might use. The result was a rock encampment that was as secure as it was isolated.

"Amazing," Aedon mumbled as the door of the camp's headquarters opened and a young man stepped outside.

His face was clean-shaven, his features sharp and clearly defined, his pale blue eyes curious and assessing as he walked forward to greet them.

"Kala!" he called out, obviously pleased to see her.

Aedon watched as the man hurried forward then reached for Kala's hand and held it to his mouth, kissing her fingertips."

You got Ginomi's message?" Kala asked, withdrawing her hand from the young man's grasp and tucking it into the pocket of her jacket.

"Yes." He looked past her to where Aedon was standing. "I admit, I didn't think it could be done."

"Korcians are notoriously good pilots." Kala stepped back and linked her arm through Aedon's. "This is Aedon Rawn. Aedon, Terk Conrad."

Terk's expression went from friendly to resentful in the blink of an eye, making Aedon wonder if he hadn't flown into an ally's camp only to find a new enemy.

Kala awoke disoriented, taking a moment to realize where she was—the Marous camp. The rock walls of the room radiated a cold that challenged the insulated sleeping bag she had cocooned herself in last night.

Not wanting to give up the warmth of the sleeping bag just yet, Kala lay quietly and remembered the current of barely controlled anger she'd sensed in Terk from the moment she'd introduced him to Aedon Rawn.

The change in Terk's usual amiable personality to a man seething with jealousy had been shocking. She had known Terk for five years, ever since he'd joined the resistance. She liked him. She admired his skills. But she'd never encouraged his affection.

Now fully awake and restless, Kala rolled over on the

hard bed, no longer able to ignore the fact that she was sleeping alone.

Rather than join her in the camp's guest room, Aedon had chosen to spend the night in the shuttle.

"I think it would be best," was all he'd said, before brushing his lips over her forehead and leaving her alone.

The words had been like his expression, blandly neutral. Kala hadn't been able to tell what emotions, if any, lay beneath the words. She only knew that his eyes hadn't been unaffected. They had burned like silver fire just before he'd turned away from her and left the room.

The question that had plagued Kala before she'd finally given into exhaustion and fallen asleep was the same question that was plaguing her now—why had Aedon chosen to sleep alone?

Was he having regrets? Guilty regrets?

Did he see their lovemaking as an insult to his wife's memory? Or had making love to her opened an old wound?

Whatever the answer, Kala wasn't happy with the decision. She had held her emotions—her affection—in reserve for years, always focused on what the resistance needed, never what she needed. She hadn't felt love, or happiness, or even sadness. The only thing she'd let herself feel passionately about was the cause of freedom.

Now, she was alive with emotion.

She was also alone.

Frustrated, Kala didn't know whether it was fate or coincidence or some cruel joke of the gods that had brought Aedon Rawn into her life.

The only thing she did know for sure was that instead of sleeping nestled in the Korcian's strong arms, she had spent the night huddled inside a solitary sleeping bag.

After a few minutes, Kala got out of bed with a groan to acknowledge the aches and pains she'd accumulated over the last forty-eight hours, then got dressed. The usual camp attire was a drab brown, insulated, uniform-like jumpsuit and a knit cap.

She walked across the rock-walled canyon to the camp's mess hall. On her way, Kala paused to take a deep breath of crisp mountain air and to cast a glance toward the shuttle.

There was no gentle sunrise at such a high altitude, no slow, leisurely arrival of morning. Instead, night ended abruptly in the high mountains. The sun vaulted over the peaks and shone down on the frozen earth. One minute it was dark. The next minute, it was brilliant—sunlight refracting off crystallized snow and ice.

"Good morning," Terk said, coming up beside her. He was a handsome man in his own right with thick sandy hair and a ruddy complexion that reddened with anger or excitement. There was an earthy quality about Terk that Kala had always liked, but not this early in the morning.

She had hoped to get a cup of coffee before having to answer the questions she knew he was impatient to ask.

"Good morning," she said in reply, wondering if Terk knew that Aedon had spent the night in the shuttle rather in her bed.

Of course, he did. Terk knew every move that was made in the hidden canyon. As camp leader, it was his job to know.

"There wasn't much conversation last night, and Ginomi's message was just as brief," Terk said abruptly. "All I know is that he'll be arriving soon to discuss a new plan of attack. What does the Korcian have to do with it?"

Kala didn't care for Terk's tone of voice. It was impatient and superior. "Aedon is here because I brought him here," she said just as abruptly.

"Why? This isn't his fight."

"I wouldn't be so sure about that."

"What can you be sure of?" Terk demanded. The words

were accompanied by cold puffs of frosty air. "What do you know about him? What's he doing on Hachyn?"

"He smuggled in a load of grenades from Pecora."

"Are the grenades in the shuttle?"

"No."

"Then what good has he done?"

The question brought Kala's chin up. "He saved my life," she said, all congeniality vanished. "Add that to the fact that he's the most skilled fighter I've ever seen, and you have all the reasons you need for him being here."

"How did you get a police shuttle?"

Kala smiled. "Aedon commandeered it. He's a *very* resourceful man."

Without warning, Terk's hand flashed out and closed around Kala's arm, holding her in place. The action told Kala how upset he was. It also told her that this wasn't the time to challenge Terk's authority by announcing that she was taking Jein's place.

"What else is he?" Terk demanded. "Your lover?"

Kala laughed when what she really wanted was to slap Terk's hand away. "You know where he slept last night, what do you think?"

His hand fell away, leaving Kala free to walk across the canyon's frozen floor to the mess hall where camp members sat at long tables, talking among themselves between sips of strong, dark tea and coffee.

She knew a few of the people in camp on a first-name basis, having only visited the canyon twice in her tenure with the resistance. Like Terk, most of them had worked and lived in the western provinces.

Their morning conversation lagged into silence as Kala entered the makeshift dining hall, forcing her to admit that the majority of the camp shared Terk's anxiety about having a newcomer in their midst.

She could understand their apprehension. Like her, they had learned to be naturally distrustful of strangers. But unlike her, they didn't know that Jein was dead, and that the cause of freedom needed every fighter it could get, Korcians included.

As she watched steaming coffee fill the mug she'd set under the spigot of a tarnished urn, Kala could only hope that Ginomi would be able to dispel any doubts the camp might have about her filling Jein's shoes.

She carried a plate of food and her cup to the closest table and sat down. The woman seated across from her was named Sy. She had joined the resistance after one of Rendhal's Honor Guards had taken a dislike to the way her parents had cheered at one of the governor's rare public appearances. The couple had been arrested, then summarily sentenced to ten years in prison. Sy's mother had died two years later. She had no idea if her father was still alive.

"I saw you come in yesterday," Sy said. "That's some pilot you're with."

"Yes, he is," Kala replied. "If we had a few more like him, we'd have Rendhal on the run."

Sy nodded, sipped her coffee, adjusted the food on her plate, then shook her head as if she'd suddenly lost her appetite. "I suppose you heard about the last team that went out."

"No. What happened?"

"Three men. Terk sent them into Gaharoff. It's a small town on the provincial border between here and the Naarca Valley. Terk intercepted a message saying that the precinct captain was being replaced. He sent the men into Gaharoff to substantiate the report. A new precinct captain could mean trouble." Sy's voice went soft as her expression saddened to the point of tears. She blinked them back. "Our men were caught and arrested, then lined up in front of the precinct building the next morning and executed as a public example of what good little Hachynites shouldn't do."

Kala pushed her plate aside. Like Sy, she had lost her appetite. "Did any of the men have families?"

"No," Sy shook her head. Her hair was dark, her eyes a soft green. "The only family any of us have is each other."

A blast of frigid wind whipped through the eating hall as the door was opened and closed. Kala shivered as the cold air found its way down the back of her jumpsuit.

"I don't think Terk is happy about having your Korcian in camp," Sy said. She was looking toward the door where Terk had just entered. Her green eyes took on a sheen that made Kala think of the way a woman looked at a man when she liked everything about him. She wondered if Terk knew that Sy had feelings for him.

"Aedon isn't *my Korcian*," she corrected Sy. "He's here because his wife and child were murdered when Rendhal's pirates raided a transport. He's a man with a score to settle."

Sy nodded, understanding all too well what it was like to want revenge for the murder of one's family. "Terk said Ginomi is coming into camp. Is that why you're here?"

"Yes." Kala took a sip of coffee. "If I'm right, there's more going on in the Naarca Valley than a change in precinct captains, but I'll let Ginomi brief the camp."

Sy stood up. "I'll see you later, then."

Kala finished her coffee, carried her plate and cup to the cleaning unit, filled two fresh mugs with coffee, and headed for the door. On her way out, she passed the table where Terk was sitting. He lifted his gaze to meet hers, but he didn't speak.

Outside the dining hall and away from the meager sleeping quarters that were home to sixty-plus people, the canyon was a patchwork of white snow and pale gray granite. On higher ground, above the deep rift that a forgotten river had cut through solid stone, cold winds lashed and heavy white clouds covered the peaks.

Kala made her way toward the shuttle. The exit hatch irised open and the entry ramp lowered to the ground as if precisely timed for her arrival. She stepped up the ramp and into the shuttle. The airship was insulated for high-altitude flights, and its interior temperature was luke-warm. Almost cozy.

Aedon was wearing one of the tunics Ginomi had pro-vided, minus sleeves he had cut off because they'd been too short and confining. The dark blue fabric hugged the planes of his chest, and Kala tried hard not to remember how he looked naked. All strong, lean muscles and bronzed skin. All man.

The rumpled state of his dark hair and the sleepy look in his eyes told her that he'd only just climbed out of his own sleeping bag.

Apart from taking one of the coffee mugs from her hand, Aedon didn't touch her. Instead, he seemed to be deliberately avoiding physical contact when he moved to the opposite side of the shuttle to sit down.

"Ginomi should be here by midafternoon," Kala said, acting as if the distance between them was perfectly nor-mal. "Terk's curious about why we're here."

"That's natural," Aedon said. "This is his camp."

"He's the camp leader, but this isn't *his* camp," Kala said. "It belongs to the resistance, to the men and women who risk their lives by simply being here."

"Take it easy. I understand."

"Understand what?" she asked, baffled by his amused tone.

"That Terk's feeling territorial."

He said it so matter-of-factly, that Kala had to smile. The gleam in Aedon's silver-blue eyes was very similar to the one she'd seen last night, just before he walked out of the room and left her alone.

Suddenly, without thinking better of it, she moved closer to where he was sitting. "Terk's territory doesn't include me."

"I know," he said, putting aside his mug.

"Then why did you sleep out here?"

"You know why."

A held breath unraveled slowly as Kala looked into eyes that had instantly darkened to the color of a winter storm. "Because you don't want the people in camp thinking that I trust you just because you're keeping my sexual appetite satisfied."

His smile went wider, before vanishing completely. "You're going to lead these people, Kala. Not Terk. Not Ginomi. I'm here to help you, but it's you they have to accept and respect, your orders they have to follow without question. I won't do anything to jeopardize that."

His understanding of things she was only beginning to realize herself released a store of emotions in Kala. Her insides went warm and her throat went dry. Without saying a word, she slipped her arms around his neck, sat down on his lap, and rested her head on his shoulder.

"I thought warrior queens were supposed to have consorts," she whispered. "Strong, virile men with nothing better to do than to satisfy their queen's every desire."

The laughter that rumbled up from inside his chest echoed in her ears. He gave her a tight squeeze. "Don't tempt me."

Any tempting Kala had in mind was postponed when the shuttle's proximity alarm sounded.

"We've got company," Aedon said. He eased her off his lap and onto her feet.

Voice activated, the hatchway opened at Aedon's command to reveal Terk standing outside. "Ginomi told me to bring Kala up to date on our operations here. Want to get started?"

Kala smiled to herself, knowing Terk had deliberately timed his appearance to interrupt them.

"No time like the present." She looked around, found Aedon's jacket, and tossed it to him. "You might as well come along. This was all your idea."

"I've never been inside one of these," Terk said. "Mind if I have a look?"

"Help yourself," Aedon said, gesturing for him to step

inside. "Nothing out of the norm as far as shuttles go. I erased the tracing program before we left Melgarr."

Terk made his way to the pilot's console and sat down. After a few minutes of study, he swirled the pilot's chair around to face them again. "With some minor modifications, this could be made to look like a transport shuttle. The guns would have to be remounted, and the police insignia removed, of course. After that, a few strategically placed dents and scuffs, and you've got a shuttle that won't draw attention."

Kala could tell from Aedon's expression that he had thought the same thing, but he seemed willing to let Terk take credit for the idea. She also knew it was because he would need Terk's expertise as a tech-rigger if his plan to get inside one of the factories was to be successful.

"How long to do the modifications?" Aedon asked. He put on his jacket, but not until a laser pistol was snugly tucked into its holster.

"Two days at the most," Terk said. "I'll get men working on it right away."

With that they left the shuttle and headed for the center of the camp's operations, a cavelike den formed from a natural rock overhang that had been artificially embellished by man. Once inside, they saw rows of computer consoles manned by an equal mix of men and women. Topographical and geological holomaps cast an eerie light against the dark stone walls.

"There are our surveillance monitors," Terk said, pointing toward the westernmost wall of the cave. "I installed sensors along every possible trail in and out of the canyon. They're monitored around the clock. There are four aerial scanners mounted on the top of the cliffs. No one is going to surprise us."

"And these?" Aedon asked, pointing toward a display of red, blue, and yellow indicators that overlaid another map.

Terk looked to Kala. His expression said he didn't like

Aedon asking all the questions and him giving all the answers.

"Aedon is in this as deep as we are, which means if he's caught he'll be executed right alongside us. I trust him. Ginomi trusts him. You can trust him."

Terk took a moment to mull over her reply. He didn't look any happier, but he answered Aedon's question. "It's a map of the Naarca Valley. The red dots are government facilities. The blue crosshatches are factories, and the yellow starbursts are villages and towns where we have safe houses."

Kala watched as Aedon studied the map. She could see his eyes narrow to dark slits as he silently counted the blue crosshatches. The intensity of his silent appraisal was almost tangible.

The Naarca Valley was a long, flat plateau that took over where the Moviash Mountains ended. Running a good thousand miles due west, until it reached a smaller, narrower range of mountains, the plateau was laced with rivers that emptied into the Jovian Sea. It was essentially an open, windswept plain stuffed full of factories. If only 20 percent of them were producing weapons, the annual output was staggering.

Kala looked at the map, then at Terk. Selwyn's betrayal was never far from her mind. "Sy told me about the men who were arrested and executed in Gaharoff. Do you think a sympathizer was turned into an informer?"

"I can't be sure of anything," Terk said. "Every day is a new lesson in survival, you know that."

Unfortunately, Kala knew only too well.

ten

ONE BY ONE, the five holograms appeared, flowing above the communication receptors like quiet, graceful ghosts.

The arrival of the Board of Directors, Sector Eight, was precisely timed to coincidence with the appearance of Hachyn's colonial governor.

Avis Rendhal sat at the end of the opaque glass conference table. He was a tall, thin man with pale azure eyes, even paler skin, and a hawkish nose. In his late forties, he had been educated at one of the finest universities in the League and personally mentored by a senior member of the Conglomerate Majority Board, the ultimate authority that oversaw the holdings of the galactic cartel.

"Good evening, gentlemen," the governor said, speaking as if the five men were seated at the table.

"Good evening," Director One replied.

Names were never used. Banker, merchant, industrialist, politician, every member of the Board was shrouded in secrecy. Powerful men engaged in nefarious and highly profitable enterprises who mixed their clandestine power with galactic finance preferred not to be known.

The Conglomerate was neither inefficient nor careless.

The four remaining directors said nothing; social niceties weren't necessary or expected. Only business was important; the ability to make governments collapse, to control markets, to manipulate economies, the power to precipitate or end wars—that was the Conglomerate's business.

And profit.

Profit above all else.

"Your production status?" Director One asked, his voice only slightly thinned by the complicated satellite relay that linked him from his home on Tobarus Four to the governor's mansion on Hachyn.

"Production is on schedule," Rendhal reported proudly. "We will move into Phase Four within the next six weeks."

"And the trading lanes," said the fourth member of the Board, a rotund middle-aged man with an angular face and the impatient eyes of a financier. His vote carried heavily in any Board decision.

"My pilots are running raids on all transport traffic," Rendhal replied with a devious smile. "In fact, they are complaining that there are fewer and fewer vessels upon which to prey. The traffic, as anticipated, is being diverted in the interest of safety."

"Excellent," Director Five responded. He had used many names in his tenure with the Conglomerate, a man in the shadows, a manipulator who knew how to keep out of sight. He was fiftyish, medium-size, with thinning hair and a raspy voice. "The transportation of the merchandise must be handled with the utmost delicately. There can be no breach in security."

"The raids will continue," Rendhal assured him. He disengaged his lean, manicured fingers and took a deep breath through his nostrils, as if he were about to deliver some unknown essential wisdom. "By the time we are ready to begin delivery, the risk of exposure will be minimal."

"And *your* rebels?" asked Director Four. He was an elderly man with silver hair and immaculate connections to the League of Planet's Trading Guild. "Are you still chasing your own tail rather than catching them?"

Nothing about the governor's expression relayed the anger he felt at having his failure thrown in his face.

Emotion was a failure unto itself.

"We arrested and executed one of their leaders only a few weeks ago," replied Rendhal. "We have also penetrated their unit here in the city. Progress is being made."

"Progress isn't enough," Director Two said flatly. "Nothing can interfere with the completion of Phase Four. *Nothing*."

"Nothing will interfere," the governor promised.

"Time is of the essence." The threat in Director One's voice came through clearly on the deep-space transmission. "You have six weeks to end your little rebellion, or we will."

Before the governor could come to his own defense the holographic images of his superiors faded into nothingness.

Rendhal pressed a button on his personal console. "Find Commander Esarell. Now!"

When Commander Denikin Esarell reached the heavy, gold-inlaid door at the end of the carpeted hall, he paused to press his right hand against the security scanning plate. The electronic lock retracted, allowing the door to slide open and allowing Esarell to pass into a new corridor, this one tiled in gleaming, white Ramoran marble.

Routine meetings of the governor's advisors were customarily held in the inner hall of the palace, but Esarell was no routine advisor. As commander of the Honor Guard, he was personally responsible for the governor's safety, both publicly and privately.

No one got within a thousand yards of the governor without first being approved by Esarell. He personally screened every employee in the palace, from the chefs to the handsomely paid females who warmed the governor's bed.

Esarell prided himself on his meticulous research almost as much as he prided himself on his consummate acting skills—his ability to project flawless loyalty to a man he loathed.

Avis Rendhal was a weakling, succumbing to his carnal appetites, yet forever hungry. He had been appointed governor by a Board of Directors that was growing increasingly impatient with his inability to bring the rebellion under control. The man who did would be looked on very favorably.

Esarell intended to be that man. And the next colonial governor of Hachyn.

When he reached the end of the second corridor, Esarell stopped again. This time, he stood perfectly still while a bioscan identified him. A scant second after the soft hum of the scanner ceased another inlaid door opened, and Esarell stepped into the governor's private suite.

The room was immense, the high ceiling ornately carved, the windows that overlooked the Jovian Sea draped in the sheerest of white silk. The ambience of the room was continued in its white leather chairs and gilded tables, as if the suggested purity of the color could erase Rendhal's sins.

At the moment, the governor was occupied with a member of his expensive harem. The naked female, paid to please, finished riding Rendhal to completion, then eased off his lap, cast Esarell a seductive smile, and exited the room.

Rendhal closed his robe over his now deflated penis and came to his feet.

"Ahh, Esarell, I've been expecting you," he said in a thin-pitched voice that could shriek like a spoiled child's when he didn't get his way. "Come in, come in. I anticipate good news, of course."

"The investigation of the precinct explosion has been completed," Esarell said. His cultured voice was laced with the inflection and cadence of a highly educated man. The glare of the room's lights reflected off the white marbled floors and walls, washing over his face, heightening the prominent cheekbones and the broad forehead. Dark brows slanted over eyes that were calm and cold.

"The results?" Rendhal prompted impatiently. "Was it the rebels?"

"Unfortunately, a definite determination cannot be made," Esarell said respectfully. "The fuel tanks had been filled only that morning. The explosion destroyed everything."

"Then it was an accident?"

"There is no evidence of an explosive device being detonated, but there is also no evidence that the tanks erupted by themselves."

Rendhal stopped short of pouring himself a drink. "What are you saying?"

"Merely that no evidence means no conclusion can be reached," Esarell explained. "Without a conclusion, there are only possibilities."

"And one of those possibilities is a rebel attack," Rendhal said angrily. He slammed his fist down on a tabletop, a crack of soft flesh against hard, cold marble.

"The police have contained most of the rebel activity in the western provinces. It stands to reason that the rebels would look to other areas to continue their campaign. The destruction of a police precinct . . ." Esarell deliberately allowed his words to fade, maximizing what they implied.

"The police are incompetent," Rendhal raged. He spoke as if exhaling, his high voice irritated. "The rebellion must be brought to an end."

Esarell said nothing, because nothing was required. His reputation had preceded him into the room—a man wholly devoid of the most elemental sense of conscience. A cold-blooded murderer. A brilliant, charismatic monster.

Esarell was not merely malicious, he had an unsurpassed gift for cruelty—not just physical pain. Anyone could inflict pain. Blood was easily drawn. But physical pain and emotional turmoil, confusion that bordered on insanity, the uncertainty of just how much pain a person could tolerate before he died was a question Esarell enjoyed answering.

Most found his methods offensive, but none could question their effectiveness.

Before coming to Hachyn, he had worked as a personal bodyguard for a Conglomerate shareholder. Esarell's previous employer had been a businessman whose stock-in-trade was contraband: women, drugs, and weapons—it mattered little to him. He was an opportunist, a trait Esarell had quickly adopted.

His name had been different then, but names were a matter of supreme indifference to Esarell's associates. It was his former employer's boasting of his bodyguard's lethal abilities that had gained Esarell an introduction to Hachyn's governor.

Rendhal stared at the commander of his personal guard. The governor's face was covered with a sheen of perspiration despite the cool breeze that blew in from the sea to fill his private suite.

"I'll not make the mistake I made with Jein," Rendhal said venomously. "I want these rebels caught and eliminated. This rebellion crushed once and for all. No imprisonment beyond what's necessary to *extract* information. Find them and kill them."

Esarell gave a rare smile. "It will be my pleasure, Excellency."

eleven

GINOMI ARRIVED AT the Marous camp as the sun was taking its westerly recline over the mountains, the last light coloring the sky in soft hues of gold and red. The perpetual mist that never left the icy peaks began to sink along with the sun, seeping down into the canyon, dampening the air and chilling the bones.

Once the senior leader of the resistance was fed and warmed with several cups of hot tea, he asked Terk to call a meeting of the entire camp.

Aedon stood in the back of the dining hall where he could observe the reactions of camp members. Curious eyes flickered over him, but their interest was short-lived once Ginomi walked to the front of the dining hall.

Kala sat at a nearby table. Aedon knew she was nervous. Although nothing about his outward appearance showed it, so was he.

If Ginomi's announcement of Jein's death and Kala's subsequent self-promotion to resistance leader wasn't well received, Aedon's mission was all but over. Terk could only be trusted to cooperate as far as he *wanted* to cooperate, especially if that cooperation meant working side-by-side with the man who had what Terk wanted—the beautiful woman named Kala.

Aedon didn't like the additional complication that had evolved from being Kala's lover, but he accepted it. He could only hope that the bonds of loyalty formed over time to the resistance outweighed Terk's personal objectives.

As Aedon looked over the men and women who had gathered to hear Ginomi's announcement, he caught the eye of a young man at one of the nearby tables. Neither spoke or acknowledged the eye contact, but the intensity wasn't diminished by its briefness.

The young man's expression mirrored the expression of others Aedon had seen since coming to the camp— humiliation at being forced to live in caves like animals, resentment at being brought to heel by a cannibalistic government, and a consuming desire to do something about it.

Aedon knew few of the resistance fighters' names, but he did know them for the independent people they were. Asking no mercy from the elements they lived in, they survived as men and women had throughout history—by sheer will. For them to be reduced to slaves was intolerable. Yet just how far they were willing to go to gain the freedom they desired was a big question. A question Aedon had no way of answering.

If Kala was accepted, and if his plan to destroy the factories was implemented, the war the resistance fighters had survived up to now would pale in comparison to the war ahead, no matter how brief the final battle.

When Ginomi reached the front table, conversation ceased. His gaze locked briefly with Kala's but only briefly.

"Fellow Hachynites," he began. "I am here to deliver the most sorrowful of news. Our loved and respected leader, Eiven Jein, is dead."

Breaths audibly drawn could be heard as the shocking news registered with the men and women assembled in the hall. Conversation began again; grunts of disbelief, tears of loss, words of confusion.

"No one is more grieved than I," Ginomi said, speaking loudly to be heard above the chaos that had erupted in the hall. "I know everyone here, myself included, would have gladly exchanged his life for Jein's, but providence decreed otherwise."

Voices calmed as the inevitable consequence of war was accepted, but grief and uncertainty continued.

Ginomi exhaled an audible breath. "As terrible as the news is, there is a small blessing. The authorities do not realize that their plot to kill Kala Char'ari and her Korcian companion resulted in Jein's death instead of theirs. As far as the governor is concerned, Eiven Jein still leads us. He is still the living, breathing inspiration that drives us forward to freedom."

Ginomi ignored the questions shouted at him and looked to Kala. He stepped back as she stood up and moved to take his place. The gesture didn't go unnoticed by Terk, or anyone else in the hall. The message was loud and clear—the old leader was giving way to the new.

Aedon kept his gaze focused on Kala, silently willing her to show the strength he knew she possessed. The strength not to ask for control, but to take it as her natural right.

She looked around the room for a long moment, rewarding each stare in full measure, silencing their questions.

"I loved Eiven Jein like a father. I will carry the grief of his death for the rest of my life," she told them. "But I ask you not to let his death become discouragement. There was no advantage that Jein sought from life more than the advantage of freedom. He coveted nothing beyond that dream, that hope. Circumstances elected us to share that dream, and circumstances force us to go on. We must continue to resist, continue to fight, and continue to hope."

"Ginomi agrees with me," Kala continued. "We must redouble our efforts, especially in the Naarca Valley."

"We've been hitting as many police patrols as we can," interrupted Terk.

"Exactly," Kala said, taking back the conversation. "The police are there to protect Governor Rendhal's interests. The Conglomerate's interest. *The factories*. The profits from those factories are Rendhal's real seat of power."

She paused to let the idea take root, and Aedon smiled to himself. He'd been right. Kala was a natural leader.

Watching her now, Aedon had to admit just how attracted to her he was—the same flinty quality that she'd shown the night he'd first met her was showing now. The same innate passion. Making love or making war, Kala Char'ari wasn't a woman who did anything halfway. Whatever she felt, she felt completely. Whatever cause she embraced, she embraced wholeheartedly.

Aedon could sense it, and so could the people in the dining hall. The very fact that they were sitting quietly, their eyes locked on the young woman standing before them, their ears attuned to her every word, spoke to her ability to lead.

"You want us to raid the factories?" Terk asked hollowly, as if he couldn't believe what he'd just heard.

"When the time is right," said Kala. "First, we plan. Then we attack."

Kala glanced away from the blurring images of the hologram to rest her eyes. She and Aedon had spent the last two hours going through every detail the camp's database had on the Naarca Valley. Much of the data was familiar; some of the analyses even reflected her own reports to

Jein from Habari, a city on the eastern edge of the valley that she'd visited two years ago.

Aedon glanced up from the console where he sat. He didn't really expect to find the answers he was looking for in the camp's database, but it gave him something to think about besides Kala's sleek body and golden-brown eyes. He looked at her over the rim of the console and smiled.

"Getting tired?"

"Bone weary is more like it," she said as she rolled her shoulders to remove the kinks. "The more I learn about the valley the more I realize how little I know about the factories."

A slight smile was Aedon's only reply. "What about Habari? You were there once, right?"

"Twice, actually," she replied, yawning. "It's a resort city built around the shore of Lake Haba. It's north of the valley, where the mountains meet the flatlands. The elite of Hachyn, which means government officials and factory managers, like to vacation there. The air is clean compared to what they breathe in the valley, and the lake sits north of the factory drainage so it's unpolluted. For the time being," she added with another yawn.

"You should get some sleep."

"Not yet. What have you found?" She came to where he was sitting and ran a hand over his shoulder.

Everyone but a sole technician, assigned to monitor the surveillance scanners while the camp slept, had left the operational center. The area where they were working was separated from the main cave by a wooden partition.

"Rest anyway," Aedon said, gently pulling her down on his lap.

Kala smiled as she looped an arm around his neck to hold herself in place. "I thought you had a rule about warrior queens and lowly knights fraternizing. Bad for morale, and all that."

Aedon laughed, doing his best to ignore the moist, sweet touch of her mouth and tongue as she kissed his throat. He wasn't very successful. When she shifted her weight to get more comfortable, he grimaced with the painful pleasure of how quickly Kala could arouse him.

"Sit still," he told her.

She gave him an innocent look, then rested her head on his shoulder.

For the next few minutes, Aedon scrutinized detailed topographic maps, grainy satellite imagery that had been stolen from the communication relays of the planet's security network, and old schematics of the factories themselves.

One structure held his attention longer than the others. It was the main power plant, the source of the energy that fueled the factories in the Naarca Valley.

As he stared at the console, Aedon felt Kala beginning to relax. The heat of her body sank into his, warming away the chill that came from sitting for hours inside a mountaintop cave. In the short time since he'd met Kala, she had managed to scale all his barriers and bypass his misgivings. Aedon knew it was her ingenuousness, her warmth, her ability to give of herself without condition or compromise.

Though Aedon savored the sweet contact of having Kala on his lap, he kept staring at the elevation mappings of the power station, his gaze moving back and forth between the overhead views and the structural blueprints, searching for any anomaly, coincidence, or pattern that would open the door to the valley.

One conclusion was inescapable: getting into the facilities in the valley was only part of the story. Infiltration was difficult, but it could be done. The tricky part was exfiltration—getting out alive.

"You're concentrating too hard," Kala whispered. The soft brush of her breath against his ear made Aedon want to rethink sleeping alone in the shuttle. She ran a delicate finger caressingly over the hard line of his jaw. "Your eyes are getting darker. Is that good or bad?"

Aedon smiled. "Bad, because we're not alone, which means I can't strip you out of those clothes and make love to you," he said, keeping his voice low so they weren't overheard. "Good, because it means the impossible might be possible after all."

His eyes narrowed as he studied the holomap again. He mentally traced the line of the maintenance tunnels that ran beneath the factories, similar to the ones Kala had introduced him to in Melgarr.

"Aedon?" she asked, sensing the intensity that had overtaken him.

Instead of answering, Aedon keyed in a request for another holomap, this one showing a secondary set of tunnels. Nearly black eyes studied the structural scenario of underground ingress and egress, cataloging the possibilities.

"You mentioned factory drainage before," he said. "Did you mean waste runoff or water?"

"Both. That's why every river and stream south of the Naarca Valley is poisoned. The pollution has already spread into the oceans. The factories are killing the planet."

Silence grew as more and more holomaps, some mere gray lines, others a rainbow of colors, were overlaid until the valley had been reconstructed from the ground up.

Aedon didn't think highly of a purely defensive mode of warfare, particularly against a superior enemy. But the situation gave him no choice.

"It might work," he mumbled under his breath.

"What might work?" Kala squirmed on his lap, trying to get a better view of the hologram images that had Aedon momentarily mesmerized. "All I see is a map dotted with factories and more precinct stations that any one valley needs."

Abruptly, Aedon sat up straighter, forcing Kala to tighten her hold around his neck or be unseated. "It's risky, but I don't see any other way."

"What?" The sleepiness had left her voice.

Her question was accompanied by a sudden whistle of cold wind through the cave and Terk's voice asking the sole technician left on duty if all was well.

Kala slipped off Aedon's lap and came to her feet a short second before Terk rounded the wooden partition. The camp leader looked as if he'd been tossing and turning instead of sleeping.

"I thought you two had already called it a night," he said, running his fingers through blond hair that had been dampened by snow. He looked at the holographic image floating above the console projector. "We studied those files all evening."

"Aedon thinks he may have a way in," said Kala, unable to hide the pride in her voice. "He was just explaining his idea to me."

Terk looked doubtful, but interested.

That interest grew as Ginomi came strolling around the corner. "Couldn't sleep," he grumbled as he dusted the snow off the shoulders of his insulated jacket. "Every time I close my eyes I see a Conglomerate army marching across the galaxy. Not the stuff of sweet dreams."

"Amen," Kala said softly.

"So what's your idea?" Terk asked, looking at the hologram instead of meeting Aedon's hard-as-steel gaze.

"The first thing we blow is the power station," Aedon said. His voice subtly shifted from the mode of gathering information to that of issuing orders. "Then we hit the factories."

"After every policeman in the valley sees the explosion," Terk scoffed. "It's a death wish."

"Not a single explosion," Aedon said, speaking with clipped precision. "The *first* explosion triggered by a relay of detonators."

"A single raid," Ginomi said, clearly impressed by the daring grandeur of the plan. "No chance for Rendhal's men to increase their vigilance after one factory falls prey.

No concern that the right factories will be hit. We take them all out of production in one night."

"That's the plan," Aedon replied. "All or nothing at all."

Terk walked to a secondary console and brought up a duplicate screen of what Aedon had been studying for hours. "How do we plant the explosives without getting caught? The maintenance tunnels are randomly searched. You never know where the security teams will be on any given day."

Aedon looked to Kala and smiled. "We won't use the maintenance tunnels. We'll use the drainage tunnels."

Ginomi slapped the console table. "Brilliant!" He looked to Terk. "Leave it to a Korcian to see tactics where everyone else sees muck and sludge."

Aedon didn't have to look very hard to see calculation flicker in Terk's eyes as he measured the threat Aedon posed to his current status as the resistance's right-hand man.

"I'll need current data to substantiate what your files show," Aedon said. "We can't go in until we know exactly what we're going to find. I'll also need a list of what precincts are responsible for what factory alarms. The most important thing is having the right operatives. I'm talking about the best you've got. There's no time to train them, so make it a team that has worked together before, but no one who can't keep up if we're discovered planting the explosives and forced to make a run for it."

"Terk, Sy, Alvaron, and Stiles," Ginomi said. "They've been teamed up for the last four years. Terk and Sy both lived and worked in the valley. Alvaron is good with explosives, and Stiles has an uncle in Habari who's very good at collecting information. But are you sure that's enough? The valley has three police precincts, two hundred men each, with another five hundred in reserve that can be called up from Melgarr on a moment's notice."

"A team of five is more than enough," Aedon assured him. "If five hundred were necessary, I'd have requested them. If I could get by with fewer than five, I would. Less people make for less complications."

"*Six* people," Kala corrected him. "Tunnels are my specialty, remember. I'm coming with you."

Aedon didn't argue for the simple reason that he didn't want to challenge Kala's newly christened authority in front of Ginomi and Terk. There'd be time enough to change her mind before the raid. And he fully intended to change her mind. His gaze told her as much, all black onyx rimmed in silver, with just a hint of angry blue.

The warrior-hardened stare would have made any man take a step back. Kala just flashed him her best smile.

"Okay," Aedon conceded for the moment. He looked to Ginomi again. "What about equipment?"

"Whatever you need, we'll get," the man from Vinsenia promised.

Aedon began reciting a list of equipment. Ginomi only smiled and nodded with each request. It only took Aedon a few seconds to realize why. To keep themselves armed, the resistance fighters had become expert thieves. The equipment they would need to destroy the factories in the Naarca Valley was going to be surreptitiously requisitioned from colonial supply depots.

Satisfied that equipment wouldn't be the issue, Aedon turned his attention to Terk. The real make-or-break factor of the raid was going to be the men, not the machinery.

"I'll need every detail you can remember about the factories before I go in," Aedon said. "I like to know what I'm blowing up."

What Aedon didn't say was that he needed to be able to give the Directorate a complete report on what Rendhal had up his sleeve. If weapons were being produced, they wouldn't be warehoused indefinitely. If there was an army being trained and equipped in the outer regions, the Directorate needed to know about it.

Terk studied the secondary console a few moments

longer, then conceded with a shrug and a voice that was slightly less skeptical than before. "It might work."

Aedon shifted his gaze back to Kala. Her eyes were bright with enthusiasm, a smile hiding her stubbornness about being included in a mission that could easily get her killed.

"It will work," she said. "And when it does, Rendhal *and* the Conglomerate Board of Directors will know that we aren't playing games. We'll fight as long as there's a world to fight for."

Aedon started to remind Kala of the harsh realities, the long odds, and the abundance of downside scenarios that went with any raid into enemy territory, but he stopped himself. At this stage, a slim hope was better than no hope at all.

twelve

THE MEMORIES WERE four years old, but they could have been yesterday's. They unspooled in Aedon's dreams, taking him back to another time, another place. Nazlean with her dark hair blowing in the wind, the sound of Cassandra's laughter as she played on the beach, the scent of a tropical jungle lush with life. Home. Happiness. Their whole lives before them.

Acdon came awake, his senses instantly alert, his mind already pushing aside the memories to focus on the here and now.

All he could hear was the silence of a room filled with the loneliness of remembrance.

Outside, the sky was caught in the gray ambiguity between night and true dawn. He got out of bed and walked to the balcony of the resort cottage that overlooked Lake Haba. With each passing moment, the sky took on more color, chasing away the shadows and wavering mists that clung to the landscape.

Ginomi had arranged everything with a spymaster's skill.

Aedon and Kala had arrived in Habari the previous afternoon and checked into the cottage. It was one of several located on the eastern side of the lake, a discreet bungalow rented out to those who preferred privacy to the crowded hotels.

Aedon's identity card showed him to be a factory manager from Ribadavia, a seaport city on the southern coast. Like most upper-level managers getting away for a few day's relaxation, he was traveling with a lovely companion.

The other four members had divided into two teams. Terk and Sy were in a hotel across the lake, Alvaron and Stiles in a safe house supplied by a Habari sympathizer.

Terk had rigged six commlinks to transmit on an archaic radio frequency that wouldn't register on the police scanners. The three teams would communicate on a preestablished schedule, but they would not meet again until everything was in place.

Standing on the balcony, Aedon looked out over the city of Habari. Like the alpine village of Vinsenia, it was a sharp contrast to the capital city, Melgarr.

Nestled at the foot of the majestic Moviash Mountains, it curved around the shores of Lake Haba. Cool white buildings with view-catching windows lined clean, smoothly paved streets. As with most resort cities, Habari was an extraordinary mix of comfortable lodgings, quaint cafés, and expensive shops.

Beyond the lake, the land gradually flattened into the infamous Naarca Valley. The winds, blowing down from the rugged peaks of the Moviashes swept the factory fumes westerly, leaving the air clean. The waters of Lake Haba were a deep blue, glistening almost amber now that the sun was rising.

As Aedon watched sunlight wash over a land that had been nothing more than a name in a Directorate report a few months ago, he tried to forget the lovely woman sleeping in the next room.

Kala hadn't complained when he'd put his gear in the second of the cottage's two bedrooms, but Aedon knew she had assumed they'd be sharing the same bed once they left the camp.

And why not? There was no one here to see where they slept. No other members of the team to notice how close they had become in so short a time.

Last night, when he'd told Kala good night and closed the bedroom door behind him, Aedon had told himself it was for her own good.

This morning, he couldn't be sure if he had played the gentlemen to protect her from heartbreak or to protect himself.

Caring again, loving again, weren't things he'd taken into consideration when he had joined the Directorate. To think about them now, in the middle of a deadly mission, was insane.

And yet, staring out at the vibrant colors of dawn, Aedon couldn't help but think of the copper blaze of Kala's hair, the catlike gleam of her eyes, and the effervescent quality of her smile. Like the bright sunrise, announcing a new day after a long, dark night, Kala was the here and now of his life.

Accepting that life's many surprises, were just that—surprises, Aedon turned away from the color streaked morning sky to find Kala standing just inside his bedroom door.

She was wearing a blue silk robe, another surprise from the camp's storeroom. With her auburn hair hanging down her back in a cascade of unbrushed curls, and her eyes still soft from sleep, she was every bit as lovely as the new day.

The way the silk smoothed over her body made Aedon's hands itch to move it aside so he could caress the soft, silky texture of her skin.

"I heard you moving around," she said sleepily.

Aedon could read the emotions in her eyes. Desire, confusion, a hint of anger because she didn't understand the blatant rejection of last night. Everything was showing, even her hesitation in greeting him.

Like an invisible current of energy, the physical distance between them surged with emotion. Excitement hovered with an edge of tension.

When Aedon didn't comment about getting up with the rising sun, Kala walked past him to the balcony beyond.

Cursing silently, Aedon stepped back onto the balcony where seeing Kala outlined in the bright shades of morning made her even more desirable.

His gaze moved over her, then away, to where the buildings of Habari were quickly emerging from the lake-induced mist that had covered them during the night.

"I've been thinking about your plan. It's genius in its simplicity," she said. "Each step is a checkpoint, each move a countermove. Brilliant, just as Ginomi said. In fact, the more I think about it, the more my gut tells me that you haven't been a freelance pilot all your life. You've been in the military. Or should I say, you *are* military."

"Every Korcian male is required to spend at least three years in military service," he said neutrally.

Kala didn't respond for a moment; instead she stared out over the lake. When she turned to meet his gaze again, her eyes had taken on a skeptical gleam.

"Three years aren't long enough for a solider to give orders as naturally as you do," she said. "You take charge too easily, too automatically. I saw it that night on the beach, at the police precinct when you stole the shuttle, and I saw it in camp, when you began organizing this raid. You're a solider to the marrow of your bones."

"I'm a Korcian. I was born and raised in a military society. I've breathed it since the day I was born."

She smiled a crooked little smile that said whatever he was hiding was on its way into the open.

When she stepped closer and ran the smooth edges of her fingernails down the length of his bare arm, Aedon tried not to notice how good the simple pleasure of her touch affected him.

He failed.

Noticing Kala was all he could do at the moment. She was standing close enough for him to breathe in the scent of her body, and to look down at the soft cleavage the robe wasn't hiding. The swell of her breasts, covered in half warm sunshine and half warm silk, were almost as tempting as her sensually curved mouth.

Taking a slow, even breath, Aedon clamped down on his body's natural response to a beautiful woman it knew it could have if only he'd return her touch.

As though there was nothing more urgent than her lazy smile and the gentle contact of her fingertips against his skin, Kala caressed him again, from elbow to hand.

"Whoever you are, whatever you are, lies aren't a part of you," she whispered lightly.

The soft tremor of her voice, and the truth in her words, was Aedon's undoing. He looked away from her beautiful face to where the brightness of a Hachynite morning ricocheted off the waters of Lake Haba.

"You're not going to tell me, are you?"

"You said that you trusted me."

She took a step back. "I'm not talking about trust, I'm talking about truth."

Aedon heard the hurt in Kala's voice and remembered the oath he had taken when he'd joined the Directorate. The clandestine nature of his life wasn't something he could share with anyone, no matter his feelings.

"The truth is that I want to help you and your people," he said. "It's the only truth that matters."

"What about me?" she asked. "Am I part of the game?"

The disdain in her voice, the blunt hint that by becoming her lover he had betrayed her as much as Selwyn had was more than Aedon could tolerate. He turned away from the glowing dawn to look into golden-brown eyes that had turned as cold as an autumn wind.

"This isn't a game," he said more angrily than he'd intended. "Meeting you wasn't part of any plan or scheme. Making love to you wasn't a ploy or a ruse to gain your cooperation. It simply happened."

"And you don't want it to happen again?" The question was more challenge than accusation.

The corner of Aedon's mouth lifted into a smile. "You're tempting me again."

The tension tightening in the pit of Kala's stomach eased with Aedon's smile. Whatever he was hiding from her wasn't dangerous to her or her people. She knew it as surely as she knew that this man had touched her in ways no other human being ever would.

There had been tragedy in his life; it was in his eyes, sometimes so clear they reflected the colors of the sky, sometimes dark and stormy. Like now.

She could demand that he tell her. Demand that he leave Hachyn immediately and take his half-truths with him, but his soft voice and dark, ardent eyes were enough for the moment. Enough to convince her that he truly cared—about her, about her people, about a future that he might or might not share.

Content with that for the moment, Kala stood in the morning sunshine and allowed herself to believe that there would be a future.

"I trust you," she said, saying the only thing that needed to be said. Saying it all in those three simple words. "And I believe that what you have told me is the truth."

Silence fell easily between them after that, broken only by the murmuring sound of lake waves against the shore. Their world wasn't sane—they were all too aware of that—yet they had found each other, and in that finding, they had discovered a bond of trust between themselves. It was a warm discovery, one to be celebrated, one that filled them with promise where uncertainty had ruled before—about life and each other.

Aedon reached out a hand to her.

Kala took it and allowed him to pull her gently toward the bed. His face was as serious and still as she'd ever seen it, his eyes intent.

Slowly, she raised up and kissed him, a gentle brush of a kiss against his full mouth. She drew back slightly, their face only inches apart. Neither had closed their eyes.

"Take off your clothes," he said.

She stepped away for a moment, perfectly aware of the provocative outline the sunlight was making of her body beneath the silk robe, reveling in his eyes upon her, in the movement of his bare chest as his breath quickened.

Watching each other shed their clothes was an act of absolution. It drained away the tension, leaving nothing but the moment.

Naked, she moved to where he was standing. He kissed her with savage tenderness, a wild, gentle longing that could not have startled him more than it did her.

Then his fingers pulled through her hair, untangling the curls. Kala stood like a statue under his touch, content to experience the raging sensations that coursed through her.

Following his lead, she rubbed his chest with her hands, snaking them around his bare back and down his hips. A low groan escaped his lips. She knew then how much he wanted her. She was only beginning to sense how much she needed him—physically and emotionally.

"You're beautiful," he said huskily.

The combination of his voice and the gentle touch of his hands was hypnotic. Kala felt sensually feline; she wanted to purr and rub herself against him.

There was a tender deference in his attitude that made her feel like a goddess, an icon being worshipped and adored. She exalted in the experience. The golden shadows of dawn filled the room, casting a mystical spell over them. He kissed her deeply once again, hungrily, and her body quivered with growing urgency.

He stretched out on the bed and drew her down, next to his side. He bent his head to her breast. His teeth grazed her nipples, and he began to suck and tease.

In a way, Kala felt strange watching him at her breast and feeling him grow hard against her thigh. She felt like a voyeur, but it excited her.

She looked at him, his weight heavy upon her, his face so close she could see the shadow of beard marring his bronzed skin. His face was flushed, his intense everchanging eyes gleaming. He kissed her again, small, sharp, biting kisses, then ran the tip of his tongue down her throat.

Kala's arms slipped around him, around his lean waist. Their bodies met with an electric jolt that brought him to full arousal. She was aware of every inch of skin, every curve of her body against his. They held each other tightly, their mouths working hotly against each other, her hips pressing upward into his, his legs nudging hers apart.

Their foreplay was slow and languorous, a sweet exploration than meandered and teased, arousing a breathless fire in both of them. It radiated through Kala in delicious waves. She caught her breath as he drew a nipple into his mouth. Tiny bursts of pleasure gathered deep inside her until she felt as if her whole being was one exquisitely tuned nerve quivering on the edge of incandescence.

His hand molded around her breasts, lifting, rolling, stroking, and her breathing grew rapid. When both of her arms tightened around him, he released her breasts and caressed her legs, then his hands moved over her thighs to her hips.

Then he wrapped his arms around her, moving her entire body against his in a long, slow caress, holding her tightly to him as they kissed. Her tongue probed the recesses of his mouth to let him know that she was ready. He softly rubbed her back and shoulders, then slowly massaged his way lower. Lower. His hands filled with her firm, full buttocks.

Her legs parted wider as his hand moved to the hot, damp center of her body. Within seconds her legs felt weak and a sweet, stinging sensation traveled from her toes to fill her head until she felt faint. She began to throb, inside, outside, the feeling growing in intensity until his mouth and hands could no longer satisfy her. She needed more.

"Now . . . there . . ." she sighed and lifted to meet the gentle probing of his fingers. "Do everything," she urged him, her body writhing under him. "Everything!"

And he did, everything that made her wild, everything that created the metamorphosis that turned her from a purring kitten into a clawing she-cat. His tongue licked and tasted, his hands rubbed and teased, leaving no inch of her untouched. No sensation unfelt. He spoke without words, his every touch telling her that she was beautiful and strong.

His lover.

His woman.

His warrior queen.

He did it all, until she arched toward him, urging him with every gesture and sound to end the sweet torment.

Only then did he join their bodies.

He held himself deep inside her, holding her against him in total intimacy. When he began to move, it was slowly, in long, smooth thrusts. Rising and falling, only to rise again, building toward a crescendo of pleasure.

Suddenly, with her nails digging into his back, Kala arched and strained as though her whole body were one long, intense, taut string that was about to snap.

And then it did, taking Aedon with her.

Over the edge, into a hot, sensual oblivion.

Her climax erupted in a flash of soul-felt, silent explosions, pulsing inside her like summer lightning.

For Kala it was like riding a wild comet. Totally out of control, unable to do anything but hang on while time and space sped by in a wild, hot wave of sensation.

For Aedon, it was a total emptying of himself. Feelings, memories, the present, the past, all emerging into one seething moment in time. A moment of completeness; it had neither beginning nor end.

Gradually, their bodies settled in gentle spasms as they completely drained the need from each other. Climax was followed by contentment and a peaceful quiet. The only sound was the soft whirl of a ceiling fan, the only movement, the gentle shift of morning shadows.

Neither spoke, fearful of spoiling the moment by speaking of a future that might never exist for them.

Kala looked up from her luncheon plate as Aedon approached. He was holding two glasses of wine. They had decided to take the midday meal on the cottage balcony rather than in the neighboring resort restaurant. Kala was pleased with the decision. Being with him was like being reborn. She felt as if the gods had decreed that the world be a place of perpetual sunshine and blue skies.

It wasn't just the physical, although being loved by Aedon was almost more than she could stand. It was the way they laughed, what they talked about, the way they slipped in and out of whispers. She had thought that she'd successfully fortified herself against an attack of emotion, but she'd been wrong.

She was powerless against the tender tug of Aedon Rawn. Powerless against the need of her own heart.

Watching Aedon's lithe walk as he stepped through the cottage door and joined her in the sunlight, she treasured every moment they shared, every moment they could steal from the demands of a dangerous mission that would begin in earnest only a few hours from now.

She'd awoken late in the morning with her head resting on Aedon's shoulder. His lovemaking had exhausted her. The intense sexuality that was as much a part of him as his Korcian eyes was both stimulating and distracting.

She should be thinking about his plan to infiltrate one of the factories as soon as it was dark. Instead she was thinking how utterly sexy he looked when he was bare-chested and smiling down at her.

Yet even as the thought came to mind, Kala realized she was reading too much into their relationship. Aedon wanted her, and she wanted him, but each day they spent together drew them closer to what could easily be the end of their lives.

Despite Aedon's passionate nature, his heart was still haunted by the memory of his wife and child. He'd come to Hachyn to seek revenge, not to give his heart to another woman.

"I thought you were thirsty," he said when she didn't reach out and take the wineglass he was offering.

Kala took the glass from his hand. "I've been to Habari before but I've never been sailing on the lake."

He smiled slightly, then checked his commlink for the time. They weren't scheduled to check in with Terk for another six hours. "Then we'll go sailing this afternoon."

An hour later they left the cottage, walking hand in hand, like a couple enjoying a relaxing summer day. Outside the sky was a clean, pristine blue dappled with wispy white clouds.

As they strolled beyond the resort's manicured gardens toward the shores of the lake, Kala tried not to think of the dangerous night ahead.

A breeze stirred vaguely, carrying the scent of the lake. "Tell me about Korcia," she said, feeling completely relaxed in his company. "What's it like?"

He led her toward a narrow, zigzagging path that tunneled through tall green foliage on its way to the lake.

They were only a few yards from the water when he stopped short, drew her into her arms, and kissed her so deeply she felt dazed.

Kala let herself be drawn into the kiss, moving instinctively to get as close to Aedon's body as their clothing allowed, seeking his heat, his touch. His passion.

When the kiss finally ended, he held her close, taking a reflective moment before answering her question. The smoldering gray color of his eyes told her that he was remembering.

"Korcia is beautiful. Lush jungles, emerald oceans, cities that glimmer like gold and silver under the sun. There's no other world like it in the galaxy," he said softly. "The mountains are almost as green as the jungle. They're covered in vines that bloom year-round. Looking at them is like seeing a living rainbow. And the people . . . We have a reputation of being unforgiving in war, but maybe that's because we treasure life so deeply."

With each breath that Kala took, Aedon's masculine strength and power broke over her, making her heart race and her body quicken. The expression on his face was relaxed. Trusting.

"You miss it, don't you?"

His eyes changed to a soft, shimmering blue. "I miss it. It's my homeworld. My people. It's who I am. Who I'll always be."

The subtle reminder of how different their worlds were, of how different their lives had been before meeting one another, only served to enforce Kala's decision to enjoy every moment she could with Aedon.

Holding the moment in her mind, because this moment, and only this moment, was all that life could promise her, Kala kissed him. She tasted him slowly, clinging to him, wanting to remember every sensation, every nuance. His arms locked around her, imprisoning her in his embrace. When their lips separated, and he spoke, she could feel his breath mingling with hers.

"Do you want to go back to the cottage?" His eyes were bright with the passion she'd come to recognize.

"Not yet," she said, smiling. "Take me sailing. I want to feel the sunshine and the water. I want to feel alive."

"You are alive," he said, kissing her with a gentleness that was at odds with the strength of his embrace. "That's what keeps me coming back for more. You're burning with life and that makes me feel more alive than I have in years."

With a sigh she pressed her cheek against his chest and listened to the echo of his heartbeat. "Then we're even, because I've never felt this alive before, either."

They rented a small sailboat at the docks. The rental office was perched on metal stilts over the water. Aedon paid the rental fee using one of the currency cards that had been given to him by Alex Ginomi. Kala added a small gratuity along with a smile. The rental clerk pocketed the gold coin, then gave them a few words of sailing advice. "I'd watch the currents on the far side of the lake, near those rocks," he said, pointing across the glassy water to where a clump of boulders resembled a large turtle sunning itself on the shore. "Keep your eyes open."

"Thanks," Kala replied. "We will."

"What was that all about?" Aedon questioned once they were seated in the small sailboat with its purple and yellow canvas catching the wind overhead. "How many people do you have in Habari?"

"Dozens," she told him.

"How many know we are here?" he asked, sounding displeased that their mission might be compromised.

"Only three. The man at the dock, the one who rented us the cottage, and Stiles's uncle."

Aedon smiled a bit grimly. "Three too many."

"Perhaps, but keep in mind that they don't know about each other. And they know even less about us. As far as the man at the docks is concerned, I'm just like him— another link in the chain."

As the boat skimmed it way over small, rippling waves, Aedon gaze swept the lake, alert to everything around them.

"There's a messenger waiting for us across the lake," she said, interpreting the boat renter's cryptic words, as she placed a wide-brimmed hat over her head to protect her face from the sun and her eyes from the bright light that reflected off the lake's glasslike, blue surface. "Probably news from Ginomi."

Kala didn't say anything more, because they both knew that the news could be bad as easily as it could be good. She simply leaned back against Aedon's thigh, allowing herself to be held captive by the gentle pitch and roll of the boat as the wind pushed it across the water.

Looking up at the sky, she saw a line of clouds blowing in from the east and wondered what else might come with them—victory perhaps.

So much had changed in such a short time. Jein's death, Aedon's appearance, and the indefinable feeling that her grand vision—freedom for her people—was actually obtainable. And all because of one man.

Aedon made the hope she had clung to for years a tangible thing. Having him with her—his support, his knowledge, his confidence—made a difference. The future didn't seem as elusive as it had a few days ago.

It took them nearly an hour to make their way across the expanse of blue water. Kala wasn't surprised by Aedon's skill at the helm. Everything he did, he did well.

She leaned over the side of the snug sailboat and dipped her hand into the gleaming water. An occasional flash of iridescent color told her that the lake was still clean enough to support aquatic life. She counted the small blessing, then looked up at Aedon.

Another blessing.

Or, perhaps, a curse. She was falling in love with him. Maybe she'd already fallen too far to stop the descent.

He looked down and smiled ruefully. "You've got something on your mind."

"Only a million or two things," she confessed, looking out over the water. The midday heat was balanced by the breeze, the peacefulness by the thought of what would come once the sun had set.

Slowly, she became aware of Aedon's intense stare.

"When I go tonight, I go alone," he said.

Kala sat up and adjusted her hat so he could see her face. "I'm not the kind of woman who sits alone in the dark worrying about the man who's fighting her battles for her. That isn't the deal."

"There isn't any deal, Kala. I can't assume responsibility for endangering your life the way I'm going to be endangering mine. There aren't any subsidiary benefits to being dead."

"That's a bit coldhearted, isn't it? I've been on recon missions before. And I'm not Jein. I have two good arms, two good legs, and a head on my shoulders. I know it's dangerous. Everything I do is dangerous."

The shore was coming up fast, the sandy beach only a few meters ahead. "We'll talk about it later."

"There's nothing to talk about." She met his gaze with one just as stubborn, just as determined. "In case you've forgotten who I am, let me introduce myself. My name is Kala Char'ari. I'm the *leader* of the Hachynite Citizens for Freedom."

Aedon smiled. "Pulling rank on me, huh?"

She glanced over her shoulder. "Since you're not military, rank has nothing to do it."

Before he could respond, Kala slipped over the side of the boat and started wading through the water on her way to shore.

thirteen

AEDON STEPPED AHEAD of Kala as they approached the clump of sun-bleached boulders near the southern shore of the lake. Beyond the rocky outcropping, pale-barked trees swayed in the breeze. Not a forest, but enough to offer shade from the afternoon sun and cover for anyone who didn't want to be seen.

A gust of fitful wind rustled the surface of the lake, but nothing else moved.

"What is it?" Kala asked, joining him on the sandy flat of land that separated the water from the wooded area.

Aedon's eyes turned to stare at the trees and underbrush. There was still no movement, only the natural shifting shadows created by sun and wind and flexing branches.

Then he saw it.

Just right of a large tree with knobby roots and silvery leaves that danced randomly in the breeze—a shadow that didn't fit. Didn't move.

But was the shadow their expected messenger or a member of the local police force?

"What is it?" Kala stepped to his side.

"We're being watched," Aedon said, keeping his voice low and shifting his gaze to Kala's face as if he were telling her how lovely she looked in the sunlight. He smiled. "Let's take a walk in the woods. Stay to my left. If it isn't the messenger, let me do the fighting."

She gave him an exasperated look. "While I do the running."

"Yes." He leaned down and kissed her. Not a long kiss, but an affectionate one. "Let's get out of the sun," he said, raising his voice just enough to be heard this time.

They walked toward the trees. Once there, the sunlight faded to a brown haze where insects buzzed around wild-flowers. They were only a few hundred feet into the woods when the rustle of underbrush and the snap of a dried twig alerted Aedon that someone was moving up behind them.

He turned in a blur of movement, simultaneously pushing Kala away. Before he had completed the turn, a laser pistol was drawn from beneath his tunic and aimed.

A startled young man held up his hands in the universal sign of surrender. "Ginomi sent me."

Kala stepped out from behind the tree where she'd taken cover. "It's okay," she said. "I recognize him. He's from Vinsenia."

The young man breathed an audible sigh of relief, but he didn't lower his hands. Young but not stupid, he wasn't about to move an inch until the angry-eyed Korcian gave him permission.

"It's okay," Kala said again. "He's one of us."

The adrenaline that had leapt into Aedon's blood-stream gave way to the soft melody of Kala's words and the laser pistol was lowered, but not holstered.

"What's the message?" Aedon asked.

The young man's lips pressed together, but not firmly enough to stop them from quivering. He was scared. Brown eyes flashed to Kala, then back to Aedon. He fidgeted, shifting his weight from one foot to another, suddenly unsure how the Korcian would receive the news. Obviously it was bad.

"What did Ginomi send you to tell us?" Kala asked, her voice reassuring.

The young man slowly lowered his hands. The fidgeting stopped, but it took several deep swallows before he was able to get the dryness out of his throat and the words out of his mouth. "Ginomi intercepted a message," he finally said. "The governor has put Commander Esarell in charge of all police activities. Effective immediately."

Kala took a step back as if she'd slapped. "Esarell!"

The young man nodded. "Ginomi said you have to be *very* careful." He looked to Aedon. "I have to get back. The patrols are being doubled on Esarell's orders."

"Then you'd better get going," Aedon said.

With that, the boy ran past them and deeper into the woods.

Warily, Aedon looked in the direction the nameless young man had taken. When the sound of insects and birds was all that could be heard, and Aedon was certain no one else was hiding in the woods, he pulled Kala into his arms, holding her until she stopped shaking from the fright that had descended at the mention of Esarell's name.

Aedon knew the commander of the governor's personal guard was considered ruthless, but there had been few facts about him in the Directorate files beyond that of a brutal reputation. The very fact that Kala's soft skin was now dampened by cold sweat was testimony enough that Esarell's reputation hadn't been overstated.

From that fact to the assumption that the governor was pulling out all the stops in an effort to end the resistance wasn't a big step.

"Esarell is inhuman," Kala said as she pulled back from Aedon's embrace so she could meet his gaze. She had already reached the same conclusion as Aedon. "He won't stop until everyone in the resistance is dead."

Aedon pulled her back into his arms. He looked over her head toward the lake, his eyes glittering like gray ice. "We'll stop him first," he promised.

Kala stood on the balcony, her hands on the railing, looking at the lake. It was past seven o'clock; the sun was dipping below the horizon, its orange rays shooting up, creating blocks of shadows over the earth—moving shadows that floated across the water like ghostly birds. The vibrant colors were hypnotic, the evening breeze refreshing.

She and Acdon had spent the afternoon hours analyzing the information Terk had given them on a particular factory site, one he had rigged to handle small electronic components.

They had worked through dinner, their thoughts never leaving the upcoming mission. Aedon was determined to go it alone, but Kala refused to let him. As the HCF's leader she had a right to strike her own blow for democracy and freedom.

Despite their differences, both worried about encountering what they had not envisioned during their planning session; the unexpected was always the most dangerous scenario.

The soft chime of the commlink she'd left on the bedside stand brought Kala out of her silent reverie.

By the time she reached the comm, Aedon was standing in the doorway of the bathroom. Water dripped down his bare chest to be absorbed by the towel that was knotted around his lean hips.

"Yes," Kala answered the comm, sticking to the rule that names were never used on open transmissions, even ones being broadcast on an archaic frequency from centuries past.

"The pumping station at the west end of the lake. Two hours," Terk's voice came back to her.

"Two hours," she said, keeping her response to a minimum.

The commlink hummed with static for a half-second before going silent.

"Where?" Aedon asked, already knowing when.

"The south end of the lake," Kala told him. "Terk will meet us there with the equipment."

Aedon cursed under his breath at the plurality of Kala's statement, but he didn't argue. He'd been doing that for the last two hours, accomplishing nothing. Determined to protect her, he gave it one last try.

"Two hours to convince you to stay here, or two hours to tie you to the bed," he said. "Which one is it going to be?"

Kala flashed him a smile as she reached for the black leggings and tunic she'd borrowed from Sy before leaving the mountain camp. "You'll never have to tie me to a bed as long as you're in it with me. As for staying here, it's a moot point. I'm going."

At first, Aedon heard only devotion and courage, but when he listened more carefully, he heard determination and demand. Insistence and intensity.

"Only as far as the valley," he conceded after a string of Korcian curses. "No one goes into the factory but me."

Kala flashed him another smile.

Two hours later, Aedon was still cursing under his breath, and Kala was still smiling. At least on the surface. Inside, her stomach had tightened into a knot. Any mission into the governor's territory was nerve-racking. The factory guards were under order to shoot first and ask questions only if their victims survived.

Kala looked to where Aedon was moving just ahead of her. As always, his body was poised for danger, ready to counter any attack. She couldn't see his eyes, but she knew they had taken on the piercing, silver-blue color of concentration.

Night had donned its black gown and the only touch of

brightness was an erratic moon lost behind a layer of clouds. They had left the cottage by way of the balcony, slipping over the side and onto the ground as silently as two black cats. Inside the cottage, dimmed lights and soft music gave the impression that the couple who had come to Habari to enjoy a romantic weekend was doing just that.

Beyond the cluster of rental cottages and walk lights the night took on an even deeper shade of black. The surrounding trees filtered the moonlight so completely that only a few muted rays reached the ground. Out of the thickness came the occasional whoop and screech of a nocturnal bird, upset at having its space invaded by people.

Silently, Aedon and Kala made their way around the lake to the southern pumping station. Used only when heavy rains threatened to damage resort property, the pumping station was a concrete bunker, built half aboveground, half below.

They stopped a few hundred feet short of the station. The lake looked more silver than blue in the moonlight, the water lapping lazily at the shore. Aedon pulled her close enough to gently brush his lips over her cheek and whispered, "Stay here while I have a look around."

Kala nodded as she slipped her laser pistol from her belt. As Aedon became just another shadow, she crouched low to the ground and waited in alert silence. With the night folding in around her, she concentrated on what she could hear instead of see, what she could sense rather than touch.

Nothing. The night was dark and still.

Several minutes passed before Aedon completed his reconnaissance and returned to her side.

"All clear," he whispered. "Let's go."

Kala took the lead as they neared the pumping station. The heels of her flat shoes sank into the damp grass until she felt the hard surface of the concrete walkway that led to the station door. There were no windows, only narrow air vents near the flat roof that stood a bare four feet above the ground.

A dim red light was affixed to the underside of the eave just above the door. Kala walked down the three steps to the metal door. Aedon was right behind her with his own weapon at the ready.

Following the predetermined signal, she tapped her knuckles lightly against the metal door twice, waited three seconds, and tapped again.

Terk opened the door and they entered the station. The red glow of emergency lighting reflected off bare concrete walls. Two large pumps, silent for now, filled all but a few square feet of the bunker.

Kala could see the equipment Aedon had requested. It was packed into two black nylon duffel bags. She looked from the equipment bags to where Terk had taken a seat on one of the outflow pipes. Sy was standing next to him.

"Ginomi got a message through to me earlier today," she told them. "He interrupted a transmission between police precincts. The governor has put Commander Esarell in charge of ferreting out the resistance. He's already doubled patrols in the western and northern provinces."

Terk's gaze didn't waver, but he reached out and gave Sy's hand a squeeze. "Nothing like the devil you know."

His deadpan humor echoed off the walls.

Sy wasn't amused. She looked at Kala, her green eyes darkened by the dim light. The shiver of unease that rippled through her was visible. "Be careful. If you're caught . . ." The words came out in a whisper but they spoke volumes.

"Getting caught isn't part of the plan," Aedon said. Everyone knew it was a ritual of self-assurance, rather than a statement of probabilities, but they accepted it as the truth, because to dwell on anything else was self-destructive.

He knelt on the floor, reached for one of the duffel bags, opened it, and began going through the contents, checking the equipment.

"At least the weather is with you," Terk said. "You're almost guaranteed heavy cloud cover for the rest of the night."

"Not a bad thing to have when you don't want to be seen," Kala replied. Her tone was light, but her eyes were serious. "We'll be back before dawn."

"Have you figured out how you're going to do this?" Terk asked Aedon.

"If the schematic you gave me is accurate, we're not talking about sophisticated monitoring, just perimeter sensors."

"One every three feet," Terk reminded him. "And at least a dozen armed guards."

"I'll squeeze through," Aedon assured him. His quick-silver eyes were a pale glitter against the dark interior of the pumping station. "What about transport? Did you get an air-scooter?"

"Waiting in the woods about two hundred yards from here," Sy said. Like Terk, she was trying to adopt a light-hearted attitude. "Stiles fined-tuned the engine. It's quiet, but not silent, so don't park on the factory doorstep. We'd also like it back. So don't go upsetting any guards and getting your asses shot off."

Aedon flashed her a smile. "Don't worry. I'm not out to introduce myself to any of Rendhal's men tonight. Just a quiet look-see, and I'm out of there."

"Then you'd better get going," Terk said. "Check in on your way back. If I haven't heard from you in ten hours—"

"If you don't hear from me in eight, move the timeline up a full twenty-four hours, get into the tunnels, and set the damn detonators," Aedon said. "Stick to the plan."

"And watch all hell break loose," Terk said.

Aedon grinned. "One way or the other."

* * *

The hills and wooded areas near Habari gradually gave way to a dark mesa as the air-scooter approached the Naarca Valley. The navigational sensors on the air-scooter had been put to the test for the first 150 kilometers, bringing them through the forest without mishap.

Now Aedon and Kala lay flat in cover across from the factory. The compound appeared quiet, the office area was shadowy and still. The main entry was closed and the transport area was deserted. Lights illuminated each building, forcing the surrounding landscape into darkness.

From their point on a nearby knoll, Aedon could hear the occasional voices of patrolling guards. Motionless, he studied the lay of the land.

The compound was several hundred acres with small outbuildings surrounding the main factory on three sides. One of the buildings housed the isolated living quarters of the guards.

"I count six guards," Kala whispered as she looked through the night visor Terk had supplied. She was laying close enough for Aedon to feel the heat of her body. "Three to the south, two north, and one just east of the office complex."

Wearing an identical visor, Aedon confirmed her count. "Twelve guards, according to Terk, working six to a twelve-hour shift," he whispered in reply. "Not enough."

"It's six too many if you ask me," Kala said. Her heart held a slow, steady beat, while tension fought to accelerate it.

She lay quietly, listening to the dark silence, fighting the urge to beg Aedon not to go in alone. She'd been on recon missions before, but she'd never lay in the dark waiting for the man she loved to live or die.

Aedon moved his head until his lips were pressing against her ear. Noise was an enemy tonight. The last weapon either one of them needed to use was their laser pistols, even though they were equipped with noise suppressors. It was a myth that suppressed laser fire was silent. It was quieter than regular fire, but the pistol still emitted a low sizzling sound as the laser blast was released.

If Aedon had to take out any of the guards, his choice would be a knife, the garrote hanging from his weapon belt, or his bare hands.

The next few moments passed in virtual silence, Kala laying still by his side, Aedon quietly scanning the area ahead.

"The compound is too big for six guards to patrol properly," he told her, his low voice only inches from her ear. "My gut is telling me that for every guard we see, there are at least three we're not seeing."

"Mine is telling me the same thing. I'm going in with you. The least I can do is watch your back."

Aedon kissed the side of her neck. "The only thing I want you watching is the compound. I don't want to bump into any surprises on my way out. Signal me on the commlink if you see anything. Otherwise, stay here."

"Promise me you'll get *out*," she said, trying not to sound worried and failing miserably.

"I promise," he said quietly. He lifted the shield of his visor, then did the same to hers, exposing her worried expression.

Looking at him, she ached with the emotions that she'd buried when they'd left the cottage. His face was shadowed by the night, his eyes a blazing silver against the bronzed texture of his skin. Kala wanted to touch him, but she didn't dare.

Danger, perhaps even death, was waiting on the other side of the fence. He couldn't afford the distraction her touch might bring, no matter how desperately she wanted to give it.

"Don't worry. This isn't the first time I've gotten in and out of someplace I'm not suppose to be," he said quietly.

"I know," she whispered, closing her eyes.

But even with her eyes closed, Kala could feel the heat of Aedon's breath as he bent his head to join their mouths. She could feel the strength of him as his body shifted alongside her. Then before she could say anything, Aedon claimed her mouth in a long, fiery kiss. It wasn't a good-bye kiss, it was a kiss of promise. And hope.

Kala returned the kiss, her lips clinging to his. His taste was hot and reckless, dangerous and daring. Life and death and everything in between.

Then he was gone, moving in a crouched position and scuttling toward the fence. Kala peered into the darkness until his black-on-black shadow disappeared from sight.

By the dull, green glow of his commlink watch, Aedon read the time—and silently swore. Less then seven hours and counting. He couldn't see the enemy, but he could sense him—out there in the darkness. Somewhere in the distance, the howling of an animal added itself to the in-sane quality of a night that was both friend and foe.

Crouched low in front of the razor-sharp fencing that edged the compound, Aedon listened, but the only sound was the soft surge of the wind as it brushed through the trees behind him. The air smelled of dew-kissed earth and industrial fumes.

Lowering himself to his belly, he pushed everything from his mind but the task at hand—disabling the perimeter sensor so he could get beyond the fence. When the sensor was disarmed, Aedon began to scoop out the dirt from under the fence. It was slow going.

Another hour passed.

When he'd finally dug a shallow hole wide enough for him to slip through without triggering the secondary alarms he was certain were built into the thin steel threads of the fence, he crawled under, emerged on the other side, and lay perfectly still to watch and listen once again.

Nothing but shadows and silence.

The factory lights cast a harsh glow on the compound; the few trees in front of the office complex were silhouetted against the pale metal and brick structure. A window on the second floor showed light.

Something or someone was silhouetted against the glass.

Aedon increased the magnification on his night visor. The silhouette was a person, leaning back in a chair, his feet crossed at the ankles and resting atop a desk, positioned as if he were watching a monitor.

Aedon watched for a full ten minutes. No movement. The guard was asleep.

Aedon forged ahead, belly-crawling his way across two acres of scrub land. The progress was slow. He used his feet and elbows, a knife in his right hand. Prickly bushes gave way reluctantly, their branches tearing at his clothing.

At last he reached a high bank of land above another less-sheltered knoll of grass. He crawled eagerly on toward the first of the outbuildings. He was forced to stop when a shadow materialized a few hundred feet to his right. A guard.

The guard was bathed in gentle moonlight, his pace that of a man whose feet were tired from endless rounds of walking the same path hour after hour.

The guard walked slowly, his head turning from left to right, as he continued his mandatory surveillance. Aedon lay flat on his belly, the tension electric as he waited, and watched, and listened. He could feel the sweat trickling down his back and chest.

Finally, the guard moved on, out of sight.

The clouds that had been building all night drifted over the moon, leaving a thin corona of light and turning the night pitch-black. Aedon took advantage of the momentary darkness and ran across the open area, then dropped into the cover of a low ditch that bordered the first outbuilding.

A stone wall, seven feet, perhaps seven and a half feet high, blocked the building's entryway. He sheathed his knife, stood up, raced toward the wall, and leaped.

Once atop the wall, he held—silent, prone; his hands gripping the sides, his body motionless—a part of the stone. He remained immobile for several seconds, then swung his weight up and over.

Aedon jumped down, slid the knife from his belt once again, and ran toward the building.

He was close enough now to read the sign posted over the building's entryway without the magnification of his night visor. He disengaged the visor, raised his left wrist to his mouth, and spoke into the commlink.

"I'm at the first outbuilding. Ready to go in," he told Kala.

"Be careful," Kala's voice came back to him. "I spotted two more guards. They're near the main factory entrance."

Aedon reached into his equipment belt and pulled out the sensory bypass card that Terk had provided. The young man had guaranteed that the card would open any of the factory doors without triggering an alarm.

Aedon was about to find out if it was true.

He ran toward the building, slid the card through the lock sensor, breathed a sigh of relief when it worked, and eased himself through the door. Beyond, the building was a hollow shell filled with bland, metal shipping containers.

Beyond the sealed containers, a cement tunnel stretched out to the main factory.

Aedon walked silently, rapidly to the end of the tunnel.

When he reached the end, the sound of indistinguishable male voices made him press himself against the wall, his knife poised for attack. The voices were coming from the factory proper, accompanied by the metallic sound of robot arms moving in synchronized, programmed gestures.

The conversation continued for several minutes before

fading—the guards had moved on in their appointed rounds.

Aedon hugged the wall as he eased himself around the corner and into the main assembly area. The complex stretched out before him, row after row of skeletally formed robots mounted alongside gigantic, slow-moving assembly lines. Machinery hummed and clicked and grunted, filling the air with abrasive noise.

The scene was surreal—robots with spindly metal appendages being fed power through thin fiber-optic tubes. Thousands of robots, working nonstop, their only respite a short disconnect for circuitry maintenance.

Aedon focused on one of the conveyor lines that was blocked from view by a bulky crane. It was used to lift the filled containers onto the transport sleds that moved back and forth through the tunnel from the factory to the holding warehouse. He watched as the nimble, humanlike fingers of the robots assembled small electronic components into a finished product.

A product that served only one purpose.

He'd spent too many years in the Fleet not to recognize the small but all-important firing mechanism used in the weapons system of a starjet.

The Conglomerate was producing starjets.

And not just a few. A *fleet* of starjets!

Aedon stared in disbelief as his mind absorbed the enormity of what he was seeing. Starjets weren't used for cargo transportation or routine interstellar travel, but they were agile, fast, and deadly when used as an attack force.

Aedon spent another hour going through the factory, forced only once to take cover from the same guards that he'd seen earlier.

The walking corridors snaked around conveyor belts and assembly frames like a dragon's tail, interrupted by an occasional lounge for the tech riggers who maintained the robots. By the time he was done touring the factory, Aedon had seen most of the navigational and guidance systems components for a starjet in their manufacturing stage.

At last he felt a cool stream of fresh air.

The ventilation shaft that Terk had marked on the building diagram—his way out.

fourteen

KALA REMAINED IN hiding just outside the fence, her body stiff from lying in the same position for hours. Where was Aedon? She'd tried to contact him twice since he'd entered the building, but all she could raise was static. The factory equipment must be interfering with the radio frequency.

Continuing the ritual of waiting and watching, Kala made one of the oldest mistakes in the world—she was so involved watching Aedon's back, she forgot about her own.

"Hello, Kala," the voice came out of the darkness behind her.

She rolled over to find a man standing a few feet away. At close range, the visor blurred vision rather than enhanced it. The intruder was little more than a black silhouette against an even blacker sky. All she could make out was his height and size—medium height, thick-chested, stocky legs. A deep voice.

And a laser rifle.

She pulled the visor off and gasped in disbelief.
Selwyn!
Kala raised her pistol and aimed it at his betraying
heart.

"Not a good idea," Selwyn said. His expression was
grim, but a small smile of genuine satisfaction played at
the corners of his mouth. "Not if you want your friend to
get out of the factory alive."

An hour later, Kala gave every indication of centering
her attention on the four walls that surrounded her. The
clean line of her jaw was marred by a purpling discol-
oration. Another mouse of color stained the skin under
her left eye—her reward for arguing with Selwyn.

"The way I see things, you owe me," the former resistance fighter said. They were in a maintenance building,
behind the factory. "I didn't sound the alarm. Your friend
got away, and I got you. Everything nice and sociable."

Kala stared at the locked door, while Selwyn bragged
about how easy it had been to catch her.

"I was doing my nightly report, and you and the Korcian popped up on the surveillance monitor. All I had to
do was sit back and wait for him to get inside. Then, down
the stairs and out the door."

What time was it? Kala wondered. At least two in the
morning, maybe later. Four hours since Aedon had crawled
under the fence. Briefly, her eyes met those of the man
opposite her. She held his gaze long enough to appear to
be interested in what he was saying.

It wasn't the knowledge that Selwyn would very likely
rape her before turning her over to the authorities, or the
likelihood that she'd die soon after that—she'd always
known it could happen. Death. What had her worried was
Aedon.

Had Selwyn really let him leave the compound, or was

he being held somewhere, being questioned by the guards? Was he even alive?

The uncertainty made her stomach clench as she met the eyes of her captor. Her voice was thick with sarcasm when she said, "So this is what you get when you betray your friends. A few coins and a job in an isolated factory with no one to talk to but guards who think you're scum and robots who can't talk back."

The blow was an open-handed slap this time, sending Kala's head sideways, leaving her ears ringing. She slid to the floor and sat there, refusing to show how terrified she was at the prospect that Aedon had been captured.

"It's better than what I had in Melgarr," Selwyn said angrily. "And it's nothing compared to what I'll be paid when I give them another resistance officer. You always lorded it over the rest of us, knowing where Jein was hiding, acting as if he couldn't survive without you. You knew him better than anyone. Esarell is going to enjoy *persuading* you to tell him everything you know."

"I don't know nearly as much as you think I do. Jein liked his secrets."

Selwyn sneered. "It doesn't matter. Esarell will win in the end. Jein knows that now."

The remark, made in the present tense, not the past tense, brought Kala's head up. "Jein is dead. He was killed when the police stormed the ruins south of Melgarr. They were after me, but they killed Jein instead."

Selwyn tossed back his head and laughed. "Jein isn't dead. He's in prison. A very special prison. One he won't escape from this time."

Kala came to her feet. Her legs were trembling so hard they barely supported her weight. "Jein is alive!"

Selwyn looked very pleased with himself. "Esarell's men dragged him out of the monastery before it exploded. He's going to be a present for the Conglomerate Board of Directors at Rendhal's going-away party."

"What are you talking about?"

This time his laugh was all-knowing, full of mockery. "Esarell has plans for Hachyn that don't include the governor."

Kala let her amber eyes lock with the murky blue ones of the man who had turned traitor. She kept her contempt from showing on her face. Time enough for that later.

Selwyn stared back, letting his gaze measure Kala from head to toe. His eyes fixed on her breasts as a smile came to his face.

Let him stare at her, Kala thought. *Let him gloat. Let him think that all he had to do was hit her to make a crying coward out of her.*

"I always wondered what you'd be like once your arrogance was stripped away," he said. "And I'm going to find out." The fingers of Selwyn's big-knuckled hand closed painfully around Kala's wrist.

Refusing to show any emotion at his cruelty, yet careful not to antagonize him, she regarded him with dark, watchful eyes.

He dragged her to her feet, then toward the back of the building, beyond the dim lights that outlined an array of tools and small equipment used to keep the factory running at peak efficiency.

"Where are you taking me?"

"Shut up!"

The fingers that imprisoned her wrist twisted, and Kala flinched at the unexpected increase in pain. Imagining no alternative that didn't involve another set of bruises, she eased her resistance.

Once they were in the rear of the building, Kala saw the metal door. Selwyn let go of her wrist and waved a laser pistol in a command for her to walk in front of him. "Inside."

Kala did as she was told and found herself standing in an unfinished extension of the maintenance building. The walls were solid concrete, the floor part enforced steel and concrete to the right, dirt to the left. Selwyn tugged her forward.

"Sit."

"On the ground?"

"Sit down." He grabbed her wrist again and twisted it to emphasize his words.

Kala sat. The dirt beneath her was oil-stained. She looked up and saw a set of chains and pulleys that had been used to set the ceiling beams.

"I'm going to leave you here for a while," Selwyn told her. "I don't want to hurt you, and you don't want the guards to hear you screaming for help, so I suggest you stay nice and quiet. I'll come back after I've checked in. We don't want to make anyone suspicious by my not keeping to my schedule. You understand what I'm saying, don't you?"

"I understand." Her voice was low and contained, hiding the hatred she vowed wouldn't show again until she was holding the laser pistol and Selwyn was begging for mercy.

Before Kala knew what he was doing, Selwyn released her wrist in exchange for an ankle. The suddenness of his gesture caught Kala off-balance. Unable to get her hands behind her quickly enough to brace herself, her head thudded onto the hard-packed dirt.

Selwyn jerked her foot up to the level of his waist, keeping her unbalanced. "Hold still," he grunted when she tried to kick her foot free.

The beam of the laser pistol played across her face.

Kala stopped fighting.

"Good girl," he said as he rested her foot against his groin and reached into his pocket.

Kala could feel the thickness of his arousal. Rape was a possibility if she didn't escape before he returned. It was exactly what Selwyn had in mind.

"This won't hurt unless you make it hurt," he said as if he were doing her a favor.

Knowing alive was better than dead, Kala lay on her back while Selwyn wrapped a cold metal band around her slim ankle. A bolt-hinge joined the two pieces of metal just above her Achilles tendon. Selwyn slipped a bolt through the matched holes drilled in the free ends of the shackles.

Once the bolt was in place, he spun the nut onto the threads until it was finger tight. Then, supporting her heel, he used a wrench to tighten the nut. A woman with fingers as her only tool would never be able to loosen it.

"Crude, but effective," he said.

Satisfied that the shackle would hold, he tossed the wrench beyond Kala's reach. Cold metal clanged as the tool bounced off the concrete wall and onto the dirt floor at the opposite end of the room.

Kala looked toward the ceiling. She knew what Selwyn had in mind. Dim light shone on the chains that hung like metal ribbons from the crane. He reached up, bunched one chain's loose end in his big fist, and pulled it toward her.

Kala felt the shackle tighten on her ankle, its sharp edges cutting into the top of her foot as Selwyn tightened the chain. He pulled the chain high, forming a loop that he secured with another bolt.

Kala scooted forward until she was directly beneath the crane's wide arm, using every inch of slack the chain offered.

Selwyn pushed a button on the crane's control panel, and it groaned as if being awakened from a deep sleep. The mechanical arm began to move and the chain was pulled even tighter.

"That should keep you out of trouble until I get back," Selwyn said. He ran his hand from her bound foot to the curve of her knee, pausing to squeeze her calf, while his eyes measured the length of her body. He licked his lips as he observed her vulnerable position. "Don't bother screaming for help. There's no one to hear you but guards, and they'd like nothing better than to find a pretty woman tied up and helpless."

Kala's dark eyes traveled the length of the chain. Flat on her back, her leg extended to its very limits, she recognized the futility of her position. So did Selwyn.

On his way to the door, he looked over his shoulder and said, "Lie there and think about all the ways a woman can pleasure a man, Kala. Because when I come back, you'd better be ready to please me, or you'll be pleasing twenty woman-hungry guards instead."

The door closed with a dull thud. Kala lay on her back in a world suddenly gone darker than she recalled it ever being before, made even darker by the possibility of never seeing Aedon again.

Aedon checked the area a second time. No sign of a struggle could be seen in the faint moonlight that made its way through the thickening clouds and protective branches of the trees. No disturbed dirt, no blood, no trampled grass except for the place where he'd left Kala lying before he'd crawled under the fence.

And yet she was gone.

Reminding himself that patience was as much a part of a warrior's arsenal as any weapon, he retraced his steps and looked again. He backtracked to where he'd hidden the air scooter. It was still there, exactly where he'd left it.

Finally, after ten tense minutes, he found a footprint. It wasn't Kala's. Whoever had made the impression in the soft earth weighed two hundred pounds or more.

A guard?

Aedon didn't think so. If a guard had stumbled upon Kala in the woods, he would have sounded an alarm. If he'd decided to enjoy her before alerting his fellow guards, there would be signs of a struggle—Kala wouldn't give in without a fight.

The conclusion that Aedon reached was simple. Kala had gone willingly with whomever had found her.

The question was who?

And where?

He stood in the darkness, staring at the lights of the compound. The sensation that enveloped him was an eerie feeling, as if he'd suddenly gone back in time, through the layers of his life, and discovered the man he'd once been.

A man capable of love.

The pirates who had killed Nazlean had been faceless men half a galaxy away. The factory guards were here now. Men he could kill if he had to, men who deserved to die if they'd harmed Kala.

He'd lost one woman to the Conglomerate. He wouldn't lose a second.

Not this time.

Not this woman.

Aedon checked his weapons, then started for the factory again. He knew what was waiting for him—at least a dozen armed guards, maybe more, and yet the only fear he felt was the fear of never holding Kala in his arms again.

Part of the numbness Kala felt in her shackled foot came from the chill of cold night air in an unheated building. But most of it, she realized, was because the circulation to her elevated foot had slowed, maybe stopped.

The bolt-locked band of metal wasn't tight enough to restrict the flow of blood. Her problem was that the imprisoned leg was suspended so that her left buttock was actually clear of the ground by a fraction of an inch. It pulled her weight down on the band, forcing the metal to cut into the top of her foot and heel. The restriction, coupled with the elevated limb, was slowing the flow of blood to her tingling foot.

For the tenth time, she shifted her position as much as the chain allowed. And again, she slid her hands open and flat beneath her trim bottom. Resting with her weight atop her hands, she was able to gain a bit of precious height and relieve some of the pressure on her foot.

This time the movement proved less successful than before. The shackle refused to slide even fractionally back along her ankle. Her foot was beginning to swell. Desperately she jiggled it. Nothing happened. The band stayed in place.

Her hands clenched under her, and she felt dirt bunch into her palms. An idea sparked, and she began to claw at the ground.

Minutes later, the tears in Kala's dark eyes were those of total frustration. With her chest heaving from her efforts, she let her bottom settle on the mound of dirt she had clawed from the stubborn floor.

Her nails were split and broken, the tips of her fingers raw and weeping blood. Her foot was bloody from its constant contact with the biting edge of the metal shackle.

She closed her eyes and took a deep breath. "Get moving," she told herself. "Ignore the pain and the blood and keep digging. It's that or Selwyn. Stop feeling sorry for yourself and think!"

She looked up at the chain. All she needed was to be able to reach high enough to get her hands on the bolt Selwyn had slipped through the two chain links. He hadn't used a wrench to tighten the second bolt. Take out the bolt, let the chain slide free of the shackle, and she'd be free. At least free enough to make her way out of the compound. Free enough to find Aedon and help him, if she could.

She felt the earthen mound she'd made. At most it was little more than a foot high. "Get back to work," she ordered herself.

The words took on a hollow sound in the isolated

room, and a trio of watching rats scurried a few feet at the sound.

Holding herself upright with her right arm, Kala fumbled for the chain with her left. Her efforts pulled the edge of the shackle into the raw cuts atop her foot. Gasping from the pain, she caught the chain above her imprisoned ankle and hung onto it with her left hand.

Taking another deep breath, she counted steadily from one to five. On the count of five, she pulled her right hand free of the mound. Lunging with all her strength, she caught the chain. Pulling upward with both hands, she awkwardly raised herself until she could get her one good foot under her.

She gave a little cry of triumph.

Once she got her balance, she stood on one foot, clutching the chain with both hands. Quickly she raised her hands along the chain to the limits of her reach.

Too low.

She couldn't reach the second bolt.

"Now what?"

She knew the next step, the only step. Asking herself the question aloud was a way to give herself time to face the inevitable.

Again she went through the deep-breathing exercise, inhaling and exhaling slowly to relieve the tension in her body and mind. After a couple of minutes, she bent her supporting leg to the limits allowed by the chain. Dreading the pain she knew was going to come next, Kala lunged upward.

She clawed at the chain links and her sore fingers slipped downward, then tightened. Clinging to the chain, clawing her way upward, Kala found herself mouthing half-formed prayers between the curses she heaped on Selwyn's head.

Finally, her trapped ankle was under her. The metal shackle slid upward on her ankle as her weight pressed down into it. With both hands tight on the chain, she hauled her body upward until she could straighten her leg. The shackle rose with her, until it caught on the swell of her calf. And there it held.

Unfortunately, Kala's weight drove the metal's edge into the front of her shin. The pain brought tears to her eyes. For a few seconds, she held tight to the chain as she supported her body's weight with her torn and bleeding hands.

The shackle bit into her shin and opened a new wound. For a moment, Kala almost laughed at the insanity of her situation. If she didn't kill herself trying to get free, Selwyn and the guards would do it for her. She clung to the chain, balanced between fear and determination.

Another emotion boiled to the surface. Anger. Anger at herself for being caught so easily.

Slowly the chain began to turn. The motion didn't bother Kala. The important thing was to reach the bolt. No matter how much her leg hurt, no matter how deeply the shackle dug into her flesh, she had to keep focused. If she let go now, there was no chance she'd have the strength to clamber up the chain a second time. The adrenaline of her struggle was wearing thin, her body was exhausted. Her heart ached at the possibility that Aedon had been captured or killed.

Finally her fingers touched the bolt.

As her bleeding fingertips slowly worked the bolt out of place, Kala fantasized about another set of chains, a rock big enough to sink to the bottom of the ocean, and a traitor named Selwyn.

Aedon was outside the office complex when he heard rapid footsteps coming toward him. The sound was incongruous. Why would someone be racing toward the office? The guards he had seen had been as lethargic as before, walking with their rifles slung over their shoulders, slow-paced, bored, wanting the night to be over. There could be a dozen reasonable explanations for someone being in a hurry at this time of night, but his instincts made him think of the unreasonable ones.

Silently, he ran to the opposite end of the building, where an intersecting corridor of concrete walls led to one of the outbuildings. He rounded the corner and pressed himself against the wall.

Since finding Kala gone, he hadn't used the commlink, all too aware that it could be used against him. If they wanted to exchange Kala for him, they'd be talking to him now.

The footsteps went silent. Then Aedon realized they hadn't disappeared, they had faded, slowed down to a normal walk—a quiet, cautious walk. And then he heard the voice. Low and gruff: whisperlike, indistinguishable. It came from around the edge of the wall, in the vicinity of the main office entrance, no more than thirty feet away.

He inched his face to the sharp, concrete corner and simultaneously readied his knife for an attack.

There was only one man, standing with his back to Aedon, facing the darkened glass of the office door. He was talking to himself.

The man turned slightly, to look toward the fence, enough for Aedon to recognize him.

Selwyn!

The man who had searched him for weapons at the park monument. The man who had earned himself a factory promotion by betraying his friends. The man who had come close to killing Kala. The man who had killed Eiven Jein instead.

Kala's disappearance suddenly made sense.

Somehow Selwyn had found her. The fact that he hadn't sounded an alarm, that the guards were still walking their posts, told Aedon volumes. None of which he liked.

He spun around the edge of wall and raced down the sidewalk that fronted the building. Aedon didn't look back;

he didn't bother to muffle his steps—it would reduce his speed. His only concern was getting his hands around Selwyn's throat so he could choke the truth out of him.

The instant Selwyn realized he wasn't alone, Aedon took a single step, his left hand reaching out to grasp the traitor's throat. He crushed his fingers into the meaty flesh and yanked Selwyn diagonally into him.

No cry emerged; Selwyn's windpipe was choked of all but enough air to form a wheezing sigh.

Aedon pushed him into the cover provided by a concrete pillar supporting the front office portico and held him there.

"Where is she?"

Selwyn tried to take a deep breath and failed. His face paled to a terrified white as he stared into Aedon's gleaming eyes and Aedon knew it was because Selwyn realized the Korcian wouldn't hesitate to kill him.

"Where?" Aedon demanded. He put the blade of his knife underneath Selwyn's ear and drew blood. "Tell me, or the point goes home. Right into your worthless brain."

Selwyn's crazed eyes darted back and forth.

Aedon relaxed his choke hold just enough for Selwyn to speak. "Where is she?"

"In the maintenance building." The words came out in a bubbling whisper of spit and fear. "I didn't hurt her. She's alive."

"What about the guards?" Aedon demanded. The knife point buried deeper. Blood flowed crimson, staining the collar of Selwyn's factory uniform.

"No one knows you're here," Selwyn insisted.

Aedon tightened his grip again. "If you aren't telling me the truth, I'll come back and cut out your lying tongue."

Selwyn looked as if he were going to faint. "She's alive," he stammered. "I swear it!"

Aedon released his choke hold, allowing Selwyn to draw a deep breath. The traitor's lungs were expanding with much-needed air when Aedon's fist crashed against his jaw with such force that Selwyn's head snapped back into the concrete pillar. He dropped to the ground like a felled tree.

Aedon wanted to finish what he'd started, but common sense prevailed. If the guards found a dead factory supervisor, they'd know the compound had been compromised. If Selwyn hadn't told them about Kala, chances were he wouldn't add insult to injury and tell them once he regained consciousness. Explaining his motives for keeping Kala locked away for himself wouldn't go down well with the authorities, much less explaining why he'd let a Korcian sympathizer into the factory—he'd lose the little he'd gained, along with his life.

Aedon dragged Selwyn's dead weight to the side of the building where the shadows would hold until first light. He removed Kala's laser pistol from the man's belt, then searched his pockets. He found a master key card, Kala's commlink, and two metal bolts that were several inches long.

He tossed the bolts into the grass, put the commlink into his pocket, and set out to find the maintenance building.

Alert, wary, his gaze swept the immediate area missing nothing. Judging from the direction Selwyn had come, the building where Kala was being held was to the rear of the factory. Aedon kept to the shadows until he reached the maintenance building.

He used the key card to open the door.

Once inside, he pressed himself against the wall and stared into the dimly lit room. To the left, a metal stairway connected the ground floor to a mesh catwalk.

Aedon crept forward, conscious of his footing, and the sound of his own breathing. His combat sense warned him there was danger ahead. His knife was held ready.

When he reached a row of metal shelving, he paused to look and listen once again.

There was movement to his right, barely discernible in the dark, but definitely movement.

"Kala?" he dared to speak aloud.

She limped to the center of the room. Her hair was matted with dirt, wild eyes stared from a grimy face, and she held a twelve-inch wrench poised to strike a skull-crushing blow.

She blinked as if she were trying to bring his face into focus. "Aedon?"

He stepped forward, allowing the dim overhead lights to illuminate him. "It's okay. I'm alone."

Slowly, hesitantly, Kala lowered the weapon. It fell beside her bloodied foot as she threw herself into his arms.

fifteen

KALA SAT STILL while Aedon freed the fabric of her leggings from the crusted cuts on her shin. Twice, as he cleaned the gouged skin on her foot, Kala flinched free of his gentle touch. And each time, she returned her foot to him without having to be told, trusting that whatever pain he was causing was regretted, but necessary.

They were at the cottage facing Lake Haba. Aedon had decided to return, confident after talking with Kala that nothing had been said to Selwyn that would give away their location or their plans.

"Jein is alive," he said, repeating what she'd told him as if he were digesting the words, deciding whether or not they were believable. "And in prison?"

"Not just any prison," Kala corrected him. "A prison he can't escape from this time."

"What does that mean to you?"

"That he's being held somewhere very special. *If* Esarell is planning to displace the governor, then it makes sense. It's been years, but Rendhal hasn't forgotten that

Jein bested him when he escaped from prison the first time. It was the beginning of the resistance movement."

Aedon had expected dissension in the ranks, but not at the level Selwyn had described to Kala. "If Esarell is planning mutiny, he must be convinced that he can gain the endorsement of the Conglomerate. That means Rendhal is hovering on the edge of disfavor. If he'd gone over the edge already, Hachyn would have a new governor. The Board doesn't waste time once it makes a decision."

"Maybe it's as simple as a sin that can never be completely forgiven," Kala said. "Rendhal's failure to kill Jein the first time is the reason the resistance is still here, causing trouble. Open an old wound instead of creating a new one."

"Maybe," Aedon conceded. "Whatever the reason, we'd be fools not to take advantage of whatever trouble is brewing in the governor's mansion. We need to strike and strike hard. And in more than one place."

"What did you find in the factory?" Kala asked.

Aedon caressed her wrist, the one Selwyn had bruised. "What I expected, but a lot more of it."

Kala rested her head against the pillow. "Selwyn said Esarell was planning the governor's going-away party. Jein is supposed to be the surprise."

"It makes sense. Stage a mutiny, toss the governor's worst mistake in his face, then sit back and soak up the applause of the Board because the elusive rebel leader had finally been caught," Aedon said. "Rendhal fails. Esarell produces results. Thus Esarell is the man you want in charge. It's not a bad strategy."

"It won't work because we can't let it work," Kala said. "Rendhal is a self-serving bastard. Esarell is a heartless monster. We have to find Jein and get him out."

There were tears in her eyes.

Aedon pulled her into his arms and held her close. "That goes without saying. But we can't do anything until we find out where he's being held." He looked down at

Kala's bruised face, at the cuts on her foot and ankle and leg, and anger welled deep inside him. He forced it aside and said, "You need a bath in rejuvenating gel."

"I'll settle for a hot bath in plain water, but only if you bathe with me."

Aedon smiled in reply. Terk and Sy wouldn't arrive for two hours. There was time to satisfy Kala and himself. He wanted to see every inch of her, to kiss every bruise, to caress the soft skin that had been abused by shackles and chains.

Looking at her, Aedon could actually feel himself falling in love. It was an odd sensation, but one that was hauntingly familiar. Years ago—on another world, in another time—his insides had roiled whenever he'd looked at Nazlean. It was the same now, and yet it was different.

Kala was different.

With Nazlean, he had been aggressive, determined to have her, bold in consummating their relationship. With Kala, he felt humbled by her trust—and her courage.

Kala exuded vitality. She wasn't afraid of life, taking the consequences along with the rewards, never looking back, always thinking of the future. She excited him in a way no other woman ever had.

Without a word, Aedon kissed her gently. Slowly his fingers slithered through her hair. When their lips parted, his mouth curved into a small smile.

"I should have tied you to the bed."

Kala smothered his face in small, wet kisses. "There was no way for you to know that Selwyn had been transferred to that particular factory. Stop feeling guilty."

Every protective instinct told Aedon just the opposite, but he kept the guilt to himself. He carried Kala into the bathroom and gently stripped her of her clothes, kissing every bruise along the way. When she was completely naked, he lifted her into his arms and set her in the circular tub where water bubbled from a dozen jets.

"I'm dirty," she said, closing her eyes against the initial painful sting and letting the warm water ease her aching body.

Aedon stripped out of his clothes, never taking his eyes off her. "Make room for a dirty man."

Kala laughed and handed him a tube of soap.

Gently, Aedon rubbed a soapy cloth over her forehead, her cheeks, her nose, her neck. He wiped her arms, turned her around and soaped her back. Turning her around again, he traced a soapy line from her neck to her abdomen, massaging her chest, encircling her breasts. Then he slid his free arm around her and kissed her.

"I can't get enough of you," he said. He continued to stroke her, exploring her body as if it were the first time.

His touch was gently sensuous and commanding, awakening a desire so strong it threatened to overwhelm them both. Kala pressed against him, matching his passion with a fervor of her own, all pain forgotten.

When the tub became too restrictive for real lovemaking, Aedon came to his feet, and dripping wet, carried Kala back to the bed. Her arms wrapped around him. Her lips sought his and expressed her eagerness in full, fiery kisses. Her body was yearning for fulfillment, but Aedon controlled the pace, building the anticipation, increasing the pleasure.

Each moment brought another voluptuous embrace, each touch a volcanic response. Every part of Aedon came alive, tingling, throbbing, elevating his senses to a pitch that was almost unbearable. Kala's hips twisted and turned, responding to his demands, making demands of her own. She was a burning, sensual fire that made him feel as if there were nothing inside him but an all-consuming heat.

They clung to each other and finally, with a burst of breathless ardor, they completed each other.

For a long time, they lay wrapped in each other's arms,

their bodies still, their lips silent, unwilling to separate, unwilling to disturb the fantasy their lovemaking had created in their minds.

"You're the most incredible man I've ever met," she whispered when their heartbeats had finally slowed to normal.

Aedon kissed her and felt his body stir to life again.

With an assertiveness he had stifled the first time, because he hadn't wanted to hurt her, he rolled, pulling Kala on top of him, kissing her in a way that eliminated all thought of talk or sleep. He nudged her legs apart, and joined their bodies again, pushing himself deep into her silky warmth.

The pleasure on Kala's face as he moved slowly in and out of her made Aedon fight for control, not of his body, but of his emotions.

He could have lost her. He'd come very close to losing her. Too damn close.

Being right didn't make a man or woman invulnerable. Aedon had buried too many loved ones to think differently.

Holding Kala now, being buried deep within her warmth, Aedon remembered how he had believed that he would have Nazlean forever. He also remembered how short forever had turned out to be.

"I want to tell you that I love you," he said in a husky voice. He looked into the golden blaze of her eyes. "But love means commitment, and I can't make promises I may not be alive to keep. Not now. Not here. Not with a war that has to be fought and won."

"I love you," Kala whispered as her mouth met his. Her voice brought him out of the past and into the present. She made a thick sound of pleasure as he rolled his hips, keeping them joined. "Neither one of us can make promises. But loving you is how I feel right now, this minute. And right now is all that life promises anyone. Don't waste it."

He smiled and returned her kiss, arching his hips until he was buried as deep inside her as he could get. Splinters of pleasure unraveled inside him. "I want you."

"Then have me," she said lovingly. "I'm yours."

Aedon awakened before the last stars had faded from the morning sky. Beyond the balcony doors, the world was coming alive. Kala stirred sleepily at his side, wrapping an arm around his waist as she snuggled in close.

Even as he told himself all the reasons why he shouldn't waken her with the same passion that had helped her to fall asleep, his hands were moving over her, pushing away the thin barrier of the bedsheet, searching for the soft, sleek center of her. Finding it, he caressed her slowly.

She moaned, then stretched like a contented cat, unconsciously pushing against his hand, wanting more of his sensual petting.

Moments later, her eyes opened, gleaming golden brown as they focused on his face.

"You're awake," she murmured, stretching again, arching her hips upward in response to his touch.

His smile was pure male. "You noticed."

"I noticed." She gasped as his fingers slid over and around the sultry core of her, finding and caressing the moist, silky flesh that was preparing to accept him.

"Good. It's more fun when I'm not making love alone."

His hand moved again, sending his touch deep inside her. Her lashes lowered as her body gave itself instinctively to the need he was arousing. She opened her legs, inviting him inside. Aedon joined their bodies completely.

The lovemaking was slow, as natural as night giving way to day. Need pricked along Aedon's spine as he worked his hips in a smooth rhythm, giving and taking as gently as sunlight taking away the shadows of a dark night.

With every breath he drew he felt himself surrendering to the need Kala had awakened in him. To the love.

When Kala couldn't hold herself back any longer, Aedon covered her mouth with his own and drank her sweet cries of pleasure as he let go of his control and poured himself into her. Her body drank his pleasure in return, silky muscles contracting to hold him in place until every drop of passion had been wrenched from him.

When Kala drifted into sleep a second time, Aedon reluctantly separated himself from her and left the bed. He dressed quickly and walked out onto the balcony.

The morning light was burning the mist from the lake, freeing it to drift lazily upward to eventually disappear completely.

As he stared out over the water, his mind's eye saw something different—the unlimited vastness of space. Dark. Cold. Immeasurable. Its beautiful blackness was interrupted only by a sporadic sprinkling of planets, asteroids, and stars.

"What are you thinking about?" Kala asked as she joined him.

Aedon drew her to his side. The silk of her blue robe slid softly against the black leather of his trousers. The gel he had spread over her cuts and bruises was doing its job—redness and bruising were slowly being replaced by the ivory tones of healthy skin.

His smile flashed briefly. "I'm thinking about star charts."

"Star charts?"

"And starjets. You don't make the components without the intention of producing a finished product. If the jets aren't being assembled here on Hachyn, the components are being shipped to another planet. The question is which one?"

Kala looked up at him. "There are a lot of factories. The starjets could be here?"

Aedon shook his head. "Starjets have to be flight tested

after assembly. That's not something you can hide easily. It means launching platforms and docking bays. And pilots."

"The only pilots on Hachyn with deep space piloting skills are Rendhal's pirates."

Aedon grinned. "Exactly."

Kala rested her hands on the balcony railing. She looked out over the lake as if she were following Aedon's line of sight as well as his line of thought. "You think the pirates are really test pilots? It's bizarre."

"Just bizarre enough to be true," he said. "And it fits the scheme of things."

Sunlight slithered over the treetops, changing the blue waters of Lake Haba to gleaming amber. Kala shivered involuntarily. "You think pirates are attacking freighters and cruise vessels and killing people because the Conglomerate wants to *test* its starjets?"

Aedon's jaw tightened. "The Fleet uses the same sort of training maneuvers, but we don't use human targets. Starjets are put through a minimum of one hundred hours of flight and target testing before they're assigned to a fighter squadron. If the Conglomerate is serious, and they are, then they'd do the same. You don't put an untested weapon into the field, and that's exactly what a starjet is. A weapon. A fast, deadly weapon."

"It's also a very recognizable one," Kala said.

"There are as many ways to disguise a space vessel as there are ways to mold a hull. The ship I docked when I arrived doesn't look like a starjet, but it is. Strip away a few bulky lines, mount the right armaments, and it's as trim and deadly as anything in the Korcian Fleet."

Kala raised her head. "I'll grant that deep space is a huge place, but a fleet of starjets is bound to catch someone's attention. We aren't that far from the Empire. Your people must monitor deep space flights."

"We do," Aedon said. His eyes darkened to a midnight blue that said he didn't like the conclusions he'd drawn.

"The pirate raids haven't left any witnesses, and only a few emergency messages got through to our patrol squads. What we do know is sketchy, but the ships are small and fast. Highly maneuverable and armed with enough munitions to blow a freighter into stardust. They strike unexpectedly, then disappear. Most of the normal shipping and transport lanes have been diverted as a result. The space between Hachyn, Pecora, and the Trinity worlds of Taza, Myamar, and Saluis has turned into a no-fly zone."

Kala looked at him, saying nothing. His eyes had changed again. Silver flecked with black, they continued to stare out at the water.

When he let go of a short, barking laugh, she stiffened at the sound. "What is it?"

"The obvious that's so clear it can't be seen unless you stumble over it," Aedon said sardonically. He smiled strangely. "A Terran would say it's the writing on the wall."

Kala grasped his meaning. "All the worlds you named are under Conglomerate control."

Aedon's breath came in hard, yet even, as cold anger congealed in the pit of his stomach. He had to admire the brutal simplicity of the Conglomerate's plan.

"Test the starjets and clear the travel corridors at the same time," he said after a moment. "Fly the finished vessels to a new base, bring the pilots back, and start all over again. Not a quick operation, but a patient approach that distracts attention from what is really happening. Brilliant."

"How many ships to do you think have gotten through?" Kala asked, trusting Aedon's conclusion as much as she trusted his warrior instincts.

"It's impossible to say. The piracy has been going on for years. A thousand ships, maybe more. But certainly enough to destroy a border station when an attack is finally launched."

"A Korcian border station."

A shrug lifted his shoulders. "We're closer to this sector of the outer regions than the League of Planets."

"That would mean war. Do you actually think the Conglomerate is ready to take on an undefeated Korcian Fleet?"

"Not yet. Then again, they don't know that anyone has caught on to their game. If I hadn't come here, if I hadn't gotten into one of those factories, no one would know now."

What Aedon didn't say was that he had to get word to the Directorate of what he'd discovered—what he thought. The fight on Hachyn was far from over. An attempt to rescue Jein had to be made. Successful or not, there was no guarantee he'd live through it. A message had to be sent, an alarm sounded.

Kala measured the intensity of Aedon's chameleon eyes, the tension that held his shoulders stiff, and the determination in his expression. She'd always known there was more to the Korcian warrior than he'd wanted to admit. She was looking at the proof now, seeing below the surface to the man who had pledged his loyalty to the Korcian Empire the same way she had pledged hers to the Hachynite Citizens for Freedom.

"But you did come here," she said, picking up on his words. "You came here because you were *sent* here. You infiltrated the factory because you were told to. You're helping us because you're under orders to help us."

Kala knew she'd just spoken the truth. It was in the sudden intake of Aedon's breath, in the flash of luminous blue that colored his eyes, in the tense line of the mouth that had kissed her so thoroughly only a short while ago.

But it wasn't betrayal Kala saw in Aedon's face. It was regret. He was looking at her as if he wished they hadn't become lovers, as if the complication of sleeping with her was getting in the way of his duty to the Empire.

Kala took a step back as her mind swirled. Had Aedon made love to her—mentioned love, only as a ploy to gain her cooperation? Did he care at all that her heart had been given without reserve, that her trust had been unconditional?

Anger flared along with a dozen other emotions. Kala thought about walking out of the cottage, walking away from the dark, dangerous stranger she'd met in a public square, but like Aedon, duty called too deeply to be ignored.

"It's true, isn't it? The Empire got wind of Rendhal's plans and sent you here to confirm them. You're a spy, or maybe even a Fleet officer. The difference is minimal from where I stand. Was your wife really killed by pirates? Did you ever have a family other than the Fleet? What does the Empire want, another planet to snuggle up to, a colony where the people are already in place with nothing left but an oath of allegiance to another unelected government?"

Her breath came in hard gasps, her words spilling out before Aedon could insert an answer. "Do you even care about the people on this world?"

The same sunlight that had burned the mist from the lake sent streamers of light over Aedon's face, transforming his silver eyes into steely pools of anger. He was looking at her as one might look at a vulnerable child being taught an uncomfortable lesson of adulthood.

"Don't judge me," he said. "And don't assume that everything is what it seems to be. You've lived under Conglomerate control long enough to know that deception is a rule of law. As for my wife, she existed. So did our child. They were my life. When they were killed, I vowed to avenge their deaths, and I *will*."

Kala took another step back. Part of her wanted to strike out, to hurt him as much as she was hurting, but she knew besting her physically would be easy. Aedon had been bred for war by a people who had never been defeated in battle. Fighting was in his blood. In his soul.

And pain was in his heart. The pain of love lost never to be regained. The pain of losing the woman he had loved.

Whatever else Kala believed, she knew Aedon wasn't lying when he said he had loved his wife and child. His eyes had darkened to a near black when he spoke of avenging their deaths.

She drew in her verbal claws and a took a deep breath. Until recently she would never have believed that the future of her homeworld could be held in the hands of one man. Not until she'd met Aedon Rawn—but now he embodied every hope of freedom she had ever dared to dream.

Freedom for her people. Freedom for herself. The freedom to love and trust, to think of a future that went beyond political victory. The fact that he didn't trust her enough to be completely honest brought a painful tightness to Kala's throat, but it didn't change his abilities—abilities the resistance needed now more than ever.

Terk and Ginomi couldn't get Jein out of prison alone. They didn't have the military genius that was as much a part of Aedon as his ever-changing Korcian eyes.

"You still haven't told me the entire truth," she said. "Will you ever?"

His brow furled and his eyes narrowed, as if he were reading something written on his mind. And in his heart.

"No," he said curtly. "You'll just have to trust me awhile longer."

sixteen

"JEIN IS ALIVE!" Terk received the news with an astonished expression. "What the hell happened last night?"

They were lunching at a lakeside restaurant—hiding in plain sight. From where they sat, Kala could see other couples who had come to the resort for a few days of secluded fun.

Kala was seated with her injured foot flat on the terrace floor. Another application of rejuvenation gel and she'd be walking without a limp. She stared out across the lake for a moment, gathering her thoughts. When she looked to Terk and Sy again, she sighed, settled back against the cushions of the high-backed chair, and told them what they were waiting to hear.

"I can't believe it," Sy said when Kala had finished. She was sitting beside Terk, looking every inch like a woman who had slept in her lover's arms last night. Several times during the meal, Kala had noticed the couple exchanging glances.

Kala wondered if she looked the same way. If Terk and

Sy knew that she and Aedon were lovers. Was Terk using Sy for physical satisfaction, or did he care for her? Perhaps she'd misjudged his previous attitude toward Aedon, labeling it jealousy when all it had been was suspicion toward an outsider.

She and Aedon had exchanged only a few words since she'd accused him of putting the Empire first. He'd said nothing to confirm or deny her accusations. Nothing beyond the fact that he'd do what he came to Hachyn to do.

With a sense of bafflement and suppressed anger, Kala knew that regardless of what she didn't *know* about Aedon, little had changed. Her gut was still telling her to trust him.

"I can't believe you let the bastard live," Terk said. He was speaking to Aedon, but his eyes were on the bruise that encircled Kalas wrist like a black-and-blue bracelet. "I would have gutted Selwyn like the pig he is."

"Selwyn is the least of our worries," Kala said. "If Aedon had killed him, doubled patrols would be tripled, and we'd lose any chance of finding Jein and freeing him. Aedon's right, Selwyn can't alert the authorities to our being in the factory compound without telling on himself. He'll keep his mouth shut."

Terk let out a frustrated breath. He poured cream into his coffee cup, then stirred it slowly. "Okay, so we know the factories are pumping out components for starjets, and we know that Esarell is going to use Jein to impress the Board of Directors. Where does that leave us?"

"With a lapful of problems," Sy said bleakly.

No one argued. None of the information Aedon and Kala had shared over lunch was good.

Aedon looked across the table to Terk. "One thing is certain. We can't blow the factories. At least not yet. Jein has to be our number-one priority. Selwyn told Kala the prison was one Jein wouldn't be able to escape from this time. Does that paint any particular picture for you?"

"There are six high-security prisons in the eastern

province alone," Terk said. "Twice that many in the south, and another four in the north. Jein could be in any one of them."

"Zahalla," Sy said, her voice low, as if the word demanded reverence.

"What's Zahalla?" Aedon asked.

"An island fortress," Terk said. "Rendhal used it for a summer palace until he got bored with being surrounded by water. He *gifted* it to Esarell when he became the Honor Guard's commander. It's a hundred kilometers off the southeast coast, totally isolated, heavily guarded, and impossible to get close to without getting your head blown off."

"A prison that offers no escape," Kala said. "I should have thought of Zahalla myself."

"You've had a lot on your mind," Aedon replied. He motioned for the waiter to refill their glasses. Nothing more was said until they could speak among themselves without being overheard.

Kala accepted the remark with a smile, knowing that Terk and Sy were watching her response. There was little comfort in the thought that she had had a lot on her mind, or that the past had taught her to stay focused on the present. It was one way to avoid making the same mistake twice. It was better to know that whatever she and Aedon shared would end one way or the other—either by one or both of them being killed, or when Aedon left Hachyn to return to his homeworld.

"Zahalla," Aedon said, repeating the name of the isolated island. "I'll need information. Architectural plans, weather maps, anything you can get your hands on."

"Done," Terk said. "What else?"

Aedon shook his head. "I can't help but think that all of our problems have a common foundation. Rendhal's been trying to shut down the resistance for years. Why wait until now to put Esarell in charge? Why the sudden urgency? Do you have anyone inside the governor's palace?"

"A few clerks and some palace staff, but no one high enough to be included in Rendhal's inner circle," Kala told him. "You think the factories are connected to Esarell being put in charge of the police forces?"

"I don't like coincidences." Aedon paused to take a drink of the white wine they'd been served with an over-priced lunch. "The Conglomerate may seem autonomous, but everything they do is connected. Every action is thought out, planned, methodically executed. It's what has kept their Board of Directors beyond the reach of any legal system in the galaxy. Things don't just happen in the corporate colonies. They're systematically analyzed before a vote is taken."

"Is the why all that important?" Kala asked tensely. Her emotions were catching up with her. She needed a few hours away from Aedon, time to think, time to console her heart and get her head on straight.

"No," Aedon agreed. "But the how and when is. Getting Jein out of prison will set off every alarm on the planet. That means we have to attack the factories simultaneously. Confusion is a weapon that's been used successfully for eons. We hit Zahalla, the Naarca Valley, and any other target Terk and Ginomi can think of—all in one night."

"Total chaos," Terk smiled benignly. He leaned back in his chair and smiled approvingly. "Rendhal's men won't know which way to run."

"Chaos or victory," Aedon said solemnly. "All or nothing at all."

"All or nothing at all." The words echoed in Kala's head as she walked along the shores of Lake Haba.

As she watched ripples of water gently caress dry land, she tried to clear her mind and heart of emotions—to focus on the facts. But the facts were unavoidably woven around one man: Aedon Rawn.

She stopped to rest, not wanting to push the overtaxed muscles of her foot and ankle too far. Sitting on a flat, flint-gray boulder near the water, she closed her eyes to the bright sunlight and let the breeze blowing down from the mountains cool her skin.

Sitting when action needed to be taken usually drove Kala crazy. Sitting silently when there was nothing else to do offered a rare opportunity, a time of forced indolence for the body and mind. This was one of those times.

Terk and Sy had returned to the Moviash camp to coordinate their efforts with Ginomi. Alvaron and Stiles were at the safe house, working on detonators and procuring any other equipment Aedon might need once he'd formulated a plan to get Jein away from the island fortress of Zahalla.

She and Aedon would remain at the resort. The weekend roster of visitors had vacated the hotels and neighboring cottages to return to their jobs in Melgarr and Lejan. The new vacationers would assume that she and Aedon were among the newly arrived guests rather than the old.

On the surface, Kala approved of the decision. Moving back and forth between the Moviash camp would take valuable time away from the other things that needed to be done if they were to free Jein and return him to the resistance. But deep inside, she dreaded the nights.

The entire lake resort had been designed for single people who didn't care to have overnight guests, except for lovers, of course.

The memories of what it had been like to sleep next to Aedon's strong body, to be held in his arms, to be loved so passionately, forced Kala to give herself a hard mental shake. She had to get hold of herself. No good would come of wasting time imagining useless possibilities. Aedon would do what he came to Hachyn to do, or die trying.

After that, he would . . . do what?

Try as she might, Kala couldn't picture Aedon giving

up a homeworld that he had pledged his life to protect for a world contaminated by corruption and neglect. It would take generations of heartfelt dedication to rebuild Hachyn after it was free.

"I thought I'd find you here."

Kala turned to find Aedon standing behind her. She glanced from his handsome face upward to the sky. The distinctive ridge of clouds that formed daily from the moisture being blown inland from the North Jovian Sea was becoming darker. The ridge was thickening into slow-moving storm clouds that promised an evening's reprieve from the summer heat.

"I needed to walk," she said, scooting down from the boulder. "And think."

"About me?"

"About Jein," she said, giving him a half-truth. "What if we can't get him out alive?"

"Then I'll die trying."

"Not you. *We*. We'll die trying," Kala said distinctly. "You may want Rendhal as cold-stone dead as the rest of us, but this isn't your war. It's ours. We'll be the ones living on this world when it's all said and done."

A brief flash of something showed in Aedon's eyes, but only for a second. "Pulling rank again?"

"We need you," she admitted. "You have the soldiering skills and the tactical ability to get us in and out of Zahalla."

He smiled without warmth. The glint in his eyes wasn't one of anger or irritation. It was ice.

"So that's all I am now. A soldier."

"It's what you've always been," Kala retorted. "Why should today be any different?"

Shimmering silver eyes darkened to match the pewter clouds that were building overhead. Frowning, he glanced toward the woods that bordered the lake. Kala had passed a routine police patrol on her way out of the resort. They had stopped to stare, but only for a moment.

"I wasn't followed," she said, sensing Aedon's unease as he scanned the wooded area for unwanted visitors. The remark also presented a way for her to avoid discussing their personal relationship.

"When you transmitted messages to Pecora, how did you do it?" he asked unexpectedly.

"Why?"

"Why do you think?" His eyes narrowed against the brilliant sunlight that momentarily escaped the thickening gray clouds.

Kala had kept a tight rein on her emotions all morning. The rein was loosening now.

"You want to warn the Empire?"

"Yes."

For a moment Kala was tempted to ignore his cool tone of voice and force him to tell her everything. But she didn't. If they traded places, she'd be doing the same thing—protecting what was important to her.

"Jein generated the transmission from the monastery to a communication station in Lejan. A *friend* of the resistance relayed it to the deep-space channel."

"What friend?"

Aedon was testing her, forcing her to prove that she still trusted him with the intricate details of the resistance's underground network.

She tilted her head to the sunlight, thinking of all the reasons she should keep what she knew to herself, and all the reasons she shouldn't. There was no straight line between right and wrong, no guarantees that any decision wouldn't be second-guessed later. Life was a series of unforeseen events. Aedon might have disappointed her emotionally, but he'd never failed to deliver on the fighting end of things. And there was a big fight ahead.

She looked to where he was standing, his body a series of coiled muscular springs, taut and contained. Her gaze swept up to his face, a face cast in unreadable stone. Then Aedon met her gaze, and the image of stone collapsed.

His eyes were alive and penetrating, forcing Kala to acknowledge him.

"His name is Montrose. He's a midlevel attaché in the Communications Bureau. He's also Yahaira's brother."

"The brothel owner."

Kala nodded, then added coolly, "I'll have to go with you. Montrose will need verification that you're with the resistance."

The sterile-looking, flat-fronted house sat on a street neighboring the Communications Bureau. Unlike Melgarr, Lejan was a new city, built less than a hundred years ago to accommodate the development of the northern provinces. The buildings were tall and modernistic. The streets were wide, well lit at night, and filled with air-taxis and scooters.

Constructed along both sides of a natural intercoastal waterway formed by the North Jovian Sea meeting the Naud River, the city served as the province's main corporate center. Uniformed police patrols were a frequent sight, accepted by the residents who were mostly government employees.

At this time of the evening there were only a small number of people in the park across from Montrose's home. Like most parks on Hachyn, the acreage was small, barely a full acre. A middle-aged man sat on a stone bench feeding red-bellied doves, one of the few remaining species of wildlife indigenous to Hachyn. The birds chirped greedily as the man tossed out a handful of unshelled seeds.

Montrose seemed oblivious to the passersby who intermittently glanced in his direction. His clothes were those of a moderately paid employee. Aedon could tell from his posture that he was shorter than most men and well rounded in the belly.

As he and Kala approached the bench, Aedon's keen

vision picked up the slight trembling of the man's hand as he reached into a foil bag, taking out seeds and scattering them, attracting scores of doves that cooed in counterpoint to their pecking of the grassy ground.

Kala stepped ahead of Aedon and sat down. Wordlessly, Montrose offered her the foil bag. Kala tossed more seeds to the encroaching doves.

Aedon stopped just short of the bench, close enough to hear what was being said, but far enough away to keep the man from getting even more nervous. It was apparent he didn't like meeting a member of the resistance face to face, even one as trusted as Kala Char'ari.

"We need to send a message," Kala said softly.

"What other reason would you have to be here?" the man replied, his voice low. The doves near his feet began to fight among themselves as another handful of seeds was tossed to the ground.

Kala returned the foil bag to his hands. "When can you send it?"

The man looked directly at Kala for the first time. His eyebrows were a shade darker than his hair. Thick and almost horizontal, they emphasized the pale blue of his eyes that reflected the languor of the summer evening.

"Not now," he said. "Esarell's men are conducting security checks. Everyone is being screened, even those of us who have perfect records. They are looking for aberrations. Strange behavior, pastimes or hobbies that appear unusual for a dedicated citizen, unexpected trips or visitors. I shouldn't even be talking to you."

"The message is necessary," Aedon said.

The man met his gaze. His expression stiffened for a moment, surprised to find that Kala's companion was a Korcian.

Several moments passed while more seed was thrown to the fluttering doves. The park began to take on shadows as the sun sank lower on the horizon.

"Very well," Montrose finally said. "But not from the Comm Bureau."

"Where and when?" Aedon asked bluntly.

Montrose hesitated for several moments, looking toward the street to make sure their conversation wasn't being observed. "We'll have to use a private station. Meet me in two hours. South of the waterfront highway. Four kilometers beyond the intercoastal bridge there's an access road . . ." He finished the directions, then stood up, tossing the last of seeds to the doves. "Make sure you aren't followed. I can access the relay frequency for five minutes. Anything longer is too dangerous."

Aedon looked around at the city that was slowly being transformed by the setting sun. Like most cities there was a rhythm to its behavior: streetlights glowed in the twilight, people were heading home after a day's work, families were inside having dinner and conversation.

As the heavy blanket of night descended, Aedon reached out and took hold of Kala's arm as she rose from the bench. She flinched, saying without words that she didn't want his touch.

His mouth flattened as his hand dropped to his side. She hadn't fought his company, but she was making it clear that their relationship was strictly business from this point on.

Aedon didn't like it, but he did understand it. They'd become comrades and lovers because she had trusted him. She still trusted him, but his refusal to tell her who had sent him to Hachyn had dampened that trust.

As they walked the short distance to a nearby tavern where they could get a drink and wait out the two hours before they were to meet Montrose, it was difficult for Aedon to dismiss his feelings for the beautiful, auburn-haired woman.

Since meeting Kala in the square, they had been constant companions. They had escaped the monastery explosion together, slept in the same bed, ate at the same table, and fought the same enemy. What they held in common outweighed their differences.

He suspected Kala felt the same way, making him want to pry beneath her sudden indifference.

"Are you hungry?" he asked as they paused to let an air-scooter whisk by them.

"Not particularly."

Aedon slanted a sideways look at her. Her eyes were staring straight ahead, her mouth set in a thin line. She was walking without a limp, but there were still bruises on her foot and leg, hidden from view by a white gauzy summer dress that swished around her ankles with every step.

The thought of Selwyn's hands on her made Aedon's blood run hot, then cold.

"How dependable is Montrose?" he asked.

"Dependable enough to be believed. Don't worry, he'll get your message through."

"I was thinking about the Comm Bureau."

She looked his way for a second. "What about it?"

"It should be one of our targets."

She made a low sound of surprise, then nodded. "You're right, of course. We could disrupt communications along the whole eastern coast if we take out the bureau in Lejan." She looked his way again. "Ginomi was right. You're a good strategist. The Empire taught you well."

Aedon refused the bait of Kala's remark.

They finished walking to the tavern in silence.

Aedon found a table near the window and ordered drinks. For a moment, his crystalline silver eyes focused completely on the young woman sitting across the table. The savage irony of finally finding a woman he could care about because he'd accepted the Directorate assignment, and knowing that the Directorate was the wedge between them, brought a crooked smile to his face.

He watched Kala staring out the window, desperately avoiding eye contact, avoiding him. Her blatant indifference tempted Aedon to reach out and touch her again, just to make her react.

Instead, he reached for his drink.

There was no point pretending their relationship wasn't in jeopardy. Aedon knew that it had been at risk since their first kiss. And yet he'd allowed the kiss to happen. Allowed it. Enjoyed it. Encouraged more kisses. He was the one who had reached for Kala last night. He couldn't blame her for feeling used today.

Desire was physical.

Trust came from the heart.

To Kala's way of thinking, he had betrayed that trust.

seventeen

AEDON AND KALA easily found the road four kilometers beyond the bridge. They walked side by side, their way illuminated by the moon and the lights that bordered the intercoastal waterway on both sides. The brackish water, slick with oil from the ships and ferries that made use of the natural passage, gleamed like licorice in the dim light.

They were approaching the comm station when voices came out of the darkness.

"Guards," Kala said, looking for someplace to take cover.

Aedon stilled her nervousness with his hand. "Running implies that we're doing something wrong," he said calmly.

Kala belittled herself for panicking. If her emotions weren't so twisted around her heart, she'd know better. She'd been living on jagged nerves all day. "Then what?"

"Two people taking an evening stroll," he answered. "Over there, by the water."

They walked casually beyond the circle of light cast by a nearby streetlight. A breeze stirred lazily, bringing the scent of the sea to mingle with the scent of the city.

"Stop looking at me as if I were the enemy," Aedon said as the guards drew nearer. "Smile. Pretend you're having a good time."

Kala laughed softly and stared up at the man who was walking so gracefully at her side. Aedon's ability to appear totally relaxed when every sense he possessed was tuned to his surroundings still amazed her. So did her ability to still be emotionally stirred by his very presence.

And yet to deny that emotion was to reject a fundamental reality of her life. She loved him.

Kala looked away. There was another reality—one just as fundamental. Just as true.

There was no guarantee either one of them would live long enough to have a future.

A few yards away, the light of the streetlamps gleamed off the polished rifles slung over the guards' shoulders.

Aedon led her down the lighted walkway that zig-zagged its way through grass and shrubs to the water's edge. He stopped, then gently pressed her against the trunk of a tree.

Kala could see his eyes narrow as they probed the darkness. His attention was on the guards, not her, but she couldn't ignore the heat of his body. They were matched length to length, his hips pressed suggestively against her, one hand braced on the trunk above her head. He was standing close enough for her to count the heartbeats pulsing in his neck.

"I'm going to kiss you," he said very softly against her ear. "Stop being angry with me and look as if you're enjoying it."

Although Kala knew the kiss was only a show for the guards, very much like their first kiss had been, she couldn't pretend not to enjoy it. The brush of Aedon's lips gently over hers was a prelude to the pleasure that would come next.

When he finally joined their mouths completely, her body instantly recognized his, softening to give whatever he wanted.

The strength and weight of Aedon's body, the scent of him, the pressure of his mouth, brought all the feelings Kala had been trying to bury all day back to the surface.

Unable to stop herself, she returned the kiss, losing her detachment as Aedon's tongue slid gently between her lips. He tasted of the whiskey he'd drunk earlier at the tavern.

Despite the danger building with each approaching footstep of the guards, the kiss was slow, undemanding. Kala found herself savoring each second, memorizing the scent and taste of him.

"They're coming this way," he said in a whisper that was more breath than words as he pulled away from her. "No. Don't move. Just relax and let me handle things."

Kala didn't have time to protest. Aedon was kissing her again, his free hand sliding over her shoulder, pausing at the curve of her breast, squeezing gently. Like his kiss, his touch was electric, unraveling her resolve. His hands continued to caress as he tasted her even more deeply.

An obscene remark came out of the darkness, and Kala stiffened.

"Trust me," Aedon whispered before stepping away from her.

The second guard mumbled something about leaving the couple be, but the guard who had made the foul remark wasn't in a benevolent mood. His next words betrayed his intentions.

"We've got orders to search anyone suspicious," he said in a malicious tone. "You take the man. I'll take the woman."

Before Kala had a chance to react, she was being pushed gently aside, away from the upcoming fight.

Aedon didn't waste any time. His eyes glittered as he faced the first of the two guards.

The man hesitated at being confronted so courageously, then crumpled to the ground as Aedon's fist rocketed into his jaw, sending him sprawling on his backside.

Kala looked for another team of guards, but the two seemed to have been patrolling alone. "Be careful," she called out to Aedon.

The second guard, who had held back, now raced forward. Used to being feared, he had been momentarily shocked by the attack. Surprised and shaken, he fumbled with his rifle. Instead of slipping down his arm, the canvas sling twisted around it.

The second guard reminded Kala of a street thug, broad and deep chested, with long arms and thick shoulders. Still not able to untangle his rifle so he could simply shoot Aedon where he stood, the guard trundled forward like a charging animal.

Aedon sidestepped him and stuck out his foot. As the guard fell to the ground, Aedon crunched a hard-fisted, power-packed blow to the man's lower back.

Then a hand shot out of the darkness, grabbing the hem of Kala's dress and dragging her to the ground. The defensive moves that were as much as part of her repertoire as her tunnel skills surfaced immediately. She went down, putting her weight on the guard's arm before rolling back to her feet. The guard's hand exchanged the hem of her dress for her ankle. Still bruised from the abuse of metal shackles, Kala grunted, then kicked at his face and chest with her good foot.

She went down again, but the guard's hands were gone. He was using them to try and stop the flow of blood from his broken nose. Kala came to her feet, along with the guard who was cursing with every breath, promising her a slow, painful death.

The profanity stopped when he saw that his fellow guard had been immobilized by Aedon's fists. A beefy arm pushed Kala away as the guard pulled a long blade from the sheathed pocket on his uniformed trouser leg. The knife flashed in the moonlight.

"Aedon!" Kala shouted.

The Korcian turned to meet his attacker.

Despite his earlier mistakes, the guard knew his business. Advancing slowly with the knife held loosely and pointed upward, he began to circle his prey. Careful, restrained movements tested Aedon's reactions without allowing a countermove.

Kala watched, breath held, as Aedon feinted to the right, just beyond the guard's reach. Kala had watched him too many times not to realize that Aedon's stumble was intentional. He pretended to miss his footing, his left foot sliding along the damp grass. The guard stepped in, his blade flashing toward Aedon's exposed throat.

The warrior shot forward, his left arm grabbing for the guard's knife hand, while his right hand balled into a fist for a shattering blow to the larynx.

But the guard was no fool. He hadn't committed himself as much as Aedon had thought, and he danced back out of reach. As Aedon's fingers closed on thin air, the knife slashed through the sleeve of his tunic. The point carved a small trickle of blood along his forearm.

The guard grinned, thinking he had won.

Kala watched as the bulky guard danced back and forth, edging Aedon closer to the water. He feinted twice, flashing his knife at the Korcian's shimmering eyes. The third time, Aedon didn't pull back.

He struck hard, his right arm smashing the knife hand aside as he stepped into the advancing guard. His left arm shot forward, palm outward. The heel of his hand connected with the guard's broken nose, flattening the already bloodied flesh and driving the bonelike cartilage into the brain case.

The knife went spinning to the ground as the guard's fingers twitched for the last time.

Kala ran toward the warrior who had just faced a lethal blade and won. Her first instinct was to wrap her arms around him, but the look on Aedon's face stopped her. His eyes were black holes of burning anger, his body still filled with pumping adrenaline from the fight.

"Are you all right?" she asked, as he bent over the dead guard.

"I'm fine," he said, not even looking at his arm. He picked up the knife.

She stared at the surviving guard. "What about him?"

Aedon checked the guard, then began rolling his body toward one of the waterside benches. "He'll be unconscious for a good hour. By the time he's thinking straight, we'll be long gone. Go on ahead. I'll catch up with you."

The comm station was a cement silo equipped with a deep-space antenna array. The few windows were high off the ground and narrow. The door, illuminated by a single light, was reinforced steel.

Kala stopped just short of the station and waited in the shadows created by a waterfront warehouse. She took deep breaths to rid her body of the anxiety that had come from watching Aedon take on a ten-inch steel blade with nothing but his bare hands.

As she leaned against the building, Kala instinctively listened for any noise that said Aedon wouldn't be the only one joining her. The only sound was the sea whispering through the reeds that grew alongside the beach. From where she was hidden by shadows, Kala could see the ocean. The wind was free over the water, stirring up choppy waves that ended in a frothing crest on the sandy shore.

Kala's thoughts quickly turned to the newly awakened sense that while her political dreams were still within reach, her personal ones seemed unattainable.

Watching Aedon fight with the guard had stirred her

emotions yet again. She analyzed the feelings, knowing there had been no premeditation in her trust, no logic in her instinct to accept his help. Only faith.

Emotions raced through Kala, forcing her to acknowledge her vulnerability. A vulnerability that had nothing to do with the physical, and everything to do with the mental. She'd been primed for Aedon by years of wishful thinking.

The facts of the matter were about as consoling as the knowledge that she had opened her heart to a man whose loyalty to the past was stronger than it was to the present.

As if an incantation had been murmured and a wish fulfilled, Aedon materialized out of the darkness. Standing just beyond the warehouse shadows that concealed her, moonlight outlined every muscular ridge of his body.

All Kala could do was look at him, praying that none of the emotions swirling beneath her bland expression showed through. She wanted to thank Aedon for defending her, but any words she could say would sound meaningless compared to the fact that he'd risked his life yet again to save hers.

She reached out and touched the sleeve of his tunic. Her fingers were immediately stained with blood. "This is the second time you've been hurt saving my life."

"How's your foot?" he asked, reminding her that he wasn't the only one who had been injured.

"I'm fine," she said, trying to mimic the blandness of his previous tone and failing. She stuck out her foot and rotated her ankle. "See?"

His eyes shone like silver fire as they traveled from her face to her breasts, then lower to where her foot now rested under her. When his gaze traveled upward again, sensations raced from Kala's breastbone to the tips of her toes. She reminded herself that while Aedon could be trusted to fight and win at any cost, he couldn't be trusted with her heart.

She also told herself that the heat pumping through her body was the aftermath of adrenaline. Not desire.

Unfortunately, Aedon's catlike eyes saw her every reaction. "You're shaking."

The words were whispered as he drew her into the protective embrace of his arms. The last place Kala wanted to be. The only place she wanted to be.

The heat of his breath against her forehead sent another shiver through her body that wasn't remotely related to fear. Her body tightened in a combination of anger, hurt, and need. Mostly need. *Let it go,* she told herself. *Let it go the same way Aedon will let it go when he returns to Korcia, if either one of you lives that long.*

The memory of just how many times she'd come close to dying since joining the resistance flashed in Kala's mind. She shoved the memory away, down into the empty space where she'd soon be forced to put Aedon Rawn.

"Can you hold on until we meet with Montrose?" he asked.

Kala smiled, albeit weakly. Aedon thought she was shivering from the fear of nearly being arrested by two of Lejan's police.

"I'm fine," she insisted, pushing against his chest, wanting to be free of the thundering need he aroused within her. "Let's go. Montrose is waiting."

Aedon wouldn't let Kala move on to the comm station until he had a thorough look at the building and its neighbors. When his silent reconnaissance was completed, he joined her in the shadows again.

"All clear," he said.

They walked to the comm station in silence.

Montrose took one look at them and asked, "What happened?"

"Nothing that hasn't been remedied," Aedon replied. "Do you have the transmitter ready?"

Montrose began pacing the comm room as if it were a cage. He paused to look at the stains on Kala's dress before shifting his gaze to the blood stains on Aedon's tunic. "If the police know you're here, I'll be arrested. Killed! I can't take the risk. You have to leave."

"Not until the message is sent," Aedon told him.

Montrose was nervous. Very nervous. But he was smart enough to know arguing with a Korcian was a waste of time. "I've set the transmit frequency to reach our friend in Pecora without being detected. From there, he'll transmit it to a relay station. Where is the message going?"

"Beyrenta," Aedon said.

"Beyrenta is *inside* the Empire," said Montrose with more than a hint of respect showing in his voice. "It could take several days to reach its destination."

Aedon looked toward the comm desk where the message would originate. "The important thing is for it to get through."

Montrose cleared his throat. "I'll attach a priority code. What's the message?"

"Set up the transmitter, I'll do the rest."

Montrose looked to Kala, who had remained silent since entering the station. "That's highly unusual. Jein requested that any transmissions be sent by me. Personally."

"This message is different," Kala replied, offering no other explanation.

Montrose started looking nervous all over again. Perspiration dotted his forehead. He wiped it away with the sleeve of his jacket, then looked at the time display on the comm console. "Once I open the relay frequency, it will take three minutes to reach Pecora. Your transmission can't exceed two minutes. One second more and it will automatically default to a screening station in Melgarr. Whatever you have to say, say it quickly."

Aedon watched as the transmitter was readied. When the time came, he replaced Montrose at the control. As his fingers moved fluidly over the keypad, Aedon knew the Korcian cryptographers in the Comm Bureau on Beyrenta would pass the information along to the Registry. From there, the rest would be up to Cullon Gavriel.

"I've never seen anything like it," Montrose commented as the code flashed across the display screen before being converted into digital impulses that would be relayed halfway across the galaxy.

"You'll never see it again," Aedon said. He entered the sign-off digit that indicated his security clearance, then shut down the console. "That's it," he said, coming to his feet. "Time to go."

Montrose cast a nervous glance at the door, but he didn't make any move to leave.

Aedon understood his meaning. "We'll go first."

He walked to the door, opened it slowly, and looked around. Nothing has changed since they'd come inside ten minutes ago. Wind was still sweeping over water. Streetlamps were still glaring down on concrete, and the night was still humid with the weight of summer.

Aedon turned to Kala. Nothing had changed there, either. She was still looking at him as if he were a stranger.

Irritated by his body's hunger for a woman who had once spoken of love, and now only wanted him for his fighting skills, Aedon turned his back and forced himself to look into the dark night with eyes as clear and hard as polished steel.

eighteen

THE CELL WAS a six-by-eight-foot cage. No windows. No visible door. The only light, dim and receded into the ceiling. Nothing but cold metal walls and silence.

Jein sat in the corner, unable to move unless he dragged himself across the floor. The pain in his head had subsided to a dull ache. His hunger and thirst were satisfied whenever a panel in the cell wall opened and food and water were put within reach.

He ate. He drank. And he waited.

Time was intangible. He had no way of knowing how long he'd been unconscious after the guards had swarmed into the monastery and taken him. He had no recollection of anything beyond a hard, crashing pain that had produced total blackness, and no gauge to measure the passing of minutes or hours or days since he'd awakened.

Unabated, memories of another prison cell rolled through his mind. Intimidation. Endless beatings. Pain mounted upon pain. Agony upon agony. The constant, ever-present threat of execution. The words echoed in his mind, sounding like a dirge, commanding Jein's psychological realm as well as his physical one.

And still he waited.

When one of the cell walls began to move, sliding silently aside, light glared down on Jein so strongly that he had to close his eyes.

"Look at me," said a tall, dark-haired man in a soothing voice.

Jein opened his eyes, blinking rapidly until his sight adjusted to the brilliant light. His captor stood before him.

Esarell smiled. There was no pity in his eyes. No compassion. They seemed scarcely human.

"The great Eiven Jein," he said. "At last we meet."

Jein said nothing. Words were unnecessary. He was the prisoner, Esarell the jailer.

Esarell continued to smile, undeterred by his prisoner's silence. He looked pointedly at Jein's lifeless legs. "Pain is a unique experience, don't you agree?"

Again, Jein said nothing.

"So is death," Esarell went on. "But I'm not here to dwell on the inevitable."

"Then why are you here?" Jein said, unaffected by a threat he had heard hundreds of times before.

"Merely to say welcome to Zahalla," Esarell replied casually. "And to let you know that I don't consider you a prisoner. Not specifically, that is. I'd rather think of you as a trophy. Something I will take out of its carefully sealed case and flaunt under Rendhal's nose when I replace him as governor."

Jein's mouth curved into a disgusted smile as he quickly realized why he was being kept alive. "You think that my capture will gain you the endorsement of the Board."

Esarell looked at him with frank admiration. "I've always thought your reputation for clear thinking was well earned. You've managed to evade Rendhal for too many years not to be an intelligent man. But you can't evade me. I'll have your head to decorate my office, and your rebels locked in chains and paraded through the streets of Melgarr when all is said and done. Rendhal is a weakling. He can only stand as long as the Board holds him up. When they remove their support . . . Again, the inevitable."

"Killing me won't end the resistance," Jein said.

Esarell fixed him with a cold stare. "On the contrary. The resistance is a few thousand people, scattered across the planet. People I can kill as easily as I'm going to kill you."

Jein looked into the commander's soulless eyes, saw the composed face that greeted the governor on a daily basis, saw the air of mastery, the tangle of ego and ambition, and something more. Hatred. Hatred for anything or anyone who stood in Esarell's way.

A chill settled over Jein's body.

"Your expression says you don't agree, but you're wrong," Esarell said proudly. "I know about your mountain encampment, and about Alexander Ginomi's unit of fighters in Vinsenia. I know about Terk Conrad and Kala Char'ari. I even know that a Korcian smuggler has joined your ranks. Surprised? Don't be. I'm a patient man, my crippled friend. A patient man who knows how to bribe informants as well as you do. The Hachynite Citizens for Freedom exists only because it serves *my* purpose to allow its meager ravings to continue. When it no longer pleases me to keep Rendhal distracted with your little games of war, the game itself will end and the governor's palace will be mine."

A mirthless laugh came from Jein. "You're a fool, Esarell. An arrogant fool. The Board of Directors doesn't promote from the lower ranks. Governors are hand-picked puppets, men groomed to take orders, not men who make executive decisions on their own. The Conglomerate may allow you to fill the gubernatorial gap, but the glory will be temporary. They will never *anoint* you into power."

Esarell laughed. "Normally, that would be the case. But these are not normal circumstances."

Jein had been interrogated too many times not to have learned from the experience. His expression showed interest, his gaze curiosity. His silence deferred to Esarell's greater knowledge.

The commander's pride did the rest.

"The Board will welcome me with open arms," Esarell explained with eloquence, elaborating on his vision of the future. "The fleet they have been building is under *my* command, the pilots personally recruited from among my Guard. Their loyalty belongs to me, not to Rendhal, and certainly not to nameless men who hide in the shadows."

A mocking smile hovered on Esarell's face as the door closed, leaving Jein in an uncomfortable, lonely silence.

nineteen

THE DINING HALL of the mountain camp had been turned into a war room.

Aedon had surprised Kala by flying the shuttle directly from Lejan to the Moviash Mountains, relegating the cottage on the shores of Lake Haba to a place that had served its purpose.

She should have been grateful that leaving the cottage behind had eliminated the worry of living and sleeping under the same roof as the handsome warrior, but Kala wasn't feeling grateful. Instead of relief, she felt tension.

Disconnected and resentful.

She felt detached from herself and everyone around her, not because she wasn't interested in every word that Aedon was saying. Because she was. Because she'd come to love the sound of his voice. Because she'd come to love the man.

Unable to deny the truth, but strong enough to admit that people somehow got through life in spite of themselves, Kala poured herself a cup of coffee and stood to the side, watching the men and women who had gathered to hear Aedon's plan.

Most of all, she watched Aedon.

Once again, he'd proven that no one knew how to stage a battle like a Korcian.

The night assault on the fortress of Zahalla was a marvel of clandestine genius. If it worked, freedom was within their grasp. If it didn't, there wouldn't be anyone alive to complain about failure.

The plan was just what Aedon had said it would be. All or nothing at all. Victory or defeat. Life or death.

"You've confirmed that Jein is being held on Zahalla?" Aedon asked Ginomi.

"Yes. We have an informant inside the Guard barracks. He's not a member of the Guard, but he's close enough to overhear their conversations. One of the lieutenants mentioned Esarell's personal *guest* and what a shame it was that the man's disabilities prevented him from enjoying Zahalla's recreational comforts. The informant was also able to confirm that Commander Esarell left for Zahalla this morning."

"How can we be certain that Jein is even alive?" Sy asked.

The question had needed to be asked. It was one every person in the room had already asked himself.

"If he were dead, there's be no reason to hide it," Aedon answered in the authoritative tone that had become commonplace since arriving in camp. "Selwyn told Kala that Jein was going to be a surprise at Rendhal's going-away party. What reason would he have to say something like that, if it wasn't true?"

Terk, who had been standing at Sy's side for most of the briefing, stepped away to refill his coffee cup before joining Aedon and Ginomi at the table. He looked at the battle map Aedon had created. The holographic images of targeted sites stared back at him; four communications stations, three launch platforms, two high-security warehouses, twenty-six factories, and the island fortress of Zahalla. If only half the targets were successfully eliminated, Rendhal's men would be working amid mass confusion.

"It will take weeks to organize a strike this big," Terk said.

"Not weeks. Days," Aedon corrected him. "Three days to be precise."

"Three days! Impossible," Terk argued. "We can't get our people in place that soon."

Aedon looked to Ginomi, then back to Terk. The elder leader's silence said Aedon was calling the shots. "Three days. The whole purpose behind striking multiple targets simultaneously is to cause as much confusion as possible. Every day we waste gives Esarell's men the upper hand. It also gives them time to use their informants against us."

"What informants?" This time the question came from Kala. She stepped closer to the table. "There's no evidence that anyone inside the resistance is feeding the governor or Esarell information."

Aedon fixed his gaze on her. As always, the ever-changing, indecipherable depths of his eyes sent a tingling awareness through Kala's body. She watched his expression soften, just enough to let her know that she wasn't going to like what he was about to say.

"A man with Esarell's reputation for getting the job done isn't going to play by the rules," Aedon said. "You have informants. Why shouldn't he?"

The question hung in the air until Ginomi nodded. "When in doubt, assume the worst. It's a logic Jein would employ. Very well. We will assume that our secrets aren't so secret. All orders to the provincial units will go through me. No one will enter or leave the camp without approval."

"Three days," Aedon said firmly, looking to the room in general. "And no ones transmits as much as a whisper unless I approve the message first. Agreed?"

Again, Ginomi nodded. "Three days. It is not a long

time, but what you ask can be accomplished. It *must* be accomplished. We have no choice."

Ginomi's acquiescence to Aedon's wishes filtered through the room. Heads nodded. Determination darkened eyes and lifted chins. Everyone who had assembled in the hall knew precisely what was at stake. Each of them had fought for years to gain what the Korcian was offering to deliver into their hands in seventy-two hours, and each thirsted for the victory.

Aedon looked to the map again, leading them through the plan of attack, starting with the broad outlines and descending to details and alternative options. As the group absorbed the mission protocol, the outside temperature began to drop. The sun sank low on the horizon, as if the very weight of the day's decision were forcing it toward the mountains.

To Kala, the end of the day was a remainder of just how little time she and Aedon had left.

Beneath that reality was the growing certainty that whatever happened, she would never respond to another man the way she responded to Aedon Rawn. Physically. Mentally. From the depths of her very soul.

The certainty filled her the same way Aedon filled her senses whenever he touched her. Completely.

Kala closed her eyes, letting the heartbreak wash through her like a slow, breaking wave. Accepting one of life's many lessons—love was as illogical as it was rare. When she opened her eyes a few seconds later, they focused on the battle map.

Once the briefing was finished, the camp members split up into small groups and set about fine-tuning the plan, bringing the schematics of the attack into line with the actuality of combatants and weapons.

Kala joined Aedon at the main table. He was reviewing a display of wind and ocean currents, while Ginomi and Terk studied a mock-up of Zahalla's fortress.

The governor's former summer palace stood two

hundred feet above the lapping waves of the Jovian Sea. Walls of reinforced steel and concrete, five feet thick, had been designed to withstand blasts from a laser cannon. The sea-facing walls were topped with watchtowers.

Terk touched a key on the portable console that was generating the holomap, pointing out features to Ginomi, then looking to Aedon. "No matter how many times I look at this, I don't see a way around the perimeter sensors."

Aedon pointed to the ocean-current map he'd been studying. "You're assuming that we'll be going *over* the walls."

"What other way is there?"

"Under them," Aedon said.

He called up a secondary map, one that showed the topographical features of the Jovian Sea. He pointed to an underwater mountain range with one peak towering above the water line—Zahalla. "Esarell's fortress isn't built on an island, it's built on the summit of an inactive volcano."

Terk looked at the map with genuine awe. "So we start at the bottom and work our way up like lava."

"These channels are large enough to support men wearing jetpacks," Aedon told him. He enlarged the holomap until the pathway used by the ancient lava eruptions became a series of dark lines leading to the surface of the island. "The channels become caves once they reach the surface."

Ginomi smiled. "Diving gear and jetpacks. No wonder the Korcian Empire has never been defeated. You take your battles seriously."

"If you don't want to win, don't get in the fight," Aedon replied.

"You do realize," Kala said, taking Aedon's attention away from ancient volcanoes and the philosophy of warfare, "that there will be at least a hundred men stationed on the island. You've only allocated six fighters to the Zahalla attack force."

"If everyone does what he's supposed to do, six will be

as good as sixty," Aedon replied, speaking in the tones of a seasoned warrior who knew the final battle would come down to skill, wits, and luck.

Kala accepted his tone and his probing gaze without question, because admitting that she was heartbroken over his lack of trust in her was something she refused to do. She lifted her chin, squared her shoulders, and met his wintry gaze with one just as cold and detached.

"We received word from Alvaron and Stiles. The charges will be put in place before morning. Alvaron will stay behind to detonate the explosions. Stiles will make his way back to camp. He's a good fighter. You might want to consider him for the Zahalla team."

"I will."

"And me."

"No."

She looked at him, measuring the anger in his eyes and the tension in his body at the same time that she remembered the gentleness of his touch and the hunger of his kiss.

Lust. Passion. A lonely and available man and woman. That's all it is, Kala told herself as she ached to reach out and touch him. Why couldn't her heart see things the way her head did?

The answer was simple. Whatever Aedon Rawn was or wasn't, he was the man she loved.

She had warned herself against the dangers of falling in love with the dark warrior, then forgotten the warning. In the end, she'd had no more control of her heart than she'd had over the weather.

"We've had this argument before," Kala reminded him, hiding her emotional nakedness behind the determined words. "We started this together. We'll finish it together."

The remaining two days preceding the attack on Zahalla were filled with more briefings. Every detail of the operation was outlined until it was imprinted on the brains of the men and women who had been selected for each task. Terk and Sy, accompanied by Stiles and a slender man named Ravier, had been selected for the Zahalla team because of their previous infiltration and mission experience. Aedon and Kala brought the count to six.

There had been no argument about her going. No words of warning. In fact, there had been few words at all. Aedon was consumed by the mission, sleeping in the shuttle the few hours he wasn't supervising everything from weapon selections to the fake uniforms that several teams would be wearing in order to gain access to the police precincts.

Ginomi transmitted the orders to the individual resistance units. Each unit assumed it was carrying out a single mission, its goal to cause as much disruption and damage as possible. The only people who knew the overall mission plan were cloistered in the mountain camp.

"Do you ever stop to think what we'll do when the fighting is over?" Sy asked as she joined Kala at one of the dining hall tables that was still used for eating.

The hall was empty except for the two women. Aedon was with Ginomi and Terk in the comm center across the compound. The remainder of the camp members had gone to bed.

Kala thought of all the dreams she had woven around the future and a tall, dark-haired Korcian warrior, and shrugged. "Sometimes. What do you plan to do?"

"Assuming we survive," Sy said laughingly. She took a moment to look around the room. "You'll probably think I'm crazy, but all I can think about is leaving this place."

"You've been in this camp for a long time. Stone walls, stone floors, arctic winds. I can't blame you for wanting a change of scenery."

"Not this camp. This planet. Hachyn," Sy said succinctly. "I was born here, but I've never been able to call it home. I want to find my father, if he's still alive. Then I want to go someplace that doesn't hold the memory of my mother dying a young woman. I can't do that here."

"And Terk?" Kala asked. "I know you care for him."

Sy avoided answering the question by asking one of her own. "What about you? From the looks of things, whatever has been brewing between you and the Korcian is still simmering."

"I don't know," Kala said honestly. "I can't imagine leaving a place I've fought so hard to keep. You see bad memories. I see potential."

"To each her own," Sy said as Terk entered the dining hall. "Gotta go."

Kala watched as the two met halfway across the room. It was apparent by the casual way that Terk slipped his arm around Sy's slender waist that their relationship had blossomed beyond friendship. To what end, only they knew. The couple spoke softly between themselves for a few minutes, then left the hall.

Kala looked down at the tea that was growing cold in her cup. Unlike Sy, she would be sleeping alone again tonight.

Maybe more cold was what she needed. A walk in the cold night air should made her appreciate the warmth of her solitary bed.

The night was a mixture of brilliant ice and snow refracting silver moonlight back into the darkness of the sky. It was high summer in the valleys below. The mountains' only concession to the season was a few melt ponds and a wind that blew briskly enough to chaff skin rather than freeze it.

Pulling up the collar of her jacket, Kala headed toward a ridge of boulders that helped to shield the camp from detection. The approach was slick and steep, the trail little more than a hollow path etched out of solid rock by eons of high-altitude winds and seasonal melts.

Above the boulders, vanilla clouds gathered like duti-
ful worshippers at the foot of the moon. Wind whistled
mournfully, scattering snow as it gushed through the
canyon.

When she could feel nothing but cold wind and see nothing but the black velvet of an endless sky, Kala stopped
walking.

She simply stood in the chill clarity and allowed her
thoughts to go where they wanted.

An old Earth proverb that had been a favorite of her father's popped into her mind. *When you find yourself in a
hole, stop digging.*

She laughed out loud, then listened as the sound
echoed back to her from the surrounding cliffs.

As a freedom fighter, she was in a hole that was very
likely to become her grave. She was there because she
was letting her pride keep her from the man she cared for
deeply, who brought out a sensuality she'd never known
existed until recently. But her sexuality wasn't all Aedon
had brought to the surface. Since meeting Aedon, a bone-
deep sense of being alive had overtaken her.

Admitting that, Kala had no choice but to also admit
that it was ludicrous to waste time worrying about what
Aedon would or wouldn't do after the attack on Zahalla.
The odds of them successfully completing the mission reduced the chance of either one of them doing anything
other than dying to near zero.

"The present, not the past. Now. Tonight. Not the future." She recited the words to herself as she slipped and
slid her way back to the canyon floor. "You've spent the
last three days dying a little bit every time you look at
him. Life is too precious to waste on regrets."

The words kept her feet moving until she reached the
shuttle. Then, confronted with what she was about to do,
Kala hesitated. What if Aedon didn't want her? What if
all he really cared about was revenge?

Uncertainly clawed at her insides.

"You should be asleep."

Kala jumped at the sound of the deep voice. She swirled around, barely able to keep her balance on the thin layer of ice that had formed on the canyon floor after sunset.

Aedon stood a few feet away, a black shadow against the dark night. His face was expressionless, as usual.

"I thought you were in the shuttle," she said.

He held up a cup from the mess hall in reply. "What are you doing out here? You're going to need all the sleep you can get."

Knowing it was now or never, truth or regret, Kala took a step toward him. Just being close to him made her warm inside and out. She drank in the sight of his finely angled features and his eyes, gleaming pure silver in the moonlight. The heart-pounding closeness of him made her heart rate increase and her blood run warm.

She felt acutely alive and deeply calm, as if everything she'd been waiting for was finally within reach.

"This could be our last night this side of eternity," she said.

Aedon saw the turbulent emotions in her eyes, heard the strain in her voice, and mistook it for the fear of the upcoming attack. "Don't think about it," he said. "You're as much of a warrior as I am. When the time comes, you'll put aside the fear and do what has to be done."

Kala tucked her trembling hands into the pockets of her insulated jacket. "I'm not talking about fear or death. I'm talking about living with regrets."

Suddenly his expression changed to the hard, primitive cast of a warrior with eyes that gleamed silver.

"Am I a regret?"

She tried to answer him, but the words stuck in her throat. All she could manage was a shake of her head.

"Kala?"

The sound of her name, spoken in a deep, husky whisper, was Kala's undoing. She shivered, but not from the cold. Emotions, released after days of second-guessing herself, shook her body.

"Let's go inside," Aedon said, taking her arm and propelling her toward the shuttle. A voice command lowered the hatchway ramp.

Once she was inside, out of the wind and cold, Kala couldn't stop shivering.

Aedon put aside his coffee cup and pulled her into his arms. "What's wrong?"

He whispered the question against her forehead. The heat of his lips against the coolness of her skin caused another shiver to cascade through Kala's body. His arms tightened, bringing her closer, sharing more of his body's heat.

"Nothing's wrong," she said raggedly. "Not as long as you're holding me."

Aedon looked into the clear depths of her eyes and saw the storm of emotions that were making her tremble. His gaze remained fixed on her face. For a long time, neither of them spoke.

"Am I a regret?" His voice was husky and low.

"No. Never." She got the words out this time. "I don't regret a single moment we've spent together."

His kiss was slow and deep, saying all the things he hadn't found the time to say.

Kala didn't need words. Not now. What she needed Aedon was already giving her. His touch. His tenderness. His need answering her own. His passion matching hers.

The kiss changed, heating to a higher intensity as Aedon's hands slid beneath her jumpsuit, greedily stroking bare skin, cupping her breasts in his hands, plying his thumbs against her sensitive nipples.

Kala's chest lifted with a sharp intake of breath, and his hold on her tightened. She could feel the tension, the savage excitement in his powerful body. She melted against him as heat shimmered through her again.

When the kiss ended, Kala burrowed her fingers through his dark mane of hair and asked, "Do you have any regrets?"

"By the stars, woman!" He took her mouth in another possessive kiss. His tongue moved into her in a thrusting rhythm that she eagerly accepted and returned.

Like a sudden storm, the atmosphere around them—between them—shifted and thickened. A sexual charge pulsed, their universe reduced to the feel and taste of one another.

Keeping his arms around her, Aedon pulled her to the floor, rejoicing in the feel of her body beneath his again. Desire burned in his veins, bringing him to full arousal.

Clothes disappeared, cast aside in a frenzied need to be as close as possible. Aedon was on his knees, looking down at her. His gaze moved hungrily over the soft curves of her body, from her breasts to the soft triangle of auburn curls at the apex of her thighs. His fingertips drew a line from her lips to the smoothness of her abdomen before trailing his fingers inexorably downward to the soft folds waiting to embrace him.

At the first contact of his intimate touch, her legs opened to give him access. He smiled, then lowered his head and pressed the wet heat of his open mouth to her breast. Her nipple tightened under the laving pressure of his tongue. Her breast swelled as his hand caressed and fondled, sending waves of tingling pleasure through her.

Aedon felt her hips begin to move, arching and retreating as his fingers caressed her. She was warm and wet, more than ready for him. The scent of her arousal came to him, sweet and faintly musky. Like no other woman, she made him acutely aware of his masculinity, his power as a man. His body throbbed to be inside her, sheathed by her satin sleek muscles.

She reached for him, her hands sliding up and over his broad chest, fingers stretching to take hold of his shoulders.

He shook his head, then came to his knees again. "I want you on your hands and knees."

Kala did as he asked, auburn hair cascading to the floor as she turned her head to look at him over her shoulder. "Like this?"

Aedon smiled as he moved in behind her, nudging her legs apart. "Just like that."

He wrapped one arm around her waist to hold her in place, using his free hand to gently cup the tantalizing curve of her bottom. He rubbed his open palm from the hollow of her hip down her thigh to her knee, then up again. When he teased the dampening curls between her legs, a soft moan escaped her lips.

The teasing continued, his fingers slowly caressing, then dipping into her, his thumb circling the point of her desire over and over. Two fingers stretched inside her, then moved in and out until she was squirming in sweet torment.

Her hips undulated, teasing him in return. Low moans and soft cries; damp flesh and straining muscles.

Aedon fitted himself to her, the hard muscles of his lower stomach against the soft curves of her bottom. Holding her hips with both hands, he filled her with one deep stroke.

He eased her gently forward, until she was resting her weight on her folded arms. His hips rocked slowly against her, building the pleasure in long, slow strokes.

He lingered over her, savoring the silkiness of her skin, the way her breasts swayed with each movement of his hips against her. He couldn't wait much longer, but he wanted to pleasure her until she collapsed beneath him, desperate for completion.

She was arching nearer and nearer to climax when he pulled out of her, turned her onto her back, lifted her legs high and wide, and mounted her again. Hard and deep.

Her eyes, darkened by passion, stared up at him as he continued to possess her. His hands slid under her to cup her bottom as he lifted her into his thrusts, working inside her until the sharp pleasure brought a gasp. She clung to him when she climaxed, whispering his name as her body convulsed.

His muscles jerked with the force of his own climax, tightening as the spasms emptied him into her silky depths. When it ended, he sank down beside her.

They were silent for a long time, each accepting that words would be an intrusion. Their lovemaking had been compelling and urgent—an affirmation of their feelings. Words weren't necessary.

Slowly, reluctantly, reality returned.

"I'll never be anything but what I am," he said, rolling onto his side so he could look down at her. He ran his fingers along the delicate line of her jaw. "Whatever secrets I have, are just that. Secrets. They can't be shared."

"I know," she said. "I may not like it, but I can accept it."

The words, finally spoken, changed their relationship once again. Lovers. Warriors. Trusted friends. They made love again, then lay in each other's arms and slept.

twenty

"IT'S LIKE THE world is holding its breath," Kala said as they exited the shuttle to find the moon hanging low in a sleeping sky. Even the wind had ceased.

Around them, granite mountains rose to a sky where stars twinkled against a blanket of black velvet. Night wouldn't begin its transformation into day for another hour.

Aedon pulled her close, wrapping an arm around her waist while they stood close, watching and listening to a night that seemed endless but wasn't.

"Have you ever been in deep space?" he asked as he leaned down to place a kiss on her upturned nose.

"No."

"Time takes on a whole new meaning. It's like flying into eternity and standing still at the same time. No barriers. No boundaries. Just endless blackness melting into itself."

Kala smiled, revealing nothing of the uneasiness that rolled through her when Aedon spoke of traveling in deep space. The Korcian Empire was half a galaxy away. Would his love of the dark beauty of space take him away from her? Would anything but being a Korcian warrior ever satisfy him?

Kala knew the answer before she asked herself the question. *"I'll never be anything but what I am."*

"I want to check the comm center," Aedon said. "The last of the units in Melgarr should be checking in before dawn."

They walked side by side, content simply to be together. Whatever they'd left unsaid would remain unsaid until another night gave way to dawn.

When the entered the comm center they found Sy sitting in front of the transmission console. Her back was to the door.

It all happened so fast, Kala couldn't be sure that it happened at all.

Before Sy could get her fingers on the keypad, Aedon was across the room, jerking her chair back and hauling her to her feet.

Green eyes went wide with surprise. "What the—"

"Who's waiting to hear our plans? The governor or Esarell?" Aedon demanded. His voice was as flat and hard as the mountain beneath his feet. When Sy didn't answer, the grip on her arm tightened until she knew there was no escaping the Korcian or his questions.

"Aedon." Kala's mouth thinned into a bleak line as she moved to where Sy was struggling to be free of the Korcian's viselike grasp. It's as far as her objection went. The transmitter console was on and ready to transmit.

Sy hadn't been receiving a message, she'd been preparing to send one.

"Sy?" Kala asked, looking at the woman she considered a friend. "I think you'd better explain."

Sy looked at the flat, metallic eyes of the Korcian holding onto her arm, then at Kala. "I don't know what you're talking about." she said. "I drew this shift. I'm supposed to be here."

"To monitor incoming messages," Aedon said. His gaze shifted to the console, then back to Sy's face. "Who were you trying to contact?"

Kala's breath came in sharply and held, but she didn't interfere. Hundreds of lives would be put at risk within the next twenty-four hours. Aedon had every right to demand an answer.

"Who?" he asked again. "Are you being paid for the information or have you been one of Rendhal's people from the start?"

Sy's expression hardened. "Let me go. I don't have to answer to you."

"Then answer to me," Kala said as disappointment and anger wrapped around her in equal measure.

It was one thing to find out after the fact that someone had betrayed you. It was something entirely different to catch him in the act.

"Why?" she asked sharply, taking away Sy's last hope that one resistance fighter would defend another's action.

"I had to."

Aedon reached behind her to disengage the transmitter. Another punch of his finger opened the commlink to Terk's quarters.

"Get over here," he said without preamble.

Terk replied to the urgency of the order. "I'm on my way."

Kala watched, still unable to believe that someone who had lost her mother to Rendhal's prisons would actually be helping him. "Why?" she asked again. "What possible reason could you have for betraying us?"

"My father!" Sy said, her eyes bright with fear. "He's alive. As long as I feed Esarell information, he'll stay alive."

Aedon released Sy and took a step back.

Sy sank into the chair. Tears were streaming down her face. She didn't say anything at first. The consequences of her actions were too heavy. Too irreversible.

Terk came rushing through the door, gathered his breath, and demanded to know what the hell was going on.

"She was sending a message."

Terk looked at Sy, then at Kala, then back to Sy. "What kind of message?"

"Terk," Sy gulped out his name. "I'm sorry."

"The reasons aren't important. How much she'd told Esarell is," Aedon intervened before the confession and accusations got out of hand.

The matter-of-factness of his tone told Kala that he hadn't been all that surprised by what they'd found.

"You've suspected her all along," she said, looking at Aedon.

"Not her. But someone. Things have been too easy."

"Easy! We've been blown into the sea and shot at by a precinct of pissed-off police. I was chained and you could have been killed looking for me. Then we were jumped—"

"By the guards in Lejan," Aedon said simply. "Just enough trouble to make things difficult, but not impossible. I shouldn't have been able to get into the factory, and I certainly shouldn't have been allowed to get out, with or without you."

"Selwyn and Sy," Kala said numbly. "Two friends. Two traitors."

Sy's face went even paler. "I had to. Esarell said he'd torture my father to death if I didn't cooperate."

"How long have you been feeding him information?" Aedon asked.

"Four years," Sy admitted.

"Esarell hasn't been in charge of the police for four weeks," Kala said angrily. "I don't understand."

"I was working in the valley," Sy muttered between sobs. "I had just met Terk. I knew he was part of the resistance, even though he hadn't said anything. I could see the resentment in his face every time a police patrol walked by."

"I didn't turn you into a traitor," Terk shouted, taking a few steps closer.

Sy flinched. "No. Esarell did. He showed me images of my father. He looked so old. So tired. Esarell said if I got into the resistance, if I passed him information, my father would get the medical attention he needed. He'd be well fed. And when the time was right, Esarell promised to release him from prison. We'd be free to leave. Free to go anywhere we wanted."

"Then he knows about this camp," Terk said. "Why hasn't he attacked? Why haven't we all been arrested?"

"I don't know!" Sy said pleadingly. "All I do is send information. Sometimes he uses it, sometimes he doesn't."

"Did you give Esarell Selwyn's name?" Kala asked.

Sy shook her head. "No. I never met Selwyn. I didn't know about him until Ginomi told us that he'd set you up in Melgarr. I didn't know he was employed at the factory. All I told Esarell was that you were going to break in and have a look around."

Kala believed her. If Esarell could blackmail one traitor, why not buy another? Or two? Or three?

"Does Esarell know we plan to blow the factories?" Aedon demanded.

"Yes."

"Does he know when?"

Sy wiped away the tears that were streaming down her face. "No. I was supposed to send him the timetable tonight. He's waiting for the message."

"What's his plan?" Terk snapped.

Sy put her face in her hands. "I don't know! I tell him what I know, he doesn't tell me."

"He must say something," Kala inserted calmly. Sy was on the verge of hysteria. "Does his voice sound angry or pleased?"

Sy looked up, meeting Kala's gaze. "When I told him about Aedon's plan to put explosives in the drainage lines, he complimented him on the idea."

"You sent a message from Lejan," Terk said accusingly. "Esarell's known all this time. What about Alvaron? Is he going to be arrested?"

"No. At least not yet," Aedon said. His eyes were the color of polished steel. "Esarell *wants* us on the offensive. We attack the factories, Rendhal has to explain his inability to protect a valuable asset to the Board of Directors, and Esarell comes out on top by finally acting on the information Sy's been feeding him for years. He brings the resistance to its knees and finishes it off with Jein's head on a platter. We destroy the factories, and Esarell gets exactly what he wants—the governor's palace."

"What difference does it make?" Terk said. "We've got to get out of camp. Warn the others. Some of the teams are already in place. They'll be walking into an ambush."

Aedon looked to where Sy was holding herself, rocking back and forth in the chair like a woman in shock. Or in mourning. Whatever she'd gained by joining the resistance had died with her confession.

"Did you have a precise time to contact Esarell?"

Sy wiped the tears from her eyes and looked at the console. "Before my shift ends."

Aedon turned the transmitter back on. "Then send your message. Only the timetable is seventy-two hours. Not twenty-four."

"You can't be serious," Terk said. His words were meant for Aedon but he hadn't been able to take his eyes off Sy. "We can't go through with it. Esarell will have his men waiting."

"Esarell is too smart to make a move before his hand is forced. Any sudden shift in guards would alert us that he knows our plans."

"What if he doesn't care? What if all he wants is as many dead freedom fighters as he can get?" Terk asked.

Aedon didn't bother with a reply. He simply looked at the console's blinking light, indicating that a relay had been opened, and then to Sy. "Make it believable," he warned her. "If you don't . . ."

The words trailed off, the threat clear.

Sy looked up at the Korcian who could kill her with one firm squeeze of his big hands around her slender throat. "What if he asks about Zahalla?"

"Tell him that we know the fortress is too well defended. We want to free Jein, but we haven't been able to figure out how to do it. Tell him that we're practical soldiers. If we can't have Jein, we want the factories. We're hungry for any victory we can get. He'll believe that much."

Sy turned toward the console, then looked over her shoulder at Kala and Terk. "What about me?"

"I don't know," Kala said softly. Honestly.

"Just do it," Terk said. Whatever affection he might have had for Sy had vanished the moment she had admitted to helping Esarell turn the resistance into pawns on a game board. "And make it convincing. You're good at that, aren't you? Pretending one thing while you do the other."

Sy didn't waste time denying Terk's accusation. She'd deceived him the most.

She looked down at the console, took a deep breath, and did the only thing left to do. She entered the transmission code Commander Esarell had given her four years ago.

Aedon motioned Kala and Terk back, away from the console and into the shadows beyond the range of the hologram transmitters. The laser pistol in the Korcian's hand told Sy that the message she was about to deliver had better be the right one.

The receptor glowed pale green as the signal was sent and whitish-blue when it was received. The matching receptor on the island of Zahalla did the same as Esarell's face appeared like a bad dream. The image wavered for a brief second before solidifying into a face-to-face confrontation with his camp informant.

"You're late," he said. "I don't like to be kept waiting."

Sy flinched as if he could reach a physical hand through the imagery and strike her. "I'm sorry," she stammered. "There's a lot going on in camp. I had to make sure everyone was asleep."

"When?" he demanded, getting right to the point.

"In three days," she told him. "The Korcian plans to strike the factories and the launch platforms in the valley at the same time."

The blue light of the holograph projector made Esarell's face glow like a nightmarish phantom. But nothing could give life to his eyes. They were as cold as a grave.

"Excellent. And Jein? Do they think they can rescue him from my evil clutches?"

"No," Sy replied. "The island is too well guarded. The Korcian can't think of a way to get in and out without a lot of people being killed. Ginomi and Terk won't risk it."

"How very humanitarian of them," Esarell replied sardonically.

Sy's voice dropped to a whisper. "What about my father?"

"Patience, my little spy. Your father is sleeping soundly in his cell. When the time is right, you will see him again."

Sy didn't look like she believed him.

Esarell didn't look like he cared.

"Seventy-two hours. Are you certain?"

"Yes," Sy replied. Her hands were gripping the edge of the console, but Esarell couldn't see how desperately she was holding on. "The factories and the launch platforms."

"Good," Esarell mumbled to himself as if he couldn't wait for the fighting to begin. "Is that all?"

"Yes."

The hologram vanished, the connection terminated at Esarell's end. No farewells. No final words of instruction. Just empty air and the unbelievable promise that Sy hadn't betrayed the resistance for nothing.

As soon as the connection went dead, Sy collapsed into the chair. Whatever strength she'd used to face Esarell one last time drained away.

Aedon pulled her to her feet. He looked to Terk. "Lock her in your quarters. If anyone asks, she slipped on the ice and sprained her ankle. Pick someone to take her place on the Zahalla team."

Terk's hand replaced Aedon's, but Sy didn't seem to notice. She was too busy looking inward with contempt and despair.

"Tell Ginomi, but don't tell anyone else," Aedon said. "There's no reason to demoralize the whole camp. And from this moment on, no ones comes into the comm center but us."

"That won't keep the camp safe once the attack begins," Terk said.

Aedon wasn't being told what he didn't already know. "We'll evacuate as soon as the shuttle is launched. Until then, keep a lid on things."

Terk nodded, then led Sy away.

Kala turned to Aedon. "Do you think Esarell believed her?"

"Why shouldn't he? Terk said himself that it would take weeks to pull off the attack. Three days will only give Esarell the impression that we're desperate."

"Aren't we?"

There was a long silence, broken only by the occasional beep of a perimeter scanner.

"I hated Selwyn the moment I realized he'd betrayed me, but I can't hate Sy," Kala finally said. "Her mother died in prison and Esarell was dangling her father's life in front of her. What choice did she have? What choice do any of us have?"

"There are always choices," Aedon said.

"I'm not so sure. I didn't choose to be born here. You didn't choose to have your wife and daughter killed."

He walked to where she was standing and pulled her

into his arms, his hands rubbing up and down her back to ease away a hurt he couldn't reach. It was too deep inside her.

"Life is making the best of the choices we're given," he said. "Right now, we can't change what Sy did. We can only make the best of it."

Kala snuggled deeper into his embrace. "I know, it's just that even after seeing it with my own eyes, I don't want to believe it. All those years. All the lies. And Terk. He and Sy were lovers. Her betrayal has to cut deep."

"Terk and Sy?"

"You didn't know? I thought you saw everything going on around you."

Aedon shook his head. "I usually do, but I assumed Terk's feelings for you—"

"Terk's a smart man," Kala said, "He knows my feelings are engaged elsewhere."

Aedon didn't answer. He just kept stroking her back until muscles tightened by anger and tension relaxed. Kala didn't argue with his blunt assessment of life. She couldn't.

Aedon was right. She couldn't undo Sy's betrayal any more than she could turn Esarell into a saint.

"I need some coffee," she said, reluctantly leaving the comfort of his arms.

They left the comm center to find the moon a white orb in a sky that was slowly changing from gray to blue.

A new day had arrived.

Kala prayed it wouldn't be their last.

twenty-one

INSPECTING WEAPONS BEFORE the battle began was a ritual as old as the warrior arts. Aedon and Kala retired to the shuttle to do the job.

When it came to the jetpacks and diving equipment that Ginomi had scavenged with incredible skill, Kala was at a loss. She sat back and watched as Aedon checked every gauge. His nimble fingers moved over the zero-porosity fabric as gently as they had moved over her skin hours earlier.

At the depths they'd be swimming, the water was cold enough to induce hypothermia in less than fifteen minutes. They'd be underwater twice that long.

When Aedon was confident the equipment would do exactly what it was supposed to do, he turned to Kala and explained the technique of using the jetpack to maneuver through water instead of the airless vacuum of space.

He made her repeat every word until he was satisfied that she could use the gear proficiently. The premise of a team was that any one member would accept personal risk to reduce the risk borne by another, but Kala knew Aedon was more worried about her than the others.

She'd never been diving before, and she'd never worn a jetpack, in space or anywhere else. She was a novice to everything but the danger involved.

"I'll be fine," she assured Aedon as he quickly disassembled and reassembled several selected weapons. Triggering mechanisms should be tight, but not too tight. Laser cartridges should slide readily into place, but with just enough resistance to ensure they stayed in place once the shooting began.

"Stay close to me," he told her as he raised the disassembled chamber of a rifle to his nose. Smelling the evidence of excessive lubricant, he used a soft rag to clean the barrel. "Diving isn't like swimming. You can lose your sense of direction when there's nothing around you but water. Keep your light focused on me in case the tether line comes loose."

Aedon's hands moved expertly while he spoke, the clicking and snapping of weaponry providing a rhythmic counterpoint to his conversation.

"I will," Kala promised.

She slid a mesh belt through the slots of the jetpack that would be strapped to her back, checking the durable fabric for any frays or irregularities. When she was done, she looked straight into Aedon's steel gray eyes. "I've never been diving before, but I know what the dark is like. I lived in it for years. My sense of direction is as good as yours, maybe better. Stop worrying. I can handle my end of things."

She reached over and placed a hand on Aedon's shoulder. "I don't want you thinking about me when you should be thinking about yourself."

Aedon's warrior eyes were surprisingly gentle as he set aside a laser rifle he'd been inspecting. "I don't want you to go, but you already know that."

"I know. What surprises me is that you haven't threatened to tie me to the bed again."

He laughed softly, the sound muffled by the pressure of his mouth against her hair. "I've thought about it, but you're right. This is your world. Your fight. I can't ask you to step back and watch."

"If you're smart enough to realize that then you're smart enough to know that nothing you do tonight can bring back your wife and daughter."

Aedon went still. "I know."

"It doesn't feel like you know," Kala said, daring to broach the subject because it meant so much. She shifted position until she could look into the darkening depths of Aedon's eyes. "I care about you. And I know that you loved your wife and child. I'm not making a comparison. I'm telling you that you can't wipe the slate clean by getting yourself killed. I like you the way you are. Alive."

Aedon kissed her. "If everything goes according to plan, we'll be spending a total of one hundred and twenty minutes on Esarell's island. After that, I plan on coming back here and making love to you until I'm too weak to breathe."

"Now that's a perfect plan," Kala said, not bothering to comment on what both of them already knew.

If they didn't get back to camp, everything that could go wrong had gone wrong.

"Excellent engineering," Aedon said admiringly. He, Kala, and Terk were standing beside the submersible that would be dropped from the low-flying shuttle into the ocean.

Whatever purpose the submersible had served before Ginomi had stolen it was unimportant. Tonight it would take a sequestered team of resistance fighters to the bottom of the Jovian Sea.

Terk ran his fingertips over the nonreflective hull of the

submersible. "It's small, but what's a little cramped space between friends."

"Nothing, if the gods are with us," said Aedon.

"Amen," Kala said. There was no mirth in her voice. As the zero hour approached, an unspoken anxiety had overtaken the camp.

The plan was simple, carried out in three stages, each phase logically evolving into the other. The shuttle was scheduled to lift off within the next ten minutes—phase one. Ginomi had dispatched the last attack team an hour ago. If they kept to schedule, the precinct launching pads would explode two minutes after the first factory went up in flames—phase two.

The comm center in Lejan would go down three minutes after that. Melgarr would go mute a few seconds later. By the time the first of twenty-six detonators had been activated, the Zahalla team's mission would be complete.

Ginomi joined them. He had accepted the news about Sy with the same gut-ripping shock as Kala and Terk. His nephew, Janson, had volunteered to fill in the gap created by Sy's sudden disability.

"Everything is on schedule," he said. "Alvaron is waiting for my signal. As soon as I know the shuttle is clear of the Lejan security net, I'll start evacuating camp."

"Where are you going to go?" Kala asked. She'd been too busy with her own preparations to ask Ginomi where he planned on hiding fifty-four resistance fighters and one spy.

"We leave in teams of ten or less," Ginomi told her. "There are plenty of places to hide."

"What about Sy?"

"She'll come with me, until we can decide what to do with her," Ginomi answered. "I don't expect a fight. Where would she run? To Esarell?"

A middle-aged man materialized out of the shadows. His name was De Vries. He'd spent eight years flying a cargo shuttle between Naarca Valley's factories and

warehouses. He was Aedon's copilot until they reached
the drop zone. After that, his orders were simple. Fly the
shuttle to a cargo platform on the southern coast near
Melgarr and wait for the signal to retrieve the Zahalla in-
sertion team and Jein.

"Be safe," Ginomi said, pulling Kala into his arms for a
fatherly embrace. He looked to Aedon. "Take care, my
Korcian friend."

"Always," Aedon assured him.

Ginomi released Kala and reached out to shake Aedon's hand. "As soon as I receive word that you have Jein
and are clear of the island, I'll issue the announcement."

"What announcement?" Kala asked, looking at the two
men.

Ginomi laughed. "We're going to tell everyone listening to the nightly comm report that Commander Esarell
has misplaced his prisoner. If Aedon is right, and I
haven't found him to be wrong yet, the news should send
our esteemed governor into a fit of rage."

Aedon couldn't hide his smile as he looked at Kala.
"With any luck Rendhal will hear the news just about the
time the factories start exploding."

Kala's smile was full of admiration. "Esarell will be
too busy covering his own ass to worry about shooting
ours off. Excellent idea."

Ginomi said his good-byes to the rest of the team, then
returned to the comm center that would continue to be the
operational nucleus for another hour.

Kala found herself alone with Aedon. There were a
thousand things she wanted to say to him, but she didn't.
Instead, she used the moment to raise up on her tiptoes
and smooth a kiss over his mouth. "For luck," she said.

Aedon held her close for a moment. "Time to go."

Once they were through the Lejan traffic net—their false
registry as a transport shuttle hadn't been questioned—and

over open water, the shuttle angled upward, banking nearly forty degrees as it turned south toward the island of Zahalla.

Aedon's piloting skills were extraordinarily smooth, anticipating and compensating for wind currents and updrafts, and the added weight of the submersible that filled the shuttle's cargo bay.

Kala sat in the shuttle's main section with Terk, Stiles, Ravier, and Janson. The four men followed the same rule as Aedon and Kala; they wore nothing reflective. As they approached the drop zone, they put on polysilk, black skull caps. Their equipment-laden vests looked lumpy beneath their wet suits, but there was no alternative. Once they were out of the water, the weapons they each carried would be critical to their survival and success.

To arrive undetected, they would have to swim several miles underwater and a full three miles up through the volcanic crevice that led to the island's underground caverns. Even with the jetpacks to propel them the going would be rough.

The water would be dark, their way guided only by the navigational comm strapped to Aedon's wrist. The weather maps confirmed that cloud cover would mask their drop from the shuttle into the ocean.

Unfortunately, the cloud cover that provided them protection also provided unpredictable winds—another enemy of precision. Under ordinary conditions, any one of a dozen complications could mean the end of the mission. Under adverse conditions, the outcome was even harder to predict.

But Kala knew, as did each of the team members, that they were only human. Mistakes could be made. Would be made.

The entire operation was in defiance of any rational calculation of the odds, but it was also Eiven Jein's only chance. Their only chance.

All or nothing at all.

At two thousand feet over a turbulent, windswept ocean, Aedon passed the shuttle's control to De Vries.

"It's time," he said, leaving the pilot's chair to join the team. He cast Kala a quick smile. "Remember. Stay together. Your tether line is your lifeline. We don't separate into teams until our feet are on dry ground."

They entered the submersible. Aedon was in alpha position, near the main hatch. Kala directly behind them. Terk and Ravier had been teamed. Janson matched to Stiles.

Comm links were checked and double-checked.

Aedon looked at Kala, switched off his comm link, and opened his visor, indicating that she should do the same.

It was the last word they'd say to one another that wouldn't be overhead by the other four members of the assault team.

"No matter what happens, stay with me," he said. His eyes were quicksilver, his words whispered.

"I will," Kala promised for the tenth time in the last twenty-four hours. She reached out and touched her gloved fingertips to his mouth. "If I haven't told you before, I'm telling you now. You're a very special man, Aedon Rawn."

He smiled, kissed the gloved fingertips covering his mouth, then lowered his visor.

"Five hundred meters and holding," De Vries called back to them from the controls. "T plus ten to eject."

Aedon closed the compact minisub's main hatch.

The command to eject was given.

The first thing Kala felt was the impact of the shuttle's powerful jet stream as it whipsawed the submersible into the air. Her seating restraints held her in place as gravity did the rest.

"Stay calm," Aedon said, speaking into his commlink.

The submersible hit the water, then skipped like a tossed stone from wave crest to wave crest. One of the men cursed, another prayed out loud. Kala kept her eyes trained on Aedon. She couldn't see his face, but she could see him. It was enough.

The submersible stopped bucking and pitching. Although there was no sensation of sinking, the calm that had enveloped them said they were under the water rather than on top of it.

"Restraints off," came the command.

Kala cleared her mind, swept away all anxieties for the time being, and did what had to be done.

Oxygen tanks and filters were checked one last time while Aedon assumed control of the submersible, this time with Terk as his copilot. They descended to five hundred feet before engaging the navigational lights.

Kala went still at the sight.

The ocean was blacker than the night had been, the strong navigational lights only able to penetrate the liquid darkness a few hundred feet. There was no sound, only the pull and tug of the current in a fluid silence that seemed strangely surreal, as if they'd been dumped into an another dimension. Another universe.

"Ten minutes until deployment," Aedon said, his deep voice more reassuring than authoritative.

Kala smiled. Her Korcian could deny being a Fleet officer all he wanted. She knew better. No one acted this serene under these conditions unless it was second nature, ingrained by training and action.

Lots of action by the way he was calmly calling out coordinates to Terk.

Kala moved to the front of the submersible, no easy task since they barely had room to turn around inside the sleek, little submarine. When she was within reach of Aedon, she put her hand on his shoulder and stared out at the ocean through the viewing portal.

Her pulse quickened. Like the hull of a sunken ship the underground mountains were slowly becoming visible. Little by little things came into perspective.

"It's beautiful," she said.

The base of the mountains seemed alive in a rainbow of colors. Coral spirals twisted and turned in a living fence around the cavern entrance, their colors iridescent when struck by the sub's lights.

"In we go," Aedon said, guiding the submersible into a giant cleft near the base of the second largest mountain.

The underwater cavern was an impenetrable black, the edges mottled by the navigation beams.

"We're down," Terk said as he settled the craft onto the cavern's floor.

A sweat-producing half hour later, they exited the submersible, laden with diving gear and jetpacks. The lights mounted on the jetpacks shone over their shoulders, offering a small reprieve from the inky blackness that enveloped them.

Kala felt cool, but not cold. Her tether line was hooked to Aedon's swimbelt, Terk's to hers, and so on, until they formed a human chain.

"Comm test," Aedon's voice came over the receptors in their diving helmets. "Alpha ready."

"Delta ready," Terk confirmed.

"Omega ready," Stiles repeated. He was the last man in the chain.

Aedon turned effortlessly in the water, switched on his jetpack, and began to swim forward.

Kala followed, her heartbeat only slightly accelerated. Darkness wasn't anything new to her. Neither were cramped spaces. As they began to swim deeper into the underwater cavern, she told herself it was nothing more than a tunnel, like dozens of tunnels that she'd maneuvered in the dark on dozens of occasions. The fact that this particular tunnel was several thousand feet below sea level wasn't something she allowed herself to dwell on. She could see Aedon ahead of her, see the trim, muscular outline of his legs as he let them float behind him. The jetpack was doing all the work.

Indigo fading to black where the lights couldn't penetrate, shades and tints and watery shadows, the volcanic crevice became a gateway into the unknown as Kala let the jetpack propel her forward.

Aedon was still in front of her, moving with the economical movements of a seasoned diver. Silver bubbles swirled from the exhaust of his jetpack, stirring the water. The sleek black fabric of his wet suit made him look like an exotic sea creature.

The water got colder the deeper they ventured into the crevice, the darkness even blacker. On three separate occasions the visibility was so poor that only the gentle tug of her tether line confirmed Aedon's presence in front of her.

It was impossible to visualize their progress as they twisted and turned, swimming through a channel created eons before the first land mammals appeared on the planet's surface.

If Kala hadn't glanced at her commlink periodically, she wouldn't have been able to gauge the passage of time. Here, as in deep space, it lost its meaning. She was swimming through darkness, a cushion of water and rock above and below her.

But even as she was propelled effortlessly through the water, Kala knew what lay ahead. An error made by any of them would imperil them all. And even if they executed their task flawlessly, any one of a thousand unpredictable circumstances could be lethal.

The cavern walls were close enough to touch in some places. Knobs of rock stuck out here and there, matched by deep seams and smaller crevices. Kala could feel the swell and tug of unseen currents as she swam by, attesting to the honeycombed nature of the mountain range.

Then, suddenly, almost without warning, the water seemed less dense. Lighter.

She could make out things more distinctly. The tunnel

wasn't as dark and forbidding as before. The rock walls took on a lighter hue, not the black volcanic color that had surrounded her for the last twenty minutes, but a deep brownish-gray color.

And sound.

The sound of water slapping and splashing against rock rather than flowing silently around it.

Then she saw Aedon's hand reaching down to her. He was standing. Standing, not swimming.

They'd made it!

Kala allowed herself to be pulled free of the water. The beam of her jetpack light bounced off the walls of the cave. She lifted her diving visor and breathed in damp, humid air that smelled of moss and brackish water.

Terk was behind her, crawling out onto the uneven floor of the cave, then turning to offer his hand to Ravier.

"That was some swim," he said a few minutes later.

"Not one I want to repeat," Stiles commented as he stripped out of his dive gear.

Aedon was busy checking equipment again, making sure that nothing had been damaged.

Kala used the time to catch her breath and to look around the cave. The sound of water dripping from the porous rock overhead combined with the distant murmurings of the surf. She knew they were near the western end of the island. The palace would be east of them, perched on a small precipice of rock that jutted out into the Jovian Sea.

The underground cave was approximately twenty feet wide and twelve feet high at its highest point. More narrow than wide, it accommodated the six team members without overcrowding.

They deposited their diving gear in one corner.

"We're ten minutes behind schedule," Aedon announced. "Let's get moving."

They exited in teams of two. The passageway leading from the cave quickly narrowed until they were forced to crawl on their hands and knees. The rock was slick with algae.

It was only a matter of minutes before the darkness of the cave gave way to the darkness of the night.

Kala crouched by Aedon at the mouth of the cave. Moonlight gleamed over tropical foliage. Despite the fugitive glitter of the stars that could be seen through a canopy of wide-branched palm trees, Kala knew the island wasn't the paradise it appeared to be.

"It's good to see the sky again," she whispered into her commlink. "If deep space is anything like what we just swam through, I'll stick to being a land mammal."

Terk agreed wholeheartedly.

"No unnecessary talking," Aedon ordered in a crisp whisper. "Let's go."

Kala looked around before following Aedon out of the cave and into the darkness. They had barely moved more than a few hundred yards when he sent her to ground with a hand signal.

It took Kala several seconds to see what he had seen—fortress walls. But instead of being outside them, they were inside. The last place, Kala sincerely hoped, where anyone would expect to find them.

twenty-two

"WEAPONS READY," AEDON said, activating the comm system that linked the six members of the team.

Aedon looked at Kala, making sure no patch of pale skin showed through her nightsuit. Black on black: the protective coloration of the night. It would help them disappear into the dimness of a deeply shadowed fortress. But by the same token, even a few inches of silvery flesh could spell disaster in the roving beam of a searchlight.

As he had emphasized during their briefings, the interior guards would no doubt be equipped with the normal technology defenses, but what they had to be the most cautious of were the senses of a vigilant human being. If something looked or sounded wrong, the guards would be alerted to a foreign presence.

For a few moments, Aedon lay perfectly still, not even breathing: just listening. There was the distant soft roar of the sea, washing at the base of the promontory. A few bird noises and, from the forest behind them, the scraping and buzzing of summer insects. It was the aural baseline of the night, one they would have to use to mask their own sound.

It was impossible to move with absolute silence: fabric slid against fabric, and soles, even those of soft rubber, registered their impact on the ground if something was crunched or broken underfoot. The night's acoustic tapestry would conceal most of their noise, but not all.

Noises that lacked explanation would prompt investigation, and that could be deadly.

Satisfied that no guards were in the immediate area, Aedon gave the order for the unit to begin moving toward the main structure.

They weaved their way through undergrowth and trees until they were within sight of the rear courtyard of the palace. Aedon knew there would be guards on duty, but their attention would be directed toward the outside world from their post in the watchtowers. The guards stationed inside the palace would be charged with the relatively trivial chores of internal discipline, mainly making sure that no one disturbed their commander's sleep.

Though they lay only a few feet from each other, Aedon murmured into his commlink. "One sentry. Southeast corner."

Terk replied in a subwhisper. "Two sentries. North veranda."

Stiles reported next. "Two sentries. Central terrace. Main entrance, Rear"

"Assume position," Aedon said, giving the command that would leave Janson and Stiles on the exterior of the palace while Terk and Ravier secured their escape route.

The shuttle would land at the far western end of the island—winds permitting.

Making sure that Kala was directly behind him, Aedon moved slowly to his left, along the palace wall, and then beneath the overhang of the veranda, walking half-crouched beneath the parapet.

He was now less than fifteen feet from the northernmost

terrace. The palace was four stories, the grand rooms on the second floor, offices on the first. Sleeping quarters and guest suites on the third. Servant and guard quarters occupied the highest level. Most of the windows were dark; dim hallway light seeped through some of them.

If the blueprints were correct, Jein's holding cell was on the first of two subterranean levels.

Aedon closed his eyes against the green display of his night visor. From this moment on the accuracy of his judgments would determine the success or failure of the mission.

His life. The lives of his team.

Kala's life.

He looked to where she was kneeling on the soft grass, close enough to touch. Behind his visor a smile softened his face.

So far, he couldn't complain about having her on the team. Despite the danger she was being exposed to, she was an asset rather than a liability. Her hands were steady, her footing sure, and her movements as graceful as the night.

Wishing they had the island to themselves, Aedon upgraded the magnification on his visor. He could see two sentries clearly now, both armed with laser pistols. He respected all weapons, but he also knew that the sentries would be unlikely to use them unless confronted. Soldiers near their sleeping commander did not make unnecessary noise without a good reason.

Aedon motioned toward the guards, indicating that he would take one, Kala the other.

Kala nodded, then lifted her laser pistol.

Two blue-light blasts of light sliced through the night.

The first guard toppled forward without a sound. The second slumped against the wall as if his legs had simply given way from under him.

Darkness returned. Untouched. Yet Aedon knew that the safety they had just gained could vanish at any moment.

He made a dash for the shadows beneath the northern veranda with Kala at his heels. They slid between the stout stone piers that supported the veranda at three-foot intervals.

According to the blueprints, the access lid was at mid-point of the northern wall, just abutting the main structure.

Aedon felt along the ground, his hands following the seam where earth and reinforced concrete met. Suddenly, he felt something. "I found it," he whispered into this commlink.

Kala crouched at his side. The grotto under their feet had been constructed for maintenance access. Beneath the metal lid, a vertical passageway, made to serve as a maintenance chute, would take them to the underground chambers of the palace.

The access lid was fashioned with handholds on either side. Aedon pulled on one, Kala the other.

"Counterclockwise," he said. "Now."

It took several moments before the lid began to give way. The metal, exposed to salt air and tropical humidity, had eroded over the years, cementing itself in place.

Aedon lifted the lid and placed it gently on the ground, out of sight.

He peered down into the hole they had uncovered. Just under the lid was a grate. And through it, he heard a welter of voices drifting up from the subterranean space.

The words were indistinct, but most of what a voice conveyed—anger, fear, scorn, excitement—was through *tone*. Words were trimming, not substance.

The sounds that drifted up were not those of a prisoner, which meant they belonged to the men guarding the holding cell.

"How many?" Kala asked.

Aedon listened again. He couldn't assume that the number of voices represented the exact number of guards. Three voices could mean twice that many men. But Aedon didn't need a visual count to know that they had to disable every man in the chamber. Any guard left standing could sound an alarm or kill Jein rather than allow him to be rescued.

"Three at the least. Maybe more," he answered.

Removing the grate required them both, and the effort needed was doubled by the imperative that it be removed noiselessly. Perspiration beaded on their faces, beneath their visors, but no matter the discomfort, nothing was rushed.

When the portcullis-like grate had joined the chute lid on the ground, Kala covered her commlink with one hand and flashed on the palace blueprints. The chute descended through several feet of concrete, angled at forty-five degrees for most of the way, then twisting and funneling down more shallowly until it reached a utility crawl space—an unusual door that led to an unpredictable pit.

"I'll go first," she said, turning around so she could slide feet first into the hole.

"As soon as you get into position, turn on your visor display," Aedon said. He hated the idea of having to put Kala in the alpha position, but her smaller size was an advantage.

The crawl space was a narrow ledge overlooking the area outside the holding cells, or so the blueprints indicated. Kala's size would make her less conspicuous.

Everything was a question until they got a look at the holding area. How many guards? The distance to Jein's cell? The position of the alarm? Would the nerve toxin they'd prepared be enough to immobilize all the guards?

If they didn't match their actions to the physical environment, the odds of a successful rescue would shift from slim to none.

Kala's pulse quickened as she made her way through the concrete chute. When she reached the crawl space, she flattened herself against the mesh grid and looked down into the palace's primary basement.

What she saw wasn't that much of a surprise.

The holding area was more corridor than room. A narrow table and two chairs were unoccupied. She turned on her visor's two-way display and whispered, "I don't see any guards."

"Can you get a better angle?" Aedon came back. "Try rolling onto your back so you can see down the length of the corridor."

Holding her breath, praying that the shift in position would be a quiet one, Kala gently maneuvered herself a full 180 degrees so she was looking down the length of her body and through the mesh grid.

Three guards.

Two standing with their backs to her, another seated at a small console that probably controlled the cell doors and the environmental conditions.

"Three," she said into her commlink. "Approximate distance twelve to fourteen feet."

"Three confirmed," Aedon replied. "The distance is closer to ten feet."

Kala didn't argue. From her point of view, they were too close for comfort.

She knew Aedon was in the chute, only a few feet behind her. The crawl space, only twenty inches wide, would be too snug a fit. He might be able to wedge himself inside, but once there, he'd be unable to maneuver freely enough to use his weapon. It was up to her.

"How are we doing on time?" she asked, allowing a soft burble of guard conversation to cover her low-pitched voice.

"Forty-five minutes before the power plant goes offline," Aedon told her. "We don't have time to wait and see if three is the usual contingent. Go for the toxin."

They had to have Jein out of his cell and into the shuttle *before* Esarell discovered that Sy had given him the wrong timetable. When the power plant in the Naarca Valley went off-line, the ensuing alarm would bring Esarell and his troops to full alert.

"Confirmed," Kala acknowledged. "I'll load the darts."

Nerve-deadening toxin rather than direct laser fire would be used on the guards inside the holding area. The reason was twofold. First, a laser pistol emitted a faint glow before the cartridge ignited. Normally, the glow wouldn't be noticeable, but in a dark, confined area it could draw attention, alerting the guards to Kala's presence. Second, a misfired dart did no collateral damage. The dart would simply embed itself in something soft or bounce harmlessly off a more solid target, barely making a sound. A misfired laser blast could burn a hole in a metal or concrete wall.

As quietly as humanly possible, Kala pulled the toxic darts from her vest. Laying the dart magazine on her stomach, she exchanged the laser cartridge in her pistol for the cartridge containing the six darts that, if properly delivered, would render the guards unconscious for several hours.

Flattening herself against the crawl space, she took aim. She would have to hit the guard at the console first. The neck or shoulders was the favored penetration point, the one that would put the guard down the fastest.

He couldn't be allowed to sound an alarm.

The surprised reaction of the other guards would give her time to deliver the next two darts.

"Easy," Aedon's voice came through her commlink. "Take a breath. Relax."

Kala closed her eyes. After a heartbeat, she opened them again, and took aim. A gentle press of her finger sent the dart through the mesh grating and down the corridor. It was stopped by the guard's left shoulder, embedding itself and ejecting the toxin in a microsecond.

The guard didn't make a sound. He simply slumped forward, covering the console with his upper body.

"Now!" Aedon urged as the two remaining guards started moving. One turned toward Kala, the other pulled his weapon and looked toward the far end of the corridor.

Kala fired twice, in rapid succession. The guard looking away from her received a dart in his upper back. His body arched, then fell to the floor.

The third guard looked toward the crawl space, then shouted something in a language Kala didn't recognize. The dart meant for him had missed by several inches. He had already pulled his weapon. He fired toward the area where he suspected someone was hiding.

A blaze of laser fire took a bite out of the concrete just above Kala's head. A second shot tore into the gridwork near her feet.

She cursed, firing again.

And missed.

Suddenly, the dimly lit corridor filled with a flare of eye-searing brightness and lethal heat as the guard began firing as quickly as his weapon would allow.

Kala sent another dart in his direction.

It struck him in the lower leg. He fired again, but the laser blasts were poorly aimed as he stumbled backward toward the alarm console.

"Put him down!" Aedon told her. "Aim for his upper body."

Kala aimed and fired, not caring where the dart embedded itself as long as it delivered the required dose of toxin.

This time the dart found its target.

A jerky hand reached, paused in midair, then fell to the guard's side.

Kala waited a few moments, making sure there was no movement from any of the guards. Then, moving swiftly, she bunched her knees as close to her chest as the crawl space allowed and gave a firm kick. The mesh bent, but it didn't give way.

Three more kicks and a section of gridwork popped off its metal latches and fell to the floor.

"Hurry," Aedon urged her on.

Kala slipped through the opening and landed on her feet, bending her knees to absorb the impact of the ten-foot drop to the concrete floor.

She toggled her visor to a standard optical view as Aedon's long legs appeared overhead. A second later he had squeezed through the opening she'd made and was standing beside her.

"Good work," he said. "Delta, we're in."

"Confirmed," Terk's voice came over the commlink. "Standing by."

Kala kept her eyes trained on the far end of the corridor and the only entryway that she could see while Aedon lifted the unconscious guard away from the console. She had replaced the almost empty nerve-toxin cartridge with a laser cartridge. Her weapon was at the ready.

For a few moments, the only audible sound was her rapid breathing while she contemplated the horror of being caught inside Esarell's high-tech dungeon.

The miniprison comprised three holding cells. The doors were almost seamless, airtight and soundproof. Esarell may have placed a dungeon beneath his feet, but he had made certain that he was spared even the faintest echo of whatever cries might come from it.

Kala glanced over her shoulder. Aedon was busy at the console, trying to open the cell doors without triggering an alarm.

They could use their laser pistols to destroy the locking mechanism, but it would almost certainly bring a palace full of guards down on their heads. The system was certain to have bypass alarms for that very reason.

"Almost there," he said as the replay scanner he'd connected to the console circuitry searched for the last code series entered.

If Jein was Esarell's only prisoner, the code should open his cell. If not, the shuttle would have additional passengers.

A few moments later Kala flinched at the sound of the mechanized door beginning to open. She turned toward the cell, holding her breath as the door slowly sank back into the wall.

The area beyond was shrouded in darkness.

Kala switched on her visor light and swept the metal cage until she saw him.

A man.

A man who didn't look glad to see them. He had flattened himself against the wall cell. One misshapen hand covered his eyes, another held him upright. As the beam illuminated him, he turned his head aside.

"Jein," Kala said softly.

She was about to step into the cell when Aedon's hand stayed her.

"Sensors," he warned her.

Kala kept her visor light trained on Jein as Aedon swept the door frame of the cell for sensory alarms.

"Jein, it's me. Kala," she said, suddenly realizing what they must look like wearing black wetsuits and skullcaps and holding drawn weapons—like guards, not saviors. "Aedon is with me. We've come to get you out of here."

twenty-three

FOR A FEW seconds, Jein remained motionless. Then he raised his face and, still huddled in the corner, looked straight into the light. Kala quickly redirected the beam to keep it out of his eyes.

What she saw broke her heart.

The hollows beneath Jein's wizard-green eyes were dark, almost purple; his once-resolute gaze was now consumed by something else—despair. As he twisted the upper half of his body around, Kala could see the small tremors that shook him; even his bushy eyebrows seemed to quiver.

"It's all right," Kala found herself saying again. "We've come for you."

Blinking as if to wake himself from a dream, Jein pitched his upper body flat against the cell wall. "Kala?"

Her name was almost incoherent, as if speaking required a greater effort than Jein had the strength to exert. His eyes held a look of bewilderment.

"Yes, Jein. It's Kala and Aedon," she said, giving him

the further reassurance that he needed as Aedon finished inspecting the door frame for sensors.

When he waved her through, Kala rushed to Jein's side. Kneeling beside him, she looked into his eyes for any sign that he had been drugged. All she could see was the trauma of being held captive in a cell where he had even been denied a view of his captors. Like anyone, he was suffering the normal confusion and disorientation of a prisoner who had been convinced there was nothing more than death in his future.

He didn't appear to have been physically abused—thank the gods—but it was apparent from his ashy complexion that days of captivity had taken their toll.

"Jein?" she said, her tone demanding his recognition this time.

He blinked, then raised a trembling hand to her face. Cold fingertips traced what wasn't covered by her visor. The touch was reassuring, Jein's eyes imploring. He cleared his throat, moistened his cracked lips, and took another deep breath. "It's impossible," he said in a familiar raspy whisper. "How?"

Kala knew that Jein was regaining his composure bit by bit, becoming himself again. His piercing eyes reminded her that this was no ordinary man. He was a natural leader, a man of integrity, a man accustomed to giving hope. He had a gift for it, a gift Hachyn needed now more than ever.

"He's okay," Kala said, looking up at Aedon.

A twitch played out on Jein's wrinkled face, and then he spoke again. "When I told you to keep her safe, Korcian, this wasn't what I had in mind."

"She's a stubborn woman," Aedon replied as he bent down and lifted Jein into his arms as though he were picking up a child. "Time to get you out of here."

Kala glanced at her commlink: any further delay would be dangerous. There was no way of knowing when the next contingent of guards would arrive to relieve the ones they had rendered unconscious.

With Jein held firmly against Aedon's chest, Kala led the way back to the crawl space. Once there, Aedon put Jein down on the floor, then still kneeling, he cupped his hands to give Kala a lift up.

With an effort, Kala put aside thoughts of them being interrupted while their backs were to the prison entryway and reached for the ledge. After pulling herself up, she turned around and reached down for Jein.

He gave her a worried look, as if she might not be able to handle his weight, then relaxed as Aedon lifted him toward Kala. She got a firm hold on his wrists. Aedon did the rest while she scooted backward, drawing herself and Jein deeper into the crawl space.

"Aedon," she said, looking through the mesh gridwork.

"Right behind you," he answered.

Kala watched as he reached for the ledge. The muscles of his shoulders and arms bunched as he pulled himself up. Then, with her in front of Jein to pull, and Aedon behind him to push, they worked their way to the chute.

"You came in through that?" Jein asked.

"It's a snug fit, but it's doable," Kala said. "Can you roll over onto your back?"

Jein managed with her help. He was in frail health, had been for years, but his weight still matched hers. The more the chute inclined, the more effort it took to move him.

Aedon saw the difficulty she was having, but there was little he could do about it. He was on his knees, like her, but his larger size gave him even less room to navigate.

After what seemed like hours, but in fact was only a few minutes, Kala could see the rim of the chute where it emptied into the courtyard. "Almost there," she told Jein.

She stopped just short of the opening, gave Jein a reassuring pat on his shoulder, before increasing the magnification on her visor. She peered over the rim. Then she watched and listened.

The only things she sensed were the distant rush of

water onto the island's rocky shore, the salty tang of a sea breeze, and the stillness of undisturbed shadows. The wind felt stronger than before, the night sky brighter. The cloud cover they had used to enter the courtyard was beginning to break up and stars were visible. So was a patch of the waxing moon.

Kala could have done without the nocturnal glow. They were out of Esarell's dungeon. But they weren't free.

Not yet.

"All clear," she reported.

Two minutes later, the three of them were on the outside.

"Fresh air," Jein mumbled, not having to be told to keep his voice low. He was lying belly-down on the ground between Kala and Aedon. "I never thought to breathe it again."

"Terk," Aedon spoke into his commlink. "Phase two complete. Package in hand. Contact shuttle. Rendezvous in five minutes."

"Confirm," Terk replied. "Five minutes."

The area immediately beneath the terrace was safer, in certain respects, than the courtyard itself. Once they left the cover provided by shadows, the moonlight became a disadvantage.

"I'm going to lift you onto my shoulder," Aedon told Jein. "Hold onto my equipment belt."

"I'll do my damnedest," the resistance leader replied, jut-jawed and determined. He was in his sixties, had been held in captivity, but his sheer force of will would see him through tonight, just as it had done years before when he'd survived another prison.

Aedon came to his knees, checked his weapon to make sure it was ready to fire, then reached down for Jein. He lifted him over his left shoulder. For the old man's sake, he didn't spell out what came next.

Nothing would be gained by telling Jein that their chance of reaching the shuttle undetected was next to none. He couldn't carry Jein and crawl to safety the way he had crawled into the courtyard. The very fact that he had a man slung over his shoulder forced Aedon to walk upright, exposing himself and Jein.

He looked to Kala, then pointed to a rock wall, fifty yards away, where the rear courtyard yielded to the natural foliage of the island. The wall itself was only a few feet high, a visual demarcation rather than a physical impediment. Once they were on the other side, it would provide some protection.

Kala pointed to her commlink. "We're running late," she said. "The plant will go off-line in less than three minutes."

Aedon's eyes scanned the darkness, looking for guards or any movement associated with palace personnel. When he didn't see anything, he gave Kala the signal.

Together they sprinted toward the rocks; Aedon slowed by Jein's weight bouncing on his shoulder.

They gained the wall without detection. Kala went over in a graceful leap. Aedon less gracefully because of the burden he carried. Once they were on the other side, he crouched as low as he could go and still hold onto Jein.

"So far, so good," Kala said.

They were both looking at the expanse of manicured yard they would have to cross before the island's thick foliage hid them from view. That darkness was their destination, their salvation. If they could reach it.

Fifty yards.

It wasn't a great distance, unless they were sighted by one of the guards on the palace seawalls.

Aedon filled his lungs with air, shifted Jein's weight to make it less cumbersome, and nodded.

They had covered almost half of the distance when a sentry from one of the battlements saw them. Light flooded the open lawn, followed by a burst of laser fire.

"Run," Aedon shouted, no longer concerned that they might be heard.

"This way," Stiles shouted back at them, revealing his position as he returned the guard's fire.

Janson joined the fight, sending a spray of laser fire toward the guard's post.

Another glare of blue-white fire, this one from a mounted laser rifle with five times the firepower of its handheld counterpart, flashed through the darkness, outlining Kala and Aedon like a floodlight from a guard tower.

"Go!" Aedon shouted. He held onto Jein with one hand and fired with the other.

"Hurry!" Kala cried out, aghast and terrified that they'd gotten this far only to be caught. "We're almost there."

A burst of rifle fire kicked up a spray of dirt at Aedon's feet. Another buzz-saw-like burst pelted the shrubbery only a few yards behind him.

Aedon fired on the run, seconds ticking by like hours. The only hope of survival lay in speed—to get to the trees and into the darkness as fast as possible.

Just when Aedon thought he wouldn't make it, a hand reached up to pull him to the ground. Jein was lifted away by either Stiles or Janson, he couldn't be sure.

"The shuttle is on its way," Stiles said as another volley of laser fire pelted the trees surrounding them. They were shots fired out of desperation, fired for show. But a stray shot could easily achieve the same as a well-aimed one. Death.

"Where's Kala?" Aedon asked urgently. Lights were on all over the compound, guards scurrying to find the intruders.

"Here," she said. "I'm right here."

Aedon looked to where she and Janson were rigging the harness they had brought to carry Jein. Stiles would do the honors. He was a stout man, shorter than Aedon, but with a strong back. He would need it. It was a good mile to the rendezvous point where the shuttle would be waiting.

A siren alarm pierced the night.

"We've got to get the hell out of here," Stiles said as he slipped into the harness and stood up, balancing Jein's weight easily enough for the time being.

"Go!" Aedon urged as he slipped a fresh laser cartridge into his weapon and turned to take aim. "Don't look back. Don't stop for anything. Get Jein to the shuttle."

Stiles and Janson slipped into the darkness.

Kala stayed with Aedon.

"You, too," he ordered.

Instead of doing what she'd been told to do, Kala knelt at Aedon's side, aimed her weapon toward a group of guards who had just appeared beneath the terrace, and began firing.

Six men fell within a matter of seconds, confirming another rule of war: the first seen were the first sacrificed.

Aedon gritted his teeth against Kala's stubbornness, and kept firing, taking down another two guards.

"Start retreating," he told her. "As soon as you get beyond sight of the palace, start running. And I mean *run*.

"Not without you," she said, tossing her used cartridge aside and reaching for another one.

"Okay. Now!"

They fired in rapid unison, walking backward into the darkness, laying down a pattern of random fire that would keep the guards from rushing them.

Orders were shouted as more guards rushed from their palace sleeping quarters, most stumbling and cursing as they struggled to get into their uniforms and ready their weapons at the same time.

The point of rendezvous was a tough, metamorphic chuck of weathered rock at the western tip of the island.

Aedon and Kala delivered one last volley of fire, then turned and raced for it.

Then, suddenly, without warning, they were looking at a guard. The man might have been walking because he couldn't sleep, or perhaps, he'd been on patrol, but regardless of the reasons, he was there now. Standing a few feet in front of them, his expression was one of momentary disbelief as he associated the shriek of the alarm with the two strangers garbed in midnight black.

The only fortunate thing about the encounter was that the guard's surprise assured Kala and Aedon that Stiles and Janson had gotten through without being detected.

The guard raised his weapon. A gratified, sadistic smile came to his face as he realized that he'd found two intruders.

Kala instantly gauged the chances of killing him without one of them being killed in return, but the thought had barely registered when Aedon's knees buckled.

She watched in awe as he dropped down to the ground, remaining perfectly erect as he bent his knees. At the same time, his right hand shot straight up, grabbing the wrist of the guard's outstretched hand.

The man's smile vanished as Aedon pulled his arm down in a powerful wrist lock, wrenching it toward his elbow and twisting it at an acute angle. Now the man bellowed in pain as his weapon dropped to the ground, the ligaments in his arm strained and torn. But Aedon was relentless, taking a long step back with his left foot and pulling the guard to the ground. He yanked on the arm with all his strength and heard a pop as the ball joint was dislocated from the socket. The guard roared again, agony mingling with disbelief at being disarmed so easily.

Aedon fell on him, bringing his weight to bear on his right knee, driving it into the guard's rib cage. The sound of breaking bone was irrefutable. The broken ribs would make simply breathing exquisitely painful.

Roused by the sound of more guards coming their way, the guard tried to free his gun arm, despite his dislocated shoulder. Aedon countered by turning his right hand into a claw that clamped around the man's throat, pulling his head back.

Kala could have fired, but she didn't dare. The flash of a laser pistol would pinpoint their location like a beacon.

She had no choice but to stand aside while Aedon choked the injured guard into unconsciousness.

"Go!" he said as soon as the knew the guard wouldn't be able to call for help.

They ran, pushing against the branches that speared their clothing, caring only about putting as much distance between themselves and the pursuing guard as humanly possible. They were in operational overtime—the mission had taken longer than planned. They had to reach the shuttle before Esarell launched his own in retaliation.

The sound of the sea grew stronger.

Muscles straining, lungs gasping for air, feet flying over rock and night-slick vegetation, they hurried toward the low whine of a shuttle fighting gravity with its thrusters.

It was hugging the shore less than a half a mile away. Then, as if the shuttle were heaving in rhythm with the waves below it, its powerful engines strained against the forces of wind and gravity and came to rest on the narrow slip of land.

There! Just ahead. Kala could see the shuttle's metallic hull reflecting moonlight. Shadow men—Stiles and Janson. They lowered Jein to the ground, then picked him up between them and carried him into the shuttle.

He was safe!

Free.

Then, when victory seemed within grasp, a flash of laser fire pocked the ground in front of them.

Aedon stumbled and fell, but not intentionally.

He'd been hit!

"No," he said, pushing her away. "Get out of here."

Kala couldn't see his injury, but the smell of scorched flesh filled her nostrils. She bent down and helped him to his feet. He outweighed her, towering over her even as he slumped in pain.

More laser fire streaked through the darkness.

"Get out of here," Aedon shouted down at the top of her head. She was wedged under his right arm, supporting him with her shoulder.

"Stop ordering me around and start moving," she snapped back. "I'm not leaving you."

Burdened, but determined, Kala turned them in the direction of the shuttle. She had no idea how badly Aedon was hurt, but leaving him behind wasn't something she even considered.

She stumbled once, struggled back to her feet, and kept moving.

Desperation gave her courage.

Love gave her strength.

Kala tuned out everything but her view of the shuttle. Twenty yards. Fifteen. Ten. She could see Stiles running toward her, feel Aedon's weight lighten as it was shared.

Terk was there, too. Shouting at her for being a damn fool, then pushing her ahead of him as he took her place.

Now, gasping and sputtering, she was inside the shuttle.

"Aedon?" she said, holding out her hands to touch him as Terk and Stiles placed him at her feet.

"Get this thing into the air," Terk ordered.

De Vries willingly obliged. Within seconds, the shuttle was ascending to an altitude beyond the range of the grounded guard's laser rifles.

Terk pulled off his visor and smiled at Kala. "He's alive. It's a leg wound."

Kala's heart squeezed hard, then harder still as she looked at Aedon's right thigh. There was little blood with a laser injury. The extreme heat of the narrow-beamed light burned through flesh and bone, cauterizing blood vessels as it went. The black polysilk of Aedon's nightsuit was melted, fused into the Korcian's flesh. It was an ugly wound.

Kala tore off her visor and reached for the medical kit Janson had produced from a shuttle bin.

She opened it, fumbled through the contents with trembling hands, and readied what she'd need. Then, gently, she removed Aedon's visor and skullcap.

His complexion was pale, the pupils of his silver-black eyes dilated in pain. His breathing was shallow, but steady.

Relief raced through her as his gaze lifted to focus on her. He was in pain. Clearly angry that she hadn't listened to him and ready to lecture her for it.

But he was alive.

"I told you to run," he said between clenched teeth.

Kala smiled down at him, then lowered her head to brush a gentle kiss across his pain-thinned mouth. "And I told you that we would finish this together. We did."

She stroked his forehead lightly, pushing sweat-dampened hair away from his face. "I'm going to give you an injection. The pain will ease in a few minutes," she told him.

"Just antibiotics," he said through clenched teeth. "I don't want to lose consciousness. We still have a lot of do."

Kala reached for the first of two syringes. One held a mammoth dose of antibiotics, the other a tranquilizing drug than would do exactly what Aedon didn't want done.

She fitted the first syringe to his upper arm and injected the antibiotics through the sleeve of his wet suit, then reached for the second.

"No," Aedon said, reaching out to wrap his hand around her wrist. "We might run into more trouble." His eyes closed, his focus momentarily lost. "I need to be able to fire a weapon."

"I can't bear seeing you in pain," Kala said shakily, aware that everyone inside the shuttle could hear their conversation, but not caring.

"How far?" he asked.

Terk answered. "Two hundred kilometers southeast of Melgarr. We'll put down in a few minutes."

"Ginomi?" he said thickly.

"He's putting out the word. By the time we have you and Jein tucked away in a safe house, Rendhal should be having that fit we talked about." Terk tapped the face of his commlink. "T minus four and counting on the first factory. After that, it's all over but the fireworks."

Kala moved so she could hold Aedon's head in her lap. "Everyone is doing exactly what you told them do," she said. "Now close your eyes and rest."

Terk had seen to Jein's comfort as best as he could considering the shuttle's limited assets. Now, he knelt down beside Aedon.

"The wound isn't as serious at it looks," he told Kala. "He's going to need rejuvenation therapy, but the tissue will heal. It didn't hit the bone."

She shuddered at the image of the laser beam slicing through Aedon's thigh bone as if it had no more density than thin air. Now that it was over, at least as much of it as Aedon could be involved in, the adrenaline of the aftermath had Kala feeling as if she'd been days without sleep rather than hours.

Sitting on the shuttle's main deck, with Aedon's head in her lap, she couldn't fight the emotions any longer. Fear. Relief. The joy of victory. Love.

They infused her soul and brought tears to her eyes.

She looked down at Aedon. His eyes were closed, his face still tight with pain. She wanted to smooth that pain away, to kiss it away, to love it away.

Would tonight's victory satisfy her avenging Korcian? Would the battles being fought in the Naarca Valley and the provinces render the blood debt owed to his wife and child paid in full?

Was freedom finally within her grasp? And if it was, would she gain it only to lose the man she loved?

As the shuttle began to circle over the landing zone,

Kala finally looked at Jein. He was strapped into one of the shuttle's eight seats. His hair was dirty, his clothes stained, his face creased with wrinkles and years of worry, but his eyes had regained their biting brilliance.

When he spoke, his voice was reedy, but clear. His eyes moist with tears. "You're a brave woman, Kala Char'ari. You humble me. All of you humble me."

Kala's smiled at her old friend. "Wait to you see what's waiting on the mainland."

twenty-four

THE GOVERNOR WAS awakened from a sound sleep by a member of the Planet Ministry.

"What?" Rendhal demanded, fumbling with his robe as he stormed out of his private bedroom and into the adjoining suite where Minister Seuret stood waiting.

The room was eye-catching in its grandeur, but its real charm lay in the accessible private entrance that enabled Rendhal's closest advisors to arrive and depart without drawing attention to themselves. The discreet meetings could take place without leaving behind any telltale logs or computerized records. They could take place without ever officially having taken place at all.

It was why Minister Seuret had chosen to use the private entrance instead of hurrying his way through the main corridors of the palace where Esarell's men stood guard. If what he had heard was true, the circumstances facing the governor's ministry and staff could be cataclysmic.

"What?" Rendhal demanded again, his voice sharp and impatient. "It's the middle of the night."

Seuret licked his dry lips. He prided himself on maintaining an outward air of serenity, no matter the circumstances. That air of serenity was close to fraying. "The power grid supplying the Naarca Valley has been disrupted."

"Disrupted? How? What in the name of Titan's three moons are you talking about?" Rendhal stomped across the room and poured himself a drink. "Well, Seuret, start explaining, I'm not telepathic."

"Before the grid went out, I was reviewing the nightly comm reports. It's part of my regular duties."

"Yes, yes. Get on with it."

Despite Seuret's high ranking and personal relationship with the governor—he was the closest thing to a friend Rendhal had—his job was analysis, not operations, and he remained an analyst to the core of his being. The ingrained mistrust that men of his ilk had toward anyone outside their normal circle was too often justified. This was one of those times.

"May I have a drink?" Seuret asked, finding his mouth unusually dry.

Rendhal flushed angrily. "Help yourself, but keep talking."

Seuret poured a splash of strong liquor into a glass, gulped it down, grimaced as it burned his throat, then turned to face a temperamental and unpredictable governor.

"As I was saying, I just finished reviewing the nightly comm reports. A message was intercepted."

"What message?" Rendhal asked, growing more impatient by the moment. "From whom, to whom? And what does a message have to do with a power plant going offline?"

"I can't be certain," Seuret told him. "The message

appears to have originated in the northern province, somewhere in the Moviash Mountains."

"Resistance fighters?"

"In all likelihood. The message was slipped in between precinct reports, injected if you like, from a compatible transmitter—"

"I don't care how it was done," said Rendhal. "I want to know what it said."

Seuret inhaled deeply then blurted out the words. "The transmission was sent from the northern province to a private residence here in the capital. It relayed the successful extraction of Eiven Jein from a prison on Zahalla."

"What?"

"The message said that Eiven Jein had been rescued. That a team of resistance fighters had infiltrated the island, freed him, and were on their way back to the mainland."

"Impossible," Rendhal said, shaking his head in disbelief at the same time the possibility of Seuret's words being true sunk in. "If Esarell had captured Jein, he would have told me."

Seuret didn't reply. The remark had been a statement, not a question.

Rendhal looked down at the marble floor, at if staring at the pristine white tiles were the same thing as looking into the all-knowing depths of a crystal ball. Gradually, his posture straightened, his shoulders stiffening. His face was flushed with anger, his eyes gleaming with hatred.

"Esarell was planning to betray me. He knows the Board is pushing me to end the rebellion. Demanding that I do it within a matter of weeks. I gave him orders. Orders to find Jein. To crush the rebellion."

"Orders he may have turned against you," Seuret said, pointing out the obvious.

Another obvious fact was that Esarell now had the entire police force at his command, courtesy of the governor's devoted trust.

Rendhal glared at Seuret. "Esarell thinks he can outwit me. He was planning on handing Jein over to the Board. He wants to make me look weak and incompetent. He wants the governorship."

"What would you have me do?" Seuret asked, knowing that in this case Esarell had underestimated Rendhal.

It was easily done. The governor appeared to be self-centered and self-serving, but underneath he was highly intelligent, greedily ambitious, and as manipulating as any member of the Board he served.

Rendhal looked toward the closed doors of the suite—doors that separated him from a palace full of Esarell's select guards.

Before he could speak, the comm panel chimed. "Excellency."

"What?" Rendhal asked, forcing his voice to its normal level and tone.

"A message from Commander Esarell," the guard outside the door announced.

"At this hour?"

"May I enter, Excellency?"

Seuret stepped back, into the darkened bedroom, out of the guard's line of sight.

"Enter," Rendhal said, giving the voice command that would be recognized by the sensors and immediately matched to his vocal imprint.

The guard walked into the room, bowed his head in respect, then said, "Commander Esarell has received word that several factories in the Naarca Valley are under attack."

"Under attack?" Rendhal sounded surprised. Looked surprised. He fumbled with the ties of his robe, deliberately projecting an image of sleepy confusion. "By whom?"

"The resistance, Excellency."

Again, Rendhal looked skeptical. "The resistance attacking factories. What purpose would it serve? Are you certain?"

The guard nodded. "The power plant supplying the valley has gone off-line. Sabotaged. Commander Esarell fears that the resistance may be planning a similar attack on the palace itself. He issued orders that you are to be escorted to Zahalla. You'll be safe there."

Safe! You mean assassinated. If I'm dead, Esarell moves into the palace and claims what is rightfully mine. But only if I let him.

"Very well, I'll get dressed," Rendhal told the guard. "You may wait outside."

As soon as the door closed behind the retreating guard, Rendhal turned to Seuret. "Power plants off-line. Factories exploding. Jein rescued when I didn't know he was being held captive. Do you think Esarell is working with the resistance against me?"

"No," Seuret said, believing he was correct. "I know Eiven Jein as well as you do. He would never partner his abilities with Esarell. I think your first conclusion was the right one. Esarell planned on using Jein against you. Perhaps the attack on the valley is a reprisal against Jein's imprisonment."

Rendhal didn't looked convinced. "Those factories . . . never mind. I'm going to need your help."

Seuret looked stunned. He was in the ministry, not the military.

"You're going with me to Zahalla," the governor announced as he tossed aside his robe and walked naked into the bedroom.

Seuret followed. "What are you planning?"

Rendhal threw clothing onto the bed, then walked to a small desk in the corner of the room. Something like a

smile played over his mouth as he deactivated the lock on
the desk drawer, then reached inside.

"Here," he said, handing Seuret a laser pistol. "You
may need this."

twenty-five

WHEN THE SHUTTLE touched down it was immediately embraced by the thick layer of fog that was the Jovian Sea's gift to the southern deltas.

"Where?" Aedon asked as another stab of pain radiated upward from his leg, consuming his entire body. The laser fire had sliced across the outer muscles of his right thigh. The blood vessels had been cauterized by heat, but not the nerve endings. They were registering pain.

Acute pain.

The sort of pain that the brain normally blocked out with unconsciousness.

"Lopreista," she told him. "You'll be safe here."

Lopreista was the seaside village that Ginomi had selected, a refuge where Jein would be welcomed and well hidden by local sympathizers. Aedon knew a physician was waiting in the safe house in case Jein required medical attention. At least his talents wouldn't go to waste.

Aedon refused to close his eyes. He stared at Kala's face, memorizing each line, remembering each kiss, each caress, each time they had made love. It helped to keep him focused, to keep his mind on something other than the pain.

There was still a lot of fighting to be done. And after that, the healing. The healing of a planet and its people. It wouldn't be a short process. Healing never was.

He also knew that Kala would be at the center of that healing, working hand in hand with Jein and the others to rebuild their world.

It was her dream.

A dream that would take a lifetime to fulfill.

Aedon knew she could do it. After tonight there wasn't any doubt in his mind—Kala Char'ari was the most incredible female he'd ever met.

What would happen between them was still an uncertainty. He was out of the fight, and would be for several days. Perhaps weeks. Rejuvenation therapy was highly effective. His leg could be returned to normal, but not immediately.

The resistance would have to succeed without him.

They had their leader back. And their confidence. They knew now that the war could be won.

Tonight had proven it.

The other members of the assault team, who had been relatively inactive since entering the shuttle, came to life as soon as the hatchway ramp was lowered. Janson and Stiles saw to Jein, unfastening the seat restraints that had held him upright during the flight, easing him into the back harness once again, then carrying him outside.

Terk, De Vries, and Ravier lifted Aedon. Kala remained at his side, holding onto his hand as they exited the shuttle and made their way toward a house shrouded in thick fog.

The safe house was the color of sand, with a tiled roof and shuttered windows. A man with tousled, straw-colored hair opened the door.

"Straight back," he instructed Aedon's bearers. "All Jein needs is food and rest."

Aedon grimaced as he was placed on a low, flat examining table. His leg was on fire, the pain constant.

"I'm staying with him," Kala told the physician.

He nodded, waved the others from the room, then activated the table's sterilizing field. It glowed a startling white beneath Aedon's black-clad body.

"I'm Dr. Cayman," the physician said.

When he met Aedon's gaze, his eyes were clear. Confident. This wasn't the first laser wound he'd treated. With an army of resistance fighters on the attack, it wouldn't be the last.

He pulled an instrument tray up to the table, then reached for a syringe. Wordlessly, he embedded the anesthesia needle in the side of Aedon's neck.

He felt the effect almost instantly.

Pain was replaced by a feeling of weightlessness, as if he had stepped off the table and into the gravity-free void of space.

Dawn was breaking, a pink tendril over the horizon. A few minutes later, the stem of color became more intense, dark violet shading swiftly into vivid cerulean. Dawn over the southern deltas of Hachyn.

Aedon watched the arrival of a new day through the window of a room that had been converted into an emergency medical station. He was alone, his naked body draped by a clean white sheet. A surgical canopy covered his thigh, intravenous tubes filled with a reddish liquid ran from therapy bags into both his arms. The anesthesia was wearing off, but he still felt drugged. Drowsy. The pain had subsided; there were drugs in the intravenous solutions.

He was straining to stay awake, fighting the sedative

effects of the drugs being dripped into his bloodstream, when the door opened and a woman walked into the room.

Not Kala.

This woman was middle-aged and blond. She was dressed casually in dark slacks and a floral hip-length tunic. She looked familiar. When she smiled at him, Aedon realized who she was.

Yahaira. The brothel owner.

Jein's former lover.

"You're awake," she said. "That's good."

"Where's Kala?" It was the first question on Aedon's mind. The only question that mattered until he got an answer.

"Melgarr or Lejan or perhaps Gaharoff, wherever she is needed the most. I can tell you that she is safe. Jein gave Terk specific orders to make sure she did nothing but monitor communications and relay messages to the units who are fighting. He loves her like a daughter. She'll be kept safe."

Aedon wanted to believe it, but he also knew how desperately Kala wanted to win this war. She'd take to the street with nothing but courage and a laser pistol if she thought it was necessary.

"And the governor?"

"He's not in the palace," Yahaira told him. "That's all we know. The entire Naarca Valley is in chaos. Factories burning, police scurrying like rodents from one building to another waiting for orders that can't arrive because the comm centers have been blacked out. It shouldn't surprise you. You planned the whole thing."

She checked the levels in the medication bags and increased the drip rate on the rejuvenation drugs. "You're a big boy, you can handle the increased dose."

Aedon remembered that Yahaira had been the one to nurse Jein back to health after his first imprisonment. He didn't question her knowledge of the rejuvenation process or her familiarity with the medical console.

When she stepped in front of the window, the morning sunlight caught her hair, making it shine as if she were twenty years younger.

"Dr. Cayman is your son, isn't he?"

She turned to look at him and smiled. "Ahh, my nursing skills."

"No. Your hair."

She raised a hand to touch the neat chignon at the nape of her neck. "You're very perceptive. Kala complimented you on that. Among other things."

"How is Jein?"

"Resting." Her expression changed, turning serious. "I know now why Kala didn't tell me about the monastery explosion. I'm not sure what I would have done. But that's the past. I've learned to live one day at a time. Jein is alive and safe. That's all that matters to me."

The drowsiness of lingering anesthesia and pain medication didn't keep Aedon from hearing the devotion in Yahaira's voice. The events that had kept her and Jein apart for years hadn't changed her feelings.

"I need to know what's happening. Have they taken Melgarr yet?" Aedon asked. The words were slurred and sluggish. The drugs were stronger than his will to stay awake.

"Good," Yahaira said, smoothing the sheet over his shoulders as if she were tucking a child into bed. "You need rest, Korcian. Sleep. Your body will heal faster."

Aedon fought it, but he couldn't stop the darkness of sedated sleep from overtaking him again. His last thought was a prayer that Kala be kept safe.

Rendhal had never cared for the isolation of Zahalla Island. He preferred the view from his balcony in the governor's palace, the view of a capital city on a planet that was his. *His,* not the Conglomerate's, and certainly not Esarell's.

He turned away from Zahalla's balcony view of the Jovian Sea, turned amber by the rising sun, to the man seated behind a large console desk.

As always, Esarell was wearing a uniform. Every crease and seam was pressed into perfection.

Seuret sat to the side of the room, his expression worried but not overly so, his hands managing his coffee cup without trembling. It was essential that Esarell not suspect there was a laser pistol hidden under his robes.

Esarell knew that Seuret was one of Rendhal's most trusted advisors. He also knew that Seuret's hard-won status was crucial to his current financial security. To his way of thinking, Seuret would side with the winner, once the winner was determined. As a financial analyst, he would detach himself from the politics and follow the money.

The exception to that line of thought was Seuret's decision that Esarell would quickly replace the members of the ministry with men of his own choosing.

Self-preservation would keep Seuret loyal to the current governor.

"Can you explain how the rebels managed to get control of three communications centers shortly after they turned the entire Naarca Valley into a fireball of ruined factories?" Rendhal demanded. "They are supposed to be, as you once put it, a gang of witless idealists."

Esarell didn't care for being called to account. It showed on his face. "I've sent a force into the Moviash Mountains. We have information, supplied by informants, that they have a base there. It will be destroyed."

Rendhal waved the remark aside with a heavy-jeweled hand. "This isn't the work of one camp. It's a military campaign. A very well-organized assault. One a gang of witless idealists shouldn't have been able to accomplish. You apparently repeated my mistake. You underestimated Eiven Jein."

Rendhal continued his verbal attack. There was no one

in the room to witness Esarell's humiliation, except Seuret, who continued to sip his coffee as if nothing that was being said concerned him. The guards had been dismissed, most ordered to the mainland before Rendhal's arrival.

"The last message from Gaharoff was sent by a hysterical precinct captain who claimed there were mobs gathering in the streets. In the streets!" Rendhal slammed his hand onto the top of Esarell's desk. "It's chaos. You've lost control, Commander."

"I intend to go to Melgarr immediately," Esarell said as if his very presence would quell the confusion. "My first concern was your safety."

Rendhal had to admire him. He was a consummate actor.

"My safety. How considerate of you," Rendhal said mockingly. He smiled, revealing a row of feral white teeth. "And how am I to be kept safe, Commander? Am I to be invited to occupy one of your private prison cells? Perhaps you'd like me to wait in the same cell as Jein? The one you confined him to before he was *liberated* by witless idealists."

Esarell's eyes flashed with anger. He reached down, as if to draw a weapon.

Seuret's coffee cup crashed to the floor as the laser pistol was drawn. At the given range, he couldn't miss. "Governor Rendhal isn't finished, Commander. If I were you, I'd be a good little soldier and stand still until the scolding is over."

"Surprised?" Rendhal shook his head pitifully. "How like you to think everyone else an idiot. From others I might expect self-delusion. But not from someone as aware as you. As intelligent. Still, you seem to be unable to grasp the current situation. Let me explain."

Rendhal glanced in Seuret's direction, his eyes sending the awaited message.

Seuret stepped closer to the desk. He raised the laser

pistol, but it was the laser pistol in Rendhal's hand that delivered the fatal blast.

When Aedon awoke the second time, voices carried him to the surface of what had been a dark void. He blinked his eyes to bring the room into focus. The shutters were closed against the sunlight, the room cast in afternoon shadows.

"Ahh, awake at last." It was Jein's voice. Soft and raspy.

Aedon turned his head to the side. Jein was seated in a gravity-chair. It wasn't as elaborate as the one he had used in the monastery, but it afforded him the mobility Esarell had stolen from him.

Yahaira stood nearby. Her son, Dr. Cayman, was busy at the medical console, monitoring Aedon's vital signs.

He left the monitors with their multicolored data lines and came to stand by the side of Aedon's bed. "Your Korcian anatomy is remarkable," he said. "Your cells are rejuvenating more quickly than I expected. A week, ten days at the most, and your leg will be as good as new. There will be some initial pain, once you start using the muscles again, but the discomfort will be minimal compared to the original injury."

"Thank you," Aedon said. His mouth and throat were dry. The intravenous fluids were feeding his body, but they couldn't quench normal thirst. He licked his lips.

"Here, let me help you to sit up," Cayman said. He returned to the console and the bed's computerized controls.

When Aedon was sitting upright, Yahaira handed him a glass of cold water. "Don't overdo," she cautioned him, then she and her son left the room.

Jein remained. He maneuvered his chair in closer. "Eager for some news, my Korcian friend?"

"Kala first. Is she safe?"

Jein smiled, then laughed.

It was a good smile. A victorious laugh.

"She's in Melgarr. Our people have taken over the ministry building. She's monitoring messages between the units fighting in the north and western provinces. We're going to win this time, Aedon. Thanks to you. Your courage is contagious. The people are joining us by the thousands. The news is spreading, and Rendhal is on the run. He's fled the palace. Every transport and freighter in the docking station is readying to leave Hachyn, laden with as many of Rendhal's officials as they can carry."

"What about Esarell?"

"Dead," Jein told him. "We got the report an hour ago. Rendhal killed him, or had him killed. The details are sketchy, but the results are the same. The Guard and the police have no master at the helm, no one to tell them what to do, or where to do it. And no communication channels to relay what few orders are being given. Precinct captains are abandoning their posts, telling their men to get out of the cities any way they can. They're running like the cowards they are."

Jein moved his chair even closer, then reached out to grip Aedon's hand. "We owe you a debt that I fear can never be repaid."

"The debt is not owed to me, it's owed to Kala and Terk and Ginomi. To the people of this world. All I did was supply the tactics. They did the real work."

Jein nodded, clearly unable to speak past the emotions of the moment.

The silence continued for several minutes, Jein thinking of a dream finally realized, Aedon thinking of where that future would take Kala and her people.

"Kala told me about the message you sent to Beyrenta, to the Empire," Jein said. "She told me what you found in the factories. Of Selwyn's betrayal and Sy's. Everything."

"If the Conglomerate is allowed to militarize, the entire galaxy will be in danger."

"I couldn't agree more," Jein said. "It was, as hindsight often reveals, predictable. Greed is a never-satisfied hunger."

"You were part of the Conglomerate bureaucracy once. You know how they think. Where would you base a small fleet of starjets?"

"In this sector?"

"Yes."

Jein rubbed a scarred hand over his mouth. "The Trinity Planets are my best guess. They are mostly unexplored. The Imperium had several mining cooperatives on Myamar, but nothing beyond a few meager settlements. The work is mainly done by drones. The other two planets are even less populated."

Aedon had come to the same conclusion. He hoped Cullon Gavriel shared his thinking. The base, wherever it was, would have to be destroyed.

"Kala thinks you were sent here to spy for the Empire," Jein injected casually. "Were you?"

"Does it matter?"

"No."

Aedon flexed his arms, causing the intravenous tubing to sway like the lifeline it was. He could already feel the rejuvenation drugs working. His leg was tingling. Healing.

"I should let you rest," Jein said. "Yahaira will not like me overtaxing your strength or mine. She's very protective of the people she loves. Like Kala."

"Kala is an incredible woman," Aedon said. He looked down at the surgical canopy that covered his leg. If she hadn't gotten him to the shuttle, he would have died.

Death.

He'd been prepared for it all his life, trained to accept it as the possibility of any battle, the consequence of a military career. He had once hoped to embrace it, to join his wife and child in whatever heaven had claimed them.

But Kala had changed all of that.

She'd turned his quest for revenge into a quest for freedom. His despair into hope.

"You trained her," Aedon said. He wasn't aware that his eyes lightened to a soft gray at the mention of her name. "All those years that she thought she was playing messenger and nursemaid, you were training her to take over."

Jein nodded. "She's a natural leader. Courageous. Compassionate. Full of life. Who better to lead us into the future?"

"You chose well," Aedon said. "She'll make a wonderful prime minister."

Jein laughed. "Anything but governor. But we're getting ahead of ourselves. Today's success must continue into tomorrow. People are shedding their fear, but the fight isn't over yet. Until it is, and for a long time thereafter, we must, as my beloved Yahaira likes to say, take our blessings where we can."

"Is Cayman your son?" Aedon asked.

With a resigned gesture, Jein leaned back in his chair. "I would like to say yes, but I can't." He looked toward the shuttered window before meeting Aedon's gaze again. "Rendhal is his father. He doesn't know. Nor does Rendhal. Yahaira lived in the palace for a short time. Afterwards, she swore me to secrecy. I owed her that and more. She was the one who told Max Branson where I was being held. She risked her life to get the information, and she risked it again when she hid me in the brothel and nursed me back to health. She's an amazing woman in her own right."

Aedon wasn't sure how to reply.

Jein smiled knowingly. "This is the outer regions, my friend. Things are rarely what they seem."

twenty-six

KALA STOOD ON the governor's balcony, overlooking Melgarr. The last place she would have ever imagined herself to be. And yet, the room behind her, once the governor's private office, was now hers. Temporarily.

Weeks of fighting had finally come to an end. The dead had been buried. The mourning would go on for years.

The city was secure, the police precincts occupied by resistance teams that were slowly bringing order back to the streets. Most of the Honor Guard and the police had fled, following Rendhal deeper into the outer regions. Those who had not, those who had been captured, were being held pending exile.

Hachyn was free of the Conglomerate.

But despite all the good news that had been pouring into Kala's temporary office, she felt burdened.

There was happiness in the victory of the HCF, exhilaration in the prospect of living on an independently governed world. And yet her heart wasn't bursting with joy.

Joy was an emotion best shared. Best celebrated with the person you loved.

Jein and Aedon were both in Melgarr, here in the palace with her and the rest of the provisional team.

Both men were regaining their strength.

Kala had passed the morning with Jein, and, as always, she had been awed by his ability to coordinate and supervise, to contribute ideas, then help to implement them into action.

The factories that hadn't been destroyed in the attack on the Naarca Valley would be retooled to produce lawful goods that could be traded in the marketplaces of the League and the Empire. The pollution would be controlled as it should have been from the beginning. The cities would be renovated, the mountains held in reserve, their wild beauty intact, for generations of Hachynites to enjoy.

A new police force would be formed, under new laws enacted to protect the people rather than to enslave them.

That was the dream.

Paying for it was the reality.

The treasury was empty, the funds transferred into a Conglomerate account before Rendhal had fled.

Hachyn was free.

It was also destitute.

If they didn't reestablish the trade routes soon, the planet would go from revolutionary freedom into financial ruin.

Kala left the balcony to sit behind her desk. Her *temporary* desk. She was certain, as was everyone, that the office should by rights belong to Jein—his election as prime minister (Kala wasn't sure when he'd decided on the name of the office) was inevitable. He was, after all, the father of the resistance. The man who had first envisioned Hachyn as a free world.

A map of the southern province was floating above the holo-projector on her desk when the comm panel chimed.

It was Yahaira.

She set a tray of food on the corner of Kala's desk. "You haven't eaten today. You can't work every minute."

"There's so much to be done," Kala said. "Jein wants to hold elections at the end of the month. That's only sixteen days away."

Yahaira wasn't moved by the urgency. "You need to rest."

Kala sank back in her chair. "The tea smells good."

Yahaira poured two cups, then sat down. "I love you as if you were my daughter. The same way Jein loves you," she said. "I found you on the streets, watched you change from a frightened, confused child into a strong woman. And yet, looking at you now, I see that same fear, the same confusion. Why?"

"Molding the future isn't as easy as it sounds. Jein is depending on me. I don't want to let him down."

Yahaira laughed softly. "You could never let Jein down. You know that. I think it's something else. Something more personal."

Kala didn't want to talk about Aedon.

It was common knowledge now that they had been lovers. *Had been.* She hadn't seen him for more than a few minutes since his arrival at the palace.

Yahaira was right. She was frightened. And confused.

She had made her feelings clear to Aedon. Told him what was in her heart.

If he cared in return, he would have insisted on seeing her. Summoned her to his side. He hadn't.

He was walking now. Awkwardly, because his leg was still healing. But he could walk.

Why hadn't he found his way to her? The distance between the guest wing and her office wasn't enough to tax his strength.

And yet, he hadn't come.

He met with Jein, and Ginomi, and Terk almost daily. They spent hours discussing the tactics of forming a new police force, of what provinces would need the most men, of securing the docking station, of regenerating the security net that protected the planet.

"It's the Korcian, isn't it?" Yahaira said.

"It's everything," Kala replied. "As strange as it may sound, I'm not sure who I am anymore. A few weeks ago, I knew what I wanted. Or at least, I thought I did."

"Men are strange creatures. They claim to be easier to understand than women, but they're not. Take Jein, for example. He hid from me all those years. Why? Because he couldn't offer me sexual satisfaction. It wasn't because he didn't love me. He did. He still does."

"There was a bounty on his head," Kala said. "He wanted to protect you."

"Just as your Korcian did his best to protect you."

"He isn't *my* Korcian."

The older woman's hazel eyes literally sparkled. "My dear, sweet, Kala. Believe me when I say that I know men. And that man is yours in every way that counts."

Twilight was bathing the city in gentle light when Kala stopped outside Aedon's suite. She announced herself, then stepped inside, unsure what would take place between them, but determined to have it happen.

Brooding was a waste of time.

So was worrying.

If Aedon wanted to leave Hachyn, he would leave. It was as simple as that.

The suite was as ornately decorated as the rest of the palace. Aedon was sitting behind a large desk, a holomap of the northern provinces floating above the receptor.

He turned off the console and stood up.

An awkward silence followed.

"You look well," Kala finally said. "I can see that Yahaira has been taking good care of you."

"Dr. Cayman gave me the last rejuvenation injection this morning."

"That's good."

A dark brow rose skeptically. "Did you come here for a medical report?"

"No." Kala hesitated, afraid to show her vulnerability. "I wanted to ask your opinion on something."

"What?"

She walked around the room for a moment, looking at the furnishings but not really seeing them.

"It's what I am. What I'll always be."

The words had haunted her for weeks. How could she change what couldn't be changed? She had fallen in love with a warrior, knowing full well that her time with him could easily be measured in hours and days.

Fighting for breath, Kala forced herself to think of a future without Aedon by her side. It was too painful to envision. So why didn't she simply ask him to stay on Hachyn? The answer was simple. If he didn't trust her enough to tell her the *whole* truth about himself, how could she entrust the rest of her life to him?

He certainly knew everything about her. And, unless he was deaf, dumb, and blind, he knew that she loved him.

No. She'd said enough. Done enough.

The next move had to be his.

Meeting his gaze, Kala realized he was waiting for her to explain why she'd come to his room. "What do you think Terk and the others will say if I recommend that Jein pardon Sy and allow her to leave with the next group of exiles? Her father is dead. According to the prison records, he died three years ago. Esarell tricked her, used her. It doesn't seem right to label her a traitor. She was forced to choose between her father and the resistance. I know I should be angry, and I am, but—"

"Your conscience won't let you see her condemned and put in prison like her parents," Aedon said.

"Yes. What purpose would it serve? She knows now that it was all for nothing. The lies. The deceit. Can you imagine carrying that weight for the rest of your life?"

Aedon walked to where she was standing.

Chills rippled through Kala's body in sensual recognition of his presence. She had thought about this moment for weeks. Dreaded it. Dreamed of it. And now, she was looking into those incredible eyes again.

Deep blue eyes. Silver eyes. Dark and brooding. Clear and strong. Always changing. Always surprising her with their clarity, their intensity, their power.

They were a dark silver now. The color of a thunderstorm flecked with black. Was he angry that she wanted to free a traitor? Or was he thinking of other things—the last time they had kissed. The last time they'd made love. It seemed a century ago, and yet it was only a few weeks. She could remember every moment of their lovemaking.

Did Aedon?

She met his gaze. Held it. "I'm sorry I haven't visited you before now. It was rude of me."

"Yes, it was." The words didn't sting because he was smiling. "As much as it bruises my Korcian pride, I know you had more important things to do."

He was getting closer.

His eyes were getting lighter. Softer. Taking on the silver-blue sheen Kala had come to recognize. They always looked that way just before he kissed her.

"Kala?"

Her name wasn't coming from Aedon, it was being spoken over the comm panel by Terk

Aedon stepped back.

"Yes," she answered, hoping whatever Terk had to say could be said through a closed door. "What is it?"

"I'm not sure," he replied. "If I hadn't heard it with my own ears, I'm not sure I would believe it myself."

Aedon opened the door. "What are you talking about?" It was apparent he didn't appreciate the interruption.

Terk looked at Kala, who was watching him with dark eyes that gave away nothing. He smiled. "We, meaning the Republic of Hachyn, just received a subspace message. The captain of a *Korcian* starcruiser is requesting permission to enter Hachynite space."

"What?"

Terk practically danced into the room. "It's true. A Korcian starcruiser, escorted by no less than eighteen Korcian starjets, and a dozen transport freighters. The captain said he has a *League* ambassador on board."

"A League ambassador on a Korcian starcruiser. Are you certain?" Kala asked. She looked at Aedon. "Does any of this surprise you?"

Aedon leaned down to give her a quick kiss. "My life has been nothing but surprises lately."

"So do I give them permission to assume orbit, or don't I?" Terk asked.

"What did Jein say?"

Terk grinned. "He said intergalactic politics was your department."

Kala did her best to look calm, as if she greeted ambassadors every day of her life. When the main door of the palace began to open, she sucked in a deep breath, let it out slowly, and prayed that she didn't embarrass herself or the newborn Republic of Hachyn.

Then, after getting a good look at the dignitaries walking toward her, all she could do was stare. The woman, wearing the white and blue ambassador robes of the League of Planets, was strikingly beautiful. Tall, slender, dark-haired and dark-eyed, she was a perfect counterpart to the tall, fierce-looking, blond-haired Korcian officer walking by her side. As he got closer, Kala watched his eyes change from golden-brown to a vivid emerald green.

"Prime Minister Char'ari," the woman said in a soft, firm voice. "It's a pleasure. My name is Danna MacFadyen, Ambassador to Korcia from the League of Planets. My escort is Colonel Gavriel. We bring good wishes to you and your people."

"Thank you," Kala replied. She looked up at the tall, imposing colonel at Ambassador MacFadyen's side. He was dressed as Aedon often was, black on black. Looking past him, at the Korcian guards who had escorted them to the surface, she saw more black uniforms.

She suddenly wished there was one more Korcian in the room, but Aedon had declined her invitation.

"*Diplomacy has rules,*" he'd insisted. "*I'm not a Hachynite citizen, or a member of the provisional government. And I'm not a Korcian officer. You don't want to insult them before you've had a chance to say hello.*"

So Kala was standing in the entry hall of the palace with Terk on her right side, and Ginomi on her left. Jein was waiting in the grand salon.

"Your arrival is a surprise," Kala said, accepting the ambassador's hand. "Totally unexpected, and thoroughly appreciated. Welcome to Hachyn."

It was after midnight before Aedon joined Cullon in his suite. Danna was with him, looking very pleased with herself.

The League of Planets had authorized her to extend whatever help was needed in reclaiming Hachyn for its true citizens.

"I see my message was well received," Aedon said. He bowed over Danna's hand, "As always, a pleasure, Madame Ambassador."

"Prime Minister Char'ari told us that you'd been injured," Danna said, looking Aedon over from head to toe. "It doesn't show."

"If you had arrived last week, you would have found me limping miserably about the palace."

Cullon offered him a drink of aged Korcian whiskey. "My personal stock," he said. "If I had a medal, I'd pin it on your chest. What you accomplished is far more than we expected."

"Only eighteen starjets, Colonel Gavriel? Surely the Empire could have spared more."

Cullon laughed. "I didn't want to frighten the new prime minister with a full battle squadron."

"Frightened Kala Char'ari? Impossible. She should have been a Korcian. She fights like one."

"An extraordinary woman," Danna said. "She was very appreciative when I told her the League authorized me to negotiate trading rights. Although I must admit some surprise at finding her appointed the provisional prime minister. One would assume that Eiven Jein—"

"It was Jein's idea. He insisted upon it." Aedon sank into one of the suite's plush chairs. "I'm glad the League is willing to finance trading routes. Rendhal stripped the treasury clean."

"Do you have any idea where he might have gone?" Cullon asked.

"I don't think it makes any difference. The Conglomerate is very good at exacting revenge. I'll wager that the Board has already sent out a team of assassins."

"And the starjets?"

Aedon made an odd sound. "It's impossible to say. Jein thinks a base on one of the Trinity Planets. I'll go to Myamar first."

Cullon shook his head. "I'm afraid not, old friend. One agent. One mission. It's something Danna and I agreed on at the start. The Directorate thanks you, the League thanks you, and the Empire thanks you. But your work here is done. Come home with us to Korcia. You can have your squadron back with a promotion to full colonel or retire a wealthy man. The choice is yours."

Aedon shook his head. "We've got unfinished business with the Conglomerate."

"It's finished as far as you're concerned," Cullon said. His tone was absolute. A superior officer giving a subordinate officer a direct order.

Aedon wasn't prepared to hear what he was hearing. It showed.

"I'll leave you two alone," Danna said. She kissed Aedon on the cheek. "Sweet dreams, Aedon Rawn. You've certainly earned them."

Aedon stared straight ahead, his thoughts inward, until he saw Danna kissing Cullon good night. It wasn't a casual kiss.

"Too bad our suites aren't adjoining," Cullon said after Danna had left for her own set of rooms. "Being on a star cruiser is almost as frustrating as diplomatic visits. Officers and crew everywhere. It's been a long three weeks."

"You and Ambassador MacFadyen."

Cullon simply smiled.

Aedon wished he could.

He had mentally prepared himself to leave Hachyn, to pursue the missing Conglomerate starjets to the ends of the galaxy if necessary. Now he was being told it was over.

"You're looking perplexed," Cullon said. "It's not a look I like to associate with a Fleet Squadron leader."

"An ex-squadron leader," Aedon corrected him. "That was my old life."

"And your new one?"

Aedon finished his whiskey. "I don't know. There's so much to be done here."

"Then do it," Cullon said. "You've had your revenge. Put it behind you. Find a woman, if you haven't already, and make a new life together. Second chances are rare."

Aedon wondered if it could be that easy.

He'd dreamed, but those dreams had been forced to take second place, behind his duty to the Directorate and the Empire. He hadn't thought himself free to promise more than the moment.

Now that he could, he wasn't sure if there would be

room in Kala's life for a husband and family. He loved her, but so did the people of Hachyn.

"What if I told you that the woman I want is very likely to be the first freely elected Prime Minister of Hachyn?" Aedon said.

"It's a dilemma I'm familiar with. If the Directorate hadn't been formed, I would have been forced to kidnap Danna to keep her on Korcia."

"Kala isn't going anywhere," Aedon said. "She fought too hard to keep this world to ever leave it."

Cullon offered Aedon a sympathetic smile and a fresh glass of whiskey.

Kala was having breakfast when Colonel Gavriel asked to meet with her privately. Dawn was only a few minutes old when he joined her on the balcony.

"I didn't mean to interrupt your meal," he said.

"You're not interrupting. Please, sit down."

He looked at her through eyes that changed to match the increasing light, growing more golden as the sun inched its way higher into the sky.

"Please express my heartfelt thanks to the High Council, Colonel Gavriel. Not only for escorting Ambassador MacFadyen to Hachyn, but for their generous aid. The freighters will be unloaded today."

"The Empire is offering more than supplies, Madame Prime Minister. I have eighteen starjets at my command. They will be left here to provide protection until Hachyn can establish its own fleet. You must realize what a corporate colony turned free republic represents to the Conglomerate."

"A threat."

"Not militarily, at least not now, but financially. And philosophically. Yes."

"I respect your candor, Colonel Gavriel, and the Empire's assistance. How long do you think it will take before our defenses are strong enough to either discourage or repel an attack?"

"Several years," Gavriel told her. "It takes more than starjets and pilots to make a good defense system. You need officers who understand the complexities of launching a planetary attack. If they can launch one, they can defend *against* one. You need a trained, disciplined military."

"Spoken like a true Korcian," Kala said. "I was a freedom fighter for most of my life, Colonel. I understand war, but I don't understand the kind of warfare you're talking about. I'm not sure any of my people do. We've been like trees, rooted to this world."

"Don't misunderstand, Madame Prime Minister. I have nothing but respect for you and your people. But when it comes to fighting, no one does it better than a Korcian."

Kala was startled by his tone. It had gone from serious to what she could only describe as amused. "I'm not sure I understand. Is the Empire offering to provide the Hachynite Republic a military consultant?"

"You already have one," Gavriel said. "If I were you, I'd convince Aedon Rawn to be my Defense Minister."

The palace sauna had become Aedon's private refuge. It was steamy and silent, like the jungles he'd played in as a child. He leaned back in the sunken marble tub and looked up through a glass dome at the stars.

His second home.

He stretched his injured leg, then relaxed it. The muscles responded without pain. The scar was already fading. Becoming a thing of the past.

"Mind if I join you?"

He turned his head to find Kala standing in a mist of

sauna steam and midnight shadows. "I thought you were in Lejan."

"Only for the day," she said. She started to undress. "The water looks relaxing."

"It is," Aedon said, watching as more and more of her slender body came into view. Water seethed gently around him as she entered the pool.

His body tightened to full arousal as she glided through the water toward him. She stopped just beyond his reach.

"Colonel Gavriel came to see me this morning," she told him. "We had a very interesting conversation."

"About what?"

She came teasingly closer. But not close enough.

"We talked about starjets and the men who fly them."

Aedon made a neutral sound. He knew Cullon would never reveal the fact that he'd once been a Squadron Commander. So what was Kala talking about? She was looking at him as if he should know. He didn't.

She swirled her hands lazily through the water. When she touched his naked leg, she trailed her hands upward, from his calf to his scarred thigh. "You told me once that you'd always be a warrior."

"I will."

"So will I," she said, smiling. "I've missed you, Aedon Rawn."

Her smile was all the temptation Aedon could take. He lunged up out of the water, grabbed her, and sank back down. Water splashed out of the sunken tub and onto gold inlaid tile.

Neither of them noticed.

They were too busy getting reacquainted.

When he'd kissed her until she was clinging to his shoulders, and touched her until she was as wet and steamy as the sauna, it was his turn to smile. "I've missed you, Kala Char'ari."

A rush of heat ran through Aedon's body as her hands found him under the water. She stroked him slowly, measuring a desire he couldn't hide. "Gavriel said I should convince you to be Jein's Minister of Defense."

She stroked him again, savoring his naked strength. "Am I convincing you?"

Aedon fitted his mouth to hers in a kiss that didn't end until she was sitting on his lap with her legs around his hips and he was buried inside her.

It was a long time before they got around to finishing the conversation.

"I won't be Jein's Minister of Defense," he said as he dried her off with a thick towel. They had been in the water for nearly an hour. The steam was soothing, but it didn't soften marble. Aedon planned on spending the rest of the night in a soft, comfortable bed—with Kala in his arms.

She went still under his touch.

Aedon watched as she drew in a deep breath and let it out slowly. He knew what she was doing. It was the way she forced herself to relax. He's seen her do it that first night in the square and a dozen times since then.

"Why not?" she asked. "Jein needs you."

Aedon looked at her and saw all the reasons why he'd never be able to leave Hachyn.

He had deceived her from the start, would continue to deceive her when it came to the Directorate and the role he had played for the sake of the Empire. But he'd be deceiving himself if he thought he could live without her.

He cupped her chin in his hand and kissed her. "You're the prime minister. Not Jein."

"Only until the provisional government is replaced by an elected one. Jein insisted or I wouldn't have done it."

He gathered her close and kissed her again. "Jein insisted because he knows that you're the best person for the job. Everyone knows it. The people love you. They look at you and see the future."

Another deep breath let out slowly. Eyes wide and questioning. Searching. Hoping. "What about your future? Am I in it?" she asked hesitantly.

"Aedon's eyes went bright as he smiled down at her. "I love you, Kala Char'ari. I can't imagine my life without you."

PRAISE FOR
EARTH FORCE RISING

"A richly detailed, highly imaginative world and a cast of clever, creative kids. Readers will be eager to bound into the next book."—Shannon Messenger, author of the Keeper of the Lost Cities series

"A joyful space adventure full of humor, friendships, and action . . . This is a great sci-fi adventure for boys and girls alike. I had so much fun reading it!" —S. J. Kincaid, author of the Insignia series and *The Diabolic*

"Fans of *Ender's Game* will feel right at home in this fast-paced debut. . . . I read it in a day, unable to put it down, and look forward to more from this promising new author!"—Wesley King, author of *The Incredible Space Raiders from Space!* and *OCDaniel*

Also by Monica Tesler

BOUNDERS
BOOK 4

HEROES THE
RETURN

MONICA TESLER

ALADDIN
New York   London   Toronto   Sydney   New Delhi

ALADDIN

An imprint of Simon & Schuster Children's Publishing Division
1230 Avenue of the Americas, New York, New York 10020
First Aladdin paperback edition December 2019
Text copyright © 2018 by Monica Tesler
Cover illustration copyright © 2018 by Owen Richardson
Also available in an Aladdin hardcover edition.
All rights reserved, including the right of reproduction in whole or in part in any form.
ALADDIN and related logo are registered trademarks of Simon & Schuster, Inc.
— For information about special discounts for bulk purchases, please contact
Simon & Schuster Special Sales at 1-866-506-1949 or business@simonandschuster.com.
The Simon & Schuster Speakers Bureau can bring authors to your live event.
For more information or to book an event, contact the Simon & Schuster Speakers Bureau
at 1-866-248-3049 or visit our website at www.simonspeakers.com.
Cover designed by Karin Paprocki
Interior designed by Mike Rosamilia
The text of this book was set in Adobe Garamond Pro.
Manufactured in the United States of America 1119 OFF
2 4 6 8 10 9 7 5 3 1
The Library of Congress has cataloged the hardcover edition as follows:
Names: Tesler, Monica, author.
Title: The heroes return / by Monica Tesler.
Description: First Aladdin hardcover edition. | New York : Aladdin, 2018. |
Series: Bounders ; book 4 | Summary: "Jasper and Mira must escape the rift and deliver a message
from the Youli to Earth Force before the war destroys their planet"— Provided by publisher.
Identifiers: LCCN 2018024629 (print) | LCCN 2018031491 (eBook) |
ISBN 9781534402492 (eBook) | ISBN 9781534402478 (hardcover)
Subjects: | CYAC: Adventure and adventurers—Fiction. | Human-alien encounters—Fiction. |
Ambassadors—Fiction. | Virtual reality—Fiction. | Science fiction. |
BISAC: JUVENILE FICTION / Action & Adventure / General. |
JUVENILE FICTION / Science & Technology. | JUVENILE FICTION / Science Fiction.
Classification: LCC PZ7.1.T447 (eBook) | LCC PZ7.1.T447 Her 2018 (print) | DDC [Fic]—dc23
LC record available at https://lccn.loc.gov/2018024629
ISBN 9781534402485 (paperback)

For Mom & Dad

WHAT ARE THE ODDS? I'VE SPENT MY whole life hearing about the Incident at Bounding Base 51 and the famous aeronauts who were lost that day. Now here I am standing right next to them.

In the rift.

Even though Gedney theorized there may be a place in the galaxy where time moved differently—almost like a rip in space itself—no one knew for sure. I guess the lost aeronauts, Mira, and I are living proof of his hypothesis.

We're living for now, at least. The longer we stay here, the more time we lose back on Earth. The aeronauts say they've been stuck in the rift for two days, but more than fourteen years have passed. Mira and I were here for at least an hour before we even found the lost aeronauts. That's got to be a couple of months back on Earth.

It's not like we can just wave our gloves and go back. For starters, my gloves were lost on Alkalinia. I managed to bring the shield down, giving Earth Force at least a fighting chance against the Alks and Youli, but then Mira bounded us out of the action. I can't believe I abandoned my friends—I abandoned my sister, Addy—on that sinister snake world, not that I would have been much help trapped at the bottom of the toxic sea. The only reason I was trapped at all was that my gloves were stuck. When we bounded, my gloves got left behind.

I doubt my gloves would make much difference here in the rift, though. Mira's gloves don't seem to work. In other words, it's not so easy to get out of here. Proof: the human bones we found a few minutes ago.

The aeronauts won't stop running their mouths. "There's no way we've been here for that long!" "Where are we any-way?" "Why on earth did the Force send *you* to rescue us?"

Even though the glum grayness of the rift swallows their voices into near nothingness, their chatter is still loud enough to obliterate any chance of me thinking things through. I get that this is a stressful situation, but competitive talking won't get us out of here.

Mira squeezes my hand. *Ignore them.*

I wish it were that easy.

"Shut up!" I finally shout.

Everyone stops talking at the same time. Their words fall slowly in the thick air, like feathers on a breeze, until they're absorbed into the spongy ground beneath our feet.

"Seriously," I continue, "if we're going to figure out how to get out of here, you need to stop freaking out! Be quiet and let me think!"

"Listen, hotshot," starts the tall aeronaut with short dark hair. I know from watching web specials that it's Bai Liu. "I don't know who you are or how you got here, but I'm not about to let a kid tell me what to do, especially one who wears the Earth Force insignia. I outrank you. Stand and salute."

"Take it down a notch, Bai," the aeronaut next to her says. "The kid's got a point. If we're all talking at once, we'll never come up with a plan." He steps in front of her and crosses his arms.

Despite how strange and unexpected all this is, I recognized Captain Denver Reddy the second I saw him. He's one of those icons who everyone knows. Tall, brown skin, lots of swagger. Mom says she and her friends used to swoon over Denver.

Bai throws up her hands but doesn't talk back. She was Denver's co-captain on the failed bound and is almost as famous as he is, but it's clear who's in charge.

If I'm being honest, I'm kind of starstruck. It's not every day that you run into the famous lost aeronauts from the Incident at Bounding Base 51.

I shake my head to clear my thoughts and take a deep breath of the stagnant, musty air. "Give me some time to think."

Time we don't have. If they've been here for fourteen years, and it only feels like two days to them, that means we're losing time at the rate of almost two days per minute. A shudder rips through me. Losing more time? It's like a sick joke after being trapped on Alkalinia. The Alks drugged us by loading us up with delicious fake food. Then they poked and prodded us with needles while we slept for days. I can't believe we managed to bound away only to get stuck here, where we're losing more time. A *lot* more time.

We go round and round with ideas but get nowhere. Meanwhile, the clock keeps ticking. Just like that, another hour slips by.

There's got to be something we can do. "Mira, can you bound? Or are you still blocked?"

"Bound?" the older aeronaut who first found us asks. "Do you see a ship around here?"

"We don't need—" I start.

Mira kicks my foot. *Quiet!* She takes my hand and pulls me from the group. The aeronauts start to fade as we retreat into the fog.

"Wait!" one of the aeronaut calls as we disappear into the gloom. "Where did you go? Don't leave us! We need—"

Let's go! Mira's fingers curl tight against the back of my hand. *We need space to think.* We walk farther from the group, our feet sinking, the aeronauts' voices fading, with each step.

The darkness swallows us up, so there's no trace of the lost aeronauts, even though they can't be more than a dozen meters away.

My mind races. How long have we been here already? How long have we been gone? I wish the answers to those questions were the same, but I know they're not. As every minute ticks by in the rift, more days pass on Earth. We've got to get out of here!

The battle on Alkalinia is long over by now. Sure, I got the shield down, but was it enough? Were the Earth Force troops able to thwart the plans of the Youli and Alkalinians? What happened to my other pod mates?

Did Addy survive?

I sink my knees to the ground. "What are we going to do?"

Mira kneels beside me. *Brain-talk.*

She's right. We don't need the lost aeronauts hearing anything that would require us to waste time educating them about stolen alien biotechnology.

I bow my head to my knees and try to clear my mind. For a second, I'm grateful for the utter desolation of this place. It swallows up sound and color and movement so completely that it feels like quicksand for the senses. I can easily forget that a crowd of lost aeronauts stands only meters away, and they're all probably expecting me to come back with an answer for how to get out of this mess, an answer that is not coming.

It's no use, I say to Mira. *We're trapped.*

She presses her palm to the back of my neck, where my Youli brain patch is implanted. A wave of feeling washes over me. Optimism. I know it's Mira's way of telling me that not all is lost.

She's obviously delusional. I close my eyes and try to push back the growing wave of panic.

A bright light shines behind my eyelids.

I bolt upright. All I can see is the brilliant glow. I jump to my feet and spin around. There's nothing but the brilliance and the sucking gray of the rift. Mira is gone.

"Mira! Where are you? Mira!"

The light shifts and solidifies. The ground shakes beside me, like something was dropped from the sky.

I turn. Mira is on her hands and knees. She tries to lift her head. Her arms collapse beneath her.

"What's wrong, Mira? What happened?" I know she wasn't here a second ago. There's no way I would have missed her.

Mira's brain alights with electricity. Something about it is different, more textured, more complex.

"Mira, are you okay? Did you bound?"

She presses her palms against the gray, squishy ground and slowly pushes herself up. I repeat my questions brain to brain, but all I sense from her is static.

The light before us fades, and I realize we're not alone. Three Youli stand directly in front of us.

My senses slam into focus, and I reach for my missing gloves. Then I jump in front of Mira to shield her from the Youli. She's still trying to stand. Her mind is sparking, but it's like she's not fully conscious.

Whatever happened to Mira must have something to do with the Youli. "Stay away from her!"

The Youli don't respond. They tip their huge heads to the side and stare at me with their bottomless black eyes, like they're carefully considering what I said. Their skin is the color of smashed peas. Their bodies pulse with the glowing beat of their alien hearts.

A razor-sharp pain drills at my temples. The loudest, shrillest noise sounds in my brain. I collapse to my knees and press my hands against my skull. How can I protect Mira when my head's about to explode? When I fear I'll lose consciousness, the pain starts to subside and a word rings in my mind, in my body, in the air. Everywhere.

Peace.

I force my gaze to the Youli standing before us. It's clear the word *peace* is coming from them. The same word they uttered on the Paleo Planet, the same word I heard on the Youli ship.

Pushing aside the last of the pain, I keep my voice low and level. "What did you do to Mira?"

Peace.

I surge to my feet and burst forward. Right into a solid wall of nothingness. I bounce backward and land on my butt. The Youli's powers obviously work here in the rift.

Next to me, Mira still struggles to stand. When she finally makes it to her feet, she braces herself against the Youli's invisible wall.

Mira! Get back!

Her brown eyes find mine and I'm flooded with emotion. I can't decipher what any of it means, but my throat turns thick. Mira's eyes fill with tears. She holds my stare, gazing at me like we've been apart for a long time.

What's wrong, Mira? What's happening?

Mira closes her eyes. She reins back her despair and shuts it inside a closed door in her mind. When she looks at me again, her mind is empty, but only for a moment. Her brain touches mine and opens wide. I hear voices, and they're not just Mira's.

Thoughts race around my head, too many thoughts to concentrate. What is going on? Why are the Youli here? What happened to Mira? Did the Youli take her? Were those Youli voices in her brain?

Even as my panic rises, waves of calm begin to swish in my skull. They must be coming from the Youli—or maybe even Mira—because there's nothing about me that feels calm. Although now . . . I'm kind of . . . maybe . . . relaxing? It's like I've just sat through an hour of Mom's meditation music, but here the effect is instantaneous.

Which means it's not real. If my time on Alkalinia taught me anything, it's that there are lots of things that aren't real.

Mira's hand is pressed against the invisible wall. Her face has that radiant, open quality I remember from way back in the cell block at the space station. As I stare at her face, searching for answers, her hand drops, and she stumbles.

The wall must be gone. I surge forward. This time, there's no wall, but one of the Youli lifts his palm and grabs my atoms, freezing me in place.

"Let go of me!" At least my mouth and vocal cords aren't frozen. One of the Youli approaches Mira, stepping right through the space in the rift that used to hold the invisible wall.

"Don't take one step closer to her!"

Brain-talk. I hear in my mind from a voice that's unmistakably Mira's. *They'll understand.*

If that's how it is, fine. I focus all my mental energy at the Youli. *Get away from her!*

They turn their large green heads toward me and gaze

upon me with their deep black eyes. Again, one word radiates from them: *Peace.*

Do they think I'm a fool? The Youli on Alkalinia weren't looking for peace. They planned to kidnap me and Mira and kill the other Bounders—they were going to murder *Addy.* I saw them shooting at Earth Force across the Alkalinian sea. I was nearly caught in the cross fire!

"Peace? You weren't saying *peace* back on Alkalinia!" I shout before remembering what Mira said about brain-talk.

I try to clear a space in my mind to form words, but my anger fills up my whole head.

Still that word rings all around: *Peace, peace, peace.*

I want to clench my fists. I want to punch the Youli in the face. But I'm frozen. All I can do is press my lips together and glare at the Youli. *There was no peace for my friends. Not on Gulaga. Not on Alkalinia. How can you bring us here and call it peace? We're trapped!*

Mira steps beside me and places her hand on my arm. Even though I can't move, I can feel her long, cold fingers through my Earth Force uniform.

I brought us here by mistake, she says. *The Youli can get us out.*

**"WHAT DO YOU MEAN, *THE YOULI CAN GET
us out?*"** I demand through gritted teeth.

Brain-talk, Mira reminds me.

"No! The Youli are not calling the shots here! I'll talk with
my voice if I want to. What happened to you? Did they take
you?"

Mira grabs my frozen hand. *I'm here. I've been right here
with you.*

That can't be true. I swear Mira vanished for a moment
right when the Youli arrived. When she reappeared, she was
overwhelmed with sadness and barely conscious. Now she
seems to be pro-Youli. When did that happen? Does she

completely forget what went down on Alkalinia a few hours ago (at least for us)?

"But I saw—"

Mira squeezes my palm and sends me an image of the lost aeronauts, who right this moment are probably just a few meters away, swallowed by the endless gloom of this place. *Quiet! They'll hear!*

Fine! I don't know what Denver, Bai, and the other aeronauts would make of this encounter with the Youli, but I doubt it would speed up our exit from the rift. No matter what's going on with Mira, it doesn't change the fact that we need to get out of the rift, and fast.

I force myself to look at the three green aliens standing in front of me. *What do you want with us?*

Peace.

As soon as the Youli thinks the word, the invisible tether that holds my body releases. I'm free to move. It must be the Youli's attempt to demonstrate trust.

I clench my fists, barely holding back from charging the Youli. *Peace, huh? What is it with you and that word? You obviously have no idea what it means!*

Mira squeezes my palm again. *Jasper! Listen to us! Please!*

Us? I shake my hand free. Seriously? She's taking their side? *They took you, didn't they? They're controlling you somehow.*

MONICA TESLER

She turns away as the Youli fill my mind with their message: *Peace.*

No! I silently scream. *I don't want to hear the word peace again! Not until I know what you did to Mira! And not until I have assurances that my sister is safe . . . that all the Bounders are safe!*

A wave of sadness and frustration fills my mind. Is that coming from Mira? Or the Youli? Or both?

As I try to process the feelings and unanswered questions, the Youli in the middle steps forward. Its voice is deep and spoken in such a melodic way it's almost like singing. *We do not speak in the same manner as you, Jasper Adams, but we have studied your kind, including your linguistics, and we will try. We cannot give you the assurances you seek, for we do not know your sister's fate. There were many casualties at the Battle of the Alkalinian Seat—Youli, Alk, and Earthling. The Youli acted without one mind, and the consequences were grave. Those who initiated the attack have been addressed, but division remains deep.*

What does he mean they "acted without one mind"? Are you saying not all the Youli wanted to fight?

Before sending me words, the Youli fills my mind with pictures, like Mira does sometimes. It's me and my pod mates on the Youli vessel right before the attack on the Gulagan space elevator. We're planting the degradation patch on the Youli systems. These images must be from the perspective of the Youli we tackled on the ship.

Your technological attack was devastating, the Youli says. *It threatens to undermine generations of peace and principled living among our people and the greater galaxy. Reunification is possible, but it comes at a price. People of both of our planets have perished. If events continue on their current course, we fear the galaxy may pay the ultimate price.*

Is he saying we were responsible for the Youli's attack on Alkalinia? That we provoked and disabled them with the degradation patch, and they were simply fighting back? No way.

Plus, nothing justifies the Youli's plans to exterminate the Bounders—*kids*—on Alkalinia.

As soon as those thoughts cross my mind, Mira turns to me and takes my other hand. She steps close, so our foreheads are almost touching. A door slams closed, a mental door, so that for a moment it's just Mira and me communicating. *The Youli didn't want to kill the Bounders*, she says. *That was the Alks' plan.*

What is going on? Mira is definitely hiding something from me. *How on earth would you know that?*

She squeezes my hands. *Trust me.*

I'm the furthest I've ever been from trusting Mira. I'm about to tell her that, but then she kicks open the confidential door, and the Youli are back in my brain.

The Youli on the left steps forward and speaks with a voice that sounds like wind chimes in my mind. *It is time we put our conflicts to rest and move our joint history into the next phase. We have a message for your people.*

I take a step back, away from the Youli, away from Mira. I turn my back to them and stare out at the gray nothingness. Mira said the Youli could get us out of here. Does that mean they know how to navigate the rift? They must. After all, they got here without a problem. It seems they were looking for us and knew exactly how and where *and when* to find us.

As much as I want to spend the next several hours yelling at these Youli about all the horrible things they've done to me and my friends, every second I waste is more time lost outside the rift. We need to escape. Accepting the Youli's help isn't just our best option, it's our only option.

I turn and face the wind chime Youli. *If I deliver your message, you'll get us out of here?*

Yes, Jasper Adams.

I take a deep breath. *What's the message?*

Peace.

Of course it is. I clasp my hands above my head and close my eyes. Peace? Really? They actually want to end the war?

We sincerely hope you choose to carry our message, the deep-voiced Youli says. *It is the most important thing you can do for* both of our peoples. *It is the greatest way to honor your sister and friends.*

Does that mean Addy's dead? I thought they said they didn't know. I clench my fists. *Don't bring my sister into this!*

Tell your people we wish to meet and discuss the requirements for your planet's entry into the Intragalactic Council, the Youli continues. *This is our gesture of peace.* The Youli extends his hand toward me. It's large and green and pulsing.

"He actually wants me to shake his hand?" I ask Mira.

He knows it's our custom, she tells me.

The other times I've touched a Youli have been extremely intense, like opening a floodgate of sensations. Still, I'm curious.

I grip the Youli's hand with my own. As soon as we touch, my body is overloaded with a million feelings and thoughts.

We both pull our hands free. The Youli stumbles back like he was pushed. They must not be too big on touching, or at least touching Earthlings.

So, we have a deal, I say. *What's next?*

Wait, Mira says. *The others.* She sends me an image of the lost aeronauts.

Oh, right. Them. They're probably only a few meters away, completely clueless to the fact that their mortal enemies have arrived.

The Youli will take them, too, she says.

"Hold on a minute," I say to her. "Why didn't they tell me

that themselves? What else have they said to you? Why are you keeping secrets from me? What happened to you?"

We're wasting time.

Something about Mira is all wrong, but what she's saying is right. The one thing we don't have is time to waste. Still, I have to know I'm not putting us and the lost aeronauts in jeopardy.

You disappeared, Mira. Where did you go?

She digs her shoe into the gray ground. *It was the only way.*

You need to tell me what happened. Now.

We went with them, she says, gazing off into the fog. *The Youli needed to understand us and—*

What do you mean "we"? I didn't go anywhere with the Youli.

Mira takes a deep breath. *I mean we need to go with them now. They'll take us to the Ezone.*

I drop her hands. *You told them about the Ezone? Doesn't that violate like a hundred Earth Force laws?*

I'm most sure of the coordinates. It was the easiest to relay.

I can't believe this. *You gave them the coordinates?*

Mira's mind swells with frustration. *How else do you think we'll get there? Or would you rather they bound us to their planet? Stop asking questions! We need to move!*

Mira never talks to me this way. There's definitely something she's not telling me. As soon as we get out of the rift, she'll have to explain what's really going on.

"Fine. Let's find the others." I start trekking through the

gray muck in the direction I think we came from. "Denver! Bai! Where are you guys?"

Soon someone returns my call. I head that way and practically collide with Bai.

She shoves me back. "Watch where you're going, plebe!"

"Sorry. Listen, I think we may have a way out of this place."

The aeronaut who found us falls to his knees. "Oh, thank God."

"What's the plan?" Denver asks.

"See, that's just it. . . . It's sort of unusual. . . . Umm . . ."

"Get back!" Bai says, throwing her arms to the side to protect the other aeronauts. Her eyes bug wide, like she's seen a ghost. "Can't you hear? Get behind me!"

I turn around. Mira and the Youli have cut through the gray haze. Since neither Mira nor our green rescue team can communicate with the aeronauts, I guess explanations are up to me.

"It's cool." I lift my palms to the side. "These guys are going to help us."

Denver steps next to Bai. "Get out of the way, kid. You don't know who you're dealing with. These aliens are our enemies."

"Yeah, I won't argue with you there. But the Youli are also our ticket out of here."

"Den, this is obviously a trap," Bai says. "These Youli scum are the reason we're here in the first place. Bounding Base 51 was under attack."

If there was ever any doubt about whether Earth Force covered up the existence of the Youli since before I was born, it was just erased.

"Listen up!" I say. "I'm no fan of the Youli, but we need to act now. While we're in here fighting, we're losing months of Earth time."

Bai angles away from me and speaks to her pod. "How do we know he's telling the truth? Why should we believe him that it's been all these years? Maybe we've only been here two days. They could be working with the Youli! They're strange kids, right? I mean, the girl doesn't even talk!"

That strikes a nerve. "Her name is Mira!" I shout, although the rift swallows most of the sound. "Here's the deal. The Youli don't care whether they include you in this rescue. The more we stand here arguing, the less I care. We're leaving the rift in one minute. You're either with us or not. Your choice."

The aeronauts huddle up and all talk at the same time. They're clearly divided about what to do. With every breath, I feel the moments pass back at home.

"What's it going to be?" I ask.

Denver places his hand on Bai's shoulder. "What choice do we have, Bai? We need to go with the kid."

"You mean with the Youli," she says.

"I mean with the kid. He's wearing the insignia. I trust him."

Denver Reddy scans the faces of his pod mates. One by one, they nod. He turns to face me. "We're in. What's the plan?"

Tell them we'll all join hands, Mira says. *I'll link with the Youli, and they'll bound us out.*

Once I relay the message to the aeronauts, Mira pulls me to the side. She weaves her fingers with mine, and looks up at me with her brown eyes. My mind fills with sadness, and this time I'm certain the sadness is hers.

"What is it?" I whisper.

She reaches her fingers to my face and gently cups my chin in her hand. Her eyes study mine. She's looking at me like she needs to memorize every detail of this moment.

"Mira?"

She bites her lip, and her face sets with a steely resolve.

You're the glue, Jasper. It has to be you. It's always been you.

What are you talking about?

I'm not going back, Jasper.

What do you mean?

I'm . . . Her mind shifts and sorts, like she's looking for the right words. *I'm leaving with the Youli.*

Wait . . . you're kidding, right? Why would you do that?

I have to.

My heart leaps in my chest. What is she saying? Why is she doing this? I can't let this happen. *No, Mira! You can't! That's not part of the deal!*

It's my choice.

No! They're making you do this!

I have to do this, Jasper. It's the only way.

That makes no sense! You need to come with me. We'll figure this out together.

Mira turns away. *I can't go with you.*

You can't or you won't?

She turns back to me, but she won't meet my gaze. *I don't want to.*

Her words punch me in the gut. She doesn't want to go with me? That can't be true. This is all wrong. Everything's happening too fast.

A hand clamps my shoulder. "Come on, kid," Denver says. "Time's a-tickin'." He breaks apart my left hand's grasp on Mira's right. Bai swoops in and clasps Mira's free palm.

Mira, no! Please!

Mira's eyes lift and linger on me for a moment. Then she turns her gaze to the center of the circle. A mental door slams closed between us. She's shut me out.

A strange sensation seizes my body, like I'm a marionette and someone is pulling the strings. Then the strangeness is replaced by the familiar discomfort of a bound.

Bam!

Slam!

My butt hits the ground. Denver still has my hand in his, but where Mira's palm was moments before, my hand hangs free.

"WHERE ON EARTH ARE WE?" ONE OF THE aeronauts asks.

Denver pushes himself up. "Are we on Earth?"

"How'd we get here?" Bai asks. "It felt like we were just ripped through space."

Pretty much.

Curling my fingers against my palm, I can almost feel Mira's skin still pressed against mine. What did you do, Mira?

"Hey, kid!" Denver says. "Where's the girl? And the Youli?"

I ignore him and look around. The room we're in is dark and disorienting. A light wind stirs the hair on my arms.

Memories tug at the corners of my mind. This is where I learned to bound.

Just like Mira said, the Youli brought us to the Ezone.

A loud noise sounds in the distance. An alarm.

Denver kicks me in the shoe. "Kid! Snap out of it and tell us what's happening!"

I push myself up to standing. "We're at the space station. This is a training room. I guess we should just head to the—"

The door bursts open, letting in a radius of light along with the wail of the alarm. Six officers rush in, weapons raised.

"What the . . . ?" the one in front shouts.

"Are you . . . ?" another says, staring at Denver and his pod.

"Jasper Adams!" A familiar face topped with bright red hair catapults at me, wrapping me up in a hug.

"Hi, Ryan!" I step back into my personal space. "How's it going?"

"*How's it going?*" he parrots back. "You're supposed to be dead, and you ask *me* how's it going? How are *you?* Where have you been all this time? How did you get here?"

"Ryan, what happened on Alkalinia? Did my sister make it? How long have—"

"Attention!" Denver Reddy claps his hands. "I am Captain Denver Reddy. Salute your senior officer!"

Ryan and all the Earth Force officers who arrived with him snap to attention. Denver turns to me. "That means you, too, kid. We're not in . . . whatever that awful place was . . . anymore."

Welcome back to Earth Force, I suppose. I resist the urge to glare at Denver and slowly lift my hand to my forehead.

Once everyone in the room other than Denver's pod is silent and standing rod straight, Denver crosses his arms against his chest. "Good. Now, no more questions. Take us to see whoever's in charge. Immediately."

The next few minutes are a total blur. The officers rush me and the lost aeronauts out of the Ezone and through the halls of the space station. As we walk, one of the officers speaks quietly into her com link. When we arrive at the chute, a dozen officers are there to greet us with starstruck looks on their faces. They salute the lost aeronauts. Some of them even bow to Denver.

Geez. The guy's not *that* awesome.

I get that it's a pretty big deal. Most of the officers at the space station were around my age when Denver and his pod disappeared. They probably watched the Incident live on the webs. Seeing Denver Reddy is like seeing someone return from the dead.

"Still using the chutes, eh?" Denver asks the young officer holding open the door to the cube.

The officer opens his mouth, but no words come out. As red rises to his cheeks, he manages to cough out, "Yes, sir, Captain Reddy, sir."

Another officer gestures for the lost aeronauts to enter the cube. She follows them in and activates the system. Denver steps up to the grate and gets sucked in. The other aeronauts follow, then the rest of the officers, until just Ryan and I are left. Now I'll finally get some answers.

"They should have let you go in the front," Ryan says. "You've been missing, too, after all." Ryan is taller, and he's not as round in the middle as he used to be. It's like someone hung him up and let gravity stretch him.

"That's okay," I say. "Ryan, how long have I been gone?"

"You don't know?" When I shake my head, Ryan's eyes go wide. "What happened?"

"Just . . . how long, Ryan?"

He scrunches up his face in thought. "The Battle of the Alkalinian Seat was close to a year ago."

A year? I suck in a breath. No wonder Ryan looks different. How much happened while I was away?

I grab Ryan's forearm. "My sister, is she okay?"

A strange look passes across his face and he flicks his eyes to the floor.

Oh God. She didn't make it. Pain pierces my chest like a twisting knife. How could I let that happen? I couldn't even protect my own sister!

"She was killed in the battle? Was it when the venom tube broke apart?"

"Oh . . . No!" Ryan shakes his head. "She survived the battle!"

Thank goodness. It feels like every muscle in my body exhales.

"It's just . . . ," Ryan continues.

Tensing up again, I tighten my grip on Ryan's arm. "Just what? Is she okay or not, Ryan?"

"She's okay—at least, I think so. The thing is, she's not here. In fact, I'm not sure where she is, although I bet she's with your pod mate Marco Romero."

Huh? What's he not telling me about Addy and Marco? And what else happened while I was away? I can't believe I was gone a whole year!

Ryan's com link buzzes, and we both jump. "Officer Walsh, please escort Officer Adams to the admiral's briefing room immediately."

He rolls his eyes and nods at the chute cube. "We've got to go. You remember how to work this thing?"

"Wait, Ryan, I don't understand. Where's my sister?"

Ryan looks both ways down the hall. "I probably shouldn't have said anything. Most of what I know is rumors. Ask the admiral. Or your buddy Cole. He has top-level clearance now. We really need to go."

As I stand on the crate waiting to be sucked into the chute, my mind spins. Mira left with the Youli, and I don't know why. Addy is gone, and I don't know where. I lost a year of my life in that horrible rift, and now it seems I may have lost even more.

Ryan stands aside to let me enter the briefing room. My heart pounds so hard, I can hardly catch my breath. And I'm exhausted. Even though adrenaline is still coursing through every centimeter of my body, I feel like I can barely stand. I was up all night, first deactivating the shield in Alkalinia, and then trying to find our way out of the rift. Now I'm back and having to wrap my head around all the time I've lost and how much has changed.

At least this room is familiar. It's the same briefing room where Admiral Eames told us that our pod would be the advance team to Alkalinia. For me, that was only a few weeks ago. For everyone else in this room, other than the lost aeronauts, a year has passed since that meeting. My mind spins. How much have I missed?

Trying to focus on one thing is a lost cause. Is Addy okay? Where is she? Why is she with Marco? Cole has top-level clearance? How did that happen? How's Lucy? What about everyone else? Did they survive the Battle of the Alkalinian Seat?

Where is Mira? Is she safe? Why did she leave with the Youli? Why did she leave *me*?

The room is almost full, and no one seemed to notice when I walked in and stood in the corner. Everyone is focused on the lost aeronauts who are in various stages of freaking out. It must be starting to set in that they've been gone for more than fourteen years—make that *fifteen* years now. A year seems like an eternity for me; I can't even imagine how they must feel. A huge chunk of life has passed them by.

Bai paces the length of the room, brushing off anyone who tries to engage her. One of the younger aeronauts begs the officers to let her contact Earth. Of course, that's not happening. Earth Force would never let this media gem get out without proper spin.

Denver is the only one who appears relatively calm. He shakes everyone's hands and smiles in a way that reminds me of Maximilian Sheek but without that weird tipped chin. After all, Denver was the face of Earth Force while Sheek was still in grade school.

"Hey, Jasper," a voice near me says. "That's your name, right?"

It's the aeronaut who first spotted us in the rift. He's leaning against the wall next to me.

I nod.

"What's happening? What are we waiting for?"

I have no idea why he's asking me when there are over a dozen high-level officers in the room. Maybe it's because

I'm the only person he knows other than his pod mates. The other officers in the room were kids when he disappeared.

I shrug. "I'm guessing the admiral is on her way. We'll know more then."

He shakes his head. "We've really been gone fifteen years, huh? This is going to be a very different homecoming than what I envisioned."

I'm not exactly sure what to say. "At least it's a homecoming, right? Everyone thought you were dead. I guess they thought I was dead, too."

"Is that why they're looking at us like we're ghosts?"

The door swings open and in walks Captain James Ridders and Cole. Everyone snaps to attention.

Cole surveys the room. His gaze passes over the lost aeronauts but doesn't stop until he spots me. When he does, his whole body seems to exhale. He dips his chin in a tiny nod.

Thank goodness! I'm finally going to get some answers. I head over to greet my friend but stop when the door opens again. Admiral Eames enters.

"What a momentous day!" she declares as she walks to the head of the table. "Welcome back!" Her voice sounds high and shaky.

Just like Cole, the admiral searches the room with her eyes, but before she finds who she's looking for, Denver Reddy plows through the crowd to reach her. "Cora!"

MONICA TESLER

He swoops her up in his arms. Her feet dangle half a meter above the floor.

For a moment—so quick I'm not even sure it happened— the admiral melts into Denver's embrace. Then she stiffens and whispers something in Denver's ear. He sets her down.

"You'll address me as *Admiral*," she says, straightening her uniform. Her cheeks are pink as she takes her seat. "At ease." She instructs her ranking officers to give up their seats for the lost aeronauts and—somewhat shockingly—me. As soon as we're seated she turns to Denver. "Captain Reddy, please tell us what happened."

"Excuse me, Admiral," Cole interjects, "but I must insist that everyone without a Code One security clearance exit the room, excluding the returning aeronauts and Officer Adams, of course."

The admiral nods.

Half a dozen officers reluctantly leave. Without them, the room is a lot less crowded. I tap my feet under the table. Let's get this started. I have a million questions that I can't wait to ask as soon as someone tells me what happened to my sister.

Denver leans forward and folds his arms on the table. He waits until the door closes and everyone still in the room is paying full attention. It's clear this guy knows how to engage a crowd.

"I'm sure you know the basics," he says. "What started out as a normal bound with live web coverage quickly went south.

As we performed the routine systems check, word came over my headset that incoming enemy was spotted within range. My first thought was to abort, but knowing that the bound was live, with cameras inside the cockpit, I continued as planned, waiting for an abort order to come from up the chain of command. Then the auto countdown initiated."

"Go on," Captain Ridders says. He stands at the admiral's side with his arms crossed.

Denver leans back. "Just before the bound, my systems went down and the cockpit was swallowed in darkness. I assumed it was engineering manually overriding and aborting the bound. Now, my best guess is our signals were scrambled by the alien vessel. The bound proceeded."

So that's the real story of the Incident at Bounding Base 51. The words that just came out of Denver Reddy's mouth explain the greatest tragedy and fascination in Earth's recent history.

"Things felt off from the moment the bound initiated," Denver continues, "like my body was being ripped in a million pieces. But thankfully we remained intact. I believe some or all of my crew was unconscious for a period of time. When we came to, we were . . . somewhere else."

"Where?" Ridders asks.

"I don't know."

"What do you mean, you don't know?" the admiral asks.

"Where have you been all this time? You've been gone for the last fifteen years, Captain Reddy."

"See, that's not exactly true."

As confused looks pass across the faces in the room, Denver turns to me. "Kid, you're the one with the answers. You explain it."

Everyone looks at me, including the admiral.

I press my fingers together beneath the table and sit up straight. "We were in the rift."

Sharp intakes of breath sound around the table. For a moment, no one speaks.

"You mean . . . a rift in space as Gedney has theorized?" Cole asks.

"Right," I say. "I mean, yes, sir." It's clear that's the correct way to address Cole in this debrief, but it feels incredibly weird to call my best friend *sir*. "And like Gedney says," I continue, "time moves differently there."

Cole, who stands on the other side of the admiral, and who doesn't react at all to my formality, braces his hands on the table and leans forward with a familiar look of curiosity. "How so?"

How do I explain? "Well, take me, for example. Ryan . . . or, umm . . . Lieutenant Walsh says I've been gone almost a year. But in my experience, I only got to the rift a few hours ago. In fact, for me, the Battle of the Alkalinian Seat was last night. I don't even know what happened. Did I get the shield down in time? Did all the Bounders survive?"

No one answers my questions, but the room erupts in chatter as everyone tries to make sense of what I said. It's hard to believe the rift exists, let alone that time moves differently there. Cole talks excitedly with Ridders. The admiral takes advantage of the distractions to lean close to Denver.

"You look so young," she says quietly. "How long were you gone?"

His face softens. "About two days."

She closes her eyes, and a pained expression paints her face. "I've aged."

He leans even closer, and I think he grabs her hand beneath the table. "You're as beautiful as ever."

She shakes her head and jerks her hands free. Placing her stacked palms on the table, she straightens in her seat. "Officer Adams, please continue," she says loudly and with enough authority to quiet the entire room. "Describe the rift, and explain how you turned up in the Ezone."

Mira . . . what on earth do I say? I can't just tell Admiral Eames that she chose to go with the Youli. I'm not even sure that's the whole truth. I'll have to be careful how I explain things.

"I'll tell you what happened," Bai interjects. "We spent two days exploring the gray no-man's-land only to have these two kids show up and—"

"*Two* kids?" Ridders interrupts.

"Yes, two, and yes, one of them is missing," she says. "In fact, I'm wondering whether the kids were in on it."

Wait, what? How could she think we were in on it?

"In on what exactly?" Admiral Eames asks.

"An enemy operation," Bai says. "Sure, we're alive and well, and that's something to celebrate, but let's not lose sight of the fact that this could be part of a massive military attack. The last time they showed up, we all know what happened."

"The last time who showed up?" Cole asks.

"The little green men!" Bai says. "Although now that I've seen them up close, they're not so little."

"Someone explain this to me," the admiral says. "Jasper, what happened?"

So much for spinning things my way. I'd better stick to the basic facts. "The only reason we're out of the rift, Admiral, is because the Youli showed up. They got us out of there."

Another round of gasps fill the room, and this time they're laced with fear.

"Sound the alarm and raise the alert level to red," the admiral says. "All weapons personnel to their posts. Scan the surrounding vectors for any sign of quantum activity."

Half of the officers in the briefing room rush out.

As Ridders and Cole drill the lost aeronauts with questions, Admiral Eames signals me. "Jasper, Officer Matheson is the only other cadet who was unaccounted for in the Battle of the Alkalinian Seat. She was with you in the rift, wasn't she?"

In the seconds that follow, I make a decision. The admiral can't know that leaving with the Youli might have been Mira's choice, not if Mira ever wants to come back.

"Yes, she was with me in the rift."

"Where is Mira now, Jasper?"

I cross my fingers beneath the table and force myself to look the admiral in the eye. "The Youli took her."

AFTER ADMIRAL EAMES QUESTIONS US
about the Youli's involvement in our rescue, she breaks up
the meeting. Apparently, it's the middle of the night at the
space station, and the admiral needs to check in with her
defensive weapons and quantum detection teams. She asks
her staff to escort the lost aeronauts to temporary quarters.
Surprisingly, she lumps me in on that request. I'd assumed
I'd be headed to the Bounder bunks, not private captain
quarters.

As her officers usher the lost aeronauts out the door, I shoot
a glance at Cole. I need to talk to him. Alone. Fortunately he
seems to understand my signal, or at least he asks the admiral

if he can walk me to my room, which means we'll have some time to talk.

Admiral Eames seems perplexed at Cole's request. Then she nods. "That's right, Captain Thompson, you were pod mates with Officer Adams during your Academy days. Of course you can escort him. Report back to me in quantum monitoring as soon as you're able."

Cole thanks the admiral and stands at my side until the room empties. When it's just the two of us, I let my shoulders slump. Finally I'm going to get some answers.

"Captain, huh?" I say, slapping Cole on the shoulder. "How did that happen?"

Cole shrugs, looking awkward for the first time since he entered the room. "I was promoted."

I laugh. "Obviously." Why am I starting to feel awkward, too? "Congratulations."

"Thanks." He stuffs his hands in his pockets. "We all thought you were dead."

Still the same Cole—he gets right to the point—although something tells me he's not exactly the same as the last time I saw him. "I'm not, but speaking of people being dead, please tell me that my sister is okay."

Cole bristles at my question. "She isn't dead, Jasper."

I exhale, relieved that Addy's alive. Still, I need details, and Cole isn't spilling. "Ryan said she's with Marco."

Cole shakes his head. "Ryan can't keep his mouth shut."

This is ridiculous. I've been gone all this time and my best friend won't even tell me what happened to my own sister. The sense of relief I had at being left with Cole is quickly evaporating. "You need to be straight with me, Cole. I have to know what's going on."

"Fine, but only because I owe you. We all owe you. If you hadn't gotten that shield down on Alkalinia, none of us would be here right now."

Only because he *owes* me? How about because he's my friend? My pod mate? "What's the situation with Addy, Cole? You need to tell me!"

He drags his foot across the floor. Is he really that uncomfortable about breaking confidentiality? She's *my* sister! Don't I have a right to know?

"She's joined the Resistance, Jasper," he finally says, "a rebel group based on Gulaga—mostly Tunnelers and disgruntled Earthlings. They're believed to be led by Jon Waters."

"Addy is with Waters?" Last time I saw her, Addy had never even met our former fearless leader. I can't believe she's with him on Gulaga. "And Marco's there, too?"

Cole glances anxiously at the door. "That's what our intelligence reports say."

When Mira and I were rescued on the Gulagan tundra, we discovered that Waters was friends with the Wackies, a group of Tunneler rebels who opposed Earth Force's control of their planet. Addy and Marco must be with them now, too. "So, Waters joined forces with Barrick and the Wackies and formed the Resistance? Are they rebelling against Earth Force? I mean, what are they *resisting?*"

Cole flicks his gaze around the room, looking anywhere but at me. "I can't say any more, Jasper. All of this is well outside your clearance. It's for your own protection. The less you know, the less likely you'll be caught up in a security sweep."

He's shutting me out? I curl my fingers into fists. "Secrets are for my safety? Why do I have a hard time believing that?"

"We've had leaks. We suspect there's a mole within the higher ranks of the Force. You don't want to be the subject of an investigation."

I can't believe this. My best friend is completely stonewalling me. "It would've been tough for me to leak information from the rift, don't you think?"

"No one is immune," Coles says, either ignoring or not catching on to my sarcasm.

"We made a pact on Gulaga not to keep secrets!" My voice shakes. I'm barely keeping it together. "It's all about the pod, remember?"

Cole stares at me, expressionless. "Our pod was disbanded."

I close my eyes. This is going nowhere. Since I left Alkalinia a few hours ago, Cole became Earth Force boss man, Mira left with the Youli, and Marco and Addy joined up with the Wackies. Who does that even leave? I take a deep breath. "What about Lucy? Is she okay? Or is that above my clearance level, too?"

Cole rolls his eyes. Apparently, we've landed on a topic he's allowed to talk about. "Lucy's fine. She's here. I'm sure she'll find you the moment she hears you've arrived at the space station." He takes a step toward the door. "We should move along. The admiral expects me by her side soon."

That's it? That's all he's going to tell me? I want my friend back. I want my *life* back. "So, you're not just a captain, you're like a really important captain, aren't you?"

"I'm the chief military strategist."

"In one year you went from cadet to chief military strategist?" Wow. To say I missed a lot would be a serious understatement. I shrug, not really knowing what else to say. "You always were the master at *Evolution of Combat*."

The bed I'm in is incredibly comfortable. It's almost as comfortable as the couches in our souped-up common room on Alkalinia, which was no more than virtual reality meant to keep us happy and stuffed and distracted so the Alks could pump us up with reptilian venom and knock us out.

My body is beyond tired. Every time I close my eyes and start to fade, my leg jerks or a shiver runs up my arm. I'm so exhausted I can't even get my body coordinated enough to sleep.

Plus, I can't turn my brain off. I keep thinking about the fact that I lost a year of my life in that horrible rift. I've only been back at the space station a few hours, and from what I can tell, everything has changed.

Every time I stop my mind from spiraling over my lost time, I zero right back in on Mira's odd behavior in the rift. My brain is on repeat, replaying her final words.

I'm leaving with the Youli.

I have to.

It's my choice.

I can't go with you.

I don't want to.

What did she mean? Did she want to leave with the Youli? Was it really her choice? Or was that part of the deal and Mira chose to shield me from it? Maybe she knew I'd never agree to let the Youli help us escape the rift if it meant Mira couldn't come with us.

If that was her reasoning, she was right.

But what if she really meant exactly what she said? She chose to go with the Youli. She said she didn't want to come with me.

Maybe the only reason I refuse to believe what she said is because it hurts too much.

When I finally manage to doze off, there's pounding at my door. I bolt upright, convinced that I'm back in Alkalinia.

Light pours into the room and something crashes onto my bed. I'm about to fend off the intruder when I realize the high-pitched voice could only be Lucy's.

"Oh my God, it's true!" she yelps. "I half thought that arrogant Cole Thompson was playing mind games with me when he confirmed the rumor that you'd returned from the dead! Oh, Jasper, not a day has gone by that you haven't been in my thoughts. You are one of the true good people in the galaxy! And to think you were almost lost forever!" With this last line, she flings herself at me, knocking us both back onto my bed.

Such drama! At least Lucy hasn't changed.

"Good to see you, too, Lucy," I say, carefully extracting myself from her hug without making her mad. Lucy can be touchy. I flip the light switch by my bed so the room is illuminated by more than just the light from the hall. "What time is it?"

"Oh, I'm so sorry. You must be exhausted. I didn't even think about how much you needed rest. I just heard first thing that you were here, and I needed to lay my own eyes on you to believe it."

Lucy looks . . . strange. Her braids and ribbons are gone. Her hair is smoothed back and secured in a knot at her neck.

She's wearing all sorts of makeup, and her lashes are so huge it looks like she's got spiders crawling out of her eyeballs.

"Um, Lucy, really, what time is it?"

"It's just past 0600."

Wow. I feel like my head just hit the pillow, and now it's already morning.

"Is it true?" Lucy asks. "Were you really stuck in the rift? And were you only gone for a few hours?"

I nod. "Two nights ago, you and I were hanging out on the couch in our Alkalinian common room."

Lucy shivers. "Don't even say the name of that horrid place! Until this morning, I thought you and Mira died there, and that I was partially to blame."

More drama. "How were you to blame?"

Lucy blinks. "Oh, you know, if I weren't so annoyed at your sister and her good-for-nothing boyfriend, maybe I could have been more helpful."

She must be talking about Marco, but boyfriend? Well, it's not like I didn't see that coming. "Come on, Lucy, that wouldn't have made any difference. The Youli were coming, no matter what we did."

"I suppose." She turns her head. A dangly diamond earring reflects the light of my bedside lamp.

It's probably a bad idea to stay on the subject of Addy and Marco given that Lucy's feelings about them don't appear to have changed, but I have to find out what she knows. "So, my sister and Marco are with Waters and the Wackies on Gulaga?"

Lucy looks around, then kicks the door closed with her foot. Fortunately, she loves to gossip, so her annoyance fades. "That's the scoop. They've joined the Resistance. Although it's on the hush hush, of course. Everything's on the hush hush around here. Word is, we have a mole." She squeezes my hand. "I'm sorry, Jasper. I'm sure you were hoping to see Addy. I can't say I'm a big fan of hers, but she was awfully broken up about your death. We all were. At the funeral, we cried in each other's arms."

"Wait. What funeral?"

"Your funeral. They had a service for you back on Earth. I delivered one of the eulogies. Mine was really spectacular— the best, by far, if I do say so myself. I may have to reenact it for you. Wouldn't that be fun? You can hear how I remember you before you even die. Actually, I'm sure we have a vid recording of it in the press archives. I'll make sure to have it retrieved this morning."

My heart clenches. I can't believe Addy had to go through that. She had to mourn a lost brother. She was already pretty anti–Earth Force by the time she reached Alkalinia. My apparent death was more than enough to push her over the edge. No wonder she bailed on Earth Force and joined up with Waters and the Resistance.

"What about my parents?" I ask.

"They were at your funeral, too, of course."

I cover my eyes with my hand. My parents held a funeral for me? I can't even imagine what that did to them. I have to contact them today. I don't care what Earth Force and its ridiculous confidentiality rules say, I can't let my parents keep thinking I'm dead.

"Speaking of death," Lucy says, "is Mira . . . ?"

"She's alive."

Lucy exhales. "Oh, thank goodness. Where is she? I'll go visit her next."

"She's not here."

Lucy looks at me quizzically.

"It's complicated. I'm sure the admiral is going to ban me from talking about this once we finish our debrief, so I might as well tell you now. The Youli rescued us from the rift, and now they have Mira."

Lucy's eyes go wide. "The Youli? I don't understand. Why would they rescue you?"

"I'm not sure, really. Waters always hinted that the Youli weren't all bad."

Lucy looks at me sideways. "How can you say that with all that's happened? Actually, I guess you don't know all that's happened. Let's just say that the war has escalated. And Earth Force has informed the public."

My eyes widen. There were rumors, sure, but now it's official knowledge. Our planet is at war. I wonder what things are like back home.

I shake my head. "I'm desperate, Lucy. I missed so much. You have to fill me in on everything. So now everyone knows about the Youli?"

"They do. I've made sure of it." Lucy smiles, bats her spider eyelashes, and tips her head to the side, freakishly like Sheek. "You're looking at the face of Earth Force—the new and improved *feminine* face."

So the comparison to Sheek was actually real? For Lucy, this must be a dream come true. She wanted to see her name on the webs ever since I met her. But how did she go from cadet to the face of Earth Force in a year? I have so many questions. "No more Sheek?"

Lucy snorts. "Oh, that clown is still around. But my ratings are sky-high. I have to think his days are numbered." She does that weird Sheek smile again and looks at me expectantly.

"Congrats. I'm sure you're great."

"Oh, I am. Speaking of which, I need to read my morning briefing notes. I bet things will be a bit chaotic over in the press room since we've raised to red alert, not to mention the unexpected return of the greatest celebrities in the history of Earth! And you, of course. We've got to determine the spin, right?"

With that, she delivers yet another Sheek smile. Then she pushes off the bed and disappears out of the room before I can answer, and before I can press her for more information about the past year.

When the door closes, I turn my light back off and throw the blanket over my head. Maybe if I burrow down I can catch another hour of sleep. Or at least maybe I can push away the thoughts that are fighting for attention in my mind.

Cole is chief military strategist and Lucy is the new face of Earth Force. What else has changed while I've been gone?

Do my parents know Addy's gone AWOL? Or do they think she's dead, too?

Why on earth did Mira leave me? What did the Youli say that made her choose to go?

I thought the only thing they wanted was peace.

The message!

I bolt up in bed.

How could I have forgotten about the message? So much has happened since I arrived at the space station that I didn't even think about speaking to Admiral Eames about the Youli's message.

I need to find the admiral right away! Giving her the message may be the only way to get Mira back. If Mira wants to come back.

MONICA TESLER

Flipping the light switch, I rummage around on the floor for my shoes then dash to the bathroom. Actually, *dash* is too strong a word. I quickly wobble to the bathroom. My legs barely feel like they're holding me up. Dark circles rim my eyes. I look pretty much what you'd expect someone who's gone through a battle, an alien rescue, and multidimensional time travel on half a night of sleep would look like—which is to say, horrible. I splash some cold water on my face then try to pat down my hair.

Once I'm dressed, I jet out of my room and instantly realize I have no idea where I am. I didn't pay attention when Cole walked us here last night, and I basically have no innate sense of direction. My internal compass is so horrible I stranded Mira and me in that VR torture chamber on Alkalinia last night. Or I guess I should say last year. We were lucky we made it out.

I take off down the hall, following the silver stripe that guides the mini spider crawlers. Hopefully that will get me out of the officers' quarters at least.

As I track the stripe around the corner, I think about my lost year and everything I learned from Cole and Lucy since I got back last night. What else did I miss? I wish Marco was here. He would have no problem filling me in, security clearance or not. I can't believe—

"Hey!" a girl's voice calls.

I stop and look up. A small girl with curly brown hair that falls just below her chin is pancaked against the wall next to the silver stripe.

She puts her hands on her hips. "You nearly plowed me down, Jasper Adams!"

"WATCH WHERE YOU'RE GOING!" THE GIRL
snaps.

"Sorry," I mumble. "I'm kind of lost. How do you know my name?"

She tilts her head and narrows her eyes at me. She must be confused how someone bright enough to be an Earth Force officer could be dumb enough to get lost at the space station. "Everyone knows your name. Your face has been plastered all across the planet for the last six months, not to mention flashed repeatedly on every web station."

"What?" I can't make sense of anything this girl just said. I take a closer look at her. She looks vaguely familiar. "Do I know you?"

"Not really. I heard you showed up last night. I work with Lucy, and she talks about you all the time." She glances down the hall before adding, "And I know your sister."

"Addy? Have you heard from her?"

The girl quickly looks around again like she's making sure no one heard me. Her eyes are so dark blue they almost look purple. "Of course not. We were juniors together. I didn't really know Addy until after the battle."

"The Battle of the Alkalinian Seat, where I supposedly perished?"

"That's the one, although apparently you didn't."

We stand there staring at each other. I'm not sure what to say. I can't seem to do much other than look at her eyes. I've never seen anyone with purple eyes before.

She blinks, and I remember why I'm here in the first place. "I need to see the admiral. Any chance you know where I can find her?"

The girl steps away from the wall, forcing me to backpedal.

"She's probably finishing up morning briefing," she says. "I'm headed that way." She waves her hand to herd me along, then takes off at a brisk pace.

"What's your name?" I ask, jogging beside her. If this girl works with Lucy, she must have access to lots of Earth Force information.

"Jayne."

"Are you like another face of Earth Force?" As soon as the words leave my lips, heat rises in my cheeks. I don't want her to think I'm saying she looks like she should be the face of Earth Force, although she kind of does, especially with the purple eyes.

She laughs. "No, that's not my thing, although I do work in public relations. Leave the cameras for Lucy and Max. I'm a copywriter. I compose what they read over the teleprompter."

"Did you just call Maximilian Sheek *Max*? He lets you call him that?"

"Of course not, but I don't see him anywhere around here, do you?"

When I don't answer, she takes off walking again. "Let's go, Jasper! I can't be late. This is going to be a big news day. Haven't you heard? The famous lost aeronauts and the Earth Force poster boy returned from the dead."

I know she's talking about me, but it doesn't feel real. Since when am I news? And the whole *returned from the dead* thing, well, that's going to take some time to sink in.

Jayne is fast. In fact, it's amazing how fast she can walk without breaking into a run. I'm half out of breath when we get to the chute cube. She holds the door and gestures with her hand. "You first."

"That's okay. You go."

"I insist. I've had way too many cadets crash into me in the tube. Something about building a human chain. We just met. I'm not ready for you to grab my ankles."

"Who said anything . . . Forget it. I'll go." Sliding past her into the cube, I stand on the chute grate with my arms folded across my chest. What's her problem with a human chain? If my pod mates were here, we'd be fighting over who got to be chain leader.

Actually, now that Cole is the military strategy god or whatever his title is, maybe he wouldn't be so quick to goof off with me, a lowly cadet. And I bet Lucy wouldn't risk messing up her new hairdo and perfect makeup.

The chute activates, and I'm sucked in. Jayne seems all right and all, but she makes me realize how much I miss the way things used to be. And from what I can tell so far, things used to be very different from how things are now.

I press my eyes closed and let the wind rush across my skin. For a moment at least, I'm anywhere I want to be. Or maybe I should say, any *when* I want to be.

As I'm dumped into the landing trough, I slam back to the here and now.

Jayne whisks in behind me.

When we exit the chute cube, she starts down the hall to the right. The hallway ends in a T. The new hall to the left is crowded with people talking and rushing between rooms. To the right, a guard stands post.

　　　　　　　　　　MONICA TESLER

"The press room is that way," Jayne says, tipping her head to the left. "Admiral Eames is down there." She nods at the guard.

"Thanks for showing me the way," I say. "I'll see you around."

"No problem. And yes, you will. I'm sure we'll be seeing lots of each other." She turns and heads up the hall, leaving me to brave Admiral Eames solo.

The guard escorts me the rest of the way to the admiral's briefing room. My palms start to sweat. Now that I'm about to see the admiral, I'm freaked. What am I going to tell her? Sure, I have a message to deliver, but what am I actually going to say? I can't exactly waltz in and say, *Peace, peace, peace,* like the Youli. That would go absolutely nowhere.

Not to mention, what am I going to tell her about Mira? I'm still not sure how I feel about the Youli, but I know how I feel about Mira. Delivering the message and cooperating with the Youli may be the only way I'll ever see her again.

I have to stay focused on my goal: bringing Mira home. That is, if she wants to come home.

We stop in front of a door. The guard points at a small bench against the wall as he speaks into his com link.

I sit down and bend over my knees, trying to shut out the hum of the florescent lights so I can come up with a plan for what to say to the admiral. When I finally push back up, the guard is no longer there. It's just me on the bench. That must mean I'm supposed to wait.

Yesterday I told the admiral that the Youli took Mira. There's no doubt she'll want me to elaborate when we talk. I could set the record straight, explain that Mira chose to go with the Youli. It's not as if I lied last night. Saying that the Youli took Mira doesn't mean it wasn't her choice. After all, the Youli had to take her, because Mira didn't know how to get out of the rift on her own. So I was technically being completely honest. Maybe the admiral would be more likely to meet with the Youli if she knew Mira had gone with them of her own free will. Maybe Mira's choice to trust the Youli would convince the admiral to trust them, too.

Somehow I doubt that.

Odds are, if I tell the admiral the truth, she'll think Mira is a traitor. She may even suspect me of being a double agent since everyone knows how close Mira and I are. I might be locked in the cell block and interrogated, especially with security so tight like Cole said. Earth Force may never trust me again. And that's not the worst of it. If I tell the truth, Mira may never be able to come home.

Maybe I shouldn't deliver the message.

The truth is, I'm not sure what to do. I wish Mira were here. She'd help me through this. She might not tell me what to do, but she'd support me as I figured it out. She'd help me find the strength to push aside my stress with all the changes from my missing year and persuade the admiral to push for peace.

Of course, the fact that Mira *isn't* here is one of the main reasons I'm sitting on this bench right now. I bury my head in my hands. My life is a mess.

Thanks, Mira. Thanks a lot for leaving me.

The door opens, and I jerk up. I have no idea how long I've been sitting on this bench. Next to me, Denver Reddy exits the admiral's briefing room. His eyes are puffy. He looks like he didn't sleep at all last night.

"I wish you'd reconsider, Cora," he says to the person on the other side of the door, who must be the admiral. "And if you do, you know where to find me." He pulls the door shut, leans against the frame, and closes his eyes.

He's obviously upset. It's kind of awkward just sitting here. I try to clear my throat to tip him off that he's not alone, but my spit goes down the wrong pipe, and I end up in a coughing fit.

Denver pulls himself together. "You okay, kid?"

I nod between coughs.

"You waiting to talk to the boss?"

I nod again as I get the coughing under control.

"Careful. She's in a mood, if you know what I mean."

Great. Just what I need. "Thanks for the heads-up. How's the reentry going?"

He shrugs. "Strange. Life kept going without me. I guess everything about that is pretty messed up. Got to go. I'm getting briefed on recent history in five minutes."

Denver takes off down the hall. Recent history? I probably need to attend that briefing, too, at least the part that covers the past year. Denver's right about one thing. Everything is pretty messed up.

"Come on in, Jasper." Admiral Eames leans against the doorframe.

I jump to my feet and raise my hand in salute. She barely seems to notice. She just disappears back into the room, which must mean she expects me to follow her.

I enter the briefing room and realize it's the same room where we had the meeting last night. Geez. My sense of direction really is awful. I had no idea that's where I was, and I certainly couldn't have made it back here without Jayne's help.

The room looks a lot different today. The lights are dimmed, and the only person present other than me is the admiral. I've never seen Admiral Eames without her entourage. Now suddenly I'm having a one-on-one meeting. This whole return from the rift experience feels like a dream. Or maybe a nightmare.

She nods at the chair beside her. I pull back the seat and perch on the edge, my back as straight as a board.

The admiral looks even more tired than Denver. I wonder

if he's one of the reasons why. I don't know what their relationship was before he was lost in the rift, but it's clear they were close. It must be super weird for her to see him after all this time. She's lived more than a dozen years longer than him. She's fought more wars, commanded more missions, watched more soldiers die.

"At ease, Jasper. It's just us."

I let my shoulders fall forward, and I scoot back in the chair. Crossing my hands on the table, I tap my thumbs together as I try to figure out what to do next.

Admiral Eames raises her eyebrows. "You were waiting outside my office, Jasper. I'm assuming you wished to speak with me."

"Oh, right. Sorry." Okay, now I need to lay it all out. "I just thought I'd follow up about my time in the rift—you know, maybe elaborate on some of the stuff we talked about last night." I twirl my thumbs in a circle to keep focused. I'm still not sure how much to say.

The admiral nods. "Great, please go ahead."

"Well, the thing is, the Youli asked me to give you a message."

She tilts her head to the side. "You communicated with the Youli?"

"Yep. I mean, yes, sir."

She narrows her eyes at me. "How?"

Inside, I kick myself. I had all morning to prepare for this meeting and didn't even plan for this question? I am such an idiot. It's basically impossible to answer without talking about my brain patch, and I really don't want the admiral to know about that. "Umm . . ."

"We know about the Youli patches implanted in yours and Officer Matheson's brain stems."

"You do?"

"Yes. And if we didn't, you were going to inform me about them in response to my question about how you communicated with the Youli, I presume." Without waiting for my confirmation, she continues, "Let's get to the point. What's the message?"

Peace. Peace. Peace.

The word rings in my mind just as it did in the rift. I can almost hear the deep voice of the Youli speaking in my brain: *Tell your people we wish to meet and discuss the requirements for your planet's entry into the Intragalactic Council. This is our gesture of peace.*

"The Youli want to talk about reaching a peace deal and Earth's entry into the Intragalactic Council," I tell her.

She laughs and shakes her head. "A peace deal? You can't be serious."

"I'm totally serious. They kept saying, *Peace, peace, peace.* They really meant it."

"And you're suddenly an excellent judge of Youli character?"

MONICA TESLER

"Well, not exactly—and I know they're, like, our mortal enemies and all—but they were really convincing. And not only that, but they rescued us. There's no way we could have escaped the rift without the Youli's help."

The admiral's expression is blank. I can't tell whether I'm managing to convince her of the Youli's commitment to peace. I need to make sure she believes me. It may be the only way to bring Mira home.

There has to be a way to reach her. But this is Admiral Eames, unreadable, and pretty much unreachable. The only time I've ever seen a crack in her exterior is last night. "They brought Denver back! He'd still be in the rift if it weren't for the Youli!"

Admiral Eames folds her hands in her lap and takes a deep breath.

Something tells me that was the wrong thing to say. I shouldn't have brought up Denver.

She locks eyes with me and says slowly, "Don't presume a thing about Captain Reddy, am I understood?"

My shoulders sink under the weight of her stare. "Yes, sir. What I mean is, the Youli said they wanted to talk peace, and to prove it, they rescued us from the rift."

"I see." The admiral steeples her fingers on the table. "What else?" Her voice is sharp and icy.

"Sir?"

"What else did you want to tell me? For example, what happened to Officer Matheson? This time, I want specifics."

"Well . . . she . . ."

"Last night you said the Youli took her."

"That's right." What do I say? How do I convince her that the Youli want to cooperate? That Mira didn't betray her people?

"You need to flesh that out, Jasper. What exactly happened?"

"I'm not sure. I think that was part of the deal. They get us out of the rift, but Mira goes with them."

"She's their hostage?"

"Yeah, I guess so."

"You think we should trust our enemy who took your friend hostage? That doesn't make sense to me, Jasper. Is there something I'm missing?"

"No." As I say the word, the hope I'd held in my heart for Mira's safe return starts to seep out. This was my one shot to get the admiral's help, and I blew it. The way she just summed up the scenario—the suggestion that we should trust an enemy who took one of our soldiers hostage—even sounds ridiculous to me.

Admiral Eames stands. "I don't think there's anything left to say on the matter." She crosses to the door and opens it, leaving no question that our meeting is over. "You'd do well to remember, Officer Adams, that disloyalty to the Force is a grave offense. Thank you for your service." She walks out, leaving me alone in her dimly lit briefing room.

Like Denver said, everything is pretty messed up, and I just made things a lot worse.

6

I DON'T KNOW HOW LONG I STAY IN THE
admiral's briefing room, but eventually I realize it's probably not the greatest idea to be sitting here on my own.
Someone's bound to come in eventually, and when they do
they'll want to know why I'm here, and I have no explanation other than I've had no energy to move since the
admiral left.

I stumble into the hall. My legs feel like jelly. At first I
think I'm just exhausted (which I am), but I begin to wonder whether it's a side effect of my travels through the rift.
Like maybe my body didn't get put back together 100 percent correctly, or maybe hanging suspended in time and then

jumping a whole year ahead just messes you up. I'll have to ask the old aeronauts how they're feeling. Their time jump was fifteen times as long as mine, so if jelly legs are a side effect, they would definitely have them.

My mind replays my conversation with the admiral. I can't believe how inept I was. Nothing I said made the admiral pause for even a moment to consider whether the Youli could be reaching out with a genuine gesture of peace. Or maybe she doesn't want to believe it. Either way, we're no closer to bringing Mira home than we were last night.

When I get to the fork in the hall, the guard nods. I still have no idea where I am. I didn't pay any attention when I was walking here this morning with Jayne. But I do know where Jayne is. She turned left for the press room when I turned right to meet with the admiral. That means if I walk straight I should run into Jayne, which hopefully means I'll also run into Lucy. And if there's one person who might be able to help me with the Mira situation, it's Lucy.

Just like this morning, tons of people buzz around the press hall reading their tablets, chatting excitedly with other officers, most of them paying zero attention to me. Some of them look up and do this weird double take when they see me, but I just keep walking.

At the end of the hall, a wide door opens to a huge room filled with dozens of monitors mounted on every wall. I head in, hoping to spot Lucy. What I see instead is my face on at least half of the screens.

"Why is my—"

"There you are!" Lucy collides with me from the side, pulling me into a tight hug. Instead of letting me go, she sort of unravels, still gripping me by my arm and unfurling her other arm wide. "Excuse me! Excuse me! All eyes and ears over here! Everyone, this is Jasper, although of course all of you know that. Jasper, this is everyone!"

This morning I thought something was different with Lucy, but now there's no mistaking. First off, she's taller—like a *lot* taller. I'm basically looking at her eye to eye. And it's not because she's grown that much. She's wearing shoes that rise up on spikes in the back. High heels, I think they're called. Second, she's wearing tons of makeup, even more than this morning. The black spider eyelashes compete for my attention with her raspberry-pink lips. And her hair is pulled back into a tight knot. Not even her uniform is the standard issue. Sure, it's still the Earth Force uniform, but it's custom-made or something. It looks more high fashion than military.

And that smell! She smells like . . . roses!

"What's with the perfume?" I ask. "You getting beauty tips from Florine?"

A couple of laughs escape around the room. Others avert their eyes so they don't look like they're eavesdropping.

Lucy glares at me. But a second later, she waves her hand, and her smile returns. She snuggles up against me. "Oh, you silly boy! I've missed you so much! Now let's head to my office, where we can have a private chat." She links her arm in mine and pulls me away from the crowd of press officers.

I glance around the room and spot Jayne in the back corner. She's sitting at a desk against the wall watching me and Lucy like everyone else in the room. When I smile, she shakes her head and gives a small wave.

Lucy leads me to a back hall. We pass an enormous office with a large desk that appears to float in the middle of the room. On the back wall, a huge painting hangs. It's the face of Maximilian Sheek, four times, each face a different color.

"Is that Sheek's office? Not much for modesty, huh?"

"Oh, that's his office, all right. He never makes it here until after lunch, though. Unless he has appearances, of course."

The next office is smaller, but not by much. Lucy pushes the door open and leads me in. Everything in the office is pink. Pink lacquer desk, pink desk chair covered in pink feathers, pink faux-fur rug, pink wallpaper with pink stripes, pink flowers in a pink vase, pink paper with pink pens, which I'm sure have pink ink.

"Well, what do you think?" she asks, twirling around.

"It's . . . pink. Is this stuff for real? It kind of reminds me of the VR in Alkalinia."

She slaps my hand. "That's a nasty thing to say. Of course it's real. I decorated myself."

"Why? I mean, why do they let you have all this stuff? And why do you need it?"

Lucy frowns. "I told you this morning, Jasper, I'm the new face of Earth Force. It's only fitting that I have an office that reflects that."

"So Earth Force's new look is pink?"

Lucy huffs. "No. This is *my* look. It's important to have a signature style, don't you think?"

"A what style?" I want to plug my nose. Her whole office reeks of roses.

"Signature. Look, Jasper, I know you've been gone a long time, and a lot has happened while you were away, but you need to understand I'm a very important person now."

"That's one of the things I want to talk to you about," I say. "You're right, I've been gone a long time, but not *that* long. How did you become the new face of Earth Force in such a short time? And how did Cole rise in the ranks so quickly?"

"Are you suggesting I don't deserve to be the face of Earth Force?"

"No, Lucy. As you always said, you were destined to be a web star. Really." Hopefully, if I tell her what I know she wants to hear, she'll answer my questions.

Lucy's lips lift in a small, unimpressed smile. "That's sweet,

Jasper. Now I know we have a lot of catching up to do, but let's get through the talking points first, shall we?" She nods at her pink guest chair, expecting me to sit. "The way I see it, the heart of the story is your hero quest. It's just amazing that someone our age—a Bounder—was the one to rescue Earth's most famous aeronauts. It really speaks to how special and important the Bounders are, wouldn't you agree?"

I have no idea what Lucy is going on about. "Talking points?"

"Yes, of course. We'll be making spin decisions imminently, and I thought we could chat first. Your inside perspective could be very helpful in creating the narrative."

"What narrative?"

She rolls her eyes. "The rescue of the lost aeronauts, of course! And you as the hero of the homecoming story! Our very own poster boy returned from the dead! You always wanted to be popular, Jasper. It's like this story is your destiny. Not to mention, it's the hugest news since I came into the position. It couldn't have come at a better time."

Jayne called me poster boy, too. "What do you mean, *poster boy?* And why is now such a good time for this news?" And why did she say I always wanted to be popular?

She waves a hand. "Oh, nothing we can't handle. Just that someone out there has been leaking information. Things can get ugly quick if we don't have control of the message."

That must be the mole Cole mentioned. "What are the leaks about?"

"You may not know this, Jasper, but Earth Force informed the public about the Youli conflict. In fact, that's what most of our press focus is about, that and the Bounders. It's very important that the public have an accurate impression of how critical Earth Force's efforts are for planetary prosperity and security."

"What about the Bounders?" Before we even left Earth for our last tour of duty, there were rumors and information leaks about the Bounders. An Earth Force officer came to our apartment and questioned Addy and me. Addy was furious. She almost joined the protestors at the Bounder launch.

Lucy gives me that fake smile again. I wonder if it's part of her signature style. "There's been some minimal backlash about Earth Force withholding information about the Bounders from the public."

As in keeping the reason for the Bounder Baby Breeding program a secret for more than thirteen years? "Minimal backlash? Are you kidding? Lucy, this is me. Jasper. We've had countless talks about how awful it was for Earth Force to keep those secrets, how they even kept our true mission a secret from us!"

"Now, really"—that smile again—"countless? I recall it coming up one or two times. But what's important is how they've handled the information once disclosed, don't you think? Not to mention that the Bounders have proven themselves invaluable in the ongoing war efforts. The public knows that many of us have risen in the ranks faster than any of the other aeronauts."

"Is that why they promoted you and Cole so—"

"Oh, I hate to interrupt, but my first daily report is about to stream. Let's watch."

She flicks her wrist at the pink wall and it morphs into a giant screen bearing the Earth Force insignia.

The insignia fades into Lucy's giant face. On the screen, she smiles and tips her head, kind of like the way Sheek always does. Then she says, "I'm Captain Lucy Dugan, and I invite you to face facts." She turns her head to the side, then glances back at the camera, batting her enormous eyelashes.

"That's my signature line," she tells me. "Get it? *Face* facts— with me as the new face of the Force. Pretty clever, right?"

The screen shifts to an image of the space station, with Lucy's voice talking over it. "Make sure to tune in later today as we bring you a breaking story that's years in the making."

"Does that blush make my face look too angular?" she asks me.

"That what?"

She waves a hand at me. "Forget it."

On the screen, the image shifts to Lucy again. She's

standing in front of a backdrop with the Earth Force insignia. She continues to hype the story breaking later today. It must be the rescue of the lost aeronauts.

The door cracks open and Jayne pops her head in. Lucy doesn't seem to notice; she's too focused on her giant face. Jayne winks at me.

"Excuse me, Captain Dugan?" Jayne says.

Lucy averts her eyes from the screen long enough to see Jayne. "What is it?" she asks impatiently.

"The image meeting is about to commence. Reddy and the other aeronauts are already in the conference room."

"Oh yes, thank you," she says, eyes still on the screen. "Is this being recorded?"

"Of course," Jayne answers. "We have the original footage we shot this morning, and we're recording the web stream as you previously requested."

Lucy extends her hand toward the screen then pauses. She gazes at her image for another second. Then she flicks her wrist and the giant Lucy disappears.

She stands. "Thank you very much, Jayne," she says without a glance in Jayne's direction. Jayne backs out of the room.

Lucy flashes a smile at me that might not be fake. "Come here, you!" She waves me over and plants a kiss on both cheeks. "We'll talk more later, okay?"

"Sure," I say to Lucy's back. She's already half out the door, and I'm left standing alone in the smelly pink room.

What happened?

I didn't get an answer to any of my questions. I never had a chance to mention Mira. I couldn't even slip in a plea to let me contact my parents.

Maybe our return is huge news, but this homecoming sucks.

Once I get out of Lucy's pink palace, my stomach starts growling. I haven't eaten anything since I arrived at the space station. In fact, I haven't eaten anything in a year if we're talking Earth time, and for weeks before that I was eating virtual Alk food. I don't even know what that stuff really was.

I need to brave the mess hall. I ask Jayne to walk me there, but she's too busy. She grabs another press officer and has him take me. Before we go, another officer snaps a dozen pictures of me against a wall with the Earth Force insignia.

My stomach is practically seizing by the time the first officer drops me off at the mess hall door. I'm greeted by the smell of day-old hot dogs. It's still disgusting, but at least some things about this place haven't changed.

As soon as I walk in, Ryan spots me. He rushes to my side and pulls me over to a table filled with familiar faces: Meggi, Annette, Desmond, Orla and Aela, even Hakim and Randall. Before I reach them, everyone at the table is on their feet clapping. Meggi runs over and wraps her arms around me. Even Hakim shakes my hand, which is weird because I can't even look at him without seeing his old pal Regis.

"When Ryan told us you were back, we could hardly believe it," Meggi says.

They give me a seat and insist I tell them what happened.

I'm sure the admiral is going to put a gag order on me soon. The true story of the rift will be classified above my own security clearance level. But as of now, no one's told me to keep quiet.

"Let me get some food first. I promise to tell you everything you want to know about the rift as long as you fill me in on everything I missed this past year."

Now I'll finally get some real answers, not rosy pink spin.

After I've choked down a grilled cheese and a couple of yogurt squeezies, I launch into the tale. As I talk, cadets from other tables gather round. The crowd hangs on every word I say.

When I reach the part where we find the lost aeronauts in the rift, Meggi reaches over and squeezes my hand. "You really are a hero, Jasper."

That's what Lucy said. Maybe she and Meggi are right. Maybe I *am* a hero.

I smile at Meggi, kick my feet up on the orange table, and go on with the story. There will be plenty of time to catch up on what I missed later.

7

JUST AS I'M DESCRIBING MY BOUND TO the Ezone with the lost aeronauts, the Bounders' com links start beeping.

"Welp, I guess that's it for lunch," Ryan says, shoving another huge bite of tater tots into his already-full mouth.

Meggi dabs her lips with a napkin, then stands with her tray. "It's so great to see you, Jasper. I can't wait to talk more later!"

"Wait a minute!" I swing my legs off the table. "Where are you guys going? I have tons of questions!"

"Duty calls." Annette's face is as expressionless as always. "That much hasn't changed."

I stand. "Seriously, where are you off to?"

"There's a captains' briefing," Hakim explains as I follow the Bounders to the tray line. I can't believe he's friends with my friends! At least Regis is still gone.

"You guys are all captains?"

"Yep," Ryan says, his mouth still full with his last bite of tater tots. "No more pod leaders, no more classes, no more kid time. We're full-fledged officers of the Force now."

"What does that even mean?"

"Pod patrol, military engagements, bounding drills—there's no time for much else," Meggi says. She and Ryan hang back, letting the other Bounders exit the mess hall first. They promise to meet up later and fill me in on what I missed. For now, I ask them to drop me at the suction chute leading to the sensory gym.

"I suppose Cole's going to be at this briefing, too?" I ask, trying not to sound too annoyed.

"He'll probably be leading the briefing," Meggi says.

"Why?" Ryan asks. "You hoping to talk to him? Good luck."

"What's that supposed to mean?"

Ryan sneers. "Only that Cole doesn't have time for the little people."

Meggi glares at Ryan then smiles sympathetically at me. "It's not like that, Jasper. Cole's just very busy these days. The best time to catch him is first thing in the morning. He wakes up super early and heads down for breakfast."

"Come on, Meggi," Ryan says. "Cole is all business these days. You should have heard his lecture about confidentiality when he found out I'd told Jasper about Addy and Marco." Ryan looks around, making sure no one heard him, then shakes his head at me. "Thanks for ratting me out, by the way."

"Really? You got in trouble for that? Sorry."

"Forget it. Just promise me you'll keep what I tell you between friends from now on."

I nod at Ryan as he and Meggi leave me at the suction chute and hurry up the hall to their briefing.

I can't believe Ryan got in trouble for telling me about my own sister. Wouldn't Cole want me to know about Addy? If Ryan hadn't tipped me off, would Cole have kept that from me?

Plus, how on earth can *keep things between friends* not include Cole?

I activate the chute and close my eyes as I'm sucked in. The wind plasters my hair to my forehead, and my hands to my sides. I try to lose myself in the rush of the chute, forget about the disaster that's my life right about now. But there's no escaping my new reality.

Me, Jasper Adams, apparent poster boy of the Bounders

(whatever that means), but otherwise useless and clueless. Sister? Missing. Friends? Busy. Life? Stolen.

That's what it feels like, anyway, like the last year was stolen from me, and all I'm left with are questions and that infuriating Youli message.

The structure that houses the sensory gym is deserted. The lights are dimmed, and all the doors in the hall are shut. It's like no one's been here in a long time. Actually, that's probably true. The main things on this side of the structure are the gym and the pod hall. It doesn't seem like the Bounders have time for the gym anymore, and they're apparently way past the need for pod leader lessons. Practically all the Bounders are captains now. Another thing I missed: a big Earth Force promotion.

I stop by the door to the pod hall and lean my eye to the scanner. A flicker of hope waves in my chest as I wait, only to hear the sour beep denying me entrance. How long ago did I first enter the pod hall? Jasper time: less than two years. Real time: way more.

I continue down the hall to the sensory gym. When I enter, the memories nearly overwhelm me. I can almost hear Mira playing piano. I close my eyes and imagine holding my clarinet in my hands, harmonizing with Mira's powerful melodies.

But there's no music today. I slowly walk to the ball pit in the corner, climb in, sink down, and disappear.

I let myself drift until I fall asleep, my mind skipping from one stressful dream to the next. Eventually, the sound of footsteps shakes me awake.

"You're a very hard person to find," a girl's voice calls.

So much for disappearing. I awkwardly push myself up through the balls to find Jayne staring back at me.

"I've never heard that before," I say. "In fact, I'm the one who's usually lost."

She crosses her arms and stares at me with her purple eyes, like she's deciding whether to believe me.

Believe me, Jayne, I'm directionally challenged.

I lie back in the ball pit, wishing I could return to disappearing. I don't have the energy to deal with people right now. "So, you found me. What do you want?"

"Geez, don't sound so thrilled." Jayne sits on the edge of the ball pit. "What's wrong?"

I shake my head. "It's nothing."

She gives me the side-eye. "It's obviously something. Talk to me. I'm a good listener."

Maybe I *will* feel better if I talk to someone. I heft myself out of the pit and sit next to her on the edge. "It's strange coming back." I stare at my shoes and force myself to keep talking. "For everyone here, life went on. They have new friends, new roles, new responsibilities. Sure, they're happy I'm back, but there's no place for me in their lives anymore."

Jayne puts her hand on my shoulder. I can feel the heat of her palm through my shirt. "I wouldn't say that, Jasper. It takes time for everyone to adjust. You included."

"I know, it's just . . ." I bite my lip, not exactly sure how to express what I'm feeling. "I'm used to certain people being around, people who know me almost better than I know myself. When they're not here, it's harder."

"Addy."

"Yeah . . . and—"

"Mira."

I nod.

"You guys were—"

"No. I mean, yes. I mean, sort of." I shake my head. "It's hard to explain."

"I was going to say 'close.'"

"Oh. Yeah, we were close."

"You know what I think you need?" Jayne pops up and shoves my shoulders, launching me back into the ball pit. Laughing, she says, "Some sensory playtime."

By the time I get my feet under me, Jayne is already across the gym, jumping on the trampoline. She hops across the springs, hurls herself in the air, and drops into the pit beside me.

"That wasn't nice!" I say with a smile. I pick up a ball in each hand and throw them at her.

"Hey!" Jayne bats the balls away then pegs me with one.

"You've got a good arm," I say, "but you won't hit me twice."

I dodge and duck the balls she hurls at me, then dive backward into the pit, letting the balls cradle my body. Jayne showers an armful of balls on my head. Then she spins around and falls beside me, giggling.

"You were right," I say. "This is what I needed." I like being with Jayne. It's easy. It's fun. And I don't need to worry about her reading my thoughts.

She stops laughing. "I'm glad, because we've got to go now."

I almost forgot that she was looking for me when she came in here. "Where?"

"To see the admiral."

By the time Jayne and I arrive at the auditorium, the first several rows are filled. Lucy is on the front stage with Maximilian Sheek. She glares at Jayne when we walk in. Jayne rushes to check in with Lucy, then takes a reserved seat near the front. From the looks of it, the entire public relations department has assembled for this meeting.

Also, all the old aeronauts are here. I slide into an empty seat next to Bai Liu.

She nods at me. "Finally a familiar face, or at least a face that hasn't aged fifteen years."

I never thought Bai Liu would think of *me* as familiar. I

guess, in a way, we're in this together. What's going on?" I ask her. "Another debrief?" I scan the room for the admiral but don't spot her.

"Hardly," Bai says, rolling her eyes. When I look at her quizzically, she adds, "You mean you haven't heard?"

"Heard what?"

The door opens before she can answer. The admiral enters, flanked on either side by Cole and Ridders. Everyone in the auditorium stands at attention. They march straight down the aisle and take seats in the front row.

Lucy approaches the podium with a humongous fake smile on her face. "Thank you all so much for coming. I'm pleased to formally announce the Lost Heroes Homecoming Tour."

The screen behind her fills with a huge graphic that reminds me of old-school video games. The letters zoom onto the screen from the left and right in bold colors. Then behind the letters, a swirling sphere comes into focus. When it slows down, I can see that it's Earth.

Old photos zoom across the image, freeze for a second in the center, then zoom away, replaced by another. They're all pictures of the lost aeronauts. Most of them are famous photos that have been all over the webs for years.

"The tour will travel to eight major sites on Earth," Lucy says. "The publicity campaign is already well under way. The public reaction to today's announcement of the lost heroes' return has already been record-setting. We'll be rolling out spots on the webs about the tour starting tomorrow. We expect turnout at the rallies to be huge, well into the tens of thousands at every location. And, of course, press coverage will be constant. In addition to EFAN filming at the rallies, we'll have cameramen with us all the time so that we can piece together a fantastic behind-the-scenes special."

Sheek pulls the mic from Lucy. Even though it's clear she's the one who put this all together, he's not about to let her take the whole spotlight. "I'll be hosting the rallies, of course."

Lucy grabs the mic back from Sheek. "We'll be cohosting them. We're not the highlight attraction, though." She turns around to look at the screen.

This is obviously a cue to whomever is running the video, because when Lucy turns, the image morphs into the face of Denver Reddy.

"I give to you . . . your lost heroes!" Lucy says with a flourish of her arm.

The audience claps as the screen moves from one lost aeronaut to the next.

Jayne catches my eye from the front. I get why she needed to be here, but why me? I would much rather be in the sensory gym than under the fluorescent lights of the auditorium.

Lucy's been talking through the whole presentation, describing each aeronaut, their home city, their greatest accomplishments. ". . . last but certainly not least . . . ," she's saying.

The screen behind her morphs into a giant picture of my face. I'm staring off to the side and look a lot younger than I am now. I have no idea where or when it was taken. The image is sort of faded in the background with these words on top: PROTECTING OUR PLANET COMES AT A PRICE.

"We can't forget the youngest hero on the Lost Heroes Homecoming Tour," Lucy continues, "Jasper Adams!"

The screen image spins. When it stops, a new picture of me smiles back. It's one of the pictures they took of me this morning in the press room. This time the words OUR HERO COMES HOME! overlay the image.

"Hero? *Me?*" I blurt out.

"Of course!" Lucy says through gritted teeth. "Although you obviously have some work to do in playing the part. Fear not, we've onboarded stylists, and I'll personally be training all of you on line delivery and stage presence beginning first thing tomorrow."

I can't believe this. They're sending me to Earth on a PR tour? How am I going to convince the admiral to talk to the Youli if I'm halfway across the galaxy?

Lucy goes on and on about the tour, but I'm not capable of listening. Everything is happening too fast. It's like the count-down for a bound that's not in my control.

Next thing I know, everyone is getting out of their seats and shuffling toward the door.

Denver claps me on the shoulder as he walks up the aisle. "Back to the future, kid. We'll be home before we know it."

"Huh?"

"You're a real zone-out, aren't you?" Bai asks as she slides by me to join Denver. "They aren't wasting time with this Lost Heroes Homecoming Tour. Our ship leaves the day after next at 0800."

"Let's go, kid," Denver says. "They need us at a secondary briefing, stat. Apparently, we need lessons on how to be heroes."

THE SECONDARY BRIEFING FOR ME AND
the lost aeronauts takes place in a large training room where
I'm pretty sure I took quantum technology with Ridders during my first tour of duty. It's basically a repeat of what was
said during the first briefing with some extra info about the
tour and our schedule for the next twenty-four hours. Midway through, plebes roll in carts of food. At first I'm pumped
because senior officer cuisine is a heck of a lot better than tofu
dogs, but then I realize I'm missing dinner in the mess hall.
I was supposed to meet up with Meggi and Ryan. They were
going to fill me in on my lost year.

"Why do I get the feeling they don't want to let us loose

at the space station?" Bai asks during our meal break.

"Because they don't want to let us loose at the space station," Denver says.

"You really think so?" I ask. "Why?"

"Information control," Bai says. "I told Den he asked too many questions during our recent history lesson this morning."

Denver shrugs. "I couldn't help it. They got it all wrong about the Tunneler treaty. Who knows what other crap they were feeding us?"

Crap? That doesn't sound too officer-like, especially when talking about the Earth Force party line. "What do you think they'd do if I tried to leave?"

"Go for it, kid." Bai nods at the door. "Be the guinea pig."

I push aside my soy nuggets and head for the door. A female officer steps in front of me. "Can I help you, Officer Adams?"

"I just need to run to the mess hall," I say. "I told my friends I'd meet them for dinner, and I want to let them know I'm not going to make it."

She smiles. "Who are your friends? I'll make sure they get the message."

"That's okay. I'll only be a minute." I dodge to the side and try to reach the door.

She's faster than me. Her body blocks the exit. "We're getting ready to resume, Officer Adams. Your friends will understand."

I back away from the door and return to the table.

As I slink into my seat, Denver leans over. "Told ya, kid."

After the briefing, we're escorted to our rooms and informed that a guard will arrive in the morning to take us to our next prep session for the Lost Heroes Homecoming Tour.

Denver and Bai were right: Earth Force is keeping tabs on us. They won't let us out of their sight. I have only slightly more freedom than the caged Youli prisoner we discovered here during our first tour of duty.

I try my door handle. At least they haven't gone so far as to lock us in our rooms. I think about heading out now and tracking down Ryan. His quarters are probably close. But the truth is, I probably only have one shot at getting out and getting answers. I need to maximize my chances.

My best chance at real answers and real results is Cole.

I set my alarm for 0445. Meggi said Cole was up early. Hopefully his version of early is earlier than the time the guard arrives at my door. And hopefully, he's willing to help out an old friend. I need answers about what happened over the last year. I have to talk to my parents. With all the press coverage, they must know by now that I'm not dead. Still, I'm sure they'd feel a lot better hearing it from me. Plus, I've got to convince Cole to persuade the admiral to talk to the Youli. Mira's future depends on it.

The next morning, I make it out of my room and to the

mess hall door without running into anyone. Two minutes later, Cole cruises down the hall in a fast, efficient clip. He's focused on the tablet he's holding. I'm betting he's going to blow right by me.

"Cole!"

He abruptly stops and jerks his head in my direction. "Jasper. Sorry, I didn't see you. What are you doing here? Why are you awake so early?"

I follow him into the mess hall. "Why are *you* up so early? I heard you eat at this time every day."

"I'm very busy, and I find the best way to maximize—"

"Forget it," I interrupt. "I didn't really mean for you to answer that." He's moving like a machine. We're already halfway through the buffet line. He stocks his plate with highly practical, protein-packed foods, like fluffed tofu and veggie nutripatties and dried fruit chunks. My plate is empty. I grab a few tater tots and a leftover yogurt squeezie from last night's dinner and tail after Cole.

"Anyway," I continue, "we haven't had a chance to catch up. I was hoping we could have breakfast together." We exit the food line and head into the seating area.

Cole stops. He stares at his plate in one hand and his tablet in the other. "I usually read the overnight briefing material during breakfast and then go directly to the fitness room."

"Does that mean 'no'?"

He stays frozen a moment longer then turns and walks toward a table near a porthole. "Let's go," he calls. "I'll skip the fitness room this morning, but I'm still on a tight schedule."

I slide into the seat across from him. "Thanks for making time for me. I know you're like a really important person these days." An awkward laugh sneaks out of my throat, and I can't think of what else to say. What is this? I'm feeling insecure around Cole? I can't afford to let that happen. Too much is at stake in this conversation.

"It's not like that," Cole says. "I function better when I stick to a schedule, that's all."

His words help me relax a little, and I toss a mushy tot into my mouth. "The food's better. At least they have choices now."

"I haven't noticed," he says. "I've gotten used to the fluffed tofu. It doesn't taste like much, but it keeps me full until lunch."

"Cool. Very efficient."

"Are you settling in?" he asks after swallowing a huge bite of tofu.

It's such a strange question, like something you'd ask a houseguest who came for an extended vacation.

"Sure. The officer digs are a real upgrade, although I'm sure that's not a permanent assignment."

"I'll see what I can do." Cole finishes his tofu and moves on to the veggie nutripatties. "I may be able to have your accommodations level permanently elevated."

"Don't worry about that," I say. "The dorm is fine. Really."

Cole nods and glances at his watch.

This breakfast definitely has a ticking clock. I need to prioritize. I can probably get someone else to fill in the blanks about my missing time. And Lucy said we'd have visiting hours for friends and family during the Lost Heroes Homecoming Tour, so I know I'll get a chance to talk to my parents soon. My first priority has to be Mira. I need to get to the Youli's message, for her sake. "There *is* something you can do for me."

Cole raises his eyebrows and mumbles, "*Hmmm,*" through his food-filled mouth.

"I need you to talk to the admiral."

He sets his fork on his plate and slowly finishes chewing. Then he takes a large gulp from his mug filled with electrolyte-probiotic water. After placing his mug on the table, he turns his gaze on me. "Jasper, you're a friend. I'm happy to listen. But you should know before you say anything that I don't practice favoritism."

Of course he doesn't. It's Cole, after all. "I would never ask you unless it was extremely important."

Cole nods for me to go ahead.

I take a deep breath. "The Youli have a message for the admiral, and—"

"You mean *peace*?" Cole whispers. "They want Earth Force

to meet for peace talks and discuss Earth's entrance to the Intragalactic Council?"

"Basically, yeah. Who told you?"

Cole rolls his eyes. "I'm the admiral's chief military strategist. I know everything. She told me yesterday afternoon. She also told me her answer: an unequivocal *no*. I agree with her wholeheartedly."

I clench my fists beneath the table. This is not going well. I have to get things back on track. "Wait a second. Hear me out. When Mira and I—"

"No. You won't change my mind. All that *peace, peace, peace* talk—the Youli said the same thing to you on their ship when we were placing the degradation patch, remember? And since then they've tried to annihilate us multiple times."

"I know you're busy, Cole, but if you just consider—"

"This has nothing to do with me being busy." Cole stands. "Come with me."

He doesn't give me a chance to respond before pushing back from the table, taking his plate to the dishwasher, and heading for the exit. I stuff the uneaten yogurt squeezie into my pocket and dash after him.

"Where are we going?" I ask once I catch up.

"My quarters. I have something to show you."

"Are you sure we can't talk about this?" I jog to keep pace with his brisk walk. He's even faster than Jayne.

Cole scans in all directions. "Certainly not in the hallway. Wait until we get to my room. Things will be a lot clearer."

We speed walk the rest of the way to the officers' quarters, and I follow Cole to the last room on the hall. He flashes his eye at the lens pad, and the door swings open.

Cole's room is huge, easily twice the size of mine. Half of the room is set up as a Spartan living space—bed, bureau, trunk—without any decoration or touch of color. I suspect Cole hasn't changed a thing since the day he was assigned these quarters.

The other half of the room, though, is something else entirely.

The walls aren't really walls but seamless screens, each one filled with data and images. Multiple projections float in the space unanchored. One is clearly Earth. It rotates on an axis, spinning by Americana East, Eurasia, and all the other mega cities visible from space.

A long, black table stretches across the room. A single chair sits behind it. The table is piled high with papers, but I can see through a gap in the clutter that the table itself is a computer console.

"Rufus," Cole says.

Uh . . . what? I'm about to ask him what he's talking about, when the room itself answers.

"Welcome back, Captain. Your morning briefing is ready."

"Thanks, Rufus," Cole says.

"You're most welcome, Captain," the voice says.

"Wait a second," I say, "Rufus is your computer? And it calls you *Captain*?"

Cole colors red and shrugs. I bet I'm the only person besides him who's ever been in here. "Rufus was the name of my avatar on my very first combat game, *Junkyard Dog Fights*."

"You never told me you played *Junkyard*."

Cole smiles, and for a moment, it's just like old times. "Of course I did. This one time, I tricked this old hound into burying his gold bone in my yard. He nearly bit my head off. In fact—"

"Captain!" Rufus interrupts. "I must remind you that your morning briefing begins in fifteen minutes."

Cole stuffs his hands in his pockets. "Anyway, that's enough about that. Let me show you why I brought you here. Rufus, run a summary vid of Youli conflicts over the last twelve months."

"Processing, Captain."

The projections fade, and the entire wall in front of us fills with an underwater image of Alkalinia. A flood of emotion washes over me. We almost died in that horrible poison sea. I brace myself against the doorframe and force myself to watch. "Where'd this vid come from?"

"We have recording devices in all the bounding ships, and many of the combat officers have cameras mounted on their helmets. I just asked Rufus to pull together a montage. I want you to see what the rest of the Youli were up to while those guys paid you a visit in the rift and asked you to deliver their message."

The video skims through one horrifying scene after another. Youli firing at Earth Force ships. Earth Force officers drowning in the Alkalinian sea. Others being seized by their atoms and ripped apart by the Youli inside the Alk port.

"The Youli in the rift told us there was division in their ranks," I say. "The degradation patch we planted caused mega damage and created a splinter in their society. How do we know the Youli who did this represent the rest of their people?"

"Keep watching," Cole says. "Ask yourself what the right call is here: Gamble the safety of your people on what the Youli told you, or defend your planet? You can't choose both, Jasper."

The image pulls away from Alkalinia into open space. As the camera zooms in on a remote bounding base, a Youli vessel materializes on-screen and starts firing. Half a dozen Earth Force officers are left dead on the bounding deck. Then it shifts to an image of the Paleo Planet and a pair of tourist hovercrafts under attack. More violence. More death. All at the hands of the Youli.

The scene shifts again, and now the space station comes into view. I take a deep breath. What on earth happened here?

But then the screen goes blank. "Captain! I must insist you leave immediately for your briefing! The admiral will not tolerate tardiness!"

"Thanks, Rufus," Cole says as he grabs his tablet. "Back to your question, Jasper. No, I won't talk to the admiral and try to convince her to engage the Youli in peace talks. I won't because I don't think we should, and hopefully now you don't either."

My mind scrambles to find something else to say, some fact or follow-up that will prolong the discussion, the one ticket I may have to seeing Mira again. Maybe that's the only way. "What about Mira?"

Cole drops his gaze and shuffles some papers on the table. "Earth Force doesn't negotiate with its enemies, Jasper, not even when a hostage is involved. Mira knew the risks when she joined Earth Force."

"It's not like she had any choice about joining Earth Force, Cole! It's not like any of us had any choice!"

Cole gathers up the papers and stacks them in a neat pile. "I don't see how that's relevant. Now if you'll excuse me, I need to get to my morning meeting with the admiral."

How can he do this to me? How can he do this to Mira? "You don't see how it's *relevant*? Come on, Cole! We've spent hours talking about this! We didn't even know they were training us to be soldiers until midway through our first tour of duty!"

"Careful, Jasper." Cole grabs the door handle. "Disloyalty to the Force is a grave offense."

That's the same thing the admiral said to me yesterday.

"Rufus, I'm leaving," Cole says to his room computer. "Initiate all security protocols."

"Aye-aye, Captain."

He pulls the handle and stands at the threshold, waiting for me to exit before him.

I know once that door closes, my chance of finding Mira will practically vanish. I have to stall. "Can we meet up later? I need to know more about what I missed."

Cole stares past me into the hall. It's clear he wants me to go. "You have a full day of training for the tour, Jasper. I'm sure you'll be told everything you need to know about last year."

I rack my brain for something to keep him talking. "Where's Gedney? I can't wait to tell him about the rift. He'll freak out, right?"

"Gedney's on Earth."

"Cool. Maybe I'll see him on the tour. Plus, I need to talk to him about my gloves. They were lost on Alkalinia." Not to mention, if Cole won't intervene with the admiral, maybe Gedney will, for Mira's sake.

"I don't think you'll be needing your gloves anytime soon."

Wait . . . what? A Bounder with no gloves is basically useless. That confirms it. I've been totally sidelined.

"You've been through quite an ordeal, Jasper," Cole continues. "You need to focus on your recovery. Now I need to—"

"Okay, just one more thing. Can I please contact my parents? I have to let them know I'm okay. They think I'm dead, Cole. They had a funeral and everything."

Cole closes his eyes for a brief moment. "I know. I was there." He checks the time. "I'll see what I can do. Thanks for meeting me for breakfast, Jasper, but I really must go."

He waits until I'm fully out of his room then closes his door and tests the lock. Without another word, he turns and heads up the hallway, walking at the same fast, efficient pace as earlier this morning.

It's like the last hour didn't change a thing.

It's like he didn't just sell out his best friend.

AS I ROUND THE CORNER TO MY HALL, I
hear banging. It doesn't take long for me to realize that I'm
the cause of the banging—indirectly, of course. An officer
stands in front of my room pounding on the door.

He doesn't hear me coming. I'm only a few meters away
when he shouts, "Officer Adams, I really must insist that you
answer your door!"

"Hey," I say.

The officer jumps. "You scared me. . . . Wait a second . . .
you are Jasper Adams."

"Yeah, I . . . uh . . . woke up early and couldn't fall back to
sleep. So I took a walk."

"You were supposed to wait for your escort."

"I'm here. You're here. What's the big deal?"

The officer shakes his head like he can't find the words. "Just come with me."

I follow him down the hall to the chute cube. It's hard to shake what just happened with Cole, but I need to focus. Since Cole's a lost cause, Lucy is probably my closest contact to the admiral. "Is Captain Dugan running the training today?"

"The training we're late to? I have no idea."

It's clear this guy isn't looking to bond. Doesn't he know I'm a hero (for whatever that's worth)? If this morning's meeting with Cole is any measure, it's not worth much.

He drops me off at the same training room we met in yesterday. It's empty other than the lost aeronauts, a few low-level officers guarding the door, and a huge breakfast spread that reminds me way too much of the fake food on Alkalinia. The Alks filled us up on our favorites at every meal, but it was all virtual—some weird combo of chemical and neurosensory input that tricked our brains into thinking we were eating chocolate chip cookies. In reality, we were chowing down on snake food laced with venom. So now I can't eat anything without a bit of skepticism.

I push aside the nasty memories and fill my plate. Things may be rotten, but that's no reason to pass up donuts. I slip into a seat next to Denver.

"Thought you'd never show, kid." He steals a strawberry donut off my plate and takes a giant bite. "I forgot how good these were."

"I told you not to eat those things," Bai says to Denver.

"The kid's eating 'em."

"The kid's a teenager. He can eat anything."

Denver shoves the rest of the donut in his mouth and raises his hands like he never had it in the first place.

"Have you been here a long time?" I ask them.

"Long enough." Bai gives Denver a knowing look.

Denver finishes chewing then takes a long swig of juice. "Whatever you have to say, you can say in front of the kid, Bai. He knows who we're dealing with."

I'm not sure what we're talking about, but I'm curious. Maybe the lost aeronauts aren't such a dead end on info after all.

"Does this have anything to do with the guards not letting us out of their sight?" I ask.

"You have Denver to thank for that," Bai says. "Like I told you yesterday, he can't keep his mouth shut, especially when he thinks someone's got the facts wrong."

Denver waves his hand dismissively. "Ignore her, kid. We'd be on lockdown no matter what. The Force can't afford to have their precious Lost Heroes get a whiff of what's really going on around here."

The door bangs open and in walks Lucy and her PR entourage. Jayne comes in last, loaded up with tablets.

"Good morning, heroes!" Lucy says to the room. She circles the table, stopping to give each of us an air kiss (except for Denver—she gives him an actual kiss, and if he hadn't turned his head at the last minute, I'm pretty sure it would have been a big, juicy smack on the lips). Jayne follows Lucy, giving each of us a tablet.

Lucy takes her place at the head of the table. "Exciting news! We worked late into the night putting the finishing touches on the script for the Lost Heroes Homecoming Tour rallies. Everything is pretty and polished! Jayne, could you please load it up on the screen so we can follow along?"

Jayne fiddles with her own tablet, and soon the wall behind Lucy flickers and fills with the Earth Force insignia. Jayne slides her finger across the screen, and the giant EF is replaced with the graphic for the Lost Heroes Homecoming Tour.

"Fabulous," Lucy says. "First things first. Every show starts with a great story. And if I do say so myself, the story of your daring rescue is one of the best we've ever created. We've already circulated this vid clip to the webs." She nods at Jayne, and the room fills with the sound of a deep male voice announcing the return of the beloved lost aeronauts.

Denver shoots me a look. What's this all about? I shrug.

The voice-over continues, recounting the story of the

Incident at Bounding Base 51. So far, this is all old news (even if the news is a bit incomplete). The screen shows images of the old aeronauts waving good-bye from the bounding deck.

Then the screen flashes through headlines from the failed bound fifteen years ago. Finally, the images fade, and what is left is an image of a Youli bounding ship. The voice picks back up: "What we know now . . . what's been revealed by our heroes . . . is that the Incident at Bounding Base 51 wasn't a terrible mistake; it was an attack by our alien enemy."

Wow. The truth finally comes out. Well, kind of. Earth Force definitely isn't owning up to knowing about the Youli attack all those years ago.

"The Youli took our beloved aeronauts hostage," the voice-over continues.

Wait a second . . . *what?*

Next to me, Denver grips the edge of the table like he's about to launch himself up and over.

"Our dear aeronauts were held prisoner on the Youli home world for fifteen years. Then the miraculous happened. The Youli attacked again, this time taking two young Bounders hostage. But these Bounders were ready. They used their skills and wielded their advanced technology to thwart the Youli. One paid the ultimate price. The other, Jasper Adams, brought the lost aereonauts home."

Denver pushes to his feet. "I've heard enough. Turn it off!"

"Come on, Den." Lucy tips her head and smiles. "This story is absolutely riveting."

"That. Did. Not. Happen." Denver's jaw is clenched, and his hands are balled into fists.

I'm still playing the words back in my head. Finally, it all clicks into place. "Paid the ultimate price? Is part of the story that Mira died?"

Lucy's lips turn down, and I swear her eyes fill with tears. "I'm so sorry, Jasper."

I jump up next to Denver. "But it's not true! She's not dead! The Youli have her!"

The door to the conference room clicks shut. "It's true now."

I turn around. Denver spins so fast, he almost loses his balance. Neither of us knew Admiral Eames was standing at the door. She must have come in when the vid clip was playing.

"Cora, this is absurd!" Denver says. "I refuse to be a part of it!"

"You'll refer to me as *Admiral*," she replies, crossing the room to join Lucy at the front. "I know this is difficult, but it's necessary. We're at war, and one of our greatest weapons is propaganda. If we're to defeat the Youli, we need the support of our people. This story is how that support is secured."

"But why not go with the truth?" I ask.

"How do you suggest we do that?" Admiral Eames asks.

"How do we explain to the Earth people why these aeronauts haven't aged a day? They know the Youli have advanced technology. They'll blame it on our enemy. It's the easiest explanation."

"Tell them about the rift!" I say.

"Absolutely not. Knowledge that the rift exists is top-level security clearance only. We may be able to use the rift for our own military purposes at some point in the future. More important, however, is that our intelligence confirms not all the Youli know how the lost aeronauts got back. You were right about one thing, Officer Adams. There's division within the Youli ranks. We're not about to hand them secrets on a silver platter."

I can't believe they want us to tell this ridiculous lie! And I can't believe that almost everyone in the room is nodding in agreement, like what the admiral said makes perfect sense! How come I get the feeling that Denver and I and maybe Bai are the only ones who think this is a horrible idea? Why don't the other lost aeronauts speak up? Is following orders more important than the truth?

"What about Mira?" I ask.

Before the admiral can reply, Lucy hops up. "It's all about the narrative! All of Earth already knows you and Mira! Having you both be featured in this story—you as the young hero, and Mira as the martyr—just adds to the drama! They'll eat it up!"

"What do you mean they already know us?"

"Like I told you, you're our poster boy, Jasper! And Mira is our poster girl!" She waves a hand at Jayne. "Pull up the images."

Jayne pokes around on her tablet. First, the screen is filled with the image I saw yesterday of me with the words PROTECTING OUR PLANET COMES AT A PRICE superimposed over my face. The image slides to the left, and a second slides in beside it. It's a picture of Mira. Her long blond braid is pulled over her left shoulder, and she stares off to the side. These three words are printed on the bottom: BEAUTY. COURAGE. SACRIFICE.

I keep rereading the words beneath Mira's face, but they don't make any sense. "What are these?"

Lucy nods at Jayne. "They're part of our pro-Bounder propaganda campaign," Jayne says quietly. "These images have been all over the webs for close to a year. Physical posters were distributed across the planet."

Oh my God.

"And now you've returned from the dead!" Lucy claps her hands. "What a story!"

"Mira's not dead," I say.

"To us, she is," Admiral Eames says before leaving the room, closing the door just as firmly as when she arrived.

I'm still shaking when they wheel in the lunch carts.

"I need a break," I tell Lucy, who's squeezed into the space next to me so she can talk to Denver.

"Perfect timing, let's eat!" She calls Jayne over. "We're breaking for lunch. Please go get those updated numbers from the press room."

"Seriously, Lucy," I say. "I need to get out of here. Let me take a walk or something. Please!"

"Jasper can come with me," Jayne says.

Lucy grimaces. I'm sure she'll say no, but then she waves a hand at Jayne. "Fine, but don't be long."

"Thanks," I say to Jayne once we exit the room. She tries to make conversation as we walk through the halls, but I can't bring myself to talk much. If I do, I'll probably start screaming about how horrible the Force is, and then they'll either lock me up or haul me back to that training room and not let me leave until our passenger craft is loaded and ready to leave for Earth.

She stops at a chute cube and opens the door. I could have sworn this led to the structure with the sensory gym, not the one with the press room, but it's not like my sense of direction is at all reliable.

"After you," she says.

That's right. Jayne refuses to go first. Just one of many things that have annoyed me since I got to the space station two days ago.

When I arrive at the trough on the other side, I'm even more sure we're nowhere near the press room. As soon as I climb out, Jayne slides in behind me.

"Where are we going?" I ask.

Jayne grins. "He speaks."

I follow her out of the chute cube and down the hall at her usual fast clip. "Are you taking me to the sensory gym?"

Jayne smiles. "Nope."

She stops at the door to the pod hall. It buzzes open after scanning her eye. We walk into the dark hall. It smells faintly of dust and gym clothes.

I'm still super irritated, but being in the pod hall makes me feel at least a tiny bit better. "How long since anyone's been in here?"

She shrugs. "A while. Shortly after the Battle of the Alkalinian Seat, Admiral Eames promoted the Bounders and overhauled the training program. Now all bounding exercises mimic military engagements and are conducted in the hangar or off-site. This pod hall hasn't been used in months. Anyhow, I thought you'd enjoy visiting a familiar spot. Waters's pod room is where the magic started, right? It's where the all-star pod first bonded."

"If you say so." A week ago I would have agreed. Now, I don't know what to think. Our pod has been ripped apart. We stand on different sides of a huge chasm. Lucy and Cole feel like strangers. I don't know when I'll see Marco again. And I may never see Mira. As far as everybody else is concerned, she's dead.

We head to the last door in the hall, and Jayne stands aside to let me enter. At least our pod room hasn't changed. There's the same green grass carpet and starry sky ceiling. The familiar lava lamps and colored sticks line the shelves. Our bright beanbags dot the floor. I fling myself down on my favorite turquoise bag.

Jayne sits cross-legged in front of me. "Okay, I'm an open book."

"What?"

"I figure we have about thirty minutes before Lucy starts trying to track me down. I know you have questions about what you missed this past year. Fire away."

"Really? What about that data from the press room?"

Jayne grins. "I downloaded it directly to my tablet during our morning session. Now, what do you want to know?"

I can't believe Jayne is making this offer. It must be incredibly risky, especially with all the paranoia about the mole. "Why are you doing this? You could get in huge trouble."

Jayne leans forward, staring at me somberly with her purple eyes. "You're not wrong, but I think you deserve some answers. But if you want me to be one hundred percent honest, I'm doing it for Addy."

"My sister? Why?"

"We're friends, Jasper. Even now I consider her a friend. I know she'd want you to know the truth."

I smile. Jayne is totally right. How many times did Addy complain about me keeping things from her, especially when it came to Earth Force? "Addy always hated secrets. Okay, so what happened on Alkalinia? Who died?"

"The whole story would take too long, but you being the hero is not just part of the Earth Force narrative. If you hadn't gotten the shield down, we probably all would have died. As it was, all of the Bounders survived—except you and Mira, although we know now that you didn't die, you were just lost in the rift. Some of the more senior Earth Force officers weren't as lucky."

Jayne goes on to list many of the men and women who died that day. Some of the names sound familiar, but most of them were combat soldiers who I didn't really know. The one exception is Chief Auxiliary Officer Wade Johnson—Bad Breath. I'm certainly not happy that Bad Breath died, but I don't feel that awful, either. I'd rather it be him than one of the Bounders.

Still, I'd rather no one had to give their lives that day. If only I could have gotten that shield down earlier.

"You must have more questions," Jayne says.

Do I ever. "Why did my sister and Marco join the Resistance?"

"I'm not sure, but I have my suspicions. They jumped

ship after your funeral, immediately after we rolled out the war campaign. Sadly, I'm pretty sure the Force told your parents that Addy is now presumed dead, too, even though they know she's with the Resistance."

I cringe. I hate to think about Addy and my parents believing I was dead, sitting through my funeral. My parents had to do that twice? They thought they'd lost both of their kids? I can't dwell on that. We don't have much time, and there's a lot more I want to know.

"Tell me about the Resistance."

Jayne folds her hands in her lap and tips her gaze to the grass-green carpet. When she finally lifts her eyes, her face is unreadable. "The Resistance opposes Earth Force. They disagree with the Force's methods, their dominion over lesser developed planets, and the war with the Youli. They're pushing for Earth's entrance into the Intragalactic Council. Your old pod leader, Jon Waters, is at the helm, and a number of Bounders and Tunnelers have joined him."

That sounds a lot like the concerns Waters has hinted at since I met him during my first tour of duty. "The Force's methods . . . Do you mean all the secrecy?"

"That's certainly part of it."

Addy was already fired up about those issues before joining Earth Force. And the truth is, I care about them, too. "When the Force informed the public about the Youli War, did they also tell them about the Resistance? Was that part of the war campaign?"

"The Resistance? No. The Force hasn't publicly acknowledged the existence of the Resistance. They did inform the people of Earth about the Youli, but let's just say it wasn't the whole truth. Lots of things were coordinated with the announcement—yours and Mira's funeral, the propaganda campaign, the planetary curfews and lockdowns, the increased military presence, the criminalization of antiwar messaging."

"So what *did* Earth Force say about the war? And why did they say anything at all?"

"There were too many rumors running around that came way too close to the truth about the Youli and the Bounder Baby Breeding Program. Earth Force needed to take control of the message. They, or I guess we should say *we*, blamed the Battle of the Alkalinian Seat on the Youli, although we didn't give any details about the battle. The story is that we were engaged in a basic military operation and were ambushed. The Youli slaughtered our officers, including two young Bounders who died valiantly defending their people and their planet."

"Me and Mira."

Jayne nods. "As you heard earlier today, we've now changed the story up a bit. You and Mira were kidnapped and went on to rescue the lost aeronauts. But back then, we turned all the panic buttons up to full volume, informing the public that all of Earth Force's might would be put to defending the planet from the Youli. We scared the public into believing that an attack on Earth soil was imminent. That way, if the Resistance launched an operation, Earth Force could blame the Youli. And if there was no violence, well, then the Force's efforts were working and deserved full support."

Wow. They really plotted it all out. The story even makes sense to me, although there's barely an ounce of truth to it. The only fact they got right is that we're at war with the Youli. "You know, I never really understood why the Youli don't attack Earth, or at least knock us down a few notches in battle. They must have the ability to annihilate us."

Jayne again drops her gaze to the grassy carpet and bites her lip. Time stretches, and I think she's not going to say anything. Maybe I stepped over some invisible line that she's not willing to cross.

"I don't know why, Jasper," she finally says, "but I have suspicions. You're right: if the Youli wanted to defeat Earth, we wouldn't be here. Our planet would have been destroyed long before we were born. The Youli's attacks are little more than a big brother's slap on the wrist. I don't think they want to destroy us. It's just that there are rules in the galaxy, and Earth isn't playing by them."

It almost sounds like Jayne is sympathetic to the Youli's position—the *Resistance's* position. Could that be true?

Before I can ask, Jayne shrugs and laughs like her comment was nothing more than a joke. "But who says the Youli get to make the rules, right? We need to assert *our* rights. Our PR campaigns help unify our planet at a time of war. That's important."

I guess, but that sounds a lot like something Lucy might say. I'm not clear at all on what Jayne actually believes, but there's no time for that now.

She answers a few more questions about what happened over the past year, but soon she checks her wristlet. We need to head back.

"Wait!" I say when Jayne stands. "Before we go, there's something else. Until Earth Force announced the Lost Heroes Homecoming Tour, my parents thought I was dead. They must be desperate to talk to me. Can you help me contact them?"

Jayne scrunches up her face. "Hmmm . . . that's tricky. There's a strict ban on outside communication." She paces the room, clearly thinking. "You know what I can do? Let's record a vid message for your parents. I'll be able to send it to them later today via our PR channels. But we need to hurry—Lucy will be wondering where we are."

I close my eyes. "That would be great. Thank you so much!"

Jayne films me as I put on a happy face and smile for the camera, assuring my parents that I'm fine and looking forward to seeing them soon in Americana East, the third stop on the Lost Heroes Homecoming Tour.

On the way back, Jayne rides in front on the chute. That must mean she's starting to trust me. That we're friends. It doesn't change the fact that things totally suck, but it does make me smile for a second before I'm sucked into the chute.

IT'S IMPOSSIBLE TO RIDE ON A PASSENGER craft and not think about my pod mates. During my very first trip to the EarthBound Academy, I bonded with Cole and Lucy, chatting about the fierceness rankings of the famous aeronauts, hitting up plebes for snacks, comparing *Evolution of Combat* stats. Since then, every time I've ridden on one of these ships, I've been with my friends.

Today, it's me and the Earth Force propaganda machine.

At least we finally made the shift to FTL. Now everything out the window is a blur. Before, I had a clear view of the dozen gunner ships escorting our passenger craft to Earth. First stop on the Lost Heroes Homecoming Tour: Eurasia East.

Jayne tried to cheer me up, but I zoned out during her many attempts at small talk, and she quickly tired of my terrible mood.

How could my attitude not be terrible? My sister and one of my best friends are AWOL and rumored to be joined up with the Resistance. My other two best friends have moved on and moved over me in Earth Force. And then there's Mira—Mira, who didn't want to come back with me, who chose the Youli over me, who left me to deal with all this mess alone.

I close my eyes and try to shut out all the noise on the passenger craft.

Mira? Can you hear me? Where are you?

I open my mind as wide as I possibly can, all the while repeating my call for Mira like a beacon across the cosmos. A lonely, unheard cry in the dark.

Puke. I sound as dramatic as Lucy.

Then I sense a presence. *Mira?*

A finger jabs my shoulder. "Scoot, kid." Denver stands in the aisle staring down at me.

I unbuckle and slide over. I can't believe I thought I'd reached Mira. I must be losing my mind.

Denver plops onto the chair I just gave up. "I've got some questions for you."

"You mean about the tour?" I haven't paid attention to anything anyone's said about the tour since the first half of our training session yesterday, and I certainly haven't read the stack of materials Lucy hand delivered to me last night before I went to bed. "See, the thing is, I have the script, but I haven't had a chance to memorize the speaking parts that Lucy—that's Lucy Dugan, the assistant press secretary—gave me, and—"

"Forget the script. We won't follow that anyway, not if I can help it."

"Do you mean you plan to tell the truth?"

"Which truth?" Denver laughs and rolls his eyes. "I don't like it any more than you, kid, but it's what has to be. Our esteemed Admiral Eames had words with me last night. Apparently, planetary security depends on me toeing the party line. I don't particularly want to be court-martialed." His voice softens. "And, truth be told, I trust her, so I'll do as she asks. I suggest you do, too."

I nod. If anything has been made crystal clear to me over the last forty-eight hours, it's that I'm expected to follow orders.

Denver crosses his leg over the opposite knee. "I'm here because I want to talk about you."

"Umm . . . okay . . ." This has taken a turn for the strange.

"Here's the thing, kid. Our fellow officers have done an admirable job bringing me up to speed on recent history, and I've spent much of my downtime reading historical web reports, but I still have questions."

"And you think *I* have the answers?" The concept that anyone would think to come to me for answers about anything is almost laugh-out-loud funny. I bite my lip so I don't accidentally let a laugh slip.

"On this subject, yes," he says. "I don't understand what you do, as a Bounder, that is. I understand the science behind quantum bounding, of course. I was one of the original aeronauts. But bounding without a ship? That's all new to me. No one has been able to explain it to me in a way that makes sense. So I figured I'd ask a Bounder, and you're the only one I know."

"You must know Lucy."

"The PR princess? Sure, but I wasn't about to subject myself voluntarily to another round of her incessant talking."

This time, I do laugh out loud. "Yeah, Lucy can be chatty."

"That's an understatement." He scans the craft until he spots Lucy in the far corner talking to some of her staff. "Do you know her well?"

A small, sad smile settles on my face. "She was my pod mate. A few days ago she was quizzing me about a crush in our quarters in Alkalinia, although that was more than a year ago in Earth time. A lot has happened since then."

"You're telling me, kid." Denver sighs and shakes his head. "Don't take me down that road. It's a slippery slope filled with potholes and black ice and roadblocks. Back to my question.

What's this shipless bounding like? Do you just wave your gloved hands and—presto?"

"Not really." How do I explain bounding to someone who has no experience with the gloves? I think back to our first time in the Ezone. "You have to merge with the gloves in a way. They become part of you and make you bigger than yourself at the same time. It's like they amplify what's already there. When I use my gloves to tap into my deeper consciousness, the universe makes sense in a way I can't explain. And it's not just that I can see and understand at a heightened level, it's that I can actually manipulate matter like I *am* the universe."

"You're the master of the universe. *Right.*"

"That's not what I mean. With the gloves, I can see what I'm made of. Literally. And I can use that knowledge to move myself, replicate myself, anywhere in the galaxy."

Denver's face is scrunched in thought. "So the gloves enable you to map and replicate atoms just like the computers on the bounding ships?"

"Yeah. Kind of." That's not how it works at all, really, but I guess it's as close as someone who has never experienced the gloves can come to understanding.

"And this is how the aliens—the Youli—magically appear places?"

"Basically," I say. "In fact, the glove technology came from them."

He sits back in his seat. "What do you mean?"

"If you ever thought your time in the rift was for nothing, you're wrong. It's above my clearance, but I think Earth Force took a Youli prisoner during the Incident at Bounding Base 51. It was after the Incident that they were able to develop the gloves. The gloves are made from Youli biotechnology."

Denver runs a hand through his hair. "That's a lot to take in. Why didn't I know this?"

"Maybe it's above your clearance level now, too."

He rolls his eyes. "A lot of things are above my clearance, and as we heard yesterday, I can't be sure anything I'm told is the truth. Never mind that now. Show me."

"Huh?"

"Show me how you bound."

I laugh. "No. Like I said, I need the gloves to bound. And even if I did have my gloves—which I don't, since they were lost on Alkalinia—I couldn't use them here. I'm sure they have bound detection activated and probably even a quantum scrambler. It's the primary defense against the Youli."

"Ah!" Denver nods. "That makes sense. If the green guys can't jump through space, it makes it a lot harder for them to sneak up on you. When are you getting new gloves?"

"I don't know." I'm sure Denver can hear the irritation in my voice. If there's one thing this conversation has brought into hyperfocus, it's the fact that I'm completely defenseless without my gloves. "I think the powers that be are worried that if I have my gloves I might be tempted to use them."

"Isn't that the whole point? You Bounders are the new front line against the Youli."

"Not while I'm on the Lost Heroes Homecoming Tour. My value as part of the Earth Force propaganda plan is more important." I cringe as soon as the words leave my mouth. Sure, Denver seems to be on the same page as me when it comes to all the Earth Force lies, but he's still one of the highest-regarded Earth Force officers of all time. I shouldn't risk bad-mouthing the Force to his face, especially now that Admiral Eames reminded him of his responsibilities. "Sorry. I shouldn't have said that."

Denver laughs. "Don't be, kid. You're exactly right. Your friend Lucy is the face of the greatest propaganda machine in the galaxy. I don't need level-one clearance to tell you that."

Despite my stubborn grumpiness, I can't help feeling happy when the image of Earth fills the front window of the craft. I'm going home.

Even though it hasn't been that long in Jasper time, it's been more than a year in Earth time, and now I can really feel how long it's been. I feel it in my bones and in my heart. It's like on some level my body registers the passage of time even though my mind can't. I hope Jayne got my message to my parents. I want them to know that I'm really okay.

Once we descend through the cloud layer, the sprawling metropolis of Eurasia East can be seen in the distance. Even closer, though, is the famous Great Wall. It stretches over twenty thousand kilometers and has been around for thousands of years. It's even visible from space! Everyone in the craft is glued to the window.

We touch down at the aeroport to the north of the city. Our tour dates and locations have been widely publicized, but our arrival details have been kept under wraps, so there's not a lot of fanfare when we exit the passenger craft—unless you count all the starstruck ground officers who can't stop staring at the lost aeronauts. They usher us to a row of waiting hovercars.

Lucy disappears into the first hover with some of the senior PR officers. Jayne is left to direct the rest of us. She refers to her tablet and waves the old aeronauts into the hover behind Lucy. The rest of the PR staff takes the next hover, leaving Jayne and me behind with the last one in line.

"Looks like you're stuck with me," she says, ducking into the hover. I climb in after her.

We zoom through the streets of what's officially called Eurasia East, but which most people call Beijing after the old Chinese city that used to be here. It's less likely to be confused with Eurasia Central, where Moscow used to be, or Eurasia

West, where Paris used to be. In most ways, Beijing looks just like Americana East—tall skyscrapers on a grid, one after the next—but there are also some differences. The gardens in the green blocks have ponds and lots of rocks, and they've preserved some of their historic buildings and temples.

But that's not the only difference. There are guards strapped with weapons on every corner and armed hovers cruise the streets. It's nothing like the Americana East I remember, but if what Jayne told me in the pod room is true, it's probably like Americana East today.

Now Earth is "officially" at war, and it needs to look the part.

"I can't believe I'm here," I say to Jayne. "I'm not sure about this tour. I don't feel like much of a hero."

"You *are* a hero, Jasper," she says. "You took the shield down on Alkalinia. Like I told you before, if you hadn't done that, Earth Force would have been destroyed. All of the Bounders would have died."

"I guess." I fiddle with the control panel on the hover's central console.

"It's true," Jayne continues. "Thanks to you, we dealt a huge blow to the Youli and the Alks. Just as important, we wiped out the Alks' venom stockpile. Without those black-market sales, the Alks are no longer a factor on the intragalactic scene."

I hit one of the buttons on the console, and the windows in the back of the hover shade to dark gray. "Admiral Eames put so much stock in our alliance with the Alkalinians. It must have been a big blow to us, too."

"True, but the Alks sold us out, Jasper. There was no avoiding that. Plus, we took captives and were able to secure a ton of intelligence." Jayne hits another button on the console, and a soundproof divider rolls up between the passenger and driver compartments. "You may not know this, but the degradation patch your pod placed on the Youli vessel worked. It caused tons of confusion with the Youli's organic communications systems, and it drove a wedge within their society. Apparently, they don't see with one mind anymore."

In other words, there's division within their ranks, just like the Youli told us in the rift. Cole wanted me to question whether that was true, or whether it really mattered. This information is definitely above my clearance level. I'm lucky Jayne is willing to bend the rules. The question is: Why?

"Oh, look!" She points out the window. "See the crowd? They're here for the heroes, Jasper. They're here for *you!*"

Up ahead, the entire city block is mobbed with people. The nucleus of the crowd is a tall building bearing the Earth Force Insignia above its main entrance. That must be where we're headed.

As our hovers approach, the crowds go wild, cheering and

shouting. They push against a blockade manned by rows of guards, all with their weapons drawn. Spectators spill to the sides of the blockade, and as our hovers part the crowd, people slam against the car, pounding on the windows, banging on the hood.

At first, I instinctively recoil and cover my head. Slowly I lower my hands and stare as desperate faces press against the windows, eager for a glimpse inside our hover. The guards push them back, clearing a path.

We glide to a stop behind the other hovers in a barricaded area in front of the building. The crowd swarms around us. Lots of people hold placards in the air. Close to half of them are posters of me—the old ones and the new ones. They wave my face in the air and scream at the hovers.

My hands shake. "I don't know if I can do this."

Jayne grins. "Get ready to be famous, Jasper Adams!" She opens the door and steps out of the hover.

"It's Jasper!" A spectator spots me in the hover and jumps the barricade. A guard dives for her, but she's too fast.

Shouts rise up and crystallize in a chant: "Jasper! Jasper! Jasper!"

The guard stops her with an electric pulse and slams her to the ground.

"Stop!" I shout, hurrying out of the hover, but I can't even hear myself over the crowd.

MONICA TESLER

Another girl hops the barricade, even though she must have seen what happened to the first. She lunges for me, throwing her arms around my neck. Guards pulls her off and drag her away, but not before she slips a piece of paper in my hand.

Earth Force officers take me by the arms and rush me to the building entrance. The noise level never dips until I'm safely inside the Earth Force headquarters.

Once I'm through the revolving doors, Lucy runs over. "Oh my goodness! This is amazing, isn't it? I knew the tour would draw crowds, but I never expected quite this amount of hoopla right at the start. What do you think? Are you enjoying being a hero?"

"It's kind of intense," I say. "How did they know we would be here? I thought only our tour dates were released."

Lucy winks. "Let's just say I thought we needed a teaser for the webs to generate buzz. Jayne did an excellent job at letting a little detail of our schedule slip out, don't you think? Did you see the cameras? I hope they caught some footage of my face. Your face, too, of course. It was just so crowded. Ha! I never imagined that being too crowded could be a problem."

When Lucy moves on to talk to someone else, I unfold the paper the girl slipped me outside. It's her web address and a handwritten note: *Message me.* The words are ringed by pink hearts.

Meanwhile, guards escort a team of cameramen in through a side door.

I fold the paper back up and stuff it in my pocket. I weave through the lobby to avoid the cameramen and look for Jayne. She's standing with some of the lost aeronauts. When she sees me, she waves me over.

She finishes talking to Bai Liu, then traces her finger down her tablet screen. "Here you are, Jasper, room 3217. That's on the thirty-second floor, just down the hall from me, actually. I'm in room 3210, so feel free to stop by if you need anything. Oh, by the way, I asked Earth Force to provide you with some toiletries and a fresh set of uniforms. The trunk should already be in your room. I'm sorry all your personal effects on Alkalinia were lost."

I shrug. Most of what I lost was Earth Force stuff anyway. The only things I really miss are my gloves.

"A guard will be by with your tablet," she continues. "It has the schedule for the tour already loaded. You'll see we have rehearsal tomorrow morning first thing. Don't be late! The lock for your room should be preprogrammed with your lens signature. See you bright and early!" She points me to the elevator and turns to help the other lost aeronauts, who are waiting for their room assignments.

The lift dings and opens. I step inside, and the doors close, leaving me pleasantly alone. After the trip from the space station and the crowds outside, I could use some alone time. I exit on the thirty-second floor and follow the hall until I reach room 3217. When I tip my eye to the scanner, the door buzzes open.

I walk in and look around. There's a small kitchenette and table in front of me and a room with a couch and a large window to the left. Then I realize someone's sitting on the couch. Did I get the room wrong?

I'm about to double-check when the person stands.

"Hello, Jasper."

It takes a few seconds for me to process, and then—

"Gedney!"

I PRACTICALLY HURDLE THE COUCH TO get to Gedney and give him a hug. He feels frail and familiar. Even though I'm used to seeing him in his lab clothes, he couldn't look more Gedney than now in an old brown coat that smells of peppermint and old books.

"What are you doing here?" I ask as we sit on the couch.

"I came to see you, of course." He pats my shoulder. "I've been worried about you, son." Leaning close, he adds in a conspiratorial tone, "And you know I couldn't resist the chance to talk to someone who's traveled to the rift and back."

Gedney was the one who'd theorized that the rift existed.

He told us about it in Alkalinia. It's not a surprise that he wants to hear about the rift from someone who's actually been there.

He winks. "Not to mention, I thought you may have a need for these." Opening his worn leather briefcase, he withdraws a small black sack and hands it to me.

"What's this?" I loosen the drawstring and reach inside. "Oh yes!" I'd know that gauzy material anywhere. I pull the gloves from the bag. "How did you find them?"

"These aren't your original gloves, I'm afraid," Gedney says. "Those were lost on Alkalinia. In a thousand years, once that ocean finally detoxifies, some fisherman will be in for a surprise when she pulls those up from the depths. I got to work on the new ones as soon as I heard you were back. I made some for Mira, as well, but I understand she wasn't so lucky."

How much should I tell Gedney about what happened to Mira? He knows about the rift, so he knows the Earth Force narrative is fiction. Even though he definitely doesn't have the clearance level for the truth, I can't let him think that Mira is dead. "Well, that's not exactly true."

He raises a hand. "You don't need to say another word, son. I already had my suspicions, and I certainly didn't come here to put you in an awkward position." Leaning back against the couch cushions, he changes the subject. "My blood sugar is a bit low. I snooped around before you arrived and found a fully stocked pantry and refrigerator. How about you pour us a glass of juice and fill me in on the rift?"

Gedney and I spend the next hour talking. He asks a million questions about the rift. I don't know the answers to most of them, like *what was the temperature?* (kind of cool, I guess), *was there water?* (the air felt damp and it was foggy, so maybe), and *did you know while you were there that you were experiencing a different time progression?* (yeah, once we found the lost aeronauts, but that's because they told us they'd only been there two days). No matter how many half answers I give, he always has another question. I don't think I've ever seen him more excited. It must be pretty cool when one of your most out-there theories ends up being true.

As I'm describing the mushy ground and the all-consuming grayness of the rift for at least the twentieth time, an enormous yawn swallows the last of my words.

Gedney puts his hands on his knees and slowly stands. I think he's even more hunched over than the last time I saw him. "It's best I let you get some rest. I'm sure they have your schedule filled."

I roll my eyes. "That's an understatement. We have rehearsal for the rallies first thing tomorrow morning, and I heard a rumor about a stylist appointment." I've been ignoring that tidbit. The last thing I want to do is be styled. I'm not even sure what that means, but I know it will be awful.

Gedney laughs. "Better you than me, son." He holds the edge of the couch for support and lowers his voice. "Jasper, before I go, there's one thing I want to discuss."

I lean closer to him. Whatever he wants to talk about sounds serious.

"As I said before," he says, "I don't want to put you in a compromising position, but there is something you should know." He waits until he's sure I'm paying attention before continuing. "Despite the many warnings to the contrary, Earth Force is not currently using a quantum scrambler on the planet's surface. They've been disabled. The Force is hoping to catch the mole red-handed (or red-gloved, if you prefer the literal), and their intelligence just revealed the culprit is likely to be on Earth at the present moment."

Why is he telling me this? As I raise my eyebrows, Gedney lowers his gaze to the black sack on my lap.

"Oh! So I can use my gloves?"

"Exactly," he whispers. "There are, however, quantum detection sensors everywhere. That much of the excessive security is the absolute truth, although the reasons have not as much to do with the war effort as they claim. So if you were to use your gloves to travel somewhere discreetly, you would want to make sure you were in a private location, somewhere you could complete your port and bound before you were identified, perhaps somewhere underground where quantum detection sensors can't quite reach. Don't spread that last piece of information around. Not many know about the sensors' limitations."

"Okay . . ." What exactly is he trying to tell me?

"And one more thing: I'm traveling from here directly back to my labs. You remember them, don't you?"

"Of course I do." How could I forget? We stayed at his labs for an entire week practicing with the BPS before our second tour of duty.

"Good. Then presumably you also recall exactly where they're located."

Before I can reply, Gedney starts for the door. Before he steps out, he turns back to me and places his hand on my shoulder. "It was great to see you, Jasper. Take care of yourself. You are one of a kind. One of the *best* kind."

The door closes behind him.

I pour another glass of juice and return to the couch. It's quiet aside from the occasional hum from the lift as it passes by the thirty-second floor. I hold my new gloves in my hands, trailing my fingers across the gauzy fabric.

What was Gedney talking about? I mean, *do I remember exactly where his laboratory is located?* Why would he ask me that? It must have been a message or have some kind of layered meaning.

Wait a second . . . that's it! He must have been asking if

I remembered the lab's exact location so that I'd be able to bound there!

But why would I need to bound there?

I'm not sure, but I'm happy to have the option.

I stuff my gloves safely back into the black drawstring bag. I need to keep these safe. And quiet.

At exactly 0600 the next morning, every light in my room turns on and Florine Statton shouts, "Time to get up! Time to get up, puhleeeze!"

What on earth? I must be having a nightmare. I squish my pillow over my head.

"Officer Adams, wake up, puh-leeeze! It's time to get up!"

If I'm not having a nightmare, that means Florine Statton is in my room.

"Get up, Officer Adams!"

I bolt up in bed and scan the room. There's no sign of anyone—definitely not Florine.

"I sense you are still in bed, Officer Adams. I must insist that you get up!" The words seem to come from the room itself.

No Florine. No whiff of roses (although that could be Lucy these days). But still, that voice!

Oh! I get it. This must be like Cole's room. Florine Statton is the voice of the room's computer.

I drop my feet to the floor.

"Officer Adams, get—"

"Shut up!" I shout. "I'm getting up." Florine must really be slipping in popularity if she's stooped to doing voice-overs for guest room computer systems. Lucy has truly taken her place as the face of Earth Force.

"Very well, Mr. Adams. You are expected downstairs in fifty-four minutes."

That means I could have slept for at least another half hour. "Hey, Florine!"

"Yes, Jasper Adams?"

"Tomorrow I only need twenty minutes to get ready, okay?"

"That will require an override."

The Force even controls when I sleep? Great.

I drag myself to the bathroom. After a hot shower, I dig through the trunk Jayne had delivered for me. It's filled with a full set of Earth Force uniforms—dress, dailies, shoes, even a new Earth Force coat. There's also a brand-new blast pack. I can't wait to use that!

I hold up the dress uniform. It looks huge, at least a size bigger than the one I used last tour. I head back to the bathroom and stand in front of the mirror. Am I really that much taller? I turn my head from side to side. My skin's not the greatest these days. There's a kind of nasty pimple on my nose. Other than that, I look exactly how I've always looked. Except maybe my jaw's a bit pointier. And maybe my shoulders are a bit wider. I drag my fingers through my messy, wet hair.

After I get dressed, I pour a glass of juice from my fridge and sit down at the small kitchen table. It's only 0615.

"Hey, Florine!"

"How may I be of service, Officer Adams?"

Florine Statton asking what she can do for *me*? I could definitely get used to this room computer. "Make that fifteen minutes."

"Noted, Officer Adams."

"So can I get that override?"

"You will need to clear that with your superiors."

Terrific. I'll have to ask Jayne if I can sleep in. It seems like I shouldn't have to ask permission for that. "Fine. Turn off . . . or . . . whatever it is you do when I'm not here. I'm going to find some breakfast."

"Understood. Have a great day, Officer Adams."

"Thanks. You, too." Geez. Now I'm talking to a computer. And not just any computer, a Florine Statton computer. I'm worse than Cole.

I pound the rest of my juice, grab my new blast pack, and am halfway out the door before I stop. Earth Force is so focused on catching the mole that I wouldn't put it past them to search rooms. I shouldn't leave my gloves here. I head back to my bedroom and extract the gloves from their soft pouch. I stuff them in a side pocket of my blast pack.

Wait . . . what if they search my blast pack? I take the gloves out of the pack and lay them on my bed. If there's anything to take from Gedney's visit, it's that these gloves might prove to be very important. Where should I put them to make sure they stay safe? I pull up my pant legs and slip one glove into each sock. It's not the most comfortable solution, but at least they're safe.

I open my door and nearly collide with Bai Liu, who's sprinting down the hall in shorts and a tank top. Her muscles are enormous. I better stay on Bai's good side.

"Morning," she says when we reach the elevator bank. "Figured I'd head out for a run before breakfast to see how much the place has changed."

"This is where you're from?" I ask.

The elevator dings, and the doors peel back.

She nods as we walk on. "It's surreal. I feel like I've been gone six months, but in reality, I haven't set foot here in fifteen years."

That must be strange. I feel pretty weird about missing a whole year. The lost aeronauts have been gone longer than I've been alive. "Do you have family coming to the visiting hour before the rally tonight?"

Bai's shoulders droop, and she stares at her shoes. "Sort of.

My mother died when I was young, and apparently my father died while I was in the rift. My wife remarried. She's coming, but I don't know if I'd call her family anymore."

I watch the numbers count down on the elevator panel. "I'm sorry."

We ride the rest of the way in silence. There's not much to say. I've been so focused on myself, I never fully realized how bittersweet this homecoming must be for the lost aeronauts. Life went on without them. Even for the ones whose *welcome homes* are better than Bai's, there's no getting around the fact that they've missed a huge chunk of life.

Bai gets off at the ground floor, and I continue on to the basement where the dining hall is located. I'm starving, and for once I feel pretty confident about what I might find to eat. After all, we're on Earth.

The dining hall is basically deserted. I head to the kitchen line and take a peek. There are noodles, tofu pudding, and three different kinds of steamed buns. I'm guessing those are traditional Eurasian foods. There's also a large vat of rice porridge with toppings like dried fruits, nuts, and honey. A huge pan of fluffed tofu sits under a heat lamp (no surprise there— Earth Force loves its fluffed tofu, the galaxy's most efficient food source). Next to the tofu, something delicious catches my eye: pancakes. I toss a steamed bun on my plate and then heap on a stack of pancakes with butter and maple syrup.

I find a table in the corner and dig in. Shivers run through my body when the sugary syrup hits my taste buds. You'd think I hadn't eaten in a year, which is kind of true. Even the greatest food will never taste quite as good as it used to, though, not after Alkalinia.

I get the feeling that someone is staring at me. I take a break from the pancakes and look around. Sure enough, an EFAN cameraman is headed my way, his lens already locked on my face. He stops on the other side of the table and adjusts his zoom lens.

"You really expect me to eat while you're filming?"

No response.

"Did you film me asking that?" Ugh. This is going to ruin a perfectly good breakfast.

"Get lost!" Jayne's bright voice calls behind me. When the cameraman doesn't react, she shoves her press badge in his face until he lowers the camera and heads to the food line where others are starting to line up for breakfast.

"Thanks," I say, covering my mouth filled with the giant bite I took while she was getting rid of the cameraman.

"Sure." She sets her tablet down on the table. "Aren't you an early riser!"

Something's different with her hair. She's tied it on the side. And she's painted her eyelids so that her eyes look even more purple. They must loosen up the Earth Force dress code for press events. She looks pretty, not that I care or anything.

"Actually, I'm not an early riser at all," I tell her. "My room computer woke me up. By the way, do they all sound like Florine Statton?"

She laughs. "Apparently, yes. Earth Force upgraded their system a few weeks ago."

"Upgrade? I'm afraid of what the computers must have sounded like before. I asked for a snooze tomorrow, but Florine said I had to get authorization."

Jayne taps on her tablet. "I'll make sure to green-light your snooze since it's clear you can get ready on the fast track."

"What's on the agenda today?"

She tips her head up. "Rehearsal, styling, and then the big rally tonight! Plus a bit of interrogation thrown in for good measure."

"Interrogation?"

"There was another intelligence leak last night. The webs are rattling with news that Earth Force has been holding back information about the aeronauts' rescue."

"You mean they know about the lost time?"

"Only rumors. You don't need to worry. They know you're not the mole. You were stuck in the rift during most of the leaks."

The smell of roses nearly makes me choke on my pancakes. "Good morning, sunshine!" Lucy plants a kiss on my cheek.

"You're just the guy I'm looking for." She slides into the seat across from me. "Are those script changes uploaded?" she asks Jayne in a much less friendly tone.

Jayne and Lucy talk briefly about the script, and then Jayne hurries out of the dining hall, leaving me and Lucy alone at the table.

"You were looking for me?" I remind Lucy. I'm ready for seconds on pancakes, but Lucy will consider it a major snub if I leave before she says what she came to say.

"Oh yes!" She leans close. I hold my breath. I don't know what's with the overdose of perfume, but she has to be taking tips from Florine (the real Florine, not the computerized version). "I saw you talking to Denver on the flight yesterday. Did he say anything about me?"

What is this about? Lucy always has an agenda with these types of questions. I think back to the ride and my conversation with Denver. "Actually, yes."

She bites her lip. "Oh my God, what was it?"

Hmmm . . . Denver and I were talking about how Lucy never shuts up. "I kind of forget."

She grabs my hand. "Think, Jasper. What did he say?"

"Not much, really. He asked me if I knew you, and I told him we used to be pod mates."

"He asked about me?" When I nod, she leans even closer. "Okay, Jasper, this is not your forte, but I need some advice. I know in some ways Denver is a lot older than me. But in other ways, he's not that much older. In fact, he was younger than Sheek is now when he went missing. So even though there's a bit of an age difference, it's not terrible, do you think?"

I have no idea what she's asking. "Do I think what?"

"Me and Denver?"

"You and Denver, what?"

She slaps my arm. "Me and Denver together. You know, as a couple. What do you think?"

I burst out laughing. "You're joking, right?"

Lucy glares at me. I guess she wasn't joking.

"Sorry," I stammer. "I must be one of those people who looks at his age the other way. He's a lot older than you, Lucy."

Lucy stands and puts her hands on her hips. "I disagree. Remember, Jasper, I have a lot more life experience than you. While you were in the rift, I was moving up the ranks of Earth Force. We stand on opposite ends of a vast maturity gap." She turns and walks across the dining hall to where the EFAN crew is filming.

I'm pretty sure Lucy just insulted me, but I don't care. I like the view from this side of the maturity gap. At least I'm free to get some more pancakes. I'm going to need them. This is lining up to be a very long day.

12

"PLACES!" LUCY SHOUTS. "PLACES, PLEASE!"

We've already run through the script for today's rally three times. I'm practically asleep on my feet. I got up too early thanks to Computer Florine, and the sugar crash from this morning's maple syrup definitely isn't helping.

"Haven't we been through this enough?" Denver asks, walking to the other side of the Earth Force conference room where we've been practicing. "And where's Max?"

Sheek, Lucy, Denver, and I are the only ones who have speaking roles at the rally. Since Sheek is a no-show (something Lucy won't shut up about), Jayne is reading his lines.

"I guess he's okay with looking like an idiot in front of

millions," Lucy replies, "but I'm not. As I always say, practice makes perfect. In fact, when I was one of the leads in the Pacific Players performance of *Dear Evan Hansen . . .*" I tune Lucy out. I've found I can use her excessive talking time to catch a short snooze.

When I open my eyes, Lucy has Denver by the hand and is walking him back to the group. "What do you say, Den? You want to be at your best tonight, don't you?"

Den? I'm convinced Lucy has extended this rehearsal just so she can spend more time with Denver.

Jayne rolls her eyes. She must have reached the same conclusion.

"One more time," Denver says. "That's it. And no more talking. Stick to the script."

Somehow Lucy turns one more time into five more times. Our rehearsal runs so late we have no break before lunch and then the mandatory Earth Force security training.

I try to hide in the back during training, but I'm not so lucky. After the introduction, we're divided into small groups, and the lost aeronauts and I are sent to a breakaway room

The young officer assigned to us is clearly overwhelmed.

"Is this really necessary?" Bai asks for the second time. Her bad mood hangs in the air like a dark cloud. She must be nervous about the visitation hour immediately after the training.

"Just give us the basics," Denver says to the officer. "All of us went through the security training protocol back at the space station, except maybe the kid, not to mention all of us were thoroughly trained fifteen years ago, when we joined the Force."

I pretend not to understand that *the kid* means me. The last thing I need is a one-on-one training session.

"The security protocol has changed," the officer says. "First, it's important that you review the updated, official Earth Force rules and positions that have been uploaded to your tablets. For example, you are not allowed to talk to your friends and family about the rift, including any mention of the time differential. Stick to the official narrative at all times."

"What am I supposed to say when my ex-wife asks why I haven't aged a day in fifteen years?" Bai asks.

The officer ignores Bai's totally legitimate question and continues reading from his notes. "Second, Earth Force wants to remind you of your confidentiality obligations. When you took your oath, you agreed to follow orders, and that includes complying with all rules pertaining to your security clearance."

"We all know there's a mole," Denver says, "and we all know it's not us. We've been lost in the rift for fifteen years, remember?" He nods at me. "Even the kid's been gone for a year."

I sink deeper into my chair, trying to disappear.

"Third," the security officer continues, "it's imperative that you follow all security precautions in place for the rallies. We are on high alert for a potential incident. Consider this an official warning."

"What kind of incident?" Bai asks.

"We have reason to believe there could be an attack by domestic terrorists."

I sit up. "You mean the Resistance?"

All eyes in the room turn in my direction. So much for disappearing.

How do I explain why I know about the Resistance without spotlighting myself for the security team? "Umm . . . I overheard one of the officers at the space station mention the Resistance. I thought maybe that's what you were talking about."

"That subject is above your clearance level," the officer says. He makes a note on his tablet, probably flagging me for future interrogations.

I don't care too much, because I'm thinking about the Resistance and what his warning might mean. I'm sure I'm the only one here who's excited about the possibility of domestic terrorism. It might help me find out exactly what's going on with my sister.

The hovers drop us off at a large, heavily guarded tower that looks exactly like every other large tower we've passed on our way here. On the outside.

When we walk in, my eyes go wide. It's like walking into Lucy's office times a billion. Everything is either gold or pink and totally over the top. The reception area has five enormous, glittering chandeliers hanging from the ceilings. The floor is covered in a pink plush rug with a twirly gold pattern. Right in the middle of the room is a circular gold desk with a pink robot receptionist.

As soon as we walk in, the robot greets us. Guess whose voice it is? That's right. Florine Statton. Not only is Florine my room computer, she's the pink robot. She must be really desperate for work.

"Greetings and welcome to the Style Gallery. Your design is our desire. How may I assist you?"

Jayne registers our arrival and seconds later we're escorted down the hall to a large room that's just as pink as the first. The ceiling is domed, and the walls are rimmed with pink plush sofas complete with pink pillows with gold tassels. I take a seat next to Denver on the closest sofa to the door, unrealistically hoping I can make a fast getaway.

Lucy is buzzing around, talking a mile a minute, giving a tour of the dome room for the EFAN cameras. She's as excited as I've ever seen her. It's like the Style Gallery was made for Lucy.

"Yoo-hoo!" Lucy calls from the center of the room. She holds her arms to the side and twirls. "Isn't this place fantastic?

You are in for a real treat! We have something super special planned for all of you! The Style Gallery helped *me* find my signature style when I became the fresh face of Earth Force. And today my stylist friends will help you find yours! As they say, your design is their desire!"

I'm pretty sure my dread levels reach record heights. Signature style? No thanks.

The next thing I know, the stylists walk in. They're all wearing pale pink pants and tight shirts striped in pink and gold. Lucy greets each of them with a triple air kiss.

"Is this for real?" Denver whispers beside me during the kissing. "Or is EFAN filming this for a candid camera show?"

"I wish. Knowing Lucy, this is as real as it gets."

Lucy squeals with delight and claps her hands. "I'm just so excited! Each of you have been assigned to one of these fantabulous stylists, who has already developed your signature glam plan! So when they call your name, come on up!"

This is a nightmare. As in, I'm pretty much convinced I'm asleep right now. My sleeping brain has mashed up pod selection from my first tour of duty with my recent visit to Lucy's pink office. That's the only explanation for the horror that's unfolding in front of me.

I pinch my forearm. It hurts. And I don't wake up.

One of the stylists steps forward. She has jet-black hair cut short to her scalp. "Bai Liu?"

Bai tentatively stands. Lucy introduces the pair, and they head off through one of the side doors. Two more aeronauts are called and exit with their stylists.

The next stylist to step forward is actually not one but two. They're virtually indistinguishable from each other. They're both tall and thin with warm brown skin and gold spiky hair that matches the tassels on the pillows.

"We have . . . ," the one on the left starts.

". . . the poster boy himself . . . ," the one on the right continues.

". . . Jasper Adams!" the one on the left finishes.

Great. Double trouble.

Denver slaps my back. "Go get 'em, kid."

I slowly walk across the wide room to where my stylists are waiting.

"Hi, Jasper!" they both say together.

"I'm Nev!"

"And I'm Dev!"

I look from one to the other and back again. "Let me guess, you're twins?"

They exchange a glance and turn back to me with wide smiles. "Bingo!" they say at the same time then erupt in giggles.

"It's obvious we're twins," one of them says, "but still, everyone has to put it out there."

I've already given up telling them apart.

"Right this way, Jasper," the other says, taking me by the arm and leading me through a side door into another room.

"Welcome to our pink palace!" they say together once the door closes behind us.

Palace is the right word. There is even more opulence in here than out there, if that's possible. More pink. More gold. More crystal. Mirrors line all the walls and the ceiling, so there aren't just two, but more like a thousand Devs and Nevs staring back at me. There's a pink table with shelves of perfumes above. There's a gold sink with gold hairbrushes and curling wands and several more styling devices I don't have the names for. There are carts piled high with makeup and hair dye and feathers and other fancy stuff.

In the center of the room is a large, pink, cushioned chaise on gold wheels.

"Will you do us the honors, Jasper?" one of the twins says, gesturing at the chaise.

"Uh, sure . . ."

"It's Dev." The twin points to a small *D* monogrammed over the heart on his shirt. I hadn't noticed it before.

"And I'm Nev," the other twin says, pointing to a monogrammed *N*.

I climb up on the chaise and sink into the soft cushions. It's so comfortable, I almost forget how pink everything is. Almost.

"What's your scent preference?" Dev asks.

"Huh?"

"Scents, aroma, perfume," Nev says. "Shall we try rose?"

I'd almost choked on Lucy's rose perfume. "Definitely not."

"Let's go with lavender," Dev says. "It's classic and relaxing."

Nev nods and retrieves a small glass bottle from the shelf. The next thing I know, lavender-infused mist is blowing through the room.

"So, Jasper," Dev says. At least I think it's Dev. I lost track of them and can't see the monogram from the chaise. "We have to ask. What's with the super-duper security?"

"It was awful," Nev says. "They questioned us all day yesterday. We didn't even get our aeronaut assignment until this morning. Can you imagine? They expected us to come up with a whole glam plan for you in just one morning!"

"There's a mole," I say. "And by the way, I'm not in need of a glam plan."

"You *so* are," Dev says.

"A mole?" Nev asks. "Do tell more."

"I'm not really supposed to talk about it," I say, remembering today's security training. "They've had problems with information leaks, and they're pretty sure there's someone on the inside. Until they find the mole, everyone's a suspect. Well, everyone but me and the lost aeronauts. We definitely weren't leaking information from the rift."

"The where?" they say at the same time.

"Oh . . . uh . . . nowhere . . . just . . . it would have been impossible to leak information while we were locked up by the Youli." The words sound flat as they fall from my mouth. I'm an awful liar. Why can't we just tell the truth? It would be easy to describe the rift to Nev and Dev. It's basically the polar opposite of their grand pink palace.

As Nev and Dev gossip about the lost aeronauts and press me for details—most of them silly things I know nothing about, like Denver's favorite hair product or Bai's exercise routine—they drape a white sheet over me and smooth back my hair with a gigantic band. Next thing I know, a bright light is aimed at my face and Nev is coming at my eye with tweezers.

A memory of the Alks and their giant neck syringe flashes in my mind. I jerk up on the chaise. "What are you doing?"

"Don't be alarmed," Nev says, guiding me back down onto the cushion. "Just a little pick and pluck. You have a few unsightly eruptions on the surface that Dev will attack next."

"Unsightly eruptions? You mean pimples? I'm thirteen. What do you expect?"

"Just try to relax, Jasper." Dev holds up two purple disks and gives them a squeeze. "These should help." He leans over me and places a disk on top of each of my eyes. They're cool and smell like Mom's chamomile tea. Within seconds I'm feeling sleepy. And then I'm slipping.

Lucy's voice jars me awake. "Don't you look like a prince!"

"That's just what Dev and I were saying!"

"Oh, Jasper Adams, you are a pretty sight," Lucy coos.

I open my eyes. Lucy is standing before me in an Earth Force uniform, but it's not the one the rest of us wear. It's a fitted skirt and jacket. And she's wearing even higher heels than she had at the space station. Her shiny hair is twisted up on top of her head, and her face is covered in makeup.

"I knew Dev and Nev would take special care of you," she says, "and I wasn't wrong. You look marvelous. Just wait until your fans see you!"

"How did you get changed so fast?" I ask. Just a few minutes ago she was introducing the stylists in the dome room.

Lucy laughs. "Oh, honey, it's been hours."

Wait a second . . . I was just on the pink chaise draped in white with Nev poking at my face and Dev placing purple disks on my eyes. Now I'm seated, no drape, and no disks. "How did I get here?"

"You took a snooze while we did our magic," Dev says.

"You drugged me?"

"We like to call it a spa nap," Nev says. "Most of our clients love it! So rejuvenating!"

I do feel refreshed. . . .

"Never mind that," Dev says, spinning my chair to face a giant mirror. "Voilà!"

It's me, obviously. But it's like me plus.

My skin has this healthy golden glow. My hair is shorter and styled in that intentionally messy look that most of the guys on the webs wear. My eyes seem to sparkle.

"Am I wearing makeup?"

"Just a bit of bronzer."

"And some clear mascara."

"Really just a touch to bring out your natural beauty."

Oh, geez. I don't know what's worse—the fact that I'm wearing makeup or the reality that I actually look pretty good with it.

"Just in time," Lucy says. "The hovers will be arriving any minute to drive us to the rally. The crowds have been gathering since last night. There are thousands there already, all waiting for a glimpse of our heroes." She squeezes my shoulder. "What do you think of that, Mr. Hero?"

I'm not used to being called a hero. Especially since I don't feel like much of one. "They've been there since last night? Do you mean they camped out?"

"Of course! What did you expect? The return of the lost aeronauts is probably the biggest story of their lifetimes."

"If only they knew the whole story," I say without really thinking.

As soon as the words slip from my mouth, Lucy's eyes bug out and she glances sideways at Nev and Dev. "Now, now don't be so dramatic, Jasper. Time to go!" She grabs me by the hand and drags me out of the chair. She blows good-bye kisses at Nev and Dev as she steers me out of the room. I mumble some thanks and jog alongside Lucy. She's a really fast walker.

"Me? Dramatic?" I say as soon as it's just us. "That's a bit of a role reversal, huh?"

Lucy stops cold. I almost trip and send us both tumbling.

"You need to think before you speak, Jasper. After all I've done for you, the least you could do is keep your mouth shut."

"What do you mean 'all you've done for me'?"

Lucy startles. "Is that a joke? I've made you into a huge superstar, Jasper, possibly more of a star than me. All you have to do is smile and say your lines. Simple. But for some reason nothing seems to be simple with you these days."

She spins on her heels and continues down the hall. I have to race to catch up.

Now I'm mad. "What's that supposed to mean?"

"Isn't this what you wanted? To be popular? Now when

you finally get what you want you keep running your mouth with all this anti–Earth Force blah, blah, blah. Do you know what happens to people who do that? No, you don't know, because you never hear from them again."

"That's what you think of me? That I just want to be popular?"

"Don't you? When Regis targeted you during our first tour of duty, and everyone started talking about you and Mira, you kept saying how you thought it would be different. How you got to the Academy and things were just as bad for you as they'd been on Earth. Don't you remember? The day you showed up Regis in the blast pack relay race was the best day of your life."

"No, it wasn't."

"It was *then*, don't deny it. And ever since, you've loved being the hero—defeating the Youli on the Paleo Planet, planting the degradation patch on the Youli vessel, taking down the shield in Alkalinia. Now you're a hero on an even grander scale. Admit it. You love it. So enjoy your popularity. And stop trying to screw it up!"

Lucy takes off down the hall, leaving me alone. She must assume I'll follow her, which I suppose I will eventually, but I can't manage to move my feet. I'm rooted to the spot as Lucy's words replay in mind. Is that what I wanted? To be popular? It seems so silly and shallow. But could she be right?

A memory flashes. I'm on the air rail the day before I leave for the EarthBound Academy. I've just met a Tunneler for the first time. I'm staring out the window and daydreaming about my trip to space, about finally finding a place where I fit.

Then I miss my stop, and my stuff spills out of my backpack right in front of Will Stevens and Dilly Epstein. Will laughs and calls me a B-wad.

At that moment, my greatest wish was to show them who I really was. A Bounder, soon to blast off and train to be an aeronaut, just like the ones on the posters, the most popular people in the galaxy.

Now *I'm* the poster boy.

As they say, be careful what you wish for.

"JASPER! THERE YOU ARE!" JAYNE RUNS
down the hall. "They're loading the hovers. Everyone's there
but you. We don't want to be late for the rally. Come on!"

She grabs my hand and drags me through the hall even
faster than Lucy. She leads us down two sets of stairs to a
parking garage where the hovers wait. An Earth Force officer
opens the rear door of the last hover, and Jayne and I slide in.
Seconds later, we're rolling.

Out the front window, I can make out our procession as we
drive up the ramp. At the front is an armored hover with the
Earth Force insignia and flashing lights.

The doors to the hover garage open, and the noise swells.

At first, I can't tell what it is, but then I realize it's scream-ing. Officers on foot hold back the crowd so our caravan can cut a path. There are so many people, I can't see where the crowd ends.

"There are thousands of people out there," I say to Jayne.

"Just wait until we get to the rally."

I press the window button, and the glass slides down. The screams intensify, and the crowd pushes against the barricade.

"We love you, Jasper!" someone shouts.

I lock eyes with a girl holding a gigantic poster. It's the new one with my face on it, but instead of the Earth Force text, the words JASPER, WILL YOU MARRY ME? are printed over my face. When she realizes I'm looking at her, she grabs her friend and starts crying.

"Can you put up your window?" Jayne asks. "We have a whole evening of this ahead of us, and I'd like a moment to catch my breath before the insanity begins again."

I roll up the glass and turn around in my seat. The noise from the crowd is still intense. I can't believe there are so many people here for us: the lost aeronauts and me. Like Lucy said, I'm beyond popular. I'm a hero.

"You okay?" Jayne asks.

"Yeah, it's just kind of bizarre."

Jayne shrugs. "It's in line with what we expected."

"Why do they even care about me?"

"We told them to, that's why. That's how propaganda works. We control the message. We hyped you and now they love you, just like Sheek, just like Lucy."

"That's it?"

"Well, it helps that you're cute."

I look at Jayne, but she's tapping on her tablet.

My face warms. Jayne thinks I'm cute? Does she think I'm cute in a propaganda way or in a cute-cute way?

Definitely a propaganda way. It's her job.

Still, she thinks I'm cute in one way or another. A smile pushes at the corner of my lips.

"Why did they make Lucy the new face of Earth Force?" I ask.

Jayne glances up from her tablet. "Isn't it obvious? It's the same reason they're hyping you now. The Force is doing everything it can to change public opinion about the Bounder Baby Breeding Program. That's been one of the most damaging leaks. Having Lucy in front of the cameras helps. It puts a friendly, pro-Force face on the Bounders."

That makes sense, I guess. I wonder who leaked the real reason Earth Force bred the Bounders after they'd managed to keep it a secret all these years. Whoever the mole is, they must be working for the Resistance.

Once we clear the crowd, the hovers make good time. Before long, our caravan slows. We're approaching the rally site, a huge open square in the center of the city, once called Tiananmen Square. The square is packed, but what really strikes me is the military presence. Earth Force officers are everywhere. Armored hovers form a solid barricade corralling the thousands of spectators. Guards stand atop the hovers, weapons drawn, scanning the crowds.

An elevated stage is set up at the gates to the ancient Forbidden City. Scaffolding surrounds the stage, and at least a hundred Earth Force officers are stationed on top.

Our hovers glide into a side building. Officers scan the vehicles top to bottom and flash mirrors beneath. They must be inspecting for bombs, or maybe even stowaways. Next, our hover passes through a sensor arch to confirm no listening devices or other electronic trackers were placed on the hovers.

I suppose the extra security should make me feel safe, but all it does is make me more nervous.

Finally we're given the signal to unload.

"You ready?" Jayne asks.

"Let me put on my hero face." I give her my best Maximilian Sheek impression.

She bursts out laughing. "Try for a more natural look, golden boy."

"Golden boy?"

"I don't know what those silly stylists did to you, but your skin is practically glowing."

The car door opens, and a guard leans down. "Each of you has a personal escort. Stay with them at all times and walk quickly. At my signal, exit the vehicle and proceed with your escort directly to the staging area."

Jayne smiles back at me before climbing out of the hover. I take a deep breath and follow her out. When we reach the door to the staging area, the guard hands me off to another Earth Force officer. She smiles and ushers me along. I follow Jayne and the lost aeronauts to a room directly beneath the stage. It's set up as a lounge with plush green couches and peacock-blue recliners. A bar and buffet line the back wall.

I'm about to head for the buffet when the officer grabs my arm.

"Hey, Jasper," she whispers. "My daughter is a huge fan. Would you mind a quick autograph?" She pulls a wristlet from her pocket.

"Um, sure." I grab the wristlet and press my thumb onto the screen. A second later, the screen reads: "Identified: Jasper Adams."

The woman beams. "Thank you so much. This will make her day!"

I nod and head to the buffet where Denver is piling buffalo chicken wings onto his plate. "Hey, kid," he says as I step beside him. "I can't get enough of these. Sure, I only felt like

I was in the rift for two days, but I'm pretty sure my stomach knows I was gone for fifteen years."

I grab some food and sit down in one of the recliners. While running my lines for the rally in my head, I devour a quesadilla and half a dozen sugar cookies with colored sprinkles, most of the time with an EFAN camera poked at my face.

Time passes, and I start to get nervous. What's the hold up? If I have to wait any longer, I'm going to forget everything I'm supposed to say. Then I'll look like a moron in front of all those people, not to mention the millions watching on the webs.

Maybe the delay is because of the terrorist threat. Could the Resistance be planning something for today's rally?

Just then, Jayne claps her hands. When she has everyone's attention, she says, "Okay, the security sweep has concluded and we're good to go. Captains Dugan and Sheek will kick off the event and introduce you like we've rehearsed. Then Captain Reddy and Officer Adams will join them at the front of the stage. Make sure to enter in the correct order so that you'll be lined up with your onstage seat. Denver, Jasper? Are both of you ready?"

Denver gives Jayne a thumbs-up. "I was born ready."

I nod, although I don't feel a bit ready. In fact, I'm worried the food I just ate will make a repeat appearance onstage.

"Okay then, let's go," Jayne says.

She waves the aeronauts out of the staging room. "You okay?" she asks, linking her arm with mine and guiding me from the room.

"Maybe? Where's Lucy?"

"She's already in the wings. She always worries that Max will try to upstage her, so she's making sure he doesn't ruin her entrance." We turn a corner and head up the stairs.

"That sounds like Lucy. And like Sheek."

She smiles. "You'll be great."

Up ahead, I can see the stage. The other aeronauts are taking their positions in the wings.

"I don't know."

"I do. And they do." Jayne coaxes me ahead and nods at the stage and the crowd beyond.

I can only see a tiny portion of the crowd from where I'm standing, but it's packed. Everyone is on their feet, clapping and whistling and shouting for us to come onstage. The air smells of sweat and excitement.

"You're sure there's no risk of an attack?"

"Trust me. I'm sure." She nods at the stage. "It's almost time."

Next thing I know, Lucy is walking across the stage from the other side, and Max glides by me to meet Lucy in the middle. The crowd roars. The sound alone nearly knocks me off my feet.

They clasp hands and walk together to the front of the stage. This is really happening.

"Welcome to the Lost Heroes Homecoming Tour!" Lucy says, waving her hand in the air.

More screams and claps and wails. The EFAN cameras pan the crowds then refocus on the stage.

I want to cover my ears.

"You know you're our first stop, right?" Sheek asks the crowd.

Even louder.

"That's because Eurasia East knows how to throw a party!"

The crowd swells in a sea of noise. I can barely hear myself think.

"You sure like your parties, Officer Dugan."

"As do you, Officer Sheek."

Their onstage banter goes on for a few more minutes. Then Jayne is tapping my shoulder and steering me into line in front of the lost aeronauts. She raises a hand and whispers, "We're a go, folks." Then she leans forward and kisses me on the cheek. "You'll be great!"

Lucy's voice rings out our cue. "Now welcome Jasper Adams and the lost aeronauts!"

Sheek and Lucy part and turn to face us. Jayne gives me a gentle push, and my feet start moving across the stage, just as we practiced in rehearsal. I focus on my breath like Mom used to make me do when I was nervous. Eight steps. Now I turn and wave at the crowd. Another breath and . . .

Oh. My. God.

I stop moving.

The crowd goes back as far as I can see. And they're screaming. For us. For me.

Denver places a hand on my shoulder. "Keep going, kid. You're doing great."

I suck in air and force my feet to move. I focus on the chair waiting for me across the stage. If I can make it there, I'll let myself look again.

I get to my chair and sink down. Denver slides in beside me. The other aeronauts fall in behind him.

Sheek is saying something, and Lucy is laughing. It's a joke they rehearsed, the joke that comes right before they introduce me and Denver.

And now they're turning and smiling at us—our cue to stand.

Denver nods at me as he rises. "Just follow my lead, kid."

When I walk past Lucy, she squeezes my wrist. "Remember, enjoy it!"

And then I'm standing in front with Denver, all the cameras pointed right at us, just a meter of stage between us and the screaming masses.

"Thank you so much for coming out today!" Denver says.

"One of the things that kept us going all those years is know-ing you were pulling for us!"

The crowd erupts in applause. Denver keeps running through the script. It's almost my turn to talk.

". . . thanks to this kid right here, Jasper Adams."

The crowd roars. I stare out at the sea of faces. A girl in the front row catches my eye. For a second, I think it's Addy. I do a double take. She's grabbing her friend's arm and screaming.

Of course it's not Addy. What would Addy think of all this? She'd hate it. She'd call it for what it is: another piece of Earth Force propaganda.

But Addy's not here. I'm here, for better or worse. So, like Lucy said, I might as well enjoy it.

I've missed my cue. I can almost hear Lucy silently scream-ing at me from behind. Fortunately, Denver was the face of Earth Force before Lucy was even born, so he knows how to get us back on track.

He swings his arm across my back. Then he balls his other fist and gives my shoulder a gentle punch. "Don't be shy, kid. They want to hear the story. Tell them how you saved us. Tell them how you brought us home." Denver sounds so genuine. No one would ever guess how hard he argued against the lie I'm about to tell.

The crowd roars again, and then they're shouting my name, over and over. My nerves start to fade as I'm lifted by the wave of their chant. I feel like I'm floating high above the crowd. They're calling to me. All I have to do is give them what they want.

I glance to the side and see Jayne. She's chanting my name, too.

Raising my hands to the sides to quiet the crowd, I take a deep breath, and then speak my line. "I was just doing my duty."

This obvious attempt at modesty stokes the crowd even more. They clap and cheer and chant my name even louder.

Denver waves them down again and says to me, "Tell them what happened, Jasper."

I launch into the carefully rehearsed story about how Earth Force was ambushed by our alien enemy. The attack was swift and deadly. The Youli executed all of our superiors and took Mira and me hostage. While imprisoned by the Youli, we made a startling discovery. The lost aeronauts from the Incident at Bounding Base 51 weren't dead, they were being held captive. Mira and I formulated a plan to break them out and bring them home. The mission was successful, but Mira paid the ultimate price. She was killed by the Youli during our heroic escape.

Behind me, a giant screen displays Mira's face, the one from the posters. It's meant to elicit sympathy from the crowd. I can't bear to look at it. If I do, I doubt I'll be able to keep up this farce.

Denver takes over, recounting their shock at our arrival. He describes how unexpected it was to be rescued after all that time, and especially by kids.

As Denver talks, I start to relax. I gaze out at the crowd, at the thousands of faces staring up at me, looking at me like I'm the hero Earth Force wants me to be.

"We owe so much to this Bounder," Denver is saying, clapping his hand on my shoulder. "It is my honor to serve with him."

"The honor is all mine," I tell the crowd. "I grew up worshipping these men and women, our lost aeronauts. They're the reason I wanted to serve in Earth Force. I am so grateful I could bring our heroes home!"

The crowd goes wild. Lucy leans over and whispers in my ear, "You're fabulous! A natural! They love you!"

Our story is fiction, but there's nothing fake about the smile spreading across my face. I wave at the crowd as Lucy, Sheek, and Denver say some parting words. Lucy grabs my hand and leads me to the wings, officially ending our first rally of the Lost Heroes Homecoming Tour. As soon as I step offstage, I'm desperate to do it again.

I CAN'T RELAX. I TRY EVERYTHING TO distract myself—web shows, snacks, a nap—but I can't keep my mind off today's rally. I can see the crowd, hear them chant my name. *Hear* isn't quite the right word. It's like I can *feel* them calling for me. I throw on my street clothes and creep down the hall to Jayne's room.

I lightly knock. No answer. I'm about to head back to my room when the door swings open. Jayne is wearing black shorts and a purple T-shirt. The front of her hair is piled on top of her head with a stylus stuck through to keep it in place.

"Hey," she says. "Everything okay?"

"Yeah, I just . . . Sorry to bother you."

"Oh, no bother. You can come in, just hold on a second." She closes the door so it's almost shut and heads back to her room.

I press on the door to sneak a peek at her room. Jayne is at her computer, collapsing a transmission projection. I only see it for a second, but something looks familiar about the location of the transmission.

She heads back to the door and waves. "Come on in."

"Who were you talking to?" I ask.

"No one important."

"Where was the transmission from?"

"The space station."

That did *not* look like the space station.

As if Jayne can read my suspicions, she adds, "I was just going over some details for the next stops on our tour."

That must have been it. "The Americanas, home of Lucy Dugan."

"Not like she'd let any of us forget it."

"Coming home to Americana West as the face of Earth Force? I honestly think Lucy's been dreaming of this her whole life. I hope it's as great as she's expecting it to be. And okay, I'll admit it, I'm pretty excited about our stop in Americana East."

Something dark crosses Jayne's face, but she quickly turns away. She grabs her projection screen and tucks it inside the pack she always carries.

I wonder why she doesn't have a blast pack like the rest of

the Bounders. Does she even know how to use one? What about the gloves? In fact, why isn't she training now? I understand why Earth Force wants Lucy and me to be on this tour—Bounder propaganda and all—but what about Jayne?

"How come you're not training with the other Bounders?"

"That question came from nowhere." Jayne pulls the stylus out, and her hair falls in curls around her face. "I used to think your mind was blank when you had a zone-out moment, but I guess it's just jumping through random topics."

I shrug. "Pretty much. Really, though, how did you get this job? Why does Earth Force have you stationed in communications rather than defense?"

"I'm kind of Lucy's understudy, actually," she says, taking a seat on the edge of her bed. "Lucy's job isn't without some risks, and I'm prepped to step in if anything happens."

"You mean a Resistance attack?" I know it's risky to ask, but Jayne brought it up when we talked in the pod room.

She scrunches up her face like she's thinking, probably deciding how much to tell me. "The Resistance is gaining strength. There are lots of people out there who would love to see Earth Force fall. That's what this tour is all about. The Force has to generate support for the war and keep people rallied around their cause."

"So Lucy's job is dangerous?" I ask, sitting down next to Jayne.

"Yes, and we have a long list of death threats to prove it." She places her hand on top of mine. "You're probably targeted, too."

"Well, that takes my mood down a few notches." Not really. I'm too focused on the feel of Jayne's hand over mine. Her fingers are warm and solid. She feels so different than Mira. Mira's hands are always cold.

Jayne jumps up and claps. "That means we need to do something fun. I'm sick of working all the time. We're in an amazing place. Let's explore!"

"You mean, like, leave the building?"

"Exactly. It's time we took an actual tour of Eurasia East. But first, hold on." Jayne runs over to her trunk and rummages through her things. When she comes back, she's holding a hat and a pair of sunglasses. "For you."

"You want me to wear those glasses? It will be dark out soon."

"I know, but people might recognize you otherwise."

"In this?" I look down at my gray sweatpants and Americana East futbol tee. I was psyched when I found them at the bottom of the trunk Jayne had sent to my room.

"You're a celebrity, Jasper! No one will have a clue who I am, so I don't have to worry about it."

I take the hat and glasses from Jayne and put them on in front of the mirror. I look ridiculous. The hat is orange. If you ask me, it makes me stand out more than blend in, and not in a good way. Plus, I would never pick these sunglasses. They're humongous. I basically look like an orange-headed bug.

"Let's go!" Jayne is already at the door.

We head down the hall and take the elevator to the lowest floor of the parking levels. That way we can skate around the area where the hovers are parked and walk out the exit ramp, hopefully avoiding the EFAN cameras, not to mention the Earth Force guards. With all the paranoia about the mole these days, they definitely wouldn't let us out to roam around Eurasia East on our own.

When we reach the top of the ramp, it's clear there's still a crowd outside. I'm guessing there will be until the guards enforce curfew. We find a side door. No one notices Jayne and me slip outside, hang a left, and head to the end of the block.

Jayne illuminates her wristlet. "If we take the air rail, we can make it to the Summer Palace in twenty minutes."

She grabs my hand and takes off running. Her grip is strong. Life pulses through Jayne. She's vibrant and grounded and more real than most people. When I'm with her, I feel confident, like everything will go our way as long as she's in charge. I can see why she connected with Addy.

We weave through the streets, trying to avoid the armed guards on every corner. When we can't avoid passing them,

I put on the hat and glasses and keep my head down, hoping they don't look too closely at us. When we finally make it the air rail stop and through the metal detectors, I slip the glasses back on and pull the brim of my hat down low. We blend into the crowd. I don't know if I've ever felt like I fit in this much in public. Before the EarthBound Academy, I was basically a nobody, but I still always felt like everybody was looking at me, like they could tell what a loser I was with just a glance.

When the next rail car arrives, we climb on and find seats. We plant our feet on the clear, plastic floor. Eurasia East spreads beneath us. It looks a lot like Americana East. Rows and rows of high rises. Still, it beats being stuck in my room with Florine Statton.

"I can't believe we're out," I say. "I was feeling pretty cooped up on the Lost Heroes Homecoming Tour."

"Not enough excitement for the big celebrity, huh?"

"Cut it out. I'm hardly a celebrity." I know that's the right thing to say, but the truth is, I *am* starting to feel like a celebrity, and I love hearing Jayne say it.

"You sure?" She pulls the glasses off my face and the hat off my head. "Just wait."

I roll my eyes. What exactly does she think is going to happen? I'm not even wearing my uniform.

At the next stop, the doors slide open and a crowd of people spill in. They fill up the other end of the rail car. Before long, one of the girls catches my eye. She whispers something to the girl next to her, and then they're both staring.

Soon, their whole group of friends is gawking at me. They giggle and steal glances.

The first girl to spot me heads in our direction. She's older than me by a few years and incredibly beautiful. She has midnight hair that hangs to her waist. Her face is a perfect oval, and her lips are painted rose red. A girl like her would never have noticed me before I returned from the rift.

"Excuse me," she asks with a shaky voice, "are you Jasper Adams?"

Before I can answer, Jayne pipes in. "Yes, he is, and I'm his publicist. Can I help you?" Her voice is so snooty and businesslike. She kind of sounds like Florine Statton.

The girl twirls her hair around her finger. "Oh no, nothing. Sorry to bother you." She glances back at her friends, then takes a deep breath. "It's just . . . can I have your autograph?" She lifts her wristlet.

"Sure." I press my thumb onto the screen. Identified: Jasper Adams.

"Oh my God!" she claps her hands and smiles. "Thank you so much!"

She runs back to her group. They giggle and squeal when she shows them my thumbprint.

"What did I tell you?" Jayne says as the air rail pulls into the next station. She hands me the hat and glasses. "This is our stop."

I follow her off the air rail, and we dash through the crowded platform. We hurry down a few city blocks until we reach a heavily guarded, brightly colored gate with ancient Chinese lettering across the top.

"How are we going to get in?" I ask.

"Leave it to me," Jayne says.

She marches up to the guards and whips her tablet out of her pack. "We're here from the Earth Force public relations department," she says, showing the guards something on her tablet. "We're scouting sites for next year's rally, and we need immediate admittance to the grounds."

The guards laugh. "Sure you are. Go home, little girl. It's almost curfew."

Jayne waves me over. "Take off the hat and glasses," she says to me then turns to the guards. "Don't you know who he is?"

The guards don't respond, but they don't mock her, either.

"Run his face through recognition. Or don't, and I'll report you directly to the admiral tomorrow."

The main guard is clearly mad at being called out by a "little girl," but he flashes his scanner at my face. Once it registers, he straightens and raises his hand in salute. "I . . . I'm sorry I didn't recognize you immediately, Officer Adams.

It's an honor to meet you. Right this way." He escorts Jayne and me to the gate. "Take as long as you need. I'll personally ensure that no one else is admitted."

Once we're inside the grounds of the Summer Palace and out of earshot of the guards, I stop Jayne. "You could have let me in on your plan."

She grins. "I could have, but that wouldn't have been as fun."

I follow her along the path leading deeper into the grounds. "This place is amazing." The Summer Palace sits on a wide lake surrounded by gardens. The buildings are all preserved in the classic Chinese architecture. The colorful, tiered structures look straight out of a fairy tale. In all my days in Americana East and even my days in space, I've never seen a human-made place that was as beautiful as this.

We walk down a long, outdoor corridor with magnificent painted ceilings. Everything is quiet except the gentle lapping of the water against the boats in the lake. Jayne and I slow down and exhale all the drama of the day, all the stress of the tour, all the expectations of the Force.

Jayne cuts off the path, but I continue, enjoying a few moments of peace.

Peace.

I haven't even thought about the Youli message today. What am I supposed to do with it anyway? Admiral Eames won't listen. Even Cole brushed me aside.

I keep walking. Soon, I'm looking at my own face. One of the old propaganda posters is tacked up on a pillar.

PROTECTING OUR PLANET COMES AT A PRICE.

Mira's face stares back from the next pillar. I stop in front of it.

Why did you leave me, Mira?

How many times have I asked that question? I'm no closer to an answer.

Or maybe I am. Maybe it's time I accepted Mira's own words. She didn't want to stay with me.

No, she *left* me. She left me to deal with all the aftermath of our lost year, and our torn-apart pod, and that ridiculous Youli message. Alone.

"Jasper!" I hear Jayne call.

I cut away from the path, and follow her voice through the trees to a garden hidden away from the lakeshore. The garden is ringed by pale, flat stones that reflect the moonlight.

"Over here," she calls.

I follow her voice to a small stone bench. She's perched on one side, staring at the sky. I sit down next to her. There's barely enough room for both of us. She leans over, ever so slightly, and our shoulders touch.

"This place is magical," she says.

"I know," I say. "It's like they transported it from another age."

"An age before space travel."

"An age without aliens."

"An age with no war."

"There's always been war," I say. "Don't you play *Evolution of Combat*?"

"Fine, then at least no alien wars." Jayne hops off the bench and sits cross-legged on the ground in front of me. "You've been through so much, Jasper. How are you doing? Really?"

I shrug. "I'm okay." I'm not going to unload my inner thoughts on Jayne anymore. I'd rather her think of me as Jasper Adams, hero, not Jasper Adams, sad and sappy dork who misses his friends. Plus, I'm starting to like this hero stuff.

"Have you been thinking about your sister?" she presses.

I guess I'm not getting out of it. "On and off. Our next stop after West is Americana East. I'll see my parents, and they're going to ask about Addy. I was supposed to look after her, you know. Great job I did at that."

Jayne places her hand on my knee. "You were saving all the Bounders and a good chunk of Earth Force. I'd say that's a pretty good explanation. Plus, you technically did save your sister."

"But I can't tell them that, can I?" My parents can't know the truth about Addy. Earth Force doesn't want anyone except level-one clearance officers to know about the Resistance. I'm definitely not allowed to talk about it with my parents.

Jayne doesn't answer. She knows what the confidentiality rules are, and she knows there's nothing I can do about it. Instead, she extends her hand.

I help her up. We stand facing each other. I should probably drop her hand, but I don't. She doesn't drop mine, either. Even in the faint light of the garden, her purple eyes shine. They're dark like the midnight sky and filled with magic like the moon.

Jayne turns her head like she can hear my thoughts and they're making her blush. But the amazing thing is, she didn't hear my thoughts. She can't. She doesn't know I was thinking about her beautiful eyes. She doesn't know I was thinking about her at all in *that way.* Which means I don't feel like a floundering mess the way I do with Mira.

The thing I love most about Mira—our intimate connection—is the thing I'm most happy is missing with Jayne. I can think about anything I want when I'm with her, and my thoughts remain my own.

Mira's face from the poster flashes through my mind, but I push it away. Remember, Jasper, Mira chose to leave. That's what she wanted. It's time I accepted that. It's time I stop looking to the past and start seeing what's right in front of me.

Jayne squeezes my hands, then pulls me deeper into the garden. The trees part, and we spill into a small clearing

MONICA TESLER

with a lotus pond. She drops my palm and kneels in front of a perfect flower. She lifts its wet, glistening petals in her fingers.

"Do you ever wonder if Addy has it right?" she whispers.

Her question takes me by surprise. I know what it sounds like she's asking—do I support the Resistance—but can that really be? Jayne works in Earth Force public relations. She knows what's expected. She knows the risk of disloyalty to the Force. I trust Jayne, but if I misinterpret her question, I could be putting both of us at risk.

I decide the safest thing to do is turn the question around. "Do you?"

"Forget I asked." Jayne stands and wipes her hands on her shorts.

But I'm not willing to forget it, risk or not. I wonder all the time whether Addy and Marco and Waters are right. Not to mention Barrick and the Wackies who saved Mira and me back on Gulaga.

"No, really," I say, grabbing her hand, "I want to know what you think about the Resistance. It's hard for me to dismiss something that Addy feels so passionately about."

She pulls her hand loose. "We should go. We need to get back before curfew." She turns and starts to walk away.

I must have said too much. As I follow Jayne out of the garden, the air hangs heavy, like there are words between us still clawing to get out. We walk in silence past the gate guards and back toward the air rail station.

Then something shifts, and the tension in the air seeps away. Jayne skips ahead, then spins back and smiles, beckoning for me to catch up. As we near the crowd waiting for the next air rail car, she squeezes my arm and cozies up against me. "Oh, Jasper! Can I have your autograph?"

I shrug her off. "Shut up."

"Don't forget your hat and glasses," she says. "I'm too tired to fend off your admirers on the way back."

THE NEXT MORNING, FLORINE WAKES ME up at 0545.

"I thought we discussed this!" I grumble, pulling the blanket over my head. "I'm low-maintenance. Let me sleep!"

"Get up, Jasper Adams! You are required to board the hover bound to the Eurasia East aeroport in fifteen minutes."

I bolt up. Jayne must have overridden the computer with a new wake-up time. That means I need to hurry.

I take a two-minute shower and stuff my gear into my trunk. Water trickles off my hair as I bend to pull the Earth Force–issued tight navy socks over my damp feet. Just as I drag my trunk into the hall, building management comes by with a huge, rolling cart to collect the luggage for the Lost Heroes Homecoming Tour. A few minutes later, I dash to the elevator then sprint through the dining hall and grab a handful of yogurt squeezies to suck down in the hover.

The aeronauts are already loaded into their vehicles when I race into the garage. A flock of EFAN cameramen turn their lenses on me as I bolt toward Jayne, who's standing in front of the last hover in line, tapping into her tablet. Terrific. There's going to be web coverage of me and my wet hair. I guess that's what Lucy meant when she said she wants them to catch us in our natural environment. Hopefully, these natural moments end up on the editing room floor.

"Nice of you to join us," Jayne says when I skid to a halt by her side.

I smile. "You kept me out late last night."

Jayne shushes me as we board. She's dressed in her Earth Force uniform, but I can still picture her in shorts and a purple tee pulling the orange hat over my head and dragging me out exploring. She said people would recognize me, and she was right. I can hardly believe that girl asked me for my autograph. That would never have happened to the old Jasper Adams. I guess it's time to accept that the new Jasper Adams—the *hero* Jasper Adams—is here to stay.

"Good morning, sunshine," Lucy coos as I climb onto the hover. Other than Jayne and me, Lucy is the only one on board.

Why on earth is Lucy riding with us? She usually insists on sitting with Denver and Max.

"We're heading home!" She squeezes her hands together and lifts them to her chest. "Americana, here we come! Just think of it, Jasper, we spent so many days dreaming of returning as celebrities, just like the aeronauts before us, and here we are! The day has finally arrived!" She pats the cushioned bench beside her, expecting me to scoot close. "Let's review our lines for the West rally. They're a bit more elaborate than our Eurasia East script, and I know you struggled with that one."

"I didn't struggle." I almost add that she may have me convinced I was once on a popularity quest, but I certainly didn't spend my days dreaming of becoming an Americana West superstar. That's signature Lucy.

Lucy smiles. "Oh, I'm not trying to make you feel bad. I know the stage is not your natural calling like it is mine. But we're on a very tight timetable. The rally's tonight, shortly after we arrive. The Americana West event is going to be huge and lots of important people are going to be there. And they're planning to film the Lost Heroes Homecoming Tour web special tonight, so it's really key that you have your part down, okay?"

It's not like I have a choice, so I just nod Lucy on.

"Great. So, when Sheek and I finish our introductions . . ."

I try to focus on what Lucy's saying—or at least I kind of do—but my mind won't stay put. I'm back onstage at last night's rally, the cheers swelling, the crowd pulsing with excitement. Are they really expecting the Americana West rally to be even bigger? Lucy's wrong. I *am* a natural. Once I settled in last night, I could have stayed onstage forever, riding the wave of elation, giving my fans exactly what they called for.

"Ow!" I pull my foot back in pain. Given the strategic placement of Jayne's shoe on the hover floor, it's clear she just stomped on my big toe. "Why'd you do that?"

Jayne just smiles and flicks her eyes at Lucy, who is glaring at me. The hover is stopped, and the Eurasia East aeroport is visible in the distance.

That was a very quick trip. I definitely zoned out.

"I *said*, do you think you have them down now?" Lucy says through gritted teeth.

She must still be talking about our lines for the Americana West rally.

"Definitely." It's always best to be definitive around Lucy. "You don't need to worry about me for a second. Jayne ran lines with me last night."

The muscles in Lucy's face relax. "Excellent. Come directly to the on-air salon once you board. Nev and Dev are waiting." She opens the door and disappears from the hover.

"Nev and Dev? *Again?*" I say to Lucy's back. She ignores me and keeps walking. "I never agreed to that!"

"Actually, you did," Jayne says. "You nodded yes to all of Lucy's questions while your mind was somewhere else."

"Great. What else did I agree to?"

"Nothing you could have gotten out of, so don't worry."

"Thanks for getting my attention at the end, but you didn't need to disfigure my foot in the process."

"You're welcome," she replies, ignoring the second half of my sentence. "Why did you lie about us running lines last night?"

"I thought it would get Lucy off my back, and it looks like it did. Why does it matter? We were together last night, weren't we?"

Jayne's lips press together in a thin line. "Yes, obviously, but that was supposed to be a secret."

"I thought us sneaking out was a secret, not us spending time together. What are you so worried about?"

"Nothing. It just wasn't on the schedule, that's all." She points at the door. "Let's go."

"Why do I get the feeling you don't want anyone to notice us alone together?"

"Don't be ridiculous. I'm worried if I get out of the hover first, you'll space and forget to unload."

"Touché." I climb out of the hover behind her. "Where are we anyway?"

"Our security team advised we use a different route to get to the aeroport. We'll take the pneumatic pipeline the rest of the way."

Jayne nods at a raised platform where the rest of our group is gathering. A long pipe extends from the platform all the way to the aeroport. In the distance, the sun rises over the Eurasia East skyline.

Something wasn't right about that exchange with Jayne, but I'm not going to waste my time trying to figure it out. If she's worried about spending time with me, who cares? These days, there are plenty of people who would kill for a few minutes with Jasper Adams.

I follow the old aeronauts onto the pipe platform. The solid doors slide back to reveal an open passenger capsule. We stream in single file, having to duck to avoid hitting the capsule's roof. I take a seat behind Bai. Seconds later, the doors slide closed and the chairs recline until we're nearly lying down. Claustrophobia creeps into my chest. I knew I wouldn't be a fan of the narrow, windowless capsule. The ceiling panel opens above me. It holds a VR visor. I pull it over my face and blink through the channels until I land on the Paleo Planet safari. That should be distracting enough to keep me from hyperventilating on the short ride to the aeroport.

The sound of an air generator fills the capsule followed by the strong sensation of forward propulsion. The VR screen flashes on, and I'm walking through the high grass, scoping a saber cat in the distance. It's so lifelike. I wonder if Cole has this visor. Playing *Evolution* on this would be outrageous.

A flock of fuchsia birds dips low to drink from the river in the distance. That might be the watering hole we visited. The place where we first battled the Youli. It took every bit of our skill to protect the other Bounders. We worked well together—me, Cole, Lucy, Marco, Mira—even when Marco decided to kamikaze the Youli on the ridge and got himself flung into a herd of mammoths. I ended up having to jump off a Youli ship as it prepared to bound.

I wonder where Marco is right now. Is Addy with him? Are they safe?

What about Mira? She could be anywhere in the galaxy right now.

I push Mira from my mind. I can't afford to get distracted before the big rally tonight. Plus, who needs Mira when there are thousands of people who are desperate just to see me onstage?

I turn off the VR headset and close my eyes.

Then I'm at the rally, gazing out at the sea of faces stretching back as far as I can see, all of them chanting my name.

There's an Earth Force officer standing at the door to the jet as we board. I recognize her from the security briefing at the space station. She's stopping everyone as they pass.

"Please place tablets and wristlets in the bin and line your bags against the wall," she says, gesturing to a circular black basket beside her. "This is a security scan. All your belongings will be returned to you upon landing."

"Are you kidding?" I ask. "I was going to play *Evolution* during the flight."

The officer raises her eyebrow. "Comply with orders, Officer Adams."

So she outranks me. So what? Doesn't me being one of the heroes on the Lost Heroes Homecoming Tour count for anything?

"Don't worry, kid," Denver says from up ahead. "You'll be spending your whole trip in styling."

The whole trip? I roll my eyes. "I thought we already went through that."

Denver shrugs. "I don't get involved in those decisions, kid. Ask your friend Lucy."

No thanks. Maybe I'll try hiding out in a corner and hope they forget about me.

I hand my tablet to the officer and lean my blast pack against the wall. I'm glad I decided to shove my gloves in my socks rather than leave them zipped in my pack. I have no idea what would happen if they discovered the gloves during the security sweep, although I can't imagine it would be good.

I follow Denver toward the passenger cabin. "What's with the security scan? They didn't do this on our other flights."

"Not sure, but it probably has something to do with the mole. I overheard some chatter this morning that we moved to red alert on the risk of a possible domestic terror event, and they think the mole is directly involved."

That must be why they rerouted us this morning. "Do they think the mole is someone on the tour?"

"Maybe? Like I said, if you want details, ask your chatty friend. My days of being in the know are in the past. Fifteen years in the past, to be exact."

I don't even get a chance to hide because Dev and Nev swoop in as soon as Denver and I step into the cabin.

"Oooh! There you are!" Dev's lavender sweater vest has a cursive *D* on the heart.

"You were fabulous at the rally!" Nev's wearing a matching vest but in lemon yellow. "You've never looked better!"

"But you will!" Dev says. "We have an enhanced glam plan ready to roll out for tonight's rally!"

"Right this way, Jasper," Nev says.

They each grab my hand, and we walk in a chain down the cabin aisle and into a back hallway. They lead me to a small room that they've done up as a salon. Everything is draped in pink cloth, and the room smells like roses. Lucy would love it.

"It's nothing compared to our salon at the Style Gallery," Nev says, "but we make do, don't we, Dev?"

"Most definitely. We would do anything for our young, handsome, oh-so-popular poster boy." Nev winks and smiles.

I force a smile. Why did they have to make everything smell like roses? "Got any of those purple eye pads?" If I have to endure this style session, I might as well sleep through it.

When I wake up, the captain is announcing our arrival at the Americana West aeronautical port. Dev spins me around in their styling chair to face a giant, rhinestone-rimmed mirror. My skin is radiant honey like last time. My hair still has that messy style, but now it's amped up with streaks of actual gold. They've done something different with my eyes, too, so they look deep and penetrating.

"So, what do you think?" Nev asks.

"I kind of look like a superhero," I reply, already picturing myself on the grand stage in Americana West.

"You're our golden boy!" Dev says. "Now hurry back to your seat and strap in before we land."

AFTER TOUCHING DOWN AT THE AEROPORT,
ten kilometers off the shores of Americana West, we take an
elevator deep below the surface of the water and board a subterranean transport, another ride with no windows. (Are they
trying to push my claustrophobia buttons? They're lucky I
don't puke!) The transport takes us right to the main hub of
Americana West, where they're holding the rally. From there,
we're escorted in a private air rail car to the rally site, where
the crowds already number in the tens of thousands and are
growing by the minute.

The air rail station stands high above the city, so when
the rail car doors open, the glamorous city spreads before us.

What was once known as the Las Vegas strip is now the central metropolis of Americana West, and the people of West have gone to great lengths to preserve the historic city.

Down on the left is a giant pyramid reaching almost as high as the air rail. Behind it is an enormous, colorful castle, and behind that, an old city skyline. On the right is the space-themed Quantum Tower, the tallest building in Americana West and the last attraction to be built on the strip. At the base of the Quantum is where the rally stage is set up. Farther ahead, a replica of the famous Eiffel Tower in Eurasia West stands next to an enormous hot air balloon. Interspersed among the sites are huge, decadent buildings with mirrored glass and cascading fountains and too many pools to count.

I can't wait to go exploring. Hopefully, Jayne is game again tonight.

Every meter of open space on the strip is jammed with people waiting for the rally or Earth Force officers ensuring their protection—at least, that's the party line.

I take a deep breath. It's still hard to believe they're all here to see us. To see me.

Lucy scoots beside me and wraps her arms around my waist. She's so excited, it feels like electricity is radiating from her skin. It's like this place was made for Lucy, and today is her grand homecoming.

How did we end up here? It seems like yesterday we were

taking the passenger craft to the EarthBound Academy for our first tour of duty. Lucy, Cole, and I were debating who was the coolest quantum aeronaut ever.

Now could it possibly be *me*?

As soon as the thought pops into my mind, I shake my head. Don't be ridiculous, Jasper. My brain buzzes in a way that reminds me of Mira laughing, probably because that's exactly what she would be doing if she could peek inside my mind right now.

But she can't. Because Mira's not here. Mira's not anywhere where she can reach me. She left me with that ridiculous Youli message that Admiral Eames didn't even want to hear.

Why do I keep letting her into my head? Mira chose to leave.

Mira chose to leave *me*.

Out there, spreading across the landmarks of Las Vegas, are tens of thousands of people who came to see *me*. Last night, Jayne chose to hang out with *me*. I may be clueless most of the time, but it's pretty clear how Jayne feels, even if she doesn't want anyone else to know.

I ball my hands into fists. Mira's not the only one with a choice. I can't keep choosing to stay in the past, obsessing over someone who chose to leave me. I need to descend to the stage and greet the thousands of screaming fans calling my name.

The choice is obvious, easy. So why does it feel so hard?

An EFAN cameraman taps me on the shoulder. Lucy squares us both to the lens and flashes a megawatt smile. Before I know it, I'm answering questions about what it feels like to be a hero and what words of wisdom I have for kids who want to grow up to be a quantum aeronaut someday, just like me.

We're herded along and vetted by security (there's still the mole to worry about, after all, not to mention the show Earth Force needs to put on to keep up planetary panic) and next thing I know we're backstage listening to the calls of the crowd.

This is it. Showtime.

Jayne squeezes my shoulder and nods: my entrance cue.

Then I'm standing onstage soaking up all the adoration.

After the rally, they usher us into the Quantum Tower and escort us to our rooms. Fortunately, my room isn't haunted by the voice of Florine Statton. The Quantum rooms are super modern, with furniture and tech that disappears into the floors and ceiling and walls when not in use. When I first walk in, I think I'm back in the VR chamber in Alkalinia because the room is totally empty. But then I happen to say out loud, "There isn't even a bed," and the wall shifts, and out drops a king-size mattress draped in silk.

I entertain myself for a good fifteen minutes shouting things at my room and watching them appear. I quickly learn that every surface can also serve as a web monitor, so soon I'm surrounded by replay images of the rally. My own face stares back at me from every direction. I have to admit, I look really good with the gold threads in my hair.

Jasper Adams, golden boy.

Soon, though, I get antsy. I'm still riding high from the energy of the crowds. I need to do something. It's time to find Jayne and explore Americana West.

When I step out of my room, Jayne is halfway down the hall, heading to her room. Perfect timing. I sprint after her.

Jayne must not hear me coming, because she doesn't even glance back. She seems totally absorbed in her thoughts, which is far more like me than Jayne.

I slam into the wall beside her, seconds before she reaches her door. "Boo!"

She jumps and lets out a little yelp. "Geez, Jasper! You scared me!"

I lean against the doorframe and tip my chin to the side the way I've seen Sheek do it a million times. If it works for him, why not for the golden boy?

She looks at me and bites her lip. Then she checks the time on her wristlet. "What's up?"

I give her my best golden boy smile. "Thought we could go exploring again, like in Eurasia East—just you and me. What do you say?"

Jayne scans the hall. "I can't. I've got work to do."

What? That's not cool. I cross my hands against my chest. "I thought we had the rest of the day off?"

She shakes her head. "Not me. Lucy has me working on a special project."

Something about this is suspicious. I narrow my eyes. "What kind of special project?"

Jayne presses her lips together. "The *none of your business* kind." She twists her doorknob and pushes past me into her room.

"What's the problem?" I ask, stepping in after her.

Jayne turns and blocks my way. A forced smile spreads across her face, and her voice comes out super sweet. "Look, Jasper, I'm sorry. I'm just in a bad mood because I have to work. We'll probably have some time tomorrow morning during the family and friends visitation hour. Maybe we can sneak out then. Sound good?"

As she talks, she places her hand on my shoulder. I don't realize it until I'm back in the hall, but she pretty much pushes me out of her room.

"Fine," I say in a way that's supposed to let her know it's really not fine at all.

I expect Jayne to keep talking—at least try to make me feel a bit better—but instead she shuts the door in my face.

I lean against the wall, my cheeks burning. Why did I pose

at her door like that? Who do I think I am? Some web star from West? Jasper Adams, golden boy, is just a fictional character. A character Jayne helped create! She probably thinks I'm a total dork. No wonder she doesn't want anything to do with me.

I shuffle down the hall to my room. I open my own door only to find my face staring back at me from all the web screens, a frozen image from the rally earlier today. Actually, I am a web star now, and if Jayne wants to blow me off, that's her loss.

"Bed!" I call to my room, standing clear as the mattress falls from the wall. I fling myself onto the silk sheets.

This sucks. It seems like everyone in West wants to be with me except Jayne.

What is she up to anyway?

She said she has to work on a secret project for Lucy. She's pretty conscientious when it comes to work, and Lucy is pretty demanding. It's probably true. Jayne's just busy.

Still, I can't shake the feeling that there was something more to Jayne's behavior. It's like she was trying to get rid of me as quickly as possible. But why?

Down the hall, the lift bell buzzes.

On a hunch, I hop up from the bed and pull the door handle just in time to see Jayne disappearing into the lift.

Secret project for Lucy . . . right.

Jayne lied.

I know it's a huge breach of trust, but I make a split-second decision to follow her. I grab the hat and glasses Jayne gave me back in Eurasia East, then dash out of my room and down the hall. I make it off the lift on the ground floor just in time to see her disappear around a corner and duck into a stairwell at the end of a back hallway.

She must be up to something.

I race to catch up and descend the stairs to the parking levels two at a time. I ease open the basement door, fingers crossed that she doesn't see me. I make it into the garage just in time to see Jayne jogging up the loading ramp.

Soon I'm tailing after her along the Las Vegas strip. I pull my hat low and slip on the sunglasses, even though it's getting dark. The city is coming alive. Everything shines with brilliant neon lights, and the crowds surge. I don't look strange at all in my sunglasses. Most of the West folks are oddly dressed—hair dyed purple or pink or turquoise, metallic clothes, lots of bright accessories. This place explains a lot about Lucy. I mean, no wonder she wants to be a star. Half the people in West seem to think they're stars whether they are or not.

There's no curfew in Americana West—something about how the city was built on a foundation of nighttime entertainment. Instead, the city is now under lockdown since the Youli war was announced. No one can enter or depart Americana West from dusk until dawn. There are also checkpoints throughout the city. In order to pass through, you need to have your eye lens scanned. Then you're uploaded into a tracker. Essentially, Earth Force watches your every move.

The weird thing is, Jayne doesn't hit a single checkpoint. Instead, we wind back and forth through streets and buildings, practically circling our steps, but slowly making our way . . . somewhere . . . without ever crossing a checkpoint. It's like she has a careful map of exactly how to avoid them.

She's hard to follow. I almost miss her hanging a left and heading for one of the classic buildings that looks more like it was transplanted from ancient Rome. I chase after her, past rows of fountains filled with sculptures of naked people shooting water out of their mouths. The ancient people of Americana West sure liked some odd stuff.

The inside of the building is just as weird and ornate as the outside. The floors are gold and slippery and filled with columns and busts with head wreaths of green leaves. Jayne leaves the main hall and darts through a crowded room filled with slot machines, all lit up with flashing lights. It instantly sends me into sensory overload.

I can't lose Jayne. I narrow my eyes to take in less of the lights and try to ignore the constant sound of clicking and bells and people shouting.

Up ahead, she turns right and picks up the pace. I follow her through a crowded hall packed with people and food.

Lines wind around the room with people piling plates full of Americana West delicacies.

My stomach grumbles, but I turn away from a banquet table stacked with cakes and pastries and keep my gaze glued to Jayne.

She ducks through double swinging doors that lead to the kitchen. When I follow her in a moment later, I nearly collide with a waiter in a tuxedo carrying champagne glasses stacked in a multitiered tower. He mutters some choice words at me, but I don't stop. On the other side of the kitchen, Jayne slips out the back door.

I make it to the door and slowly pull back the handle. It opens to an alley behind the building. I edge out as stealthily as possible, knowing that Jayne must be close.

Once I ease the door closed, I look around. Jayne is at the other end of the alley. I tiptoe behind a nearby dumpster that hopefully will give me some cover.

Jayne glances around anxiously and checks her wristlet.

What is she doing?

Seconds later, a figure emerges from the darkness.

I'm too far away to make out the details. There's another dumpster halfway between me and Jayne. If I stay low, I can probably make it there without them spotting me.

I crouch and scurry the distance to the second dumpster, crossing my fingers that Jayne and the mystery person don't hear me. I slide in behind the dumpster then carefully peek over. They're deep in conversation. I don't think they heard me.

I'm still too far away to hear what they're saying, but I have a much better view of what's happening. Jayne is talking to a guy with his back to me. He's dressed in dark canvas pants and a gray sweatshirt with the hood pulled over his head.

Who is that guy? Could he be part of Lucy's special project? Or is he a friend of Jayne's? Someone she'd rather spend time with than me? My chest tightens, but I shake it off. What is she up to? I need to know who that guy is.

Both Jayne and her mystery man activate their wristlets. They must be transferring data.

Jayne glances around. I duck. The next time I chance a glance, they're shaking hands. It looks like their meeting is over.

When they break apart, they shift positions so the man is faced in my direction. He starts heading my way, probably exiting at the other end of the alley.

I flatten myself against the wall and hope he doesn't see me.

When he darts past, I get a good look at him.

He's not a man. He's a boy. My age. A face I'd know anywhere.

Regis.

I BARGE INTO JAYNE'S ROOM AT THE
Quantum Tower. "I know it's you! You're the mole! I can
hardly believe it, but I saw it with my own eyes! The only
reason I'm telling you first is that I want to hear you say it. As
soon as you do, I'm marching out of here and reporting you."

Panic flicks across Jayne's face, but only for an instant. "I
have no idea what you're talking about." She turns back to her
tablet and deactivates the projection. The table where she'd
been working disappears into the wall.

"You're lying." I fold my arms tightly against my chest.
"You know exactly what I'm talking about."

Jayne crosses the small room. "Look, Jasper, I don't know

what you think you saw, but you've got it all wrong."

"I'm not going to debate it with you, Jayne. You're the mole. As soon as I report you, I'm sure the Force will be able to confirm it. No one can cover all their tracks."

"Calm down. Let's talk about this. Couch!" A sofa rises up from the floor.

I retreat to the door. I'm about to walk out and go straight to the security officer, but I can't bring myself to leave without an answer. I spin around. "What I don't understand, Jayne, is how on earth can you work with him?"

"Who?" Jayne's voice is guarded, but it's clear she's starting to freak.

I spit out the name like it's poison on my lips. "Regis."

She closes her eyes and shakes her head. When she opens them, she whispers, "You followed me, didn't you?"

"I can't believe you, Jayne! He's the absolute worst! He's worse than the worst! He's the only cadet ever ejected from the EarthBound Academy!"

"Jasper, I've heard the stories. I know he was awful when he was in the Force, but he's changed. He's a good guy."

I choke out a laugh. I can't believe she's saying this. "Right. Regis, the epitome of good guy."

"I'm serious. I know he had some anger issues, but—"

"Some anger issues? Are you kidding me? He tried to *kill* me. Multiple times."

"Okay, some major behavioral issues. But he's getting help. And in the meantime, he's been a new-wave Resistance fighter for more than two years now."

"Regis is in the Resistance?" That can't be possible. Everything I know about the Resistance is contrary to what Regis stands for, unless he's just out for revenge against the Force for booting him from the Academy.

"Yes." Jayne tentatively touches my forearm. "I know I'm taking a chance here, Jasper, but I also know you're sympathetic to our cause."

"*Our* cause? So you're *in* the Resistance? You're not just selling secrets to the highest bidder?"

She scoffs. "Of course not! Your old pod leader, Jon Waters, is our top general. Your pod mate Marco Romero heads up the guerilla regiment. Addy is with us. I know that in your heart, *you* are with us, too. You said yourself that you have a hard time opposing something your sister feels so strongly about."

I sink to the couch. "That's not what I said. You're putting words in my mouth."

"I'm not. Marco told me you agreed that Earth was exploiting developing planets like Gulaga and the Paleo Planet. He said you'd want Earth to join the Intragalactic Council and abide by the code of planetary citizens. That's what the Resistance is fighting for." Jayne sits down beside me. "I know you, Jasper," she pleads. "I know you don't agree with what

Earth Force is doing. You hate having to go along with their lies. They're using you, Jasper."

I get it now. Jayne's not only the mole. She's not only working with Regis. She was ordered to convert me, to get close to me and turn me for the Resistance. Everything that's passed between us has been part of the Resistance's agenda.

"You don't know me," I say. "I'm just some ridiculous celebrity to you, like Sheek. You've spent this entire time leading me on so I'd eventually join your side." I square my jaw and stare her down. "That's it, right? You weren't going to spring it on me yet, but that's the plan, isn't it, Jayne?"

Jayne shakes her head. "It's not like that, Jasper. I like you. Really, I do."

"Sure." I scoot to the far end of the couch.

She reaches for my hand. "We're friends, Jasper."

"Right, friends." I pull my palm free.

"Yes, friends." Jayne's voice rises. "What did you think? I'm not out to steal somebody's boyfriend."

"What are you talking about?"

"I know about you and Mira, Jasper. Everyone knows."

Why is she talking about Mira? She has nothing to do with this! "Mira is not my girlfriend! How many times do I have to say that? And even if she were, she's halfway across the galaxy right now! She chose the Youli over me, okay? So I guess the joke's on me twice."

I bury my head in my hands. I can't believe this is happening. The few times I thought about joining the Resistance, this is not how I saw this moment going down. I envisioned Waters shaking my hand and welcoming me with Addy and Marco by his side. The last thing I pictured was Regis. I hate everything about him. How can we both stand for the same thing? How can Jayne stand to be around him? To be allied with him?

Plus, I still feel torn in two. I was destined to be in Earth Force since before I was born. Could I really oppose them? Fight for the other side? And what about the Youli? The images Cole showed me were powerful. The Youli has brought tremendous pain and suffering to our people. They aren't innocent. They may want peace, but they're not peaceful.

"Look, Jasper—"

"Don't even start. I don't want to hear any more of your lies. There's only one thing I want to know. Why were you meeting with Regis?"

"I can't tell you that," Jayne says quietly.

I push up from the couch, rage burning just beneath the surface of my skin. I'm sick of feeling like a pawn, to Earth Force, to Waters, and now even to Jayne. "Yes, you *can* tell me, and you *will*. If you don't, I'm turning you in."

Jayne stands and matches my gaze. Silence stretches between us. I don't break eye contact. She needs to know I won't yield on this.

Finally, her shoulders sink and she plops back down on the couch. "There's going to be an incident in Americana East," she whispers. "We're planting bombs—"

Bombs? "You can't! My parents are in Americana East! They'll be at the rally!"

"No one will get hurt. They're smoke bombs. Once they're detonated, the Resistance plans to grab one of the aeronauts."

It takes me a minute to process what she's saying. In my mind, I see my parents running scared in a cloud of smoke. "You mean you're going to take a hostage?"

"We don't look at it that way." From the way she says *we*, I can tell she believes in the Resistance, that she's dedicated to the cause. "We'll smuggle the aeronaut off the planet and over to Gulaga to connect with the Resistance."

"And you think this aeronaut is just going to go with you? Do your bidding?"

"We believe they will once they find out the whole truth about what Earth Force has been up to all these years."

"And you really think you can get them off the planet? How?"

"I don't know all the details, but I have confidence in the plan."

I laugh. "That makes one of us."

"Trust me."

I practically choke on another laugh. "*Trust* you? Really? You've been lying to me since the day we met."

"Sometimes deception is necessary, Jasper. Maybe I haven't been totally honest with you, but I haven't outright lied."

"Yes, you did! You lied today when you went to meet Regis!"

"Okay, fine, but only because it was absolutely necessary."

I used to think that secrets were justified sometimes. Mira and I kept our brain patches secret from the rest of our pod for most of our time on Gulaga. We did it at Waters's request, just like Jayne. "You sound like him," I tell her.

"Who?"

"Waters."

"He cares about you, Jasper."

"Right."

"Join us."

Jayne looks up at me. Despite the lies, I still feel the connection between us. I don't want to feel it, but it's there. Maybe she's being honest about us being friends. Maybe. All I know is I don't want to hurt her. If Earth Force finds out she's the mole, she'll be locked up and probably tortured.

"I need time to think," I tell Jayne.

"We don't have much time." She lets that sink in, then adds, "Joining us will help keep Addy safe, Jasper."

Now she's using my sister to justify her actions, to make me do what she wants? My eyes narrow, and I turn my head to the side. "What is this? A bribe? Blackmail?"

Jayne presses her lips together. "It's a fact, Jasper, plain and simple. Addy needs you. The Resistance needs you."

"Why do I need to choose sides? If the Resistance supports Earth's entry into the Intragalactic Council, they should try to persuade the admiral. If they were willing to compromise, I'm sure—"

"No." Jayne's eyes are cold, and her hands are clenched. "The Resistance won't compromise. We're done cowering before the Force."

I shake my head. Why doesn't anyone want to find a solution? Why is everyone so convinced that their way is the only way? "What do you want with *me*, then? You told me your plan, and it doesn't involve me."

"Go to Addy, Jasper. Join the Resistance in Gulaga."

"Oh sure, no problem. I'll just bound right over."

"You met with Gedney in Eurasia East, didn't you?"

How does she know that? "Wait . . . is Gedney in the Resistance, too?"

She doesn't answer my question. "If you met with Gedney, then you know what to do."

Huh? Oh . . . wait . . . when Gedney visited me in Eurasia, he asked if I remembered where his labs were located. Jayne must be saying I should go there first.

She takes a step back and crosses her arms against her

chest. "And Jasper, I'm sure Admiral Eames would be very interested to learn that Mira *chose* the Youli over you, like you said. That doesn't sound like a hostage situation now, does it? Of course, if what I've heard about your relationship is true, I'm sure you'd go to great lengths to protect Mira, even if she's not your girlfriend."

Now, *that is* blackmail.

In my small room on one of the highest floors of the Quantum Tower, I lie on my bed and slip the thin, gauzy material over my fingers. It's so tempting to tap in and feel the connection with the world around me. How fitting it would be to quantum bound in the very tower named for the technology. Of course, it's named after the quantum bounding ships that Earth developed through the normal course of technological advancement, not the bounding gloves that were developed based on stolen Youli technology.

Despite the temptation, I know I can't bound. Gedney said that Earth Force had quantum detection scanners in all the cities. If I even tapped in to the brain connection and started manipulating matter, a team of guards would rush in here and confiscate my gloves within minutes. I'm sure they'd arrest me. I doubt it would go much further than that, though. Admiral Eames would probably have a tough talk with me and send me back out on tour. They wouldn't dare disrupt the Lost Heroes Homecoming Tour, not with all the effort they've put into making me their star.

Instead, I close my eyes and feel the gauze against my skin. I told Jayne I needed time to think. The truth is, I'm confused, and not just about whether to join the Resistance. I'd do anything to have Mira here with me, to have her help me sort through all the chaos in my mind.

The familiar pain of Mira's absence stirs in my gut like a twisting knife. This time, though, instead of running from the pain, I face it.

I keep reliving our rescue from the rift as Mira leaving me, of Mira choosing the Youli over me, but is that just the story I keep telling myself? I've learned enough about stories from Earth Force to know that they're not always the truth.

I replay my moments with Mira in the rift—our relief that we'd survived the Battle of the Alkalinia Seat, the realization that we were trapped, the discovery of the lost aeronauts, the arrival of the Youli.

The more I think about it, the more I realize I have more questions than answers about why Mira left. Yes, she said it was her choice, that she wanted to go. But she also said she had to leave with the Youli, that it was *the only way*, whatever that means.

It's not like she rolled her eyes and said something like

I'm so sick of you, Jasper, that I decided to give up my friends, my planet, my entire life *to go live with our mortal enemy.*

What she did say is this: *You're the glue, Jasper. It has to be you. It's always been you.*

And while that's still pretty cryptic, it doesn't exactly sound like something someone would say as an explanation for why they just didn't want to hang out anymore.

That's simply not the truth.

This is the truth: ever since I escaped the rift, I've been having a giant pity party for myself. And while some of that is probably warranted—after all, Mira is missing, my sister is AWOL, all my friends moved on, and I lost a whole year—it's certainly not helping me move forward with my life.

So, time's up. No more pity party. I have to stop framing everything with me in the center. The world doesn't revolve around me, even if Earth Force would like the public to think so.

I'm not sure why Mira left, but what if . . . maybe . . . it wasn't because of me? What if it was because she believed in the Youli's message of peace and, for reasons I don't yet understand, her leaving was part of that?

Jayne's a Resistance fighter. Her actions aren't motivated by me. They're motivated by her cause. I don't have to look past the risks she's taking within Earth Force to see that.

Marco and Addy didn't abandon me. They thought I was dead. They joined the Resistance to fight for what they believe in, just like Jayne.

Cole and Lucy didn't leave me behind. They just got on with their lives.

And me? Is that my problem—that I can't get on with my life? Is part of me stuck in the limbo of the rift, wondering why all my friends have moved on?

Who would believe that? I've only been out of the rift a few weeks, and I'm already one of the biggest celebrities on the planet.

I rub my gloved hands together, feeling the friction of the material start to build, resisting the temptation to tap in. It's time I stop focusing on others' actions and motivations and turn the spotlight on my own. What do *I* want? What do *I* believe?

I'm still not sure who has it right. Earth Force wants to protect our planet, but their actions hurt others, and they keep the truth from the public. The Resistance wants Earth to become a better planetary citizen, but they're not willing to compromise to get there. The Youli say they want peace, but their actions don't add up.

Somewhere there's a middle ground, and I need to find it. I'm through with being someone else's pawn. It's time to seize control of my own narrative.

For now, that means I need to find my sister and reconnect with Marco.

I need to travel to Gulaga to engage with the Resistance.

I need to tell Waters about the Youli message and hope it's enough for him to see that peace is the only way forward, and we can't get there without compromise. Our future—the future of our planet—depends on it.

18

AS OUR CRAFT TOUCHES DOWN AT AMERICANA East, my hands are shaking. Since the rift warped the passage of time for me, I'll be seeing my parents sooner than I would have if our third tour had gone as planned. But for my parents, it's been close to two years since we were together. They spent most of that time thinking I was dead. Jayne told me that the Force informed my parents that Addy was also missing in action and presumed dead. So even though I'm sure they'll be excited to see me, they'll also want to hear about my sister. At least Jayne was able to get them my video message that we taped in the pod room.

Before we get off the craft, Jayne reviews the tour stop

itinerary with everyone. After the old aeronauts exit the cabin, she catches my eye. We haven't talked since last night. I know she wants to know what I'm thinking, whether I've made a decision about joining the Resistance, but I'm not ready to talk to her. Even though I've made my decision, I'm not ready to forgive her for lying to me.

I cut up a side aisle and head to the exit. Water shuttles wait to take us across the channel. It wasn't long ago that I rode in one with my family and listened to the protestors chant from their barges. Today a different kind of crowd greets us at the landing dock.

Just like at our last two stops, there are tons of people with posters, many of them with images of me and the lost aeronauts. I spot at least a dozen JASPER, WILL YOU MARRY ME? signs. Even if I'm kind of getting used to this celebrity stuff, those signs still make my cheeks warm.

In the middle of the crowd there's some jostling, and soon half a dozen new signs wave in the air: NO MORE WAR!, TELL THE TRUTH!, BOUNDERS HAVE RIGHTS! I bet some of the same protestors were on those water barges when we left for the Academy. Addy had wanted to join them. If only I could tell them what she's up to now. Addy would be their hero.

There's more chaos and confusion in the crowd, and soon the people part, admitting a group of guards with riot gear and raised shields. They zero in on the protestors, who hold their ground. Soon they're literally on the ground, tased and then cuffed.

I guess Jayne wasn't kidding when she told me antiwar messaging had been outlawed.

We're hurried off the shuttles and into hovers for the ride to the Earth Force complex, where we'll be staying. That's where I'll meet up with my parents later tonight during the family and friends visiting hour.

As we drive through the familiar streets of Americana East, I press my hand against the glass. We glide past the green block where Addy, Cole, and I caught our breath after taking the lift for a joyride. Two blocks to the left is my school. Above us, the air rail zooms by. How many times did I sit on a rail car and stare out to sea, waiting for the day I could finally leave for the Academy, the one place in the world where I thought I'd fit in?

Wow. I didn't know what I didn't know.

As soon as I unload from the hover in the garage, I chase down Lucy so I can escape from Jayne and her questioning eyes.

"Hey!" I dodge in front of Lucy and walk backward. "Do you think we can talk about the rally later?"

She narrows her eyes. "You've been doing everything you can to avoid talking to me about these rallies. What's changed?"

Aside from me not wanting to talk to Jayne right now? "I thought I might take on a bigger role. After all, this is my hometown."

Lucy flashes a megawatt smile and throws her arms around me. "Oh, Jasper, you make me so happy! I knew you'd embrace your role as a true celebrity! And I know just how to expand your speaking part. I hope Denver doesn't mind that we'll have to cut his comments short. He'll just have to deal. Tomorrow is your day, Jasper! We're going to make it extra special!"

She slips my hand under her arm and practically drags me across the garage to the lift as she keeps talking about her ideas to make me even more center stage. I glance back to make sure I'm far away from Jayne. Good, she's stuck talking to Sheek. That means she'll be tied up for a while. His list of demands for star treatment grows with each stop.

Once I'm given my room assignment, I take off, eager for some alone time. When I get to my room, I realize how exhausted I am from staying up half the night thinking about what to do. I plan to close my eyes for just a few minutes, but the next thing I know, the room computer is shouting at me.

"Jasper Adams, your guests have arrived. Please proceed to the lounge area."

The good news? The room computer doesn't sound a thing like Florine Statton.

The bad news? I feel totally unprepared to see my parents.

I sit up in bed and look around my room. I don't even remember arriving here. In fact, my mind feels like mush. My palms are sweating. And my feet won't move. Why am I so nervous?

The last time I saw them, they were saying good-bye to me on the flight deck before I left on my third tour of duty. It was Addy's first trip to the EarthBound Academy. My parents asked only one thing of me: to watch over my sister.

How did that go?

I force myself out of my room and down to the lobby. The visitation room is already crowded when I enter, but Mom spots me immediately. She barrels into me from the side and wraps me up in her arms.

"Oh my God," she says, tears streaming down her face. "I can't believe it's really you. I thought we'd never see you again." She buries her head against my shoulder, then pulls back and ruffles my hair. A small cluster of lines frames the corners of her eyes. Those weren't there the last time I saw her.

I'm enveloped in a second hug from behind. "We're so glad to see you, Jasper!" Dad's voice warms me like a blanket.

When they withdraw from the hug, they each grip one of my arms and won't let go.

"Let's find a place to talk." I guide us to a corner with an open love seat and armchair. Mom and I sit together, and Dad sits in the chair.

Across the room, Denver catches my eye. He's sandwiched on a small couch between two much older women. I don't know if they're sisters or friends or something else, but it reminds me that my reunions are not nearly as difficult as Denver's. At least I'm not coming back to find my parents fifteen years older.

"We were stunned when we got the news that you were alive," Mom says, wiping away fresh tears. "When we were first notified that you were missing, we held on to hope, even after your funeral, but as the months passed, we started accepting that we'd really lost you."

"It's so wonderful to see you, Jasper," Dad says. "We never thought this day would come." He leans over and places his palm on my knee. Mom clutches Dad's other hand, so we're all connected.

"It's really good to see you guys," I say.

Dad leans even closer. He looks tired. They both do. "Jasper, we have to ask. Do you have any information about your sister? Could she be alive, too?"

I hesitate. I can't bring myself to lie to my parents about Addy. They deserve to know the truth.

"She is, isn't she?" Mom asks, her voice shaking and rising with each word. "She's alive, but you're not allowed to say anything!"

Heads swing around to stare at us.

"Emma, be quiet!" Dad whispers. "You're attracting attention." He squeezes in beside us on the love seat and lowers his voice. "Can you at least tell us whether she's alive?"

I can't lie. Not about this. Not to my parents. They have a right to know.

I stare directly at my dad and tip my chin just a bit. That's all I can risk. There's too much at stake. The last thing I need is to be on the security team's radar. That would make it nearly impossible for me to ditch away at the rally tomorrow morning.

"What does that mean?" Mom asks. She's trying to be quiet but failing miserably. "Richard, what is Jasper saying?" she asks my dad.

"Is everything all right over here?" a guard asks from behind me.

I stand. "Everything's fine. My parents were asking about how I rescued the lost aeronauts. I was just explaining that the details of the mission are classified."

The guard nods. It's understandable that my parents would be curious. "All you need to know, Dr. and Mr. Adams, is that your son is a hero." He extends his hand to my father.

My father stands and shakes his hand. "Thank you, Officer. We couldn't be more proud of Jasper." He returns to his seat in the armchair.

The rest of the visit is strained. Mom wrestles back tears, and it's clear she's struggling not to ask more about Addy. Dad tells me news from our apartment building, and he fills me in on a new research study that Mom is leading at the hospital, but I can tell he's hoping I can slip them more information about my sister.

Every few minutes, we're interrupted by one of the guests asking for an autograph or a picture with me. At first, my parents are impressed, but then they get annoyed having to share my attention. Before we know it, the visitation hour is up.

"Are you going to the rally tomorrow?" I ask my parents. I know they'll be there, even though I wish they'd stay home. Jayne promised the Resistance was only planting smoke bombs, but something could go wrong. If anything happens to my parents, I'll never be able to forgive myself.

"Of course we'll be there," Mom chokes out, pulling me into a hug.

"We wouldn't miss it," Dad says, joining us again on the love seat and waiting his turn for a hug.

I want to warn them to stay away, but I know I can't. It's too risky. If word got out, the Resistance's plans would be foiled. Not to mention, there's nothing I could say that would convince them not to come—certainly nothing I could say under the watch of all these guards. Jayne better be right about the smoke bombs.

One of the guards catches my eye and nods at the door. It's time for my parents to go.

As I escort them to the exit, Jayne appears out of nowhere.

Great, exactly the person I was hoping to avoid.

"Mr. and Mrs. Adams," she says to my parents. "My name is Jayne. I'm part of the Earth Force public relations team."

I can't believe she'd corner my parents just so she could talk to me.

"It's such a privilege to meet you," she continues. "I wanted to let you know that your daughter, Adeline, is one of the most extraordinary people I've ever met."

What? I mean, Addy's great and all, but that's what she came to say? I fix my eyes on Jayne. She seems totally genuine. I look around to see if anyone is listening. Even bringing Addy's name up is a risk, one I'm surprised Jayne would take.

Mom can't even talk through her tears, so instead she pulls Jayne into a hug.

Dad shakes her hand. "Thank you so much, Jayne. That means the world to us."

After saying good-bye to my parents, Jayne gives me a sad smile. Then she walks away.

So I guess that wasn't about me either.

I DIDN'T THINK IT WAS POSSIBLE, BUT
the crowds seem even bigger here as the hovers cut through
Americana East, transporting me and the old aeronauts to
the seaside stage where we'll hold the rally. They bring us in
through a rear entrance and hurry us to a backstage lounge,
where we'll wait for our cue. The air is thick with the sounds
of thousands waiting for us to appear.

As soon as I walk in, Jayne pulls me aside.

She glances around the lounge then narrows her eyes at
me. "Are you in?"

I nod.

"You have your gloves?"

I bend down and act like I'm scratching my ankle. Lifting my pant leg, I show Jayne the gauzy fabric peeking out of the top of my sock.

"Good." She turns and heads for the exit.

I grab her arm. "Wait! What's the plan?"

She shakes her head. She still has no intention of telling me. "Just do your part."

She's not even going to confirm where I'm going? What if I get it wrong? What if my attempts at guessing what the Resistance wants me to do fall flat? Things are moving way too fast. "What about you?"

"I can take care of myself."

"Will I see you on Gulaga?"

Jayne's eyes almost bug out of her head. She glances around to make sure no one heard me, then drags me out of the lounge and into the empty hall. "No."

"You're staying on the tour? What if you're caught?"

Jayne shakes her head. "I knew the risks, Jasper. You and I are part of a much larger puzzle. Focus on your piece and nothing more."

"But, what if—"

"It's almost time to take our places." She grabs my arm and steers us back into the lounge, closing out any chance I had at getting answers.

It's not like I trust Jayne after all her lies, but I definitely preferred feeling like we were in this together.

Now I'm on my own, and mostly in the dark.

I hope I know what I'm doing.

We've been lined up backstage for almost fifteen minutes, and there's still no sign of Lucy.

Sheek flicks his hair and lets out an exasperated sigh. "Let's just get on with it. It's not like I've never hosted something on my own. Of course, if *I* were missing, it would be catastrophic."

Jayne checks her tablet. She's stressed. Most people probably think she's stressed because Lucy is missing, but I know what's really wrong. We're minutes away from the biggest attack the Resistance has ever launched on Earth soil. I'm sure they've timed their actions to the rally script. Without Lucy up there saying her lines, the timing will be off.

"Jasper! Coming through! Jasper!" Lucy is gasping for breath when she reaches me. Dev and Nev trail behind her, touching up her hair and makeup.

"Where have you been?" Jayne demands. "We were scheduled to go on ten minutes ago."

Lucy waves her off. "Jasper, my magic worked! With almost zero planning and no preparation, I was able to assemble most of your classmates for a memory walk as you make your entrance! Isn't that amazing?"

"What's a memory walk?" I ask. "Wait a second . . . did you say my old *classmates* are here?" A lump forms in the base of my throat, followed by an even bigger lump in the pit of my stomach.

"We need to move, people!" Jayne says. Her eyes are drilling into me. If we don't stay on schedule the Resistance's plans might be a bust.

"Yes!" Lucy says, answering my question. "They're assembling on the other side right now! Immediately before your entrance, they'll march onstage, and then you can walk the line and greet them while everyone cheers. It will be magical! It's the big extra you were looking for! And it will remind the crowd that a few years ago you were just another schoolkid in Americana East! Jasper Adams, boy next door–turned–Earth Force hero!"

How did I get myself into this? The only reason I asked Lucy for a bigger role was because I was trying to avoid Jayne the day we arrived. The last thing I want is a memory walk with my old classmates. I hated my school in Americana East. The other kids called me Klutz most of the time. I bet half of them didn't even know my name until they heard about the Lost Heroes Homecoming Tour.

"Are we going to do this or stand around talking about it all day?" Sheek asks as he surveys his perfectly manicured fingernails.

"He's right," Jayne says. "We can't delay any longer!" She's looking at me as she talks. Actually, everyone is looking at me. I guess tonight is my night.

I nod. "Let's do this."

Lucy smiles, and her eyes sparkle. For a moment, I see her as she used to be: my dramatic, chatty friend with her hair tied back in colorful ribbons. I've missed Lucy, even the new Lucy. I can tell by how happy she is about what she's planned that she's missed me, too. The memory walk might not be what I wanted, but it's Lucy's way of trying to bridge the gap back to me.

It's too bad I'll never get to cross that bridge. Before the night is over, I'll be long gone, first across the continent to Gedney's labs, then hopefully across the galaxy to Gulaga.

Lucy blows me a kiss and takes Sheek's arm to walk onstage. The roar of the crowd swells, and when it finally calms, they say their opening lines.

I strain to see the opposite wing. A group of kids waits for their cue. The lump in my throat thickens as I try to find some familiar faces.

"Please welcome students from Americana East, District Eight!" Lucy turns to their wing and claps.

My former classmates cross the stage in one long line. They're led by a pretty, petite girl with a huge smile. Dilly Epstein. Even when most of the kids were awful, Dilly was always kind to me.

Jayne gently nudges my shoulder. "It's go time."

I step onstage with my own smile plastered on. I pause a moment to wave to the crowd, then I turn to my former classmates and their starstruck faces.

"Hi, Dilly," I say.

"I always knew you were special, Jasper." She leans in and kisses my cheek.

My feet freeze. I can't believe Dilly Epstein just kissed me. Somehow I get moving again, shaking hands with the next kid in line, snagging hugs and collecting kisses.

Next thing I know, I'm face to face with Will Stevens. His hand is on my shoulder and he's smiling and saying congratulations just like he always expected this would happen.

But he never expected this would happen. The day before I left for the space station he laughed in my face and called me a B-wad.

I smile back and shake his hand even as a slew of unkind words race through my mind. *You always thought you were so great, Will. Now look who's on top of the world.*

Then I'm greeting the last kid in line, and my classmates are clapping, and Denver is joining me onstage. He marches me to the front, and I stand before my city, Americana East, as one of the biggest celebrities in the world.

Down in the VIP section in front of the stage, I spot my parents smiling up at me. In the wings, Jayne gives me a thumbs-up. We're seconds away from the attack. She's counting on me to do what's right.

But how do I know what's right? Last night I felt confident that I was making the right decision, but now that the moment's arrived, I'm not so sure. Dilly said she always knew I was special. Maybe she's right. Maybe I *am* special and I'm meant to use my fame and celebrity status to change things for the better.

If I thwarted the Resistance, I'd be even more of a hero than I am now. I'd be even more popular.

All I'd have to do is warn everyone. Instead of saying my next line, I could announce that an attack was planned and urge the crowd to take cover.

Denver says his lines, describing his time in the rift. Soon it will be my turn to talk.

I scan the crowd, looking for signs of the Resistance. All I see are smiling faces.

Lucy elbows me in the rib cage. It's my line.

If I don't say something, they'll skip over me and improvise. My chance to warn the crowd will be lost.

My parents stare up at me, beaming with pride. Right now, they think I'm a hero. What will they think if I join the Resistance?

"I said, what do you think, Jasper?" Denver asks.

I swallow hard. "I think . . . I think . . ." I steal a glance at the wing. Jayne's no longer there. In the VIP section, someone is running through the crowd, shoving past my parents, heading for the exit. Earth Force officers spill out the side doors, weapons raised.

"Watch out!"

Bombs blast in near unison across the sea of faces below. A cloud of smoke billows across the stage as guards storm from the wings, pushing us away from the crowd. I fight through their ranks to the edge of the stage to see what's happening.

Smoke fills the air and the sound of gun fire rings all around. The crowd is in chaos.

This is my chance. All I need to do is run for the exit.

But what about my parents? They're down there. Somewhere.

There wasn't supposed to be violence!

I drop down off the stage and jump the rope into the VIP section. I wade through the thick smoke, searching for my parents.

There are people everywhere. I nearly trip over a small girl who must have been separated from her family. Seconds later, a woman cries with relief and scoops the girl into her arms.

I push on, scanning the soot-covered faces. Finally I spot a man on the ground. There's something familiar about his body, his posture. I lunge in that direction.

My dad is kneeling with my mom in his arms. Her clothes are soaked in blood. My dad presses a ripped cloth against her shoulder.

"Mom! Are you okay? I'll go get help!" This is all my fault. How could I let this happen?

"You need to get to safety, Jasper," Dad says. "You might be a target."

"I'm not," I tell him. "Let me get help!"

"She'll make it," he says, pushing me away. "I think it's just a surface wound. Please, take cover!"

"Jasper," Mom whispers. She stretches her hand toward my cheek.

"Quiet, Emma," Dad says. "Don't strain yourself."

I lean close. "I'm here, Mom."

"Find your sister."

My resolve hardens. I lock eyes with my mom and nod.

Then I run for the exit.

Crowds pour out of the stadium onto the streets. I duck into the first alley I pass. I swing my blast pack around and pull out the hat and glasses. Then I strip off my Earth Force shirt and stuff it into my pack.

I can't believe I left my mom! I should go back. She could be dying. Jayne promised there wouldn't be violence. Why did I believe her?

Mom said to find Addy. That needs to be my focus now. I

stay close to the buildings and sprint as fast as I can, but it's a lot of stops and starts as I dodge the crowd. Soon the crowds start to thin, as I manage to outrun most of the spectators. By now, Earth Force is probably realizing that I'm missing. I wonder if one of the lost aeronauts is missing, too, if the Resistance's plan was successful. I wonder who they took.

I keep running. There's only three more blocks to my apartment building. When I finally reach it, I race down the ramp to the parking garage and keep on running to the lower level.

I race to the back where the storage rooms are. I find the one that Addy and I used for our secret meeting before she left with me for the Academy. I try the door. It doesn't budge. Please don't be locked. I shove against it with my shoulder, and it swings open.

A cloud of dust rises to greet me as I close the door and flip the light switch. Dust quickly coats my nose and throat. I try to cough it out, but that only stirs up more dust.

The weird dolls with the red lips look at me. I try not to pay attention to their unblinking stares. Instead, I dig my gloves out of my socks. I slide them onto my blood-covered hands and fit the fingers. They feel exactly like my old gloves. I hope they work the same.

I pull my shirt up over my nose and mouth and take a deep breath. Gedney better be right about the quantum detection scanners not working underground. What if he's wrong?

What if there's actually a quantum scrambler in use? Those work underground. They used them in Gulagaven. And they don't block bounds, they just scatter your atoms across the universe if you attempt a bound. That would make a quick end to this whole Jasper-finding-Addy plan.

Here goes nothing.

I drop my hands to my sides and close my eyes. Then I reach out with my mind and feel instantly alive. My skin tingles with excitement. I sense every atom in the room, then in the garage, then in my building, then in all of Americana East. I expand my consciousness until I feel I could fill the whole universe and bend every atom to my will.

But that's not why I'm here. I'm a trained soldier, and now I fight for my own cause.

Flexing my fingers, I raise my hands and draw atoms like metals to a magnet. They crystallize into a great ball of energy, swirling and swelling until my port is complete.

I pull up an image of Waters's and Gedney's labs.

Then I bound.

MY HIP STRIKES THE PAVEMENT OF THE
helipad halfway across the American continent. My landings still need work. No wonder I never healed right after my fall in the hangar during my first tour of duty. The new gloves aren't the problem, although they are a bit quick on the takeoff.

An alarm is sounding—probably a quantum detection scanner announcing my arrival. I push myself up on my hands and knees.

A few moments later, Gedney shuffles out the lab door.

"Welcome, Jasper! I'm so glad you made it." He extends his palm, but I get the rest of the way up on my own. I brush the dust from the basement closet off my uniform and pull off my gloves, my hands still covered with my mom's blood.

"There wasn't supposed to be violence!" I shout at him. "My mom was shot!"

Gedney's face winces in alarm. "I'm so sorry. Things didn't go exactly as planned."

I bend over and rest my hands on my knees, catching my breath and trying to slow my racing heart. I can't believe I left my mom at the rally. What if she doesn't make it? What if there's more violence? What if they're caught in the cross fire? Sobs build in my chest. I swallow them down. "I think she'll be okay," I say, mostly trying to convince myself. "My dad said it was a surface wound."

Gedney nods. "I'll try to have someone check on her as soon as possible. I'm sorry, son."

I'm furious with the Resistance, and I'm annoyed that Gedney wasn't being honest about his role with them when he visited me on the Lost Heroes Homecoming Tour. But even so, I'm happy to see him. "I guess you were expecting me."

Gedney tips his head. "Let's say I was hoping you'd come."

"I didn't know you were working with the Resistance." We might as well clear the air about that up front.

"It's best to be discreet, don't you think? At any rate, you seem to have found out on your own." He turns and hobbles back where he came from, calling over his shoulder, "Come in. We have much to catch up on."

I follow Gedney into the kitchen of the lab building where one of his assistants is at the stove, stirring a huge silver pot with an old wooden spoon.

"You remember Jasper Adams?" Gedney leans over the pot and inhales the fragrant smell of garlic and onions and spice.

"Of course," the woman says. "Nice to see you, Jasper. The chili is ready. Eat up."

After she leaves the kitchen, Gedney points at a chair. "Sit. I'll dish it out." He pulls two white bowls from the cupboard and ladles chili into both. "You can speak freely in front of my staff. They're loyal to Jon—and to me, I suppose, although it's Jon who brought them on."

"Have you been working with Waters all this time?"

"Not exactly." He places a steaming bowl of chili on the table in front of me alongside a tall glass of water. "Jon and I had a falling-out on Gulaga. I strongly disagreed with his decision to implant the Youli brain patches in you and Mira, as you know. Then so much went wrong on the tour: the disastrous meeting with the Youli, the alliance with the Alks, the unexpected Earth Force offensive at the intragalactic summit. Some of the blame belongs to Jon. He knows it, but it took a while for him to see his part. It took even longer before we were ready to talk it out. But in the end, we want the same things—for you kids, for Earth, for the greater galaxy."

"Why aren't you on Gulaga?"

"It's important to have members of the Resistance every-where, don't you think? That way we can more effectively do what our name suggests: resist. Here at the labs I'm still doing important research. Yes, it may benefit Earth Force in the short run, but it will benefit Earth in the long run. Waters understands that. Of course, the real value of me staying in place is my ability to pass information and . . . other things, if you will."

"So you're a spy like Jayne?" I cringe as I say her name. What if Jayne was injured at the rally, too? In my mind I see my dad holding my mom, both of them covered in her blood.

"I wouldn't use that word, but if it helps you to frame it that way, so be it."

I press my eyes shut, trying to erase the picture of my parents. I need to focus. Jayne wasn't willing to give me any answers. Hopefully Gedney is. "What do you want from me?"

"You're in a unique position, Jasper. You're one of the few humans alive who has talked with the Youli directly."

I swirl the chili around the bowl with my spoon. I suppose there's no reason to hold back with Gedney. "The Youli gave me a message in the rift. They want peace."

Gedney bows his head and takes a long breath. "That is good news." He sits back in his chair. "You have doubts?"

He must see the confusion written on my face. "Cole doesn't think we should listen to the Youli. He showed me vids of the Battle of the Alkalinian Seat and other clashes with the Youli that happened while I was stuck in the rift. How can the Youli seek peace but still attack our people?"

He folds his hands on the table. "It's complex. We dealt a blow to the Youli when you kids placed the degradation patch on their vessel. It divided them."

"That's what the Youli who helped us escape from the rift told us."

"It's true, and such division is particularly challenging for a species used to acting with a collective mind. Some of their people believed that Earth should be stopped and were willing to do whatever it took to make that happen. But recent reports suggest they've healed their internal differences, and that they're ready to move forward. That's why now is the perfect time to negotiate a peace between our planets and finally join the vast intragalactic community."

Gedney's explanation makes sense and squares with the other facts I've gathered since returning from the rift, but I'm still not clear why the Resistance is so eager for me to join them. They risked blowing Jayne's cover in hopes she'd convert me, and I don't even think they knew about the Youli message. "Where do I fit in?"

He doesn't answer at first. Instead, he studies my face,

then slowly smiles. "We've always said the Bounders are the future, but you kids never understand how important you are, do you?"

When I don't reply, he continues, "The Youli know you can communicate with them, Jasper. They've known since they first encountered you on the Paleo Planet, long before you had the brain patch implanted. Now they've entrusted you with an important message. Don't forget you also have relationships with leaders in both Earth Force and the Resistance. I'd say it's clear how you fit in. And that's not even counting your relationship with Miss Matheson."

My heart jumps. "Do you have news about Mira?"

He shakes his head. "Only whispers, I'm afraid. I've heard she's alive and safe. I believe in my heart that she is critical to the peace process."

I almost wish he hadn't said that. It makes me think—it makes me *hope*—that Mira will come back, that her absence is part of the larger workings of the galaxy that I just don't understand right now. Mira always sensed that kind of stuff. Maybe her leaving with the Youli had all to do with that and nothing to do with me. "I wish she were here. She'd know what to do." And she'd help me calm down. How am I supposed to play an important part in the peace process—how am I even supposed to track down my sister—when I don't know if my mom is okay?

Gedney leans forward and lays his frail hand on my shoulder. "Perhaps Mira will be back someday soon, Jasper. For now, you need to trust in yourself, and something tells me you know what to do, too."

I try not to think any more about Mira or my mom. There's no time for a pity party. Like Gedney said, I need to trust myself and do what needs to be done: get to Gulaga, talk to Waters, and find Addy. "I can't make a difference from here. We both know where I need to go."

Gedney nods. "I was hoping you'd feel that way."

"But first," I say, "I need to know what happened on Gulaga. During our tour of duty, it was clear a lot of Tunnelers weren't fans of Earth Force, and we knew about the Wackies, but all of that was still pretty underground. Literally, underground." I choke out a laugh at my bad joke.

"Good one." Gedney chuckles. He takes my chili bowl and refills it at the stove. When he returns to the table, his tone is serious. "After the space elevator snapped, unrest grew on Gulaga. Waters stayed behind and mobilized the rebels. Earth Force miscalculated. They left repairs in the hands of the Tunnelers, so when the Resistance rose up, there weren't many who were willing to stand and fight for Earth Force. In fact, almost every Tunneler was proud to fight with the Resistance. Soon, the remaining Earth Force loyalists were forced off the planet or . . ."

He doesn't finish the sentence. "Killed," I say.

Gedney nods. "No matter how you look at it, Jasper, this is war."

"That's why we need peace. Too many have died already. I have to carry the Youli message to the Resistance. What's the plan?"

"As soon as the escort arrives with the seized aeronaut, you'll be stowed away on a cargo ship bound for the Nos Redna Space Port. From there, our operative will fly you to Gulaga."

I'd almost forgotten that the smoke bombs at the rally were just a distraction for the Resistance to kidnap an aeronaut. "The plan worked? Things turned ugly and violent pretty quick. I figured the Resistance really botched things up."

Shaking my head free of images from the rally, I ball my hands into fists. When I get to Gulaga, I'm going to have some choice words for Waters about the Resistance and its tactics. It's almost like they're taking lessons from Earth Force, even if their positions are at odds.

"Again, son, I'm so sorry about your mother." Gedney speaks softly, obviously aware of how upset I am. "We believe the Force picked up on our plans at the last minute, but we managed to carry out the operation. If we tuned into the webs, you'd quickly learn that you and Denver Reddy are missing."

My mouth falls open. "It's Denver?"

Gedney nods.

"That's a huge blow to Earth Force!"

"Everything came together, even with the breach in intelligence."

"You're sending us both to Gulaga?"

"That's the plan." He smiles and pats my hand. "Now finish your chili and relax. You probably won't have much good food or rest for a while." He scrapes his bowl and takes it to the sink.

We talk for a few minutes about the logistics of my stay. He promises to check on my mother as soon as he can. Then he leaves the kitchen to return to his laboratory.

I can't believe I'm going back to Gulaga, back to a diet of forage and fungi and BERF bars. It's time to stockpile Earth food. I force down a third bowl of chili, even though I'm way past full. Maybe Gedney will let me bring a duffel filled with snacks to Gulaga.

After I eat, I refill my glass with clean, cold water. I take a long sip and let it trickle down my throat. I try not to think about much—my brain is tired of thinking,—but whenever my mind starts to relax, I see my mom on the ground covered in blood.

I have to trust that she's okay, that the wound wasn't serious, that her friends and colleagues at the hospital are giving her good care.

But even if she's not okay, I'm doing exactly as she asked. I'm going to find my sister.

The next morning, I wake to the cutting swish of helicopter blades out the window. Gedney told me last night that the helicopter pilot is an agent for the Resistance, even though he works for Earth Force. Every week he does an authorized supply run for the laboratory, which often includes a lot of unauthorized information and materials for the Resistance. Today, his cargo is a bit different. If Gedney is right, Denver Reddy should be on board.

I pull on the pair of sweatpants one of the lab assistants gave me last night and head for the helipad.

Gedney's already waiting outside. "Your traveling companions have arrived."

The helicopter touches down and the blades start to slow.

I'm not sure what I'll say to Denver. I can't imagine he's in a very good mood after being kidnapped. Plus, I have no idea what they've told him about me, if they told him anything.

The pilot hops out of the cockpit and crouches to avoid the blades. Then he opens the back door and leans inside. Next thing I know, he's pulling Denver out by his bound wrists.

Denver bends low and jogs alongside the pilot to clear the helicopter. When he looks up, his eyes find mine.

His face is a mix of fury and confusion. "I wasn't expecting to see *you* here, kid. You were in on this?"

"Not exactly," I say. "I had no idea you were part of it. I wasn't sure *I* was until a few days ago."

"You're going to have to explain that," Denver says.

Before I can reply, Gedney claps Denver on the shoulder. "Everything will be explained soon, Captain Reddy. We apologize for the manner in which you've been brought here, but it was necessary to—"

Gedney keeps talking, but I can't focus on his words. Someone else is climbing out of the helicopter and running toward the labs.

A dark knot twists in my belly—because even though he's hunched over and wearing a hat, I can tell from the way he moves that it's Regis.

I grab Gedney by the arm and pull him around the side of the lab building. When we're out of view of the others, I turn on him. "You didn't tell me Regis was coming!"

"I wasn't sure he was until this very moment." Gedney keeps calm, even though I'm clearly furious, and even though I just forcefully dragged him across the compound. "The Resistance employs several different escorts, and identities of those on specific missions are divulged on a need-to-know basis."

I clench my fists. "But you knew it was possible."

"I also knew you might not agree to come if I told you Regis would be traveling to Gulaga."

"He's going to Gulaga? With me?" I laugh, if you can call the nasty, stupefied croak that forces its way out of my throat a laugh. "Then you're right, Gedney. If Regis is going, I'm not." I turn away from him, walk the long way around the laboratory buildings, and kick open the gate of the compound. Without a glance back, I jog across the field of wildflowers where I once lay with Mira counting stars and listening to crickets. I shake my head free of the memory and push forward up the mountain.

I'VE BEEN CLIMBING AT A BRISK PACE
for several minutes when I hear footsteps crunching dry
leaves on the path behind me.

"Hey!" Regis yells. "Wait up!"

The dark knot in my gut twists tighter. I can name it now
as the particular mix of anger and wariness that I associate
with Regis. I won't let him see my fear, but I wish I were wearing my gloves.

"Why would I wait for you?" I call over my shoulder.
"What could you possibly have to say to me?"

"Please, Jasper!"

Please, Jasper? Those are words I never thought I'd hear from Regis. I turn around and plant my feet.

Regis stops and bends over his knees, out of breath. It's clear he's been running to catch me. "Give me a sec," he says between gasps.

Smart Jasper would turn his back on Regis and keep heading up the path, but I'm not thinking smart right now. I'm actually curious what on earth he's going to say to try to bridge the chasm that exists between us—a chasm at least as deep and dark as the one he forced Mira and me off in Gulagaven. If it weren't for Mira's quick thinking, he would have killed us both.

Regis takes a huge gulp of air. "Look, I was a jerk, I get it."

"You were a *jerk*? You *get* it? What exactly do you *get*, Regis?"

"I have a lot of regrets, okay?" Regis stands and clasps his hands above his head, still breathing hard. "But it was a long time ago, and I've been working really hard to show I've changed."

I laugh. "You have an odd definition of 'long time.'"

He drops his hands and starts to close the distance between us. "I know it must seem that way to you."

Right. From Regis's perspective, our tour in Gulaga was a year and a half ago. For me, it wasn't half that long.

Regis keeps on talking. "Getting booted from the Academy

was the best and worst thing that happened to me. I blamed you at first, Jasper. I knew it was Gedney who arranged for my dismissal, and I had a hunch you put him up to it. But shortly after I got home, Gedney reached out to me. He explained that some of my behavior has to do with my genetics—I have these impulses that are hard to control. It's not an excuse, but it helps explain things."

"You're right; it's not an excuse."

Regis keeps going like he didn't hear me. "Gedney's been great. He's helped me develop strategies to stay calm and focused."

I curl my fingers tight against my palms. "You've been working with Gedney all this time? You were in touch with him during my mission to Alkalinia?" I talked to Gedney about Regis the day before we left for that slimy, underwater planet. How could he look me straight in the face and talk about Regis's dismissal from the Academy and not mention that he was helping him get all zen or whatever?

"Yes. I'd been leaking information on behalf of the Resistance for months by then."

Wait . . . before Addy and I left for the Academy, there was an anonymous informant who was pumping the webs with Earth Force secrets. The Force was doing everything it could to contain the leak, and promising swift and serious discipline for anyone caught divulging secrets, including

Bounders. Addy and I were interrogated. I was convinced our apartment was bugged. That's why Addy and I had to talk in our building's basement storage room, the dusty old closet with the freaky dolls where I bounded from yesterday. Could Regis have been the leak?

I tip my head and look Regis in the eyes. "Were you the one who tipped off the media about the Bounders and the Youli war?"

Regis nods with a satisfied smile.

"How'd you do it? You managed to keep leaking secrets even when Earth Force swept the planet on a major manhunt for the mole."

"What can I say? I've always been creative in my plans. Remember Florine and the tofu noodles? At least this time I'm fighting for the right side rather than just fighting."

The image of Florine in the trough with the noodles in her hair forces a smile onto my face. "Those noodles were awesome."

"Yeah." Regis laughs and shakes his head. "She was drowning in those things!"

"All you could see were her pink fingernails reaching out for help!"

"Help me! Puh-leeeze!"

Regis's Florine impression is so spot-on, I burst out laughing.

Wait a second! I am *not* sharing a laugh with Regis. No way!

"How about we head back to the labs?" Regis asks, trying to take advantage of our chummy moment.

I backpedal up the path. "Are you kidding? I'm not heading anywhere with you!" The pitch of my voice rises. "It doesn't matter what line of fluff you give me, and I don't care what Gedney says, you can't erase the past! I almost died because of you! Mira almost died! There is no coming back from that!"

Regis takes a deep breath, and this time it's not from running up the mountain. He balls his fists, then flexes his fingers. The seconds pass. I can almost hear him counting to ten in his head.

"I'm trying very hard, Jasper," he says through a clenched jaw. "I want to do what's right."

"Great. Do what's right. If the Resistance wants a civil war, they're going to need soldiers. More bodies can only help."

"That's not what I mean, and you know it!" Regis shouts. "I've spent the last eighteen hours with that has-been aeronaut Denver Reddy and all his arrogant blather. I'm not going to take it from you!"

"You kidnapped Denver. What did you expect? And what on earth did you expect me to do? Hold your hand all the way to Gulaga?"

"I've come to escort you to the headquarters of the Resistance, and you're going to come with me whether you like it or not!"

I stop backpedaling, and instead march right up to Regis. "Are you threatening me?"

He lunges forward, stopping just inches from my face. "What if I am?"

I keep my voice low and level. "I'd say, I'm right. You haven't changed a bit."

Regis deflates. He takes a step back. His face is red, and he won't look at me. "I'm going back to the labs," he whispers. "Please think about this, Jasper. The Resistance needs you. I don't want to be the one who prevents that."

Instead of responding, I turn around and head up the mountain. My muscles are tense, like they're bracing for impact. I'm half convinced Regis is going to plow up the path and tackle me. That's definitely what the old Regis would do.

I can't believe the Resistance is entrusting such an important mission to Regis. First the attack gone wrong at the rally, and now this? I almost died because of Regis and my mom almost died because of the Resistance. Why did I go AWOL to help a bunch of rebels who are just as bad as Earth Force, maybe even worse?

As I climb, the sounds of the forest soon replace the heavy fall of Regis's shoes on the path. Up ahead, a bird whistles—three shrill calls. His mate answers from the left, high in the trees. Every few steps, the brush stirs as a critter scurries to get out of my way.

I want to stay mad, but the calmness of the forest seeps in and relaxes me. I love this place. There aren't many spots left on Earth where you can simply be in harmony with the natural world.

That's why Earth is so obsessed with the Paleo Planet. It reminds us what our planet used to be like. Of course, we're stripping the nature away there as well. They've probably even amped up the occludium mining operations since the Resistance ousted Earth Force from Gulaga.

I can't believe Gedney expects me to travel there with Regis. He knows our history. It's not fair to even ask me to go with him.

Still, what if what Regis said about genetics is true? Could his "behavioral issues," as Jayne called them, be due to his Bounder genes? If so, is it fair to hold him solely accountable? And what if it's possible that he's changed?

I shake the thoughts from my head. I am *not* going to Gulaga with Regis.

For the rest of the climb, I push myself hard. I focus on the burn in my muscles and the strain in my lungs as I climb higher up the mountain. With every step, I get farther away from everything weighing me down and holding me back.

The forest starts to fade and rocks dot the landscape. Soon I emerge on the ridge where my pod mates and I ate lunch when we reunited here before our second tour of duty.

I hunt around until I spot the cairn we built. The tower of rocks still stands, memorializing the strength of our pod. I can almost hear our voices ring out.

It's all about the pod.

So much has changed.

How did things break apart?

Can we ever come back together?

I pound on the laboratory door until Gedney finally hobbles into view.

"Patience, patience, my boy," he says, pulling back the door. "You'll wake the whole compound."

I put my palm against the door and push. It flies open and slams into the wall. "I thought you were all about hurry, hurry, hurry."

Gedney turns around and slowly makes his way to the other side of the laboratory—past the glass aquariums filled with Youli appendages and various other alien body parts used to develop stolen biotechnology. I follow Gedney to the small alcove in the back of the lab, where a metal table is pushed against a side wall. On the opposite wall is Waters's desk. On top of the desk is the glass orb—now empty—that used to store the Youli brain patches Waters implanted in me and Mira.

Gedney drags a rolling desk chair to the metal table and gestures to a nearby stepladder, presumably suggesting I sit.

I don't.

"I can see you're upset," he says.

"To put it mildly."

"Good news, son. We were able to confirm that your mother is doing well. She's already home from the hospital."

Something inside of me unclenches, and I let out a deep breath.

Gedney points again at the stepladder. "Please."

I sit down and immediately regret it. He's already managed to bend me to his will. I'm sure in his mind he's only a few moves away from getting me to agree to go with Regis.

Gedney folds his hands in his lap. "What's on your mind, Jasper?"

"You lied to me."

"I did not."

"You told us you got Regis kicked out of the Academy. Meanwhile, you'd already recruited him for your secret work with the Resistance. How is that not lying?"

"That's exactly what I did," Gedney says calmly, "and I never lied to you about it."

I spring up from the stepladder. "Don't try to trip me up on technicalities! How could you do this? You knew what Regis did to me and Mira!"

Gedney steeples his fingers. "I will always put the interests of the Bounders first. Regis is a Bounder."

"And a psychopathic would-be killer."

"I don't see it that way. Yes, Regis has a history of violence, but isn't that partially Earth Force's fault? We reintroduced the Bounder genes without any support despite knowing that they brought along challenges as well as strengths. If we had intervened with Regis when he young, he may have learned to express his passions in other ways."

"His passions? You sound like he likes to paint or collects vintage comic books! Plotting my death is not a passion!"

Gedney locks his eyes with mine. "I do not excuse Regis's behavior, Jasper, but I do believe in him as a member of the Resistance. People can change. Do you not feel you've changed since entering the Academy?"

Here he goes again, trying to outwit me, and it's working. Lucy's words ring in my mind. *All you wanted, Jasper, was to be popular.* I've tried to convince myself that Lucy was wrong. But what if she wasn't? Maybe that's exactly who I was when I arrived at the Academy. If I've changed for the better, could Regis?

It doesn't matter. "I could never trust him."

"*Never* is an extreme word, but I didn't ask you to trust him. I asked you to go with him to Gulaga. Trust . . . well, that's something for another day. Maybe Regis will prove himself to you and you'll come to trust him."

I laugh. That's the funniest thing I've heard in a long time, ten times funnier than Florine Statton and the tofu strings. Anyone who thinks I might come to trust Regis is out of their mind.

"Will you go with him?" Gedney asks.

I don't answer.

Gedney spins his chair and withdraws a tablet from a file under the table. "That's why you came down here, isn't it? To help make up your mind?" He sets the tablet on the table.

I sit back down on the stepladder. "Can't I go without him?"

"No. Regis has made this trip before, and he knows what to do. You don't. And you certainly don't while smuggling an unwilling hostage."

"Denver."

Gedney nods and turns back to face me. "Jasper, I've said this already. You're critical not only to the Resistance, but to the bigger picture—the movement for peace. For starters, we're going to need Denver's cooperation, and you're the only one who's spent time with him since he escaped the rift. I'm sure your presence will go some distance in ensuring Denver's reunion with Jon isn't a total disaster."

"Denver knows Waters?"

"Of course. The last time they saw each other, they weren't on the best of terms. I'll leave that for you to hear directly from the two of them."

My gaze is drawn back to the glass orb on Waters's desk. I wasn't on the best of terms with Waters when I saw him last either, and now I'm considering joining him in the Resistance. Maybe this whole thing is a bad idea.

"I knew this would be difficult for you, Jasper," Gedney says, "so I enlisted help to convince you." He glides his finger across the tablet. A projection flashes in the air above and then crystallizes around an image of my sister.

"Addy?" I lean forward, trying to get a better view, but the image quality is pretty poor. Even so, I can see that Addy looks different, older. "When was this filmed?"

"Earlier today. We took a great risk with the transmission." He presses the play icon and Addy jumps to life.

"Jasper!" Addy raises her hand to the camera, almost like she can touch me across the stars. "I'm so relieved you're alive! After what happened on Alkalinia, I thought I'd never see you again!" She glances to the side, then bites her lip and nods. Someone outside the camera angle must be giving her directions. She leans closer to the lens. "Jasper, I don't have much time. Just please do as Gedney says and come here right away! We need you. *I* need you. I love you, J! I'll see you real soon!" She lifts her hand again, and the image freezes.

My eyes fill with tears that struggle to escape. Even though I'd been assured that Addy was alive, that she'd survived the Battle of the Alkalinian Seat, I'd never felt 100 percent sure until this very moment. Her message had to have been recorded earlier today, otherwise it wouldn't make any sense. I raise my palm to the projection and hold it against my sister's frozen fingers.

Addy is alive.

She needs me.

And I promised Mom I'd find her.

Okay, Gedney, you win.

"Fine . . . I'll go."

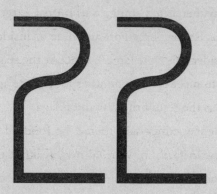

22

REGIS, DENVER, AND I STAND SIDE BY
side in the hangar, staring at the small crate.

"You can't be serious," Denver says.

"I'm not excited about it, either," Regis says, "but we have no choice and very little time, so shut your mouth and climb in."

The crate is roughly a meter and a half square on the bottom, and not nearly as high. The three of us won't even be able to sit up straight once we're inside. How on earth will we make it all the way to the space port in that?

This morning at the compound, Gedney laid out the plan as we ate breakfast. The pilot, who doubled as a Resistance operative, would pick us up in the helicopter and transport us to a seldom-used freight hangar at the nearby Earth Force base. From there, he'd smuggle us onto a cargo craft bound for the Nos Redna Space Port and hide us inside a large crate (they consider this crate large?). Once at the space port, we're supposed to meet up with another Resistance agent who will transport us the rest of the way to Gulaga.

"I thought Gedney said there'd be food," I say, not that I'm hungry. In fact, I'm worried my breakfast might make a reappearance the second we're sealed into the crate. I'm just trying to stall.

Regis points at a duffel bag by his feet. "There are the supplies."

"The crate's not even big enough for us and our blast packs!" I say. "Where are we supposed to put that duffel?"

Regis glares at me. "You're worse than Denver. Both of you, get in!"

"Not unless you make me, tough guy," Denver says, "which really means, not unless you make *us*." He lifts his right hand, taking my left along for the ride, and shakes it at Regis.

This morning, when Gedney cuffed Denver to me, I protested. Even if Denver is a flight risk, he's not my problem. He's not my prisoner. Gedney wasn't interested in my opinion. Apparently, Denver couldn't be cuffed to Regis because

Regis needs his hands free in case he needs to use his gun.

That's right. I'm traveling in confined quarters with Regis, who is armed, while I'm handcuffed to an unwilling captive. Nothing could possibly go wrong.

"Yeah, that's what I thought," Denver says to Regis, who's getting angrier by the millisecond. "You just talk tough."

Regis balls his fists as his face turns from pink to pinker to bright, flaming red. Then he closes his eyes and takes a deep breath. His mouth forms words, though no sounds come out. He's counting to ten, one of his calm-down strategies courtesy of Gedney.

Denver laughs. "Keep counting. You're a ticking time bomb."

Regis's eyes fly open, and he jumps forward, shoving Denver in the chest. My arm jerks back as Denver falls to the hangar floor. I land on top of him. Regis knocks me off and sticks the gun in Denver's face. Denver keeps right on laughing.

I glance at my watch. If what Regis said before is true, we only have a few minutes before the pilot comes back with the crew to load the craft. If I'm going to see Addy, I need to get in that crate now.

"Stop letting him provoke you," I say to Regis as I push myself to my knees and yank Denver by the cuff. "Let's go."

Denver doesn't give me too much of a fight, not with Regis's gun now jabbed between his shoulder blades. We haul ourselves up on the loading rack and climb into the crate. I swing my blast pack off my free arm and sink down. There's just enough room for me to sit with my knees bent. Once the lid is on, I'll have to duck my head.

Regis tosses in the duffel then climbs in next to me. There is literally no room between us. We're packed like sardines.

Great. I'm sandwiched between Regis and Denver for the entire trip. This is going to be the longest few hours of my life.

Technically, I guess my hours in the rift were the longest in my life—a whole year long—but something tells me this trip will feel even longer.

A moment later, we hear footsteps, then the pilot's head appears over the crate. "All set?" he whispers. "Nighty-night."

He slides the lid over the crate, leaving us in almost total darkness. The only light comes from four slits carved into the corners, our source of fresh air for the journey. Next, a drill buzzes. He's sealing us in.

My breath comes fast. I'm not good in small places. The tight walls of the crate get even tighter, like they're going to flatten me into a pancake. I close my eyes, but all I can feel is the sensation of being suffocated. I'm back on Alkalinia with a gazillion gallons of water pressing down on me.

I. Can't. Breathe.

"Settle down, kid," Denver whispers. "You've got to stop hyperventilating. It's going to be a long ride. Take a tip from your friend here and try some deep breaths."

"Shut up," Regis says.

"He's not my friend," I say between gasps for air.

"Seriously, shut up, both of you," Regis says. "Don't make a sound until we take off. We can't risk anyone in the crew hearing us."

I focus on slowing my breath and try to send my mind to a different place. Just yesterday I ran through the field of wild flowers where Mira and I lay side by side and counted stars before leaving for Gulaga. I relax my mind and go back to that field. I see the vast sky dotted with tiny pinpricks of light. I hear the insects buzzing between blades of grass. I feel Mira's long fingers weaving with my own.

The crate jerks, and I slide into Regis, even though I didn't know there was any room left to slide. The crate is at an incline; we must be on a loading belt. Once we level out, we're hefted into the air and jostled. When we're set down, I assume it's for good, but then the crate is shoved even deeper into the craft. We must be flush against some other crates, because the small amount of light we have is dimmed in two corners.

"Do you think they blocked the air slits?" I whisper. "If we can't breathe, we're goners."

"Shhh!" Regis says. "You're fine! Keep dreaming about Magic Mira and be quiet."

I clench my fists and bite down on my lip. I want to rail at Regis, but he's right that we need to be quiet. I can't believe he guessed (correctly) that I was thinking about Mira. I can't give him an excuse to say anything more about her. If he does, Denver's bound to ask questions about Mira and how she came to leave the rift with the Youli, a topic I've somehow managed to avoid with him so far.

We're quiet for a long time. At first, I'm convinced we're running out of air, but then I forget to worry about it, and I'm still breathing, so I guess it's not a problem. But what is a problem: the heat. It's getting hotter by the second. And it stinks. I don't know what this crate is typically used for, but it smells like old cheese. I try to breathe out of my mouth, but that's worse. I can still smell cheese, only now I can pretty much taste it, too.

If I could just move around, I might be able to take my mind off the smell and the sweat that's pooling in every crease of my skin. But there's nowhere to go. I shift my legs. Denver shoves my shin. My legs fall the other way. Regis knocks my knees with his own. I keep my eyes closed and try not to think about the absolutely horrible, utterly unfathomable situation I'm in.

Why on earth did I agree to do this?

We haven't even left the ground, and I'm losing it.

A loud noise sounds, and the light in the crate dims even more.

"They've sealed the door," Regis says. "We're probably about to leave."

"Thanks for that nugget of wisdom," Denver says. "We never would have guessed."

"Regis is super smart like that," I say.

Regis elbows me in the rib cage.

"Ow!" I shove him back.

He elbows me again.

Denver slaps my forehead with his cuff-free hand. "Stop it! Both of you! The only thing worse than being locked in this crate for a whole day is being locked in here with you two!"

"You don't need to tell me." My forehead stings, but not enough to distract me from the foul cheese smell.

"Apparently, I do, kid, because you and your pal keep making things even more unbearable."

"I told you, he's not my pal," I say.

"Fine, whatever you say. There's obviously history between you. What's all the bad blood?"

"Regis tried to kill me," I answer matter-of-factly.

Denver exhales in a long whistle. "That would do it."

"I thought we weren't going to bring up the past," Regis grumbles.

"I never agreed to that, nor will I ever. I said I'd try to move on, but that doesn't mean I'm going to forget what happened."

Regis slams his fist against the side of the crate. At least it wasn't the side of my head.

"Why don't you count to ten like they taught you in reform school or wherever they sent you to make you somewhat human?" I ask.

Regis slams his fist again.

"New topic," Denver says. "How long have you been working with the Resistance, kid? Is that why you pulled us out of the rift in the first place?"

"What? No. I'm not working for the Resistance. Or, well, not formally. I didn't even know the plan in Americana East until a few days ago, when Jayne—"

Regis elbows me in the ribs again. This time, I deserved it.

"Jayne is part of the Resistance?" Denver asks. "I never would have guessed. She seems so rah-rah Earth Force."

"Forget I said anything."

"You suck, Jasper," Regis says.

"Since it's already out there," I say, "I have to know: Is Jayne okay? Was her cover blown?"

"Not until right now," Regis says.

Yeah, I suck. "The point is, I have friends on both sides," I tell Denver. "My sister is with the Resistance. I haven't seen her in a long time."

"So all of this is about a family reunion for you?" Denver asks.

"No, there's a lot more to it." There is, but I'm not sure how to explain it to Denver. I rub my head with my free hand. "I agree with the Resistance's principles. And I think they have the best shot at negotiating peace."

"Peace? Are you kidding?" Denver asks. "They attacked us at the rally! They kidnapped me, and now they're shipping us halfway across the galaxy! What does that have to do with peace?"

"Everything," Regis whispers.

Denver leans forward so he can see me and Regis. "No, seriously, both of you, I want to know about the Resistance. I've hardly gotten any answers from Earth Force—not that I'm surprised—and what they have told me has me questioning who the bad guys really are."

That's a pretty bold thing to say—some may even say treasonous. Maybe Gedney was right. Maybe Denver *can* be swayed toward the Resistance.

"And what's more," Denver continues, "there's no way Admiral Eames is going to let that attack go unanswered. So, here's the thing: I'm willing to listen to the Resistance and consider helping you defend against Earth Force's inevitable counterattack, but you'd better start talking."

I take a deep breath of the stale, cheesy air. "A lot has

happened since you got stuck in the rift, Denver, a lot more than they taught you in your recent history classes. You know how they made us lie about our rescue from the rift? That's just the beginning. . . ."

23

OBVIOUSLY, DENVER KNOWS ABOUT THE
Incident at Bounding Base 51, but he only knows his part—
the part with the failed bound that leaves him and his fellow
aeronauts trapped in the rift for more than fifteen years. So I
figure that's a pretty good place to start.

I tell him how the Incident changed everything. In its wake,
all of Earth's space programs and militaries were formally
merged under Earth Force. Space programs make sense—in
fact, the space program that oversaw all quantum aeronautics
was already called Earth Force—but did anyone question why
Earth Force needed to control the military? It's clear now, obviously, but what about then? Didn't it seem suspicious?

My mind is transported back to our pod room during the first tour of duty when we sat on bean bags and listened to Waters talk about the history of the Bounders. Shortly after the Incident, the Bounder Baby Breeding Program was announced. All male-female couples, like my parents, were tested for the Bounder genes. If they carried the genes and planned to procreate, well, let's just say the end results were Bounder babies like me and Addy.

"Yeah, yeah, yeah," Denver interrupts as I go through the history, "because the Bounders are the only humans who can use the alien technology. I thought you were going to tell me something I didn't know."

"They told you all that at the space station?" I'm surprised his clearance level was that high.

"No. It's old news, kid. We knew Earth Force was study-ing the Youli's biochemistry and comparing it to the human genome back before the Incident. They wanted to expand their research and conduct experiments on an actual alien. That's one of the reasons we engaged in the training exercise the day we got trapped in the rift. We hoped to lure the Youli in and capture one."

"Why did they film it live, then?" Regis asks.

"Who knows? Arrogance? It's not like they planned to stream the alien capture part, just the dashing aeronauts boarding their bounding ships. We filmed all the bounds in those days. Nothing ever went wrong, and the public couldn't get enough of us, which kept the funds rolling in. You think you're a celebrity now, kid? It's nothing compared to back then." Denver shifts, jerking my cuffed arm to the left. "Anyhow, the lure worked too well. The aliens showed up before we expected, and they disrupted our bound. But I understand it wasn't all in vain. Earth Force apparently snagged a little green man, and Waters and Gedney worked their magic. Add fifteen years, and here we are."

"What do Waters and Gedney have to do with any of this?" I ask, tugging my arm back to the right.

"You really don't know? It was their research! Jon Waters was the one who wanted the Youli taken prisoner! Even before they captured one, he and Gedney had hypothesized that alien DNA could be used as a bioweapon, but only certain people would be able to wield it. That's why the Bounder Baby Breeding Program was ultimately started."

Denver's words fall into place in my mind, connecting dots that had dangled far too long. "They reintroduced the Bounder genes because they were similar enough to parts of the Youli genome that we'd be able to use their biotech," I say, thinking out loud.

"Bingo, kid. It's all in the genes."

"And Waters and Gedney were the masterminds from the beginning."

Denver claps his hands, pulling my left hand along for the ride. "You got it! Waters is just a jerk. He thinks he knows everything. But Gedney is the real deal. We used to call him Einstein."

"I used to think Waters knew everything, too," I say. "Now I know he's just another adult with an agenda. For him, the end always justifies the means."

"Think what you want about Waters," Regis says, "just don't lose sight of the real enemy: Earth Force."

Regis asks some more questions about the Incident at Bounding Base 51 and the Bounder Baby Breeding Program, but I tune them out. It's mostly stuff I already know. Plus, I need some time to process what Denver just said about Waters and Gedney. After all this time, neither of them ever confirmed that they were personally involved with the Bounder Baby Breeding Program, let alone that it was their brainchild. I guess I should have known. The signs were all there—Gedney knows more about the gloves than anyone— but I didn't want to believe it. Was the Youli prisoner being held at the space station during our first tour of duty just another one of their science experiments?

The craft lurches forward as it shifts to Faster Than Light Speed, and we end up in a pile at one end of the craft.

"FTL," I mutter.

"I can think of a few different acronyms I'd use to describe that," Denver says, pushing his way off of us and back to his corner.

"It's no treat sharing this crate with you, either," Regis says.

"You're the last person I ever wanted to be in close quarters with," I say to Regis.

"The feeling's mutual."

"Enough," Denver says. "Your bickering is exhausting. Let's get back to the topic. So, you're saying that Earth Force kept the Youli war and the reason for the Bounder Baby Breeding Program a secret all these years?"

Regis must have added those gems while I zoned out.

"That's right," Regis says. "Now here's what I want to know: How did the Youli war start?"

Denver takes a deep breath. "Some things happened before I joined Earth Force, so for the old stuff, I only know what I was told, and we all know how loose the Force is with the truth. But the way it was said to me is like this: Shortly after Earth developed Faster Than Light technology, we were exploring an up-until-then-unknown sector of the galaxy when we were hailed by the Youli. This is known in high-security circles as first contact. As the story goes, it was no accident that we encountered the Youli. The Youli had been watching Earth for a long time and waiting until we achieved space travel technology that took us outside the confines of our solar system. Once we had that, the Youli reached out and basically offered to take us under their wing in the greater goings-on of the galaxy. For a while, we all played nice."

"We started out as friends?" I ask.

"Sort of," Denver says. "It was more like a mentor relationship. The Youli civilization is far older and more advanced than ours, and they never let us forget it. In the greater order of the galaxy, there are rules and ethical standards that have to be followed. Of course, one of the signature features of Earth and its people is our collective arrogance. We don't like other folks' rules and standards, even when those folks are much older and wiser. I guess Earth is like a meta version of your pod leader, Jon Waters. We think we know everything, and that arrogance is always our downfall."

"The Youli war," I say.

"I'm getting there," Denver says. "I was pretty junior when a lot of this was happening, but I'd put it this way: Earth had a *take what we like* approach to Youli mentorship and our introduction on the galactic scene. We took the trade deals and technology transfers, and we ignored some of the other stuff."

"Like what?" Regis asks.

"The Intragalactic Council does not allow interaction with developing planets who haven't reached FTL capacity."

Now we're getting somewhere. "The Tunnelers."

"Exactly," Denver says.

"You were on Gulaga when Earth Force negotiated the terms of the Tunneler alliance, right?" I ask.

"Negotiated? Alliance?" Denver laughs. "Is that what the Force told you?"

I always wondered what really happened on Gulaga. "That's not how it went down? There's so little information."

"No, and I was there," Denver says. "Cora and I were the two youngest pilots deployed."

"Cora?" Regis asks. "You mean Admiral Eames?"

"Um . . . yeah." Denver laughs again, but there's no amusement in it. It's the kind of laugh that masks pain. "Cora has done quite well for herself."

If the rumors circulating at the space station are true, Denver and Admiral Eames had been in love when he disappeared into the rift. Only a few months after the Incident, she stepped up as the admiral of the consolidated Earth Force. How did she have the focus and drive to do that after losing Denver? How was she able to put it all aside and lead her planet in the defense of a secret alien war?

From what I can tell, Denver's homecoming has been strange and strained for both of them.

"You could say that," Regis says. "What actually happened on Gulaga?"

"We wanted to expand our bounding program," Denver continues, seemingly relieved to get back to the facts, "but we needed more occludium. We tried to trade for it, but the Intragalactic Council blocked us—something about keeping our development at a sustainable pace. Earth Force wasn't having it. So when our sensors located occludium ore on Gulaga, we set out to claim it.

"Frankly, when we arrived, we didn't take much notice of the Tunnelers. They barked and bowed when we landed on their planet, but we thought they were just a primitive species. Pests, really. Only later, when we learned that they'd built an expansive civilization underground and had been mining occludium for hundreds of years, did we realize their utility. We wouldn't even need to set up a mining operation on Gulaga. One already existed, along with a people who could run it."

"Free labor," Regis says.

"That's right," Denver says. "We commandeered them."

"So there *was* bloodshed?" I'd always guessed there was more to the story.

"To put it lightly. When the Tunnelers tried to resist us taking over, we showed them they had no choice. The fighting didn't last long. Our military might and technology far surpassed anything the Tunnelers had ever seen. But they fought admirably. Some of those Tunnelers are the bravest beings I've ever encountered."

The Wackies. I picture grizzly old Barrick with the scar

running across his face. There's no doubt he was leading the charge against Earth. In fact, he's still fighting us.

"The truth is," Denver says quietly, "I've never felt right about it. When I heard you were taking me to Gulaga, I stopped resisting so hard. I'm intrigued to go back. I feel I owe something to its people."

"You're going willingly?" I ask.

"I wouldn't say that," Denver says, "but if I'd really been trying to ditch you guys, I'd be long gone by now."

"What is this? Some tactic to get us to uncuff you?" Regis asks. "Because it's not going to work."

"Why? You don't trust me?"

Regis laughs.

"What about you, kid?" Denver asks.

"I'm not sure."

"Do you trust him?" Denver asks, obviously referring to Regis.

"No," I answer without a second thought.

"Well, then it looks like we all have trust issues."

I don't realize I've fallen asleep until the crate is hefted off the floor of the craft, knocking me into Regis, who kicks me in the shin.

I raise my eyebrows. Where are we?

Nos Redna Space Port, Regis mouths.

I nod. We need to be quiet or risk being discovered.

Voices from outside the box reach us. They're not speaking English. In fact, it doesn't even sound like language. The closest I can relate is the Tunneler bark, but this sounds more like chirping. Seconds later, a translator kicks in. It's hard to hear the specifics, but I think they're asking our pilot for cargo papers.

"Is there a problem?" I whisper.

"Routine," Regis answers and lifts a finger to his lips.

Several seconds pass with nothing happening. Then the chirping starts back up. This time, there's no translation and no sound of our pilot. The crate is hefted up and placed on a transporter that whisks us across the landing bay.

"Still routine?" Denver asks.

Regis nods.

"Where are they taking us?" I ask.

"We usually unload in a private storage bay. I'm guessing that's where we're headed now."

Doors clang shut, and chirping comes from all sides. There must have been a whole bunch of those aliens waiting for us in the private storage bay.

"That's . . . odd," Regis whispers.

"What?" Denver and I say at the same time.

"I don't know why those chirping dudes are still around. Usually we're unloaded by Tunnelers, occasionally by Earthlings, but never by . . . whoever these guys are."

A hush falls in the bay, and then the doors open and close once more. The chirping starts again, but this time it's loud and formal (or at least as formal as chirping can sound). Then the translator kicks in, except that it doesn't translate into English.

The translation is robotic and strange but also familiar.

I look at Regis. He shrugs.

Once I hear the reply, there's no mistaking the language they're speaking.

It's the signature hiss of Alkalinians.

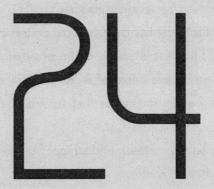

I MUST HAVE GASPED, BECAUSE BOTH
Denver and Regis elbow me hard in the ribs. I bend over and
try not to yelp in pain.

"We're in trouble," I whisper. "Those are Alks."

"That means nothing to me, kid," Denver says.

My heart races, and my breath comes fast. This crate never
felt so suffocating. "The Alks are the aliens who sold us out
to the Youli. I bounded to the rift in the middle of the battle
on their planet."

"Are you sure those are Alkalinians?" Regis asks.

I hush them so I can listen. Outside the box, the chirpers

chirp away. I hold my breath and wait for the translation and reply, hoping I was wrong.

Again, the sinister hiss of Alkalinian fills the bay.

A shiver seizes my body as the terrible reality sets in. The Alks are here, and there can be only one reason why. They're here for us, and they've already got us locked up.

We need to move. I lean forward and grab my blast pack. "Do our gloves work here?" I ask Regis.

He yanks his own blast pack into his lap. "Yes. There's no scrambler."

"Good," I say, already pulling my gloves from my pack, "because they're probably our only chance to get out of this."

Denver yanks my left hand by our shared cuff. Regis hands me the key, and I detach us.

"I don't have any gloves." Denver waves his now free hands in the air. "But I'm an excellent shot." He points at the gun strapped to Regis's waist.

"Don't even think about it," Regis says.

"You'd rather get killed than let me help?"

"He's right, Regis. Give him the gun." I fit my gloves on my fingers. When Regis doesn't move, I add, "Now!"

Regis unholsters the gun and hands it to Denver. Then he pulls on his gloves.

"Plan?" Denver says, disengaging the gun's safety. "What can you guys actually do with those things?"

"You'll find out soon enough," I say. "We need to act fast while we still have the element of surprise. I'll pop off the lid, and you get ready to fire. Regis, you and I will try to immobilize anyone who's armed."

"How?" Regis's voice shakes.

I slap his leg, trying to inject a dose of confidence that I don't feel myself. "However you can. Fling their weapons away. You remember the pillow fight our first tour."

"That didn't go my way," Regis whispers.

I look him in the eyes. "This time it will."

Regis nods.

Denver looks up at the lid of the crate. "Let's do this."

I close my eyes and tap into the energy of my gloves. The familiar current courses through me. Once I've aligned with the source, I point my fingertips at the crate's lid. I take a deep breath, then force all my mental effort into blowing the top of the crate to the roof.

The lid flies off, and fresh air rushes into the crate. The light is so bright after being shut in all day, I have to squint. And I have to move. Denver springs to a squat and starts firing. Regis and I both leap off the sides and take cover behind the crate. My muscles scream from being cramped in a crate all day, but I let the adrenaline surge through me, forcing my limbs to obey.

"How many?" Regis shouts over the sound of weapons

firing. He holds his palms out in front of him. I can almost see the energy radiating from his fingers.

"I'll check." Peeking around the side of the crate, I count five Alks, none of them close enough to see if I know them from Alkalinia. There are also about a dozen other aliens in the bay, who I assume are the chirpers. They're tall and skinny and have three sets of mini wings around their midriff. They don't fly, exactly, but they leap in the air and flutter, making them hard for Denver to target.

Luckily, only about half of the chirpers are armed, and most of them share tandem rifles.

Denver quickly takes out four of them.

The buzz of a laser nearly gives me a haircut. I duck back behind the crate. "Five Alks and about a dozen chirpers."

Regis nods and flutters his gloved fingers. "Now or never."

I steady my breath, and the world shifts into that slow-motion mode like when we placed the degradation patch on the Youli vessel or when I brought the shield down in Alkalinia.

Every minute, every moment of every minute, means life or death right now.

"On my count." I raise a finger . . . one, two, *three*.

I pivot out from behind the box and raise both hands. I whip my right palm at the closest group of chirpers and seize control of their atoms. With my left, I condense the air around me into a viscous bubble that hopefully will slow down incoming fire. I fling the chirpers against the far wall and fix my sights on the Alks.

Two of them are firing at Denver, and three others hover near the door. I dash behind a stack of empty shipping containers and seize control of the flying throne of the nearest Alk. Focusing my intentions, I flip the seat, and the Alk tumbles to the ground and tries to slither out of range. I seize him by his cyborg arm and send him flying across the bay. On the other side of the hangar, Regis takes out two chirpers and their tandem rifle.

"Behind you!" Denver shouts from the top of the crate.

I swing around just in time to fend off another chirper duo.

Denver trades shots with an Alk wielding a laser staff. "Help me out, kid!" he hollers, nodding at a pair of chirpers targeting him with their rifle.

I grab the atoms of the chirper on the left and toss him to the edge of the bay. Then I fling the other one up in the air. He collides with the ceiling and crashes down. His long, skinny body bends in a bad way on the ground; his paper-thin wings flitter to a stop.

"Yeah, kid!" Denver shouts. He dives into the crate as his Alk adversary lets loose a laser beam from his staff.

Sparks ricochet off the crate and ding across the port,

sending more chirpers for the door. Regis uses the distraction to dash across the bay and take cover behind a stack of empty crates. Now our offensive has the remaining Alks and chirpers pinned in.

Regis freezes the Alk firing at Denver, leaving Denver free to take him out with the gun.

"Nice trick!" I shout.

That leaves a final group of chirpers and a single Alk left to immobilize. As he closes in, his features come into focus. It's Steve, our guide from Alkalinia.

The chirpers break for the door. Regis and I use the same strategy to freeze the chirpers, and Denver picks them off one by one with the gun.

Until Steve is the only one left.

Denver aims the gun.

"Wait!" I raise my gloved hand at Denver. "He's mine."

Steve's back is to me as he races for the exit. I seize his throne and slowly rein it in. Then I spin him like a top until he's facing me.

Anger rises in my chest. My eyes swim with rage at the memory of Addy and Marco racing through the venom tube, Serena sliding in to help them, all of her abandoned babies rushing to greet her and ripping the tube in two.

I pull Steve's throne to the floor then throw it back in the air, launching Steve from his velvet cushion. Before he hits the ground, I grab his scaly Alk body and tear his cyborg arm clean off. He drops to the floor and wriggles for the door.

I don't even bother using my gloves. I run across the bay and step on Steve's tail. Then I bend over my old Alk guide. "Hello, Sss-Steve. Tell Sss-Seelok I say hello."

He hisses at me, but his translator is nowhere in sight. "Grab a voice box from one of those chirpers!" I shout at Regis.

When I have the box, I shove it under Steve's scaly chin. "How did you know we'd be here?"

Steve clicks and hisses. "Sss-silly boy, don't you know what Alksss do? We deal in sss-secretsss. Nothing is off-limitsss at the right price-sss."

"Who sold us out?"

"Molesss are everywhere, Jasss-per, even in the Resss-issstanssse."

Denver walks up behind me. "We need to go, kid."

"Someone squealed. We need answers."

"No time. They'll be on us in seconds if we don't move." Denver grabs my arm.

I shake free. "Not yet." I lift my gloved hand and seize the atoms around Steve's scrawny neck. He struggles to breathe, his hisses leaking from his throat in a weak stutter. All it would take is a bit more pressure. Just a little squeeze. He deserves it. If he'd had his way, I'd be dead. All the Bounders would be dead.

"Let's go!" Regis calls.

Denver gently places his hand on my wrist and lowers my gloved hand to my side.

"He could warn the others," I say to Denver. Why shouldn't we finish what we started? We already took out the chirpers and the other Alks.

Denver stoops over Steve and brings the butt of the gun down hard on his head, knocking him out. "Not anymore."

I scan the bay and take stock. Part of me still wants Steve dead, but I know it's not necessary. If I killed him now, I'd be no better than the Alks.

Regis stands by a rear exit, waving his arms. "This way!"

Denver and I jog across the bay and follow Regis into a dark hallway. We pick our way through the back halls, trying to avoid contact with anyone. Soon, though, the hall fills with chirpers flitting swiftly by, carrying dirty plates and glasses and paying absolutely zero attention to us.

"What's that smell?" I ask. "It's like a mash-up of red licorice and dirty sneakers."

"Where did you come up with that?" Denver asks.

Regis stops us. "We're almost at the kitchens. Beyond them is the bar. That's where we'll meet our ride."

Denver nods and starts back down the hall.

MONICA TESLER

Regis grabs his arm. "Not so fast." He points to the gun. "Hand it over."

Denver dangles the gun in Regis's face. When Regis reaches for it, Denver laughs and shoves it in his waistband. "Not a chance. This gun is mine now."

"No way." Regis balls his hands into fists.

Denver keeps right on laughing. "What are you going to do, fight me for it?"

"Forget it, Regis," I say. "He saved our butts back there. I guess we all need to practice more trust."

Regis shakes his head. "Fine." He flips the hood of his sweatshirt up, then pulls some hats out of the duffel and hands them to me and Denver. "You're two of the most wanted guys in the galaxy. Put these on and keep a low profile. And put your gloves away, Jasper. We don't want to raise any red flags."

As I slip off my gloves and zip them into my blast pack, I think about what Regis said. There are probably a few bounty hunters in that bar who could make a pretty penny bringing Denver and me back to Earth. Maybe Regis was right to ask for the gun back. With our gloves stowed, Denver is the only one of us who's armed. There's not much stopping him from marching us up to the head of the port and turning us in. I'm sure he could catch a ride back to Earth in no time.

Hopefully our heart-to-heart in the crate counts for something.

We follow Regis into the bar. It's shaped in a circle with the bartenders in the center, counter seats surrounding them, and a ring of tables on the rim. The place throbs with a rapid bass beat and whistles with the sound of electronic music blaring a reed setting in a minor key.

It's packed. I'm trying to keep my head down and not attract attention, but I steal a few glances. The chirpers are working the tables. A tall dude who looks kind of like a twig with lots of arms is bartending. And there are dozens of species of aliens I've never seen before. Gedney wasn't kidding when he described the intragalactic scene as vast.

Fortunately, I don't spot any Alks or Youli, but I'm pretty sure I spy a table of Tunnelers in the back. There are lots of humanoid-like aliens with different-colored skins and odd appendages, but there are also aliens I don't even have words to describe and that I never would have imagined existed if I weren't staring at them right now with my own two eyes. Like the giant slug-looking thing that's driving around in a motorized cart, or the table filled with tiny creatures that look more like ants than any alien I've ever seen.

Regis jerks his head toward a table in the corner. We follow him and slide into seats. Seconds later, one of the chirpers flits to our table. She has silver chains wrapped around her body, with coins jangling from hooks. Her wings are dyed purple and pierced with multicolored crystals.

MONICA TESLER

She chirps at us, then presses a button on her translator. A husky woman's voice booms out, "What'll it be, boys?"

Denver laughs. "Who programmed that voice box?"

"Low profile," Regis mutters under his breath. Then he smiles at the chirper. "Three sour ticklers."

"Coming right up, honey." She reaches into her apron and pulls out a handful of small foil packages. "Enjoy your nuts."

I peel back the foil and out roll a bunch of black rocks. I'm about to pick one up when it jumps on the table. I jerk back. "What are those?"

Regis pops all of his in his mouth at once. "Hoppers. They're imported from one of the nearby planets. They taste kind of like soy nuggets."

Denver smells one of the hoppers, then bites it in half. "They're not bad."

"Not bad" is not good enough for me to even try. I push the foil-wrapped nuts over to Regis. "Have mine."

My stomach grumbles. I dig in my bag and pull out a protein bar.

"Not in here!" Regis says. "It's rude!"

"Since when do you care about being rude?"

Denver swipes my bar and shoves it in the duffel. "If you're hungry, eat your hoppers, kid."

I'm about to protest when the chirper arrives with our

drinks—they're blue and frothy and releasing teal steam into the air.

A long, curly straw sticks out of the glass. I take a tiny sip. My lips pucker. It tastes like jelly beans and sour peach candy mixed together. So, in other words, I love it.

Denver tries his drink and makes a face. I guess I'm not the only picky one. "What are we supposed to do? Just sit here and wait for our ride to show up?"

"Don't worry," Regis says, scanning the bar. "She'll show. She's probably just waiting until it's safe. I'm sure security has found our trail of carnage by now."

"Speaking of that," I say, "what if they figure out that we were behind that? We're basically sitting ducks right here."

"Which is why we need to keep a low profile," Regis says.

As soon as the words "low profile" leave his mouth, a fit of barking erupts at my back.

I spin around just as a voice box starts to spit out a long stream of words.

"Oh! Oh! Oh! I was so very worried! Especially when I heard the rumors. And oh! Oh! Oh! They're true! They're true! Jasper Adams! I didn't know if I would ever see you again! But oh! You're here! Give me a hug!"

Neeka throws her furry Tunneler arms around my neck before the voice box finishes translating.

"NEEKA! I HAD NO IDEA YOU WERE GOING
to be here!" I free myself from her furry arms but keep hold
of her paw. My Tunneler friend is wearing an emerald-green
tunic that makes the green of her eyes shine. Gone are the
days of the burlap sack—standard Tunneler attire under
Earth Force control.

"Neither did I," Regis says.

Neeka growls. "Oh! Shut up! You know I didn't come here
for you."

Denver leans back in his seat and folds his arms across his
chest. "Your little reunion is quite possibly the furthest thing

from low profile." Nodding at Neeka, he adds, "Isn't someone going to introduce us?"

"Oh! Captain Reddy!" Neeka says through the voice box. She drops my hand and offers her paw to Denver, who shakes it a little awkwardly. "I do apologize. I am so very sorry! Oh! I was ever so rude! I told myself before I got here that the very first thing I—"

"Hey!" Denver holds up his hands. "Stop talking for a minute! Start off by telling me who you are."

"Oh! Oh! You are oh so right! Where are my manners? Oh!"

Denver looks at me. "On second thought, kid, you tell me who your friend is."

"Denver, meet Neeka." I put my arm across her shoulders. She wraps herself around me and squeezes. "She was our pod's junior ambassador on Gulaga, and she's awesome."

Neeka smiles up at me. "Your sister can't wait to see you."

"You've met Addy?"

She nods.

A swell of emotion rises in my chest, making me feel lightheaded and heavy on my feet at the same time. I'm going to see Addy. I'm here with Neeka. Yes, there's a war. And yes, we'll try to push for peace. But it's also about family and friends, the things that matter most in life.

"We should go," Regis says quietly.

MONICA TESLER

"I don't take orders from you," Neeka barks back.

"He's right," I say to her. "We had a run-in with some old friends back in the cargo hold."

"Friends?" Neeka asks.

"Kidding," I say. "They were Alks, and they had a heads-up we were coming."

"Someone's going to want to know who left the mess," Denver says.

"Plus," I say, grinning at Neeka, "I can't wait to see Addy."

We follow Neeka out of the bar and back through the rear hallways until we reach a hangar crowded with small ships. Pilots and crew hang about chatting, cleaning their crafts, loading cargo. Neeka leads us across the hangar, greeting almost everyone we pass. She stops in front of the most banged-up, piece-of-junk ship in the hangar.

"Oh! Here's my baby," she says, patting the ship with her paw.

"This thing flies?" Denver asks.

"Barely," Regis grumbles.

Neeka swats him. "Oh! Excuse me? This beauty is a ruby in the rough. Isn't that how your cliché goes?"

"Diamond, but who's listening to me?" Regis says.

"No one, as usual." She places her paw on the lock sensor, and the loading bridge drops down. "All aboard! Oh! I can't wait to fly you to Gulaga, Jasper! It's where you belong!"

We climb onto Neeka's ship, which looks just as bad inside as out. Once we strap in, she flips a bunch of switches, backs us up, and steers us out of the hangar into open space. While we fly, Denver peppers her with questions about the Resistance. From the way Neeka's talking, it's clear she's a pretty high-ranking rebel. After her dad died during the battle with the Youli, she sought out Barrick and volunteered for the Resistance, and she's taken every chance she can to prove herself and rise in the ranks.

"Commander Krag was your father?" Denver asks. Apparently, he met Krag when he came with Admiral Eames and the other Earth Force officers to hammer out the Earth-Tunneler treaty. "I remember him. He was a fierce and loyal advocate for his people, even when we were much younger. I'm sorry for your loss."

"Thank you," Neeka says. "Even though it's been a year and a half since my dad died, the wound feels fresh. Sometimes I can almost hear him whispering to me." She doesn't ask Denver any questions about his time in Gulaga twenty years ago. She must have already known he was there and accepts that we need to move forward. Plus, the fact that Denver's voice sounded heavy with guilt probably helps.

"I'm sure your dad would be very proud of you, Neeka," I say.

"Definitely," Regis says.

Neeka snaps at him. "Oh! Don't you dare try to ingratiate yourself with me, Regis!"

"You don't want me to kiss your furry butt?"

She hops up barking. "Out! Get out of my sight! Go strap in by the engine and stay there until we land!"

"Gladly," Regis says. He undoes his harness and disappears to the back of the craft.

"What's your deal with him?" I ask once he's gone.

"Oh! What is *my* deal?" Neeka barks, her temper still sizzling. "What is *your* deal? How could you forgive him for all the evils he caused? Do you not remember what happened on Gulaga? He almost killed you and Mira more than once!"

"That explains a lot," Denver says.

"I definitely wouldn't say I've forgiven him. It's complicated."

Neeka doesn't respond. She checks some of the gauges on the ship and prepares for the shift to FTL. Once that's done, she asks in a much calmer voice, "How is Mira?"

Denver perked up as soon as Neeka mentioned Mira's name a moment ago. Now he's practically sitting on the edge of his seat, waiting for my answer. I've intentionally avoided the topic with him. I have no idea what his Earth Force buddies told him about her.

"I haven't seen Mira in a while," I say. "The Youli have her."

"Mira's the girl from the rift, right?" Denver asks. "What

happened? Why did she leave with them? Was that part of the deal—she went with them to save us?"

I ask myself those same questions every day, and I'm still no closer to an answer. I don't know how to respond.

"Kid?"

I decide to stick to the truth. "All I know is she had to leave with them, but also she said it was her choice to go."

We don't talk much for the rest of the ride. Denver dozes off. I'm exhausted, but I can't get Mira off my mind, and I'm too excited to see Addy and Marco to fall asleep. I close my eyes and try to call up happy memories. I'm reliving the epic pillow fight during our first tour when we slam out of FTL.

Out the window, the planet of Gulaga is in our sights, along with the wreckage of the space elevator. A long spire stretches from the surface of the planet out into space. Construction crafts surround the tip of the spire, and repair robots work on a large platform suspended in space. A dozen defense ships dot the perimeter.

"They're rebuilding the space elevator?" I ask.

"Oh! No! It's far too much of a risk. We learned that the hard way, didn't we? We are disassembling what remains of the elevator and bringing the scrap to the surface. We need all the space-worthy building materials we can find."

"Are you building ships with the scrap?" Denver asks.

Neeka's ship isn't the only one that looks like she bought

MONICA TESLER

it at the junkyard. Almost all the Resistance ships look like pieces of junk because, according to Neeka, they mostly are junk. When the Youli snapped the space elevator, much of the Gulagan fleet was lost or destroyed. Later, when the Resistance ousted Earth Force, the Force left with any ship that could fly, hoping to strand the Gulagans on the planet. Fortunately, some of the Tunneler engineers had learned enough from Earth Force during the occupation that they were able to piece together some new ships out of scrap metal and broken-down Force ships that had been abandoned in a repair facility on the surface.

"What's that silvery gauze around Gulaga?" Denver asks.

"That's the occludium shield," I say. "No bounding to the surface."

"Ah!" he says. "I should have guessed. Occludium-based technology has come a long way since I was stranded in the rift."

"Good news, Jasper," Regis says as he returns to the front of the craft. "The Resistance deactivated the scramblers on the surface."

"So we can bound wherever we want?"

When Regis nods, a smile stretches across my face. That is definitely good news. No more getting stuck on the tundra. No more crossing narrow bridges in Gulagaven. No more flying my blast pack without my gloves.

As we cut through the atmosphere and prepare to land at Gulagaven, Neeka calls down to the surface for them to lower the standard force field that now protects the main settlement.

"I can't wait to see Addy," I say. "Will she be there when we touch down?"

"I'm sorry, no," Neeka says. "They keep the exact itinerary of the transports a secret for security purposes, but I'll take you to her as soon as we land. Speaking of landing, we'll be exiting the craft outside. There are parkas stocked in the aft cabin. You'll need to put those on for the short walk into the tunnels."

"I could never forget how frigid your planet is," Denver says. "I almost lost my fingers on my first visit to Gulaga."

"I almost lost my life when I was trapped outside overnight, thanks to Regis," I say.

Regis shakes his head. "Please stop bringing that up."

"I told you before, Regis, I might be able to forgive you eventually, but I'll never forget what you did. And I'm going to make sure you don't forget, either."

"Fine," he says. "Since we're bringing up memories, every time I land in Gulaga, I remember when you put burning foot powder in my boots."

"That was a joke."

"I wasn't laughing."

"And I wasn't laughing when you threw those bugs in my bed. In fact—"

Neeka waves her paws in the air. "Oh! Oh! No! Enough!"

"I'm with her," Denver says. "Shut it until we land. Then the two of you can find an isolated underground burrow and yell at each other all you want."

I'm half-frozen by the time we make it down the entrance ramp. Once we pass through the two containment doors and into the Outfitters, a Tunneler trades our coats for some human-size parkas. I strip the too-small Tunneler coat off and don the parka as fast as I can, but I still feel like I was dipped in an ice pond. Denver, Regis, and I huddle together shivering until Neeka finishes shutting down her ship and joins us.

My excitement grows with each step as we wind our way down into the heart of Gulagaven. I can't believe I'm really about to see my sister. When we reach the central chasm, I place my hand against the mud wall and keep walking. Soon, I have to stoop to stop from bumping my head.

"Were the ceilings always so low in this part of Gulagaven?" I ask. "I don't remember having to bend over until we reached the branch halls."

Neeka laughs. "You're oh-so-much taller than the last time you were here."

"Even I remember these low ceilings," Denver says. "And

how could I forget the bottomless pit? That thing still makes my heart race." He keeps his hand on the wall, too.

After a few turns around the central chasm, we begin to encounter other Tunnelers. Almost all of them have traded their drab brown-and-gray tunics for colorful garb like we saw across the tundra in the Wacky headquarters during my tour of duty. I bet that's how Tunnelers dressed before Earth Force showed up in the first place.

It's not just their clothes that seem different, though. The Tunnelers greet Neeka cheerfully, and many of them smile at Denver, Regis, and me. Some of them give us a far-less-than-friendly stare, which I can understand given their history with Earth. The point is that almost all of them look us in the eye, and that's a huge change from the last time I was here.

We pass through the central market, and it's even louder and rowdier than I remember. Tunnelers bark and wave their paws as they trade for goods and clothes and treats—not that I'd call those creepy crawlies treats. The smell alone is enough to make my stomach turn. I don't bother asking Regis if the Tunneler cuisine has improved since Earth Force left, because I'm 99 percent sure I don't want to know the answer, and I'm going to find out soon enough anyway.

Once we pass the market, Regis cuts off on his own, mumbling something about changing his clothes and taking a nap. We certainly don't try to stop him. All of us are happy to be free of him, at least for now. Maybe Regis has changed, but bad blood runs thick, and he's still annoying, even if he's not actively trying to kill me.

Finally, we find ourselves at the once ornate, carved doors of the Tunneler Parliamentary Chamber. The relief carvings on the doors are filled over with mud, probably because the carvings depict scenes from the Tunnelers' first contact with Earth.

When I stood before these doors during my tour of duty, the Bounders were booed. A disgruntled Tunneler even threw eggs at us. Now, though, there is no sign of protest. I'm hoping these doors and the chamber beyond have regained their status as a place of reverence and pride for the Tunnelers.

Neeka greets the door guards. "Brother, sister, salutations. I bow to your service and fortitude." She tips her head down.

"And we also bow to you, sister," they both respond, inclining their heads.

"Will you grant us access to the chamber?" Neeka asks.

"We will, sister," the one on the right answers.

Both of the guards grip a handle and pull the doors back. As we pass through, they say in unison, "May your days be peaceful and productive, and may your nights provide shelter from the cold."

I step into the large chamber filled with dozens of tiny carrels carved into the high walls where Tunnelers have participated in their government throughout the generations. This is where I first saw an Alkalinian. This is where Admiral Eames rallied the Bounders to fight the Youli. And hopefully, this is where I'll be reunited with my sister.

The chamber floor is packed with humans and Tunnelers, all dressed in brightly colored tunics like Neeka. They're crowded around a projection table. Graphs and charts and pictures rotate in the air above the table.

I scan the room for my sister. She spots me first.

"Jasper!" Addy cuts through the crowd and tackle-hugs me, nearly knocking us both to the ground.

26

I HOLD MY SISTER LIKE SHE'S THE GRAVITY
keeping me on the ground. Now that we're back together, I'm
too afraid to let go. Eventually, Addy untangles herself from
me and cups my cheek with her palm. "I thought I'd never
see you again."

I place my hand on hers. "I thought you were dead. The
Battle of the Alkalinian Seat . . ."

"I know." She hugs me again. "Thank goodness we're both
alive. And thank God you made it here safely."

A hand clamps on my shoulder and gently pulls Addy and
me apart.

"Ace, I thought you'd never show."

I grip Marco's palm and pull him in for a hug. "Good to see you, Marco."

"*So* good, J-Bird. Welcome back from the land of the dead."

"You just can't get rid of me."

Neeka runs over and corrals us all in her furry arms. "Oh! Together again! Happy day!"

When we break apart, another familiar face stands behind Neeka.

"Welcome, Jasper," Jon Waters says. "I'm so glad you chose to join us." He looks the same: tall, wrinkled shirt, tweed blazer.

I expected to feel something more when I saw Waters—anger, I hoped, or intimidation, I feared. Instead, I'm oddly detached, like he doesn't have quite as strong a spell over me as before.

Next to me, Denver clears his throat. "Not all of us had a choice." I was so caught up in my reunion with Addy, I'd forgotten about Denver. His arms are crossed against his chest, and his cold stare makes clear he's not thrilled to see Waters. Two armed Tunnelers stand just behind him.

"Good to see you again, Denver," Water says, extending his palm.

Denver doesn't shake. "I'm not going to say the same. Under the right circumstances, I suppose I might enjoy grabbing a whiskey and talking old times, but those circumstances don't include being kidnapped and shipped across the galaxy in a crate with two kids."

"As I understand it," Waters says, trying to sound friendly while matching Denver's cold stare, "one of those kids—one of *my* students—deserves the credit for you being back in the galaxy in the first place."

Denver clasps my shoulder. "Jasper and I have spent a lot of time together, Jon. I know how he feels about you, and I guarantee you deserve none of the credit for any of his actions."

Okay, so that's out there.

Waters shoots me a glance, then drops his gaze. "Point taken. Now, if you'll excuse me, I need to return to the briefing. They'll see you both to your quarters, where you can rest and change. We'll talk more later." He nods at the two Tunneler guards behind Denver and heads back to the group.

"Mr. Waters," I call after him. I might as well get to the point of why I came halfway across the galaxy, other than seeing my sister, of course: the Youli's message.

He turns around.

"I need to speak with you."

"I'll find you after the briefing, Jasper." He turns to my sister. "Addy, Marco, you're needed over here."

Addy holds tight to my hand. "I haven't seen my brother in almost a year."

Waters stares down my sister. She doesn't budge.

"Fine, you have an hour, but then I need you back."

"Thanks," Addy says, already dragging me to the door. "Oh, and Marco's coming with us."

Marco runs ahead, not waiting for Waters's response.

Soon we're in the hall, beyond earshot of the guards, and it's just me, my sister, and one of my best friends in the whole galaxy. It feels like every millimeter of my body exhales.

"I'm exhausted," I say. "And starving. Is the food any better here?"

Marco laughs. "There's a BERF bar with your name on it just waiting for you in the cantina."

My face falls. "And I'm betting some tasty green forage, too?"

"Don't worry," Addy says. "I have a secret stash of decent snacks. Let's go!"

When we cut down the hall that takes us to the old Earth Force wing, Addy stops. "The fruit balls are in my room. Head to the Nest, and I'll meet you there in a few." She jogs ahead and hangs a left at the next hallway.

Marco and I keep going until we reach a familiar door. He pulls an old-fashioned key from his pocket.

"Since when are the baths locked?" I ask.

"Gotta keep our private hideout private," he says.

"I thought the scrambler was turned off."

"It is. Only Bounders are allowed in. In fact, I rarely use this key. We usually just bound, but I thought I'd treat you to a formal entrance."

"How very kind and un-Marco-like of you."

"I've grown up while you've been gone, Ace. Don't worry, nothing too dramatic, but I can act my age occasionally. Your sister has been a good influence."

I follow him into the baths. The entry looks just like we left it. Puffy stools line the walls, and a desk is on the back wall. That's where the two old Tunnelers sat when they brought us here from the trash tunnel. No wonder they hated us. We stunk!

We cut through the empty shower stalls to the back room—a.k.a. the Nest. The place looks even more homey than I remembered. There are papers scattered around with drawings labeled in my sister's handwriting. There's also a blanket, some pillows, and an overflowing waste bin filled with protein bar and fruit ball wrappers.

I sit down on the bench and kick up my feet. "Speaking of my sister . . ." I leave the words dangling, hoping he'll fill in the blank.

"Yeah, umm, about that . . ." He doesn't finish his sentence, either, but he doesn't need to. He fiddles with a string on his sleeve.

"It's cool." It's not like I didn't assume Marco was Addy's

boyfriend. Their connection was growing back in Alkalinia, and that was close to a year ago.

"Addy and I have been through a lot together, Ace."

I nod, and for a while, we don't say anything more. I lie back and hang my arm off the bench, dragging my fingers through the thick carpet made of mold. The last time I was in the Nest, the whole pod was together.

"You see Lucy and Cole?" Marco asks. He must have been thinking the same thing.

"They've changed."

Marco snorts. "Understatement."

"Cole is this military strategy genius, which I guess was kind of predictable."

"If you say so. He did have mad skills at *Evolution of Combat*."

"Remember that time we synced up and charged Normandy?"

"Epic."

I close my eyes and try to go back to a simpler time when my ranking at *Evolution* was an important focus of my life. It doesn't work. "I spent a lot of time with Lucy."

Marco groans. "It's impossible to watch the webs for more than two minutes without seeing her huge eyes staring back at you."

"She was pretty annoyed with you and Addy the last time we were all together."

Silence filled with things unsaid hangs in the air between us.

"What happened?" I finally ask. I've been wanting to know since I escaped the rift, and for the first time, I might actually get an answer.

Marco shrugs. "It's hard to explain."

"I traveled across the galaxy in a box with Regis to get here, Marco. The least you can do is tell me what I missed while I was trapped in the rift."

Marco laughs. "You make a fair point, Ace." He sits up on one of the mushroom-shaped stools and crosses his legs. He looks eerily like Waters.

"Alkalinia sucked," he says. "After the shield blew, it was a free-for-all. Addy and I were running through the lower levels of the Seat, dodging Alks as they tore about on their scooters. We finally made it up to the siphon bay. It was outright war. Earth Force and Youli were ripping each other apart. We didn't stick around for long because we needed to get to the other Bounders.

"Once we made it to the quarters hall, we were blocked. Steve and a bunch of his throne-riding Alk groupies were holding their position. Steve was hissing orders. Not much of it went through the translators, but one of the Alks had his on, and I'm pretty sure he was telling them to kill all the Bounders.

"We knew we had to do something fast. Addy and I had

our gloves out, but they were useless with the scrambler on. The other Bounders were no help. The ones who were awake were so groggy from the venom they could barely stand. Some of the Alks had those yellow vials. I think they were going to overdose our friends. If it hadn't been for Cole and Lucy, they probably would have."

It's weird to hear what happened to my friends while Mira and I were trapped in the rift. If I hadn't gotten that shield down, they'd be dead. "What did Cole and Lucy do?"

"During the chaos, Cole hacked the system and deactivated the scrambler. They came at the Alks from behind. I'm sure it was Cole's mastermind plan, but Lucy was able to wrangle the other Bounders into our quarters while Cole used his gloves to immobilize the Alks who were fighting off Addy and me from the other side. Once the Bounders were safely in, Cole retreated and sealed the doors."

"How?"

Marco shrugs. "Cole figured out some tech thing. Anyway, they survived the battle, which is a lot more than I can say about a lot of the Earth Force soldiers who fought that day. Eventually the Youli retreated, and a handful of Alks got off the planet on their vessel."

"I know. We ran into Steve at the space port."

"Seriously? What happened?"

"I'll tell you later. Go on with the story."

MONICA TESLER

Marco explained how Cole was hailed as a military hero for saving the Bounders and quickly moved up the ranks. Lucy used her recognition to talk her way into a press position and rose from there.

"What about you and Addy? It sounds like the two of you deserved some credit."

"Yeah, well, Addy—"

As if on cue, my sister bounds into the room. Literally bounds.

"I'm back!" she says, flopping cross-legged to the floor.

"You've been practicing with the gloves," I say.

She winks. "It's been a while since you saw me, J. I'm a bounding expert now. What did I miss?" She tosses me a pack of strawberry fruit balls.

"Actually, I was telling J-Bird what *he* missed when he was trapped in the rift."

"About that . . . ," Addy says, ripping open her own pack of fruit balls. "Time moves differently in the rift, huh?"

I nod. "It was like I was only gone for a couple of hours. The lost aeronauts were only there for two days."

"So, let me get this straight," she says, "you lived for a few hours in the rift while I lived for almost a year in the real world, right?"

I shrug. "I guess."

Addy hops up. "That makes me older than you!"

Umm . . . no. I shake my head and stare down my sister. "It does not."

"Oh yes, it does! And don't forget it!" She twirls around the room chanting, "I'm your big sister! I'm your big sister!"

She eventually sits down beside me on the bench and nudges me with her shoulder. "Seriously, though, what happened in the rift? Where's Mira? All we've heard are rumors."

I tell them about the Youli, their message, and Mira's departure. A thick lump forms in my throat while I talk. Sharing it with my sister makes the wound feel fresh.

"The Youli and their peace talk," Marco says, "that's old news. Isn't that what that guy said to you on top of his spaceship on the Paleo Planet? And then again when we planted the degradation patch on their systems during the intragalactic summit?"

"This was different."

"How?" Addy asks.

"I don't know how to explain it. It *felt* different."

Addy places her hand on my shoulder. "Maybe it just felt different because Mira went with them."

"No, that wasn't it," I say, "and anyway, why are you guys fighting me on this?"

Marco and Addy exchange glances.

"We're not fighting you, Ace. It's just . . . peace can be dangerous. For us."

That makes zero sense. "Peace is the opposite of dangerous."

"Maybe for most," Addy says. "But what about the Bounders? Someone has to look out for our interests."

"We were born to be soldiers," Marco says. "We were bred for war, not peace. If there's peace, there are no more Bounders."

I laugh. "Come on. It's not like they're going to kill us off."

"In a way, I think they will, Jasper," my sister says, "unless the Bounders have a voice at the table." I'm sure she can tell by my face that I don't understand.

"If there's no more need for Bounders," she explains, "no more *military* need, there's no more need for the Bounder Baby Breeding Program, at least how things are currently constructed on Earth."

"I'm still not sure I understand."

"It's like this, J-Bird. Addy and I and the other Bounders in the Resistance, we've had almost a year to reflect on the Battle of the Alkalinian Seat. Yes, we want peace, but we want a say in what that peace looks like. Earth needs to change. We need a planet—a civilization—that has room for all types of people, one where Bounders are welcome and born not because of military need but because it's right." He offers his hand to Addy. They stand together, staring down at me. "If this war has taught us one thing, it's that in our differences lie our strengths."

"And while we're open to talking about our planet's entry into the Intragalactic Council," Addy says, "it can't be on just the Youli's terms. The Resistance needs a voice. The Bounders need a voice."

As I stare at my sister, I'm struck again by how much time I lost in the rift. Addy has always been willful and strong, but the person I'm looking at isn't my kid sister. She's a leader, a warrior.

"Will you fight with us, Jasper?" she asks. "Will you join the Resistance?"

They're both looking at me, waiting for my answer. It would be so easy to say yes, to let Addy and Marco take over, to follow their direction and fight alongside Waters again. The truth is, I do think they stand on the right side of the conflict, even if Waters doesn't always do the right thing. Since my first tour of duty when I learned the depth of Earth Force's deception, I've known in my gut that what the Force is doing is wrong. Plus, there's no one in the galaxy I trust more than Addy and Marco.

The problem is, when I really think about it, I trust Cole and Lucy, too. What Cole showed me about the Youli was really troubling, even with Gedney's explanation about the Youli division. Cole's 100 percent on board with Earth Force, and he has the best strategic instincts of anyone I know. Then there's Lucy. She may be annoying sometimes, but there's no one who has a bigger heart, who cares more about her friends. I know she thinks she's doing the right thing.

Could there be a middle ground? Is there a road to peace that brings everyone together? That unites Earth Force and the Resistance?

"I have to talk to Waters first," I tell them. I need to speak to him directly about the Youli's message and his intentions.

The air next to Addy shimmers. Half a second later, Regis appears.

I recoil. Maybe I was starting to tolerate Regis, but that definitely doesn't mean I was ready to invite him to the Nest. Unfortunately, it seems someone already issued an invitation.

"What's up?" Marco asks him.

"Waters asked me to get you guys," Regis says. "He needs all the captains in the Parliamentary Chamber, stat."

"*Captains*," I say. "So the Bounders in the Resistance were promoted just like in Earth Force."

"It's nothing like Earth Force, J. Just wait and see." He turns to Addy. "We should go."

"In a sec," she says. "You go ahead."

Marco shrugs, then bounds away with Regis.

Addy sits on the floor and pats the ground beside her. I slide off the bench and plop down next to my sister.

She wraps me up in a giant hug. "I can't believe you're really here, J. I spent so many nights lying on this rug, trying to imagine you somewhere in the galaxy, alive. Everyone kept saying there was no way you survived, but I wouldn't accept it. I *couldn't* accept it. A world without you just wasn't something I could get my head around."

"When I got to the rift," I say, "all I could think about was watching the venom tube rip open into the deadly waters with you and Marco inside it. I could actually picture your sinking corpse."

"That's gruesome." Addy starts laughing. "Everything about Alkalinia was gruesome. It was so horrible it's actually funny."

I'm laughing, too. "Do you remember how freaked Marco was when he met Serena's babies?"

Addy falls back on the carpet. "So freaked! I mean, who wouldn't be freaked wading across a futbol field filled with tiny, venomous snakes?"

"Welcome to the EarthBound Academy!" I say, lying down beside her. "Was it all you thought it would be?"

"And more!" She giggles. "I nearly died along with all my new Bounder friends, and my brother was lost in a timeless rift! It's awesome!"

Our laughs fade, and the memories recede, and I'm left again with the reality of my post-rift life. "Marco was telling me what happened while I was stuck in the rift. You showed up before he got to the part where you and he joined the Resistance."

"They had a funeral for you, Jasper," Addy says quietly. "It was the worst day of my life. Tons of people spoke, including Admiral Eames. While she talked, a giant screen rose up behind her with a picture of you and the words PROTECTING OUR PLANET COMES AT A PRICE scrawled in cursive letters across your face. That very day, Earth Force posted the picture on the webs and distributed posters across the planet. Your death became their propaganda campaign."

Jasper Adams: poster boy. The way Lucy tells it, everything about the campaign was a huge success. As with most things, though, there's another side.

"I was so appalled," she continues, "I never reported back to duty. Neither did Marco. Neither did a lot of the Bounders."

So that's how so many Bounders ended up with the Resistance. In some weird way, it's because of me. "Is that why things got so bad with my pod? Because Cole and Lucy supported the propaganda campaign?"

"No, that wasn't it. . . ." She props up on one elbow and looks down at me. "Don't you see? Your pod was already growing apart back on Alkalinia. And then you were gone. You were the only thing holding the pod together, Jasper."

"I don't believe that. It can't be that simple."

"Sometimes it is. Bonds break."

Mira's words from the rift come back to me. *You're the glue, Jasper.*

Addy sits up and crosses her legs on the rug. She reaches over and squeezes my hand. "Friends come and go, J. But family is forever."

A sad smile lifts my lips. I'm so relieved to be back with Addy. She's not only family, she's one of my dearest friends. Wait . . . family . . . our parents.

I push myself up. "I saw Mom and Dad."

Addy raises her hands to her face. "Really? How are they?"

"They're worried about you, Addy. They thought you were dead, too, you know."

"Did you tell them I'm alive?"

"I hinted at it."

"Good. I know we're supposed to be all secretive in the Resistance, but I hate keeping them in the dark."

"There's something else, Ads." I scoot my back against the bench. "Mom was injured in the Resistance attack."

Alarm crosses Addy's face. "No! Everything went wrong! It was supposed to be nonviolent. We think someone must have tipped off Earth Force. Tell me she's okay, Jasper!"

"Gedney's sources said she was released from the hospital. But I'm not going to lie, she was badly hurt." I can see Mom's face, staring up at me through blood and tears. "She pushed me to search for you, Addy."

She blinks back tears. "None of that was supposed to happen. It's all our fault."

Silence stretches between us. In many ways, it *is* the Resistance's fault. They may have the ultimate goal of peace, but they're willing to cross a lot of lines to get there. I wish I could tell Addy that everything will be fine, but we'd both know it wasn't the truth.

"It's hard to predict what might happen when you're at war," I finally say, "even when you have the best intentions. I believe in the Youli's message, Addy. Peace is the answer."

She smooths her bounding gloves and rises to her feet. "I don't disagree with you, J, but we need to fight for the kind of peace that protects everyone."

27

ADDY WALKS ME TO THE BOUNDER BURROW
before heading to the Parliamentary Chamber. She suggested we bound there, but I insisted on taking the long way around. I wanted a few more minutes with my sister.

The Burrow—the old Bounders dormitory—is cavernous and empty. The silver glow of the occludium-powered lights casts a glare on the glossy walls. I run my fingers along the shellacked mud. I can almost hear Lucy and Neeka talking about clear nail polish. I wonder if Neeka misses Lucy. The old Lucy.

I walk all the way to the last bunk, the one Marco, Cole, and I shared with Regis and his pod mates during our tour of duty. It's empty. The beds are stripped, and there's no sign that anyone has stayed here in a long time. It's probably been empty since we left.

There were stacks of bedrolls by the front of the Burrow, but I'm too tired to go all the way back. Plus, everything aches. My body is screaming at me for spending a whole day curled up in a dark box.

I climb up to the top bunk, the one that used to be mine, the one that Regis tossed the creepy crawlies in during our tour. I close my eyes, expecting to fall asleep instantly, but I can't. Instead, I think about what Addy and Marco said about the Bounders, which makes me worry about the talk I need to have with Waters, which reminds me of the Youli's visit to the rift. And Mira.

Why did you leave with the Youli, Mira?

Do you miss me as much as I miss you?

Will I ever see you again?

I must eventually doze off, because the next thing I know, someone is barking in my ear.

I shoot up in bed and almost fall out of the bunk.

"Didn't think I'd see you again," the monotone voice box translates.

I get a look at the source of the bark: an old Tunneler with a scar across his furry face.

"You scared me half to death, Barrick. Don't do that again!"

"It's good for you. Keeps the reflexes sharp. Let's go." He makes some growly noises that don't translate and starts walking toward the exit.

"What do you mean? Go where?" I grab my blast pack and follow him across the Burrow.

"I said, let's go. Waters is waiting," he calls over his shoulder.

"Why didn't he come himself?" I ask once I catch up with Barrick.

"He's very busy."

"Sure."

"I'm sure he's busier than you," he barks. "I just found you asleep."

He has a point. "Why are you still using that old beta-version voice box?"

"Why are you still asking annoying questions?"

Barrick is as grumpy as ever. He saved my life, so he's not all bad, but he's not the best for friendly strolls through Gulagaven. When he had to escort Mira and me back here from the Wacky base, you'd think he was forced to eat an entire plate of those creepy crawlies (although who knows, maybe Barrick likes those things). He couldn't ditch us fast enough.

I follow Barrick through the halls and into another open

chasm. He keeps walking right onto one of the narrow bridges with no guard rails.

I freeze. There's no way I'm crossing that bridge. Mira and I nearly plunged to our deaths off one of those the last time I was here, thanks to Regis. I unzip my blast pack and dig for my gloves.

Barrick stops and turns around on the middle of the bridge. My stomach quakes just looking at him out there.

"What are you doing?" he asks.

"Give me a minute." I shake out my gloves and slip them on my fingers.

"Not in here!" he shouts.

"The scrambler is off."

"Don't care. Don't like those darn things."

I can't bound because he doesn't like my gloves? Tough luck.

I tap in, build a port, and bound, beating Barrick to the other side of the bridge.

He growls at me. I don't need the voice box to tell me he's mad.

"What is wrong with you?" the translation confirms. "I told you not to do that!"

I stand strong. "I don't follow orders from you, Barrick! And let me give you a preview of my meeting with Waters: I don't follow orders from him, either!"

Barrick passes me and heads down the hall. "We'll see about that," he barks over his shoulder.

I follow a few paces behind him. The ceiling gets lower with each step. Soon I'm more hunched over than Gedney on a bad day. I have a horrible sense of direction, but if I had to guess, I'd say we're near the bar where we first met Barrick.

He stops in front of a door guarded by a very large, very well-armed Tunneler. He has at least three guns strapped to his furry body.

Barrick nods at the guard, and he steps aside. I follow Barrick into a wide alcove. At the far end of the room is a long, stone table with a desk chair behind it. A few cushy stools are arranged in front. Maps and diagrams are tacked up all over the walls, and stacks of paper and tech crowd the floor around the table.

Waters is standing in the center of the room, spinning a projection of a galaxy sector. When we enter, he snaps his fingers, and the projection vanishes.

"Ah! Jasper! Come in. Have a seat. The stools look funny, I know, but they're actually quite comfortable. Feel free to take your shoes off. The carpet is incredibly soft. Believe it or not, it's made from—"

"Mold," I interrupt. "I've been here before, remember?"

Waters narrows his eyes and nods. "Yes, of course I do. Please sit." He sinks down on one of the mushroom stools. Barrick leans against the doorframe and crosses his arms.

"I'd like to talk with you alone," I say.

Waters looks at Barrick, who shakes his head.

"Whatever you have to say, you can say in front of Barrick."

"Are you, like, co-leaders or something?"

"We're not co-anything," Barrick says. "You got your meeting. Talk."

I sit on a mushroom and clasp my hands. I don't like this dynamic. I don't like that Barrick isn't sitting. I don't like that I feel like this is two against one, especially since I'd hoped to leave the room feeling like we were on the same page, united.

"Before you start, Jasper," Waters says, "I need to know more about Mira."

At the mention of her name, my heart jumps. "Have you heard something?"

"Only that she's with the Youli."

"Is she okay?"

Waters shakes his head. "I have no idea. I hoped you would shed some light on what happened."

Something inside of me falls, like a piece of glass crashing and shattering into a million tiny pieces. For a moment, I had dared to hope that Waters might have news about Mira. But he doesn't know anything more than I do. In fact, I'm probably his source, indirectly. I told Jayne, who probably told her handler in the Resistance, who probably told Waters.

Or maybe Gedney just called him up and told him the whole story since they're buds again now.

I push aside my emotions and try to hold a neutral expression while I talk to Waters. "I'm sure you heard we were trapped in the rift after the Battle of the Alkalinian Seat."

He nods me on.

I recount how we found the lost aeronauts and learned that time moved differently in the rift. Then I explain how the Youli arrived and offered us a deal. They'd help us escape the rift if we delivered a message. Of course, the "we" was really "me," because Mira didn't come back.

"What's the message?" Barrick asks.

I keep my eyes on Waters.

He taps his foot. "Go ahead, Jasper. Give us the message."

"Peace," I say. "The Youli want us to work toward peace together and discuss Earth's admission to the Intragalactic Council."

Waters steeples his fingers and raises them to his chin. I hold my breath. So much depends on his reaction.

Just when I start to think he's with me, he presses against his thighs and stands. "That message wasn't for me."

I look down at the moldy rug. I need to keep this going in the right direction. I need Waters to agree to work toward peace, and that starts with a peaceful resolution to his conflict with Earth Force. "They didn't specify who it was for."

"Jasper," Waters starts, pacing the alcove as he talks, "we're fighting on the same side as the Youli. I've been fighting on their side for years. We want to stop Earth Force from exploiting early developing planets. We want Earth to be invited to join the Intragalactic Council. As long as we have a meaningful voice on the Council, our interests are aligned with the Youli. We want peace. You are preaching to the converted with your so-called message."

This is not going the way I hoped, but I'm not going to let him run me over with his teacher tone. "You may support the Youli's agenda, Mr. Waters, but you're not practicing peace. The Resistance is openly fighting Earth Force now. You smoke-bombed a rally, and people got hurt, my mom included! And you kidnapped Denver Reddy and shipped him across the galaxy against his will!"

Waters doesn't respond to what I said. Instead he sits back down and leans close. "You talked to Admiral Eames first, didn't you? What did she say?"

Why does he have to be so good at reading the situation?

"She's not interested in peace."

"No, she's not," Barrick says. "She's interested in occludium. We have it, and they want it."

"Don't you think that oversimplifies things?" I ask.

"Usually the obvious answer is the right one," Waters says.

The anger I thought would come when I first saw Waters

starts to simmer beneath my skin. "Who are *you* to talk about what's right?" I say, my voice growing louder with each word. "You can't keep defending your actions that way! The ends do not always justify the means!"

"Let's keep the focus on the topic at hand, Jasper."

"No! I'm done doing what you say. I know the truth now, Mr. Waters. I know what really happened at the Incident at Bounding Base 51. You kidnapped a Youli so that you could conduct experiments on him. That's what caused the Incident. It's *your* fault Denver and the other aeronauts were lost in the rift all those years!"

Waters crosses his legs and tries his best to look unruffled. "I can see Denver has been telling stories. Yes, a Youli was taken prisoner that day, but I didn't order that."

I push to my feet. "But you admit you experimented on him!"

"Gedney and I were scientists instructed by Earth Force to research an alien life-form. Not only did we have no real choice in the matter, it was also a tremendous opportunity for the human race."

"And then you started the Bounder Baby Breeding Program! It was *you* who decided to breed kid soldiers!"

"No!" Waters jumps up. "That is not how it happened! I established a relationship with the Youli. Through him and his collective mind link, I was able to learn that Earth had

MONICA TESLER

essentially doomed its development by weeding out certain genes from the population. I argued to reintroduce those genes for the future of our species."

"And you needed a rationale. . . ." Standing up, I see I'm not that much shorter than Waters now.

"Yes, I emphasized the potential military benefit, but it was necessary."

"Again, the end justifies the means."

"What would you have me say, Jasper? That I'd rather the Bounders not be born? That I'd rather *you* not be born?"

I ignore his questions, even though he's baiting me with the same issue Marco and Addy explained in the Nest. Is he the one who planted that seed in their minds? "What about the other Youli prisoner? The one at the space station during our first tour of duty?"

"That wasn't my doing."

"You didn't know about him? Come on!"

"Of course I knew about him, but it wasn't my idea to take him. It ended up being a stroke of luck, though. I was able to communicate with the Youli through him and further our peace talks. You put a real roadblock in those talks with that stunt you pulled at the Wacky outpost."

I throw up my hands. This has gone far enough. "Nice, Mr. Waters! Blame it all on the kid! Way to turn the tables. I'm going to find my sister." I head for the door. Barrick blocks my exit.

"Before you go, Jasper," Waters says calmly, "let's bring things back to the Youli message."

I turn around.

Waters waits until he's sure he has my full attention. "If you're interested in peace, like the Youli, like me, then know that Earth Force is on the wrong side of that line." He snaps his fingers, and the projection reappears in the center of the room showing an image of the space station that housed the EarthBound Academy during my first tour of duty. "Thirty Earth Force gunner ships have just left that space station. Our intelligence indicates they're headed for Gulaga."

"What?"

"See for yourself." Waters flicks his fingers, and the image zooms out, showing a larger galactic snapshot of the space station. He points to a cluster of pinpricks of light moving steadily away from the station. If he's telling the truth, that's the Earth Force fleet. "It seems we've forced the admiral's hand. Eames is launching a full-scale attack. She was embarrassed in front of the whole world when we nabbed you and Denver. She couldn't let that stand."

"You planned this?" A wave of nausea curls from my belly up my throat. Denver said Eames couldn't let his kidnapping go unanswered.

"It's not possible to plan your enemy's behavior," Waters says, "but I'm awfully good at predicting it."

"Why did you provoke her like this?"

"I'm not interested in peace with Earth Force, Jasper, not in the short term. I've tried that route. Now I'm convinced that the only way to achieve long-term peace is to rid the galaxy of the Force once and for all. We need a new government in place to usher in our future as full members of the Intragalactic Council."

"With you at the helm?"

"If necessary, for a time, but that's not my goal. There are plenty of young leaders who share my ideals and who would do incredible things for our planet and the greater galaxy. Your sister, for one, Jasper." He smiles. "Maybe even you."

If what he's saying is true, Gulaga will be under attack in a matter of hours. "So, what exactly are you planning to do?"

"You'll see."

28

THE CHAMBER FLOOR IS PACKED WITH
Tunnelers and Earthlings. Almost every carrel climbing the walls is filled. The room hums with excitement. It's a totally different kind of energy from when I stood here as Admiral Eames rallied Earth Force for Operation *Vermis*. Then, it was rage, entitlement. We had a common enemy: the Youli. Now everyone in this room has a common cause. Unity. Independence. Ultimately, peace—and they're willing to do whatever it takes to get there.

Waters stands at the podium. He stands for Gulagan freedom, Bounders' rights, the greater galactic community. He stands for things I believe in.

Then why is it so hard for me to join him? Especially when joining him means joining Addy and Marco?

"Listen up!" Water says. "Our intelligence indicates that Earth Force will move into position and commence an aerial assault within the next hour. In addition, we must assume they have bounding ships positioned to enter our airspace at a moment's notice. Yes, we have the occludium shield in place, but don't forget that the shield doesn't prevent Earth Force landing on the surface in regular spacecraft."

A smaller group of Tunnelers and Earthlings stands with Waters on the front stage. I'm guessing they're the captains. Many of them I recognize: Addy, Marco, Neeka, Grok (another one of the junior ambassadors during our tour of duty), Minjae (one of the juniors in Addy's pod), even Regis.

Barrick stands next to Waters. "What's the update on fortifications?" he barks. From the way he asks, it's clear he's one of the leaders, outranking probably everyone but Waters.

Grok steps forward. "We reinforced the standard force field around Gulagaven yesterday to prepare for the attack. It should hold."

"For how long?" Marco asks. "Earth Force has far superior artillery. We're outgunned."

"It shouldn't come to that," Waters says. "All we want to do is bait them for a fight."

"Are you sure it's going to work after what happened at

the Lost Heroes Homecoming Tour rally?" Addy asks. "There were injuries, casualties. Admiral Eames has even more at stake." What she doesn't say is that our mother was one of those injured in the Resistance attack.

"She won't risk it," Waters says, "not with the world watching. And after what happened at the rally, you know they'll be watching."

Denver elbows me. "Any idea what the grand plan is, kid?" We're hiding out in one of the carrels on the first level, although we're not really hiding since Denver can't go anywhere without two Tunneler guards on his heels.

I shake my head. "No clue."

"Your friend is right," he whispers. "The Resistance is outgunned. I don't see how your old pod leader can eke out a victory here."

"Still," Waters continues from the podium, "we'll prepare our defensive as a precaution. You all know your roles. Everyone except captains is dismissed to their ready positions. It's a go, friends." Waters pumps his fist, then inclines his head. "Brothers, sisters, I bow to your service and fortitude."

The crowd bows and calls back, "And we also bow to you, brother."

It's the same exchange Neeka had with the chamber guards when we first arrived. I wonder if it's a traditional Tunneler custom.

Waters raises his arms and shouts, "May your days be peaceful and productive, and may your nights provide shelter from the cold."

The crowd cheers and floods out of the carrels, most of them headed for the exit. We join the masses, but before we reach the doors, Denver's guards block our path. They're not wearing voice boxes, but the one on the right raises a paw toward the stage, where Waters, Barrick, and the captains are continuing with the briefing.

"Moment of truth, kid," Denver says. "Something tells me we're about to find out why they shipped me across the galaxy."

"Then why do they need *me*?"

"If you don't think you're part of his grand plan by now, you don't know Jon Waters as well as you think."

Denver marches straight up to Waters. I join Addy and Marco and the other captains. I already know Waters was hoping I'd join the Resistance. He'll take as many Bounders as he can get. After all, another Bounder in the Resistance is one less in Earth Force. But could Denver be right? Could he want me for something more than that? Do I play a part in his grand plan?

Waters and Barrick hear reports from all the captains about armed crafts, artillery, defense, tunnel security—the list goes on and on without any mention of Denver or me. Finally

Waters dismisses the majority of his captains to their posts. All pilots, including Neeka, are instructed to board their crafts and wait for the launch signal.

Soon, the only ones left in the chamber are me, Denver, Addy, Marco, Regis, Barrick, and a handful of other officers, most of whom are strapped with guns. I'm guessing they're here to enforce whatever Waters is about to say.

Once the doors close behind the departing captains, Waters clasps his hands. "I'm sure all of you have had a chance to meet our guests, Denver Reddy and Jasper Adams. I trust your—"

"Get on with it, Jon," Denver interrupts. "I'm not your guest. I'm your prisoner. What I want to know is why."

Waters purses his lips. "Very well. Earth Force relies heavily on its media campaign to control public opinion and support. Right now, the population of our home planet is carefully waiting to see how Admiral Eames will respond to your . . . disappearance, if you will. As of now, rumors run rampant, but the Force hasn't confirmed that the Resistance is behind what occurred. In fact, we strongly believe that, once again, Earth Force will blame this on the Youli. As you know, the Force hasn't confirmed the existence of the Resistance at all, although reports are all over the webs." Waters pauses, letting his words sink in.

"And?" Denver asks impatiently.

"And that's about to change."

He walks to the center of the stage and activates a projection. This time, we're seeing Gulaga. He flicks his fingers, and the image zooms out until we can see the Earth Force fleet closing in. For several moments, he doesn't speak. He lets us watch the fleet as it gets closer and closer. He lets the gravity of the situation sink in.

"I need you to stop this," he finally says.

"How exactly do you propose we do that?" Denver asks.

"You are two of the most recognizable, popular people on the planet. I need you to tell Earth that you stand with the Resistance, and that the Resistance stands for peace. I need you to convince them that it's time to move beyond Earth Force and usher in a new era as members of the Intragalactic Council. I need you to tell Earth Force to stand down."

He needs *me* to do that? Why did he factor me into this? How did he know for sure I would come? The Resistance kidnapped Denver, but I came by choice.

"How on earth is that even possible?" Denver asks.

"It's all set up. We have a high-level contact in Earth Force public relations. She's arranged for the broadcast to stream globally. Once it's out, the webs will run with it. Earth Force won't be able to shut it down."

"Jayne," I say.

"That's right," Waters says. "Jayne is an extremely valuable asset of the Resistance, as I believe you already know, Jasper."

Waters must have been the one who told Jayne to bring me into the fold. He sent Gedney to see me on the tour. He made the recording of Addy begging me to join them. He knew I would come, and he knew I would be a far more willing participant in his plan if I thought I came by choice. And he knew I could help get Denver on board.

"As for timing," Waters continues, "we'll wait until the Earth Force fleet is within range, perhaps even draw combat. That way, we'll have excellent footage of the Force's savagery to include with the broadcast."

Wait a second. This is moving too fast. I may agree with the Resistance's objectives, but I don't approve of all their methods, including this one. There's way too much that could go wrong.

"You're risking everyone on Gulaga for this?" Denver asks.

"It's a calculated risk. I'm confident Admiral Eames will cave. Once she knows that you're on Gulaga, Denver, she'll call it off. We both know she wouldn't do anything that might result in your death."

Denver throws up his hands. "That's ridiculous. You've never understood how the military works, Jon. Cora is a soldier. She'll prioritize the mission, not her personal feelings. And trust me, her personal feelings are no longer a factor."

"You've been gone a long time, Denver. I understand the military. And I know Cora. Trust *me*."

Denver clenches his jaw and starts to shake. Every muscle in his body is coiled tight, like he's about to spring on Waters. His Tunneler guards take a step closer.

I'm no expert on Admiral Eames, but no matter how she reacts there's a lot that could go wrong. I have a very bad feeling about this. I glance at Addy. She bites her lip and looks away.

Barrick's com link buzzes. He relays the report to Waters. The first Earth Force vessels have been detected on standard satellite. They should be in Gulagan airspace within minutes.

"Excellent," Waters says. "We'll watch the initial engagement. Then we'll broadcast live. Regis, please oversee the setup for filming, load the script into the teleprompter, and confirm Jayne is ready to go."

Regis nods and exits the chamber.

We crowd around the projection, watching as the Earth Force fleet closes in. When they're within striking distance, Waters gives the order to send the Resistance ships out to meet them. Sweat beads on my forehead. I clasp and unclasp my palms, watching for the first sighting of the Gulagan vessels.

"You're sending those heaps of junk out there?" Denver asks. "That's a suicide mission."

"They're trained in evasive tactics," Waters says. "We won't keep it up for long."

"Neeka is piloting one of those?" I ask my sister, remembering the ride in Neeka's craft and how the inside looked like it was held together with duct tape and wire.

"Yes," she says gravely, still not meeting my gaze.

How did it come to this? We're out of options. Earth Force is retaliating for the Resistance's attack at the rally. Their counterattack was predictable. All of this is part of Waters's plan. And our only shot at calling off the fleet is Waters's broadcast.

If it's the only way, we might as well minimize the risk. "Can't we just broadcast now instead of—" I start.

Waters raises his hand. "Timing is everything."

Regis comes back into the chamber with a group of Tunnelers. At the far end of the stage, they set up two chairs and a small recording device on a tripod in front. Now that I see the setup, I realize it must be the same place they filmed Addy's message to me.

Marco elbows me in the ribs and points to the projection. A dozen Tunneler crafts zoom out of the atmosphere in a V formation, preparing to engage the Earth Force fleet. I'm pretty sure Neeka's craft is the leader.

The Tunnelers shoot, then roll out on the sides, circling back to form a perimeter. Earth Force returns fire, but the Tunnelers shuffle position, evading the brunt of the assault. All the while, they rain fire on the Force ships.

"Earth Force isn't taking damage from those hits," I say.

"They're shielded," Marco says. "Our shots are all deflected."

"Well, how do we expect—" My words are cut short when a burst of orange light showers across the projection. One of the Resistance ships was hit. It spirals away from the others. A second round of fire finds its target, and the Tunneler craft explodes.

"No!" I shout.

"Is everything prepared for the broadcast?" Waters asks Regis, his voice low and urgent.

Once Regis confirms, he looks at me and Denver. "Okay. It's time." He crosses the stage in long, swift strides, headed to the area set up for the broadcast.

Denver folds his arms against his chest. "No."

Waters stops. "What did you say?"

"I said no. It doesn't matter what you do, Jon. Torture me, if you want. I'm not doing your broadcast. I am not your pawn. I'm not going to read your words to the people of Earth. I may not agree with Earth Force, but that doesn't mean I agree with you."

Waters waves his arm at the projection. "You see what's happening out there, and I know you're sympathetic to our cause!" He marches over to Denver. "You're not going to stand here and do nothing while countless Tunnelers die. *Again.* You don't have a choice!"

"There's always a choice, Jon. You miscalculated. Threats may work on Eames, but they won't work on me. I have nothing to live for. Life passed me by while I was stuck in the rift."

"You couldn't save the Tunnelers before, Denver, but you can save them today!" Waters shouts. "If you don't, their blood is on your hands!"

"Do you still not get it, Jon?" Denver shouts back. "Their blood is on *your* hands!"

29

"THEY'RE NOT GOING TO MAKE IT!" I plead with Denver. "We have to stop this!"

"It's not our job, kid. We didn't start this, and crowning Jon Waters the winner is not going to end it."

"My friends are going to die!" For all I know, Neeka is already dead.

"This is war, kid. That's what happens. If you want it to stop, convince your pod leader to raise a white flag and admit defeat."

"And . . . what? Keep fighting a war with the Youli that will ultimately destroy us?" I ask. "Allow Earth Force to decide the future of our planet? Even *you* know that's a horrible idea!

Please!" When Denver shakes his head, I turn back to Waters. "Mr. Waters, you've got to do something!"

Waters doesn't hear me. He's fixed on the projection. Three more Resistance ships have taken hits. Two have disengaged with engine failure. Meanwhile, the Earth Force ships continue to press without any sign of damage.

A second ship explodes in a crater of light. My breath catches in my throat. When the image clears, half of the Earth Force ships are no longer visible on the projection.

"They've entered the atmosphere," Addy says. "We need to get out there!"

"The Bounders need to stop them on the ground," Marco says. "If they make it through the force field, we're done for!"

My sister and Marco stare at Waters, waiting for their orders.

Waters nods at Barrick.

"Romero, Adams," Barrick barks, "gather the other Bounders, get in position, and await further orders."

Adams . . . not me, my sister. He's sending her into battle. "Let me do the broadcast on my own!" I beg.

"No," Waters says, he takes a deep breath, then softens his voice, probably to sound less threatening, more like a friend explaining a plan, but his expression oozes with desperation as he turns to face me and Denver. "It needs to be both of you on the broadcast, or it won't work. The people of Earth know you both were taken. If you don't appear together, Earth Force will be able to spin the story their way. They'll likely claim you're responsible for the kidnapping, Jasper, that you're working with the Youli."

Denver grabs my arm. "Don't let him manipulate you like this, kid. There has to be another way."

"There is no other way!" Waters shouts at Denver.

"Surrender!" Denver shouts back.

"You know we can't do that!"

Barrick refocuses the projection. At least ten Earth Force vessels are nearly on the ground. He barks into his com link. "The Bounders are ready to engage," he relays to Waters.

"Give the order," Waters says, then turns back to me and Denver. "Are you really going to send Jasper's sister into the line of fire?"

I look at Denver, hands clenched to my chest.

"The Bounders have departed," Barrick reports.

Denver shakes his head. "I'm not doing it, kid. I'm sorry."

"Convince him," Waters says to the armed guards.

The Tunnelers drag Denver across the stage.

"Stop it!" The Tunnelers ignore me. I run after them. "I said stop!"

Denver takes the first two punches standing up, then hits the chamber floor. The Tunnelers kick him in the ribs, flip him, and kick him in the back. I wrap my arms around my waist and rock back and forth. All I can do is watch in horror as they beat him to a pulp.

But it doesn't really matter what they do. They need Denver to cooperate or this won't work. They can't put Denver on a live broadcast with a gun to his head. That would make the Resistance look like the bad guys. It would justify Earth Force's actions.

Another one of Waters's plans backfires, and we're left paying the price.

Barrick's bark calls me back to the moment. "The Bounders are taking fire."

I spin back to the projection, expecting to see bounding ships engaging the Earth Force gunners on the ground. Instead, my jaw drops as I process what I'm witnessing on the projection. Addy, Marco, and the other Bounders don't have ships. They're out there on foot, engaging Earth Force on the frozen Gulagan tundra, fighting with their gloved hands.

"Are you insane?" I scream at Waters. "They're going to get killed!"

"Bounders are a priceless commodity," he replies. "I doubt Earth Force will fire on them."

"You *doubt* it?" I shout. "I'm done gambling on your guesses, Mr. Waters!"

I pace back and forth in front of the projection. Every second wasted is a second closer to Addy's inevitable death. I can't believe I came all the way to Gulaga only to watch my sister be slaughtered.

"Do something!" I scream.

No one responds. Waters and Barrick urge on their guards trying to beat sense into Denver.

Regis grabs my arm and bends close. "Let's go."

"Where?"

"Where do you think?" He nods at the projection. "They need us out there."

He wants to fight with Addy, Marco, and the other Bounders? I glance back at Waters and Denver—that's hopeless. Regis is right. My best bet is to join the fight. I nod.

Regis takes off running. Once we pass through the doors of the chamber, he loosens the control straps on his blast pack and lifts off. I'm right behind him.

We weave through the narrow tunnels of Gulagaven, slowly making our way to the surface. Regis is flying because of me. He could just as easily bound to the force field—after all, the scramblers are off—but I don't know the way.

I push myself faster and suddenly my brain seizes on a memory. I'm racing Regis in the hangar during our first tour of duty. More than anything I wanted to humiliate him. My hatred fueled me.

Now, as I race to help my sister and friends, I'm fueled by determination. If anything, Regis and I have a common enemy. And maybe, as much as I don't want to admit it, maybe Regis isn't the enemy anymore.

He touches down and darts forward. He hurries us through a door into a small outfitter and tosses me a bundle of outerwear. I shove my arms and legs into the suit, don the helmet, and force my feet into boots. Regis is ready by the time I'm dressed.

"Right through these doors!" He activates the sliders, and we pour into the first exit chamber. The door slides closed behind us. One more door and we're in the battle.

"Hey," I say to Regis. "Thanks."

He looks at me and nods. "The Bounders will be the ones who end this."

He lowers his visor and seals his helmet. The door slides back, the frigid air rushes in, and Regis and I take off across the Gulagan tundra.

Up ahead, the Earth Force gunner ships close in. The Bounders hold them back with their gloves. Regis breaks left, but I bolt straight ahead toward the point where I spotted Addy on the screen.

My mind is a jumble. I'm clenched in fury over Waters's failed threats and riddled with fear that my sister and friends are going to get killed. Plus, I probably know some of the soldiers in the Earth Force vessels. They might be Bounders. For all I know, Ryan or Meggi or even Cole might be right here on the tundra. I don't want them to die either. There must be another way to force Admiral Eames to call off the attack. If I could only clear my head enough to think.

The thing is . . . Waters isn't wrong. Threats *will* work on Admiral Eames—the threat of exposing her propaganda campaign and the threat that Denver's life is at stake.

What if all we needed to do was lay down the threats?

We don't actually need to broadcast, we just need to *threaten* to broadcast.

What comes after the threats is what's important. And if I can get Waters and Denver to buy into the next steps, we might be able to stop this.

Voices swirl in my head.

Regis's words from moments ago: *The Bounders will be the ones who end this.*

Addy's words from the Nest: *The Bounders need a voice.*

Mira's words from the rift: *You're the glue, Jasper. It has to be you. It's always been you.*

I skid to a halt.

This needs to stop.

And *I* need to be the one to end it. I *want* to be the one to end it.

I'm one of the most popular people on Earth right now. I thought that no longer meant much to me, but the truth is, it does. It does because it might help me end this and finally achieve peace for our planet.

I spot Addy up ahead. I lock in visual contact and bound to her side.

"What are you doing out here?" she screams. Her arms are raised. She's trying to block the fighter guns of the nearest Earth Force ship. I raise my gloved hands and help. Slowly we're able to turn the metal so that the gun is pointed in upon the ship.

"Listen, I have a plan. I think I can convince Waters, but it will take a few minutes. Bound back with me."

Addy targets the second gun on the ship. "No way. We're outnumbered, J. Without my help, we're doomed, if we're not already."

I scan the line of Bounders. There are far too few. No matter how powerful we are with the gloves, they stand no chance against this artillery, especially when the other Earth Force ships land. The best they can do is buy us time.

Which means I need to hurry.

I nod at Addy. "I'll be as quick as I can."

Pulling up a mental image of the Parliamentary Chamber, I build my port and bound, landing half a meter away from Denver.

"Where were you, kid?" he asks with a strained voice. The guards have kept his face free of bruises, but his insides are a different story.

I unseal my helmet and throw it on the chamber floor. "I have an idea. Please listen."

Denver locks eyes with me. At first, I don't think he'll agree. Then he dips his chin in a small nod.

I jump to my feet and run to the projection, where Waters stands with Barrick. "There's another way!"

Waters spins. "Where were you?"

"There's no time to explain. My idea will save us."

"Unless you can talk sense into Reddy, don't waste my time."

"Hear him out, Jon." Denver pushes to standing, wincing from the beating.

Waters narrows his eyes at me. "Ten seconds."

"You don't have to broadcast live. You just have to threaten to do it. Get Admiral Eames on the line. Tell her what you plan to do. Make her call off the invasion."

Waters's face crinkles and his gaze drops as he processes what I said.

"The most that gets us is a cease-fire," he says.

"For now, that's enough! They're dying out there!"

Denver nods, catching on to my idea. "The kid's right. Start with a cease-fire and move on to diplomacy. Someone needs to negotiate, Jon, and by 'someone,' I do *not* mean you."

"Well, if you think I'm sending you—"

"Send me!" I shout. They all turn to me, one face more incredulous than the next. "Send the Bounders!"

Suddenly the Youli's message resonates in stunning tone.

Their message wasn't for Earth Force. It wasn't for the Resistance, either. It was for me, and I know exactly what needs to be done. "I've spoken to you, Mr. Waters, and I've talked to Admiral Eames. Neither of you is capable of reaching terms. You need fresh voices. Like you said, there are plenty of young leaders who share your ideals, who would do incredible things for the galaxy, who can move Earth toward peace." Regis knew exactly what he was talking about. "The Bounders will be the ones to end this."

"What exactly are you suggesting?" Waters asks.

"Both sides send representatives to a neutral location to negotiate—Cole Thompson and Lucy Dugan for Earth Force, Marco Romero and Adeline Adams for the Resistance." I swallow hard before continuing. ". . . as long as all of them are still alive. I'll facilitate the discussion."

Waters laughs. "Don't be ridiculous. You're just kids."

Denver places his hand on my shoulder. "Maybe so, Jon. But this kid rescued me from the rift, helped lead a publicity campaign across his planet, and talked sense to me in a cramped crate. Not to mention that much of what you're fighting over is technology that only the Bounders are capable of wielding. I'd say our futures lie with these kids."

Waters closes his eyes and rubs his chin.

"They're closing in on the force field!" Barrick barks.

We're out of time.

"Your plan has a major flaw, Jasper," Waters says. "Earth Force will never agree to it."

"That's where you're wrong, Jon," Denver says. "Get me a secure line to Cora. I'll get her on board."

30

THE SECONDS TICK BY AS WATERS TRIES
to secure a channel to Admiral Eames. On the projection, the
battle intensifies.

Addy and Marco work together. They manage to stop one
of the ships from progressing, but it's clearly draining them.
Minjae and another Bounder arrest a second ship, but the rest
of the gunners continue their advance.

"We need to hurry!" I shout. "What's taking so long?"

"They've nearly breached the force field," Barrick says.

As soon as the words squeak from Barrick's voice box, the closest gunner ship fires at the invisible wall, the only thing separat-
ing Earth Force from Gulagaven and the heart of the Resistance.

One of the Bounders runs to the front to defend the force field, trying to knock away the laser fire with the power of his gloves.

He's too close. He can't hold back that kind of firepower.

I see the moment when his energy gives out. One second, he has control of the laser with his gloves; the next, his arms collapse inward. Then he's lying in a heap on the cold ground, his protective gear burned through and steaming in the cold Gulagan air.

Only now can I clearly see his face.

Regis.

"No!" I slam my fists into the projection and stumble forward, nearly falling to the ground.

"Denver!" Waters shouts. "Get over here now! I've got Cora on the line!"

No matter how quickly Denver manages to convince Admiral Eames, it might not be fast enough to save the Bounders. Every second counts.

I grab my helmet. "I'm bounding out there."

Barrick grumbles and dodges for me. I duck out of the way. "Don't you dare—" his voice box is translating, but I build my port and bound before it finishes.

I land half a meter from Addy. My skin burns. I didn't have time to seal the coat sleeves tight against my gloves. And I don't have time to worry about that now. I aim my gloves at the advancing gunner ship and help my sister hold it off.

"What's happening?" Addy asks with a strained voice. She's tired. The Bounders can't keep this up for long.

"Denver is negotiating with Admiral Eames. We're hoping for a cease-fire."

Please let it work. Please. Everything I've done, all the choices I've made, have led me to this moment. If I'm wrong, I might as well go lie down next to Regis.

Addy turns back to the ship. I feel her command of the atoms slipping. This isn't going to work.

"We need to make them defend from both sides," I say. "That will buy us time."

"But the force field . . ."

"All we need is a few minutes, Ads. If it takes longer than that, we're goners no matter what."

She nods and refocuses her energy at the ship. "Go!"

I bound to the flank, where Marco and Minjae are holding back another gunner.

"Come with me—attack from the rear!" I shout.

Marco gives a thumbs-up and nods at Minjae. The three of us open ports.

I hit the frozen ground behind the middle gunner, the same ship my sister fights from the front. I flash my gloves at its thrusters. The ship jerks back. I grab the straps of my blast pack and shoot up in the air, barely avoiding getting run over. Addy darts to the side to target another ship.

"Good one!" Marco calls, copying my move on the thrusters of another ship. We're disrupting their attack plan and causing confusion. Some of the ships try to turn around; others stop firing. If we can keep up the disruption for a few more minutes, hopefully Eames will stop the advance.

I shift my focus to the ship advancing on Addy. She disarms one of the guns, but the ship still edges forward. Her arms bend inward. She collapses to her knees.

"No!" I grab the ship by its right wing and fling it with all my might. It spins in a circle and comes to rest facing me.

Lasers blast from its remaining gun. I bank right in my blast pack then zoom low to the ground out of firing range. I touch down and turn, raising my palms.

This is it. Give me all you've got.

I brace for the impact of the lasers, hoping my new gloves and my wavering strength are enough to shield myself. Otherwise, I'll end up fried on the ground like Regis.

But the shots don't come.

The ship drops its rocket vents and lifts off. It slowly rises above the frozen ground until it's high enough to shift its engine and blast through the Gulagan atmosphere.

The other Earth Force vessels follow, departing the surface.

Oh my God. It must have worked. Eames must have agreed to a cease-fire.

Soon, all of the Earth Force ships are gone, and only the slim line of Bounders remain.

I run across the tundra and sweep up Addy in a huge hug. Marco collides with us from behind, and we fall to the ground in a giant pig pile.

I'm freezing and crying and so tired I might never get back up.

But we're alive.

We're wonderfully, blissfully, gratefully alive.

For now.

What comes next is up to the Bounders.

It's all set. Denver talked Admiral Eames into a cease-fire, and she agreed to send Lucy and Cole to negotiate, as long as they're allowed to talk with her before reaching an agreement. Waters isn't too happy with the plan, but he's going along with it. After all, what choice does he have (other than to be soundly beaten by Earth Force in a costly battle)?

Funny how it turns out that Waters is the one with no choice, although nothing about today is really funny.

Was it only this morning that I climbed into a crate with Regis? That we battled Alks and chirpers side by side? And now his body lies on the tarmac, frozen, covered in a tarp and awaiting a final trip home to Earth. He'll be traveling in a different kind of box this time.

I won't ever forget the way Regis treated me at the Academy, the way he treated Mira. But I do forgive him. He acknowledged his wrongs, and he did right in the end.

Twenty Tunnelers lost their lives in the space fight. Only two Resistance ships made it home. I feel guilty being happy that Neeka was spared, but I am. She piloted her hunk-of-junk craft to the surface on the other side of Gulaga once her first engine was hit, saving her from the brunt of the battle. A ground crew is crossing the tundra now to bring her home.

Other than Regis, the Bounders all survived, but a lot of them sustained injuries. I'm one of the lucky ones. My only battle scars are the patches of skin on both of my forearms that were exposed to the Gulagan air. They're covered in salve and wrapped in gauze. The painkillers they gave me in the infirmary seem to be working.

I can't afford to dwell on the day's losses. I need to focus on the negotiation. The meet is set to convene at Bounding Base 32, the place our pod went on our first bounding trip. The base is evacuating right now. Addy's never been there, but the Resistance has a BPS, so she can scan the coordinates pre-bound.

Since I'm going to serve as an impartial facilitator, I left Addy and Marco to talk strategy with Waters and Barrick. Denver and I are sitting in the cantina. I didn't even bother getting food. He filled a plate with forage and fungi, and has spent most of the time pushing it around his tray with a spork.

Shortly before I'm supposed to join Addy and Marco in the Parliamentary Chamber, Waters walks into the cantina.

"I need to speak with you privately, Jasper."

Denver raises his eyebrows. He'll stay if I want him to. I shake my head, letting him know I'm okay. He leaves the table and heads to the other side of the cantina, clutching his side as he walks. He's pretty banged up from the Tunneler beating.

Waters pulls back a chair and sits. He waits until Denver is out of earshot, then leans his arms on the table. "We've been contacted by the Youli. We know they monitor most of our communications, and apparently today was no exception."

I nod for him to go on.

"They intercepted the call between Denver and Admiral Eames. The Youli know about the meet, Jasper, and they want to send a representative."

Include the Youli in our negotiations? Eames would never agree to that. Plus, it doesn't fit the spirit of the meet: young leaders taking their planet in a new direction.

"No way," I tell Waters. "My pod knows one another, and they know Addy. They may not all trust one another now, but the seeds of trust are still there. Injecting a Youli into this would erode all that."

Waters pushes Denver's tray away. He sits up straight and looks me in the eye. The silence is heavy, because I know he has more to say.

"It's Mira."

My breath catches in my throat so badly I almost gag. "Mira? How?"

"Easy. She'll bound there, just like you."

"Yes, but how did this come about?" I swallow hard. "And how is she?"

Waters leans back in the chair. "I haven't spoken to her, but I have no reason to suspect she's been harmed. The Youli likely suggested they send Mira because they know it's the only way we'd agree."

"So it wasn't her idea?" This probably has nothing to do with Mira wanting to see me. The Youli are probably making her do this.

"I really don't know any more than what I've already told you, Jasper."

What if she doesn't even want to go? She may not care if she ever sees me again.

I know I should tell Waters that Mira can't come. She'll make me jittery, and it's not like she's going to persuade the others of anything—at least, not with words. On the other hand, Mira's a keen judge of a situation. Maybe having her there will be helpful.

Who am I kidding? Would I ever turn down a chance to see Mira again? Of course not.

"Tell the Youli she can come."

I expect Waters to leave, but he sits there staring at me.

"Can I ask you a question?" he finally asks.

I shrug. The last thing I want is to keep talking to Waters, but I know he's going to ask no matter what I say.

"Do the brain patches actually work?"

After everything that happened today, that's what he wants to know? I can't think of a good reason to lie anymore. "Yeah, they work, although they have a range. It's not like I can talk to her right now."

"Hmmm." Waters runs his hand through his hair. "You know, Jasper, I never wanted things to go the way they did. I messed up. I guess I keep messing up. But I'm trying to do the right thing. People are counting on me."

I shake my head. What is he expecting me to say? "Is that an apology?"

"Not a good one. How's this: I'm sorry."

Too little, too late. His words don't even touch me. I sit back in my chair and cross my arms. "How's this: There's nothing you could say that would make me fully trust you again. You used me. You used my friends."

Waters nods. "That's fair."

Fair? Who cares about fair? I grab the table and lean

forward. "What part of this war is fair, particularly to the Bounders?"

"Look, Jasper," Waters says, pushing away, "I said I was sorry, and I meant it. But let's get one thing straight between us: I don't regret what I'm fighting for."

I lower my voice and narrow my eyes. "Neither do I."

We lock eyes, and I know he's expecting me to turn away first. The Jasper who showed up at the EarthBound Academy for his first tour of duty would have. Not anymore.

Eventually Waters drops his gaze. A tiny part of me feels victorious, but there's too much at stake today to care for long.

"I need to respond to the Youli," he says.

I nod.

He stands and places a hand on my shoulder before leaving the cantina. That used to be comforting. Now it just feels like another weight on my back.

"YOU READY?" I ASK ADDY.

"I've used the BPS before," she says. "Stop big-brothering me. I'm the older sibling now, remember?"

"Very funny," I say.

"We need to go," Marco says.

"Remember, we'll be available via com link the whole time," Waters says, "and you need to return and confer before reaching a deal. Jasper, per the terms Captain Reddy negotiated, you need to bound in first."

I give Addy a quick hug then tap in and build my port. I pull up a clear image of Bounding Base 32 and *bam!*

My knees buckle as I hit the flight deck. Another botched landing.

As we agreed, the bounding base is deserted. It's downright creepy to be standing alone on an empty building in space. Beyond the flight deck, the endless blackness is dotted by stars light-years away.

A shimmer next to me announces the next arrival.

Bam! Lucy bounds in.

As soon as she gets her bearings, she charges at me, fists raised. "I can't believe you, Jasper Adams! After all I did for you! I made you a star! You were breaking hearts across the planet. And then you betray me? I'll tell you what, Jasper, you broke *my* heart! You—"

"Lucy! Stop!" I grab her wrists to stop her pounding on my chest. "I didn't know what the Resistance had planned until right before it happened." That's not entirely true, but it's not wildly far off, either. "Please understand, Lucy. I had to see my sister."

Addy bounds in.

Lucy takes a step back. She adjusts her uniform and wipes a makeup-filled tear from her cheek.

"Hello, Lucy," Addy says.

Lucy smiles the fakest smile I've ever seen. "Adeline." She looks Addy up and down, taking in her bright,

Tunneler-inspired clothes. Her lip turns up in disgust. "What are you wearing?"

Addy glares at Lucy. "Why? Does my outfit offend the new face of Earth Force?"

Geez. Things aren't going well. Maybe this was a bad idea. Maybe I was wrong to assume we could move past everything that happened while I was in the rift. I don't even know all that went down. I should have made Addy give me the gritty details before this meet.

Cole bounds in next. He stands rod straight in his perfectly pressed Earth Force uniform. He commands an authority I never could have imagined when I first met Cole. He nods at me and Addy.

When Marco arrives, Lucy raises her clenched fists again. Fortunately, this time she doesn't charge.

"Hey, Wiki, DQ!" Marco says.

"Don't you dare." Lucy's voice is a grumbled whisper filled with menace.

I have to keep things under control. I kick Marco's foot. "No nicknames."

"Whatever you say, Ace."

"I see you haven't changed, Marco," Lucy says.

Before Marco can respond, I step forward. "See, that's one of the reasons I pushed for this meet. We know one another really well. If there's anyone capable of hashing out a truce, it's us." I take a deep breath, hoping one of them will jump in and at least agree with the idea that this meet could work.

Silence.

Eventually Cole nods. "Let's get started, then."

"In a second," I say. "We're waiting on one more person."

"What do you mean?" Lucy says. "We agreed to a specific attendance list! If you're already breaking the negotiated rules, we're going to leave. In fact—"

The air between us shimmers, and a second later, Mira is standing on the deck.

Her blond hair hangs loose around her shoulders and glistens like real gold. She's wearing a long white dress that catches the light with a faint iridescence. Her bare hands glow.

I try to keep my expression blank. Inside, my heart hops against my ribs.

"Oh my God!" Lucy shouts. She runs across the flight deck and throws her arms around Mira. "How is this possible? We all thought you were dead!"

I almost remind Lucy that she made up the story about Mira being dead, but I decide it probably won't advance our talks. "The Youli intercepted the communication between Captain Reddy and Admiral Eames," I explain. "They insisted that Mira come to the meet."

"We should have been informed," Cole says.

"Actually, you were." I try to keep my voice from shaking.

"We said we wanted the pod here. Mira's been staying with the Youli, but she's every bit a member of this pod." I swallow hard. I can't believe Mira is standing a few meters away.

I steal a glance at her. She turns. As soon as our eyes meet, a whole world opens in my mind. Love, joy, and comfort pour in, but a layer of sadness and longing hangs at the edges.

Mira smiles. *Hello, Jasper.*

I take a deep breath. "Hi, Mira."

"I'm okay with Mira being present," Cole says, "but I must insist that there be no brain-talk. That's not fair to the rest of us."

"And it's not fair to Mira to disallow it," I say. "We both know Mira doesn't speak in the customary Earth way."

"Then *you* can't brain-talk, Jasper," Marco says to me, "and if Mira does, you have to translate everything she says." He turns to Cole. "Does that work for you?"

Cole nods.

"Everyone else?" I ask.

Addy and Lucy nod.

"Mira?"

Yes. I've missed you so much.

I take another deep breath. Everything in me wants to reach out and touch her, make sure that she's real. For now, though, I'll have to settle with letting our minds touch. I take a moment to feel her familiar presence inside my brain. Now I need to stay on track.

"She says she agrees," I say. "Should we go inside? I asked the officers at the bounding base to leave some food for us in the cantina."

Marco laughs. "Why is it always about food with you?"

The joke doesn't reach Cole. "We'll stay out here."

"Fine," I say. So much for keeping things casual.

I stand up straight and launch into the remarks I prepared on Gulaga. "So to start, I'll remind everyone that Cole and Lucy are here on behalf of Earth Force, Marco and Addy are here for the Resistance, Mira is here for the Youli who consider themselves an interested party, and I'm here to act as a neutral facilitator. I'm hoping we can keep our discussions as informal as possible. Who would like to speak first?"

Glances flicker around our circle. Is no one going to talk? I shoot a glance at my sister. I traveled halfway across the galaxy for her. The least she could do is help me out now.

Addy steps forward. "I know I'm kind of the outsider, here, so why don't I start?" She side-eyes Marco, who nods her on. "I've always admired your pod. You're all so different, but you achieved so much together. I know things were difficult after the Battle of the Alkalinian Seat. I know I certainly wasn't on my best behavior. I said things I regret, things I didn't mean. I'm sorry for that. But here's the thing: you guys, your pod, you're the best thing about Earth. It doesn't get better than you. I hope you know that, and I hope we can talk together and get on the same page about moving forward."

Lucy puts her hands on her hips. "I don't know where that speech came from, little sister, but don't think for a minute that you can excuse your behavior by writing it off as emotional distress. I'm emotionally distressed every day, and it doesn't stop me from showing up and doing my job for Earth Force. Do you think you were the only ones reeling from Jasper's death? I was devastated and charged with rolling out Earth Force's biggest PR campaign since the launch of the Bounder Baby Breeding Program. The two of you went AWOL when I needed you most!"

"Lucy," Marco starts—I think it may be the first time I've ever heard him use her actual name—"we were all devastated, and we all had different ways of dealing with it. But that's not where the divisions in the pod began, and it's not when our views split with the Force. Even in Alkalinia, we didn't see eye to eye on the Force's tactics. I don't expect us to agree on everything today, either, but I do think we can reach a reasonable solution to our immediate problem."

"I'd prefer if we kept emotions out of this," Cole starts.

Like that has any chance of success.

"Let me summarize why we're here," he continues. "Our

fleet is positioned to destroy Gulaga. You have Denver Reddy, and he's prepared to publicly declare support for the Resistance with Jasper by his side. We're at a standoff, and we're here to see if we can stand down."

Lucy is dramatic but reasonable, Mira says. *She understands the media dynamics. Tell her that the Resistance has no desire to air the broadcast if Earth Force agrees to terms.*

"Mira thinks we can reach a deal," I say. "The Resistance won't air the broadcast as long as we can reach an agreement, which obviously includes Earth Force's immediate exit from Gulagan space."

"Any deal must include Denver's return," Lucy says. "And you, Jasper."

I anticipated this. "Neither Denver nor I are Earth Force prisoners."

"No," Lucy says, "you're hostages of the Resistance."

"Actually, they're not," Addy says. "They've both decided to stay on Gulaga of their own free will."

"Remind me why you're here again?" Lucy says to Addy. "You were not in our pod. And frankly, you add nothing to this discussion!"

"She's right, Lucy," I say. "Denver and I don't want to go back. That's our choice."

"Let's leave," Cole says to Lucy and begins building a port. I'm almost sure he's bluffing, but I can't risk it. "Wait!

Maybe there's a middle ground. I'd be willing to return to Earth to finish out the Lost Heroes Homecoming Tour if it meant we could reach an agreement today."

"And Denver?" Lucy asks.

"We will discuss it during our caucus," Addy replies.

"Even if Captain Reddy agrees," Cole says, "it's not good enough. The Resistance must answer for its attack at the rally."

Addy balls her fists and puffs her chest, the same stance she'd always take before pummeling me over taking the last chocolate chip cookie Mom baked. "And Earth Force must answer for shooting down more than half our ships today!"

Lucy takes an angry step toward my sister.

"Hey!" I say. "We're here to find a way forward, not dwell in the past. Let's cool things down."

"How can I cool things down when you destroyed my narrative?!" Lucy shouts at me. "Any solution we reach has to address the publicity nightmare you left us!"

"We'll get to that, Lucy, if we can agree to some preliminaries. For starters, no more violence. Both sides stand down. Earth Force leaves Gulagan airspace. The Resistance ceases all attacks on Earth. We'll discuss whether Denver and I are willing to return."

"No way, J—" Marco starts.

"It's reasonable, Marco," I say. "If we're going to reach a compromise, both sides have to give something up."

"That's what *compromise* means, in case you didn't know," Lucy says to Marco.

"Don't start with me, Lucy," Marco says.

"What are *they* giving up?" Addy says through gritted teeth.

"Our ships are poised to destroy you," Cole says. "We're willing to discuss letting you live."

They would never destroy Gulaga. They value the occludium ore too much.

"Mira rightly points out that you'd never risk the destruction of the occludium or the mining operations on Gulaga, Cole, so please stop bluffing. It's getting us nowhere."

"Then what do you want?" Cole asks.

"Publicly acknowledge the Resistance and formally listen to our demands," Addy says.

Lucy laughs. "If you think Admiral Eames will agree to that, you're dumber than I thought."

"Agree to return Captain Reddy permanently, and I'll present that to her," Cole says.

"We already said no," Marco says. "Denver doesn't want to go. The best we *might* be able to do is convince him to finish out the tour."

"Then I don't see how we move forward," Cole says. He lifts his gloves.

"Wait," Addy says. "We'll ask him."

"Okay, then," I say. "I know Admiral Eames and Captain

Reddy discussed this already, but any deal reached today must include an agreement for both sides to meet within the next month with their leaders and the delegates here today—meaning us—to hammer out a formal deal and next steps. Understood?" They nod in acknowledgment. "Great. We'll break and reconvene here in twenty minutes." That didn't go the best, but I suppose it could have gone a lot worse.

"We'll be back," Cole says to Addy and Marco. "Make sure you are, too." He builds a port and bounds away.

Seconds later, Lucy vanishes.

"You coming?" Marco asks me.

Stay.

"No," I say. "I'm supposed to be neutral in all of this. I'll wait here."

Addy and Marco bound back to Gulaga, leaving Mira and me alone on the flight deck.

32

MIRA LOOKS SO BEAUTIFUL THAT I HAVE
to shade my eyes. I don't want her to know my thoughts—
although it's not as if covering my face and twisting my neck
will make a difference in her ability to read my mind.

Even though I'm not watching, I feel her take a step closer,
then another.

I can't help it. I turn back to her.

Words don't flow from Mira, but feelings do, a full spectrum of feelings. She encapsulates us in a bubble of contradic-
tions: joy and sorrow, hope and despair, love and resentment.

"You left me." I blink, spilling tears onto the flight deck.
"You said you didn't want to come back with me."

I'm sorry.

"Why?"

I can't explain.

"You can't say that! You can't just disappear with the Youli and then refuse to tell me why. That's not how friendship works, Mira!"

What I don't say—what I know she hears anyway—is that I thought we were more than friends.

Mira takes a step closer. She raises her palm, her long fingers spread wide like a sea star. Then she places her hand on my heart.

A sizzling current seizes my body. My head falls back as my chest juts forward against Mira's palm. The current intensifies. Our connection strengthens. For a moment it isn't me and Mira, two separate people. It's *us*, together, merged in a place beyond time and space.

She curls her fingers and lowers her hand, severing the connection.

I fall to my knees. My hips strike the flight deck. I'm empty. It feels like Mira grabbed my heart and ripped it right out of my rib cage.

Mira kneels beside me. *Okay?*

No, I'm not okay! I want her hand on my chest. I want her arms wrapped around me. I want to bury my head in her neck and cry.

MONICA TESLER

I want her to stay.

I shouldn't ask. I shouldn't dare hope, but I can't help it.

I watch her face until her eyes meet mine. *Will you stay?*

She drops her gaze to the flight deck. *No.*

No? It feels like my heart is ripped out all over again. *Why not?* I slam my hands against the flight deck. "Why not, Mira?!" My words spill out through tears and clenched teeth. "Oh, wait, that's right . . . you can't explain. You're not going to explain, you're just going to abandon your friends again, is that it? You're going to abandon *me* again, Mira!"

It's not about what I want. This is just what has to be.

Maybe she thinks she can't come back. Maybe she thinks Admiral Eames would lock her up or even execute her for joining the Youli. She might be right.

I stand and gather her hands, pulling her to her feet. *It's okay, Mira, you can come back. You can come to Gulaga with me. Waters would love for you to join the Resistance. There's a place for you, Mira. There will always be a place for you.*

Mira jerks her hands away and walks to the edge of the flight deck. In the light of the stars, her golden hair seems to glow.

I don't need her words to know her answer. It doesn't matter what I say, she's not staying.

Please, Mira.

She turns back to me. *I will try to explain, but not here, not now.*

"When, then?"

When you come.

An image forms in my mind of a huge crystal city glistening under the light of a trio of suns, its buildings stretching like thin fingers to the sky.

Is that the Youli home world? I ask.

I can't wait to show it to you. We can be together there, Jasper, at least for a little while.

What on earth does that mean? Why is she talking in riddles?

A flicker of light flashes in my peripheral vision, followed by a second. By the time I turn around, Cole and Lucy are standing on the flight deck. Addy and Marco arrive seconds later.

I straighten and try to calm my insides. There's no time to decipher what Mira is saying, not when so much depends on this meet. It's time to finish what we came here to do.

"Have both sides had a chance to talk with their leaders?" My voice trembles as I ask my pod mates. They confirm that they have. "What do you think of the terms?"

"We have a question for you, Jasper," Addy says. "Are you sure you're willing to finish out the Lost Heroes Homecoming Tour?"

I look from Addy and Marco to Cole and Lucy. "If it means we leave here today with an agreement, then yes."

"Captain Reddy agrees to return for the tour as long as Jasper does," Marco says.

"And after?" Lucy asks.

"That's up to him," Addy says. "Captain Reddy hasn't made a decision about what to do after the tour. As you all know, he just rejoined society after being stranded in the rift for fifteen years. He would like time to weigh his options, and he wants free passage back to Gulaga after the tour ends if that's what he decides."

"We can live with that," Lucy says and nods at Cole.

"Earth Force will withdraw its troops from Gulagan space," Cole says, "as long as the Resistance stops all attacks."

Marco nods. "Agreed."

"Then it looks like we have a deal," I say, relieved that something productive is actually going to come from this meet.

Wait.

Mira walks into the middle of our group—Addy and Marco to her right, Cole and Lucy to her left, me directly in front. She raises her arms, and her palms shine with a golden light

Then she's in my brain. But more than that, I can tell from the expressions on Addy's and my pod mates' faces that Mira is in their brains, too.

The Youli also have a demand.

"Are you hearing this?" Cole asks.

Marco taps his head. "Loud and clear, Wiki."

"I don't think it's Mira," I tell them, remembering what Waters said about the collective Youli mind. "I think it's the Youli talking."

Mira's face is blank, but the words continue to flow from her into our minds. *Earth must present itself before the Intragalactic Council. We have selected the five of you as representatives of your planet.*

"We can't just agree to that," I say.

"How are you speaking to us?" Lucy asks Mira. "Did you learn this from the Youli?"

"Is this what brain-talk always feels like?" Addy asks me.

You have one Earth month. Then we will meet here again and travel together to the Youli home world to meet with the Council.

"What if we don't?" I ask.

As soon as the words leave my mouth, the space around the bounding base illuminates and three silver spheres appear. They spin faster than light, and as they do, they unfurl into giant saucers, just like the Youli ship we saw on the Paleo Planet.

Earth Force may be poised to destroy Gulaga, but the Youli are positioned to destroy Earth and all its peoples. You have not yet witnessed the extent of our power. We have tolerated Earth's unethical acts long enough. You must appear and negotiate your planet's admission to the Intragalactic Council. It is time Earth understands its role as a planetary citizen of the galaxy.

Mira's words fade. The Youli ships begin to spin. They circle back into spheres. In a flash of light, they're gone. For the briefest moment, Mira's eyes meet mine.

And then she is gone, too.

The five of us are left behind on the flight deck.

Marco and Addy exchange glances. So do Cole and Lucy. Then Cole looks at Marco, who shrugs. Addy and Lucy both look like they're about to laugh. And then we're all communicating silently, without words, almost like Mira. Even though something unexpected and dangerous just happened, it kind of feels like old times. Because . . . really . . . the threat of the Youli annihilating us is nothing new.

I push aside the well of emotions bubbling inside me and break the silence. "So I guess we have a deal. Or, at least, Earth Force and the Resistance do. As for the Youli, you should talk to your leaders, but I suspect I'll be seeing you back here in a month." Even though that sounds totally bizarre, it also sounds somehow right.

Is that the only reason Mira came? To threaten us into appearing before the Intragalactic Council? Was she happy to see me? If it was up to her, would she have stayed?

All I know is she's gone, like before, and I'm left with more questions than answers.

"Thank you, Jasper," Cole says, nodding formally.

"Yes, thank you." Lucy gives me a hug. "I love you even though I'm still mad."

I squeeze Lucy tight. Love is a strange thing. I think I love Mira. But I also love Addy—in a different way, of course. In fact, I love everyone standing on this flight deck.

Marco slaps his hand on my back. "Thanks, Ace. Now, didn't you say something about food?"

Addy smiles. "Why not? Anything is better than BERF."

"Blah!" Lucy says, pretending to puke. "You couldn't force me to eat that stuff again!"

Despite the drama, Lucy heads for the base and the rest of us follow like it's the most normal thing in the world.

With each step, the stiffness seems to seep out of Cole. "I can't believe you went back to Gulaga, Jasper, not with all the forage and fungi."

Marco swings his arm over Cole's shoulder. "He just wanted to pay a visit to the trash worm, Wiki. If I remember right, you had a close-up view of his insides."

Lucy pretends to vomit again. "Leave it to you guys to gross me out twice."

"Nothing's as gross as your signature scent," I say. "I left your office smelling like a rose garden."

"I love roses," Addy says, glancing cautiously at Lucy.

Lucy looks surprised for a moment, and then her expression

388   MONICA TESLER

softens. "Thanks for coming to my defense, sweetie," she says to Addy. "Us girls need to stick together."

Once we're in the mess hall, we pull up seats around an old metal table. Marco fills a tray with tater tots and slides it into the center.

Soon we'll have to get back. Waters will wonder where we are, and I'm sure Admiral Eames is just as antsy about Cole and Lucy. But for now, even if it's strained, even if it's fleeting, even if it requires a whole tray of tater tots to keep it going, we're a pod again.

And I don't think any of us want to let that go.

Not yet.

Acknowledgments

The last few years have been a whirlwind of writing, marketing, and interacting with incredible booksellers, teachers, librarians, publishing professionals, authors, and, of course, readers. I have so much gratitude for those who have supported me, worked alongside me, and taught me by example since I first sent the Bounders series out into the world.

With the publication of *The Heroes Return*, special thanks are owed to my fabulous editor, Sarah McCabe, and the entire team at Simon & Schuster/Aladdin. Also, I will be forever grateful to my agent, David Dunton, and my first editor, Michael Strother, who both saw the potential in the Bounders series from the beginning.

I draw my inspiration from many places, but no place greater than my own family. My husband, Jamey, and our children, Nathan and Gabriel, will forever have my heart and gratitude. Thank you so much for your continued support and love on this journey.

Creativity needs to be nurtured. Fortunately, I come from a family that celebrates and supports my creativity. My parents,

Lynne and Richard Swanson, have always been my biggest fans, whether it be at a piano recital, a theater performance, or a book launch party. Thank you, Mom and Dad, for helping me fill the creative well from which I continue to draw. This book is for you.

Don't miss Jasper's final adventure
in the EarthBound Academy!

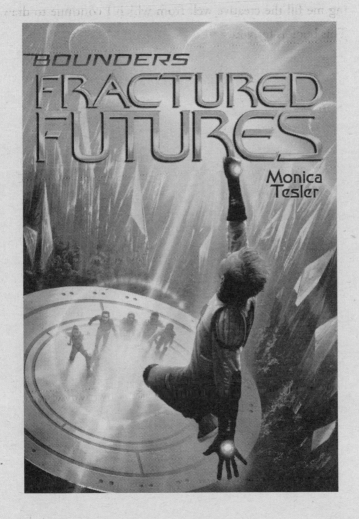

BOUNDERS

FRACTURED
FUTURES

Monica
Tesler

WE SHIFT INTO FASTER-THAN-LIGHT SPEED, leaving the cold and rocky surface of Gulaga behind. I grip the hand rests and focus my gaze out the front window. Everything's a haze, but I still know the other ships are there, the five Earth Force fighter crafts sent to escort Denver Reddy and me back to Earth and the Last Heroes Homecoming Tour.

Our craft is nearly empty—only the captain, a few crew members, and two passengers. Or maybe I should say three passengers. We're bringing Regis back to Earth. His casket is in the cargo hold.

"It's weird," I say to Denver, who's stretched out on the row in front of me. His arms are slung over his face, probably to block the light. "Regis traveled here in a box, and now he travels home in one." On our way to Gulaga, Denver, Regis, and I were packed like sardines into a shipping crate and then attacked by Alkalinians before we could rendezvous with Neeka, our Tunneler junior ambassador–turned–Resistance fighter, for the ride to the planet's surface. We were lucky Regis and I had our gloves. I rub my hands against the secret glove pocket Addy helped me sew into my jacket. I'll never go anywhere without my gloves again.

"At least we're not in a box with him this time," comes Denver's muffled reply. I definitely don't disagree with that. After what went down on Gulaga, I'm lucky not to be in a casket myself.

The last time I saw Regis alive was out on the Gulagan tundra during the battle with Earth Force. Minutes earlier, we'd raced to join the fight. Together. I never thought I'd willingly do anything with Regis, and now I never will again.

"I feel guilty." I'm talking to Denver, but I really just need to say the words out loud.

He sits up and stretches as he turns to face me. "Why?"

I shrug and look down at the worn carpet beneath my feet. "I've secretly wished for this moment. I mean, not this *exact* moment, but something close."

Denver waves his hand. "The demise of your nemesis? Who hasn't fantasized about that? It doesn't mean you caused it, kid. You're not a god, despite what your million screaming fans on Earth think." He turns back around and closes his eyes. "There's work to be done. That's where your head needs to be. And where my head needs to be is in dreamland. Wake me up when the Lost Heroes Homecoming Tour is over, will ya?"

A few minutes later, his breath is loud and steady—not quite a snore, but he's definitely asleep. How can he sleep when there's so much at stake? I could barely string together a few hours of shut-eye the last few days on Gulaga. Rejoining the homecoming tour doesn't stress me out—not that I'm looking forward to it or anything—but what comes after does. Formal talks between Earth Force and the Resistance. A visiting delegation to the Youli home world. Another reunion with Mira.

As Regis and I raced through the Gulagan tunnels to join the battle, he turned to me and said, "Bounders will be the ones who end this." His words inspired my strategy that led to a cease-fire between Earth Force and the Resistance. Now that truce is so fragile, it could unravel with a simple tug on the strings that hold it together.

Before we reached that strained peace, we were nearly annihilated. If I hadn't convinced Waters to get on board with my plan—and Denver hadn't persuaded Admiral Eames—Addy would be dead. I'd probably be dead, too. Instead, my pod mates, my sister, and I met off-site at a bounding base to hammer out the beginnings of a peace deal. It's strange that we're the ones starting to bridge the gap between Earth Force and the Resistance, but somehow both Waters and Eames agreed, thanks to Denver's urging. Since the alternative was total destruction (the Resistance) or a worldwide televised outing of your generations of lies (Earth Force), I guess you could say we had a lot of leverage.

Even though the off-site meet at the bounding base was my idea, I never could have predicted that Mira would show up on behalf of the Youli. Almost a week has passed since the meet, but I can still feel Mira's hand on my heart. I wish that moment could have lasted forever. Oddly, it almost felt like it did, like it defied time and space.

In the minutes we were alone together at the bounding base, the past and future didn't matter. I temporarily forgot how Mira left with the Youli when we were stranded in the rift. I lost the urge to beg her to stay. We were just there, together in space, sharing the most intense connection in the galaxy.

But of course it didn't last. Mira was there for a reason. She issued an ultimatum from the Youli. We would need to travel to the Youli home world as representatives of Earth.

Our planet was required to appear before the Intragalactic Council and answer for its actions. The Youli wasn't messing around. As soon as Mira stated their demands, three Youli ships showed up, armed and ready for battle.

When the ships spun into spheres and bounded away, Mira left, too. It felt like she ripped my heart out and took it with her. I can still feel a hole in my chest, a bottomless cavern that can't be filled, no matter what.

The good news (sort of) is that I've had zero time to obsess about Mira. As soon as we returned from the bounding base, we went into prep mode. Earth Force and the Resistance had to hammer out the details of their cease-fire. Waters reached out to his Youli contacts to clarify and flesh out their demands. Although the primary focus is the Intragalactic Summit that is scheduled to take place in less than a month at an as-yet-undisclosed location, the Youli have insisted that Earth first send ambassadors to their planet. They've been very clear who those ambassadors should be: everyone present at the bounding base meet and absolutely no one else. That means Addy, my pod mates, and I are heading to the Youli home world on our own. I'm kind of surprised Waters and Eames agreed, but since both of them want us to get the inside scoop on the Youli prior to the Summit and neither of them are willing to waste their negotiating power on the issue of adult chaperones, we're going.

For now, though, we're broken into camps. Earth Force on one side, the Resistance on the other, and Denver and I caught in the middle. So we're headed back to Earth. Part of the truce between Earth Force and the Resistance is that Denver and I have to finish out the Lost Heroes Homecoming Tour. It helps the Force save face with the public. I hated leaving Addy, Marco, and the rest of my friends behind on Gulaga, especially when I'm diving headfirst into the awkwardness and animosity that comes with going AWOL during your own homecoming tour.

Maybe it won't be so bad. The Force's culture of secrecy might work in my favor this time. Admiral Eames might have kept the truth about Denver's and my involvement with the Resistance to a small circle of confidantes, leaving most of the Force in the dark as to why we've been missing for a week and the tour visits had to be rescheduled. For all I know, everyone without a level-one security clearance has been fed the public narrative (the Force's feel-good word for *lie*) that Denver and I were injured in the attack at the rally in Americana East.

Two people who definitely know the truth? Cole and Lucy. By the time we said good-bye at the bounding base, some of the tension in the pod had faded. Still, there's no way they've forgiven me for bailing on the tour, going to Gulaga, and fighting with the Resistance.

Since we're traveling at FTL, it won't be long until we're

back on Earth and back on the tour. Soon, Denver and I will know who buys into the Earth Force narrative, and we'll be the ones onstage repeating the lies to thousands of screaming fans.

The smoke clears, and the Eurasia West skyline comes into view out the front window. The Eiffel Tower rises high above the other buildings. When we were little, Mom read Addy and me a book about Paris. It described the city from hundreds of years ago, when you could buy bread and pastries from a corner baker and visit museums with tons of real paintings hanging on the walls. All that's gone now, but the Eiffel Tower still points to the sky, just like it did in the book.

Mira is from Eurasia West, although not from Paris specifically. She grew up in a northern district. Still, she must have left from here to travel to the Americanas. I wonder what she thought of the Eiffel Tower. Maybe she had a copy of the Paris book, too. Maybe her family will be at the rally later, hoping to hear firsthand how her daughter died during our infamous rescue of the lost aeronauts. That's a lie I particularly hate.

We make our way to the exit ramp. A motorcade is waiting to escort us back to the tour. A group of Earth Force officers stands at attention. Off to the side is a familiar woman wearing a formal black suit and enormous sunglasses.

Why is Florine Statton here? The last thing I knew, she'd been banished to hotel voice-over work.

"Who's the suit?" Denver asks me. When I tell him, he shrugs. "Never heard of her."

He really has been missing for a long time. "Don't tell *her* that."

We make our way across the tarmac. I smell Florine long before I reach her. She's still going overboard with the rose perfume. Lucy isn't a fan of Florine, but she follows her taste in fragrance and nail polish.

Florine extends a limp hand to Denver and then to me. Her nails shine, pink and glossy. She goes through the introductions in her typical bored voice, but then she leans forward and whispers in a conspiratorial tone, "I have a business proposal to discuss later. I think you could make a fortune in celebrity appearances."

"No thanks," Denver says.

Florine laughs like she thinks he's joking.

The officers wave us toward the waiting hovers, but something catches my eye on the other side of the craft. A man and a woman in civilian clothes are waiting by a large commercial hover that isn't nearly as new and shiny as the Earth Force vehicles. The woman is crying. Her shoulders bob up and down. Her hands are wrapped tightly around her middle. The man stands stiffly with his hand placed on the woman's back.

Something about the man is . . . familiar.

The crew is unloading the craft. The cargo plank rises on the accordion lift and lowers with baggage and goods. The next time it rises, crew from the craft push a familiar box onto the lift: Regis's casket. As soon as it comes into view, the woman bursts into sobs.

The realization hits me as his casket is lowered to the ground. That's why the man looks familiar. He looks like Regis. Those must be his parents.

Two men in suits exit the civilian hover and cross to the casket. As they wheel it back, the woman races over. She drapes herself across the box that contains her son's remains. Her sobs are loud now. Her body shudders. Her shoulders heave. Regis's father is trying to coax her away so the casket can be loaded onto the waiting hover.

An officer's hand is on my arm, steering me to the motorcade. "Let's go, Adams."

I shake him off and dart across the tarmac.

It won't do me any favors in the Earth Force popularity department, but I can't turn my back.

"Excuse me," I say, nearly slamming into the casket as I skid to a stop in front of Regis's parents.

"Yes?" the man says. He must recognize me from the webs. My face was plastered everywhere since I returned from the rift with the lost aeronauts. I can see the confusion on his face. Why is an Earth Force hero talking to the parents of the only student ever expelled from the EarthBound Academy?

Now that I'm here, I'm not sure what to say. "I . . . uh . . . I'm . . . sorry about your son."

The woman steps away from the casket and turns to face me. Tears still stream down her face, but her crying is quiet now. "Did you know Regis?" she chokes out.

I'm not sure what to say. That yes, I knew her son, and I hated him. He tried to kill me multiple times, and that's why he was booted from the Academy. I don't think those sentiments would add anything to this horrible moment. Plus, in the end, did I really hate the person Regis had become?

"Regis and I were . . . well, we . . . he and I . . . we fought together." I take a deep breath and search for the right words. "And no matter what anyone else tells you, I want you to know that he died admirably." I stick out my hand to Regis's father. He stares at it for a second, then quickly clasps and releases my palm.

His mother grips my shoulders and then pulls me in for a hug. It's a gesture that's so motherly it makes me miss my own mom. Before she steps back, she whispers in my ear, "Thank you."

I nod at them both, then turn and jog back to the waiting motorcade, wiping away a few stray tears that I don't want anyone in Earth Force to see. I ignore the glares from the officers and slide into my seat next to Denver.

He gives my knee a slap. "Good on you, kid. You're one of the best kind."

Looking for another great book?
Find it
IN THE MIDDLE.

Fun, fantastic books for kids
in the in-be**TWEEN** age

IntheMiddleBooks.com

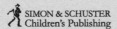